MW00562791

EPIC

BEASTS &
CREATURES
MYTHS & TALES
ANTHOLOGY OF CLASSIC TALES

Foreword by Dr. Tok Thompson

FLAME TREE PUBLISHING

TALES

This is a FLAME TREE Book

Publisher & Creative Director: Nick Wells
Editorial Director: Catherine Taylor
Special thanks to Tim Leng and Federica Ciaravella

FLAME TREE PUBLISHING
6 Melbray Mews, Fulham,
London SW6 3NS, United Kingdom
www.flametreepublishing.com

First published 2022
Copyright © 2022 Flame Tree Publishing Ltd

· 22 24 26 25 23
3 5 7 9 10 8 6 4 2

ISBN: 978-1-83964-883-0
Special ISBN: 978-1-83964-998-1

The cover image is created by Flame Tree Studio
based on artwork courtesy of Shutterstock.com, including by Neba.

Incidental motif images courtesy of Shutterstock.com:
moj0j0 and Lifeking.

A copy of the CIP data for this book is available from the British Library.

Printed and bound in China

EPIC

BEASTS & CREATURES MYTHS & TALES

ANTHOLOGY OF CLASSIC TALES

Foreword by Dr. Tok Thompson

FLAME TREE PUBLISHING

TALES

Contents

CREATURES FROM THE DEPTHS

Dragons & Serpents

SUPERNATURAL BEASTS & BEINGS

LITTLE CREATURES & TINY FOLK

Foreword

COMPRISED OF CLASSIC OFFERINGS drawn from some of the most famous folklorists and other writers of the nineteenth and early twentieth centuries, this compendium offers windows into other worlds: worlds of fantastic creatures, strange and supernatural beings and stories that have withstood the test of time. All cultures around the world maintain traditions of supernatural others, a wondrous display of the diversity of human cultural ingenuity. Within those traditions one may have believers and non-believers; those that have encountered them or those that have not; yet there is commonly agreement in each culture about what the possibilities are, what sorts of spirits and creatures are said to exist, and what the relationship is between humans and these others.

The others – the beasts, creatures, spirits, supernatural people – are often helpful, yet also often destructive. Perhaps most common is an ambivalent relationship, one open to changes and vagaries depending on the interactions between them and humans. For many of these stories, their appearance in writing long ago moved from the realm of belief into the realm of fantasy and fiction, yet the figures mentioned in fiction often contain long lineages, with ties to ancient societies, magic practices, occult knowledge and spirits and gods of long ago. In many ways, these others are both of long ago, and of right now, joining our lives with those of ancient people as the themes, plots, motifs and stories echo down the centuries, if not millennia. These stories contain worlds within worlds, secret knowledges tucked away and treasure trails for the aspiring folklorist to follow.

But the stories are not confined to the past, as our contemporary world maintains and changes old beliefs, reinvigorating some and neglecting others, and inserting brand-new characters (take modern 'extra-terrestrials' for example), who often seem to reflect and represent those that came before. Even with all the epochal changes in human culture, many creatures and beasts have persisted, taking on new forms, appearing in new stories and other genres, all the while maintaining ancient and at times divinely connected aspects. Fantastic creatures might be shrunken deities, or connected to ancient ethnic others, or perhaps a bit of both (were the Greeks influenced by the horse-riding Scythians in forming the fearsome centaur, or were the centaurs descended from Gods, as other accounts suggest?). Beasts, creatures and spirits clearly reflect human concerns, fears, hopes, aspirations and worldviews, straddling the boundary between us and them, humans and animals, natural and supernatural, gods and demons. They can function as community symbols, such as the strong affection given to Sasquatch in the Pacific Northwest of today. They can represent the unknown, like the sea monsters populating the edges of the known world in early maps. They offer a chance for bravery, adventure, danger and excitement. They frequently teach of moral considerations. They represent local culture, and local beliefs, yet, at the same time, can be linked to stories in wide swaths of the globe, as in the figure of the dragon. Stories of fantastic creatures have always been and continue to be a vibrant part of the human cultural experience, guiding our thoughts and actions with their insights into the unknown.

Tok Thompson, PhD
Professor of Anthropology and Communication
University of Southern California

Publisher's Note

AS TALES FROM MYTHOLOGY AND FOLKLORE are principally derived from an oral storytelling tradition, their written representation depends on the transcription, translation and interpretation by those who heard them and first put them to paper. They also vary depending on whether they were directly sourced from original first-hand accounts, are versions re-told in the author's own words and style, or even are more modern fictional tales inspired by aspects of fantastical legend. The stories in this book are a mixture of these, a mixture of myths, legends, folklore, fairy tales and some classic fiction, and you can learn more about the authors and their works at the back of the book. This collection presents a thoughtfully selected cross-section of stories from all over the world, though some countries may seem more heavily represented than others since their cultures have more readily conjured up beasts and creatures to demonstrate moral or fabulistic points, or to explain natural and social phenomenon.

Though discretion has been used to alter the text in some instances (mainly alterations to spellings and punctuation, for the sake of a degree of consistency), some words, names and diacritical marks vary from story to story and have been left as they were so as to not undermine the original source.

We also ask the reader to remember that while the essence of the myths and tales in this anthology are timeless, much of the factual information, opinions regarding the nature of countries and their peoples, as well as the style of writing and way of presenting speech patterns, are of the era during which they were written and must not be taken as a reflection of modern standards.

If after reading this collection your appetite is not sated, we refer the reader to our companion title *Gods & Monsters Myths & Tales*, for even more wondrous tales of beasts and creatures – especially the monstrous kind.

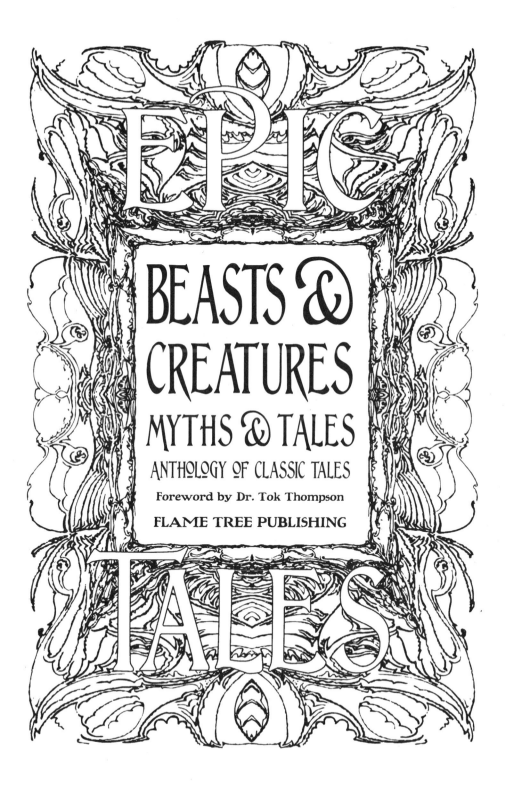

EPIC

BEASTS & CREATURES

MYTHS & TALES

ANTHOLOGY OF CLASSIC TALES

Foreword by Dr. Tok Thompson

FLAME TREE PUBLISHING

TALES

BEASTS & CREATURES IN FOLKLORE & IMAGINATION

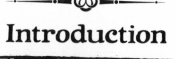

Introduction

AS IF THE ANIMAL KINGDOM were not big and varied enough already, it has been imaginatively expanded down the centuries by human storytellers. They have come up with a whole menagerie of mythical creatures. Some are benign and beautiful, others cruel and monstrous (or merely mischievous), but all add to the richness of our lives. The Bird With Nine Heads of Chinese myth (page 123) or the Scylla of classical Greek tradition could never have been anything other than imaginary. Others, like the Japanese Vampire Cat (page 125) or India's Giant Crab (page 209), are ordinary animals with an extraordinary dimension. Such creatures bring the natural and supernatural worlds together in a way that makes us wonder exactly what and who we are ourselves.

Speaking Volumes

'I wish you could talk,' says the little boy in Abbie Phillips Walker's story 'The Good Sea Monster' (1917, page 208). 'I can … No one ever wished it before,' the beast replies. He is wrong, of course: for as long as anyone can remember, in whatever culture we care to name, people have craved a conversation with animals. They have longed to learn their wisdom, to understand their existences as mammals, birds, reptiles, insects or other creatures – and to have an alternative, external perspective on human life. And so, in myth, in folk tale, in fairy tale and romance, animals are often endowed with the gift of speech – or selected individuals granted the gift of understanding them.

The truth is, though, that even in the routine of everyday life animals do 'talk' to us. They may not directly address us in words, but they still have much to say and they communicate it. In this respect, even the most 'ordinary' animal is enchanted. By their very existence (real or imaginary) they seem to speak.

As the art critic and novelist John Berger (1926–2017) noted, animals are simultaneously 'like and unlike' us – and it is in both these aspects that they speak to us. Like us they are living, breathing, feeling things which suffer from mortality – and the ever-present fear that brings. Yet their difference brings home to us the strangeness of our world. Even the most beloved pet is profoundly alien to us in this respect: close as we may be, we are divided by an unbridgeable gulf.

Symbiosis and Symbolism

Animals have evolved alongside us, with archaeological evidence indicating that they have always played a role in our lives – at least peripherally, but for the most part much more centrally. Whether we hunted or herded animals, or kept them as household friends, they have been there with us. Berger describes how in their most 'primitive' state human beings were first set apart from the animals by a capacity to think symbolically – yet it was animals that humans took as their first symbols. 'What distinguished men from animals was born of their relationship with them,' Berger explains.

At some level we always understood this – even if we arguably misunderstood that relationship. For most of our history humans have assumed a divinely ordained superiority over the animal kingdom. We had to, in order to make sense of our place in the universal order.

As human societies first emerged – scattered far and wide in small, nomadic hunter-gatherer communities – we seem to have seen our fellow creatures in fraternal terms. In this Paleolithic ('Old Stone Age') period, which began around 2.5 million years ago, we relied on animals for meat and had to kill them to survive. Even so, we appear to have admired them for many of their attributes, as well as appreciating them for the sustenance they gave. Certain species were singled out: totem creatures with whom we particularly identified and to whose power, beauty, grace or cunning we aspired.

Hence the appeal of Mad Buffalo (page 113) – not a beast himself, in fact, but a Native American hunter. In legend he took on the name (along with the courage and the strength) of the giant buffalo he overcame. Mad Buffalo gained his name through this heroic exploit, but his place in mythic history was won by driving out the destructive Thunderbird from the territory of his tribe.

Domestication and Domination

With the advent of agriculture and the domestication of livestock in the Neolithic ('New Stone Age') some 12,000 years ago, however, our entire standpoint with regard to Nature was transformed. Nowadays we associate farming and pastoralism with peace, rural living with calm contentment.

Yet the first farmers lived in something like a state of war with the world. They saw Nature as something to be subdued, suppressed and tamed. Rivers were dammed, ditches dug for irrigation, forests felled and wildernesses cleared for cultivation.

Animals, of course, were wooed with food into closer companionable relationships (like dogs or cats), formed into flocks or herds for fleece and milk, or brought to bridle to be beasts of burden or of haulage. Nomadism no longer made sense. People now sought to be sedentary; they lived in permanent settlements to be near their fields and supplies. . These were certainly not cities by modern standards but, small as they were, they represented the beginnings of urban life.

It was inevitable that these – literally epoch-making – changes would find a place in the folk memory. In one richly-imagined form or another, the transformation wrought by the 'Neolithic Revolution' is recalled in some of the world's most ancient and important myths. In the Bible's Book of Genesis, for instance, when Adam and Eve are expelled from the Garden of Eden, they are told that they'll have to produce their own food by their own hard work. Their sons, Cain and Abel, famously fall out and fight – whereupon Cain commits humankind's first murder. What modern readers are slower to note, as products of an essentially urban civilization, is that Cain and Abel's quarrel is a clash of lifestyles too. Cain is a farmer: he tills the soil, we're told; Abel a pastoralist who tends sheep.

A Frightful Femininity

Not that pastoralism is necessarily peaceful. The giant Cyclops in the Odyssey is a case in point. He may be big and fierce, but for the 'Father of Psychoanalysis' Sigmund Freud his fury was feminine; his single eye symbolically a vagina. Odysseus' battle with him symbolized the hero's struggle to assert his male strength and instinct for order over a wild and wilful – and essentially feminine – primal state. This opposition was to be rehearsed just about endlessly in the mythology of subsequent civilizations, whether as an underlying tension or an active conflict.

Take the 'Vampire Cat' of Japanese legend (page 125), which kills the fair Princess and takes her place in the unwitting Prince's bed. Caressing and fondling him, she beguiles the Prince, draining his blood away amidst his bliss. She could hardly represent more clearly the sinister strength of female sexuality: 'pussy power' at its most seductive and destructive.

Freud was fascinated by the Gorgon myth, which he saw as dramatizing the masculine fear of female sexuality. The monstrous sisters' hair might appear phallic in its writhing, hissing, snakelike strands, but in the mass it stood out scarily like female pubic hair.

Their petrifying look (literally so in legend: a single glance would turn the viewer into stone) reflected the shock of the young boy who saw that his mother had no penis – the source, Freud suggested, of a 'castration anxiety' that would haunt him from then on. Such horrors lie far beneath the surface in the urbane, child-friendly Victorian version of the story told by the famous American novelist Nathaniel Hawthorne (page 37), but they lend a certain special frisson none the less.

Shocking Sexuality

Not that the masculine principle could not be unsettling in its own way. A man with a horse's body, the classical centaur (page 27) represents the 'animal' physicality and predatory impulses of the human male. So in his different way does the Minotaur (page 49): half-man, half-bull and wholly emblematic of the damage to be done to defenceless maidens by the male sex-drive.

In such a context, we can see that the kind of idealized (arguably infantilized) 'innocence' that self-consciously 'civilized' society yearned to see in its young women did not adapt well to the realities of the lives they would have to lead. This is the problem faced by Beauty in the famous fairy tale 'Beauty and the Beast' (page 128). Psychoanalysts see the story as a dramatization of the process (sometimes slow and painful, but necessary) by which a growing daughter learns to transfer her affections from her father to a potential partner. A well-ordered society needed its young girls to be emphatically un-sexual, but it also required them to slide smoothly into their roles as wives and mothers upon marriage.

Beyond Our Comprehension

At the very least, these extraordinary beasts reflect back to us the extravagance of our imagination, our ability to make a strange world even more strange. While this is a tribute to our creativity as a species, it also testifies to a cast of mind that draws us to the obscure and the occult. Eager as we are to understand our universe, a part of us is concerned that too clear a comprehension will prove reductive. ('Philosophy will clip an angel's wings,' wrote Keats.) For all our curiosity, our determination to sound the scientific depths, humans are just as desperate to find them unfathomable.

Hence the appeal of the Unicorn (page 137) which, though celebrated for its beauty and purity, is valued almost as much for its scarcity and elusiveness. Father Jerome Lobo, a Portuguese Jesuit who claimed to have seen one during his travels in the mountains of Ethiopia, aptly characterized it as 'that beast so much talked about and so little known'. Though in some places it was said to 'abound', these were invariably regions of the earth where Europeans had seldom ventured: the unicorn was the embodiment of unfamiliarity, in other words.

The Phoenix (page 36), for its part, was not just rare: it was unique. Quite literally, as there was only ever one. This magnificent bird – 'partly red and partly golden' and about the size of an eagle – lived in the remotest reaches of the vast Arabian desert. It lived for 500 years, then immolated itself on the altar of a holy temple. The bird burned itself up completely, the fire perfumed by the sacred balms placed upon it by attendant priests, before arising, reborn and rejuvenated, from its own ashes.

Riotous Assemblage

Monsters such as the Minotaur or Centaur, as we have seen, hint at something menacing in male sexuality – but they also attest to the human instinct to cut and paste, to make a montage out of what they know. So it is with the eagle-headed, lion-bodied Griffin (page 104) in the Western tradition and the Samébito in the Japanese story (page 205), who has the body of a man, a demon's face and a dragon's ruffled beard.

Along with the instinct to mix and match goes a still more ambitious impulse to synthesize life itself: to put together the parts that might make up another being. The ultimate example of this occurs in 'The Rabbi's Bogey-man' (page 322). Created in the Ghetto of Prague by a Jewish scholar who wants a servant to take the strain during his Sabbath day of rest, this mechanical being was to find fame as the 'Golem' – an early version of (and possible inspiration for) Frankenstein's Monster.

Grimly grotesque, such monsters as the Cyclops (page 23), the Trolls of the Hedale Woods (page 87) or Bigfoot (page 118) can clearly be seen to emblematize deeper human fears. Yet we should not forget that they are also human creations. Perhaps we find that our ability to conjure up such terrors, then by and large envisage their eventual defeat, helps to reassure us that we have at least some control over our lives.

All at Sea

The ocean, of course, has a symbolism and imagery all of its own. Its waters can be inexpressibly gentle – wavelets lapping placidly against a beach or jetty on a calm and sunny day – or enormously, irresistibly violent in the force of a storm. Likewise, while they may start clear and light in their shallows, they quickly become impossibly deep and dark. Who knows what mysteries may lurk in such depths? Our unsettling sense of its vastness somehow sets off the wariness we feel about other aspects of our existence; our uneasy feeling of being more generally 'out of our depth'.

As with the ocean, so with its creatures, coloured (and frequently magnified) by myth. The dreadful Kraken (page 147) is a case in point. It does not take Sigmund Freud to see that the 'murky depths' in which it dwells resemble those of our own psyches; its eruption into daylight a breaking-through of terrors we normally suppress. That is before we even get to the size and strangeness of the squidlike beast itself, with its entangling arms and its clinging, sucking tentacles.

Washed Up

The 'Sea Raiders' that H.G. Wells imagined attacking the Devon coast (page 157) were also giant cephalopods. Ashore, outside their normal habitat, they appear even more grotesque – precisely because they *are* outside their natural home. It feels incongruous even to see them there. Furthermore here, without the water's support and weighed down by the effects of gravity, the cephalopods spill over themselves like so much suppurating slime.

For the depths of the sea are remote from us in a way that even the most distant desert cannot be. Different forces of gravity, buoyancy and pressure prevail there. Near the ocean floor, temperatures do not change and light fails to penetrate: a completely alien fauna has evolved. It is not too difficult for us to believe that the narrator in the 'Demons of the Sea', William Hodgson's eerie tale (page 151), would have been shocked to find himself confronted with 'the most horrible creatures I had ever seen'.

> *Their bodies had something of the shape of a seal's, but of a dead, unhealthy white. The lower part of the body ended in a sort of double-curved tail on which they were able to shuffle about. In place of arms, they had two long, snaky feelers, at the end of which were two very humanlike hands, which were equipped with talons instead of nails.*

They are, as he sums up himself, appalling 'parodies' of human beings. To some extent, many mythical sea-monsters are.

Love Beneath the Waves

This is by no means always the case, however. In classical tradition, every object ashore had its own equivalent beneath the sea. Similar ideas have prevailed in many mythologies around the world. The lives and loves of Mermaids (to a lesser extent Mermen too) often closely resemble those of mortals.

Indeed, these emotions often span the boundaries between their worlds. Mermaids or mermen tend to fall in love with mortals they meet along the water's edge. 'The Little Mermaid' of Hans Christian Andersen is only the most famous example of a sizeable genre of stories in which sea-dwelling spirits fall in love with those living on land and try to create new lives for themselves ashore. Or vice versa, as with Maurice Connor, the blind piper in the Irish tale 'The Wonderful Tune', who follows a mermaid to a new life beneath the waves.

In Jonas Lie's enchanting fairy tale 'Finn Blood' (1893, page 172), the beautiful daughter of the *draug* or merman takes the mortal boy she loves on an eerie voyage beneath the waves. She leads him through another world, one in which the ghostly bodies of those who have drowned flit among shipwrecked hulks. Lost at sea, they have had to go unburied and are thus unable to find peace.

Worm of Water

The idea of the *nicor* or 'water-wyrm' was well-known in Anglo-Saxon England as a sort of dragon, but it has an odd – and even counterintuitive – ring to us today. To some extent it did in its own day too, since this monster – which lurked in 'bottomless' pools, emerging occasionally to snatch unwary wayfarers – represented the survival of an older idea of the dragon, long since displaced to the mythic margins.

For many centuries – in the West, at any rate – the archetypal dragon has been a scaly, four-footed creature that breathes fire. Neither recognizably a 'worm' nor in any way watery, in other words. In the most archaic traditions, however – as in Chinese folk culture to this day – the dragon did indeed resemble an oversized worm or snake in shape.

Or, to be more symbolically exact, an exaggerated phallus. This dragon's association with water embraced not just the fertilizing rain that allowed the crops to grow and feed us, but also the seminal fluid enabling us to reproduce.

From Rain to Fire

This ancient tradition seems to have taken a turn somewhere in the Indo-European past – perhaps taking a line through the lightning bolts that accompanied the greatest rainstorms. Early Greek writings, such as those of Hesiod mention flame-breathing dragons of our modern sort, while the Bible's Book of Isaiah also refers to 'fiery flying serpents'.

These Western dragons changed in other aspects too. In Freudian terms these monsters no longer seem to symbolize fertility, with its capacity to refresh and replenish, but instead an anally-retentive urge to covet and possess, close up, accumulate and hoard. Nowadays the best-known dragon of this kind is probably Smaug, in J.R.R. Tolkien's famous fantasy *The Hobbit*. He lies in the midst of his mountain, jealously guarding his great mound of gold. But Smaug has his analogues in the dragon that guards the hoard of the Nibelung in the Old Norse story of Sigurd (page 223) and the defender of the Golden Fleece in the ancient Greek legend of 'Medea' (page 218).

That the association with water did not disappear completely is clear not only from the Anglo-Saxon examples, but also from others such as 'The Prince and the Dragon' (page 253). This Serbian story features a dragon who breathes fire in the customary European way, even though his lair lies at the bottom of a lake. The monster in the Spanish legend of 'The Treasure of the Dragon' (page 244) is described as being half-fish, half-lion, with enormous wings. Though he has amassed an immense quantity of gold and jewels, it is the imprisoned princess who arrests the hero's awestruck gaze. While the dragon lived she was a statue. Many other victims lay around his lair, transformed into precious stones. Only with the dragon's death could they be released, as his black magic was dissolved.

In Man's Clothing

Next come what the early anthropologist Frank Hamel was to call 'human animals', the most notorious of which is undoubtedly the Werewolf. Lycanthropy, as Hamel notes (page 284), has an exceedingly ancient pedigree, appearing in the classical works of Petronius and Pliny. The 'meaning' of such a creature seems self-evident. The Jekyll-and-Hyde transition of an outwardly respectable man into a wild and feared predatory animal quite obviously underlines the idea that civilization is a mere veneer over our savage nature.

Too obviously, perhaps. It is hard for us to get a clear perspective on how attitudes to this condition have evolved and changed over so many centuries. Our perceptions cannot but be coloured by the fact that what we read now has been filtered through the perceptions of more recent writers on whose researches we rely. What strikes us now about the earliest Werewolf stories is how un-'Gothic' they are. Many are remarkably matter-of-fact in their acceptance of lycanthropy and show little horror at the whole idea. As described by classical writers, for example, the condition is little more than a curiosity – intriguing for sure, but not unduly disturbing.

The Threat to Faith

Did the coming of Christianity change this? It does not really appear so. In the 'Lay of the Bisclavaret' by the twelfth-century French poet Marie de France (page 286), the werewolf is kept imprisoned in his animal form by his faithless wife. She takes his hidden clothing so he cannot change back to human shape. Ferocious as this wolf is in his attacks on her, he remains mild and gentle to all others, impressing the king with his courtly grace. The werewolf's inward character has not changed at all: his monstrous appearance is rather a reproach to his treacherous wife who, with all her elegance and beauty, is stained with sin. From our twenty-first-century standpoint, it's hard to imagine Werewolf-ism being incidental to a story about something else – but this tale is clearly about wifely loyalty and love.

Maybe this should not seem so surprising. It is broadly true that pre-Reformation Europe was more tolerant of the occult and offbeat than we might readily assume. Despite the bloodthirsty zeal with which it persecuted 'heretics' who offered alternatives to its doctrines, the Catholic Church did not concern itself too much about what we would see as darker dangers. The 'Age of Faith' was sufficiently self-confident to be unfazed by folk beliefs – spanning everything from fairies to fortune-telling. Such foolishness might just, conceivably, be genuinely the work of the Devil – but he was no match for God, nor any threat to his Church on Earth. It was the advent of modernity that brought the great wave of witch-hunts and the crackdown on 'black magic': a little enlightenment is a dangerous thing, it seems.

Romantic Outcast

If the Reformation recoiled in horror from the wildness the Werewolf represented, Romanticism reimagined the creature's role as a glamorous outsider. As described by the nineteenth-century American writer Eugene Field (page 294), the Werewolf is a 'hero' along the lines of Lord Byron's Manfred or Emily Brontë's Heathcliff. His very cruelty reveals his alluring depth:

Nowhere was there pity for the wolf; what mercy, thus, should I, the werewolf, show? The curse was on me and it filled me with a hunger and thirst for blood.

Other stories of changing states can be seen to follow a broadly similar trajectory. The idea that human nature is profoundly ambivalent may be a constant, but the way in which it is appreciated evolves. The Fairy Changeling who usurps the baby's place in the story of 'Wee Johnnie in the

Cradle' (page 319) is, both in his general boorishness and his entrancing singing voice, a comic exemplar for human nature at its best and worst. So, in its way, is the shapeshifting 'Kildare Pooka' (page 321).

But we find more melancholy, thoughtful reflections too. Pale, gaunt and cold, the woman who comes back to sleep with her husband in 'The Dead Wife Among the Fairies' (page 315) both is and is not the love that he lost: her story makes us think about what it is to be ourselves. The invisible body that attacks the narrator in Sheridan LeFanu's eerie tale 'What Was It?' is clearly emblematic of all those darker things he cannot understand in his own nature.

You and Me in Miniature

Which is where the Little People come in. If animals are, as Berger said, both 'like and unlike' us, how much more true is that for the various fairies, goblins, brownies, dwarfs, imps and elves that have so abounded in the mythologies of the world? The idea that such quasi-human creatures might exist seems somehow to underscore our sense of our own reality. 'He was always saying "That's so",' we're told of 'The Leprechaun of Ardmore Tower' (page 376): an ontological statement of a sort.

At their simplest, stories of these creatures account for the random little accidents of life – the stew that fails to thicken; the plate that turns up broken; the spilled cream. More seriously, though, they may help to regulate us morally; we're told that the Kabouters of Dutch legend, for example, 'help the good and wise people to do things better, but ... plague and punish the dull folks' (page 408). Or they may hold up a mirror to mortal foibles and faults, as does the 'Yellow Dwarf' (page 379). His rejection by the Princess highlights human disloyalty and lack of faith.

The Little People may also embody human weaknesses, of course – sometimes to a spectacular degree. In (half-)comically exaggerated form, the female inhabitants of Sri Lanka's 'Goblin City' (page 394) exemplify an untrammelled sexual voracity traditionally attributed by men to womankind. One way and another, however, it seems fair to say that these beings help us to see ourselves from a fresh perspective. The same might also be said of all the other mythical beasts in this book.

Creatures of
Myth & Legend

Introduction

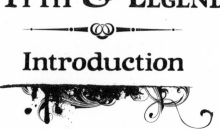

THE MYTHICAL GREEK HERO had a torrid time of it on his way back to his island home of Ithaca after the Trojan War. Homer recorded the details in his epic, *The Odyssey*, and these gripping stories have been remembered and re-told ever since. Legendary he may be, but Odysseus is also an 'Everyman': which of us will not find trials and challenges lying in wait for us along life's journey? Not perhaps (or so we hope!) a ravening giant like the Cyclops or a 'gluttonous and evil creature' like the Scylla, but setbacks and crises that will test our mettle even so.

The Twelve Labours of Heracles were explicitly imposed as a punishment – and for a genuinely dreadful crime. Even so, they can be seen as tests as well. Through his courage and resourcefulness in handling them, Heracles showed that he had rehabilitated himself as a hero. It was nevertheless no coincidence that so many of his tasks involved the taming or the slaying of monstrous beasts. Heracles' ability to stamp his authority on Nature was at this time the measure of the man – complemented by his ability to assert a male authority over women. Perseus, another Greek hero, also showed this when he secured the Gorgon Medusa's head.

Ultimately, though, the 'meaning' of these mythic creatures is not so obscure. They stand collectively for all those things we do not and cannot know. If the trolls of the Old Norse tradition represent the menace lurking in the dark depths of the forest, the Unicorn reminds us that the world is wider, more mysterious and arguably more beautiful than we frequently assume.

The Cyclopes

ODYSSEUS AND HIS MEN sailed until they were forced to stop for food and fresh water. A small island appeared in the distance, and as they drew nigh, they saw that it was inhabited only by goats, who fed on the succulent, sweet grass which grew plentifully across the terrain. Fresh water cascaded from moss-carpeted rocks, and tumbled through the leafy country. The men's lips grew wet in anticipation of its cold purity.

As they clambered aboard shore, the fresh air filling their lungs, the men felt whole once more, and when they discovered, in their travels, an inviting cave filled with goats' milk and cheese, they settled down to feast. Their bellies groaning, and faces pink with pleasure, Odysseus and his men settled back to sleep on the smooth face of the cave, warmed by the hot spring that pooled in its centre, and sated by their sumptuous meal.

They were woken abruptly by heavy footfall, which shook the ground with each step. Eyeing one another warily, the tired men stayed silent, barely alert, but overwhelmingly fearful. Into the cave burst a flock of snow-white sheep and behind them the frightful giant Polyphemus, a Cyclops with one eye in the centre of his face. Polyphemus was the son of Poseidon, and he lived on the island with his fellow Cyclopes, existing peacefully in seclusion. He had not seen man for many years, and his single eyebrow raised in anticipation when he came upon his visitors. Odysseus took charge.

"Sire, in the name of Zeus, I beg your hospitality for the night. I've weary men who…"

His words were cut off. The Cyclops laughed with outrage and reaching over, plucked up several of Odysseus's men and ate them whole. The others cowered in fear, but Odysseus stood firm, his stance betraying none of the fear that surged through his noble blood.

"I ask you again," he began. But Polyphemus merely grunted and turned to roll a boulder across the opening to the cave. He settled down to sleep, his snores lifting the men from the stone floor of the cave, and forbidding them sleep. They huddled round Odysseus, who pondered their plight.

When he woke, Polyphemus ate two more men, and with his sheep, left the cave, carefully closing the door on the anxious men. They moved around their prison with agitation, wretched with fear. It was many hours before the Cyclops returned, but the men could not sleep. They waited for the sound of footsteps, they sickened at the thought of their inescapable death.

But the brave Odysseus feared not. His cunning led him through the maze of their predicament, and carefully and calmly he formed a plan. He was waiting when Polyphemus returned, and sidled up to the weary Cyclops with his goatskin of wine.

"Have a drink, ease your fatigue," he said quietly, and with surprise the giant accepted. Unused to wine, he fell quickly into confusion, and laid himself unsteadily on the floor of the cave.

"Who are you, generous benefactor," he slurred, clutching at the goatskin.

"My name is No one," said Odysseus, a satisfied smile fleeting across his face.

"No one…" the giant repeated the name and slipped into a deep slumber, his snores jolting the men once more.

Odysseus leapt into action. Reaching for a heavy bough of olive-wood, he plunged in into the fire and moulded its end to a barbed point. He lifted it from the fire, and with every ounce of strength and versatility left in his depleted body, he thrust it into Polyphemus' single eye, and stepped back, out of harm's way.

The Cyclops' roar propelled him through the air, momentarily deafening him. The men shuddered in the corner, shrieking with terror as the giant fumbled wildly for his torturers, grunting and shrieking with the intense pain. Soon his friends came running, and when they enquired the nature of his troubles, he could only cry, "No one has blinded me" at which they returned, perplexed to their homes.

The morning came, cool and inviting, and hearing his sheep scrabbling at the door to get out to pasture, Polyphemus rose, and feeling along the walls, he found his boulder, and moved it. A smug look crossed his tortured features, and he stood outside the cave, his hands moving across the sheep as they left.

"You cannot leave this cave," he taunted. "You cannot escape me now." He giggled with mirth at his cleverness, but his smile faded to confusion and then anger when he realized that the sheep had exited, and the cave was now empty. The men were gone.

Odysseus and his men laughed out loud as they unstrapped themselves from the bellies of the sheep, and racing towards their ships, Odysseus called out, "Cyclops. It was not No one who blinded you. It was Odysseus of Ithaca," and with that he lifted their mooring and set out for sea.

The torment of the giant rose in a deluge of sound and fury, echoing across the island and wakening his friends. Tearing off slabs of the mountainside, Polyphemus hurled them towards the escaping voice, which continued to taunt him. He roared a prayer to his father Poseidon, begging for vengeance, and struggled across the grass towards the sea.

But Odysseus had left, his ship surging across the sea to join with the rest of the fleet. Odysseus had escaped once more, and the sea opened up to him and his men, and they continued homewards, unaware that Poseidon had heard the cries of his son, and had answered them. Vengeance would be his.

Scylla and Charybdis

CIRCE HAD WARNED ODYSSEUS of the dangers that would beset him and his crew should they choose to ignore the words of wise Tiresias. The next part of their journey would take them though a narrow strait, peopled by some of the most fearsome monsters in all the lands. Odysseus was to guide the ship through the narrow passage, through fierce and rolling waters, looking neither up nor down, embodying all humility.

But the pride of Odysseus was more deeply rooted than his fear, and ignoring Circe's words, he took a stand on the prow of his ship, heavily armoured and emboldened by the support of his men. Here he stood as they passed the rocks of Charybdis, the hateful daughter of Poseidon, who came to the surface three times each day in order to belch out a powerful whirlpool, drawing into her frothing gut all that came back with it. There was no sign of her now, the waters suspiciously stilled. Ahead lay an island, drenched in warm sunlight, beckoning to the weary sailors. They must just make it through.

Odysseus had kept the details of this fearsome strait from his men. They had been weakened by battle, and by the horrific sights which had met their eyes since leaving Troy. They were so close to Ithaca, he dared not cast their hopes and anticipation into shadow. And so it was that only Odysseus knew of the next monster who was to be thrust upon them in that dangerous channel, only Odysseus who knew that she was capable of tasks more gruesome than any of them had seen in all their travels.

For Scylla was a gluttonous and evil creature that haunted the strait, making her home in a gore-splattered den where she feasted on the remains of luckless sailors. She was, they said, a nymph who had been the object of Glaucus's attentions. Glaucus was a sea-god who had been turned into a merman by a strange herb he had unwittingly swallowed. And as much as he adored Scylla, so he was loved by Circe who, in a jealous rage, had turned Scylla into a terrible sea-monster with six dog's heads around her waist. She lived there in the cliff face in the straits of Messina, and devoured sailors who passed. She moved silently. Odysseus was loath to admit it, but the silent danger she represented placed more fear in his heart than the bravest of enemies.

Odysseus and his men passed further into the quiet strait, their mouths dry with fear. A silence hung over them like a shroud. And then it was broken by a tiny splash, and tinkle of water dripping, and up, with a mighty roar, came Scylla, the mouths on each head gaping open, their lethal jaws sprung for one purpose alone. Smoothly she leaned forward and in a flash of colour, of torn clothing and hellish screams, six of his best men were plucked from their posts aboard ship and drawn into the mouth of her cave. Their cries rent at the heart, at the conscience of Odysseus, and he turned helplessly to his remaining crew who looked at him with genuine fear, distrust and anger. A mutinous fever bubbled at the edges of their loyalty, and Odysseus knew he had lost them. He looked back at the cave where Scylla had silenced his hapless men, and signalled the others to row faster. A repeat of her attack would leave him with too few men to carry on. They rowed towards the shores of the great three-cornered island, Thrinacie, where the herds of the Sun-god Helius grazed peacefully on the hilltops.

The Wanderings

THE FIRST STOP ON JASON'S VOYAGE was the island of Lemnos, off the coast of Asia Minor. Lemnos was an island blighted by the gods. Aphrodite, annoyed by the womenfolk's lack of veneration, punished them by imbuing their bodies with a nauseating smell that repelled their husbands. The Lemnian men therefore started to turn to other women, stoking the fury of their neglected wives. Maddened with yearning and anger, the women of Lemnos killed all the male inhabitants of the islands, and lived on under the rule of their queen, Hypsipyle.

The Argonauts' stay at Lemnos would not be a short one. In return for the right to land, Hypsipyle made Jason promise that they would stay for some duration before departing. In the end, Lemnos was home to the warrior crew for a full year – all except Heracles and a small contingent of more disciplined men, who stayed on the Argo. The women, grateful for the male company, lauded the men with pageant and dance, fragrant sacrifices and exquisite foods. Days rolled into weeks, and weeks into months. Some of the warriors even had children with these women; Jason himself had two children with the queen. The Argo sat listlessly at its anchorage under an impassive sun, until Heracles expressed his wrath, and awakened the sense of purpose once more. Jason made his farewells to Hypsipyle, and soon the Argo was on its way east once more.

The experience on Lemnos had lapped at the Argonauts' moral strength. A test of physical and martial strength would face them at their next port of call, the Cyzicus peninsula. Here King Cyzicus of the Doliones welcomed them enthusiastically, but with his own hidden purpose. The Doliones were being terrorized by a tribe of fearsome six-armed giants, the Gegeines, who lived in the land beyond Bear Mountain. King Cyzicus evoked the physical delights of this land, while omitting to mention its earth-shaking inhabitants. Meanwhile, the Gegeines themselves – spurred by greed – had spotted the Argo at anchorage and plotted to raid her. At the moment when most of the crew were ashore, the Gegeines rushed down from the hillside, expecting easy plunder. What they found was the iron resistance and swift muscle of Heracles and a small group of other warriors, who fought the giants with no thought of the struggle being unequal. The Gegeines suffered grievously, many of them killed before the return of the rest of the Argo's crew put the survivors into rout.

Tragedy followed, however. Once the celebrations of victory had died down, Jason put his ship to sea once more, but night-time, smarting rain and capricious winds drove them back to Cyzicus. As they landed, the Doliones confused them with Pelasgian raiders, and fierce battle ensued. Their eyes seeing only a muted world of half shapes, Jason and the king fought a battle, in which Cyzicus was slain. When morning revealed a horror of sword-hewn bodies, and a dead king, the lamentations were compounded by the suicide of the king's daughter, who hanged herself in grief.

Angry storms kept the Argo at anchor until the gods were appeased, then the ship set sail once again, still far from Colchis. Fate then dealt another adverse hand, when Heracles broke an oar, his muscles greater in strength than the oak he gripped. The ship landed at Cius to find a replacement. Heracles' beloved servant Hylas here wandered off on his own, hoping to find water for the evening meal. He happened upon a pool which gave up no reflection when he faced its haunting surface. Instead, he saw the sensuous, floating grace of the water nymphs, creatures with a magnetizing beauty, bodies curving ceaselessly and effortlessly in the water. Hylas was never seen again, drawn down into the nymph's depthless world. Heracles, when he discovered the loss, was distraught, and left the Argo for good to search for Hylas. Jason had lost one of his stalwart warriors.

The events of the recent past focused Jason's thoughts on what might be to come. Thus he took the ship to Salmydessus in Thrace, seeking out the counsel of Phineus, king of Thrace and a seer of unmatched vision. Phineus had been blinded by an offended Zeus, and his misery was multiplied tenfold by the shrill visitations of the Harpies, winged monsters with the head of a haggard woman and the body of a decrepit, razor-clawed bird. Sickening, stinking creatures, the Harpies would prey on Phineus every time he tried to eat, snatching or defiling his food. Half-starved, Phineus pleaded with the Argonauts to help, and they succeeding in freeing him from this torture. Phineus, in his gratitude, told Jason how to pass through the Symplegades ('Clashing Rocks').

The Symplegades were, since the foundation of the Earth, granite guardians at the entrance to the Black Sea. To prevent passage through the straits, these towering rocks, opposing one another, would snap shut in a split second rush, accompanied by a sonorous crack and a tsunami-like displacement of water. Even swift-swimming sea creatures such as dolphins could not always escape the vice-like rocks, and many ships were splintered to destruction. Phineus suggested that Jason release a dove as he approached the rocks; the Symplegades would snap shut on the bird, then the Argo could pass through as they reopened.

It remained to be seen whether Phineus's vision would work in practice. The crew sat in cold fear under the shadow of the rocks as the dove was released. With explosive force, the Symplegades smashed their faces together, just nipping out the tail feathers of the dove as it passed through. Now was the Argo's chance, yet the swelling waves pushed the ship back, delaying its movement forward for crucial seconds. As the Argo moved into the kill zone, the Symplegades towered above them like hammers of death, and a rumbling signalled their imminent crushing movement. Seeing disaster unfold, the goddess Athene herself intervened, holding back one of the rocks with her left hand, while pushing the Argo through the straits. Even the strength of a goddess eventually gave way to the clashing rocks; they smashed together with a roar that seemed to shatter heaven, clipping off the tip of the Argo's stern – but the ship was safe.

The now-weary crew pushed on towards Colchis, enduring further challenges. On the way, their spirits were chilled by the screams of Prometheus, the Titan sentenced to punishment by Zeus. His agony was to be tied to a rock, and each day a mighty eagle would swoop in to tear open his belly and feast on his liver. Prometheus, body arched in torment, back scraped on the sun-bleached coastal rock, did not die; his liver reformed after each ordeal, only to be gouged from him again the next day, and every day thereafter. Near the Caucasian mountains, the Argonauts saw the rush of wind from the eagle's wings billow the sails, and heard its wing beat disturb the air above the clouds. Then came the dire screams of Prometheus, as he experienced his daily torture. Slowly the cries faded into the distance, and the Argo eventually came to its destination. Colchis drew into view and the anchor thumped into the still coastal waters. The Golden Fleece was now the goal.

How the Centaur Trained the Heroes on Pelion

HERE FOLLOWS a tale of heroes who sailed away into a distant land, to win themselves renown forever, in the adventure of the Golden Fleece.

And what was that first Golden Fleece? The old Hellens said that it hung in Colchis, which we call the Circassian coast, nailed to a beech-tree in the war-God's wood; and that it was the fleece of the wondrous ram who bore Phrixus and Helle across the Euxine sea. For Phrixus and Helle were the children of the cloud-nymph, and of Athamas the Minuan king. And when a famine came upon the land, their cruel step-mother Ino wished to kill them, that her own children might reign, and said that they must be sacrificed on an altar, to turn away the anger of the Gods. So the poor children were brought to the altar, and the priest stood ready with his knife, when out of the clouds came the Golden Ram, and took them on his back, and vanished. Then madness came upon that foolish king, Athamas, and ruin upon Ino and her children. For Athamas killed one of them in his fury, and Ino fled from him with the other in her arms, and leaped from a cliff into the sea, and was changed into a dolphin, such as you have seen, which wanders over the waves for ever sighing, with its little one clasped to its breast.

But the people drove out King Athamas, because he had killed his child; and he roamed about in his misery, till he came to the Oracle in Delphi. And the Oracle told him that he must wander for his sin, till the wild beasts should feast him as their guest. So he went on in hunger and sorrow for many a weary day, till he saw a pack of wolves. The wolves were tearing a sheep; but when they saw Athamas they fled, and left the sheep for him, and he ate of it; and then he knew that the oracle was fulfilled at last. So he wandered no more; but settled, and built a town, and became a king again.

But the ram carried the two children far away over land and sea, till he came to the Thracian Chersonese, and there Helle fell into the sea. So those narrow straits are called 'Hellespont,' after her; and they bear that name until this day.

Then the ram flew on with Phrixus to the north-east across the sea which we call the Black Sea now; but the Hellens call it Euxine. And at last, they say, he stopped at Colchis, on the steep Circassian coast; and there Phrixus married Chalciope, the daughter of Aeetes the king; and offered the ram in sacrifice; and Aeetes nailed the ram's fleece to a beech, in the grove of Ares the war-God.

And after awhile Phrixus died, and was buried, but his spirit had no rest; for he was buried far from his native land, and the pleasant hills of Hellas. So he came in dreams to the heroes of the Minuai, and called sadly by their beds, "Come and set my spirit free, that I may go home to my fathers and to my kinsfolk, and the pleasant Minuan land."

And they asked, "How shall we set your spirit free?"

"You must sail over the sea to Colchis, and bring home the golden fleece; and then my spirit will come back with it, and I shall sleep with my fathers and have rest."

He came thus, and called to them often; but when they woke they looked at each other, and said, "Who dare sail to Colchis, or bring home the golden fleece?"

And in all the country none was brave enough to try it; for the man and the time were not come.

Phrixus had a cousin called Aeson, who was king in Iolcos by the sea. There he ruled over the rich Minuan heroes, as Athamas his uncle ruled in Boeotia; and, like Athamas, he was an unhappy man. For he had a step-brother named Pelias, of whom some said that he was a nymph's son, and there were dark and sad tales about his birth. When he was a babe he was cast out on the mountains, and a wild mare came by and kicked him. But a shepherd passing found the baby, with its face all blackened by the blow; and took him home, and called him Pelias, because his face was bruised and black. And he grew up fierce and lawless, and did many a fearful deed; and at last he drove out Aeson his step-brother, and then his own brother Neleus, and took the kingdom to himself, and ruled over the rich Minuan heroes, in Iolcos by the sea.

And Aeson, when he was driven out, went sadly away out of the town, leading his little son by the hand; and he said to himself, "I must hide the child in the mountains; or Pelias will surely kill him, because he is the heir."

So he went up from the sea across the valley, through the vineyards and the olive groves, and across the torrent of Anauros, toward Pelion the ancient mountain, whose brows are white with snow.

He went up and up into the mountain, over marsh, and crag, and down, till the boy was tired and footsore, and Aeson had to bear him in his arms, till he came to the mouth of a lonely cave, at the foot of a mighty cliff.

Above the cliff the snow-wreaths hung, dripping and cracking in the sun; but at its foot around the cave's mouth grew all fair flowers and herbs, as if in a garden, ranged in order, each sort by itself. There they grew gaily in the sunshine, and the spray of the torrent from above; while from the cave came the sound of music, and a man's voice singing to the harp.

Then Aeson put down the lad, and whispered:

"Fear not, but go in, and whomsoever you shall find, lay your hands upon his knees, and say, 'In the name of Zeus, the father of Gods and men, I am your guest from this day forth.'"

Then the lad went in without trembling, for he too was a hero's son; but when he was within, he stopped in wonder to listen to that magic song.

And there he saw the singer lying upon bear-skins and fragrant boughs: Cheiron, the ancient centaur, the wisest of all things beneath the sky. Down to the waist he was a man, but below he was a noble horse; his white hair rolled down over his broad shoulders, and his white beard over his broad brown chest; and his eyes were wise and mild, and his forehead like a mountain-wall.

And in his hands he held a harp of gold, and struck it with a golden key; and as he struck, he sang till his eyes glittered, and filled all the cave with light.

And he sang of the birth of Time, and of the heavens and the dancing stars; and of the ocean, and the ether, and the fire, and the shaping of the wondrous earth. And he sang of the treasures of the hills, and the hidden jewels of the mine, and the veins of fire and metal, and the virtues of all healing herbs, and of the speech of birds, and of prophecy, and of hidden things to come.

Then he sang of health, and strength, and manhood, and a valiant heart; and of music, and hunting, and wrestling, and all the games which heroes love: and of travel, and wars, and sieges, and a noble death in fight; and then he sang of peace and plenty, and of equal justice in the land; and as he sang the boy listened wide-eyed, and forgot his errand in the song.

And at the last old Cheiron was silent, and called the lad with a soft voice.

And the lad ran trembling to him, and would have laid his hands upon his knees; but Cheiron smiled, and said, "Call hither your father Aeson, for I know you, and all that has befallen, and saw you both afar in the valley, even before you left the town."

Then Aeson came in sadly, and Cheiron asked him, "Why camest you not yourself to me, Aeson the Aeolid?"

And Aeson said:

"I thought, Cheiron will pity the lad if he sees him come alone; and I wished to try whether he was fearless, and dare venture like a hero's son. But now I entreat you by Father Zeus, let the boy be your guest till better times, and train him among the sons of the heroes, that he may avenge his father's house."

Then Cheiron smiled, and drew the lad to him, and laid his hand upon his golden locks, and said, "Are you afraid of my horse's hoofs, fair boy, or will you be my pupil from this day?"

"I would gladly have horse's hoofs like you, if I could sing such songs as yours."

And Cheiron laughed, and said, "Sit here by me till sundown, when your playfellows will come home, and you shall learn like them to be a king, worthy to rule over gallant men."

Then he turned to Aeson, and said, "Go back in peace, and bend before the storm like a prudent man. This boy shall not cross the Anauros again, till he has become a glory to you and to the house of Aeolus."

And Aeson wept over his son and went away; but the boy did not weep, so full was his fancy of that strange cave, and the centaur, and his song, and the playfellows whom he was to see.

Then Cheiron put the lyre into his hands, and taught him how to play it, till the sun sank low behind the cliff, and a shout was heard outside.

And then in came the sons of the heroes, Aeneas, and Heracles, and Peleus, and many another mighty name.

And great Cheiron leapt up joyfully, and his hoofs made the cave resound, as they shouted, "Come out, Father Cheiron; come out and see our game."

And one cried, "I have killed two deer;" and another, "I took a wild cat among the crags;" and Heracles dragged a wild goat after him by its horns, for he was as huge as a mountain crag; and

Coeneus carried a bear-cub under each arm, and laughed when they scratched and bit, for neither tooth nor steel could wound him.

And Cheiron praised them all, each according to his deserts.

Only one walked apart and silent, Asclepius, the too-wise child, with his bosom full of herbs and flowers, and round his wrist a spotted snake; he came with downcast eyes to Cheiron, and whispered how he had watched the snake cast its old skin, and grow young again before his eyes, and how he had gone down into a village in the vale, and cured a dying man with a herb which he had seen a sick goat eat.

And Cheiron smiled, and said, "To each Athene and Apollo give some gift, and each is worthy in his place; but to this child they have given an honour beyond all honours, to cure while others kill."

Then the lads brought in wood, and split it, and lighted a blazing fire; and others skinned the deer and quartered them, and set them to roast before the fire; and while the venison was cooking they bathed in the snow-torrent, and washed away the dust and sweat.

And then all ate till they could eat no more (for they had tasted nothing since the dawn), and drank of the clear spring water, for wine is not fit for growing lads. And when the remnants were put away, they all lay down upon the skins and leaves about the fire, and each took the lyre in turn, and sang and played with all his heart.

And after a while they all went out to a plot of grass at the cave's mouth, and there they boxed, and ran, and wrestled, and laughed till the stones fell from the cliffs.

Then Cheiron took his lyre, and all the lads joined hands; and as be played, they danced to his measure, in and out, and round and round. There they danced hand in hand, till the night fell over land and sea, while the black glen shone with their broad white limbs and the gleam of their golden hair.

And the lad danced with them, delighted, and then slept a wholesome sleep, upon fragrant leaves of bay, and myrtle, and marjoram, and flowers of thyme; and rose at the dawn, and bathed in the torrent, and became a schoolfellow to the heroes' sons, and forgot Iolcos, and his father, and all his former life. But he grew strong, and brave and cunning, upon the pleasant downs of Pelion, in the keen hungry mountain air. And he learnt to wrestle, and to box, and to hunt, and to play upon the harp; and next he learnt to ride, for old Cheiron used to mount him on his back; and he learnt the virtues of all herbs and how to cure all wounds; and Cheiron called him Jason the healer, and that is his name until this day.

The Twelve Labours of Heracles

SON OF ZEUS, father of the Greek Gods, and Alcmene, a human, Heracles was born a mortal who could feel pain, but was possessed with immense strength, courage and intelligence; a man who bridged the gap between mortals and gods. As such, tales of his extraordinary life are legendary and his twelve labours rank as the most incredible of all. As penance for the murder of his children in a fit of insanity brought on by Hera – Zeus's queen who was jealous of Heracles – Heracles was forced to serve his cousin, the spiteful and cowardly King Eurystheus of Argos, for 12 years, performing any tasks that were asked of him, no matter how deadly and perilous. If Heracles could do this, his soul would be purified and he would earn immortality.

The Nemean Lion

Heracles' first task was to defeat the ferocious lion of Nemea and bring its skin – invulnerable to weapons – back to Eurystheus. The formidable lion terrorized the village and seized its inhabitants to feast upon at will. Armed with a bow and arrow, sword of bronze and his beloved club, which he had fashioned from an olive tree that he uprooted and tore apart, Heracles threw himself into his first labour with vigour, never one to turn away from a challenge.

Tracking the lion to its cave, Heracles shot at his prey with his bow, but the arrows just bounced off its impenetrable skin. Trying a different tactic, Heracles waited until the lion retreated into its cave, then blocked off one of the entrances, leaving only one. Bravely entering the cave, armed with his club, he felt his way through the darkness, managing to stun the lion with one almighty blow. Heracles then vanquished the powerful lion by throttling it with his bare hands.

But his quest was not yet concluded. Try as he might, Heracles could not remove the precious skin from the lion. His blade proved useless, as did the sharp stones on the cave's floor. It was not until Athene, the goddess of inspiration and invention, told him to use the lion's own claws that he was able to remove the skin.

Heracles returned to Argos to present the lion skin to Eurystheus, who was astonished that Heracles had defeated the beast. Entering the palace with the lion skin slung over his person, its head protecting his own, Heracles struck terror into the timorous heart of Eurystheus. From then on, Eurystheus took care not to underestimate his illustrious cousin, even having a huge bronze jar built, in which to hide from the indomitable hero.

The Lernaean Hydra

For his second task, Heracles had to defeat the dreaded hydra, a creature made by Hera to rid herself from him once and for all. The multi-headed monster dwelled deep in the swamps of Lerna, from which it would rise up and attack the villagers. Heracles travelled to Lerna with his nephew and charioteer, Iolaus. He used flaming arrows to lure the monster out into the open, hoping to lessen the effects of its poisonous breath.

Heracles then set about attacking its heads with his mighty club and hacking them off with his sword. But his efforts were to no avail. Every time he succeeded in removing one head, two more would grow in its place. Again and again Heracles attacked, hoping that the hydra's regenerative powers would fail, but even his great strength began to wane. The hydra had wrapped itself around his body, slowly crushing his bones, while its merciless heads kept on attacking him.

But Heracles was not defeated. Summoning up his remaining strength, he called for his nephew's aid, tasking him with cauterizing the bloody stump of every head he could sever. Summoning up his courage, Iolaus did as Heracles commanded and one by one the heads fell, with nothing able to grow in their place. Soon, the hydra was left with only one head; the immortal head. Using the bronze sword given to him by Athene, Heracles lopped off the head in a single vigorous strike. The monster was defeated. Taking no chances, Heracles buried the immortal head under a giant rock.

He then dipped the tips of his arrows into the hydra's venomous blood, making them poisonous. Because Heracles had only defeated the Hydra with Iolaus' assistance, Eurystheus stated that this task did not count.

The Ceryneian Hind

With two labours completed, Eurystheus and Hera – who had been scrutinizing Heracles' progress – realized that not even a monster was capable of defeating the warrior. They devised a new undertaking that would be even more onerous. Heracles was tasked with catching the Ceryneian hind, a female deer. Sometimes known as a stag because of its golden antlers, the nimble creature also had bronze hooves and could run faster than an arrow in flight. Eurystheus had made the task even more deadly by choosing the pet creature of Artemis, the goddess of the hunt. Even if Heracles did manage to capture the hind, Artemis would likely take vengeance on him for harming her beloved animal.

Heracles gave chase for one whole year, yet the hind never tired. Along the banks of the river Ladon in Arcadia, as the hind slowed to take drink from the cooling waters, Heracles managed to bring it down with an arrow fired between its forelegs, causing the hind to falter and stumble without drawing blood. This way, Heracles captured the fleet-footed beast without provoking the anger of Artemis.

Heracles bound the animal, then explained to Artemis that he had been forced into this ill-treatment as one of his labours. She graciously forgave his impudence and allowed him to leave unharmed as long as he promised to return the treasured hind.

Taking the prize to Eurystheus, Heracles kept his bargain with Artemis by telling Eurystheus that he needed to take the hind from him with his own hands. Reluctantly, Eurystheus emerged from the safety of his palace to see the fabled Ceryneian hind for himself. Reaching for it eagerly, just before he could grasp her fur, Heracles let go and she raced back to Artemis, escaping with ease.

The Eurymanthian Boar

Travelling through the mountains to capture the Eurymanthian boar for Eurystheus, Heracles took respite with his old friend Pholus, the centaur. Over a shared meal, Heracles asked for wine. Pholus reluctantly opened a jar, which had been a present from Dionysus, the god of wine, meant for all the centaurs. This attracted the other centaurs – proud and noble creatures – who were angry that their gift had been dishonoured and drank. In a frenzied rage, they attacked Heracles. Heracles defended himself with his bow and arrows, which, coated in the hydra's venom, caused many deaths.

Chiron, a centaur who had tutored Heracles, was wounded in the fray. Pholus, curious as to why the arrows had caused such devastation, picked one up to inspect it. It slipped from his hand and pierced his foot, letting in the deadly venom that killed him.

Heavy at heart at the loss of his friend and the difficult task ahead, Heracles continued his quest. Reaching the mountains, he began tracking and chasing his quarry. Following Chiron's advice about trapping the boar, Heracles drove it into a heavy snow drift. He then trapped the wildly struggling boar in a net, tied it snugly, threw it over his shoulder and carried it back to Eurystheus, freeing the villagers from the constant terror the brutal boar had caused. Eurystheus cowered in fear in the bronze jar, increasingly awed by the resilience and courage of his cousin.

The Augean Stables

Concocting an even more arduous task for Heracles, Eurystheus now determined to defeat and humiliate the hero in one repugnant labour. King Augeas of Elis owned massive stables filled with immortal cattle, which had not been cleaned for over thirty years. It was Heracles' task to clean out the stables and he only had one day to do it. Eurystheus was convinced that even the stupendous strength of Heracles was not up to this insurmountable task.

But he did not reckon with Heracles' wisdom. Heracles went to King Augeas and offered to clean his stables in a single day if Augeas would give him one-tenth of the herd as payment. The king readily agreed, believing the task to be impossible. Heracles then headed for the stables. There, he tore great holes in two facing walls of the stables. Digging trenches leading directly to these holes, he redirected the course of two rivers – the Alpheus and the Peneus – straight through the stable, where the rapid flow of water surged through, washing away all the muck and dirt that had built up over thirty years.

Astounded that Heracles had managed his task, Augeas refused to honour their agreement, saying that he never promised Heracles any reward. Heracles responded in anger and pledged to take what was owed to him. Augeas' son, Phyleus, interceded and settled the matter between them. This was the second task that Eurystheus refused to count, saying that Heracles had used the river to do the work and been well paid for his labours.

The Stymphalian Birds

For his sixth task, Heracles was pitted against the ferocious Stymphalian birds. A huge flock of the diabolical fowl had gathered at a lake near Stymphalos, where they were quickly breeding, causing despair and death to the countryside and population. The birds would devour anything – including human flesh – and were able to attack their prey by shooting razor-sharp brass feathers at them. Their beaks were made of bronze and could easily peck right through flesh. Heracles was vastly outnumbered and, to make matters worse, he could not get near enough to the birds to harm them. The swampy lake would not bear his weight and if he tried to force his way through it, he would sink and drown.

Athene, who watched over Heracles, had been observing him try to reach the vile birds. Pledging her assistance, she gave Heracles a pair of clappers made from bronze. These noisemakers had been forged by Hephaistos and, when Heracles shook them, they created a terrible, deafening din that shocked the birds and made them take flight from their impregnable roost. Taking advantage of their fear and confusion, Heracles began to shoot them down with his trusty bow. He dispatched dozens of the creatures and those remaining bolted in terror, never to return. The town was safe and Heracles was now half way through his labours. The menacing birds would later torment the brave souls accompanying Jason and his Argonauts.

The Cretan Bull

Minos, the King of Crete, was a powerful and tyrannical ruler who wanted to secure his throne with the help of the gods. He had made a promise to Poseidon that he would sacrifice anything the god sent him from the sea. However, when Poseidon sent a handsome snow-white bull, Minos killed another in its place because he was awed by the strength and savagery of Poseidon's bull. Furious that a mere mortal would try to deceive him, Poseidon made Minos' wife, Queen Pasiphae, fall in love with the bull. She later sired the Minotaur, a monster with the head of a bull and the body of a man. This monstrous being had to be trapped within a maze known as the Labyrinth where it could wander forever without finding his way out.

Poseidon's massive bull also needed controlling, rampaging across Crete, leaving a wake of death and destruction wherever it went. When Heracles arrived to capture the bull, Minos was delighted. He even offered help, but Heracles refused, knowing he had to entrap the east alone. This he did quite easily, by tracking the bull, then wrapping his unyielding arms around its gigantic neck and, slowly but surely, squeezing until it surrendered. Heracles then tethered the bull securely around its neck and rode the creature back to Eurystheus. Having no idea what to do with the ferocious beast, Eurystheus released the bull, where it roamed around Greece, continuing to terrorize people until Theseus, another hero and acolyte of Heracles, caught up to the bull in Marathon. He killed the satanic swine, offering it as a sacrifice to the gods and ridding Greece from the chaos it provoked. Theseus – himself a demi-god sired by Poseidon and a human woman – would later prove his own strength when he subdued the Minotaur.

The Mares of Diomedes

With Heracles now on his eighth labour, Eurystheus was concerned that he would never outfox the great warrior. For his next diabolical trial, Heracles was set the task of stealing the mares of Diomedes, the King of Thrace. Diomedes was a savage giant, who ruled a sadistic tribe of warriors called the Bistones. The perverse King kept his four mares chained to a manger of bronze and fed them an unnatural diet of human flesh, from unwitting travellers to the region. The barbarous mares had to be safely tethered, as they had been driven mad by their diet, needing more and more flesh to keep them satiated.

Heracles travelled to Thrace with a band of followers to plunder the mares for Eurystheus. In the midst of dispatching the grooms who fed the horses, Heracles' men were set upon by the Bistones. One of Heracles' followers, a youth named Abderos, was left to watch the mares while Heracles and his men crushed their attackers. But Abderos was no match for the frenzied violence of the horses and, on Heracles' return, he found only pieces of his dear friend remained. Devastated at the loss of Abderos, Heracles sought bloody vengeance. The warrior met and fought Diomedes, who was a powerful warrior and as untamed as his mares. Despite his ferocity, he was no match for Heracles, who annihilated his foe. Still mourning Abderos, Heracles then fed Diomedes to his own mares. The flesh of their master satisfied their blood-lust and Heracles was able to take them back to Argos. Even though they were much calmer, Eurystheus feared the feral horses. Set free, they roamed Greece until reaching Mount Olympus, where they were savaged by wild beasts, Zeus having rejected the sacrifice of their unholy flesh.

Hippolyte's Belt

For his ninth task, Heracles was set the challenge of retrieving the belt of Hippolyte, Queen of the Amazons. This race of female warriors, who had invented and perfected the art of fighting on horseback, were renowned for their bravery and fighting skills. Hippolyte was the strongest and bravest of all the Amazons. For this, Ares, the god of war, awarded her with a leather belt, believed to give power to its wearer. Hippolyte wore this belt to carry her weapons. Eurystheus wanted the belt for his daughter, Admete, who had always coveted it.

Taking his followers – including Theseus – Heracles travelled to the land of the Amazons, deep in the Caucasus mountains, to bring back the fabled belt for Admete. When the ship docked, Hippolyte herself came down the mountain to meet the famous band of champions. Heracles explained why they had come and that he was under oath to complete his tasks. Hippolyte, who had been swayed by many tales of Heracles' strength and prowess in battle, said that she would gladly give her belt to him so that he could complete his tasks.

But the ever-vengeful Hera, who was dismayed that Heracles would not have to do battle for the belt, manipulated the Amazons into believing that the strangers intended to carry off their

Queen. Furious at the deception, the Amazons laid siege to Heracles and his men. A mighty battle erupted, ending only when Heracles struck the killing blow to Hippolyte and took her belt. In some versions, it was Theseus who subdued the great Amazon Queen, carrying her off and marrying her just as Hera prophesised. Heracles returned to Argo and gave the enchanted belt to Eurystheus for his daughter, fulfilling yet another of his legendary labours.

The Cattle of Geryon

To bring back the cattle of Geryon was Heracles' next endeavour. Geryon was a giant monster with three heads and three sets of arms and legs. He was also a fearsome warrior. His cattle were renowned and Eurystheus thought that he had finally given Heracles an unmanageable task, as stealing them would be hard enough, but herding them all the way back to Argos was nigh on impossible.

Undaunted, Heracles set off for Erythia, passing through the desert of Libya on the way. It was here, frustrated by the intense, relentless heat, that Heracles discharged an arrow from his bow directly into Helios, the Sun god. Helios was impressed by Heracles' valour and presented him with use of the golden cup in which he sailed every night across the sea to his home in the east. Heracles used this cup to sail to Erythia. As soon as he landed, he was brutally attacked by Orthrus, Geryon's vicious two-headed dog who guarded the famous cattle. With but one glorious swing of his club, Heracles killed Orthrus and then dispatched Eurytion, the herdsman, in the same way.

But the odious Geryon would not be so easily quelled. Roaring with rage, he flew at Heracles. The two fought evenly until Heracles shot Geryon through one of his heads with his venomous arrows. After that, it was relatively easy to take the cattle, and head back to Argos. It was only when the vindictive Hera sent a gadfly to irritate the herd, causing them to scatter in every direction, that Heracles encountered any trouble. So fast and so numerous was the herd that it took Heracles the best part of a year to track them down. Next, Hera caused a flood to overfill a river, meaning that there was no way for the cattle to cross. Again, Heracles bested her, filling the river with stones so that the cattle could walk across without being swept away. In a galling put down to all his efforts, when Heracles successfully brought the herd before Eurystheus, he sacrificed them to the spiteful Hera.

The Apples of the Hesperides

Now nearing the end of his labours, Eurystheus had devised what he felt sure was an impossible task. Heracles was to fetch him the golden apples that Gaia, the earth mother, had given to Hera and Zeus on their wedding day. They were safely hidden in a garden under the guard of a fierce dragon called Ladon and the Hesperides, the nymph daughters of Atlas. One of the last Titans, Atlas, had been condemned by Zeus to forever hold up the heavens on his shoulders.

Heracles headed west in search of the garden, his quest taking him through most of Greece. On the way, he killed the abhorrent eagle that tormented Prometheus by daily tearing out his liver. In gratitude, Prometheus related to Heracles that Atlas was the only person who could successfully retrieve the apples. Heracles eventually found the garden by forcing Nereus, the shape-shifting old man of the sea, to reveal its location by holding him in a vice-like grip, no matter what he turned himself into.

To convince Atlas to help him, Heracles acquiesced to shoulder his burden, of which Atlas had grown deathly weary of carrying. Instantly agreeing to help, Atlas easily retrieved the apples from his daughters. However, on his return, Atlas decided he did not want to take back his burden.

Heracles was trapped with the heavens on his shoulders and no way of freeing himself. Just as Atlas was taking his leave, Heracles asked the titan if he would temporarily take back the world while Heracles made himself more comfortable. Agreeing, Atlas set down the apples and took back the heavens, only for Heracles to abandon him to his burden.

Returning to Argos, Heracles presented the stunned King with the apples. Being the property of the gods, Heracles eventually had to return the apples to Athene, who replaced them in the garden. This labour is sometimes known as Heracles' last, but he still had one final challenge to fulfill before gaining immortality and the peace he so dearly craved.

Cerberus

For his final labour, Heracles was set his most hazardous challenge by far, which would send him into the Underworld itself to bring Cerberus, the hound of hell, back to Eurystheus alive. Cerberus was a demonic three-headed dog with writhing, hissing snakes as his tail who guarded the gates of Hades. Even entering the Underworld was a task of extreme bravery, as no one who did so had ever escaped alive. Heracles first went to Eleusis, where he was initiated into the Eleusinian Mysteries. Their sacred ceremonies would enable him to travel safely through – and out of – the afterlife.

Heracles then entered the gates of Hades, escorted by Athene and Hermes, the god of boundaries. Before he could reach Cerberus, Heracles had to cross the River Styx. Charon, the ferryman, demanded payment from every passenger: a coin placed in the dead person's mouth. He would also only carry those who were dead. Heracles could meet neither request, but by the sheer force of his anger, Charon relented and rowed Heracles deep into the Underworld to meet the King, Hades.

Hades agreed that Heracles could take Cerberus to Eurystheus, but only on the condition that he overpowered the massive hound without the use of his weapons. Heracles duly surrendered his trusty bow, sword and club, which had been with him since the start of his labours and, unarmed, headed onwards to claim his prize. When Heracles cornered Cerberus by the River Aucheron, he overpowered the beast by wrestling it until it surrendered. Heracles then bound and dragged Cerberus out of Hades, presenting him to Eurystheus.

Finally outdone, Eurystheus fled in terror at the sight of the monstrous hound, begging Heracles to return Cerberus to the Underworld. In return, Eurystheus released Heracles from his service, earning him immortality and freedom.

The Phœnix

IN FORMER TIMES, when hardly anybody thought of travelling for pleasure, and there were no Zoological Gardens to teach us what foreign animals and birds were really like, men used to tell each other stories about all sorts of strange creatures that lived in distant lands. Sometimes these tales were brought by the travellers themselves, who loved to excite the wonder of their friends at home, and knew there was nobody to contradict them. Sometimes they may have been invented by people to amuse their children; but, anyway, the old books are full of descriptions of birds and beasts very interesting to read about.

One of the most famous of these was the Phœnix, a bird whose plumage was, according to one writer, "partly red and partly golden," while its size was "almost exactly that of the eagle." Once in five hundred years it "comes out of Arabia," says one old writer, "all the way to Egypt, bringing the parent bird, plastered over with myrrh, to the Temple of the Sun (in the city of Heliopolis), and then buries the body. In order to bring the body, they say, it first forms a ball of myrrh as big as it can carry, puts the parent inside, and covers the opening with fresh myrrh; the ball is then exactly the same weight as at first; thus it brings the body to Egypt, plastered over as I have said, and deposits it in the Temple of the Sun." This is all that the writer we have been quoting seems to know about the Phœnix; but we are told by someone else that its song was "more beautiful than that of any other bird," and that it was "a very king of the feathered tribes, who followed it in fear, while it flew swiftly along, rejoicing as a bull in its strength." Flashing its brilliant plumage in the sun, it went its way till it reached the town of Heliopolis. "In that city," says another writer, whose account is not quite the same as the story told by the first, "there is a temple made round, after the shape of the Temple at Jerusalem. The priests of that temple date their writings from the visits of the Phœnix, of which there is but one in all the world. And he cometh to burn himself upon the altar of the temple at the end of five hundred years, for so long he liveth. At the end of that time the priests dress up their altar, and put upon it spices and sulphur, and other things that burn easily. Then the bird Phœnix cometh and burneth himself to ashes. And the first day after men find in the ashes a worm, and on the second day they find a bird, alive and perfect, and on the third day the bird flieth away. He hath a crest of feathers upon his head larger than the peacock hath, his neck is yellow and his beak is blue; his wings are of purple colours, and his tail yellow and red in stripes across. A fair bird he is to look upon when you see him against the sun, for he shineth full gloriously and nobly."

It is very hard to believe that the man who wrote this had not actually seen this beautiful creature, he seems to know it so well, and perhaps sometimes he really fancied that one day it had dazzled his eyes as it darted by. The Phœnix was a living bird to old travellers and those to whom they told their stories, although they are not quite agreed about its habits, or even about the manner of its death. Sometimes, as we have seen, the Phoenix has a father, sometimes there is only one bird. In general it burns itself on a spice-covered altar; but, according to one writer, when its five hundred years of life are over it dashes itself on the ground, and from its blood a new bird is born. At first it is small and helpless, like any other young thing; but soon its wings begin to show, and in a few days they are strong enough to carry the parent to the city of Heliopolis, where, at sunrise, it dies. The new Phœnix then flies back home, where it builds a nest of sweet spices – cassia, spikenard and cinnamon; and the food that it loves is another spice, drops of frankincense.

The Gorgon's Head

PERSEUS WAS THE SON OF DANAE, who was the daughter of a king. And when Perseus was a very little boy, some wicked people put his mother and himself into a chest, and set them afloat upon the sea. The wind blew freshly, and drove the chest away from the shore, and the uneasy billows tossed it up and down; while Danae clasped her child closely to her bosom, and dreaded that some big wave would dash its foamy crest over them both. The chest sailed on, however, and neither sank nor was upset; until, when night was coming, it floated so near an island that it got entangled in a fisherman's nets, and was drawn out high and dry upon the sand. The island was called Seriphus, and it was reigned over by King Polydectes, who happened to be the fisherman's brother.

This fisherman, I am glad to tell you, was an exceedingly humane and upright man. He showed great kindness to Danae and her little boy; and continued to befriend them, until Perseus had grown to be a handsome youth, very strong and active, and skilful in the use of arms. Long before this time, King Polydectes had seen the two strangers – the mother and her child – who had come to his dominions in a floating chest. As he was not good and kind, like his brother the fisherman, but extremely wicked, he resolved to send Perseus on a dangerous enterprise, in which he would probably be killed, and then to do some great mischief to Danae herself. So this bad-hearted king spent a long while in considering what was the most dangerous thing that a young man could possibly undertake to perform. At last, having hit upon an enterprise that promised to turn out as fatally as he desired, he sent for the youthful Perseus.

The young man came to the palace, and found the king sitting upon his throne.

"Perseus," said King Polydectes, smiling craftily upon him, "you are grown up a fine young man. You and your good mother have received a great deal of kindness from myself, as well as from my worthy brother the fisherman, and I suppose you would not be sorry to repay some of it."

"Please your Majesty," answered Perseus, "I would willingly risk my life to do so."

"Well, then," continued the king, still with a curving smile on his lips, "I have a little adventure to propose to you; and, as you are a brave and enterprising youth, you will doubtless look upon it as a great piece of good luck to have so rare an opportunity of distinguishing yourself. You must know, my good Perseus, I think of getting married to the beautiful Princess Hippodamia; and it is customary, on these occasions, to make the bride a present of some far-fetched and elegant curiosity. I have been a little perplexed, I must honestly confess, where to obtain anything likely to please a princess of her exquisite taste. But, this morning, I flatter myself, I have thought of precisely the article."

"And can I assist your Majesty in obtaining it?" cried Perseus, eagerly.

"You can, if you are as brave a youth as I believe you to be," replied King Polydectes, with the utmost graciousness of manner. "The bridal gift which I have set my heart on presenting to the beautiful Hippodamia is the head of the Gorgon Medusa, with the snaky locks; and I depend on you, my dear Perseus, to bring it to me. So, as I am anxious to settle affairs with the princess, the sooner you go in quest of the Gorgon, the better I shall be pleased."

"I will set out to-morrow morning," answered Perseus.

"Pray do so, my gallant youth," rejoined the king. "And, Perseus, in cutting off the Gorgon's head, be careful to make a clean stroke, so as not to injure its appearance. You must bring it home in the very best condition, in order to suit the exquisite taste of the beautiful Princess Hippodamia."

Perseus left the palace, but was scarcely out of hearing before Polydectes burst into a laugh; being greatly amused, wicked king that he was, to find how readily the young man fell into the snare. The news quickly spread abroad, that Perseus had undertaken to cut off the head of Medusa with the snaky locks. Everybody was rejoiced; for most of the inhabitants of the island were as wicked as the king himself, and would have liked nothing better than to see some enormous mischief happen to Danae and her son. The only good man in this unfortunate island of Seriphus appears to have been the fisherman. As Perseus walked along, therefore, the people pointed after him, and made mouths, and winked to one another, and ridiculed him as loudly as they dared.

"Ho, ho!" cried they; "Medusa's snakes will sting him soundly!"

Now, there were three Gorgons alive, at that period; and they were the most strange and terrible monsters that had ever been since the world was made, or that have been seen in after days, or that are likely to be seen in all time to come. I hardly know what sort of creature or hobgoblin to call them. They were three sisters, and seem to have borne some distant resemblance to women, but were really a very frightful and mischievous species of dragon. It is, indeed, difficult to imagine what hideous beings these three sisters were. Why, instead of locks of hair, if you can believe me, they had each of them a hundred enormous snakes growing on their heads, all alive, twisting, wriggling, curling, and thrusting out their venomous' tongues, with forked stings at the end! The teeth of the Gorgons were terribly long tusks; their hands were made of brass; and their bodies were all over scales, which, if not iron, were something as hard and impenetrable. They had wings, too, and exceedingly splendid ones, I can assure you; for every feather in them was pure, bright, glittering, burnished gold, and they looked very dazzlingly, no doubt, when the Gorgons were flying about in the sunshine.

But when people happened to catch a glimpse of their glittering brightness, aloft in the air, they seldom stopped to gaze, but ran and hid themselves as speedily as they could. You will think, perhaps, that they were afraid of being stung by the serpents that served the Gorgons instead of hair – or of having their heads bitten off by their ugly tusks – or of being torn all to pieces by their brazen claws. Well, to be sure, these were some of the dangers, but by no means the greatest, nor the most difficult to avoid. For the worst thing about these abominable Gorgons was, that, if once a poor mortal fixed his eyes full upon one of their faces, he was certain, that very instant, to be changed from warm flesh and blood into cold and lifeless stone!

Thus, as you will easily perceive, it was a very dangerous adventure that the wicked King Polydectes had contrived for this innocent young man. Perseus himself, when he had thought over the matter, could not help seeing that he had very little chance of coming safely through it, and that he was far more likely to become a stone image than to bring back the head of Medusa with the snaky locks. For, not to speak of other difficulties, there was one which it would have puzzled an older man than Perseus to get over. Not only must he fight with and slay this golden-winged, iron-scaled, long-tusked, brazen-clawed, snaky-haired monster, but he must do it with his eyes shut, or, at least, without so much as a glance at the enemy with whom he was contending. Else, while his arm was lifted to strike, he would stiffen into stone, and stand with that uplifted arm for centuries, until time, and the wind and weather, should crumble him quite away. This would be a very sad thing to befall a young man who wanted to perform a great many brave deeds, and to enjoy a great deal of happiness, in this bright and beautiful world.

So disconsolate did these thoughts make him, that Perseus could not bear to tell his mother what he had undertaken to do. He therefore took his shield, girded on his sword, and crossed over from the island to the mainland, where he sat down in a solitary place, and hardly refrained from shedding tears.

But, while he was in this sorrowful mood, he heard a voice close beside him.

"Perseus," said the voice, "why are you sad?"

He lifted his head from his hands, in which he had hidden it, and, behold! all alone as Perseus had supposed himself to be, there was a stranger in the solitary place. It was a brisk, intelligent, and remarkably shrewd-looking young man, with a cloak over his shoulders, an odd sort of cap on his head, a strangely twisted staff in his hand, and a short and very crooked sword hanging by his side. He was exceedingly light and active in his figure, like a person much accustomed to gymnastic exercises, and well able to leap or run. Above all, the stranger had such a cheerful, knowing, and helpful aspect (though it was certainly a little mischievous, into the bargain), that Perseus could not help feeling his spirits grow livelier, as he gazed at him. Besides, being really a courageous youth, he felt greatly ashamed that anybody should have found him with tears in his eyes, like a timid little school-boy, when, after all, there might be no occasion for despair. So Perseus wiped his eyes, and answered the stranger pretty briskly, putting on as brave a look as he could.

"I am not so very sad," said he; "only thoughtful about an adventure that I have undertaken."

"Oho!" answered the stranger. "Well, tell me all about it, and possibly I may be of service to you. I have helped a good many young men through adventures that looked difficult enough beforehand. Perhaps you may have heard of me. I have more names than one; but the name of Quicksilver suits me as well as any other. Tell me what your trouble is, and we will talk the matter over, and see what can be done."

The stranger's words and manner put Perseus into quite a different mood from his former one. He resolved to tell Quicksilver all his difficulties, since he could not easily be worse off than he already was, and, very possibly, his new friend might give him some advice that would turn out well in the end. So he let the stranger know, in few words, precisely what the case was – how that King Polydectes wanted the head of Medusa with the snaky locks as a bridal gift for the beautiful Princess Hippodamia, and how that he had undertaken to get it for him, but was afraid of being turned into stone.

"And that would be a great pity," said Quicksilver, with his mischievous smile. "You would make a very handsome marble statue, it is true, and it would be a considerable number of centuries before you crumbled away; but, on the whole, one would rather be a young man for a few years, than a stone image for a great many."

"O, far rather!" exclaimed Perseus, with the tears again standing in his eyes. "And, besides, what would my dear mother do, if her beloved son were turned into a stone?"

"Well, well; let us hope that the affair will not turn out so very badly," replied Quicksilver, in an encouraging tone. "I am the very person to help you, if anybody can. My sister and myself will do our utmost to bring you safe through the adventure, ugly as it now looks."

"Your sister?" repeated Perseus.

"Yes, my sister," said the stranger. "She is very wise, I promise you; and as for myself, I generally have all my wits about me, such as they are. If you show yourself bold and cautious, and follow our advice, you need not fear being a stone image yet awhile. But, first of all, you must polish your shield, till you can see your face in it as distinctly as in a mirror."

This seemed to Perseus rather an odd beginning of the adventure; for he thought it of far more consequence that the shield should be strong enough to defend him from the Gorgon's brazen claws, than that it should be bright enough to show him the reflection of his face. However, concluding that Quicksilver knew better than himself, he immediately set to work, and scrubbed the shield with so much diligence and good-will, that it very quickly shone like the moon at harvest-time. Quicksilver looked at it with a smile, and nodded his approbation. Then, taking off his own short and crooked sword, he girded it about Perseus, instead of the one which he had before worn.

"No sword but mine will answer your purpose," observed he; "the blade has a most excellent temper, and will cut through iron and brass as easily as through the slenderest twig. And now we will set out. The next thing is to find the Three Grey Women, who will tell us where to find the Nymphs."

"The Three Grey Women!" cried Perseus, to whom this seemed only a new difficulty in the path of his adventure; "pray, who may the Three Grey Women be? I never heard of them before."

"They are three very strange old ladies," said Quicksilver, laughing. "They have but one eye among them, and only one tooth. Moreover, you must find them out by starlight, or in the dusk of the evening; for they never show themselves by the light either of the sun or moon."

"But," said Perseus, "why should I waste my time with these Three Grey Women? Would it not be better to set out at once in search of the terrible Gorgons?"

"No, no," answered his friend. "There are other things to be done, before you can find your way to the Gorgons. There is nothing for it but to hunt up these old ladies; and when we meet with them, you may be sure that the Gorgons are not a great way off. Come, let us be stirring!"

Perseus, by this time, felt so much confidence in his companion's sagacity, that he made no more objections, and professed himself ready to begin the adventure immediately. They accordingly set out, and walked at a pretty brisk pace; so brisk, indeed, that Perseus found it rather difficult to keep up with his nimble friend Quicksilver. To say the truth, he had a singular idea that Quicksilver was furnished with a pair of winged shoes, which, of course, helped him along marvellously. And then, too, when Perseus looked sideways at him, out of the corner of his eye, he seemed to see wings on the side of his head; although, if he turned a full gaze, there were no such things to be perceived, but only an odd kind of cap. But, at all events, the twisted staff was evidently a great convenience to Quicksilver, and enabled him to proceed so fast, that Perseus, though a remarkably active young man, began to be out of breath.

"Here!" cried Quicksilver, at last – for he knew well enough, rogue that he was, how hard Perseus found it to keep pace with him – "take you the staff, for you need it a great deal more than I. Are there no better walkers than yourself, in the island of Seriphus?"

"I could walk pretty well," said Perseus, glancing slyly at his companion's feet, "if I had only a pair of winged shoes."

"We must see about getting you a pair," answered Quicksilver.

But the staff helped Perseus along so bravely, that he no longer felt the slightest weariness. In fact, the stick seemed to be alive in his hand, and to lend some of its life to Perseus. He and Quicksilver now walked onward at their ease, talking very sociably together; and Quicksilver told so many pleasant stories about his former adventures, and how well his wits had served him on various occasions, that Perseus began to think him a very wonderful person. He evidently knew the world; and nobody is so charming to a young man as a friend who has that kind of knowledge. Perseus listened the more eagerly, in the hope of brightening his own wits by what he heard.

At last, he happened to recollect that Quicksilver had spoken of a sister, who was to lend her assistance in the adventure which they were now bound upon.

"Where is she?" he inquired. "Shall we not meet her soon?"

"All at the proper time," said his companion. "But this sister of mine, you must understand, is quite a different sort of character from myself. She is very grave and prudent, seldom smiles, never laughs, and makes it a rule not to utter a word unless she has something particularly profound to say. Neither will she listen to any but the wisest conversation."

"Dear me!" ejaculated Perseus; "I shall be afraid to say a syllable."

"She is a very accomplished person, I assure you," continued Quicksilver, "and has all the arts and sciences at her fingers' ends. In short, she is so immoderately wise, that many people call her wisdom personified. But, to tell you the truth, she has hardly vivacity enough for my taste; and I think you would scarcely find her so pleasant a travelling companion as myself. She has her good points, nevertheless; and you will find the benefit of them, in your encounter with the Gorgons."

By this time it had grown quite dusk. They were now come to a very wild and desert place, overgrown with shaggy bushes, and so silent and solitary that nobody seemed ever to have dwelt or journeyed there. All was waste and desolate, in the grey twilight, which grew every moment more obscure. Perseus looked about him, rather disconsolately, and asked Quicksilver whether they had a great deal farther to go.

"Hist! Hist!" whispered his companion. "Make no noise! This is just the time and place to meet the Three Grey Women. Be careful that they do not see you before you see them; for, though they have but a single eye among the three, it is as sharp-sighted as half a dozen common eyes."

"But what must I do," asked Perseus, "when we meet them?"

Quicksilver explained to Perseus how the Three Grey Women managed with their one eye. They were in the habit, it seems, of changing it from one to another, as if it had been a pair of spectacles, or – which would have suited them better – quizzing-glass. When one of the three had kept the eye a certain time, she took it out of the socket and passed it to one of her sisters, whose turn it might happen to be, and who immediately clapped it into her own head, and enjoyed a peep at the visible world. Thus it will easily be understood that only one of the Three Grey Women could see, while the other two were in utter darkness; and, moreover, at the instant when the eye was passing from hand to hand, neither of the poor old ladies was able to see a wink. I have heard of a great many strange things, in my day, and have witnessed not a few; but none, it seems to me, that can compare with the oddity of these Three Grey Women, all peeping through a single eye.

So thought Perseus, likewise, and was so astonished that he almost fancied his companion was joking with him, and that there were no such old women in the world.

"You will soon find whether I tell the truth or no," observed Quicksilver. "Hark! Hush! Hist! Hist! There they come, now!"

Perseus looked earnestly through the dusk of the evening, and there, sure enough, at no great distance off, he descried the Three Grey Women. The light being so faint, he could not well make out what sort of figures they were; only he discovered that they had long grey hair; and, as they came nearer, he saw that two of them had but the empty socket of an eye, in the middle of their foreheads. But, in the middle of the third sister's forehead, there was a very large, bright, and piercing eye, which sparkled like a great diamond in a ring; and so penetrating did it seem to be, that Perseus could not help thinking it must possess the gift of seeing in the darkest midnight just as perfectly as at noonday. The sight of three persons' eyes was melted and collected into that single one.

Thus the three old dames got along about as comfortably, upon the whole, as if they could all see at once. She who chanced to have the eye in her forehead led the other two by the hands, peeping sharply about her, all the while; insomuch that Perseus dreaded lest she should see right through the thick clump of bushes behind which he and Quicksilver had hidden themselves. My stars! it was positively terrible to be within reach of so very sharp an eye!

But, before they reached the clump of bushes, one of the Three Grey Women spoke.

"Sister! Sister Scarecrow!" cried she, "you have had the eye long enough. It is my turn now!"

"Let me keep it a moment longer, Sister Nightmare," answered Scarecrow. "I thought I had a glimpse of something behind that thick bush."

"Well, and what of that?" retorted Nightmare, peevishly. "Can't I see into a thick bush as easily as yourself? The eye is mine, as well as yours; and I know the use of it as well as you, or may be a little better. I insist upon taking a peep immediately!"

But here the third sister, whose name was Shakejoint, began to complain, and said that it was her turn to have the eye, and that Scarecrow and Nightmare wanted to keep it all to themselves. To end the dispute, old Dame Scarecrow took the eye out of her forehead, and held it forth in her hand.

"Take it, one of you," cried she, "and quit this foolish quarrelling. For my part, I shall be glad of a little thick darkness. Take it quickly, however, or I must clap it into my own head again!"

Accordingly, both Nightmare and Shakejoint stretched out their hands, groping eagerly to snatch the eye out of the hand of Scarecrow. But, being both alike blind, they could not easily find where Scarecrow's hand was; and Scarecrow, being now just as much in the dark as Shakejoint and Nightmare, could not at once meet either of their hands, in order to put the eye into it. Thus (as you will see, with half an eye, my wise little auditors), these good old dames had fallen into a strange perplexity. For, though the eye shone and glistened like a star, as Scarecrow held it out, yet the Grey Women caught not the least glimpse of its light, and were all three in utter darkness, from too impatient a desire to see.

Quicksilver was so much tickled at beholding Shakejoint and Nightmare both groping for the eye, and each finding fault with Scarecrow and one another, that he could scarcely help laughing aloud.

"Now is your time!" he whispered to Perseus.

"Quick, quick! before they can clap the eye into either of their heads. Rush out upon the old ladies, and snatch it from Scarecrow's hand!"

In an instant, while the Three Grey Women were still scolding each other, Perseus leaped front behind the clump of bushes, and made himself master of the prize. The marvellous eye, as he held it in his hand, shone very brightly, and seemed to look up into his face with a knowing air, and an expression as if it would have winked, had it been provided with a pair of eyelids for that purpose. But the Grey Women knew nothing of what had happened; and, each supposing that one of her sisters was in possession of the eye, they began their quarrel anew. At last, as Perseus did not wish to put these respectable dames to greater inconvenience than was really necessary, he thought it right to explain the matter. "My good ladies," said he, "pray do not be angry with one another. If anybody is in fault, it is myself; for I have the honour to hold your very brilliant and excellent eye in my own hand!"

"You! you have our eye! And who are you?" screamed the Three Grey Women, all in a breath; for they were terribly frightened, of course, at hearing a strange voice, and discovering that their eyesight had got into the hands of they could not guess whom. "O, what shall we do, sisters? what shall we do? We are all in the dark! Give us our eye! Give us our one, precious, solitary eye! You have two of your own! Give us our eye!"

"Tell them," whispered Quicksilver to Perseus, "that they shall have back the eye as soon as they direct you where to find the Nymphs who have the flying slippers, the magic wallet, and the helmet of darkness."

"My dear, good, admirable old ladies," said Perseus, addressing the Grey Women, "there is no occasion for putting yourselves into such a fright. I am by no means a bad young man. You shall have back your eye, safe and sound, and as bright as ever, the moment you tell me where to find the Nymphs."

"The Nymphs! Goodness me! sisters, what Nymphs does he mean?" screamed Scarecrow. "There are a great many Nymphs, people say; some that go a hunting in the woods, and some that live inside of trees, and some that have a comfortable home in fountains of water. We know nothing at all about them. We are three unfortunate old souls, that go wandering about in the dusk, and never had but one eye amongst us, and that one you have stolen away. O, give it back, good stranger! – whoever you are, give it back!"

All this while the Three Grey Women were groping with their outstretched hands, and trying their utmost to get hold of Perseus. But he took good care to keep out of their reach.

"My respectable dames," said he – for his mother had taught him always to use the greatest civility – "I hold your eye fast in my hand, and shall keep it safely for you, until you please to tell me where to find these Nymphs. The Nymphs, I mean, who keep the enchanted wallet, the flying slippers, and the what is it? – the helmet of invisibility."

"Mercy on us, sisters! what is the young man talking about?" exclaimed Scarecrow, Nightmare, and Shakejoint, one to another, with great appearance of astonishment. "A pair of flying slippers, quoth he! His heels would quickly fly higher than his head, if he were silly enough to put them on. And a helmet of invisibility! How could a helmet make him invisible, unless it were big enough for him to hide under it? And an enchanted wallet! What sort of a contrivance may that be, I wonder? No, no, good stranger! we can tell you nothing of these marvellous things. You have two eyes of your own, and we have but a single one amongst us three. You can find out such wonders better than three blind old creatures, like us."

Perseus, hearing them talk in this way, began really to think that the Grey Women knew nothing of the matter; and, as it grieved him to have put them to so much trouble, he was just on the point of restoring their eye and asking pardon for his rudeness in snatching it away. But Quicksilver caught his hand.

"Don't let them make a fool of you!" said he. "These Three Grey Women are the only persons in the world that can tell you where to find the Nymphs; and, unless you get that information, you will never succeed in cutting off the head of Medusa with the snaky locks. Keep fast hold of the eye, and all will go well."

As it turned out, Quicksilver was in the right. There are but few things that people prize so much as they do their eyesight; and the Grey Women valued their single eye as highly as if it had been half a dozen, which was the number they ought to have had. Finding that there was no other way of recovering it, they at last told Perseus what he wanted to know. No sooner had they done so, than he immediately, and with the utmost respect, clapped the eye into the vacant socket in one of their foreheads, thanked them for their kindness, and bade them farewell. Before the young man was out of hearing, however, they had got into a new dispute, because he happened to have given the eye to Scarecrow, who had already taken her turn of it when their trouble with Perseus commenced.

It is greatly to be feared that the Three Grey Women were very much in the habit of disturbing their mutual harmony by bickerings of this sort; which was the more pity, as they could not conveniently do without one another, and were evidently intended to be inseparable companions. As a general rule, I would advise all people, whether sisters or brothers, old or young, who chance to have but one eye amongst them, to cultivate forbearance, and not all insist upon peeping through it at once.

Quicksilver and Perseus, in the mean time, were making the best of their way in quest of the Nymphs. The old dames had given them such particular directions, that they were not long in finding them out. They proved to be very different persons from Nightmare, Shakejoint, and Scarecrow; for, instead of being old, they were young and beautiful; and instead of one eye amongst the sisterhood, each Nymph had two exceedingly bright eyes of her own, with which she looked very kindly at Perseus. They seemed to be acquainted with Quicksilver; and when he told them the adventure which Perseus had undertaken, they made no difficulty about giving him the valuable articles that were in their custody. In the first place, they brought out what appeared to be a small purse, made of deer-skin, and curiously embroidered, and bade him be sure and keep it safe. This was the magic wallet. The Nymphs next produced a pair of shoes, or slippers, or sandals, with a nice little pair of wings at the heel of each.

"Put them on, Perseus," said Quicksilver. "You will find yourself as light-heeled as you can desire, for the remainder of our journey."

So Perseus proceeded to put one of the slippers on, while he laid the other on the ground by his side. Unexpectedly, however, this other slipper spread its wings, fluttered up off the ground, and would probably have flown away, if Quicksilver had not made a leap, and luckily caught it in the air.

"Be more careful," said he, as he gave it back to Perseus. "It would frighten the birds, up aloft, if they should see a flying slipper amongst them."

When Perseus had got on both of these wonderful slippers, he was altogether too buoyant to tread on earth. Making a step or two, lo and behold! upward he popt into the air, high above the heads of Quicksilver and the Nymphs, and found it very difficult to clamber down again. Winged slippers, and all such high-flying contrivances, are seldom quite easy to manage, until one grows a little accustomed to them. Quicksilver laughed at his companion's involuntary activity, and told him that he must not be in so desperate a hurry, but must wait for the invisible helmet.

The good-natured Nymphs had the helmet, with its dark tuft of waving plumes, all in readiness to put upon his head. And now there happened about as wonderful an incident as anything that I have yet told you. The instant before the helmet was put on, there stood Perseus, a beautiful young man, with golden ringlets and rosy cheeks, the crooked sword by his side, and the brightly polished shield upon his arm – a figure that seemed all made up of courage, sprightliness, and glorious light. But when the helmet had descended over his white brow, there was no longer any Perseus to be seen! Nothing but empty air! Even the helmet, that covered him with its invisibility, had vanished!

"Where are you, Perseus?" asked Quicksilver.

"Why, here, to be sure!" answered Perseus, very quietly, although his voice seemed to come out of the transparent atmosphere. "Just where I was a moment ago. Don't you see me?"

"No, indeed!" answered his friend. "You are hidden under the helmet. But, if I cannot see you, neither can the Gorgons. Follow me, therefore, and we will try your dexterity in using the winged slippers."

With these words, Quicksilver's cap spread its wings, as if his head were about to fly away from his shoulders; but his whole figure rose lightly into the air, and Perseus followed. By the time they had ascended a few hundred feet, the young man began to feel what a delightful thing it was to leave the dull earth so far beneath him, and to be able to flit about like a bird.

It was now deep night. Perseus looked upward, and saw the round, bright, silvery moon, and thought that he should desire nothing better than to soar up thither, and spend his life there. Then he looked downward again, and saw the earth, with its seas, and lakes, and the silver courses of its rivers, and its snowy mountain-peaks, and the breadth of its fields, and the dark cluster of its woods, and its cities of white marble; and, with the moonshine sleeping over the whole scene, it was as beautiful as the moon or any star could be. And, among other objects, he saw the island of Seriplius, where his dear mother was. Sometimes, he and Quicksilver approached a cloud, that, at a distance, looked as if it were made of fleecy silver; although, when they plunged into it, they found themselves chilled and moistened with grey mist. So swift was their flight, however, that, in an instant, they emerged from the cloud into the moonlight again. Once, a high-soaring eagle flew right against the invisible Perseus. The bravest sights were the meteors, that gleamed suddenly out, as if a bonfire had been kindled in the sky, and made the moonshine pale for as much as a hundred miles around them.

As the two companions flew onward, Perseus fancied that he could hear the rustle of a garment close by his side; and it was on the side opposite to the one where he beheld Quicksilver, yet only Quicksilver was visible.

"Whose garment is this," inquired Perseus, "that keeps rustling close beside me, in the breeze?"

"O, it is my sister's!" answered Quicksilver. "She is coming along with us, as I told you she would. We could do nothing without the help of my sister. You have no idea how wise she is. She has such eyes, too! Why, she can see you, at this moment, just as distinctly as if you were not invisible; and I'll venture to say, she will be the first to discover the Gorgons."

By this time, in their swift voyage through the air, they had come within sight of the great ocean, and were soon flying over it. Far beneath them, the waves tossed themselves tumultuously in mid-sea, or rolled a white surf-line upon the long beaches, or foamed against the rocky cliffs, with a roar that was thunderous, in the lower world; although it became a gentle murmur, like the voice of a baby half asleep, before it reached the ears of Perseus. Just then a voice spoke in the air close by him. It seemed to be a woman's voice, and was melodious, though not exactly what might be called sweet, but grave and mild.

"Perseus," said the voice, "there are the Gorgons."

"Where?" exclaimed Perseus. "I cannot see them."

"On the shore of that island beneath you," replied the voice. "A pebble, dropped from your hand, would strike in the midst of them."

"I told you she would be the first to discover them," said Quicksilver to Perseus. "And there they are!"

Straight downward, two or three thousand feet below him, Perseus perceived a small island, with the sea breaking into white foam all around its rocky shore, except on one side, where there was a beach of snowy sand. He descended towards it, and, looking earnestly at a cluster or heap of brightness, at the foot of a precipice of black rocks, behold, there were the terrible Gorgons! They lay fast asleep, soothed by the thunder of the sea; for it required a tumult that would have deafened everybody else to lull such fierce creatures into slumber. The moonlight glistened on their steely scales, and on their golden wings, which drooped idly over the sand. Their brazen claws, horrible to look at, were thrust out, and clutched the wave-beaten fragments of rock, while the sleeping Gorgons dreamed of tearing some poor mortal all to pieces. The snakes that served them instead of hair seemed likewise to be asleep; although, now and then, one would writhe, and lift its head, and thrust out its forked tongue, emitting a drowsy hiss, and then let itself subside among its sister snakes.

The Gorgons were more like an awful, gigantic kind of insect – immense, golden-winged beetles, or dragon-flies, or things of that sort –at once ugly and beautiful – than like anything else; only that they were a thousand and a million times as big. And, with all this, there was something partly human about them, too. Luckily for Perseus, their faces were completely hidden from him by the posture in which they lay; for, had he but looked one instant at them, he would have fallen heavily out of the air, an image of senseless stone.

"Now," whispered Quicksilver, as he hovered by the side of Perseus – "now is your time to do the deed! Be quick; for, if one of the Gorgons should awake, you are too late!"

"Which shall I strike at?" asked Perseus, drawing his sword and descending a little lower. "They all three look alike. All three have snaky locks. Which of the three is Medusa?"

It must be understood that Medusa was the only one of these dragon-monsters whose head Perseus could possibly cut off. As for the other two, let him have the sharpest sword that ever was forged, and he might have hacked away by the hour together, without doing there the least harm.

"Be cautious," said the calm voice which had before spoken to him. "One of the Gorgons is stirring in her sleep, and is just about to turn over. That is Medusa. Do not look at her! The sight would turn you to stone! Look at the reflection of her face and figure in the bright mirror of your shield."

Perseus now understood Quicksilver's motive for so earnestly exhorting him to polish his shield. In its surface he could safely look at the reflection of the Gorgon's face. And there it was – that terrible countenance – mirrored in the brightness of the shield, with the moonlight falling over it, and displaying all its horror. The snakes, whose venomous natures could not altogether sleep, kept twisting themselves over the forehead. It was the fiercest and most horrible face that ever was seen or imagined, and yet with a strange, fearful, and savage kind of beauty in it. The eyes were closed, and the Gorgon was still in a deep slumber; but there was an unquiet expression disturbing her features, as if the monster was troubled with an ugly dream. She gnashed her white tusks, and dug into the sand with her brazen claws.

The snakes, too, seemed to feel Medusa's dream, and to be made more restless by it. They twined themselves into tumultuous knots, writhed fiercely, and uplifted a hundred hissing heads, without opening their eyes.

"Now, now!" whispered Quicksilver, who was growing impatient. "Make a dash at the monster!"

"But be calm," said the grave, melodious voice, at the young man's side. "Look in your shield, as you fly downward, and take care that you do not miss your first stroke."

Perseus flew cautiously downward, still keeping his eyes on Medusa's face, as reflected in his shield. The nearer he came, the more terrible did the snaky visage and metallic body of the monster grow. At last, when he found himself hovering over her within arm's length, Perseus uplifted his sword, while, at the same instant, each separate snake upon the Gorgon's head stretched threateningly upward, and Medusa unclosed her eyes. But she awoke too late. The sword was sharp; the stroke fell like a lightning-flash; and the head of the wicked Medusa tumbled from her body!

"Admirably done!" cried Quicksilver. "Make haste, and clap the head into your magic wallet."

To the astonishment of Perseus, the small, embroidered wallet, which he had hung about his neck, and which had hitherto been no bigger than a purse, grew all at once large enough to contain Medusa's head. As quick as thought, he snatched it up, with the snakes still writhing upon it, and thrust it in.

"Your task is done," said the calm voice. "Now fly; for the other Gorgons will do their utmost to take vengeance for Medusa's death."

It was, indeed, necessary to take flight; for Perseus had not done the deed so quietly, but that the clash of his sword, and the hissing of the snakes, and the thump of Medusa's head as it tumbled upon the sea-beaten sand, awoke the other two monsters. There they sat, for an instant, sleepily rubbing their eyes with their brazen fingers, while all the snakes on their heads reared themselves on end with surprise, and with venomous malice against they knew not what. But when the Gorgons saw the scaly carcass of Medusa, headless, and her golden wings all ruffled, and half spread out on the sand, it was really awful to hear what yells and screeches they set up. And then the snakes! They sent forth a hundred-fold hiss, with one consent, and Medusa's snakes answered them out of the magic wallet.

No sooner were the Gorgons broad awake, than they hurtled upward into the air, brandishing their brass talons, gnashing their horrible tusks, and flapping their huge wings so wildly, that some of the golden feathers were shaken out, and floated down upon the shore. And there, perhaps, those very feathers he scattered, till this day. Up rose the Gorgons, as I tell you, staring horribly about, in hopes of turning somebody to stone. Had Perseus looked them in the face, or had he fallen into their clutches, his poor mother would never have kissed her boy again! But he took good care to turn his eyes another way; and, as he wore the helmet of invisibility, the Gorgons knew not in what direction to follow him; nor did he fail to make the best use of the winged slippers, by soaring upward a perpendicular mile or so. At that height, when the screams of those abominable creatures sounded faintly beneath him, he made a straight course for the island of Seriphus, in order to carry Medusa's head to King Polydectes.

I have no time to tell you of several marvellous things that befell Perseus, on his way homeward; such as his killing a hideous sea-monster, just as it was on the point of devouring a beautiful maiden; nor how he changed an enormous giant into a mountain of stone, merely by showing him the head of the Gorgon. If you doubt this latter story, you may make a voyage to Africa, some day or other, and see the very mountain, which is still known by the ancient giant's name.

Finally, our brave Perseus arrived at the island, where he expected to see his dear mother. But, during his absence, the wicked king had treated Danae so very ill, that she was compelled to make her escape, and had taken refuge in a temple, where some good old priests were extremely kind to her. These praiseworthy priests, and the kind-hearted fisherman, who had first shown hospitality to Danae and little Perseus when he found them afloat in the chest, seem to have been the only persons on the island who cared about doing right. All the rest of the people, as well as King Polydectes himself, were remarkably ill-behaved, and deserved no better destiny than that which was now to happen.

Not finding his mother at home, Perseus went straight to the palace and was immediately ushered into the presence of the king. Polydectes was by no means rejoiced to see him; for he had felt almost certain, in his own evil mind, that the Gorgons would have torn the poor young man to pieces, and have eaten him up, out of the way. However, seeing him safely returned, he put the best face he could upon the matter and asked Perseus how he had succeeded.

"Have you performed your promise?" inquired he. "Have you brought me the head of Medusa with the snaky locks? If not, young man, it will cost you dear; for I must have a bridal present for the beautiful Princess Hippodamia, and there is nothing else that she would admire so much."

"Yes, please your Majesty," answered Perseus, in a quiet way, as if it were no very wonderful deed for such a young man as he to perform. "I have brought you the Gorgon's head, snaky locks and all!"

"Indeed! Pray let me see it," quoth King Polydectes. "It must be a very curious spectacle, if all that travellers tell about it be true!"

"Your Majesty is in the right," replied Perseus. "It is really an object that will be pretty certain to fix the regards of all who look at it. And, if your Majesty think fit, I would suggest that a holiday be proclaimed, and that all your Majesty's subjects be summoned to behold this wonderful curiosity. Few of them, I imagine, have seen a Gorgon's head before, and perhaps never may again!"

The king well knew that his subjects were an idle set of reprobates, and very fond of sight-seeing, as idle persons usually are. So he took the young man's advice, and sent out heralds and messengers, in all directions, to blow the trumpet at the street-corners, and in the market-places, and wherever two roads met, and summon everybody to court. Thither, accordingly, came a great multitude of good-for-nothing vagabonds, all of whom, out of pure love of mischief, would have been glad if Perseus had met with some ill-hap, in his encounter with the Gorgons. If there were any better people in the island (as I really hope there may have been, although the story tells nothing about any such), they stayed quietly at home, minding their own business, and taking care of their little children. Most of the inhabitants, at all events, ran as fast as they could to the palace, and shoved, and pushed, and elbowed one another, in their eagerness to get near a balcony, on which Perseus showed himself, holding the embroidered wallet in his hand.

On a platform, within full view of the balcony, sat the mighty King Polydectes, amid his evil counsellors, and with his flattering courtiers in a semicircle round about him. Monarch, counsellors, courtiers, and subjects, all gazed eagerly towards Perseus.

"Show us the head! Show us the head!" shouted the people; and there was a fierceness in their cry as if they would tear Perseus to pieces, unless he should satisfy them with what he had to show. "Show us the head of Medusa with the snaky locks!"

A feeling of sorrow and pity came over the youthful Perseus.

"O King Polydectes," cried he, "and ye many people, I am very loath to show you the Gorgon's head!"

"Ah, the villain and coward!" yelled the people, more fiercely than before. "He is making game of us! He has no Gorgon's head! Show us the head, if you have it, or we will take your own head for a football!"

The evil counsellors whispered bad advice in the king's ear; the courtiers murmured, with one consent, that Perseus had shown disrespect to their royal lord and master; and the great King Polydectes himself waved his hand, and ordered him, with the stern, deep voice of authority, on his peril, to produce the bead.

"Show me the Gorgon's head, or I will cut off your own!"

And Perseus sighed.

"This instant," repeated Polydectes, "or you die!"

"Behold it, then!" cried Perseus, in a voice like the blast of a trumpet.

And, suddenly holding up the head, not an eyelid had time to wink before the wicked King Polydectes, his evil counsellors, and all his fierce subjects were no longer anything but the mere images of a monarch and his people. They were all fixed, forever, in the look and attitude of that moment! At the first glimpse of the terrible head of Medusa, they whitened into marble! And Perseus thrust the head back into his wallet, and went to tell his dear mother that she need no longer be afraid of the wicked King Polydectes.

The Minotaur

IN THE OLD CITY OF TRŒZENE, at the foot of a lofty mountain, there lived, a very long time ago, a little boy named Theseus. His grandfather, King Pittheus, was the sovereign of that country, and was reckoned a very wise man; so that Theseus, being brought up in the royal palace, and being naturally a bright lad, could hardly fail of profiting by the old king's instructions. His mother's name was Æthra. As for his father, the boy had never seen him. But, from his earliest remembrance, Æthra used to go with little Theseus into a wood, and sit down upon a moss-grown rock, which was deeply sunken into the earth. Here she often talked with her son about his father, and said that he was called Ægeus, and that he was a great king, and ruled over Attica, and dwelt at Athens, which was as famous a city as any in the world. Theseus was very fond of hearing about King Ægeus, and often asked his good mother Æthra why he did not come and live with them at Trœzene.

"Ah, my dear son," answered Æthra, with a sigh, "a monarch has his people to take care of. The men and women over whom he rules are in the place of children to him; and he can seldom spare time to love his own children as other parents do. Your father will never be able to leave his kingdom for the sake of seeing his little boy."

"Well, but, dear mother," asked the boy, "why cannot I go to this famous city of Athens, and tell King Ægeus that I am his son?"

"That may happen by and by," said Æthra. "Be patient, and we shall see. You are not yet big and strong enough to set out on such an errand."

"And how soon shall I be strong enough?" Theseus persisted in inquiring.

"You are but a tiny boy as yet," replied his mother. "See if you can lift this rock on which we are sitting?"

The little fellow had a great opinion of his own strength. So, grasping the rough protuberances of the rock, he tugged and toiled amain, and got himself quite out of breath, without being able to stir the heavy stone. It seemed rooted into the ground. No wonder he could not move it; for it would have taken all the force of a very strong man to lift it out of its earthy bed.

His mother stood looking on, with a sad kind of a smile on her lips and in her eyes, to see the zealous and yet puny efforts of her little boy. She could not help being sorrowful at finding him already so impatient to begin his adventures in the world.

"You see how it is, my dear Theseus," said she. "You must possess far more strength than now before I can trust you to go to Athens, and tell King Ægeus that you are his son. But when you can lift this rock, and show me what is hidden beneath it, I promise you my permission to depart."

Often and often, after this, did Theseus ask his mother whether it was yet time for him to go to Athens; and still his mother pointed to the rock, and told him that for years to come, he could not be strong enough to move it. And again and again the rosy-cheeked and curly-headed boy would tug and strain at the huge mass of stone, striving, child as he was, to do what a giant could hardly have done without taking both of his great hands to the task. Meanwhile the rock seemed to be sinking farther and farther into the ground. The moss grew over it thicker and thicker, until at last it looked almost like a soft green seat, with only a few grey knobs of granite peeping out. The overhanging trees, also, shed their brown leaves upon it, as often as the autumn came; and at its base grew ferns and wild flowers, some of which crept quite over its surface. To all appearance, the rock was as firmly fastened as any other portion of the earth's substance.

But, difficult as the matter looked, Theseus was now growing up to be such a vigorous youth, that, in his own opinion, the time would quickly come when he might hope to get the upper hand of this ponderous lump of stone.

"Mother, I do believe it has started!" cried he, after one of his attempts. "The earth around it is certainly a little cracked!"

"No, no, child!" his mother hastily answered. "It is not possible you can have moved it, such a boy as you still are!" Nor would she be convinced, although Theseus showed her the place where he fancied that the stem of a flower had been partly uprooted by the movement of the rock. But Æthra sighed, and looked disquieted; for, no doubt, she began to be conscious that her son was no longer a child, and that, in a little while hence, she must send him forth among the perils and troubles of the world.

It was not more than a year afterwards when they were again sitting on the moss-covered stone. Æthra had once more told him the oft-repeated story of his father, and how gladly he would receive Theseus at his stately palace, and how he would present him to his courtiers and the people, and tell them that here was the heir of his dominions. The eyes of Theseus glowed with enthusiasm, and he would hardly sit still to hear his mother speak.

"Dear mother Æthra," he exclaimed, "I never felt half so strong as now! I am no longer a child, nor a boy, nor a mere youth. I feel myself a man! It is now time to make one earnest trial to remove the stone."

"Ah, my dearest Theseus," replied his mother, "not yet! not yet!"

"Yes, mother," said he, resolutely, "the time has come."

Then Theseus bent himself in good earnest to the task, and strained every sinew, with manly strength and resolution. He put his whole brave heart into the effort. He wrestled with the big and sluggish stone, as if it had been a living enemy. He heaved, he lifted, he resolved now to succeed, or else perish there, and let the rock be his monument forever! Æthra stood gazing at him, and clasped her hands, partly with a mother's pride, and partly with a mother's sorrow. The great rock stirred! Yes, it was raised slowly from the bedded moss and earth, uprooting the shrubs and flowers along with it, and was turned upon its side. Theseus had conquered!

While taking breath, he looked joyfully at his mother, and she smiled upon him through her tears.

"Yes, Theseus," she said, "the time has come and you must stay no longer at my side! See what King Ægeus, your royal father, left for you, beneath the stone, when he lifted it in his mighty arms, and laid it on the spot whence you have now removed it."

Theseus looked, and saw that the rock had been placed over another slab of stone, containing a cavity within it; so that it somewhat resembled a roughly-made chest or coffer, of which the upper mass had served as the lid. Within the cavity lay a sword, with a golden hilt, and a pair of sandals.

"That was your father's sword," said Æthra, "and those were his sandals. When he went to be king of Athens, he bade me treat you as a child until you should prove yourself a man by lifting this heavy stone. That task being accomplished, you are to put on his sandals, in order to follow in your father's footsteps, and to gird on his sword, so that you may fight giants and dragons, as King Ægeus did in his youth."

"I will set out for Athens this very day!" cried Theseus.

But his mother persuaded him to stay a day or two longer, while she got ready some necessary articles for the journey. When his grandfather, the wise King Pittheus, heard that Theseus intended to present himself at his father's palace, he earnestly advised him to get on board of a vessel, and go by sea; because he might thus arrive within fifteen miles of Athens, without either fatigue or danger.

"The roads are very bad by land," quoth the venerable king; "and they are terribly infested with robbers and monsters. A mere lad, like Theseus, is not fit to be trusted on such a perilous journey, all by himself. No, no; let him go by sea!"

But when Theseus heard of robbers and monsters, he pricked up his ears, and was so much the more eager to take the road along which they were to be met with. On the third day, therefore, he bade a respectful farewell to his grandfather, thanking him for all his kindness; and, after affectionately embracing his mother, he set forth, with a good many of her tears glistening on his cheeks, and some, if the truth must be told, that had gushed out of his own eyes. But he let the sun and wind dry them, and walked stoutly on, playing with the golden hilt of his sword, and taking very manly strides in his father's sandals.

I can tell you only a few of the adventures that befell Theseus on the road to Athens. It is enough to say, that he quite cleared that part of the country of the robbers, about whom

King Pittheus had been so much alarmed. One of these bad people was named Procrustes; and he was indeed a terrible fellow, and had an ugly way of making fun of the poor travellers who happened to fall into his clutches. In his cavern he had a bed, on which, with great pretence of hospitality, he invited his guests to lie down; but if they happened to be shorter than the bed, this wicked villain stretched them out by main force; or, if they were too tall, he lopped off their heads or feet, and laughed at what he had done, as an excellent joke. Thus, however weary a man might be he never liked to lie in the bed of Procrustes. Another of these robbers, named Scinis, must likewise have been a very great scoundrel. He was in the habit of flinging his victims off a high cliff into the sea; and, in order to give him exactly his deserts, Theseus tossed him off the very same place. But if you will believe me, the sea would not pollute itself by receiving such a bad person into its bosom, neither would the earth, having once got rid of him, consent to take him back; so that, between the cliff and the sea, Scinis stuck fast in the air, which was forced to bear the burden of his naughtiness.

After these memorable deeds, Theseus heard of an enormous sow, which ran wild, and was the terror of all the farmers round about; and, as he did not consider himself above doing any good thing that came in his way, he killed this monstrous creature, and gave the carcass to the poor people for bacon. The great sow had been an awful beast, while ramping about the woods and fields, but was a pleasant object enough when cut up into joints, and smoking on I know not how many dinner tables.

Thus, by the time he reached his journey's end, Theseus had done many valiant feats with his father's golden-hilted sword, and had gained the renown of being one of the bravest young men of the day. His fame travelled faster than he did, and reached Athens before him. As he entered the city, he heard the inhabitants talking at the street corners, and saying that Hercules was brave, and Jason too, and Castor and Pollux likewise, but that Theseus, the son of their own king, would turn out as great a hero as the best of them. Theseus took longer strides on hearing this, and fancied himself sure of a magnificent reception at his father's court, since he came thither with Fame to blow her trumpet before him, and cry to King Ægeus, "Behold your son!"

He little suspected, innocent youth that he was, that here, in this very Athens, where his father reigned, a greater danger awaited him than any which he had encountered on the road. Yet this was the truth. You must understand that the father of Theseus, though not very old in years, was almost worn out with the cares of government, and had thus grown aged before his time. His nephews, not expecting him to live a very great while, intended to get all the power of the kingdom into their own hands. But when they heard that Theseus had arrived in Athens, and learned what a gallant young man he was, they saw that he would not be at all the kind of person to let them steal away his father's crown and sceptre, which ought to be his own by right of inheritance. Thus these bad-hearted nephews of King Ægeus, who were the own cousins of Theseus, at once became his enemies. A still more dangerous enemy was Medea, the wicked enchantress; for she was now the king's wife, and wanted to give the kingdom to her son Medus, instead of letting it be given to the son of Æthra, whom she hated.

It so happened that the king's nephews met Theseus, and found out who he was, just as he reached the entrance of the royal palace. With all their evil designs against him, they pretended to be their cousin's best friends, and expressed great joy at making his acquaintance. They proposed to him that he should come into the king's presence as a stranger, in order to try whether Ægeus would discover in the young man's features any likeness either to himself or his mother Æthra, and thus recognize him for a son. Theseus consented; for he fancied that his father would know him in a moment, by the love that was in his heart. But, while he waited at the door, the nephews ran and told King Ægeus that a young man had arrived in Athens who, to their certain knowledge, intended to put him to death, and get possession of his royal crown.

"And he is now waiting for admission to your majesty's presence," added they.

"Aha!" cried the old king, on hearing this. "Why, he must be a very wicked young fellow indeed! Pray, what would you advise me to do with him?"

In reply to this question, the wicked Medea put in her word. As I have already told you, she was a famous enchantress. According to some stories, she was in the habit of boiling old people in a large cauldron, under pretence of making them young again; but King Ægeus, I suppose, did not fancy such an uncomfortable way of growing young, or perhaps was contented to be old, and therefore would never let himself be popped into the cauldron. If there were time to spare from more important matters, I should be glad to tell you of Medea's fiery chariot, drawn by winged dragons, in which the enchantress used often to take an airing among the clouds. This chariot, in fact, was the vehicle that first brought her to Athens, where she had done nothing but mischief ever since her arrival. But these and many other wonders must be left untold; and it is enough to say, that Medea, amongst a thousand other bad things, knew how to prepare a poison, that was instantly fatal to whomsoever might so much as touch it with his lips.

So, when the king asked what he should do with Theseus, this naughty woman had an answer ready at her tongue's end.

"Leave that to me, please your majesty," she replied. "Only admit this evil-minded young man to your presence, treat him civilly, and invite him to drink a goblet of wine. Your majesty is well aware that I sometimes amuse myself with distilling very powerful medicines. Here is one of them in this small phial. As to what it is made of, that is one of my secrets of state. Do but let me put a single drop into the goblet, and let the young man taste it; and I will answer for it, he shall quite lay aside the bad designs with which he comes hither."

As she said this, Medea smiled; but, for all her smiling face, she meant nothing less than to poison the poor innocent Theseus, before his father's eyes. And King Ægeus, like most other kings, thought any punishment mild enough for a person who was accused of plotting against his life. He therefore made little or no objection to Medea's scheme, and as soon as the poisonous wine was ready, gave orders that the young stranger should be admitted into his presence. The goblet was set on a table beside the king's throne; and a fly, meaning just to sip a little from the brim, immediately tumbled into it, dead. Observing this, Medea looked round at the nephews, and smiled again.

When Theseus was ushered into the royal apartment, the only object that he seemed to behold was the white-bearded old king. There he sat on his magnificent throne, a dazzling crown on his head, and a scepter in his hand. His aspect was stately and majestic, although his years and infirmities weighed heavily upon him, as if each year were a lump of lead, and each infirmity a ponderous stone, and all were bundled up together, and laid upon his weary shoulders. The tears of both joy and sorrow sprang into the young man's eyes; for he thought how sad it was to see his dear father so infirm, and how sweet it would be to support him with his own youthful strength, and to cheer him up with the alacrity of his loving spirit. When a son takes his father into his warm heart, it renews the old man's youth in a better way than by the heat of Medea's magic cauldron. And this was what Theseus resolved to do. He could scarcely wait to see whether King Ægeus would recognize him, so eager was he to throw himself into his arms.

Advancing to the foot of the throne, he attempted to make a little speech, which he had been thinking about, as he came up the stairs. But he was almost choked by a great many tender feelings that gushed out of his heart and swelled into his throat, all struggling to find utterance together. And therefore, unless he could have laid his full, overbrimming heart into the king's hand, poor Theseus knew not what to do or say. The cunning Medea observed what was passing in the young man's mind. She was more wicked at that moment than ever she had been before; for (and it makes me tremble to tell you of it) she did her worst to turn all this unspeakable love with which Theseus was agitated, to his own ruin and destruction.

"Does your majesty see his confusion?" she whispered in the king's ear. "He is so conscious of guilt, that he trembles and cannot speak. The wretch lives too long! Quick! offer him the wine!"

Now King Ægeus had been gazing earnestly at the young stranger, as he drew near the throne. There was something, he knew not what, either the white brow, or in the fine expression of his mouth, or in his beautiful and tender eyes, that made him indistinctly feel as if he had seen this youth before; as if, indeed, he had trotted him on his knee when a baby, and had beheld him growing to be a stalwart man, while he himself grew old. But Medea guessed how the king felt, and would not suffer him to yield to these natural sensibilities; although they were the voice of his deepest heart, telling him, as plainly as it could speak, that here was our dear son, and Æthra's son, coming to claim him for a father. The enchantress again whispered in the king's ear, and compelled him, by her witchcraft, to see everything under a false aspect.

He made up his mind, therefore, to let Theseus drink off the poisoned wine.

"Young man," said he, "you are welcome! I am proud to show hospitality to so heroic a youth. Do me the favour to drink the contents of this goblet. It is brimming over, as you see, with delicious wine, such as I bestow only on those who are worthy of it! None is more worthy to quaff it than yourself!"

So saying, King Ægeus took the golden goblet from the table, and was about to offer it to Theseus. But, partly through his infirmities, and partly because it seemed so sad a thing to take away this young man's life, however wicked he might be, and partly, no doubt, because his heart was wiser than his head, and quaked within him at the thought of what he was going to do – for all these reasons, the king's hand trembled so much that a great deal of the wine slopped over. In order to strengthen his purpose, and fearing lest the whole of the precious poison should be wasted, one of his nephews now whispered to him –

"Has your majesty any doubt of this stranger's guilt? There is the very sword with which he meant to slay you. How sharp, and bright, and terrible it is! Quick! – let him taste the wine; or perhaps he may do the deed even yet."

At these words, Ægeus drove every thought and feeling out of his breast, except the one idea of how justly the young man deserved to be put to death. He sat erect on his throne, and held out the goblet with a steady hand, and bent on Theseus a frown of kingly severity; for, after all, he had too noble a spirit to murder even a treacherous enemy with a deceitful smile upon his face.

"Drink!" said he, in the stem tone with which he was wont to condemn a criminal to be beheaded. "You have well deserved of me such wine as this!"

Theseus held out his hand to take the wine. But, before he touched it, King Ægeus trembled again. His eyes had fallen on the gold-hilted sword that hung at the young man's side. He drew back the goblet.

"That sword!" he exclaimed; "how came you by it?"

"It was my father's sword," replied Theseus, with a tremulous voice. "These were his sandals. My dear mother (her name is Æthra) told me his story while I was yet a little child. But it is only a month since I grew strong enough to lift the heavy stone, and take the sword and sandals from beneath it, and come to Athens to seek my father."

"My son! my son!" cried King Ægeus, flinging away the fatal goblet, and tottering down from the throne to fall into the arms of Theseus. "Yes, these are Æthra's eyes. It is my son."

I have quite forgotten what became of the king's nephews. But when the wicked Medea saw this new turn of affairs, she hurried out of the room, and going to her private chamber, lost no time in setting her enchantments at work. In a few moments, she heard a great noise of hissing snakes outside of the chamber window; and, behold! there was her fiery chariot, and four huge winged serpents, wriggling and twisting in the air, flourishing their tails higher than the top of the palace, and all ready to set off on an aerial journey. Medea staid only long enough to take her son with her, and to steal the crown jewels, together with the king's best robes, and whatever other valuable things she could lay hands on; and getting into the chariot, she whipped up the snakes, and ascended high over the city.

The king, hearing the hiss of the serpents, scrambled as fast as he could to the window, and bawled out to the abominable enchantress never to come back. The whole people of Athens, too, who had run out of doors to see this wonderful spectacle, set up a shout of joy at the prospect of getting rid of her. Medea, almost bursting with rage, uttered precisely such a hiss as one of her own snakes, only ten times more venomous and spiteful; and glaring fiercely out of the blaze of the chariot, she shook her hands over the multitude below, as if she were scattering a million curses among them. In so doing, however, she unintentionally let fall about five hundred diamonds of the first water, together with a thousand great pearls, and two thousand emeralds, rubies, sapphires, opals, and topazes, to which she had helped herself out of the king's strong box. All these came pelting down, like a shower of many-coloured hailstones, upon the heads of grown people and children, who forthwith gathered them up, and carried them back to the palace. But King Ægeus told them that they were welcome to the whole, and to twice as many more, if he had them, for the sake of his delight at finding his son, and losing the wicked Medea. And, indeed, if you had seen how hateful was her last look, as the flaming chariot flew upward, you would not have wondered that both king and people should think her departure a good riddance.

And now Prince Theseus was taken into great favour by his royal father. The old king was never weary of having him sit beside him on his throne, (which was quite wide enough for two,) and of hearing him tell about his dear mother, and his childhood, and his many boyish efforts to lift the ponderous stone. Theseus, however, was much too brave and active a young man to be willing to spend all his time in relating things which had already happened. His ambition was to perform other and more heroic deeds, which should be better worth telling in prose and verse. Nor had he been long in Athens before he caught and chained a terrible mad bull, and made a public show of him, greatly to the wonder and admiration of good King Ægeus and his subjects. But pretty soon, he undertook an affair that made all his foregone adventures seem like mere boy's play. The occasion of it was as follows:

One morning, when Prince Theseus awoke, he fancied that he must have had a very sorrowful dream, and that it was still running in his mind, even now that his eyes were open. For it appeared as if the air was full of a melancholy wail; and when he listened more attentively, he could hear sobs, and groans, and screams of woe, mingled with deep, quiet sighs, which came from the king's palace, and from the streets, and from the temples, and from every habitation in the city. And all these mournful noises, issuing out of thousands of separate hearts, united themselves into one great sound of affliction, which had startled Theseus from slumber. He put on his clothes as quickly as he could, (not forgetting his sandals and gold-hilted sword,) and hastening to the king, inquired what it all meant.

"Alas! my son," quoth King Ægeus, heaving a long sigh, "here is a very lamentable matter in hand! This is the woefulest anniversary in the whole year. It is the day when we annually draw lots to see which of the youths and maidens of Athens shall go to be devoured by the horrible Minotaur!"

"The Minotaur!" exclaimed Prince Theseus and like a brave young prince as he was, he put his hand to the hilt of his sword. "What kind of a monster may that be? Is it not possible, at the risk of one's life, to slay him?"

But King Ægeus shook his venerable head, and to convince Theseus that it was quite a hopeless case, he gave him an explanation of the whole affair. It seems that in the Island of Crete there lived a certain dreadful monster, called a Minotaur, which was shaped partly like a man and partly like a bull, and was altogether such a hideous sort of a creature that it is really disagreeable to think of him. If he were suffered to exist at all, it should have been on some desert island, or in the duskiness of some deep cavern, where nobody would ever be tormented by his abominable aspect. But King Minos, who reigned over Crete, laid out a vast deal of money in building a habitation for the Minotaur, and took great care of his health and comfort, merely for mischief's sake. A few years before this time, there had been a war between the city of Athens and the island of Crete, in which the Athenians were beaten and compelled to beg for peace. No peace could they obtain, however, except on condition that they should send seven young men and seven maidens, every year, to be devoured by the pet monster of the cruel King Minos. For three years past, this grievous calamity had been borne. And the sobs, and groans, and shrieks, with which the city was now filled, were caused by the people's woe, because the fatal day had come again, when the fourteen victims were to be chosen by lot; and the old people feared lest their sons or daughters might be taken, and the youths and damsels dreaded lest they themselves might be destined to glut the ravenous maw of that detestable man-brute.

But when Theseus heard the story, he straightened himself up, so that he seemed taller than ever before; and as for his face, it was indignant, despiteful, bold, tender, and compassionate, all in one look.

"Let the people of Athens, this year, draw lots for only six young men, instead of seven," said he. "I will myself be the seventh; and let the Minotaur devour me, if he can!"

"O my dear son," cried King Ægeus, "why should you expose yourself to this horrible fate? You are a royal prince, and have a right to hold yourself above the destinies of common men."

"It is because I am a prince, your son, and the rightful heir of your kingdom, that I freely take upon me the calamity of your subjects," answered Theseus. "And you my father, being king over this people, and answerable to Heaven for their welfare, are bound to sacrifice what is dearest to you, rather than that the son or daughter of the poorest citizen should come to any harm."

The old king shed tears, and besought Theseus not to leave him desolate in his old age, more especially as he had just begun to know the happiness of possessing a good and valiant son. Theseus, however, felt that he was in the right, and therefore would not give up his resolution. But he assured his father that he did not intend to be eaten up, unresistingly, like a sheep, and that, if the Minotaur devoured him, it should not be without a battle for his dinner. And finally, since he could not help it, King Ægeus consented to let him go. So a vessel was got ready, and rigged with black sails; and Theseus, with six other young men, and seven tender and beautiful damsels, came down to the harbour to embark. A sorrowful multitude accompanied them to the shore. There was the poor old king, too, leaning on his son's arm, and looking as if his single heart held all the grief of Athens.

Just as Prince Theseus was going on board, his father bethought himself of one last word to say.

"My beloved son," said he, grasping the prince's hand, "you observe that the sails of this vessel are black; as indeed they ought to be, since it goes upon a voyage of sorrow and despair. Now, being weighed down with infirmities, I know not whether I can survive till the vessel shall return. But, as long as I do live, I shall creep daily to the top of yonder cliff, to watch if there be a sail upon the sea. And, dearest Theseus, if by some happy chance, you should escape the jaws of the Minotaur, then tear down those dismal sails, and hoist others that shall be bright as the sunshine. Beholding them on the horizon, myself and all the people will know that you are coming back victorious, and will welcome you with such a festal uproar as Athens never heard before." Theseus promised that he would do so. Then, going on board, the mariners trimmed the vessel's black sails to the wind, which blew faintly off the shore, being pretty much made up of the sighs that everybody kept pouring forth on this melancholy occasion. But by and by, when they had got fairly out to sea, there came a stiff breeze from the northwest, and drove them along as merrily over the white-capped waves as if they had been going on the most delightful errand imaginable. And though it was a sad business enough, I rather question whether fourteen young people, without any old persons to keep them in order, could continue to spend the whole time of the voyage in being miserable. There had been some few dances upon the undulating deck, I suspect, and some hearty bursts of laughter, and other such unseasonable merriment among the victims, before the high, blue mountains of Crete began to show themselves among the far-off clouds. That sight, to be sure, made them all very grave again.

Theseus stood among the sailors, gazing eagerly towards the land; although, as yet, it seemed hardly more substantial than the clouds, amidst which the mountains were looming up. Once or twice, he fancied that he saw a glare of some bright object, a long way off, flinging a gleam across the waves.

"Did you see that flash of light?" he inquired of the master of the vessel.

"No, prince; but I have seen it before," answered the master. "It came from Talus, I suppose."

As the breeze came fresher just then, the master was busy with trimming his sails, and had no more time to answer questions. But while the vessel flew faster and faster towards Crete, Theseus was astonished to behold a human figure, gigantic in size, which appeared to be striding, with a measured movement, along the margin of the island. It stepped from cliff to cliff, and sometimes from one headland to another, while the sea foamed and thundered on the shore beneath, and dashed its jets of spray over the giant's feet. What was still more remarkable, whenever the sun shone on this huge figure, it flickered and glimmered; its vast countenance, too, had a metallic lustre, and threw great flashes of splendour through the air. The folds of its garments, moreover, instead of waving in the wind, fell heavily over its limbs, as if woven of some kind of metal.

The nigher the vessel came, the more Theseus wondered what this immense giant could be and whether it actually had life or no. For though it walked, and made other lifelike motions, there yet was a kind of jerk in its gait, which, together with its brazen aspect, caused the young prince to suspect that it was no true giant, but only a wonderful piece of machinery. The figure looked all the more terrible because it carried an enormous brass club on its shoulder.

"What is this wonder?" Theseus asked of the master of the vessel, who was now at leisure to answer him.

"It is Talus, the man of Brass," said the master.

"And is he a live giant, or a brazen image?" asked Theseus.

"That, truly," replied the master, "is the point which has always perplexed me. Some say, indeed, that this Talus was hammered out for King Minos by Vulcan himself, the skilfulest of all workers in metal. But who ever saw a brazen image that had sense enough to walk round an island three times a day, as this giant walks round the Island of Crete, challenging every vessel that comes nigh the shore? And, on the other hand, what living thing, unless his sinews were made of brass, would not be weary of marching eighteen hundred miles in the twenty-four hours, as Talus does, without ever sitting down to rest? He is a puzzler, take him how you will."

Still the vessel went bounding onward; and now Theseus could hear the brazen clangour of the giant's footsteps, as he trod heavily upon the sea-beaten rocks, some of which were seen to crack and crumble into the foamy waves beneath his weight. As they approached the entrance of the port, the giant straddled clear across it, with a foot firmly planted on each headland, and uplifting his club to such a height that its butt-end was hidden in a cloud, he stood in that formidable posture, with the sun gleaming all over his metallic surface. There seemed nothing else to be expected but that, the next moment, he would fetch his great club down, slam bang, and smash the vessel into a thousand pieces, without heeding how many innocent people he might destroy; for there is seldom any mercy in a giant, you know, and quite as little in a piece of brass clockwork. But just when Theseus and his companions thought the blow was coming, the brazen lips unclosed themselves, and the figure spoke.

"Whence come you, strangers?"

And when the ringing voice ceased, there was just such a reverberation as you may have heard within a great church bell, for a moment or two after the stroke of the hammer.

"From Athens!" shouted the master in reply.

"On what errand?" thundered the Man of Brass.

And he whirled his club aloft more threateningly than ever, as if he were about to smite them with a thunderstroke right amidships, because Athens, so little while ago, had been at war with Crete.

"We bring the seven youths and the seven maidens," answered the master, "to be devoured by the Minotaur!"

"Pass!" cried the brazen giant.

That one loud word rolled all about the sky, while again there was a booming reverberation within the figure's breast. The vessel glided between the headlands of the port, and the giant resumed his march. In a few moments, this wondrous sentinel was far away, flashing in the distant sunshine, and revolving with immense strides around the Island of Crete, as it was his never-ceasing task to do.

No sooner had they entered the harbour than a party of the guards of King Minos came down to the water side, and took charge of the fourteen young men and damsels. Surrounded by these armed warriors, Prince Theseus and his companions were led to the king's palace, and ushered into his presence. Now, Minos was a stern and pitiless king. If the figure that guarded Crete was made of brass, then the monarch, who ruled over it, might be thought to have a still harder metal in his breast, and might have been called a man of iron. He bent his shaggy brows upon the poor Athenian victims. Any other mortal, beholding their fresh and tender beauty, and their innocent looks, would have felt himself sitting on thorns until he had made every soul of them happy, by bidding them go free as the summer wind. But this immitigable Minos cared only to examine whether they were plump enough to satisfy the Minotaur's appetite. For my part, I wish he himself had been the only victim; and the monster would have found him a pretty tough one.

One after another, King Minos called these pale, frightened youths and sobbing maidens to his footstool, gave them each a poke in the ribs with his sceptre, (to try whether they were in good flesh or no,) and dismissed them with a nod to his guards. But when his eyes rested on Theseus, the king looked at him more attentively, because his face was calm and brave.

"Young man," asked he, with his stern voice, "are you not appalled at the certainty of being devoured by this terrible Minotaur?"

"I have offered my life in a good cause," answered Theseus, "and therefore I give it freely and gladly. But thou, King Minos, art thou not thyself appalled, who, year after year, hast perpetrated this dreadful wrong, by giving seven innocent youths and as many maidens to be devoured by a monster? Dost thou not tremble, wicked king, to turn thine eyes inward on thine own heart? Sitting there on thy golden throne, and in thy robes of majesty, I tell thee to thy face, King Minos, thou art a more hideous monster than the Minotaur himself!"

"Aha! do you think me so?" cried the king, laughing in his cruel way. "To-morrow, at breakfast time, you shall have an opportunity of judging which is the greater monster, the Minotaur or the king! Take them away, guards; and let this free-spoken youth be the Minotaur's first morsel!"

Near the king's throne (though I had no time to tell you so before) stood his daughter, Ariadne. She was a beautiful and tender-hearted maiden, and looked at these poor doomed captives with very different feelings from those of the ironbreasted King Minos. She really wept, indeed, at the idea of how much human happiness would be needlessly thrown away, by giving so many young people, in the first bloom and rose blossom of their lives, to be eaten up by a creature who, no doubt, would have preferred a fat ox, or even a large pig, to the plumpest of them. And when she beheld the brave, spirited figure of Prince Theseus bearing himself so calmly in his terrible peril, she grew a hundred times more pitiful than before. As the guards were taking him away, she flung herself at the king's feet, and besought him to set all the captives free, and especially this one young man.

"Peace, foolish girl!" answered King Minos. "What hast thou to do with an affair like this? It is a matter of state policy, and therefore quite beyond thy weak comprehension. Go water thy flowers, and think no more of these Athenian caitiffs, whom the Minotaur shall as certainly eat up for breakfast as I will eat a partridge for my supper."

So saying, the king looked cruel enough to devour Theseus and all the rest of the captives, himself, had there been no Minotaur to save him the trouble. As he would hear not another word in their favour, the prisoners were now led away, and clapped into a dungeon, where the jailer advised them to go to sleep as soon as possible, because the Minotaur was in the habit of calling for breakfast early. The seven maidens and six of the young men soon sobbed themselves to slumber. But Theseus was not like them. He felt conscious that he was wiser, and braver, and stronger than his companions, and that therefore he had the responsibility of all their lives upon him, and must consider whether there was no way to save them, even in this last extremity. So he kept himself awake, and paced to and fro across the gloomy dungeon in which they were shut up.

Just before midnight, the door was softly unbarred, and the gentle Ariadne showed herself, with a torch in her hand.

"Are you awake, Prince Theseus?" she whispered.

"Yes," answered Theseus. "With so little time to live, I do not choose to waste any of it in sleep."

"Then follow me," said Ariadne, "and tread softly."

What had become of the jailer and the guards, Theseus never knew. But, however that might be, Ariadne opened all the doors, and led him forth from the darksome prison into the pleasant moonlight.

"Theseus," said the maiden, "you can now get on board your vessel, and sail away for Athens."

"No," answered the young man; "I will never leave Crete unless I can first slay the Minotaur, and save my poor companions, and deliver Athens from this cruel tribute."

"I knew that this would be your resolution," said Ariadne. "Come, then, with me, brave Theseus. Here is your own sword, which the guards deprived you of. You will need it; and pray Heaven you may use it well."

Then she led Theseus along by the hand until they came to a dark, shadowy grove, where the moonlight wasted itself on the tops of the trees, without shedding hardly so much as a glimmering beam upon their pathway. After going a good way through this obscurity, they reached a high, marble wall, which was overgrown with creeping plants, that made it shaggy with their verdure. The wall seemed to have no door, nor any windows, but rose up, lofty, and massive, and mysterious, and was neither to be clambered over, nor, so far as Theseus could perceive, to be passed through. Nevertheless, Ariadne did but press one of her soft little fingers against a particular block of marble, and, though it looked as solid as any other part of the wall, it yielded to her touch, disclosing an entrance just wide enough to admit them. They crept through, and the marble stone swung back into its place.

"We are now," said Ariadne, "in the famous labyrinth which Dædalus built before he made himself a pair of wings, and flew away from our island like a bird. That Dædalus was a very cunning workman; but of all his artful contrivances, this labyrinth is the most wondrous. Were we to take but a few steps from the doorway, we might wander about all our lifetime, and never find it again. Yet in the very centre of this labyrinth is the Minotaur; and, Theseus, you must go thither to seek him.

"But how shall I ever find him," asked Theseus, "if the labyrinth so bewilders me as you say it will?"

Just as he spoke, they heard a rough and very disagreeable roar, which greatly resembled the lowing of a fierce bull, but yet had some sort of sound like the human voice. Theseus even fancied a rude articulation in it, as if the creature that uttered it were trying to shape his hoarse breath into words. It was at some distance, however, and he really could not tell whether it sounded most like a bull's roar or a man's harsh voice.

"That is the Minotaur's noise," whispered Ariadne, closely grasping the hand of Theseus, and pressing one of her own hands to her heart, which was all in a tremble. "You must follow that sound through the windings of the labyrinth, and, by and by, you will find him. Stay! take the end of this silken string; I will hold the other end; and then, if you win the victory, it will lead you again to this spot. Farewell, brave Theseus."

So the young man took the end of the silken string in his left hand, and his gold-hilted sword ready drawn from its scabbard, in the other, and trod boldly into the inscrutable labyrinth. How this labyrinth was built is more than I can tell you. But so cunningly contrived a mizmaze was never seen in the world, before nor since. There can be nothing else so intricate, unless it were the brain of a man like Dædalus, who planned it, or the heart of any ordinary man; which last, to be sure, is ten times as great a mystery as the labyrinth of Crete. Theseus had not taken five steps before he lost sight of Ariadne; and in five more his head was growing dizzy. But still he went on, now creeping through a low arch, now ascending a flight of steps, now in one crooked passage, and now in another, with here a door opening before him, and there one banging behind, until it really seemed as if the walls spun round, and whirled him along with them. And all the while, through these hollow avenues, now nearer, now farther off again, resounded the cry of the Minotaur; and the sound was so fierce, so cruel, so ugly, so like a bull's roar, and withal so like a human voice, and yet like neither of them, that the brave heart of Theseus grew sterner and angrier at every step, for he felt it an insult to the moon and sky, and to our affectionate and simple Mother Earth, that such a monster should have the audacity to exist.

As he passed onward, the clouds gathered over the moon, and the labyrinth grew so dusky that Theseus could no longer discern the bewilderment through which he was passing. He would have felt quite lost, and utterly hopeless of ever again walking in a straight path, if, every little while, he had not been conscious of a gentle twitch at the silken cord. Then he knew that the tender-hearted Ariadne was still holding the other end, and that she was fearing for him, and hoping for him, and giving him just as much of her sympathy as if she were close by his side. O, indeed, I can assure you, there was a vast deal of human sympathy running along that slender thread of silk. But still he followed the dreadful roar of the Minotaur, which now grew louder and louder, and finally so very loud that Theseus fully expected to come close upon him, at every new zigzag and wriggle of the path. And at last, in an open space, at the very centre of the labyrinth, he did discern the hideous creature.

Sure enough, what an ugly monster it was! Only his horned head belonged to a bull; and yet, somehow or other, he looked like a bull all over, preposterously waddling on his hind legs; or if you happened to view him in another way, he seemed wholly a man, and all the more monstrous for being so. And there he was, the wretched thing, with no society, no companion, no kind of a mate, living only to do mischief, and incapable of knowing what affection means. Theseus hated him, and shuddered at him, and yet could not but be sensible of some sort of pity; and all the more, the uglier and more detestable the creature was. For he kept striding to and fro, in a solitary frenzy of rage, continually emitting a hoarse roar, which was oddly mixed up with half-shaped words; and, after listening a while, Theseus understood that the Minotaur was saying to himself how miserable he was, and how hungry, and how he hated everybody, and how he longed to eat up the human race alive.

Ah, the bull-headed villain! And O, my good little people, you will perhaps see, one of these days, as I do now, that every human being who suffers anything evil to get into his nature, or to remain there, is a kind of Minotaur, an enemy of his fellow-creatures, and separated from all good companionship, as this poor monster was.

Was Theseus afraid? By no means, my dear auditors. What! a hero like Theseus afraid! Not had the Minotaur had twenty bull heads instead of one. Bold as he was, however, I rather fancy that it strengthened his valiant heart, just at this crisis, to feel a tremulous twitch at the silken cord, which he was still holding in his left hand. It was as if Ariadne were giving him all her might and courage; and, much as he already had, and little as she had to give, it made his own seem twice as much. And to confess the honest truth, he needed the whole; for now the Minotaur, turning suddenly about, caught sight of Theseus, and instantly lowered his horribly sharp horns, exactly as a mad bull does when he means to rush against an enemy. At the same time, he belched forth a tremendous roar, in which there was something like the words of human language, but all disjointed and shaken to pieces by passing through the gullet of a miserably enraged brute.

Theseus could only guess what the creature intended to say, and that rather by his gestures than his words; for the Minotaur's horns were sharper than his wits, and of a great deal more service to him than his tongue. But probably this was the sense of what he uttered:

"Ah, wretch of a human being! I'll stick my horns through you, and toss you fifty feet high, and eat you up the moment you come down."

"Come on, then, and try it!" was all that Theseus deigned to reply; for he was far too magnanimous to assault his enemy with insolent language.

Without more words on either side, there ensued the most awful fight between Theseus and the Minotaur that ever happened beneath the sun or moon. I really know not how it might have turned out, if the monster, in his first headlong rush against Theseus, had not missed him, by a hair's breadth, and broken one of his horns short off against the stone wall. On this mishap, he bellowed so intolerably that a part of the labyrinth tumbled down, and all the inhabitants of Crete mistook the noise for an uncommonly heavy thunder storm. Smarting with the pain, he galloped around the open space in so ridiculous a way that Theseus laughed at it, long afterwards, though not precisely at the moment. After this, the two antagonists stood valiantly up to one another, and fought, sword to horn, for a long while. At last, the Minotaur made a run at Theseus, grazed his left side with his horn, and flung him down; and thinking that he had stabbed him to the heart, he cut a great caper in the air, opened his bull mouth from ear to ear, and prepared to snap his head off. But Theseus by this time had leaped up, and caught the monster off his guard. Fetching a sword stroke at him with all his force, he hit him fair upon the neck, and made his bull head skip six yards from his human body, which fell down flat upon the ground.

So now the battle was ended. Immediately the moon shone out as brightly as if all the troubles of the world, and all the wickedness and the ugliness that infest human life, were past and gone forever. And Theseus, as he leaned on his sword, taking breath, felt another twitch of the silken cord; for all through the terrible encounter, he had held it fast in his left hand. Eager to let Ariadne know of his success, he followed the guidance of the thread, and soon found himself at the entrance of the labyrinth.

"Thou hast slain the monster," cried Ariadne, clasping her hands.

"Thanks to thee, dear Ariadne," answered Theseus, "I return victorious."

"Then," said Ariadne, "we must quickly summon thy friends, and get them and thyself on board the vessel before dawn. If morning finds thee here, my father will avenge the Minotaur."

To make my story short, the poor captives were awakened, and, hardly knowing whether it was not a joyful dream, were told of what Theseus had done, and that they must set sail for Athens before daybreak. Hastening down to the vessel, they all clambered on board, except Prince Theseus, who lingered behind them, on the strand, holding Ariadne's hand clasped in his own.

"Dear maiden," said he, "thou wilt surely go with us. Thou art too gentle and sweet a child for such an iron-hearted father as King Minos. He cares no more for thee than a granite rock cares for the little flower that grows in one of its crevices. But my father, King Ægeus, and my mother, Æthra, and all the fathers and mothers in Athens, and all the sons and daughters too, will love and honour thee as their benefactress. Come with us, then; for King Minos will be very angry when he knows what thou hast done."

Now, some low-minded people, who pretend to tell the story of Theseus and Ariadne, have the face to say that this royal and honourable maiden did really flee away, under cover of the night, with the young stranger whose life she had preserved. They say, too, that Prince Theseus (who would have died sooner than wrong the meanest creature in the world) ungratefully deserted Ariadne, on a solitary island, where the vessel touched on its voyage to Athens. But, had the noble Theseus heard these falsehoods, he would have served their slanderous authors as he served the Minotaur! Here is what Ariadne answered, when the brave prince of Athens besought her to accompany him:

"No, Theseus," the maiden said, pressing his hand, and then drawing back a step or two, "I cannot go with you. My father is old, and has nobody but myself to love him. Hard as you think his heart is, it would break to lose me. At first, King Minos will be angry; but he will soon forgive his only child; and, by and by, he will rejoice, I know, that no more youths and maidens must come from Athens to be devoured by the Minotaur. I have saved you, Theseus, as much for my father's sake as for your own. Farewell! Heaven bless you!"

All this was so true, and so maiden-like, and was spoken with so sweet a dignity, that Theseus would have blushed to urge her any longer. Nothing remained for him, therefore, but to bid Ariadne an affectionate farewell, and to go on board the vessel, and set sail.

In a few moments the white foam was boiling up before their prow, as Prince Theseus and his companions sailed out of the harbour, with a whistling breeze behind them. Talus, the brazen giant, on his never-ceasing sentinel's march, happened to be approaching that part of the coast; and they saw him, by the glimmering of the moonbeams on his polished surface, while he was yet a great way off. As the figure moved like clockwork, however, and could neither hasten his enormous strides nor retard them, he arrived at the port when they were just beyond the reach of his club. Nevertheless, straddling from headland to headland, as his custom was, Talus attempted to strike a blow at the vessel, and, overreaching himself, tumbled full length into the sea, which splashed high over his gigantic shape, as when an iceberg turns a somerset. There he lies yet; and whoever desires to enrich himself by means of brass had better go thither with a diving bell, and fish up Talus.

On the homeward voyage, the fourteen youths and damsels were in excellent spirits, as you will easily suppose. They spent most of their time in dancing, unless when the sidelong breeze made the deck slope too much. In due season, they came within sight of the coast of Attica, which was their native country. But here, I am grieved to tell you, happened a sad misfortune.

You will remember (what Theseus unfortunately forgot) that his father, King Ægeus, had enjoined upon him to hoist sunshiny sails, instead of black ones, in case he should overcome the Minotaur, and return victorious. In the joy of their success, however, and amidst the sports, dancing, and other merriment, with which these young folks wore away the time, they never once thought whether their sails were black, white, or rainbow coloured, and, indeed, left it entirely to the mariners whether they had any sails at all. Thus the vessel returned, like a raven, with the same sable wings that had wafted her away. But poor King Ægeus, day after day, infirm as he was, had clambered to the summit of a cliff that overhung the sea, and there sat watching for Prince Theseus, homeward bound; and no sooner did he behold the fatal blackness of the sails, than he concluded that his dear son, whom he loved so much, and felt so proud of, had been eaten by the Minotaur. He could not bear the thought of living any longer; so, first flinging his crown and sceptre into the sea, (useless baubles that they were to him now!) King Ægeus merely stooped forward, and fell headlong over the cliff, and was drowned, poor soul, in the waves that foamed at its base!

This was melancholy news for Prince Theseus, who, when he stepped ashore, found himself king of all the country, whether he would or no; and such a turn of fortune was enough to make any young man feel very much out of spirits. However, he sent for his dear mother to Athens, and, by taking her advice in matters of state, became a very excellent monarch, and was greatly beloved by his people.

The Símúrgh in the Shah Nameh

Zál, the Son of Sám

ACCORDING TO THE traditionary histories from which Firdusi has derived his legends, the warrior Sám had a son born to him whose hair was perfectly white. On his birth the nurse went to Sám and told him that God had blessed him with a wonderful child, without a single blemish, excepting that his hair was white; but when Sám saw him he was grieved:

> *His hair was white as goose's wing,*
> *His cheek was like the rose of spring*
> *His form was straight as cypress tree—*
> *But when the sire was brought to see*
> *That child with hair so silvery white,*
> *His heart revolted at the sight.*

His mother gave him the name of Zál and the people said to Sám, "This is an ominous event, and will be to thee productive of nothing but calamity; it would be better if thou couldst remove him out of sight.

> *"No human being of this earth*
> *Could give to such a monster birth;*
> *He must be of the Demon race,*
> *Though human still in form and face.*
> *If not a Demon, he, at least,*
> *Appears a party-coloured beast."*

When Sám was made acquainted with these reproaches and sneers of the people, he determined, though with a sorrowful heart, to take him up to the mountain Alberz, and abandon him there to be destroyed by beasts of prey. Alberz was the abode of the Símúrgh or Griffin, and, whilst flying about in quest of food for his hungry young ones, that surprising animal discovered the child lying alone upon the hard rock, crying and sucking its fingers. The Símúrgh, however, felt no inclination to devour him, but compassionately took him up in the air, and conveyed him to his own habitation.

> *He who is blest with Heaven's grace*
> *Will never want a dwelling-place*
> *And he who bears the curse of Fate*
> *Can never change his wretched state.*
> *A voice, not earthly, thus addressed*
> *The Símúrgh in his mountain nest—*
> *"To thee this mortal I resign,*
> *Protected by the power divine;*
> *Let him thy fostering kindness share,*
> *Nourish him with paternal care;*
> *For from his loins, in time, will spring*
> *The champion of the world, and bring*
> *Honour on earth, and to thy name;*
> *The heir of everlasting fame."*

The young ones were also kind and affectionate to the infant, which was thus nourished and protected by the Símúrgh for several years.

The Dream of Sám

It is said that one night, after melancholy musings and reflecting on the miseries of this life, Sám was visited by a dream, and when the particulars of it were communicated to the interpreters of mysterious warnings and omens, they declared that Zál was certainly still alive, although he had been long exposed on Alberz, and left there to be torn to pieces by wild animals. Upon this interpretation being given, the natural feelings of the father returned, and he sent his people to the mountain in search of Zál, but without success. On another night Sám dreamt a second time, when he beheld a young man of a beautiful countenance at the head of an immense army, with a banner flying before him, and a Múbid on his left hand. One of them addressed Sám, and reproached him thus:

> *Unfeeling mortal, hast thou from thy eyes*
> *Washed out all sense of shame? Dost thou believe*
> *That to have silvery tresses is a crime?*
> *If so, thy head is covered with white hair;*
> *And were not both spontaneous gifts from Heaven?*
> *Although the boy was hateful to thy sight,*
> *The grace of God has been bestowed upon him;*
> *And what is human tenderness and love*
> *To Heaven's protection? Thou to him wert cruel,*
> *But Heaven has blest him, shielding him from harm.*

Sám screamed aloud in his sleep, and awoke greatly terrified. Without delay he went himself to Alberz, and ascended the mountain, and wept and prayed before the throne of the Almighty, saying:

> *"If that forsaken child be truly mine,*
> *And not the progeny of Demon fell,*

O pity me! forgive the wicked deed,
And to my eyes, my injured son restore."

His prayer was accepted. The Símúrgh, hearing the lamentations of Sám among his people, knew that he had come in quest of his son, and thus said to Zál: – "I have fed and protected thee like a kind nurse, and I have given thee the name of Dustán, like a father. Sám, the warrior, has just come upon the mountain in search of his child, and I must restore thee to him, and we must part." Zál wept when he heard of this unexpected separation, and in strong terms expressed his gratitude to his benefactor; for the Wonderful Bird had not omitted to teach him the language of the country, and to cultivate his understanding, removed as they were to such a distance from the haunts of mankind. The Símúrgh soothed him by assuring him that he was not going to abandon him to misfortune, but to increase his prosperity; and, as a striking proof of affection, gave him a feather from his own wing, with these instructions: – "Whenever thou art involved in difficulty or danger, put this feather on the fire, and I will instantly appear to thee to ensure thy safety. Never cease to remember me.

"I have watched thee with fondness by day and by night,
And supplied all thy wants with a father's delight;
O forget not thy nurse – still be faithful to me—
And my heart will be ever devoted to thee."

Zál immediately replied in a strain of gratitude and admiration; and then the Símúrgh conveyed him to Sám, and said to him: "Receive thy son – he is of wonderful promise, and will be worthy of the throne and the diadem."

The soul of Sám rejoiced to hear
Applause so sweet to a parent's ear;
And blessed them both in thought and word,
The lovely boy, and the Wondrous Bird.

He also declared to Zál that he was ashamed of the crime of which he had been guilty, and that he would endeavor to obliterate the recollection of the past by treating him in future with the utmost respect and honor.

When Minúchihr heard from Zábul of these things, and of Sám's return, he was exceedingly pleased, and ordered his son, Nauder, with a splendid istakbál, to meet the father and son on their approach to the city. They were surrounded by warriors and great men, and Sám embraced the first moment to introduce Zál to the king.

Zál humbly kissed the earth before the king,
And from the hands of Minúchihr received
A golden mace and helm. Then those who knew
The stars and planetary signs, were told
To calculate the stripling's destiny;
And all proclaimed him of exalted fortune,
That he would be prodigious in his might,
Outshining every warrior of the age.

Delighted with this information, Minúchihr, seated upon his throne, with Kárun on one side and Sám on the other, presented Zál with Arabian horses, and armor, and gold, and splendid garments, and appointed Sám to the government of Kábul, Zábul, and Ind. Zál accompanied his father on his return; and when they arrived at Zábulistán, the most renowned instructors in every art and science were collected together to cultivate and enrich his young mind.

In the meantime Sám was commanded by the king to invade and subdue the Demon provinces of Karugsár and Mázinderán; and Zál was in consequence left by his father in charge of Zábulistán. The young nursling of the Símúrgh is said to have performed the duties of sovereignty with admirable wisdom and discretion, during the absence of his father. He did not pass his time in idle exercises, but with zealous delight in the society of accomplished and learned men, for the purpose of becoming familiar with every species of knowledge and acquirement. The city of Zábul, however, as a constant residence, did not entirely satisfy him, and he wished to see more of the world; he therefore visited several other places, and proceeded as far as Kábul, where he pitched his tents, and remained for some time.

The Seven Labours of Rustem

Later on in the Shah Nameh, *is retold the story of the seven labours of Rustem. Before they even attempt to seize the city of Mázinderán, the Iranian king Kai-káús and his army are defeated, blinded and captured. Kai-káús sends a plea for help to fellow king Zál, whose brave young son Rustem sets out to liberate the captives by the quickest route – this route, however, is 'full of dangers and difficulty, and lions, and demons, and sorcery', not to mention a 'monstrous dragon-serpent'...*

FIRST STAGE. He (Rustem, the hero of the *Shah Nameh*) rapidly pursued his way, performing two days' journey in one, and soon came to a forest full of wild asses. Oppressed with hunger, he succeeded in securing one of them, which he roasted over a fire, lighted by sparks produced by striking the point of his spear, and kept in a blaze with dried grass and branches of trees. After regaling himself, and satisfying his hunger, he loosened the bridle of Rakush, and allowed him to graze; and choosing a safe place for repose during the night, and taking care to have his sword under his head, he went to sleep among the reeds of that wilderness. In a short space a fierce lion appeared, and attacked Rakush with great violence; but Rakush very speedily with his teeth and heels put an end to his furious assailant. Rustem, awakened by the confusion, and seeing the dead lion before him, said to his favorite companion:

> *"Ah! Rakush, why so thoughtless grown,*
> *To fight a lion thus alone;*
> *For had it been thy fate to bleed,*
> *And not thy foe, my gallant steed!*
> *How could thy master have conveyed*

> *His helm, and battle-axe, and blade,*
> *Kamund, and bow, and buberyán,*
> *Unaided, to Mázinderán?*
> *Why didst thou fail to give the alarm,*
> *And save thyself from chance of harm,*
> *By neighing loudly in my ear;*
> *But though thy bold heart knows no fear,*
> *From such unwise exploits refrain,*
> *Nor try a lion's strength again."*

Saying this, Rustem laid down to sleep, and did not awake till the morning dawned. As the sun rose, he remounted Rakush, and proceeded on his journey towards Mázinderán.

Second Stage. After travelling rapidly for some time, he entered a desert, in which no water was to be found, and the sand was so burning hot, that it seemed to be instinct with fire. Both horse and rider were oppressed with the most maddening thirst. Rustem alighted, and vainly wandered about in search of relief, till almost exhausted, he put up a prayer to Heaven for protection against the evils which surrounded him, engaged as he was in an enterprise for the release of Kai-káús and the Persian army, then in the power of the demons. With pious earnestness he besought the Almighty to bless him in the great work; and whilst in a despairing mood he was lamenting his deplorable condition, his tongue and throat being parched with thirst, his body prostrate on the sand, under the influence of a raging sun, he saw a sheep pass by, which he hailed as the harbinger of good. Rising up and grasping his sword in his hand, he followed the animal, and came to a fountain of water, where he devoutly returned thanks to God for the blessing which had preserved his existence, and prevented the wolves from feeding on his lifeless limbs. Refreshed by the cool water, he then looked out for something to allay his hunger, and killing a gor, he lighted a fire and roasted it, and regaled upon its savory flesh, which he eagerly tore from the bones.

When the period of rest arrived, Rustem addressed Rakush, and said to him angrily:

> *"Beware, my steed, of future strife.*
> *Again thou must not risk thy life;*
> *Encounter not with lion fell,*
> *Nor demon still more terrible;*
> *But should an enemy appear,*
> *Ring loud the warning in my ear."*

> *After delivering these injunctions, Rustem laid down to sleep, leaving*
> *Rakush unbridled, and at liberty to crop the herbage close by.*

Third Stage. At midnight a monstrous dragon-serpent issued from the forest; it was eighty yards in length, and so fierce, that neither elephant, nor demon, nor lion, ever ventured to pass by its lair. It came forth, and seeing the champion asleep, and a horse near him, the latter was the first object of attack. But Rakush retired towards his master, and neighed and beat the ground so furiously, that Rustem soon awoke; looking around on every side, however, he saw nothing – the dragon had vanished, and he went to sleep again. Again the dragon burst out of the thick darkness, and again Rakush was at the pillow of his master, who rose up at the alarm: but anxiously trying to penetrate the dreary gloom, he saw nothing – all was a blank; and annoyed at this apparently vexatious conduct of his horse, he spoke sharply:

> *"Why thus again disturb my rest,*
> *When sleep had softly soothed my breast?*
> *I told thee, if thou chanced to see*
> *Another dangerous enemy,*
> *To sound the alarm; but not to keep*
> *Depriving me of needful sleep;*
> *When nothing meets the eye nor ear,*
> *Nothing to cause a moment's fear!*
> *But if again my rest is broke,*
> *On thee shall fall the fatal stroke,*
> *And I myself will drag this load*
> *Of ponderous arms along the road;*
> *Yes, I will go, a lonely man,*
> *Without thee, to Mázinderán."*

Rustem again went to sleep, and Rakush was resolved this time not to move a step from his side, for his heart was grieved and afflicted by the harsh words that had been addressed to him. The dragon again appeared, and the faithful horse almost tore up the earth with his heels, to rouse his sleeping master. Rustem again awoke, and sprang to his feet, and was again angry; but fortunately at that moment sufficient light was providentially given for him to see the prodigious cause of alarm.

> *Then swift he drew his sword, and closed in strife*
> *With that huge monster. – Dreadful was the shock*
> *And perilous to Rustem; but when Rakush*
> *Perceived the contest doubtful, furiously,*
> *With his keen teeth, he bit and tore away*
> *The dragon's scaly hide; whilst quick as thought*
> *The Champion severed off the ghastly head,*
> *And deluged all the plain with horrid blood.*
> *Amazed to see a form so hideous*
> *Breathless stretched out before him, he returned*
> *Thanks to the Omnipotent for his success,*
> *Saying – "Upheld by thy protecting arm,*
> *What is a lion's strength, a demon's rage,*
> *Or all the horrors of the burning desert,*
> *With not one drop to quench devouring thirst?*
> *Nothing, since power and might proceed from Thee."*

Fourth Stage. Rustem having resumed the saddle, continued his journey through an enchanted territory, and in the evening came to a beautifully green spot, refreshed by flowing rivulets, where he found, to his surprise, a ready-roasted deer, and some bread and salt. He alighted, and sat down near the enchanted provisions, which vanished at the sound of his voice, and presently a tambourine met his eyes, and a flask of wine. Taking up the instrument he played upon it, and chanted a ditty about his own wanderings, and the exploits which he most loved. He said that he had no pleasure in banquets, but only in the field fighting with heroes and crocodiles in war. The song happened to reach the ears of a sorceress, who, arrayed in all the charms of beauty, suddenly approached him, and sat down by his side. The champion put up a prayer of gratitude for having been supplied with food and wine, and music, in the desert of Mázinderán, and not knowing that the enchantress was a demon in disguise, he placed in her hands a cup of wine in the name of God; but at the mention of the Creator, the enchanted form was converted into a black fiend. Seeing this, Rustem threw his kamund, and secured the demon; and, drawing his sword, at once cut the body in two!

Fifth Stage.

> *From thence proceeding onward, he approached*
> *A region destitute of light, a void*
> *Of utter darkness. Neither moon nor star*
> *Peep'd through the gloom; no choice of path remained,*
> *And therefore, throwing loose the rein, he gave*
> *Rakush the power to travel on, unguided.*
> *At length the darkness was dispersed, the earth*
> *Became a scene, joyous and light, and gay,*
> *Covered with waving corn – there Rustem paused*
> *And quitting his good steed among the grass,*
> *Laid himself gently down, and, wearied, slept;*
> *His shield beneath his head, his sword before him.*

When the keeper of the forest saw the stranger and his horse, he went to Rustem, then asleep, and struck his staff violently on the ground, and having thus awakened the hero, he asked him, devil that he was, why he had allowed his horse to feed upon the green corn-field. Angry at these words, Rustem, without uttering a syllable, seized hold of the keeper by the ears, and wrung them off. The mutilated wretch, gathering up his severed ears, hurried away, covered with blood, to his master, Aúlád, and told him of the injury he had sustained from a man like a black demon, with a tiger-skin cuirass and an iron helmet; showing at the same time the bleeding witnesses of his sufferings. Upon being informed of this outrageous proceeding, Aúlád, burning with wrath, summoned together his fighting men, and hastened by the directions of the keeper to the place where Rustem had been found asleep. The champion received the angry lord of the land, fully prepared, on horseback, and heard him demand his name, that he might not slay a worthless antagonist, and why he had torn off the ears of his forest-keeper! Rustem replied that the very sound of his name would make him shudder with horror. Aúlád then ordered his troops to attack Rustem, and they rushed upon him with great fury; but their leader was presently killed by the master-hand, and great numbers were also scattered lifeless over the plain. The survivors running away, Rustem's next object was to follow and secure, by his kamund, the person of Aúlád, and with admirable address and ingenuity, he succeeded in dismounting him and taking him alive. He then bound his hands, and said to him:

> *"If thou wilt speak the truth unmixed with lies,*
> *Unmixed with false prevaricating words,*
> *And faithfully point out to me the caves*
> *Of the White Demon and his warrior chiefs—*

And where Káús is prisoned – thy reward
Shall be the kingdom of Mázinderán;
For I, myself, will place thee on that throne.
But if thou play'st me false – thy worthless blood
Shall answer for the foul deception."
"Stay,
Be not in wrath," Aúlád at once replied—
"Thy wish shall be fulfilled – and thou shalt know
Where king Káús is prisoned – and, beside,
Where the White Demon reigns. Between two dark
And lofty mountains, in two hundred caves
Immeasurably deep, his people dwell.
Twelve hundred Demons keep the watch by night
And Baid, and Sinja. Like a reed, the hills
Tremble whenever the White Demon moves.
But dangerous is the way. A stony desert
Lies full before thee, which the nimble deer
Has never passed. Then a prodigious stream
Two farsangs wide obstructs thy path, whose banks
Are covered with a host of warrior-Demons,
Guarding the passage to Mázinderán;
And thou art but a single man – canst thou
O'ercome such fearful obstacles as these?"

At this the Champion smiled. "Show but the way,
And thou shalt see what one man can perform,
With power derived from God! Lead on, with speed,
To royal Káús." With obedient haste
Aúlád proceeded, Rustem following fast,
Mounted on Rakush. Neither dismal night
Nor joyous day they rested – on they went
Until at length they reached the fatal field,
Where Káús was o'ercome. At midnight hour,
Whilst watching with attentive eye and ear,
A piercing clamor echoed all around,
And blazing fires were seen, and numerous lamps
Burnt bright on every side. Rustem inquired
What this might be. "It is Mázinderán,"
Aúlád rejoined, "and the White Demon's chiefs
Are gathered there." Then Rustem to a tree
Bound his obedient guide – to keep him safe,
And to recruit his strength, laid down awhile
And soundly slept.
When morning dawned, he rose,
And mounting Rakush, put his helmet on,
The tiger-skin defended his broad chest,
And sallying forth, he sought the Demon chief,

Arzang, and summoned him with such a roar
That stream and mountain shook. Arzang sprang up,
Hearing a human voice, and from his tent
Indignant issued – him the champion met,
And clutched his arms and ears, and from his body
Tore off the gory head, and cast it far
Amidst the shuddering Demons, who with fear
Shrunk back and fled, precipitate, lest they
Should likewise feel that dreadful punishment.

Sixth Stage. After this achievement Rustem returned to the place where he had left Aúlád, and having released him, sat down under the tree and related what he had done. He then commanded his guide to show the way to the place where Kai-káús was confined; and when the champion entered the city of Mázinderán, the neighing of Rakush was so loud that the sound distinctly reached the ears of the captive monarch. Káús rejoiced, and said to his people: "I have heard the voice of Rakush, and my misfortunes are at an end;" but they thought he was either insane or telling them a dream. The actual appearance of Rustem, however, soon satisfied them. Gúdarz, and Tús, and Báhrám, and Gíw, and Gustahem, were delighted to meet him, and the king embraced him with great warmth and affection, and heard from him with admiration the story of his wonderful progress and exploits. But Káús and his warriors, under the influence and spells of the Demons, were still blind, and he cautioned Rustem particularly to conceal Rakush from the sight of the sorcerers, for if the White Demon should hear of the slaughter of Arzang, and the conqueror being at Mázinderán, he would immediately assemble an overpowering army of Demons, and the consequences might be terrible.

"But thou must storm the cavern of the Demons
And their gigantic chief – great need there is
For sword and battle-axe – and with the aid
Of Heaven, these miscreant sorcerers may fall
Victims to thy avenging might. The road
Is straight before thee – reach the Seven Mountains,
And there thou wilt discern the various groups,
Which guard the awful passage. Further on,
Within a deep and horrible recess,
Frowns the White Demon – conquer him – destroy
That fell magician, and restore to sight
Thy suffering king, and all his warrior train.
The wise in cures declare, that the warm blood
From the White Demon's heart, dropped in the eye,
Removes all blindness – it is, then, my hope,
Favored by God, that thou wilt slay the fiend,
And save us from the misery we endure,
The misery of darkness without end."

Rustem accordingly, after having warned his friends and companions in arms to keep on the alert, prepared for the enterprise, and guided by Aúlád, hurried on till he came to the Haft-koh, or Seven Mountains. There he found numerous companies of Demons; and coming to one of the caverns, saw it crowded with the same awful beings. And now consulting with Aúlád, he was informed that the most advantageous time for attack would be when the sun became hot, for then all the Demons were accustomed to go to sleep, with the exception of a very small number who were appointed to keep watch. He therefore waited till the sun rose high in the firmament; and as soon as he had bound Aúlád to a tree hand and foot, with the thongs of his kamund, drew his sword, and rushed among the prostrate Demons, dismembering and slaying all that fell in his way. Dreadful was the carnage, and those who survived fled in the wildest terror from the champion's fury.

Seventh Stage. Rustem now hastened forward to encounter the White Demon.

> *Advancing to the cavern, he looked down*
> *And saw a gloomy place, dismal as hell;*
> *But not one cursed, impious sorcerer*
> *Was visible in that infernal depth.*
> *Awhile he stood – his falchion in his grasp,*
> *And rubbed his eyes to sharpen his dim sight,*
> *And then a mountain-form, covered with hair,*
> *Filling up all the space, rose into view.*
> *The monster was asleep, but presently*
> *The daring shouts of Rustem broke his rest,*
> *And brought him suddenly upon his feet,*
> *When seizing a huge mill-stone, forth he came,*
> *And thus accosted the intruding chief:*
> *"Art thou so tired of life, that reckless thus*
> *Thou dost invade the precincts of the Demons?*
> *Tell me thy name, that I may not destroy*
> *A nameless thing!" The champion stern replied,*
> *"My name is Rustem – sent by Zál, my father,*
> *Descended from the champion Sám Súwár,*
> *To be revenged on thee – the King of Persia*
> *Being now a prisoner in Mázinderán."*
> *When the accursed Demon heard the name*
> *Of Sám Súwár, he, like a serpent, writhed*
> *In agony of spirit; terrified*
> *At that announcement – then, recovering strength,*
> *He forward sprang, and hurled the mill-stone huge*
> *Against his adversary, who fell back*
> *And disappointed the prodigious blow.*
> *Black frowned the Demon, and through Rustem's heart*
> *A wild sensation ran of dire alarm;*
> *But, rousing up, his courage was revived,*
> *And wielding furiously his beaming sword,*
> *He pierced the Demon's thigh, and lopped the limb;*
> *Then both together grappled, and the cavern*
> *Shook with the contest – each, at times, prevailed;*
> *The flesh of both was torn, and streaming blood*
> *Crimsoned the earth. "If I survive this day,"*
> *Said Rustem in his heart, in that dread strife,*

"My life must be immortal." The White Demon,
With equal terror, muttered to himself:
"I now despair of life – sweet life; no more
Shall I be welcomed at Mázinderán."
And still they struggled hard – still sweat and blood
Poured down at every strain. Rustem, at last,
Gathering fresh power, vouchsafed by favouring Heaven
And bringing all his mighty strength to bear,
Raised up the gasping Demon in his arms,
And with such fury dashed him to the ground,
That life no longer moved his monstrous frame.
Promptly he then tore out the reeking heart,
And crowds of demons simultaneous fell
As part of him, and stained the earth with gore;
Others who saw this signal overthrow,
Trembled, and hurried from the scene of blood.
Then the great victor, issuing from that cave
With pious haste – took off his helm, and mail,
And royal girdle – and with water washed
His face and body – choosing a pure place
For prayer – to praise his Maker – Him who gave
The victory, the eternal source of good;
Without whose grace and blessing, what is man!
With it his armor is impregnable.

The Champion having finished his prayer, resumed his war habiliments, and going to Aúlád, released him from the tree, and gave into his charge the heart of the White Demon. He then pursued his journey back to Káús at Mázinderán. On the way Aúlád solicited some reward for the services he had performed, and Rustem again promised that he should be appointed governor of the country.

"But first the monarch of Mázinderán,
The Demon-king, must be subdued, and cast
Into the yawning cavern – and his legions
Of foul enchanters, utterly destroyed."

Upon his arrival at Mázinderán, Rustem related to his sovereign all that he had accomplished, and especially that he had torn out and brought away the White Demon's heart, the blood of which was destined to restore Kai-káús and his warriors to sight. Rustem was not long in applying the miraculous remedy, and the moment the blood touched their eyes, the fearful blindness was perfectly cured.

The champion brought the Demon's heart,
And squeezed the blood from every part,
Which, dropped upon the injured sight,
Made all things visible and bright;
One moment broke that magic gloom,
Which seemed more dreadful than the tomb.

The monarch immediately ascended his throne surrounded by all his warriors, and seven days were spent in mutual congratulations and rejoicing. On the eighth day they all resumed the saddle, and proceeded to complete the destruction of the enemy. They set fire to the city, and burnt it to the ground, and committed such horrid carnage among the remaining magicians that streams of loathsome blood crimsoned all the place.

Káús afterwards sent Ferhád as an ambassador to the king of Mázinderán, suggesting to him the expediency of submission, and representing to him the terrible fall of Arzang, and of the White Demon with all his host, as a warning against resistance to the valor of Rustem. But when the king of Mázinderán heard from Ferhád the purpose of his embassy, he expressed great astonishment, and replied that he himself was superior in all respects to Káús; that his empire was more extensive, and his warriors more numerous and brave. "Have I not," said he, "a hundred war-elephants, and Káús not one? Wherever I move, conquest marks my way; why then should I fear the sovereign of Persia? Why should I submit to him?"

This haughty tone made a deep impression upon Ferhád, who returning quickly, told Káús of the proud bearing and fancied power of the ruler of Mázinderán. Rustem was immediately sent for; and so indignant was he on hearing the tidings, that "every hair on his body started up like a spear," and he proposed to go himself with a second dispatch. The king was too much pleased to refuse, and another letter was written more urgent than the first, threatening the enemy to hang up his severed head on the walls of his own fort, if he persisted in his contumacy and scorn of the offer made.

As soon as Rustem had come within a short distance of the court of the king of Mázinderán, accounts reached his majesty of the approach of another ambassador, when a deputation of warriors was sent to receive him. Rustem observing them, and being in sight of the hostile army, with a view to show his strength, tore up a large tree on the road by the roots, and dexterously wielded it in his hand like a spear. Tilting onwards, he flung it down before the wondering enemy, and one of the chiefs then thought it incumbent upon him to display his own prowess. He advanced, and offered to grasp hands with Rustem: they met; but the gripe of the champion was so excruciating that the sinews of his adversary cracked, and in agony he fell from his horse. Intelligence of this discomfiture was instantly conveyed to the king, who then summoned his most valiant and renowned chieftain, Kálahúr, and directed him to go and punish, signally, the warrior who had thus presumed to triumph over one of his heroes. Accordingly Kálahúr appeared, and boastingly stretched out his hand, which Rustem wrung with such grinding force, that the very nails dropped off, and blood started from his body. This was enough, and Kálahúr hastily returned to the king, and anxiously recommended him to submit to terms, as it would be in vain to oppose such invincible strength. The king was both grieved and angry at this situation of affairs, and invited the ambassador to his presence. After inquiring respecting Káús and the Persian army, he said:

> "And thou art Rustem, clothed with mighty power,
> Who slaughtered the White Demon, and now comest
> To crush the monarch of Mázinderán!"
> "No!" said the champion, "I am but his servant,
> And even unworthy of that noble station;
> My master being a warrior, the most valiant
> That ever graced the world since time began.
> Nothing am I; but what doth he resemble!
> What is a lion, elephant, or demon!
> Engaged in fight, he is himself a host!"

The ambassador then tried to convince the king of the folly of resistance, and of his certain defeat if he continued to defy the power of Káús and the bravery of Rustem; but the effort was fruitless, and both states prepared for battle.

The engagement which ensued was obstinate and sanguinary, and after seven days of hard fighting, neither army was victorious, neither defeated. Afflicted at this want of success, Káús grovelled in the dust, and prayed fervently to the Almighty to give him the triumph. He addressed all his warriors, one by one, and urged them to increased exertions; and on the eighth day, when the battle was renewed, prodigies of valor were performed. Rustem singled out, and encountered the king of Mázinderán, and fiercely they fought together with sword and javelin; but suddenly, just as he was rushing on with overwhelming force, his adversary, by his magic art, transformed himself into a stony rock. Rustem and the Persian warriors were all amazement. The fight had been suspended for some time, when Káús came forward to inquire the cause; and hearing with astonishment of the transformation, ordered his soldiers to drag the enchanted mass towards his own tent; but all the strength that could be applied was unequal to move so great a weight, till Rustem set himself to the task, and amidst the wondering army, lifted up the rock and conveyed it to the appointed place. He then addressed the work of sorcery, and said: "If thou dost not resume thy original shape, I will instantly break thee, flinty-rock as thou now art, into atoms, and scatter thee in the dust." The magician-king was alarmed by this threat, and reappeared in his own form, and then Rustem, seizing his hand, brought him to Káús, who, as a punishment for his wickedness and atrocity, ordered him to be slain, and his body to be cut into a thousand pieces! The wealth of the country was immediately afterwards secured; and at the recommendation of Rustem, Aúlád was appointed governor of Mázinderán. After the usual thanksgivings and rejoicings on account of the victory, Káús and his warriors returned to Persia, where splendid honors and rewards were bestowed on every soldier for his heroic services. Rustem having received the highest acknowledgments of his merit, took leave, and returned to his father Zál at Zábulistán.

Suddenly an ardent desire arose in the heart of Káús to survey all the provinces and states of his empire. He wished to visit Túrán, and Chín, and Mikrán, and Berber, and Zirra. Having commenced his royal tour of inspection, he found the King of Berberistán in a state of rebellion, with his army prepared to dispute his authority. A severe battle was the consequence; but the refractory sovereign was soon compelled to retire, and the elders of the city came forward to sue for mercy and protection. After this triumph, Káús turned towards the mountain Káf, and visited various other countries, and in his progress became the guest of the son of Zál in Zábulistán where he stayed a month, enjoying the pleasures of the festive board and the sports of the field.

The disaffection of the King of Hámáverán, in league with the King of Misser and Shám, and the still hostile King of Berberistán, soon, however, drew him from Ním-rúz, and quitting the principality of Rustem, his arms were promptly directed against his new enemy, who in the contest which ensued, made an obstinate resistance, but was at length overpowered, and obliged to ask for quarter. After the battle, Káús was informed that the Sháh had a daughter of great beauty, named Súdáveh, possessing a form as graceful as the tall cypress, musky ringlets, and all the charms of Heaven. From the description of this damsel he became enamoured, and through the medium of a messenger, immediately offered himself to be her husband. The father did not seem to be glad at this proposal, observing to the messenger, that he had but two things in life valuable to him, and those were his daughter and his property; one was his solace and delight, and the other his support; to be deprived of both would be death to him; still he could not gainsay the wishes of a king of such power, and his conqueror. He then sorrowfully communicated the overture to his child, who, however, readily consented; and in the course of a week, the bride was sent escorted by soldiers, and accompanied by a magnificent cavalcade, consisting of a thousand horses and mules, a thousand camels, and numerous female attendants. When Súdáveh descended from her litter, glowing with beauty, with her rich dark tresses flowing to her feet, and cheeks like the rose, Káús regarded her with admiration and rapture; and so impatient was he to possess that lovely treasure, that the marriage rites were performed according to the laws of the country without delay.

The Sháh of Hámáverán, however, was not satisfied, and he continually plotted within himself how he might contrive to regain possession of Súdáveh, as well as be revenged upon the king. With this view he invited Káús to be his guest for a while; but Súdáveh cautioned the king not to trust to the treachery which dictated the invitation, as she apprehended from it nothing but mischief and disaster. The warning, however, was of no avail, for Káús accepted the proffered hospitality of his new father-in-law. He accordingly proceeded with his bride and his most famous warriors to the city, where he was received and entertained in the most sumptuous manner, seated on a gorgeous throne, and felt infinitely exhilarated with the magnificence and the hilarity by which he was surrounded. Seven days were passed in this glorious banqueting and delight; but on the succeeding night, the sound of trumpets and the war-cry was heard. The intrusion of soldiers changed the face of the scene; and the king, who had just been waited on, and pampered with such respect and devotion, was suddenly seized, together with his principal warriors, and carried off to a remote fortress, situated on a high mountain, where they were imprisoned, and guarded by a thousand valiant men. His tents were plundered, and all his treasure taken away. At this event his wife was inconsolable and deaf to all entreaties from her father, declaring that she preferred death to separation from her husband; upon which she was conveyed to the same dungeon, to mingle groans with the captive king.

> *Alas! how false and fickle is the world,*
> *Friendship nor pleasure, nor the ties of blood,*
> *Can check the headlong course of human passions;*
> *Treachery still laughs at kindred; – who is safe*
> *In this tumultuous sphere of strife and sorrow?*

How Obassi Osaw Proved the Wisdom of Tortoise

OBASSI OSAW MARRIED MANY WIVES. Among these was the daughter of Tortoise. She was so proud of her father that she annoyed Obassi by exclaiming, "Oh, my father, you have more sense than any other person!" whenever the least thing happened, even if she only knocked her foot or felt surprised.

Obassi determined to find out for himself if Tortoise was really so very wise. He therefore built a room without doors or windows. Into this he secretly let down eight persons, and sent to Tortoise to come at once and tell him what was within.

Tortoise sent back a message that he would certainly come next day, but in such a way that no one should see him enter, for he was surely the wisest of men, and none could know how he came. Obassi was still more displeased when he heard this.

Now the daughter went and told Tortoise that her husband was annoyed with her for constantly praising her father's wisdom. "Perhaps," said she, "it is to prove this that he has sent for you." Tortoise answered, "It is well."

Next morning Obassi sent other messengers to bid his father-in-law hasten, but, when the men arrived, Tortoise was nowhere to be found. His wife said that he had gone hunting, so the messengers had better not wait. They agreed to this, and set out once more. The woman ran after them with a parcel and said, "Will you please take this to my daughter?"

This the men promised, and gave the parcel to the girl, not knowing that it was Tortoise whom they carried. She bore the packet before Obassi, set it on the ground and unfastened the tie-tie, when out stepped – what? Tortoise himself.

Obassi was very much surprised, and bade the guest go and stay in his daughter's house till next morning. So they went off together.

At night, when all was quiet, Tortoise made a small hole in the wall of the room which Obassi had built. Then he took a stick and dipped it into some foul-smelling stuff. The men who were inside noticed the bad odour, and began calling to each other by name, asking its cause.

In this way Tortoise heard that there were eight men in the secret room, and also learned their names. He was very careful to fill up the little hole which he had made, and afterwards went back to bed.

Next morning a great company was gathered together to witness the shame of Tortoise when he should fail to answer the question of their Lord.

Obassi stood in the middle of the audience room and said very loudly that Tortoise must now tell him what was hidden in the windowless house, or suffer death if he could not do so.

Then Tortoise rose and said that there were eight men shut up within, and, to the surprise of all the people, he repeated their names, thus proving himself to be wiser than all his fellows, just as his daughter had said.

Obassi was so vexed that he ordered his men to seize Tortoise, sharpen a stick, and drive it through this overwise creature, so as to fasten him to the ground at a place where cross-roads meet. He also ordered that the beast should be fixed upright, so as to look at his judge on high. Obassi decreed further that, whenever a man wished to make him a sacrifice, Tortoise should be offered in this way. That is why we often see Tortoise impaled before Jujus, or at cross-roads.

The Grinding-Stone that Ground Flour by Itself

THERE HAD BEEN another great famine throughout the land. The villagers looked thin and pale for lack of food. Only one family appeared healthy and well. This was the household of Anansi's cousin. Anansi was unable to understand this, and felt sure his cousin was getting food in some way. The greedy fellow determined to find out the secret.

What had happened was this: Spider's cousin, while hunting one morning, had discovered a wonderful stone. The stone lay on the grass in the forest and ground flour of its own accord. Near by ran a stream of honey. Kofi was delighted. He sat down and had a good meal. Not being a greedy man, he took away with him only enough for his family's needs.

Each morning he returned to the stone and got sufficient food for that day. In this manner he and his family kept well and plump, while the surrounding villagers were starved and miserable-looking.

Anansi gave him no peace till he promised to show him the stone. This he was most unwilling to do – knowing his cousin's wicked ways. He felt sure that when Anansi saw the stone he would not be content to take only what he needed. However, Anansi troubled him so much with questions that at last he promised. He told Anansi that they would start next morning, as soon as the women set about their work. Anansi was too impatient to wait. In the middle of the night he bade his children get up and make a noise with the pots as if they were the women at work. Spider at once ran and wakened his cousin, saying, "Quick! It is time to start." His cousin, however, saw he had been tricked, and went back to bed again, saying he would not start till the women were sweeping. No sooner was he asleep again than Spider made his children take brooms and begin to sweep very noisily. He roused Kofi once more, saying, "It is time we had started." Once more his cousin refused to set off – saying it was only another trick of Spider's. He again returned to bed and to sleep. This time Spider slipped into his cousin's room and cut a hole in the bottom of his bag, which he then filled with ashes. After that he went off and left Kofi in peace.

When morning came the cousin awoke. Seeing no sign of Spider he very gladly set off alone to the forest, thinking he had got rid of the tiresome fellow. He was no sooner seated by the stone, however, than Anansi appeared, having followed him by the trail of ashes.

"Aha!" cried he. "Here is plenty of food for all. No more need to starve." "Hush," said his cousin. "You must not shout here. The place is too wonderful. Sit down quietly and eat."

They had a good meal, and Kofi prepared to return home with enough for his family. "No, no!" cried Anansi. "I am going to take the stone." In vain did his friend try to overcome his greed. Anansi insisted on putting the stone on his head, and setting out for the village.

> *"Spider, Spider, put me down, said the stone.*
> *The pig came and drank and went away,*
> *The antelope came and fed and went away:*
> *Spider, Spider, put me down."*

Spider, however, refused to listen. He carried the stone from village to village selling flour, until his bag was full of money. He then set out for home.

Having reached his hut and feeling very tired he prepared to put the stone down. But the stone refused to be moved from his head. It stuck fast there, and no efforts could displace it. The weight of it very soon grew too much for Anansi, and ground him down into small pieces, which were completely covered over by the stone. That is why we often find tiny spiders gathered together under large stones.

The Three Billy-Goats Gruff

ONCE ON A TIME there were three Billy-goats, who were to go up to the hill-side to make themselves fat, and the name of all three was 'Gruff.'

On the way up was a bridge over a burn they had to cross; and under the bridge lived a great ugly Troll, with eyes as big as saucers, and a nose as long as a poker.

So first of all came the youngest billy-goat Gruff to cross the bridge.

"Trip, trap; trip, trap!" went the bridge.

"WHO'S THAT tripping over my bridge?" roared the Troll.

"Oh! it is only I, the tiniest billy-goat Gruff; and I'm going up to the hill-side to make myself fat," said the billy-goat, with such a small voice.

"Now, I'm coming to gobble you up," said the Troll.

"Oh, no! pray don't take me. I'm too little, that I am," said the billy-goat; "wait a bit till the second billy-goat Gruff comes, he's much bigger."

"Well! be off with you," said the Troll.

A little while after came the second billy-goat Gruff to cross the bridge.

"TRIP, TRAP! TRIP, TRAP! TRIP, TRAP!" went the bridge.

"WHO'S THAT tripping over my bridge?" roared the Troll.

"Oh! it's the second billy-goat Gruff, and I'm going up to the hill-side to make myself fat," said the billy-goat, who hadn't such a small voice.

"Now, I'm coming to gobble you up," said the Troll.

"Oh, no! don't take me, wait a little till the big billy-goat Gruff comes, he's much bigger."

"Very well! be off with you," said the Troll.

But just then up came the big billy-goat Gruff.

"TRIP, TRAP! TRIP, TRAP! TRIP, TRAP!" went the bridge, for the billy-goat was so heavy that the bridge creaked and groaned under him.

"WHO'S THAT tramping over my bridge?" roared the Troll.

"IT'S I! THE BIG BILLY-GOAT GRUFF," said the billy-goat, who had an ugly hoarse voice of his own.

"Now, I'm coming to gobble you up," roared the Troll.

> *Well, come along! I've got two spears,*
> *And I'll poke your eyeballs out at your ears;*
> *I've got besides two curling-stones,*
> *And I'll crush you to bits, body and bones.*

That was what the big billy-goat said; and so he flew at the Troll and poked his eyes out with his horns, and crushed him to bits, body and bones, and tossed him out into the burn, and after that he went up to the hill-side. There the billy-goats got so fat they were scarce able to walk home again; and if the fat hasn't fallen off them, why they're still fat; and so:

> *Snip, snap, snout,*
> *This tale's told out.*

Soria Moria Castle

THERE WAS ONCE UPON A TIME a couple of folks who had a son called Halvor. Ever since he had been a little boy he had been unwilling to do any work, and had just sat raking about among the ashes. His parents sent him away to learn several things, but Halvor stayed nowhere, for when he had been gone two or three days he always ran away from his master, hurried off home, and sat down in the chimney corner to grub among the ashes again.

One day, however, a sea captain came and asked Halvor if he hadn't a fancy to come with him and go to sea, and behold foreign lands. And Halvor had a fancy for that, so he was not long in getting ready.

How long they sailed I have no idea, but after a long, long time there was a terrible storm, and when it was over and all had become calm again, they knew not where they were, for they had been driven away to a strange coast of which none of them had any knowledge.

As there was no wind at all they lay there becalmed, and Halvor asked the skipper to give him leave to go on shore to look about him, for he would much rather do that than lie there and sleep.

"Dost thou think that thou art fit to go where people can see thee?" said the skipper; "thou hast no clothes but those rags thou art going about in!"

Halvor still begged for leave, and at last got it, but he was to come back at once if the wind began to rise.

So he went on shore, and it was a delightful country; whithersoever he went there were wide plains with fields and meadows, but as for people, there were none to be seen. The wind began to rise, but Halvor thought that he had not seen enough yet, and that he would like to walk about a little longer, to try if he could not meet somebody. So after a while he came to a great highway, which was so smooth that an egg might have been rolled along it without breaking. Halvor followed this, and when evening drew near he saw a big castle far away in the distance, and there were lights in it. So as he had now been walking the whole day and had not brought anything to eat away with him, he was frightfully hungry. Nevertheless, the nearer he came to the castle the more afraid he was.

A fire was burning in the castle, and Halvor went into the kitchen, which was more magnificent than any kitchen he had ever yet beheld. There were vessels of gold and silver, but not one human being was to be seen. When Halvor had stood there for some time, and no one had come out, he went in and opened a door, and inside a Princess was sitting at her wheel spinning.

"Nay!" she cried, "can Christian folk dare to come hither? But the best thing that you can do is to go away again, for if not the Troll will devour you. A Troll with three heads lives here."

"I should have been just as well pleased if he had had four heads more, for I should have enjoyed seeing the fellow," said the youth; "and I won't go away, for I have done no harm, but you must give me something to eat, for I am frightfully hungry."

When Halvor had eaten his fill, the Princess told him to try if he could wield the sword which was hanging on the wall, but he could not wield it, nor could he even lift it up.

"Well, then, you must take a drink out of that bottle which is hanging by its side, for that's what the Troll does whenever he goes out and wants to use the sword," said the Princess.

Halvor took a draught, and in a moment he was able to swing the sword about with perfect ease. And now he thought it was high time for the Troll to make his appearance, and at that very moment he came, panting for breath.

Halvor got behind the door.

"Hutetu!" said the Troll as he put his head in at the door. "It smells just as if there were Christian man's blood here!"

"Yes, you shall learn that there is!" said Halvor, and cut off all his heads.

The Princess was so rejoiced to be free that she danced and sang, but then she remembered her sisters, and said: "If my sisters were but free too!"

"Where are they?" asked Halvor.

So she told him where they were. One of them had been taken away by a Troll to his castle, which was six miles off, and the other had been carried off to a castle which was nine miles farther off still.

"But now," said she, "you must first help me to get this dead body away from here."

Halvor was so strong that he cleared everything away, and made all clean and tidy very quickly. So then they ate and drank, and were happy, and next morning he set off in the grey light of dawn. He gave himself no rest, but walked or ran the livelong day. When he came in sight of the castle he was again just a little afraid. It was much more splendid than the other, but here too there was not a human being to be seen. So Halvor went into the kitchen, and did not linger there either, but went straight in.

"Nay! do Christian folk dare to come here?" cried the second Princess. "I know not how long it is since I myself came, but during all that time I have never seen a Christian man. It will be better for you to depart at once, for a Troll lives here who has six heads."

"No, I shall not go," said Halvor; "even if he had six more I would not."

"He will swallow you up alive," said the Princess.

But she spoke to no purpose, for Halvor would not go; he was not afraid of the Troll, but he wanted some meat and drink, for he was hungry after his journey. So she gave him as much as he would have, and then she once more tried to make him go away.

"No," said Halvor, "I will not go, for I have not done anything wrong, and I have no reason to be afraid."

"He won't ask any questions about that," said the Princess, "for he will take you without leave or right; but as you will not go, try if you can wield that sword which the Troll uses in battle."

He could not brandish the sword; so the Princess said that he was to take a draught from the flask which hung by its side, and when he had done that he could wield the sword.

Soon afterwards the Troll came, and he was so large and stout that he was forced to go sideways to get through the door. When the Troll got his first head in he cried: "Hutetu! It smells of a Christian man's blood here!"

With that Halvor cut off the first head, and so on with all the rest. The Princess was now exceedingly delighted, but then she remembered her sisters, and wished that they too were free. Halvor thought that might be managed, and wanted to set off immediately; but first he had to help the Princess to remove the Troll's body, so it was not until morning that he set forth on his way.

It was a long way to the castle, and he both walked and ran to get there in time. Late in the evening he caught sight of it, and it was very much more magnificent than either of the others. And this time he was not in the least afraid, but went into the kitchen, and then straight on inside the castle. There a Princess was sitting, who was so beautiful that there was never anyone to equal her. She too said what the others had said, that no Christian folk had ever been there since she had come, and entreated him to go away again, or else the Troll would swallow him up alive. The Troll had nine heads, she told him.

"Yes, and if he had nine added to the nine, and then nine more still, I would not go away," said Halvor, and went and stood by the stove.

The Princess begged him very prettily to go lest the Troll should devour him; but Halvor said, "Let him come when he will."

So she gave him the Troll's sword, and bade him take a drink from the flask to enable him to wield it.

At that same moment the Troll came, breathing hard, and he was ever so much bigger and stouter than either of the others, and he too was forced to go sideways to get in through the door.

"Hutetu! what a smell of Christian blood there is here!" said he.

Then Halvor cut off the first head, and after that the others, but the last was the toughest of them all, and it was the hardest work that Halvor had ever done to get it off, but he still believed that he would have strength enough to do it.

And now all the Princesses came to the castle, and were together again, and they were happier than they had ever been in their lives; and they were delighted with Halvor, and he with them, and he was to choose the one he liked best; but of the three sisters the youngest loved him best.

But Halvor went about and was so strange and so mournful and quiet that the Princesses asked what it was that he longed for, and if he did not like to be with them. He said that he did like to be with them, for they had enough to live on, and he was very comfortable there; but he longed to go home, for his father and mother were alive, and he had a great desire to see them again.

They thought that this might easily be done.

"You shall go and return in perfect safety if you will follow our advice," said the Princesses.

So he said that he would do nothing that they did not wish.

Then they dressed him so splendidly that he was like a King's son; and they put a ring on his finger, and it was one which would enable him to go there and back again by wishing, but they told him that he must not throw it away, or name their names; for if he did, all his magnificence would be at an end, and then he would never see them more.

"If I were but at home again, or if home were but here!" said Halvor, and no sooner had he wished this than it was granted. Halvor was standing outside his father and mother's cottage before he knew what he was about. The darkness of night was coming on, and when the father and mother saw such a splendid and stately stranger walk in, they were so startled that they both began to bow and curtsey.

Halvor then inquired if he could stay there and have lodging for the night. No, that he certainly could not. "We can give you no such accommodation," they said, "for we have none of the things that are needful when a great lord like you is to be entertained. It will be better for you to go up to the farm. It is not far off, you can see the chimney-pots from here, and there they have plenty of everything."

Halvor would not hear of that, he was absolutely determined to stay where he was; but the old folks stuck to what they had said, and told him that he was to go to the farm, where he could get both meat and drink, whereas they themselves had not even a chair to offer him.

"No," said Halvor, "I will not go up there till early tomorrow morning; let me stay here tonight. I can sit down on the hearth."

They could say nothing against that, so Halvor sat down on the hearth, and began to rake about among the ashes just as he had done before, when he lay there idling away his time.

They chattered much about many things, and told Halvor of this and of that, and at last he asked them if they had never had any child.

"Yes," they said; they had had a boy who was called Halvor, but they did not know where he had gone, and they could not even say whether he were dead or alive.

"Could I be he?" said Halvor.

"I should know him well enough," said the old woman rising. "Our Halvor was so idle and slothful that he never did anything at all, and he was so ragged that one hole ran into another all over his clothes. Such a fellow as he was could never turn into such a man as you are, sir."

In a short time the old woman had to go to the fireplace to stir the fire, and when the blaze lit up Halvor, as it used to do when he was at home raking up the ashes, she knew him again.

"Good Heavens! is that you, Halvor?" said she, and such great gladness fell on the old parents that there were no bounds to it. And now he had to relate everything that had befallen him, and the old woman was so delighted with him that she would take him up to the farm at once to show him to the girls who had formerly looked down on him so. She went there first, and Halvor followed her. When she got there she told them how Halvor had come home again, and now they should just see how magnificent he was. "He looks like a prince," she said.

"We shall see that he is just the same ragamuffin that he was before," said the girls, tossing their heads.

At that same moment Halvor entered, and the girls were so astonished that they left their kirtles lying in the chimney corner, and ran away in nothing but their petticoats. When they came in again they were so shamefaced that they hardly dared to look at Halvor, towards whom they had always been so proud and haughty before.

"Ay, ay! you have always thought that you were so pretty and dainty that no one was equal to you," said Halvor, "but you should just see the eldest Princess whom I set free. You look like herds-women compared with her, and the second Princess is also much prettier than you; but the youngest, who is my sweetheart, is more beautiful than either sun or moon. I wish to Heaven they were here, and then you would see them."

Scarcely had he said this before they were standing by his side, but then he was very sorrowful, for the words which they had said to him came to his mind.

Up at the farm a great feast was made ready for the Princesses, and much respect paid to them, but they would not stay there.

"We want to go down to your parents," they said to Halvor, "so we will go out and look about us."

He followed them out, and they came to a large pond outside the farmhouse. Very near the water there was a pretty green bank, and there the Princesses said they would sit down and while away an hour, for they thought that it would be pleasant to sit and look out over the water, they said.

There they sat down, and when they had sat for a short time the youngest Princess said, "I may as well comb your hair a little, Halvor."

So Halvor laid his head down on her lap, and she combed it, and it was not long before he fell asleep. Then she took her ring from him and put another in its place, and then she said to her sisters: "Hold me as I am holding you. I would that we were at Soria Moria Castle."

When Halvor awoke he knew that he had lost the Princesses, and began to weep and lament, and was so unhappy that he could not be comforted. In spite of all his father's and mother's entreaties, he would not stay, but bade them farewell, saying that he would never see them more, for if he did not find the Princess again he did not think it worth while to live.

He again had three hundred dollars, which he put into his pocket and went on his way. When he had walked some distance he met a man with a tolerably good horse. Halvor longed to buy it, and began to bargain with the man.

"Well, I have not exactly been thinking of selling him," said the man, "but if we could agree, perhaps—"

Halvor inquired how much he wanted to have for the horse.

"I did not give much for him, and he is not worth much; he is a capital horse to ride, but good for nothing at drawing; but he will always be able to carry your bag of provisions and you too, if you walk and ride by turns." At last they agreed about the price, and Halvor laid his bag on the horse, and sometimes he walked and sometimes he rode. In the evening he came to a green field, where stood a great tree, under which he seated himself. Then he let the horse loose and lay down to sleep, but before he did that he took his bag off the horse. At daybreak he set off again, for he did not feel as if he could take any rest. So he walked and rode the whole day, through a great wood where there were many green places which gleamed very prettily among the trees. He did not know where he was or whither he was going, but he never lingered longer in any place than was enough to let his horse get a little food when they came to one of these green spots, while he himself took out his bag of provisions.

So he walked and he rode, and it seemed to him that the wood would never come to an end. But on the evening of the second day he saw a light shining through the trees.

"If only there were some people up there I might warm myself and get something to eat," thought Halvor.

When he got to the place where the light had come from, he saw a wretched little cottage, and through a small pane of glass he saw a couple of old folks inside. They were very old, and as grey-headed as a pigeon, and the old woman had such a long nose that she sat in the chimney corner and used it to stir the fire.

"Good evening! good evening!" said the old hag; "but what errand have you that can bring you here? No Christian folk have been here for more than a hundred years."

So Halvor told her that he wanted to get to Soria Moria Castle, and inquired if she knew the way thither.

"No," said the old woman, "that I do not, but the Moon will be here presently, and I will ask her, and she will know. She can easily see it, for she shines on all things."

So when the Moon stood clear and bright above the tree-tops the old woman went out. "Moon! Moon!" she screamed. "Canst thou tell me the way to Soria Moria Castle?"

"No," said the Moon, "that I can't, for when I shone there, there was a cloud before me."

"Wait a little longer," said the old woman to Halvor, "for the West Wind will presently be here, and he will know it, for he breathes gently or blows into every corner."

"What! have you a horse too?" she said when she came in again. "Oh! let the poor creature loose in our bit of fenced-in pasture, and don't let it stand there starving at our very door. But won't you exchange him with me? We have a pair of old boots here with which you can go fifteen quarters of a mile at each step. You shall have them for the horse, and then you will be able to get sooner to Soria Moria Castle."

Halvor consented to this at once, and the old woman was so delighted with the horse that she was ready to dance. "For now I, too, shall be able to ride to church," she said. Halvor could take no rest, and wanted to set off immediately; but the old woman said that there was no need to hasten. "Lie down on the bench and sleep a little, for we have no bed to offer you," said she, "and I will watch for the coming of the West Wind."

Ere long came the West Wind, roaring so loud that the walls creaked.

The old woman went out and cried:

"West Wind! West Wind! Canst thou tell me the way to Soria Moria Castle? Here is one who would go thither."

"Yes, I know it well," said the West Wind. "I am just on my way there to dry the clothes for the wedding which is to take place. If he is fleet of foot he can go with me."

Out ran Halvor.

"You will have to make haste if you mean to go with me," said the West Wind; and away it went over hill and dale, and moor and morass, and Halvor had enough to do to keep up with it.

"Well, now I have no time to stay with you any longer," said the West Wind, "for I must first go and tear down a bit of spruce fir before I go to the bleaching-ground to dry the clothes; but just go along the side of the hill, and you will come to some girls who are standing there washing clothes, and then you will not have to walk far before you are at Soria Moria Castle."

Shortly afterwards Halvor came to the girls who were standing washing, and they asked him if he had seen anything of the West Wind, who was to come there to dry the clothes for the wedding.

"Yes," said Halvor, "he has only gone to break down a bit of spruce fir. It won't be long before he is here." And then he asked them the way to Soria Moria Castle. They put him in the right way, and when he came in front of the castle it was so full of horses and people that it swarmed with them. But Halvor was so ragged and torn with following the West Wind through bushes and bogs that he kept on one side, and would not go among the crowd until the last day, when the feast was to be held at noon.

So when, as was the usage and custom, all were to drink to the bride and the young girls who were present, the cup-bearer filled the cup for each in turn, both bride and bridegroom, and knights and servants, and at last, after a very long time, he came to Halvor. He drank their health, and then slipped the ring which the Princess had put on his finger when they were sitting by the waterside into the glass, and ordered the cup-bearer to carry the glass to the bride from him and greet her.

Then the Princess at once rose up from the table, and said, "Who is most worthy to have one of us – he who has delivered us from the Trolls or he who is sitting here as bridegroom?"

There could be but one opinion as to that, everyone thought, and when Halvor heard what they said he was not long in flinging off his beggar's rags and arraying himself as a bridegroom.

"Yes, he is the right one," cried the youngest Princess when she caught sight of him; so she flung the other out of the window and held her wedding with Halvor.

Origin of Tiis Lake

A TROLL HAD ONCE TAKEN UP HIS ABODE near the village of Kund, in the high bank on which the church now stands, but when the people about there had become pious, and went constantly to church, the troll was dreadfully annoyed by their almost incessant ringing of bells in the steeple of the church. He was at last obliged, in consequence of it, to take his departure, for nothing has more contributed to the emigration of the troll-folk out of the country, than the increasing piety of the people, and their taking to bell-ringing. The troll of Kund accordingly quitted the country, and went over to Funen, where he lived for some time in peace and quiet. Now it chanced that a man who had lately settled in the town of Kund, coming to Funen on business, met this same troll on the road.

"Where do you live?" asked the troll.

Now there was nothing whatever about the troll unlike a man, so he answered him, as was the truth –

"I am from the town of Kund."

"So?" said the troll, "I don't know you then. And yet I think I know every man in Kund. Will you, however," said he, "be so kind as to take a letter for me back with you to Kund?"

The man, of course, said he had no objection.

The troll put a letter into his pocket and charged him strictly not to take it out until he came to Kund church. Then he was to throw it over the churchyard wall, and the person for whom it was intended would get it.

The troll then went away in great haste, and with him the letter went entirely out of the man's mind. But when he was come back to Zealand he sat down by the meadow where Tiis lake now is, and suddenly recollected the troll's letter. He felt a great desire to look at it at least, so he took it out of his pocket and sat a while with it in his hands, when suddenly there began to dribble a little water out of the seal. The letter now unfolded itself and the water came out faster and faster, and it was with the utmost difficulty the poor man was able to save his life, for the malicious troll had enclosed a whole lake in the letter.

The troll, it is plain, had thought to avenge himself on Kund church by destroying it in this manner, but God ordered it so that the lake chanced to run out in the great meadow where it now stands.

The Trolls in Hedale Woods

UP AT A PLACE IN VAAGE, in Gudbrandsdale, there lived once on a time in the days of old a poor couple. They had many children, and two of the sons who were about half grown up had to be always roaming about the country begging. So it was that they were well known with all the highways and by-ways, and they also knew the short cut into Hedale.

It happened once that they wanted to get thither, but at the same time they heard that some falconers had built themselves a hut at Mæla, and so they wished to kill two birds with one stone, and see the birds, and how they are taken, and so they took the cut across Longmoss. But you must know it was far on towards autumn, and so the milkmaids had all gone home from the shielings, and they could neither get shelter nor food. Then they had to keep straight on for Hedale, but the path was a mere track, and when night fell they lost it; and, worse still, they could not find the falconers' hut either, and before they knew where they were, they found themselves in the very depths of the forest. As soon as they saw they could not get on, they began to break boughs, lit a fire, and built themselves a bower of branches, for they had a hand-axe with them; and, after that, they plucked heather and moss and made themselves a bed. So a little while after they had lain down, they heard something which sniffed and snuffed so with its nose; then the boys pricked up their ears and listened sharp to hear whether it were wild beasts or wood trolls, and just then something snuffed up the air louder than ever, and said –

"There's a smell of Christian blood here!"

At the same time they heard such a heavy foot-fall that the earth shook under it, and then they knew well enough the trolls must be about.

"Heaven help us! what shall we do?" said the younger boy to his brother.

"Oh! you must stand as you are under the fir, and be ready to take our bags and run away when you see them coming; as for me, I will take the hand-axe," said the other.

All at once they saw the trolls coming at them like mad, and they were so tall and stout, their heads were just as high as the fir-tops; but it was a good thing they had only one eye between them all three, and that they used turn and turn about. They had a hole in their foreheads into which they put it, and turned and twisted it with their hands. The one that went first, he must have it to see his way, and the others went behind and took hold of the first.

"Take up the traps," said the elder of the boys, "but don't run away too far, but see how things go; as they carry their eye so high aloft they'll find it hard to see me when I get behind them."

Yes! the brother ran before and the trolls after him, meanwhile the elder got behind them and chopped the hindmost troll with his axe on the ankle, so that the troll gave an awful shriek, and the foremost troll got so afraid he was all of a shake and dropped the eye. But the boy was not slow to snap it up. It was bigger than two quart pots put together, and so clear and bright, that though it was pitch dark, everything was as clear as day as soon as he looked through it.

When the trolls saw he had taken their eye and done one of them harm, they began to threaten him with all the evil in the world if he didn't give back the eye at once.

"I don't care a farthing for trolls and threats," said the boy, "now I've got three eyes to myself and you three have got none, and besides two of you have to carry the third."

"If we don't get our eye back this minute, you shall be both turned to stocks and stones," screeched the trolls.

But the boy thought things needn't go so fast; he was not afraid for witchcraft or hard words. If they didn't leave him in peace he'd chop them all three, so that they would have to creep and crawl along the earth like cripples and crabs.

When the trolls heard that, they got still more afraid and began to use soft words. They begged so prettily that he would give them their eye back, and then he should have both gold and silver and all that he wished to ask. Yes! that seemed all very fine to the lad, but he must have the gold and silver first, and so he said, if one of them would go home and fetch as much gold and silver as would fill his and his brother's bags, and give them two good cross-bows beside, they might have their eye, but he should keep it until they did what he said.

The trolls were very put out, and said none of them could go when he hadn't his eye to see with, but all at once one of them began to bawl out for their goody, for you must know they had a goody between them all three as well as an eye. After a while an answer came from a knoll a long way off to the north. So the trolls said she must come with two steel cross-bows and two buckets full of gold and silver, and then it was not long, you may fancy, before she was there. And when she heard what had happened, she too began to threaten them with witchcraft. But the trolls got so afraid, and begged her beware of the little wasp, for she couldn't be sure he would not take away her eye too. So she threw them the cross-bows and the buckets and the gold and the silver, and strode off to the knoll with the trolls; and since that time no one has ever heard that the trolls have walked in Hedale wood snuffing after Christian blood.

How Tyr Lost His Hand

TYR WAS GENERALLY SPOKEN OF and represented as one-armed, just as Odin was called one-eyed. Various explanations are offered by different authorities; some claim that it was because he could give the victory only to one side; others, because a sword has but one blade. However this may be, the ancients preferred to account for the fact in the following way:

Loki married secretly at Jotunheim the hideous giantess Angur-boda (anguish boding), who bore him three monstrous children – the wolf Fenris, Hel, the parti-coloured goddess of death, and Iormungandr, a terrible serpent. He kept the existence of these monsters secret as long as he could; but they speedily grew so large that they could no longer remain confined in the cave where they had come to light. Odin, from his throne Hlidskialf, soon became aware of their existence, and also of the disquieting rapidity with which they increased in size. Fearful lest the monsters, when they had gained further strength, should invade Asgard and destroy the gods, Allfather determined to get rid of them, and striding off to Jotunheim, he flung Hel into the depths of Niflheim, telling her she could reign over the nine dismal worlds of the dead. He then cast Iormungandr into the sea, where he attained such immense proportions that at last he encircled the earth and could bite his own tail.

None too well pleased that the serpent should attain such fearful dimensions in his new element, Odin resolved to lead Fenris to Asgard, where he hoped, by kindly treatment, to make him gentle and tractable. But the gods one and all shrank in dismay when they saw the wolf, and none dared approach to give him food except Tyr, whom nothing daunted. Seeing that Fenris daily increased in size, strength, voracity, and fierceness, the gods assembled in council to deliberate how they might best dispose of him. They unanimously decided that as it would desecrate their peace-steads to slay him, they would bind him fast so that he could work them no harm.

With that purpose in view, they obtained a strong chain named Laeding, and then playfully proposed to Fenris to bind this about him as a test of his vaunted strength. Confident in his ability to release himself, Fenris patiently allowed them to bind him fast, and when all stood aside, with a mighty effort he stretched himself and easily burst the chain asunder.

Concealing their chagrin, the gods were loud in praise of his strength, but they next produced a much stronger fetter, Droma, which, after some persuasion, the wolf allowed them to fasten around him as before. Again a short, sharp struggle sufficed to burst this bond, and it is proverbial in the North to use the figurative expressions, 'to get loose out of Laeding,' and 'to dash out of Droma,' whenever great difficulties have to be surmounted.

The gods, perceiving now that ordinary bonds, however strong, would never prevail against the Fenris wolf's great strength, bade Skirnir, Frey's servant, go down to Svartalfaheim and bid the dwarfs fashion a bond which nothing could sever.

By magic arts the dark elves manufactured a slender silken rope from such impalpable materials as the sound of a cat's footsteps, a woman's beard, the roots of a mountain, the longings of the bear, the voice of fishes, and the spittle of birds, and when it was finished they gave it to Skirnir, assuring him that no strength would avail to break it, and that the more it was strained the stronger it would become.

Armed with this bond, called Gleipnir, the gods went with Fenris to the Island of Lyngvi, in the middle of Lake Amsvartnir, and again proposed to test his strength. But although Fenris had grown still stronger, he mistrusted the bond which looked so slight. He therefore refused to allow himself to be bound, unless one of the Aesir would consent to put his hand in his mouth, and leave it there, as a pledge of good faith, and that no magic arts were to be used against him.

The gods heard the decision with dismay, and all drew back except Tyr, who, seeing that the others would not venture to comply with this condition, boldly stepped forward and thrust his hand between the monster's jaws. The gods now fastened Gleipnir securely around Fenris's neck and paws, and when they saw that his utmost efforts to free himself were fruitless, they shouted and laughed with glee. Tyr, however, could not share their joy, for the wolf, finding himself captive, bit off the god's hand at the wrist, which since then has been known as the wolf's joint.

Deprived of his right hand, Tyr was now forced to use the maimed arm for his shield, and to wield his sword with his left hand; but such was his dexterity that he slew his enemies as before.

The gods, in spite of the wolf's struggles, drew the end of the fetter Gelgia through the rock Gioll, and fastened it to the boulder Thviti, which was sunk deep in the ground. Opening wide his fearful jaws, Fenris uttered such terrible howls that the gods, to silence him, thrust a sword into his mouth, the hilt resting upon his lower jaw and the point against his palate. The blood then began to pour out in such streams that it formed a great river, called Von. The wolf was destined to remain thus chained fast until the last day, when he would burst his bonds and would be free to avenge his wrongs.

While some mythologists see in this myth an emblem of crime restrained and made innocuous by the power of the law, others see the underground fire, which kept within bounds can injure no one, but which unfettered fills the world with destruction and woe. Just as Odin's second eye is said to rest in Mimir's well, so Tyr's second hand (sword) is found in Fenris's jaws. He has no more use for two weapons than the sky for two suns.

The worship of Tyr is commemorated in sundry places (such as Tübingen, in Germany), which bear more or less modified forms of his name. The name has also been given to the aconite, a plant known in Northern countries as 'Tyr's helm.'

Beowolf

I
How Beowulf Overcame the Ogre and the Water-Witch

LONG AGO, THERE LIVED IN DANELAND A KING, beloved of all, called Hrothgar. He was valiant and mighty in war, overcoming all his foes and taking from them much spoil. Looking upon his great treasure, King Hrothgar said, "I will build me a great hall. It shall be vast and wide, adorned within and without with gold and ivory, with gems and carved work. It shall be a hall of joy and feasting."

Then King Hrothgar called his workmen and gave them commandment to build the hall. They set to work, and becoming each day more fair, the hall was at length finished. It stood upon a height, vast and stately, and as it was adorned with the horns of deer, King Hrothgar named it Hart Hall. The King made a great feast. To it his warriors young and old were called, and he divided his treasure, giving to each rings of gold. And so in the hall there was laughter and song and great merriment. Every evening when the shadows fell, and the land grew dark without, the knights and warriors gathered in the hall to feast. And when the feast was over, and the great fire roared upon the hearth, the minstrel took his harp and sang. Far over dreary fen and moorland the light glowed cheerfully, and the sound of song and harp awoke the deep silence of the night. Within the hall was light and gladness, but without there was wrath and hate. For far on the moor there lived a wicked giant named Grendel, prowling at night to see what evil he might do.

Very terrible was this ogre Grendel to look upon. Thick black hair hung about his face, and his teeth were long and sharp, like the tusks of an animal. His huge body and great hairy arms had the strength of ten men. He wore no armour, for his skin was tougher than any coat of mail that man or giant might weld. His nails were like steel and sharper than daggers, and by his side there hung a great pouch in which he carried off those whom he was ready to devour. Day by day the music of harp and song was a torture to him and made him more and more mad with jealous hate.

At length he crept through the darkness to Hart Hall where the warriors slept after feast and song. Arms and armour had been thrown aside, so with ease the ogre slew thirty of the bravest. Howling with wicked joy he carried them off and devoured them. The next night, again the wicked one crept stealthily through the darkening moorland until he reached Hart Hall, stretched forth his hand, and seized the bravest of the warriors. In the morning each man swore that he would not again sleep beneath the roof of the hall. For twelve years it stood thus, no man daring, except in the light of day, to enter it.

And now it came to pass that across the sea in far Gothland the tale of Grendel and his wrath was carried to Beowulf the Goth, who said he would go to King Hrothgar to help him. Taking with him fifteen good comrades, he set sail for Daneland.

When Hrothgar was told that Beowulf had come to help him, he said, "I knew him when he was yet a lad. His father and his mother have I known. Truly he hath sought a friend. I have heard that he is much renowned in war, and hath the strength of thirty men in the grip of his hand. I pray Heaven he hath been sent to free us from the horror of Grendel. Bid Beowulf and his warriors to enter."

Guided by the Danish knight, Beowulf and his men went into Hart Hall and stood before the aged Hrothgar. After friendly words of greeting Beowulf said, "And now will I fight against Grendel, bearing neither sword nor shield. With my hands alone will I grapple with the fiend, and foe to foe we will fight for victory."

That night Beowulf's comrades slept in Hart Hall. Beowulf alone remained awake. Out of the mists of the moorland the Evil Thing strode. Loud he laughed as he gazed upon the sleeping warriors. Beowulf, watchful and angry, curbed his wrath. Grendel seized one of the men, drank his blood, crushed his bones, and swallowed his horrid feast. Then Beowulf caught the monster and fought till the noise of the contest was as of thunder. The knights awoke and tried to plunge their swords into the hide of Grendel, but in vain. By enchantments he had made himself safe. At length the fight came to an end. The sinews in Grendel's shoulder burst, the bones cracked. The ogre tore himself free, leaving his arm in Beowulf's mighty grip.

Sobbing forth his death-song, Grendel fled till he reached his dwelling in the lake of the water-dragons, and there plunged in. The dark waves closed over him and he sank to his home. Loud were the songs of triumph in Hart Hall, great the rejoicing, for Beowulf had made good his boast. He had cleansed the hall of the ogre. A splendid feast was made and much treasure given to Beowulf by the King and Queen.

Again did the Dane lords sleep in the great hall, but far away in the water-dragons' lake the mother of Grendel wept over the dead body of her son, desiring revenge. Very terrible to look upon was this water-witch. As the darkness fell she crept across the moorland to Hart Hall. In she rushed eager for slaughter. A wild cry rang through the hall. The water-witch fled, but in doing so carried off the best beloved of all the King's warriors.

Quickly was Beowulf called and he rode forth to the dark lake. Down and down he dived till he came to the cave of the water-witch whom he killed after a desperate struggle. Hard by on a couch lay the body of Grendel. Drawing his sword he smote off the ogre's head. Swimming up with it he reached the surface and sprang to land, and was greeted by his faithful thanes. Four of them were needed to carry the huge head back to Hart Hall.

His task being done Beowulf made haste to return to his own land that he might seek his own King, Hygelac, and lay before him the treasures that Hrothgar had given him. With gracious words the old King thanked the young warrior, and bade him to come again right speedily. Hygelac listened with wonder and delight to all that had happened in Daneland and graciously received the splendid gifts.

For many years Beowulf lived beloved of all, and when it befell that Hygelac died in battle, the broad realm of Gothland was given unto Beowulf to rule. And there for fifty years he reigned a well-loved King.

II
How the Fire Dragon Warred with the Goth Folk

And now when many years had come and gone and the realm had long time been at peace, sorrow came upon the people of the Goths. And thus it was that the evil came.

It fell upon a time that a slave by his misdeeds roused his master's wrath, and when his lord would have punished him he fled in terror. And as he fled trembling to hide himself, he came by chance into a great cave.

There the slave hid, thankful for refuge. But soon he had cause to tremble in worse fear than before, for in the darkness of the cave he saw that a fearful dragon lay asleep. Then as the slave gazed in terror at the awful beast, he saw that it lay guarding a mighty treasure.

Never had he seen such a mass of wealth. Swords and armour inlaid with gold, cups and vessels of gold and silver set with precious stones, rings and bracelets lay piled around in glittering heaps.

For hundreds of years this treasure had lain there in secret. A great prince had buried it in sorrow for his dead warriors. In his land there had been much fighting until he alone of all his people was left. Then in bitter grief he gathered all his treasure and hid it in this cave.

"Take, O earth," he cried, "what the heroes might not keep. Lo! good men and true once before earned it from thee. Now a warlike death hath taken away every man of my people. There is none now to bear the sword or receive the cup. There is no more joy in the battle-field or in the hall of peace. So here shall the gold-adorned helmet moulder, here the coat of mail rust and the wine-cup lie empty."

Thus the sad prince mourned. Beside his treasure he sat weeping both day and night until death took him also, and of all his people there was none left.

So the treasure lay hidden and secret for many a day.

Then upon a time it happened that a great dragon, fiery-eyed and fearful, as it flew by night and prowled seeking mischief, came upon the buried hoard.

As men well know, a dragon ever loveth gold. So to guard his new-found wealth lest any should come to rob him of it, he laid him down there and the cave became his dwelling. Thus for three hundred years he lay gloating over his treasure, no man disturbing him.

But now at length it chanced that the fleeing slave lighted upon the hoard. His eyes were dazzled by the shining heap. Upon it lay a cup of gold, wondrously chased and adorned.

"If I can but gain that cup," said the slave to himself, "I will return with it to my master, and for the sake of the gold he will surely forgive me."

So while the dragon slept, trembling and fearful the slave crept nearer and nearer to the glittering mass. When he came quite near he reached forth his hand and seized the cup. Then with it he fled back to his master.

It befell then as the slave had foreseen. For the sake of the wondrous cup his misdeeds were forgiven him.

But when the dragon awoke his fury was great. Well knew he that mortal man had trod his cave and stolen of his hoard.

Round and round about he sniffed and searched until he discovered the footprints of his foe. Eagerly then all over the ground he sought to find the man who, while he slept, had done him this ill. Hot and fierce of mood he went backwards and forwards round about his treasure-heaps. All within the cave he searched in vain. Then coming forth he searched without. All round the hill in which his cave was he prowled, but no man could he find, nor in all the wilds around was there any man.

Again the old dragon returned, again he searched among his treasure-heap for the precious cup. Nowhere was it to be found. It was too surely gone.

But the dragon, as well as loving gold, loved war. So now in angry mood he lay couched in his lair. Scarce could he wait until darkness fell, such was his wrath. With fire he was resolved to repay the loss of his dear drinking-cup.

At last, to the joy of the great winged beast, the sun sank. Then forth from his cave he came, flaming fire.

Spreading his mighty wings, he flew through the air until he came to the houses of men. Then spitting forth flame, he set fire to many a happy homestead. Wherever the lightning of his tongue struck, there fire flamed forth, until where the fair homes of men had been there was naught but blackened ruins. Here and there, this way and that, through all the land he sped, and wherever he passed fire flamed aloft.

The warfare of the dragon was seen from far. The malice of the worm was known from north to south, from east to west. All men knew how the fearful foe hated and ruined the Goth folk.

Then having worked mischief and desolation all night through, the fire-dragon turned back; to his secret cave he slunk again ere break of day. Behind him he left the land wasted and desolate.

The dragon had no fear of the revenge of man. In his fiery warfare he trusted to find shelter in his hill, and in his secret cave. But in that trust he was misled.

Speedily to King Beowulf were the tidings of the dragon and his spoiling carried. For alas! even his own fair palace was wrapped in flame. Before his eyes he saw the fiery tongues lick up his treasures. Even the Gift-seat of the Goths melted in fire.

Then was the good King sorrowful. His heart boiled within him with angry thoughts. The fire-dragon had utterly destroyed the pleasant homes of his people. For this the war-prince greatly desired to punish him.

Therefore did Beowulf command that a great shield should be made for him, all of iron. He knew well that a shield of wood could not help him in this need. Wood against fire! Nay, that were useless. His shield must be all of iron.

Too proud, too, was Beowulf, the hero of old time, to seek the winged beast with a troop of soldiers. Not thus would he overcome him. He feared not for himself, nor did he dread the dragon's war-craft. For with his valour and his skill Beowulf had succeeded many a time. He had been victorious in many a tumult of battle since that day when a young man and a warrior prosperous in victory, he had cleansed Hart Hall by grappling with Grendel and his kin.

And now when the great iron shield was ready, he chose eleven of his best thanes and set out to seek the dragon. Very wrathful was the old King, very desirous that death should take his fiery foe. He hoped, too, to win the great treasure of gold which the fell beast guarded. For already Beowulf had learned whence the feud arose, whence came the anger which had been so hurtful to his people. And the precious cup, the cause of all the quarrel, had been brought to him.

With the band of warriors went the slave who had stolen the cup. He it was who must be their guide to the cave, for he alone of all men living knew the way thither. Loth he was to be their guide. But captive and bound he was forced to lead the way over the plain to the dragon's hill.

Unwillingly he went with lagging footsteps until at length he came to the cave hard by the seashore. There by the sounding waves lay the savage guardian of the treasure. Ready for war and fierce was he. It was no easy battle that was there prepared for any man, brave though he might be.

And now on the rocky point above the sea King Beowulf sat himself down. Here he would bid farewell to all his thanes ere he began the combat. For what man might tell which from that fight should come forth victorious?

Beowulf's mind was sad. He was now old. His hair was white, his face was wrinkled and grey. But still his arm was strong as that of a young man. Yet something within him warned him that death was not far off.

So upon the rocky point he sat and bade farewell to his dear comrades.

"In my youth," said the aged King, "many battles have I dared, and yet must I, the guardian of my people, though I be full of years, seek still another feud. And again will I win glory if the wicked spoiler of my land will but come forth from his lair."

Much he spoke. With loving words he bade farewell to each one of his men, greeting his dear comrades for the last time.

"I would not bear a sword or weapon against the winged beast," he said at length, "if I knew how else I might grapple with the wretch, as of old I did with Grendel. But I ween this war-fire is hot, fierce, and poisonous. Therefore I have clad me in a coat of mail, and bear this shield all of iron. I will not flee a single step from the guardian of the treasure. But to us upon this rampart it shall be as fate will.

"Now let me make no more vaunting speech. Ready to fight am I. Let me forth against the winged beast. Await ye here on the mount, clad in your coats of mail, your arms ready. Abide ye here until ye see which of us twain in safety cometh forth from the clash of battle.

"It is no enterprise for you, or for any common man. It is mine alone. Alone I needs must go against the wretch and prove myself a warrior. I must with courage win the gold, or else deadly, baleful war shall fiercely snatch me, your lord, from life."

Then Beowulf arose. He was all clad in shining armour, his gold-decked helmet was upon his head, and taking his shield in hand he strode under the stony cliffs towards the cavern's mouth. In the strength of his single arm he trusted against the fiery dragon.

No enterprise this for a coward.

III
How Beowulf Overcame the Dragon

Beowulf left his comrades upon the rocky point jutting out into the sea, and alone he strode onward until he spied a great stone arch. From beneath the arch, from out the hillside, flowed a stream seething with fierce, hot fire. In this way the dragon guarded his lair, for it was impossible to pass such a barrier unhurt.

So upon the edge of this burning river Beowulf stood and called aloud in anger. Stout of heart and wroth against the winged beast was he.

The King's voice echoed like a war-cry through the cavern. The dragon heard it and was aroused to fresh hate of man. For the guardian of the treasure-hoard knew well the sound of mortal voice. Now was there no long pause ere battle raged.

First from out the cavern flamed forth the breath of the winged beast. Hot sweat of battle rose from out the rock. The earth shook and growling thunder trembled through the air.

The dragon, ringed around with many-coloured scales, was now hot for battle, and, as the hideous beast crept forth, Beowulf raised his mighty shield and rushed against him.

Already the King had drawn his sword. It was an ancient heirloom, keen of edge and bright. Many a time it had been dyed in blood; many a time it had won glory and victory.

But ere they closed, the mighty foes paused. Each knew the hate and deadly power of the other.

The mighty Prince, firm and watchful, stood guarded by his shield. The dragon, crouching as in ambush, awaited him.

Then suddenly like a flaming arch the dragon bent and towered, and dashed upon the Lord of the Goths. Up swung the arm of the hero, and dealt a mighty blow to the grisly, many-coloured beast. But the famous sword was all too weak against such a foe. The edge turned and bit less strongly than its great king had need, for he was sore pressed. His shield, too, proved no strong shelter from the wrathful dragon.

The warlike blow made greater still the anger of the fiery foe. Now he belched forth flaming fire. All around fierce lightnings darted.

Beowulf no longer hoped for glorious victory. His sword had failed him. The edge was turned and blunted upon the scaly foe. He had never thought the famous steel would so ill serve him. Yet he fought on ready to lose his life in such good contest.

Again the battle paused, again the King and dragon closed in fight.

The dragon-guardian of the treasure had renewed his courage. His heart heaved and boiled with fire, and fresh strength breathed from him. Beowulf was wrapped in flame. Dire was his need.

Yet of all his comrades none came near to help. Nay, as they watched the conflict they were filled with base fear, and fled to the wood hard by for refuge.

Only one among them sorrowed for his master, and as he watched his heart was wrung with grief.

Wiglaf was this knight called, and he was Beowulf's kinsman. Now when he saw his liege lord hard pressed in battle he remembered all the favours Beowulf had heaped upon him. He remembered all the honours and the wealth which he owed to his King. Then could he no longer be still. Shield and spear he seized, but ere he sped to aid his King he turned to his comrades.

"When our lord and King gave us swords and armour," he cried, "did we not promise to follow him in battle whenever he had need? When he of his own will chose us for this expedition he reminded us of our fame. He said he knew us to be good warriors, bold helmet-wearers. And although indeed our liege lord thought to do this work of valour alone, without us, because more than any man he hath done glorious and rash deeds, lo! now is the day come that hath need of strength and of good warriors. Come, let us go to him. Let us help our chieftain although the grim terror of fire be hot.

"Heaven knoweth I would rather the flame would blast my body than his who gave me gold. It seemeth not fitting to me that we should bear back our shields to our homes unless we may first fell the foe and defend the life of our King. Nay, it is not of the old custom of the Goths that the

King alone should suffer, that he alone should sink in battle. Our lord should be repaid for his gifts to us, and so he shall be by me even if death take us twain."

But none would hearken to Wiglaf. So alone he sped through the deadly smoke and flame, till to his master's side he came offering aid.

"My lord Beowulf," he cried, "fight on as thou didst in thy youth-time. Erstwhile didst thou say that thou wouldst not let thy greatness sink so long as life lasteth. Defend thou thy life with all might. I will support thee to the utmost."

When the dragon heard these words his fury was doubled. The fell wicked beast came on again belching forth fire, such was his hatred of men. The flame-waves caught Wiglaf's shield, for it was but of wood. It was burned utterly, so that only the stud of steel remained. His coat of mail alone was not enough to guard the young warrior from the fiery enemy. But right valiantly he went on fighting beneath the shelter of Beowulf's shield now that his own was consumed to ashes by the flames.

Then again the warlike King called to mind his ancient glories, again he struck with main strength with his good sword upon the monstrous head. Hate sped the blow.

But alas! as it descended the famous sword Nægling snapped asunder. Beowulf's sword had failed him in the conflict, although it was an old and well-wrought blade. To him it was not granted that weapons should help him in battle. The hand that swung the sword was too strong. His might overtaxed every blade however wondrously the smith had welded it.

And now a third time the fell fire-dragon was roused to wrath. He rushed upon the King. Hot, and fiercely grim the great beast seized Beowulf's neck in his horrid teeth. The hero's life-blood gushed forth, the crimson stream darkly dyed his bright armour.

Then in the great King's need his warrior showed skill and courage. Heeding not the flames from the awful mouth, Wiglaf struck the dragon below the neck. His hand was burned with the fire, but his sword dived deep into the monster's body and from that moment the flames began to abate.

The horrid teeth relaxed their hold, and Beowulf, quickly recovering himself, drew his deadly knife. Battle-sharp and keen it was, and with it the hero gashed the dragon right in the middle.

The foe was conquered. Glowing in death he fell. They twain had destroyed the winged beast. Such should a warrior be, such a thane in need.

To the King it was a victorious moment. It was the crown of all his deeds.

Then began the wound which the fire-dragon had wrought him to burn and to swell. Beowulf soon found that baleful poison boiled in his heart. Well knew he that the end was nigh. Lost in deep thought he sat upon the mound and gazed wondering at the cave. Pillared and arched with stone-work it was within, wrought by giants and dwarfs of old time.

And to him came Wiglaf his dear warrior and tenderly bathed his wound with water.

Then spake Beowulf, in spite of his deadly wound he spake, and all his words were of the ending of his life, for he knew that his days of joy upon this earth were past.

"Had a son been granted to me, to him I should have left my war-garments. Fifty years have I ruled this people, and there has been no king of all the nations round who durst meet me in battle. I have known joys and sorrows, but no man have I betrayed, nor many false oaths have I sworn. For all this may I rejoice, though I be now sick with mortal wounds. The Ruler of Men may not upbraid me with treachery or murder of kinsmen when my soul shall depart from its body.

"But now, dear Wiglaf, go thou quickly to the hoard of gold which lieth under the hoary rock. The dragon lieth dead; now sleepeth he for ever, sorely wounded and bereft of his treasure. Then haste thee, Wiglaf, for I would see the ancient wealth, the gold treasure, the jewels, the curious gems. Haste thee to bring it hither; then after that I have seen it, I shall the more contentedly give up my life and the kingship that I so long have held."

Quickly Wiglaf obeyed his wounded lord. Into the dark cave he descended, and there outspread before him was a wondrous sight. Treasure of jewels, many glittering and golden, lay upon the ground. Wondrous vessels of old time with broken ornaments were scattered round. Here, too, lay old and rusty helmets, mingled with bracelets and collars cunningly wrought.

Upon the walls hung golden flags. From one a light shone forth by which the whole cavern was made clear. And all within was silent. No sign was there of any guardian, for without lay the dragon, sleeping death's sleep.

Quickly Wiglaf gathered of the treasures all that he could carry. Dishes and cups he took, a golden ensign and a sword curiously wrought. In haste he returned, for he knew not if he should find his lord in life where he had left him.

And when Wiglaf came again to where Beowulf sat he poured the treasure at his feet. But he found his lord in a deep swoon. Again the brave warrior bathed Beowulf's wound and laved the stricken countenance of his lord, until once more he came to himself.

Then spake the King: "For this treasure I give thanks to the Lord of All. Not in vain have I given my life, for it shall be of great good to my people in need. And now leave me, for on this earth longer I may not stay. Say to my warriors that they shall raise a mound upon the rocky point which jutteth seaward. High shall it stand as a memorial to my people. Let it soar upward so that they who steer their slender barks over the tossing waves shall call it Beowulf's mound."

The King then took from his neck the golden collar. To Wiglaf, his young thane and kinsman, he gave it. He gave also his helmet adorned with gold, his ring and coat of mail, and bade the warrior use them well.

"Thou art the last of our race," he said. "Fate hath swept away all my kinsmen, all the mighty earls. Now I too must follow them."

That was the last word of the aged King. From his bosom the soul fled to seek the dwellings of the just. At Wiglaf's feet he lay quiet and still.

The Story of Conn-Eda
or, The Golden Apples of Lough Erne

IT WAS LONG BEFORE the time the western districts of *Innis Fodhla* had any settled name, but were indiscriminately called after the person who took possession of them, and whose name they retained only as long as his sway lasted, that a powerful king reigned over this part of the sacred island. He was a puissant warrior, and no individual was found able to compete with him either on land or sea, or question his right to his conquest. The great king of the west held uncontrolled sway from the island of Rathlin to the mouth of the Shannon by sea, and far as the glittering length by land. The ancient king of the west, whose name was Conn, was good as well as great, and passionately loved by his people. His queen was a *Breaton* (British) princess, and was equally beloved and esteemed, because she was the great counterpart of the king in every respect; for whatever good qualification was wanting in the one, the other was certain to indemnify the omission. It was plainly manifest that heaven approved of the career in life of the virtuous couple; for during their reign the earth produced exuberant crops, the trees fruit ninefold commensurate with their usual bearing, the rivers, lakes, and surrounding sea teemed with abundance of choice fish, while herds and flocks were unusually prolific, and kine and sheep yielded such abundance of rich milk that they shed it in torrents upon the pastures; and furrows and cavities were always filled with the pure lacteal produce of the dairy. All these were blessings heaped by heaven upon the western districts of *Innis Fodhla*, over which the benignant and just Conn swayed his sceptre, in approbation of the course of government he had marked out for his own guidance. It is needless to state that the people who owned the authority of this great and good sovereign were the happiest on the face of the wide expanse of earth. It was during his reign, and that of his son and successor, that Ireland acquired the title of the 'happy isle of the west' among foreign nations. Con Mór and his good Queen Eda reigned in great glory during many years; they were blessed with an only son, whom they named Conn-eda, after both his parents, because the Druids foretold at his birth that he would inherit the good qualities of both. According as the young prince grew in years, his amiable and benignant qualities of mind, as well as his great strength of body and manly bearing, became more manifest. He was the idol of his parents, and the boast of his people; he was beloved and respected to that degree that neither prince, lord, nor plebeian swore an oath by the sun, moon, stars, or elements, except by the head of Conn-eda. This career of glory, however, was doomed to meet a powerful but temporary impediment, for the good Queen Eda took a sudden and severe illness, of which she died in a few days, thus plunging her spouse, her son, and all her people into a depth of grief and sorrow from which it was found difficult to relieve them.

The good king and his subjects mourned the loss of Queen Eda for a year and a day, and at the expiration of that time Conn Mór reluctantly yielded to the advice of his Druids and counsellors, and took to wife the daughter of his Arch-Druid. The new queen appeared to walk in the footsteps of the good Eda for several years, and gave great satisfaction to her subjects. But, in course of time, having had several children, and perceiving that Conn-eda was the favourite son of the king and the darling of the people, she clearly foresaw that he would become successor to the throne after the demise of his father, and that her son would certainly be excluded. This excited the hatred and inflamed the jealousy of the Druid's daughter against her step-son to such an extent, that she resolved in her own mind to leave nothing in her power undone to secure his death, or even exile from the kingdom. She began by circulating evil reports of the prince; but, as he was above suspicion, the king only laughed at the weakness of the queen; and the great princes and chieftains, supported by the people in general, gave an unqualified contradiction; while the prince himself bore all his trials with the utmost patience, and always repaid her bad and malicious acts towards him with good and benevolent ones. The enmity of the queen towards Conn-eda knew no bounds when she saw that the false reports she circulated could not injure him. As a last resource, to carry out her wicked projects, she determined to consult her *Cailleach-chearc* (hen-wife), who was a reputed enchantress.

Pursuant to her resolution, by the early dawn of morning she hied to the cabin of the *Cailleach-chearc*, and divulged to her the cause of her trouble.

"I cannot render you any help," said the *Cailleach*, "until you name the *duais*" (reward).

"What *duais* do you require?" asked the queen, impatiently.

"My *duais*," replied the enchantress, "is to fill the cavity of my arm with wool, and the hole I shall bore with my distaff with red wheat."

"Your *duais* is granted, and shall be immediately given you," said the queen. The enchantress thereupon stood in the door of her hut, and bending her arm into a circle with her side, directed the royal attendants to thrust the wool into her house through her arm, and she never permitted them to cease until all the available space within was filled with wool. She then got on the roof of her brother's house, and, having made a hole through it with her distaff, caused red wheat to be spilled through it, until that was filled up to the roof with red wheat, so that there was no room for another grain within. "Now," said the queen, "since you have received your *duais*, tell me how I can accomplish my purpose."

"Take this chess-board and chess, and invite the prince to play with you; you shall win the first game. The condition you shall make is, that whoever wins a game shall be at liberty to impose whatever *geasa* (conditions) the winner pleases on the loser. When you win, you must bid the prince, under the penalty either to go into *ionarbadh* (exile), or procure for you, within the space of a year and a day, the three golden apples that grew in the garden, the *each dubh* (black steed), and *coileen con na mbuadh* (hound of supernatural powers), called Samer, which are in the possession of the king of the Firbolg race, who resides in Lough Erne. Those two things are so precious, and so well guarded, that he can never attain them by his own power; and, if he would rashly attempt to seek them, he should lose his life."

The queen was greatly pleased at the advice, and lost no time in inviting Conn-eda to play a game at chess, under the conditions she had been instructed to arrange by the enchantress. The queen won the game, as the enchantress foretold, but so great was her anxiety to have the prince completely in her power, that she was tempted to challenge him to play a second game, which Conn-eda, to her astonishment, and no less mortification, easily won.

"Now," said the prince, "since you won the first game, it is your duty to impose your *geis* first."

"My *geis*" said the queen, "which I impose upon you, is to procure me the three golden apples that grow in the garden, the *each dubh* (black steed), and *cuileen con na mbuadh* (hound of supernatural powers), which are in the keeping of the king of the Firbolgs, in Lough Erne, within the space of a year and a day; or, in case you fail, to go into *ionarbadh* (exile), and never return, except you surrender yourself to lose your head and *combead beatha* (preservation of life)."

"Well, then," said the prince, "the *geis* which I bind you by, is to sit upon the pinnacle of yonder tower until my return, and to take neither food nor nourishment of any description, except what red-wheat you can pick up with the point of your bodkin; but if I do not return, you are at perfect liberty to come down at the expiration of the year and a day."

In consequence of the severe *geis* imposed upon him, Conn-eda was very much troubled in mind; and, well knowing he had a long journey to make before he would reach his destination, immediately prepared to set out on his way, not, however, before he had the satisfaction of witnessing the ascent of the queen to the place where she was obliged to remain exposed to the scorching sun of the summer and the blasting storms of winter, for the space of one year and a day, at least. Conn-eda being ignorant of what steps he should take to procure the *each dubh* and *cuileen con na mbuadh*, though he was well aware that human energy would prove unavailing, thought proper to consult the great Druid, Fionn Dadhna, of Sleabh Badhna, who was a friend of his before he ventured to proceed to Lough Erne. When he arrived at the bruighean of the Druid, he was received with cordial friendship, and the *failte* (welcome), as usual, was poured out before him, and when he was seated, warm water was fetched, and his feet bathed, so that the fatigue he felt after his journey was greatly relieved. The Druid, after he had partaken of refreshments, consisting of the newest of food and oldest of liquors, asked him the reason for paying the visit, and more particularly the cause of his sorrow; for the prince appeared exceedingly depressed in spirit. Conn-eda told his friend the whole history of the transaction with his stepmother from the beginning to end.

"Can you not assist me?" asked the Prince, with downcast countenance.

"I cannot, indeed, assist you at present," replied the Druid; "but I will retire to my *grianan* (green place) at sun-rising on the morrow, and learn by virtue of my Druidism what can be done to assist you."

The Druid, accordingly, as the sun rose on the following morning, retired to his *grianan*, and consulted the god he adored, through the power of his *draoidheacht*. When he returned, he called Conn-eda aside on the plain, and addressed him thus:

"My dear son, I find you have been under a severe – an almost impossible – *geis* intended for your destruction; no person on earth could have advised the queen to impose it except the Cailleach of Lough Corrib, who is the greatest Druidess now in Ireland, and sister to the Firbolg, King of Lough Erne. It is not in my power, nor in that of the Deity I adore, to interfere in your behalf; but go directly to Sliabh Mis, and consult *Eánchinn-duine* (the bird of the human head), and if there be any possibility of relieving you, that bird can do it, for there is not a bird in the western world so celebrated as that bird, because it knows all things that are past, all things that are present and exist, and all things that shall hereafter exist. It is difficult to find access to his place of concealment, and more difficult still to obtain an answer from him; but I will endeavour to regulate that matter for you; and that is all I can do for you at present."

The Arch-Druid then instructed him thus: – "Take," said he, "yonder little shaggy steed, and mount him immediately, for in three days the bird will make himself visible, and the little shaggy steed will conduct you to his place of abode. But lest the bird should refuse to reply to your queries, take this precious stone (*leag lorgmhar*), and present it to him, and then little danger and doubt exist but that he will give you a ready answer." The prince returned heartfelt thanks to the Druid, and, having saddled and mounted the little shaggy horse without much delay, received the precious stone from the Druid, and, after having taken his leave of him, set out on his journey. He suffered the reins to fall loose upon the neck of the horse according as he had been instructed, so that the animal took whatever road he chose.

It would be tedious to relate the numerous adventures he had with the little shaggy horse, which had the extraordinary gift of speech, and was a *draoidheacht* horse during his journey.

The Prince having reached the hiding-place of the strange bird at the appointed time, and having presented him with the *leag lorgmhar*, according to Fionn Badhna's instructions, and proposed his questions relative to the manner he could best arrange for the fulfilment of his *geis*, the bird took up in his mouth the jewel from the stone on which it was placed, and flew to an inaccessible rock at some distance, and, when there perched, he thus addressed the prince, "Conn-eda, son of the King of Cruachan," said he, in a loud, croaking human voice, "remove the stone just under your right foot, and take the ball of iron and *corna* (cup) you shall find under it; then mount your horse, cast the ball before you, and having so done, your horse will tell you all the other things necessary to be done." The bird, having said this, immediately flew out of sight.

Conn-eda took great care to do everything according to the instructions of the bird. He found the iron ball and *corna* in the place which had been pointed out. He took them up, mounted his horse, and cast the ball before him. The ball rolled on at a regular gait, while the little shaggy horse followed on the way it led until they reached the margin of Lough Erne. Here the ball rolled in the water and became invisible.

"Alight now," said the *draoidheacht* pony, "and put your hand into mine ear; take from thence the small bottle of *ice* (all-heal) and the little wicker basket which you will find there, and remount with speed, for just now your great dangers and difficulties commence."

Conn-eda, ever faithful to the kind advice of his *draoidheacht* pony, did what he had been advised. Having taken the basket and bottle of *ice* from the animal's ear, he remounted and proceeded on his journey, while the water of the lake appeared only like an atmosphere above his head. When he entered the lake the ball again appeared, and rolled along until it came to the margin, across which was a causeway, guarded by three frightful serpents; the hissings of the monsters was heard at a great distance, while, on a nearer approach, their yawning mouths and formidable fangs were quite sufficient to terrify the stoutest heart.

"Now," said the horse, "open the basket and cast a piece of the meat you find in it into the mouth of each serpent; when you have done this, secure yourself in your seat in the best manner you can, so that we may make all due arrangements to pass those *draoidheacht peists*. If you cast the pieces of meat into the mouth of each *peist* unerringly, we shall pass them safely, otherwise we are lost." Conn-eda flung the pieces of meat into the jaws of the serpents with unerring aim.

"Bare a benison and victory," said the *draoidheacht* steed, "for you are a youth that will win and prosper." And, on saying these words, he sprang aloft, and cleared in his leap the river and ford, guarded by the serpents, seven measures beyond the margin.

"Are you still mounted, prince Conn-eda?" said the steed.

"It has taken only half my exertion to remain so," replied Conn-eda.

"I find," said the pony, "that you are a young prince that deserves to succeed; one danger is now over, but two others remain."

They proceeded onwards after the ball until they came in view of a great mountain flaming with fire. "Hold yourself in readiness for another dangerous leap," said the horse. The trembling prince had no answer to make, but seated himself as securely as the magnitude of the danger before him would permit. The horse in the next instant sprang from the earth, and flew like an arrow over the burning mountain.

"Are you still alive, Conn-eda, son of Conn-mór?" inquired the faithful horse.

"I'm just alive, and no more, for I'm greatly scorched," answered the prince.

"Since you are yet alive, I feel assured that you are a young man destined to meet supernatural success and benisons," said the Druidic steed. "Our greatest dangers are over," added he, "and there is hope that we shall overcome the next and last danger."

After they had proceeded a short distance, his faithful steed, addressing Conn-eda, said, "Alight, now, and apply a portion of the little bottle of *íce* to your wounds." The prince immediately followed the advice of his monitor, and, as soon as he rubbed the *íce* (all-heal) to his wounds, he became as whole and fresh as ever he had been before. After having done this, Conn-eda remounted, and following the track of the ball, soon came in sight of a great city surrounded by high walls. The only gate that was visible was not defended by armed men, but by two great towers that emitted flames that could be seen at a great distance.

"Alight on this plain," said the steed, "and take a small knife from my other ear; and with this knife you shall kill and flay me. When you have done this, envelop yourself in my hide, and you can pass the gate unscathed and unmolested. When you get inside you can come out at pleasure; because when once you enter there is no danger, and you can pass and repass whenever you wish; and let me tell you that all I have to ask of you in return is that you, when once inside the gates, will immediately return and drive away the birds of prey that may be fluttering round to feed on my carcass; and more, that you will pour any drop of that powerful *íce*, if such still remain in the bottle, upon my flesh, to preserve it from corruption. When you do this in memory of me, if it be not too troublesome, dig a pit, and cast my remains into it."

"Well," said Conn-eda, "my noblest steed, because you have been so faithful to me hitherto, and because you still would have rendered me further service, I consider such a proposal insulting to my feelings as a man, and totally in variance with the spirit which can feel the value of gratitude, not to speak of my feelings as a prince. But as a prince I am able to say, come what may – come death itself in its most hideous forms and terrors – I never will sacrifice private friendship to personal interest. Hence, I am, I swear by my arms of valour, prepared to meet the worst – even death itself – sooner than violate the principles of humanity, honour, and friendship! What a sacrifice do you propose!"

"Pshaw, man! Heed not that; do what I advise you, and prosper."

"Never! never!" exclaimed the prince.

"Well, then, son of the great western monarch," said the horse, with a tone of sorrow, "if you do not follow my advice on this occasion, I tell you that both you and I shall perish, and shall never meet again; but, if you act as I have instructed you, matters shall assume a happier and more pleasing aspect than you may imagine. I have not misled you heretofore, and, if I have not, what need have you to doubt the most important portion of my counsel? Do exactly as I have directed you, else you will cause a worse fate than death to befall me. And, moreover, I can tell you that, if you persist in your resolution, I have done with you for ever."

When the prince found that his noble steed could not be persuaded from his purpose, he took the knife out of his ear with reluctance, and with a faltering and trembling hand essayed experimentally to point the weapon at his throat. Conn-eda's eyes were bathed in tears; but no sooner had he pointed the Druidic *scian* to the throat of his good steed, than the dagger, as if impelled by some Druidic power, stuck in his neck, and in an instant the work of death was done, and the noble animal fell dead at his feet. When the prince saw his noble steed fall dead by his hand, he cast himself on the ground, and cried aloud until his consciousness was gone. When he recovered, he perceived that the steed was quite dead; and, as he thought there was no hope of resuscitating him, he considered it the most prudent course he could adopt to act according to the advice he had given him. After many misgivings of mind and abundant showers of tears, he essayed the task of flaying him, which was only that of a few minutes. When he found he had the hide separated from the body, he, in the derangement of the moment, enveloped himself in it, and proceeding towards the magnificent city in rather a demented state of mind, entered it without any molestation or opposition. It was a surprisingly populous city, and an extremely wealthy place; but its beauty, magnificence, and wealth had no charms for Conn-eda, because the thoughts of the loss he sustained in his dear steed were paramount to those of all other earthly considerations.

He had scarcely proceeded more than fifty paces from the gate, when the last request of his beloved *draoidheacht* steed forced itself upon his mind, and compelled him to return to perform the last solemn injunctions upon him. When he came to the spot upon which the remains of his beloved *draoidheacht* steed lay, an appalling sight presented itself; ravens and other carnivorous birds of prey were tearing and devouring the flesh of his dear steed. It was but short work to put them to flight; and having uncorked his little jar of *íce*, he deemed it a labour of love to embalm the now mangled remains with the precious ointment. The potent *íce* had scarcely touched the inanimate flesh, when, to the surprise of Conn-eda, it commenced to undergo some strange change, and in a few minutes, to his unspeakable astonishment and joy, it assumed the form of one of the handsomest and noblest young men imaginable, and in the twinkling of an eye the prince was locked in his embrace, smothering him with kisses, and drowning him with tears of joy. When one recovered from his ecstasy of joy, the other from his surprise, the strange youth thus addressed the prince:

"Most noble and puissant prince, you are the best sight I ever saw with my eyes, and I am the most fortunate being in existence for having met you! Behold in my person, changed to the natural shape, your little shaggy *draoidheacht* steed! I am brother of the king of the city; and it was the wicked Druid, Fionn Badhna, who kept me so long in bondage; but he was forced to give me up when you came to *consult* him, for my *geis* was then broken; yet I could not recover my pristine shape and appearance unless you had acted as you have kindly done. It was my own sister that urged the queen, your stepmother, to send you in quest of the steed and powerful puppy hound, which my brother has now in keeping. My sister, rest assured, had no thought of doing you the least injury, but much good, as you will find hereafter; because, if she were maliciously inclined towards you, she could have accomplished her end without any trouble. In short, she only wanted to free you from all future danger and disaster, and recover me from my relentless enemies through your instrumentality. Come with me, my friend and deliverer, and the steed and the puppy-hound of extraordinary powers, and the golden apples, shall be yours, and a cordial welcome shall greet you in my brother's abode; for you will deserve all this and much more."

The exciting joy felt on the occasion was mutual, and they lost no time in idle congratulations, but proceeded on to the royal residence of the King of Lough Erne. Here they were both received with demonstrations of joy by the king and his chieftains; and, when the purpose of Conn-eda's visit became known to the king, he gave a free consent to bestow on Conn-eda the black steed, the *coileen con-na-mbuadh*, called Samer, and the three apples of health that were growing in his garden, under the special condition, however, that he would consent to remain as his guest until he could set out on his journey in proper time, to fulfil his *geis*. Conn-eda, at the earnest solicitation of his friends, consented, and remained in the royal residence of the Firbolg, King of Lough Erne, in the enjoyment of the most delicious and fascinating pleasures during that period.

When the time of his departure came, the three golden apples were plucked from the crystal tree in the midst of the pleasure-garden, and deposited in his bosom; the puppy-hound, Samer, was leashed, and the leash put into his hand; and the black steed, richly harnessed, was got in readiness for him to mount. The king himself helped him on horseback, and both he and his brother assured him that he might not fear burning mountains or hissing serpents, because none would impede him, as his steed was always a passport to and from his subaqueous kingdom. And both he and his brother extorted a promise from Conn-eda, that he would visit them once every year at least.

Conn-eda took leave of his dear friend, and the king his brother. The parting was a tender one, soured by regret on both sides. He proceeded on his way without meeting anything to obstruct him, and in due time came in sight of the *dún* of his father, where the queen had been placed on the pinnacle of the tower, in full hope that, as it was the last day of her imprisonment there, the prince would not make his appearance, and thereby forfeit all pretensions and right to the crown of his father for ever. But her hopes were doomed to meet a disappointment, for when it had been announced to her by her couriers, who had been posted to watch the arrival of the prince, that he approached, she was incredulous; but when she saw him mounted on a foaming black steed, richly harnessed, and leading a strange kind of animal by a silver chain, she at once knew he was returning in triumph, and that her schemes laid for his destruction were frustrated. In the excess of grief at her disappointment, she cast herself from the top of the tower, and was instantly dashed to pieces. Conn-eda met a welcome reception from his father, who mourned him as lost to him for ever, during his absence; and, when the base conduct of the queen became known, the king and his chieftains ordered her remains to be consumed to ashes for her perfidy and wickedness.

Conn-eda planted the three golden apples in his garden, and instantly a great tree, bearing similar fruit, sprang up. This tree caused all the district to produce an exuberance of crops and fruits, so that it became as fertile and plentiful as the dominions of the Firbolgs, in consequence of the extraordinary powers possessed by the golden fruit. The hound Samer and the steed were of the utmost utility to him; and his reign was long and prosperous, and celebrated among the old people for the great abundance of corn, fruit, milk, fowl, and fish that prevailed during this happy reign. It was after the name Conn-eda the province of Connaucht, or *Conneda*, or *Connacht*, was so called.

The Griffin

THERE WAS ONCE upon a time a King, but where he reigned and what he was called, I do not know. He had no son, but an only daughter who had always been ill, and no doctor had been able to cure her. Then it was foretold to the King that his daughter should eat herself well with an apple. So he ordered it to be proclaimed throughout the whole of his kingdom, that whosoever brought his daughter an apple with which she could eat herself well, should have her to wife, and be King.

This became known to a peasant who had three sons, and he said to the eldest, "Go out into the garden and take a basketful of those beautiful apples with the red cheeks and carry them to the court; perhaps the King's daughter will be able to eat herself well with them, and then thou wilt marry her and be King."

The lad did so, and set out.

When he had gone a short way he met a little iron man who asked him what he had there in the basket, to which replied Uele, for so was he named, "Frogs' legs."

On this the little man said, "Well, so shall it be, and remain," and went away.

At length Uele arrived at the palace, and made it known that he had brought apples which would cure the King's daughter if she ate them. This delighted the King hugely, and he caused Uele to be brought before him; but, alas! When he opened the basket, instead of having apples in it he had frogs' legs which were still kicking about. On this the King grew angry, and had him driven out of the house.

When he got home he told his father how it had fared with him. Then the father sent the next son, who was called Seame, but all went with him just as it had gone with Uele. He also met the little iron man, who asked what he had there in the basket.

Seame said, "Hogs' bristles," and the iron man said, "well, so shall it be, and remain."

When Seame got to the King's palace and said he brought apples with which the King's daughter might eat herself well, they did not want to let him go in, and said that one fellow had already been there, and had treated them as if they were fools. Seame, however, maintained that he certainly had the apples, and that they ought to let him go in. At length they believed him, and led him to the King. But when he uncovered the basket, he had but hogs' bristles. This enraged the King most terribly, so he caused Seame to be whipped out of the house.

When he got home he related all that had befallen him, then the youngest boy, whose name was Hans, but who was always called Stupid Hans, came and asked his father if he might go with some apples.

"Oh!" said the father, "thou wouldst be just the right fellow for such a thing! If the clever ones can't manage it, what canst thou do?"

The boy, however, did not believe him, and said, "Indeed, father, I wish to go."

"Just get away, thou stupid fellow, thou must wait till thou art wiser," said the father to that, and turned his back.

Hans, however, pulled at the back of his smock-frock and said, "Indeed, father, I wish to go."

"Well, then, so far as I am concerned thou mayst go, but thou wilt soon come home again!" replied the old man in a spiteful voice. The boy, however, was tremendously delighted and jumped for joy.

"Well, act like a fool! Thou growest more stupid every day!" said the father again. Hans, however, did not care about that, and did not let it spoil his pleasure, but as it was then night, he thought he might as well wait until the morrow, for he could not get to court that day. All night long he could not sleep in his bed, and if he did doze for a moment, he dreamt of beautiful maidens, of palaces, of gold, and of silver, and all kinds of things of that sort. Early in the morning, he went forth on his way, and directly afterwards the little shabby-looking man in his iron clothes came to him and asked what he was carrying in the basket. Hans gave him the answer that he was carrying apples with which the King's daughter was to eat herself well.

"Then," said the little man, "so shall they be, and remain."

But at the court they would none of them let Hans go in, for they said two had already been there who had told them that they were bringing apples, and one of them had frogs' legs, and the other hogs' bristles. Hans, however, resolutely maintained that he most certainly had no frogs' legs, but some of the most beautiful apples in the whole kingdom. As he spoke so pleasantly, the door-keeper thought he could not be telling a lie, and asked him to go in, and he was right, for when Hans uncovered his basket in the King's presence, golden-yellow apples came tumbling out.

The King was delighted, and caused some of them to be taken to his daughter, and then waited in anxious expectation until news should be brought to him of the effect they had. But before much time had passed by, news was brought to him: but who do you think it was who came? It was his daughter herself! As soon as she had eaten of those apples, she was cured, and sprang out of her bed. The joy the King felt cannot be described! But now he did not want to give his daughter in marriage to Hans, and said he must first make him a boat which would go quicker on dry land than on water.

Hans agreed to the conditions, and went home, and related how it had fared with him. Then the father sent Uele into the forest to make a boat of that kind. He worked diligently, and whistled all the time. At midday, when the sun was at the highest, came the little iron man and asked what he was making?

Uele gave him for answer, "Wooden bowls for the kitchen."

The iron man said, "So it shall be, and remain."

By evening Uele thought he had now made the boat, but when he wanted to get into it, he had nothing but wooden bowls. The next day Seame went into the forest, but everything went with him just as it had done with Uele. On the third day Stupid Hans went. He worked away most industriously, so that the whole forest resounded with the heavy strokes, and all the while he sang and whistled right merrily.

At midday, when it was the hottest, the little man came again, and asked what he was making?

"A boat which will go quicker on dry land than on the water," replied Hans, "and when I have finished it, I am to have the King's daughter for my wife."

"Well," said the little man, "such a one shall it be, and remain."

In the evening, when the sun had turned into gold, Hans finished his boat, and all that was wanted for it. He got into it and rowed to the palace. The boat went as swiftly as the wind.

The King saw it from afar, but would not give his daughter to Hans yet, and said he must first take a hundred hares out to pasture from early morning until late evening, and if one of them got away, he should not have his daughter. Hans was contented with this, and the next day went with his flock to the pasture, and took great care that none of them ran away.

Before many hours had passed came a servant from the palace, and told Hans that he must give her a hare instantly, for some visitors had come unexpectedly. Hans, however, was very well aware what that meant, and said he would not give her one; the King might set some hare soup before his guest next day. The maid, however, would not believe in his refusal, and at last she began to get angry with him. Then Hans said that if the King's daughter came herself, he would give her a hare. The maid told this in the palace, and the daughter did go herself.

In the meantime, however, the little man came again to Hans, and asked him what he was doing there?

He said he had to watch over a hundred hares and see that none of them ran away, and then he might marry the King's daughter and be King.

"Good," said the little man, "there is a whistle for thee, and if one of them runs away, just whistle with it, and then it will come back again."

When the King's daughter came, Hans gave her a hare into her apron; but when she had gone about a hundred steps with it, he whistled, and the hare jumped out of the apron, and before she could turn round was back to the flock again. When the evening came the hare-herd whistled once more, and looked to see if all were there, and then drove them to the palace.

The King wondered how Hans had been able to take a hundred hares to graze without losing any of them; he would, however, not give him his daughter yet, and said he must now bring him a feather from the Griffin's tail. Hans set out at once, and walked straight forwards. In the evening he came to a castle, and there he asked for a night's lodging, for at that time there were no inns.

The lord of the castle promised him that with much pleasure, and asked where he was going?

Hans answered, "To the Griffin."

"Oh! To the Griffin! They tell me he knows everything, and I have lost the key of an iron money-chest; so you might be so good as to ask him where it is."

"Yes, indeed," said Hans, "I will do that."

Early the next morning he went onwards, and on his way arrived at another castle in which he again stayed the night. When the people who lived there learnt that he was going to the Griffin, they said they had in the house a daughter who was ill, and that they had already tried every means to cure her, but none of them had done her any good, and he might be so kind as to ask the Griffin what would make their daughter healthy again?

Hans said he would willingly do that, and went onwards. Then he came to a lake, and instead of a ferry-boat, a tall, tall man was there who had to carry everybody across.

The man asked Hans whither he was journeying?

"To the Griffin," said Hans.

"Then when you get to him," said the man, "just ask him why I am forced to carry everybody over the lake."

"Yes, indeed, most certainly I'll do that," said Hans.

Then the man took him up on his shoulders, and carried him across. At length Hans arrived at the Griffin's house, but the wife only was at home, and not the Griffin himself.

Then the woman asked him what he wanted?

Thereupon he told her everything; that he had to get a feather out of the Griffin's tail, and that there was a castle where they had lost the key of their money-chest, and he was to ask the Griffin where it was? That in another castle the daughter was ill, and he was to learn what would cure her? And then not far from thence there was a lake and a man beside it, who was forced to carry people across it, and he was very anxious to learn why the man was obliged to do it.

Then said the woman, "But look here, my good friend, no Christian can speak to the Griffin; he devours them all; but if you like, you can lie down under his bed, and in the night, when he is quite fast asleep, you can reach out and pull a feather out of his tail, and as for those things which you are to learn, I will ask about them myself."

Hans was quite satisfied with this, and got under the bed. In the evening, the Griffin came home, and as soon as he entered the room, said, "Wife, I smell a Christian."

"Yes," said the woman, "one was here today, but he went away again"; and on that the Griffin said no more.

In the middle of the night when the Griffin was snoring loudly, Hans reached out and plucked a feather from his tail. The Griffin woke up instantly, and said, "Wife, I smell a Christian, and it seems to me that somebody was pulling at my tail."

His wife said, "Thou hast certainly been dreaming, and I told thee before that a Christian was here today, but that he went away again. He told me all kinds of things that in one castle they had lost the key of their money-chest, and could find it nowhere."

"Oh! The fools!" said the Griffin; "the key lies in the wood-house under a log of wood behind the door."

"And then he said that in another castle the daughter was ill, and they knew no remedy that would cure her."

"Oh! The fools!" said the Griffin; "Under the cellar-steps a toad has made its nest of her hair, and if she got her hair back she would be well."

"And then he also said that there was a place where there was a lake and a man beside it who was forced to carry everybody across."

"Oh, the fool!" said the Griffin; "if he only put one man down in the middle, he would never have to carry another across."

Early the next morning the Griffin got up and went out. Then Hans came forth from under the bed, and he had a beautiful feather, and had heard what the Griffin had said about the key, and the daughter, and the ferry-man. The Griffin's wife repeated it all once more to him that he might not forget it, and then he went home again. First he came to the man by the lake, who asked him what the Griffin had said, but Hans replied that he must first carry him across, and then he would tell him. So the man carried him across, and when he was over Hans told him that all he had to do was to set one person down in the middle of the lake, and then he would never have to carry over any more.

The man was hugely delighted, and told Hans that out of gratitude he would take him once more across, and back again. But Hans said no, he would save him the trouble, he was quite satisfied already, and pursued his way. Then he came to the castle where the daughter was ill; he took her on his shoulders, for she could not walk, and carried her down the cellar-steps and pulled out the toad's nest from beneath the lowest step and gave it into her hand, and she sprang off his shoulder and up the steps before him, and was quite cured.

Then were the father and mother beyond measure rejoiced, and they gave Hans gifts of gold and of silver, and whatsoever else he wished for, that they gave him. And when he got to the other castle he went at once into the wood-house, and found the key under the log of wood behind the door, and took it to the lord of the castle. He also was not a little pleased, and gave Hans as a reward much of the gold that was in the chest, and all kinds of things besides, such as cows, and sheep, and goats.

When Hans arrived before the King, with all these things – with the money, and the gold, and the silver and the cows, sheep and goats, the King asked him how he had come by them. Then Hans told him that the Griffin gave everyone whatsoever he wanted. So the King thought he himself could make such things useful, and set out on his way to the Griffin; but when he got to the lake, it happened that he was the very first who arrived there after Hans, and the man put him down in the middle of it and went away, and the King was drowned.

Hans, however, married the daughter, and became King.

The Twelve-Headed Griffin

I

ONCE UPON A TIME there lived a King and Queen whose greatest blessing from God was an only child of fifteen, named Theodor.

This boy from his childhood had learnt to ride, and to shoot with the bow, and had become a great proficient in both arts.

One day while practising archery, one of his arrows shot out of sight. The boy having marked the direction which it took, went to his father to request his swiftest horse, and money to go in search of his arrow.

His father gave him money, and permission to take the best horse in his stables.

With joy the boy mounted swiftly, and set off at a gallop.

After riding long and far, so far that the sun was disappearing from the horizon, he found himself in a vast prairie full of flowers. Stopping his horse, standing up in his stirrups, and shading his eyes with his hand, he perceived his arrow sticking in the ground. Dismounting he went quickly to the spot, seized the arrow with both hands, and with difficulty drew it out, leaving a great hole in the earth where it had penetrated. On looking down this hole, he saw at the bottom of it, a fine bull, and on the bull's back, a sword and a letter.

In great surprise at all these strange surroundings, he opened the letter and read, "Whomsoever will take this bull and will give it three pecks of wheat and a gallon of wine, and continue to do so daily, the bull will have power to bring back to life the man who does this, no matter how many times he may die. This sword will turn into stone any living or inanimate object."

Leading the bull, and strapping on the sword, the boy went on his way.

Towards night he reached a city and asked food and shelter of an old woman whom he met with. For himself a draught of water, for the bull a gallon of wine. The old woman fed him and his animals, and gave the requisite wine to the bull. Water she said she had none, for in the whole city there was but one fountain, and that at the outskirts of the town; and that this fountain was guarded by a twelve-headed monster. Whomsoever needed water must sacrifice a young maiden to his appetite.

She told him that the next day it was the King's turn to give his daughter, and that this said King had made a proclamation to the effect, that whosoever would kill this monster and save his daughter, immense riches, and the hand of his daughter in marriage would be the reward.

The youth hearing all this, requested the old woman to awake him very early next morning, and to give him her water-jars, saying he would fill them without giving anything to the monster. She promised this, and he soon fell into a sound sleep.

According to promise the next morning she aroused him, and taking his sword, his bow and arrows, and the water-jars, set off for the well. Arrived there, he found the King's daughter weeping, and waiting to be eaten by the monster. Said the youth to her, "I have come to deliver you from the fangs of the monster, on one condition, that is, that you let me sit down by your side, lay my head on your lap, and if I should fall asleep, not to awake me until the monster shows himself."

The young girl acquiesced with joy, and sitting clown beside her, the youth laid his head on her lap, and soon fell asleep. When the monster made his appearance, the girl was so overwhelmed with terror that she could not awake the youth, but cried so plentifully that the scalding tears fell on his face. Jumping up, he saw the monster before him. Charging his bow, he placed himself in front of the maiden; the monster seeing this, exclaimed, "Stand aside, and let me take my right," but the youth refused, it the same time drew the string of his bow and sent an arrow into the head which was stretched forth for his destruction.

The monster writhed with pain, and projected a second head, and then began a terrible strife. The youth's only defence was his courage and his bow, but the monster had his twelve heads, and his poisoned breath.

All that long summer's day they fought until evening; as night fell the boy could hardly stand from fatigue, had broken his bow, and had but one arrow in his quiver. But, on the other hand, the monster remained with only one head left out of the twelve.

At length, the youth took from the maiden's head, a long mesh of her rich hair – she, more dead than alive from terror, and with it bound his broken bow together, and the fight recommenced. Eventually the youth was victorious, but fell down faint from loss of blood.

While both these young creatures lay fainting by the well side, there came up a Tzigan, in the service of the King, to fetch water. Seeing the monster annihilated, he sought the young Princess, and finding that she was not dead, but only in a swoon, he threw water over her, and she quickly returned to her senses. The Tzigan enquired of her who had killed the monster, and the maiden pointed to the apparently dead Theodor. Quick as thought the Tzigan seized the youth's sword, and cut his body into hundreds of pieces.

Then, collecting the twelve heads and tongues of the monster, and charging the maiden not to tell to the King who had performed this mighty deed, he accompanied her to her father's palace.

Without the knowledge of the Tzigan, the maid let fall a ring, and a handkerchief, beside the remains of the slaughtered youth.

When the King saw his daughter approach, he was overwhelmed with joy, and demanded the name of her deliverer. "I, mighty King," replied the Tzigan, with pride. "Can this be true?" enquired the King. "It is true," said his daughter, tremulously.

Though the King was sorely grieved that the deliverer of his child was a gipsy, and a slave, yet he felt bound to fulfil the promise that she should be given him to wife.

II

While Theodor was lying hewed in morsels, by the side of the well, the old woman, his hostess, went to her stable to feed and give drink to the Bull. On seeing her, he refused all nourishment, telling her that "he was thirsting after water, and not after wine, and that she must lead him to the public well; as now that the monster existed no longer, all the world could drink water in peace." He bade her take with them a lump of salt, and soon they arrived at the well.

When the woman saw the morsels of what had once been the brave youth, she began to cry aloud; but the bull said to her, "Don't distress yourself in that way, but do as I tell you: take up piece by piece, limb by limb, and place them together, as they were in life." Obeying him, she put the different members once more together again. The bull licked well the lump of salt, then breathed over, and licked the youth. Wherever his tongue passed over, the marks of the sword disappeared, and when he once more breathed into his face, Theodor opened his eyes and exclaimed: "Have I slept long?" "You would have slept longer," said the woman, "if your bull had not brought you to life."

All was as a dream to him, and it was only after the bull had explained all that had occurred, that he understood why the maiden was no longer by his side.

On looking around him he saw the ring and the handkerchief which she had dropped; he took possession of them, and they returned to the old woman's dwelling.

The following day the King caused a proclamation to be issued to the effect that the nuptials of his beloved daughter, with Burcea, the Tzigan, would take place in eight days. Burcea her deliverer, inviting the neighbouring Kings and Nobles to come and do honour to the ceremony.

He sent for the court tailor, and commanded for his future son-in-law, clothing befitting his new rank. He ordered his treasurer to pay to Burcea any sum of money which he might demand.

On the appointed day, the guests were assembled in the Imperial Palace; but all were melancholy, and angry, that an ugly, uneducated gipsy, should have gained such a high-born, lovely bride.

Amongst them all, the King was the most grieved, with the exception, perhaps, of his daughter, who reproached herself for not having told the truth to the King, her father.

Burcea, the Tzigan, alone, was joyful.

In those days, it was the custom at the marriage of a King's daughter, for each subject to offer a present, according to his means; so Theodor begged the old woman to make him a cake, which she should take to the palace as his offering. She willingly agreed, and began to make the cake. When it was ready for the oven, the youth slipped the ring into the middle of the cake, and covered the paste over it.

The cake was baked, and wrapped in a clean napkin, and taken by the old woman to the gate of the palace. Her dress was so old and so patched, that the servants forbade her to enter; but the Princess looking from the window, gave orders that she should be admitted, and brought into her presence.

This was quickly done, and the cake was offered with humble wishes for her future happiness. The Princess took the cake and broke it; imagine her surprise when she found her ring in the middle of it! "Where is the person who put this ring here?" asked she of the old woman. "It must be the handsome boy that is at my cottage," said she, "he who was hewn to pieces by your slave, and was restored to life and health by his friendly bull."

"Take this purse of money for yourself," said the Princess," and return quickly to your home, tell my deliverer to come here, for I am awaiting him."

The woman sped swiftly on her errand. Full of joy, the youth seized his sword, and taking the handkerchief, set off for the Imperial palace.

On reaching the reception ball, he saw a crowd of nobles, and in their centre, Burcea the Tzigan, swelling with pride, and thinking himself as powerful as a Grand Vizier.

The youth passed speedily on, until he reached an apartment where the Princess was reclining. Seeing him, she sprang up, and flung herself into his arms, crying out, "this is my deliverer, this is my deliverer."

A crowd quickly surrounded them, and Theodor, in a clear voice, said: "It is true that I am the deliverer of this maiden, who would have been eaten by the monster of the well. I killed him, and she was free; but faint from fatigue and loss of blood, when a slave of the King's, coming to the well, and seeing me in this state, hewed me to pieces with my own sword, and threatened the maiden with death, if she avowed the truth. At the same time he possessed himself with the proofs of the monster's destruction. Had it not been for a bull, endowed with a miraculous power of bringing the dead to life, I should now be ready for my grave. Seeing that many wise men are here, and knowing that there is wisdom in numbers, I entreat all present to judge and condemn the one who is guilty."

"To death! to death!" cried the crowd.

The Emperor, calling his servants, ordered them to bring two horses from his stables, one bred in the mountains, the other bred in the plains, and to tie the limbs of Burcea, the Tzigan, to these two animals; his order was obeyed, the horses were let loose, and setting off in a galop in different directions, the body of the slave was torn limb from limb.

And now, indeed, there was a real rejoicing; but the marriage, and the court festivities were all postponed, until the arrival of the parents of Theodor, who embraced him, and wept for joy and pride, that he had so nobly distinguished himself.

They built for him, and his young bride, a magnificent palace; at the entrance to the court-yard, there was also a well of purest water, apparently guarded and watched over by a gigantic bull in marble.

Bosh-kwa-dosh, or The Mastodon

THERE WAS ONCE A MAN who found himself alone in the world. He knew not whence he came, nor who were his parents, and he wandered about from place to place, in search of something. At last he became wearied and fell asleep. He dreamed that he heard a voice saying, "Nosis," that is, my grandchild. When he awoke, he actually heard the word repeated, and looking around, he saw a tiny little animal hardly big enough to be seen on the plain. While doubting whether the voice could come from such a diminutive source, the little animal said to him, "My grandson, you will call me Bosh-kwa-dosh. Why are you so desolate? Listen to me, and you shall find friends and be happy. You must take me up and bind me to your body, and never put me aside, and success in life shall attend you." He obeyed the voice, sewing up the little animal in the folds of a string, or narrow belt, which he tied around his body, at his navel. He then set out in search of some one like himself, or other object. He walked a long time in the woods without seeing man or animal. He seemed all alone in the world. At length he came to a place where a stump was cut, and on going over a hill he descried a large town in a plain. A wide road led through the middle of it; but what seemed strange was, that on one side there were no inhabitants in the lodges, while the other side was thickly inhabited. He walked boldly into the town.

The inhabitants came out and said: "Why here is the being we have heard so much of – here is Anish-in-á-ba. See his eyes, and his teeth in a half circle – see the Wyaukenawbedaid! See his bowels, how they are formed;" – for it seems they could look through him. The king's son, the Mudjékewis, was particularly kind to him, and calling him brother-in-law, commanded that he should be taken to his father's lodge and received with attention. The king gave him one of his daughters. These people (who are supposed to be human, but whose rank in the scale of being is left equivocal) passed much of their time in play and sports and trials of various, kinds. When some time had passed, and he become refreshed and rested, he was invited to join in these sports. The first test which they put him to, was the trial of frost. At some distance was a large body of frozen water, and the trial consisted in lying down naked on the ice, and seeing who could endure the longest. He went out with two young men, who began, by pulling off their garments, and lying down on their faces. He did likewise, only keeping on the narrow magic belt with the tiny little animal sewed in it; for he felt that in this alone was to be his reliance and preservation. His competitors laughed and tittered during the early part of the night, and amused themselves by thoughts of his fate. Once they called out to him, but he made no reply. He felt a manifest warmth given out by his belt. About midnight, finding they were still, he called out to them, in return, "What!" said he, "are you benumbed already? I am but just beginning to feel a little cold." All was silence. He, however, kept his position till early day break, when he got up and went to them. They were both quite dead, and frozen so hard, that the flesh had bursted out under their finger nails, and their teeth stood out. As he looked more closely, what was his surprise to find them both transformed into buffalo cows. He tied them together, and carried them towards the village. As he came in sight, those who had wished his death were disappointed, but the Mudjékewis, who was really his friend, rejoiced. "See!" said he, "but one person approaches – it is my brother-in-law." He then threw down the carcasses in triumph, but it was found that by their death he had restored two inhabitants to the before empty lodges, and he afterwards perceived that every one of these beings, whom he killed, had the like effect, so that the depopulated part of the village soon became filled with people.

The next test they put him to, was the trial of speed. He was challenged to the race ground, and began his career with one whom he thought to be a man; but everything was enchanted here, for he soon discovered that his competitor was a large black bear. The animal outran him, tore up the ground, and sported before him, and put out its large claws as if to frighten him. He thought of his little guardian spirit in the belt, and wishing to have the swiftness of the Kakake, i.e. sparrowhawk, he found himself rising from the ground, and with the speed of this bird he outwent his rival, and won the race, while the bear came up exhausted and lolling out his tongue. His friend the Mudjékewis stood ready, with his war-club, at the goal, and the moment the bear came up, dispatched him. He then turned to the assembly, who had wished his friend and brother's death, and after reproaching them, he lifted up his club and began to slay them on every side. They fell in heaps on all sides; but it was plain to be seen, the moment they fell, that they were not men, but animals – foxes, wolves, tigers, lynxes, and other kinds, lay thick around the Mudjékewis.

Still the villagers were not satisfied. They thought the trial of frost had not been fairly accomplished, and wished it repeated. He agreed to repeat it, but being fatigued with the race, he undid his guardian belt, and laying it under his head, fell asleep. When he awoke, he felt refreshed, and feeling strong in his own strength, he went forward to renew the trial on the ice, but quite forgot the belt, nor did it at all occur to him when he awoke, or when he lay down to repeat the trial. About midnight his limbs became stiff, the blood soon ceased to circulate, and he was found in the morning a stiff corpse. The victors took him up and carried him to the village, where the loudest tumult of victorious joy was made, and they cut his body into a thousand pieces, that each one might eat a piece.

The Mudjékewis bemoaned his fate, but his wife was inconsolable. She lay in a state of partial distraction, in the lodge. As she lay here, she thought she heard some one groaning. It was repeated through the night, and in the morning she carefully scanned the place, and running her fingers through the grass, she discovered the secret belt, on the spot where her husband had last reposed. "Aubishin!" cried the belt – that is, untie me, or unloose me. Looking carefully, she found the small seam which inclosed the tiny little animal. It cried out the more earnestly, "Aubishin!" and when she had carefully ripped the seams, she beheld, to her surprise, a minute, naked little beast, smaller than the smallest new-born mouse, without any vestige of hair, except at the tip of its tail; it could crawl a few inches, but reposed from fatigue. It then went forward again. At each movement it would pupowee, that is to say, shake itself like a dog, and at each shake it became larger. This it continued until it acquired the strength and size of a middle sized dog, when it ran off.

The mysterious dog ran to the lodges, about the village, looking for the bones of his friend, which he carried to a secret place, and as fast as he found them arranged all in their natural order. At length he had formed all the skeleton complete, except the heel bone of one foot. It so happened that two sisters were out of camp, according to custom, at the time the body was cut up, and this heel was sent out to them. The dog hunted every lodge, and being satisfied that it was not to be found in the camp, he sought it outside of it, and found the lodge of the two sisters. The younger sister was pleased to see him, and admired and patted the pretty dog, but the elder sat mumbling the very heel-bone he was seeking, and was surly and sour, and repelled the dog, although he looked most wistfully up in her face, while she sucked the bone from one side of her mouth to the other. At last she held it in such a manner that it made her cheek stick out, when the dog, by a quick spring, seized the cheek, and tore cheek and bone away and fled.

He now completed the skeleton, and placing himself before it, uttered a hollow, low, long-drawn-out howl, when the bones came compactly together. He then modulated his howl, when the bones knit together and became tense. The third howl brought sinews upon them, and the fourth, flesh. He then turned his head upwards, looking into the sky, and gave a howl, which caused every one in the village to startle, and the ground itself to tremble, at which the breath entered into his body, and he first breathed and then arose. "Hy kow!" I have overslept myself, he exclaimed; "I will be too late for the trial." "Trial!" said Bosh-kwa-dosh, "I told you never to let me be separate from your body, you have neglected this. You were defeated, and your frozen body cut into a thousand pieces, and scattered over the village; but my skill has restored you. Now I will declare myself to you, and show who and what I am!"

He then began to Pupowee, or shake himself, and at every shake, he grew. His body became heavy and massy, his legs thick and long, with big clumsy ends, or feet. He still shook himself, and rose and swelled. A long snout grew from his head, and two great shining teeth out of his mouth. His skin remained as it was, naked, and only a tuft of hair grew on his tail. He rose up as high as the trees. He was enormous. "I should fill the earth," said he, "were I to exert my utmost power, and all there is on the earth would not satisfy me to eat. Neither could it fatten me or do me good. I should want more. The Great Spirit created me to show his power when there were nothing but animals on the earth. But were all animals as large as myself, there would not be grass enough for food. But the earth was made for man, and not for beasts. I give some of those great gifts which I possess. All the animals shall be your food, and you are no longer to flee before them, and be their sport and food." So saying, he walked off with heavy steps and with fierce looks, at which all the little animals trembled.

How Mad Buffalo Fought
the Thunder-Bird

ONCE UPON A TIME the Indians owned all the land around the Big Sea Water. The Good Spirit had smoked the pipe of peace at the Red-stone quarry and called all the nations to him. At his command they washed the war-paint from their faces, buried their clubs and tomahawks and made themselves pipes of red sand-stone like the one that he had fashioned. They, too, smoked the peace-pipe, and there was no longer war among the nations, but each dwelt by its own river and hunted only the deer, the beaver, the bear, or the bison.

In those happy days there lived on that shore of the Big Sea Water, which is directly under the hunter's star, an Indian whom all his nation trusted, for there were none like him in courage, wisdom, and prudence. From his early childhood they had looked to him to do some great deed.

He had often mastered the grizzly bear and the strong buffalo. Once he captured a buffalo ox, so large and so strong that a dozen arrows did not kill it, and from that day he was known as Mad Buffalo.

When the magic horns were needed for medicine for the people, Mad. Buffalo went forth in the Moon of Flowers and by cunning, not by magic, cut them from the head of the Great Horned Serpent. For this the people loved him and he sat with the oldest and the wisest of the tribe.

Their greatest trouble in those days was the mysterious thunder-bird, which was often seen flying through the air. It had black and ragged wings, and as it moved swiftly overhead they darkened all the earth. On moonlight nights no harm came; but when it passed in the daytime, or when the Moon-princess was journeying to see her brother, the Sun-prince, and her shining lodge was hidden by the beautiful red, the thunder-bird did evil to all who fell under its shadow.

Great curiosity existed as to its nest, but no one had dared to follow it, nor had any hunter discovered a place where it seemed likely that it could hide. Some thought it lived in a hollow tree, others that its home was in the sandstone caverns, but it had never been seen to alight.

One day in the winter, Mad Buffalo set out in search of food for his family. He had to travel to the lodge of the beavers across the Big Sea Water and far up the river. He trapped a fat beaver, slung it over his shoulder and started for home just as the full moon showed through the tree-tops.

While crossing the lake, when he was in sight of his own wigwam, a great shadow passed before him, shutting out all light. After it had gone he looked about him for the cause. The night was clear and the moon so bright that the hunter's star could be seen but faintly, but objects about him were as plain as in the day.

At first he saw nothing, for the thunderbird was directly over his head; but as it circled he caught sight of it. It made a swift movement downwards, pounced upon him and lifted him with all he had into the air.

He felt himself rising slowly till he was far above the earth, yet not so far as to prevent him seeing what was going on in the village. He could even see his own wigwam and his children in the doorway. They saw him and were terribly frightened. Their mother failed to comfort them, for they knew by heart all the dreadful tales that were told of the thunder-bird. They themselves had seen the beautiful birch tree which they had often climbed, torn up by the roots and lie black and dead in the forest. And the oak tree where the warriors assembled was split to its base by this terrible creature. The yellow cedar whose boughs were used for the canoe that sailed on the Big Sea Water was scorched and blighted by the thunder-bird.

Mad Buffalo's heart did not fail him. He grasped his spear firmly and waited his chance to do battle with the monster. Faster and faster they went towards the north, straight across the Big Sea Water, rising higher and higher in the air.

At last they came to a great mountain where no trees grew. The top was a solid, bare, rugged rock, while the sides were formed of sharp boulders, with here and there a small patch of coarse grass and a few stunted furze bushes. In a cleft of the highest rock overhanging the water was the nest of the thunder-bird. It was made of the tendons of human beings, woven with their scalp locks and the feathers they had worn when living.

Still Mad Buffalo was not afraid. As the bird neared its home it croaked and muttered, and the sound was echoed and re-echoed till the noise was deafening. Worse than this, the creature tried to dash him against the rock, driving him towards it with its wings; and when these struck him his flesh stung and smarted as if touched by coals of fire.

By violently wrenching himself and balancing his spear, he managed to escape uninjured. At length with one powerful blow the bird drove him into its nest. It then flew away.

Mad Buffalo was stunned, but only for a moment. On coming to himself he heard a low crackling noise of thunder and found that he was left to the mercy of a brood of wild, hungry young thunders, for whose food he had probably been brought. They began at once to pick at his head, uttering croaks like the old bird, only not so loud; but as they were many the sound was, if possible, more dreadful.

Seeing that they were young birds, Mad Buffalo supposed they would be helpless; and when the old bird was out of sight he ventured to fight them. Raising himself as well as he could, he struck at one with his spear. Thereupon they all set upon him, beating him with their wings and blinking at him with their long, narrow, blood-red eyes, from which darted flashes of lightning that scorched his hands and face. In spite of the pain he fought bravely; though, when they struck him with their sharp wings, it was like the prick of a poisoned arrow or the sting of a serpent.

One by one their strength failed them and they were beaten down into the nest. Mad Buffalo took hold of the largest and strongest, wrung its neck and threw it over the precipice. On seeing this the others crept close together and did not offer to touch him again.

He seized another, pulled out its heart, threw the body away and spread the skin over the edge of the nest to dry. Then filling his pipe from a pouch of wolf skin suspended from his belt, he sat down to smoke. While resting he wrung the necks of the other birds and threw them into the Big Sea Water, saving only their hearts and claws.

When he had killed them all he took four short whiffs at his pipe, pointing as he did so to the kingdoms of the four winds, and asking them for assistance. Then he got inside the dry skin, fastened it round him with the claws he had saved, put the hearts of the young thunders on his spear and started to roll down the side of the mountain.

As he tumbled from rock to rock the feathers of the skin flashed like fire-insects. When he was about half way down he straightened himself out and, lifting the wings with his arms, found that he could fly. He moved slowly at first, but was soon used to the motion and went as fast as the great bird could have done.

He crossed the Big Sea Water and winged his way over the forest until he came to the place from which he had been taken ten days before. There he alighted, tore off the bird's skin and started homewards.

His wife and children could hardly believe that it was he; for they supposed the young thunders had long ago picked his bones. He broiled the hearts of the birds, which crackled and hissed so that they could be heard a mile from the wigwam, but the meat was juicy and tender.

The old bird was never seen again in that part of the country. Hunters who came from the Rocky Mountains say that it built a nest on the highest peak, where it raised another brood that sometimes came down towards the earth, despoiling the forests and the grain fields. But they flew higher than formerly, and from the day that Mad Buffalo fought them they never interfered with men. Their nest henceforth was made of the bones of the, mountain goat and the hair of his beard.

Now when Indian children hear the fire crackling they say it is the hearts of the young thunders; for all their nations know of the brave deed of Mad Buffalo.

Great Head and the Ten Brothers

IN A REMOTE INDIAN VILLAGE at the edge of the forest, an orphaned family of ten boys lived in a small lodge with their uncle. The five elder brothers went out to hunt every day, but the younger ones, not yet ready for so rigorous a life, remained at home with their uncle, never daring to venture too far from their home.

One day, the group of elder brothers, who had been away deer-hunting, failed to return at the usual hour. As the evening wore on, there was still no sign of them, and by nightfall their uncle had become extremely worried for their safety. It was agreed among the remaining family that the eldest boy should go out on the following morning in search of his brothers. He readily accepted the challenge and he set off after sunrise, confident that he would locate them before long. But the boy did not return, and his disappearance caused even greater consternation among the household.

'We must find out what is happening to them,' said the next in line. 'Though I am young and ill-prepared for adventure, I cannot bear to picture any of my family lying wounded in some fearful, hostile place.'

And so, having obtained his uncle's permission, he too set off enthusiastically, though he was not so self-assured as his brother before him. Just like the others, however, the youth failed to reappear, and an identical fate awaited the two more after him who took it upon themselves to go out in search of the lost hunters. At length, only one small brother remained with his uncle at the lodge, and fearing he might lose the last of his young nephews, the old man became very protective of him, turning a deaf ear to his persistent pleas to be allowed take his turn in the search.

The youngest brother was now obliged to accompany his uncle everywhere. He was even forced to walk with the old man the short distance to the wood-pile, and he longed for the day when adventure would come knocking on his door. He had almost resigned himself to the fact that this would never happen when, one morning, as the pair stooped to gather firewood, the young boy imagined he heard a deep groan coming from the earth beneath his feet. He called upon his uncle to listen and the sound, unmistakably a human groan, soon repeated itself. Both were deeply shocked by the discovery and began clawing frantically at the earth with their bare hands. Shortly afterwards, a human face revealed itself and before long, they had uncovered the entire body of a man, caked in mould and scarcely able to breathe.

Carefully, they lifted the unfortunate creature from the soil and carried him into their lodge where they rubbed his skin down with bear oil until he slowly began to revive. It was several hours before the man could bring himself to speak, but then, at last, he began mouthing a few words, informing his hosts that he had been out hunting when his mind had suddenly become entirely blank. He could remember nothing more, he told them, neither his name, nor the village he had come from. The old man and his nephew begged the stranger to stay with them, hoping that soon his memory would be restored and that then, perhaps, he could help them in their own search.

The days passed by, but after only a very short time, the young boy and his uncle began to observe that the person they had rescued was no ordinary mortal like themselves. He did not eat any of the food they served him, but his strength increased daily none the less. He had no need of sleep, and often when it rained he behaved very strangely, tossing restlessly in his chair and calling aloud in a curious language.

One night, a particularly violent storm raged outside. As the rain pelted down and the winds howled fiercely, the boy and his uncle were awoken by the loud cries of their guest:

'Do you hear that noise?' he yelled. 'That is my brother, Great Head, riding on the wind. Can you not hear him wailing?'

'Yes, we can,' said the old man. 'Would you like us to invite him here? Would he come if you sent for him?'

'I would certainly like to see him,' replied the strange guest, 'but he will not come unless I bring him here by magic. You should prepare for him a welcoming meal, ten large blocks of maple-wood, for that is the food he lives on.' And saying this, the stranger departed in search of his brother, taking with him his bow and a selection of arrows, carved from the roots of a hickory-tree.

At about midday, he drew near to Great Head's dwelling and quickly transformed himself into a mole, so that his brother would not notice his approach. Silently, he crept through the grass until he spotted Great Head up ahead, perched on a cliff-face, glowering fiercely at an owl.

'I see you!' shouted Great Head, 'now you shall die.' And he lunged forward, ready to devour the helpless creature.

Just at that moment, the mole stood up, and taking aim with his bow, shot an arrow in Great Head's direction. The arrow became larger and larger as it sped through the air towards the monstrous creature, but then, when it had almost reached its target, it turned back on itself and returned to the mole, regaining its normal size. Great Head was soon in pursuit, puffing and snorting like a hurricane as he trampled through the trees. Once more, the mole shot an arrow and again it returned to him, luring Great Head further and further onwards towards the lodge where the young boy and his uncle nervously awaited their arrival.

As soon as the door to their house burst open, its terrified occupants began attacking Great Head with wooden mallets. But the more vigorously they struck him, the more Great Head broke into peals of laughter, for he was not only impervious to pain, but the sight of his brother standing before him had put him in the best of moods. The two embraced warmly and Great Head sat down to his meal of maple-blocks which he devoured with great relish.

When he had done, he thanked his hosts for their hospitality and enquired of them how he might return their kindness. They began telling him the story of their missing relatives, but had only uttered a few words before Great Head interrupted them:

'You need tell me no more,' he said to them, 'I know precisely what has become of them. They have fallen into the hands of a woodland witch. Now if this boy will accompany me, I will point out her dwelling and show him the bones of his brothers.'

Although reluctant to release him, the uncle perceived how anxious his nephew was to learn the fate of his brothers. Finally, he gave his consent, and the young boy started off with Great Head, smiling broadly at the thought of the adventure which lay ahead.

They did not once pause for rest and after a time they came upon a ramshackle hut, in front of which were strewn dry bones of every size and description. In the doorway sat a crooked old witch, rocking back and forth, singing to herself. When she looked up and saw her visitors, she flew into a rage and began chanting her spell to change the living into dry bones. But her magic had no effect on Great Head, and because his companion stood in his shadow, he too was protected from the charm. The youth sprang forward and began to attack the frail, old witch, beating her with his fists until she fell lifeless to the ground. As soon as she lay dead, a loud shriek pierced the silence, and her flesh was transformed into black-feathered birds that rose squawking into the air.

The young boy now set about the task of selecting the bones of his brothers. It was slow and difficult work, but, at last, he had gathered together nine white mounds. Great Head came forward to examine each of them and when he was satisfied that no bone was missing he spoke to his young companion:

'I am going back to my rock,' he told him. 'But do not despair or think I have abandoned you, for soon you will see me again.'

The boy stood alone, guarding the heaps of bones, trying to decide whether he should make his way back home before daylight faded. Looking upwards, he noticed that a huge storm was gathering and began walking towards the hut for shelter. The hail beat on his back even as he walked the short distance and soon sharp needles of rain pricked his skin all over. The thunder now clashed and lightning struck the ground wherever he attempted to step. The young boy grew fearful and flung himself to the earth, but suddenly he heard a familiar voice calling to him, and lifting his eyes, he saw Great Head riding at the centre of the storm.

'Arise you bones,' Great Head yelled, 'I bid you come to life.' The hurricane passed overhead in an instant, as rapidly as it had first appeared. The young boy felt certain that he must have been dreaming, but then, he observed that the mounds had disappeared. In a moment he was surrounded by his brothers and huge tears of relief and joy flooded down his cheeks.

A Bigfoot 'Goblin Story' Told to Roosevelt

FRONTIERSMEN ARE NOT, as a rule, apt to be very superstitious. They lead lives too hard and practical, and have too little imagination in things spiritual and supernatural. I have heard but few ghost stories while living on the frontier, and these few were of a perfectly commonplace and conventional type.

But I once listened to a goblin story which rather impressed me. It was told by a grisled, weather-beaten old mountain hunter, named Bauman, who was born and had passed all his life on the frontier. He must have believed what he said, for he could hardly repress a shudder at certain points of the tale; but he was of German ancestry, and in childhood had doubtless been saturated with all kinds of ghost and goblin lore, so that many fearsome superstitions were latent in his mind; besides, he knew well the stories told by the Indian medicine men in their winter camps, of the snow-walkers, and the spectres, and the formless evil beings that haunt the forest depths, and dog and waylay the lonely wanderer who after nightfall passes through the regions where they lurk; and it may be that when overcome by the horror of the fate that befell his friend, and when oppressed by the awful dread of the unknown, he grew to attribute, both at the time and still more in remembrance, weird and elfin traits to what was merely some abnormally wicked and cunning wild beast; but whether this was so or not, no man can say.

When the event occurred Bauman was still a young man, and was trapping with a partner among the mountains dividing the forks of the Salmon from the head of Wisdom River. Not having had much luck, he and his partner determined to go up into a particularly wild and lonely pass through which ran a small stream said to contain many beaver. The pass had an evil reputation because the year before a solitary hunter who had wandered into it was there slain, seemingly by a wild beast, the half-eaten remains being afterwards found by some mining prospectors who had passed his camp only the night before.

The memory of this event, however, weighed very lightly with the two trappers, who were as adventurous and hardy as others of their kind. They took their two lean mountain ponies to the foot of the pass, where they left them in an open beaver meadow, the rocky timber-clad ground being from thence onwards impracticable for horses. They then struck out on foot through the vast, gloomy forest, and in about four hours reached a little open glade where they concluded to camp, as signs of game were plenty.

There was still an hour or two of daylight left, and after building a brush lean-to and throwing down and opening their packs, they started up stream. The country was very dense and hard to travel through, as there was much down timber, although here and there the sombre woodland was broken by small glades of mountain grass.

At dusk they again reached camp. The glade in which it was pitched was not many yards wide, the tall, close-set pines and firs rising round it like a wall. On one side was a little stream, beyond which rose the steep mountain-slopes, covered with the unbroken growth of the evergreen forest.

They were surprised to find that during their short absence something, apparently a bear, had visited camp, and had rummaged about among their things, scattering the contents of their packs, and in sheer wantonness destroying their lean-to. The footprints of the beast were quite plain, but at first they paid no particular heed to them, busying themselves with rebuilding the lean-to, laying out their beds and stores, and lighting the fire.

While Bauman was making ready supper, it being already dark, his companion began to examine the tracks more closely, and soon took a brand from the fire to follow them up, where the intruder had walked along a game trail after leaving the camp. When the brand flickered out, he returned and took another, repeating his inspection of the footprints very closely. Coming back to the fire, he stood by it a minute or two, peering out into the darkness, and suddenly remarked: "Bauman, that bear has been walking on two legs." Bauman laughed at this, but his partner insisted that he was right, and upon again examining the tracks with a torch, they certainly did seem to be made by but two paws, or feet. However, it was too dark to make sure. After discussing whether the footprints could possibly be those of a human being, and coming to the conclusion that they could not be, the two men rolled up in their blankets, and went to sleep under the lean-to.

At midnight Bauman was awakened by some noise, and sat up in his blankets. As he did so his nostrils were struck by a strong, wild-beast odour, and he caught the loom of a great body in the darkness at the mouth of the lean-to. Grasping his rifle, he fired at the vague, threatening shadow, but must have missed, for immediately afterwards he heard the smashing of the underwood as the thing, whatever it was, rushed off into the impenetrable blackness of the forest and the night.

After this the two men slept but little, sitting up by the rekindled fire, but they heard nothing more. In the morning they started out to look at the few traps they had set the previous evening and to put out new ones. By an unspoken agreement they kept together all day, and returned to camp towards evening.

On nearing it they saw, hardly to their astonishment, that the lean-to had been again torn down. The visitor of the preceding day had returned, and in wanton malice had tossed about their camp kit and bedding, and destroyed the shanty. The ground was marked up by its tracks, and on leaving the camp it had gone along the soft earth by the brook, where the footprints were as plain as if on snow, and, after a careful scrutiny of the trail, it certainly did seem as if, whatever the thing was, it had walked off on but two legs.

The men, thoroughly uneasy, gathered a great heap of dead logs, and kept up a roaring fire throughout the night, one or the other sitting on guard most of the time. About midnight the thing came down through the forest opposite, across the brook, and stayed there on the hill-side for nearly an hour. They could hear the branches crackle as it moved about, and several times it uttered a harsh, grating, long-drawn moan, a peculiarly sinister sound. Yet it did not venture near the fire.

In the morning the two trappers, after discussing the strange events of the last thirty-six hours, decided that they would shoulder their packs and leave the valley that afternoon. They were the more ready to do this because in spite of seeing a good deal of game sign they had caught very little fur. However, it was necessary first to go along the line of their traps and gather them, and this they started out to do.

All the morning they kept together, picking up trap after trap, each one empty. On first leaving camp they had the disagreeable sensation of being followed. In the dense spruce thickets they occasionally heard a branch snap after they had passed; and now and then there were slight rustling noises among the small pines to one side of them.

At noon they were back within a couple of miles of camp. In the high, bright sunlight their fears seemed absurd to the two armed men, accustomed as they were, through long years of lonely wandering in the wilderness to face every kind of danger from man, brute, or element. There were still three beaver traps to collect from a little pond in a wide ravine nearby. Bauman volunteered to gather these and bring them in, while his companion went ahead to camp and made ready the packs.

On reaching the pond Bauman found three beaver in the traps, one of which had been pulled loose and carried into a beaver house. He took several hours in securing and preparing the beaver, and when he started homewards he marked with some uneasiness how low the sun was getting. As he hurried towards camp, under the tall trees, the silence and desolation of the forest weighed on him. His feet made no sound on the pine needles, and the slanting sun rays, striking through among the straight trunks, made a grey twilight in which objects at a distance glimmered indistinctly. There was nothing to break the ghostly stillness which, when there is no breeze, always broods over these sombre primeval forests.

At last he came to the edge of the little glade where the camp lay, and shouted as he approached it, but got no answer. The camp fire had gone out, though the thin blue smoke was still curling upwards. Near it lay the packs, wrapped and arranged. At first Bauman could see nobody; nor did he receive an answer to his call. Stepping forward he again shouted, and as he did so his eye fell on the body of his friend, stretched beside the trunk of a great fallen spruce. Rushing towards it the horrified trapper found that the body was still warm, but that the neck was broken, while there were four great fang marks in the throat.

The footprints of the unknown beast-creature, printed deep in the soft soil, told the whole story.

The unfortunate man, having finished his packing, had sat down on the spruce log with his face to the fire, and his back to the dense woods, to wait for his companion.While thus waiting, his monstrous assailant, which must have been lurking nearby in the woods, waiting for a chance to catch one of the adventurers unprepared, came silently up from behind, walking with long, noiseless steps, and seemingly still on two legs. Evidently unheard, it reached the man, and broke his neck by wrenching his head back with its forepaws, while it buried its teeth in his throat. It had not eaten the body, but apparently had romped and gambolled round it in uncouth, ferocious glee, occasionally rolling over and over it; and had then fled back into the soundless depths of the woods.

Bauman, utterly unnerved, and believing that the creature with which he had to deal was something either half human or half devil, some great goblin-beast, abandoned everything but his rifle and struck off at speed down the pass, not halting until he reached the beaver meadows where the hobbled ponies were still grazing. Mounting, he rode onwards through the night, until far beyond the reach of pursuit.

A Sasquatch in British Columbia
Deposition by Mr. William Roe

FROM THE CITY OF EDMONTON, Alberta. An affidavit by William Roe. To the Agassiz, Harrison Advance, Printers & Publishers, Drawer O, Agassiz, B.C.; Attention Mr. John W. Green. From the legal Department of Allen F. MacDonald, B.A., L.L.B., City Solicitor., H. F. Wilson, B.A., Asst. City Solicitor and R. N. Saunders, Claims Agent.

Dear Sir:

Re. Affidavit of Mr. William Roe, on August 26th, 1957. Mr. Wm. Roe approached the writer requesting the swearing out of An Affidavit in regard to a strange animal he had seen in British Columbia.

The affidavit was drawn up by a member of our legal department and sworn to in the usual manner by the writer.

I cannot state as to the creditability of the story.

We trust the foregoing information will be of assistance.

Yours truly,

(signed) W. H. Clark

Asst. Claims Agent

Affidavit

I, W. Roe, of the City of Edmonton, in the province of Alberta make oath and say,

(1) That the exhibit A attached to this, my affidavit, is absolutely true and correct in all details.

Sworn before me in the City of Edmonton, Province of Alberta, this 26th day of August, A.D. 1957,

(signed) Wm. Roe and then

signed by Clark under a

numbering D.D. 2822

Exhibit A

Ever since I was a small boy back in the forests of Michigan, I have studied the lives and habits of wild animals. Later when I supported my family in northern Alberta by hunting and trapping,

I spent many hours just observing the wild things. They fascinated me. The most incredible experience I ever had with a wild creature occurred near a little place called Tete Jaune Cache, B.C., about 80 miles west of Jasper, Alberta.

I had been working on the highway near this place, Tete Jaune Cache, for about two years. In October 1955, I decided to climb five miles up Mica Mountain to an old deserted mine, just for something to do. I came in sight of the mine about three o'clock in the afternoon after an easy climb. I had just come out of a patch of low brush into a clearing, when I saw what I thought was a grizzly bear in the brush on the other side. I had shot a grizzly near that spot the year before. This one was only about 75 yards away, but I didn't want to shoot it, for I had no way of getting it out. So I sat down on a small rock and watched, with my rifle in my hand.

I could just see part of the animal's head and the top of one shoulder. A moment later it raised up and stepped out into the opening. Then I saw it wasn't a bear.

This to the best of my recollection is what the creature looked like and how it acted as it came across the clearing directly towards me. My first impression was of a huge man about six feet tall, almost three feet wide, and probably weighing near 300 pounds. It was covered from head to foot with dark brown, silver-tipped hair. But as it came closer I saw by its breasts that it was female.

And yet, its torso was not curved like a female's. Its broad frame was straight from shoulder to hip. Its arms were much thicker than a man's arms and longer, reaching almost to its knees. Its feet were broader proportionately than a man's, about five inches wide in the front and tapering to much thinner heels. When it walked it placed the heel of its foot down first, and I could see the grey-brown skin or hide on the soles of its feet.

It came to the edge of the bush I was hiding in, within 20 feet of me, and squatted down on its haunches. Reaching out its hands it pulled the branches of bushes towards it and stripped the leaves with its teeth. Its lips curled flexibly around the leaves as it ate. I was close enough to see that its teeth were white and even. The head was higher at the back than at the front. The nose was broad and flat. The lips and chin protruded farther than its nose. But the hair that covered it, leaving bare only the parts of its face around the mouth, nose and ears, made it resemble an animal as much as a human. None of this hair, even on the back of its head, was longer than an inch, and that on its face much shorter. Its ears were shaped like a human's ears. But its eyes were small and black like a bear's. And its neck also was unhuman, thicker and shorter than any man's I have ever seen.

As I watched this creature I wondered if some movie company was making a film in this place and that what I saw was an actor made up to look partly human, partly animal. But as I observed it more I decided it would be impossible to fake such a specimen. Anyway, I learned later there was no such company near that area. Nor, in fact, did anyone live up Mica Mountain, according to the people who lived in Tete Jaune Cache.

Finally, the wild thing must have got my scent, for it looked directly at me through an opening in the brush. A look of amazement crossed its face. It looked so comical at that moment I had to grin. Still in a crouched position, it backed up three or four short steps, then straightened up to its full height and started to walk rapidly back the way it had come. For a moment it watched me over its shoulder as it went, not exactly afraid, but as though it wanted no contact with anything strange.

The thought came to me that if I shot it I would possibly have a specimen of great interest to scientists the world over. I had heard stories about the Sasquatch, the giant hairy 'Indians' that live in the legend of the Indians of British Columbia and also, many claim are still, in fact, alive today. Maybe this was a Sasquatch, I told myself.

I levelled my rifle. The creature was still walking rapidly away, again turning its head to look in my direction. I lowered the rifle. Although I have called the creature 'it,' I felt now that it was a human being, and I knew I would never forgive myself if I killed it.

Just as it came to the other patch of brush it threw its head back and made a peculiar noise that seemed to be half laugh and half language, and which I could only describe as a kind of a whinny. Then it walked from the small brush into a stand of lodge-pole pines.

I stepped out into the opening and looked across a small ridge just beyond the pine to see if I could see it again. It came out on the ridge a couple of hundred yards away from me, tipped its head back again, and again emitted the only sound I had heard it make, but what this half laugh, half language was meant to convey I do not know. It disappeared then, and I never saw it again.

I wanted to find out if it lived on vegetation entirely or ate meat as well, so I went down and looked for signs. I found it in five different places, and although I examined it thoroughly, could find no hair or shells or bugs or insects. So I believe it was strictly a vegetarian.

I found one place where it had slept for a couple of nights under a tree. Now, the nights were cool up the mountain, at this time of year especially, and yet it had not used a fire. I found no signs that it possessed even the simplest of tools. Nor did I find any signs that it had a single companion while in this place.

Whether this creature was a Sasquatch I do not know. It will always remain a mystery to me unless another one is found.

I hearby declare the above statement to be in every part true, to the best of my powers of observation and recollection.

Signed William Roe
Witnessed

The Bird with Nine Heads

LONG, LONG AGO, there once lived a king and a queen who had a daughter. One day, when the daughter went walking in the garden, a tremendous storm suddenly came up and carried her away with it. Now the storm had come from the bird with nine heads, who had robbed the princess, and brought her to his cave. The king did not know whither his daughter had disappeared, so he had proclaimed throughout the land: "Whoever brings back the princess may have her for his bride!"

Now a youth had seen the bird as he was carrying the princess to his cave. This cave, though, was in the middle of a sheer wall of rock. One could not climb up to it from below, nor could one climb down to it from above. And as the youth was walking around the rock, another youth came along and asked him what he was doing there. So the first youth told him that the bird with nine heads had carried off the king's daughter, and had brought her up to his cave. The other chap knew what he had to do. He called together his friends, and they lowered the youth to the cave in a basket. And when he went into the cave, he saw the king's daughter sitting there, and washing the wound of the bird with nine heads; for the hound of heaven had bitten off his tenth head, and his wound was still bleeding. The princess, however, motioned to the youth to hide, and he did so. When the king's daughter had washed his wound and bandaged it, the bird with nine heads felt so comfortable, that one after another, all his nine heads fell asleep. Then the youth stepped forth from his hiding-place, and cut off his nine heads with a sword. But the king's daughter said: "It would be best if you were hauled up first, and I came after."

"No," said the youth. "I will wait below here, until you are in safety." At first the king's daughter was not willing; yet at last she allowed herself to be persuaded, and climbed into the basket. But before she did so, she took a long pin from her hair, broke it into two halves and gave him one and kept the other. She also divided her silken 'kerchief with him, and told him to take good care of both her gifts. But when the other man had drawn up the king's daughter, he took her along with him, and left the youth in the cave, in spite of all his calling and pleading.

The youth now took a walk about the cave. There he saw a number of maidens, all of whom had been carried off by the bird with nine heads, and who had perished there of hunger. And on the wall hung a fish, nailed against it with four nails. When he touched the fish, the latter turned into a handsome youth, who thanked him for delivering him, and they agreed to regard each other as brothers. Soon the first youth grew very hungry. He stepped out in front of the cave to search for food, but only stones were lying there. Then, suddenly, he saw a great dragon, who was licking a stone. The youth imitated him, and before long his hunger had disappeared. He next asked the dragon how he could get away from the cave, and the dragon nodded his head in the direction of his tail, as much as to say he should seat himself upon it. So he climbed up, and in the twinkling of an eye he was down on the ground, and the dragon had disappeared. He then went on until he found a tortoise-shell full of beautiful pearls. But they were magic pearls, for if you flung them into the fire, the fire ceased to burn and if you flung them into the water, the water divided and you could walk through the midst of it. The youth took the pearls out of the tortoise-shell, and put them in his pocket. Not long after he reached the sea-shore. Here he flung a pearl into the sea, and at once the waters divided and he could see the sea-dragon. The sea-dragon cried: "Who is disturbing me here in my own kingdom?" The youth answered: "I found pearls in a tortoise-shell, and have flung one into the sea, and now the waters have divided for me."

"If that is the case," said the dragon, "then come into the sea with me and we will live there together." Then the youth recognized him for the same dragon whom he had seen in the cave. And with him was the youth with whom he had formed a bond of brotherhood: He was the dragon's son.

"Since you have saved my son and become his brother, I am your father," said the old dragon. And he entertained him hospitably with food and wine.

One day his friend said to him: "My father is sure to want to reward you. But accept no money, nor any jewels from him, but only the little gourd flask over yonder. With it you can conjure up whatever you wish."

And, sure enough, the old dragon asked him what he wanted by way of a reward, and the youth answered: "I want no money, nor any jewels. All I want is the little gourd flask over yonder."

At first the dragon did not wish to give it up, but at last he did let him have it, after all. And then the youth left the dragon's castle.

When he set his foot on dry land again he felt hungry. At once a table stood before him, covered with a fine and plenteous meal. He ate and drank. After he had gone on a while, he felt weary. And there stood an ass, waiting for him, on which he mounted. After he had ridden for a while, the ass's gait seemed too uneven, and along came a wagon, into which he climbed. But the wagon shook him up too, greatly, and he thought: "If I only had a litter! That would suit me better." No more had he thought so, than the litter came along, and he seated himself in it. And the bearers carried him to the city in which dwelt the king, the queen and their daughter.

When the other youth had brought back the king's daughter, it was decided to hold the wedding. But the king's daughter was not willing, and said: "He is not the right man. My deliverer will come and bring with him half of the long pin for my hair, and half my silken 'kerchief as a token." But when the youth did not appear for so long a time, and the other one pressed the king, the king grew impatient and said: "The wedding shall take place tomorrow!" Then the king's daughter went sadly through the streets of the city, and searched and searched in the hope of finding her deliverer. And this was on the very day that the litter arrived. The king's daughter saw the half of her silken handkerchief in the youth's hand, and filled with joy, she led him to her father. There he had to show his half of the long pin, which fitted the other exactly, and then the king was convinced that he was the right, true deliverer. The false bridegroom was now punished, the wedding celebrated, and they lived in peace and happiness till the end of their days.

The Vampire Cat

THE PRINCE OF HIZEN, a distinguished member of the Nabeshima family, lingered in the garden with O Toyo, the favourite among his ladies. When the sun set they retired to the palace, but failed to notice that they were being followed by a large cat.

O Toyo went to her room and fell asleep. At midnight she awoke and gazed about her, as if suddenly aware of some dreadful presence in the apartment. At length she saw, crouching close beside her, a gigantic cat, and before she could cry out for assistance the animal sprang upon her and strangled her. The animal then made a hole under the verandah, buried the corpse, and assumed the form of the beautiful O Toyo.

The Prince, who knew nothing of what had happened, continued to love the false O Toyo, unaware that in reality he was caressing a foul beast. He noticed, little by little, that his strength failed, and it was not long before he became dangerously ill. Physicians were summoned, but they could do nothing to restore the royal patient. It was observed that he suffered most during the night, and was troubled by horrible dreams. This being so his councillors arranged that a hundred retainers should sit with their lord and keep watch while he slept.

The watch went into the sick-room, but just before ten o'clock it was overcome by a mysterious drowsiness. When all the men were asleep the false O Toyo crept into the apartment and disturbed the Prince until sunrise. Night after night the retainers came to guard their master, but always they fell asleep at the same hour, and even three loyal councillors had a similar experience.

During this time the Prince grew worse, and at length a priest named Ruiten was appointed to pray on his behalf. One night, while he was engaged in his supplications, he heard a strange noise proceeding from the garden. On looking out of the window he saw a young soldier washing himself. When he had finished his ablutions he stood before an image of Buddha, and prayed most ardently for the recovery of the Prince.

Ruiten, delighted to find such zeal and loyalty, invited the young man to enter his house, and when he had done so inquired his name.

"I am Ito Soda," said the young man, "and serve in the infantry of Nabeshima. I have heard of my lord's sickness and long to have the honour of nursing him; but being of low rank it is not meet that I should come into his presence. I have, nevertheless, prayed to the Buddha that my lord's life may be spared. I believe that the Prince of Hizen is bewitched, and if I might remain with him I would do my utmost to find and crush the evil power that is the cause of his illness."

Ruiten was so favourably impressed with these words that he went the next day to consult with one of the councillors, and after much discussion it was arranged that Ito Soda should keep watch with the hundred retainers.

When Ito Soda entered the royal apartment he saw that his master slept in the middle of the room, and he also observed the hundred retainers sitting in the chamber quietly chatting together in the hope that they would be able to keep off approaching drowsiness. By ten o'clock all the retainers, in spite of their efforts, had fallen asleep. Ito Soda tried to keep his eyes open, but a heaviness was gradually overcoming him, and he realised that if he wished to keep awake he must resort to extreme measures. When he had carefully spread oil-paper over the mats he stuck his dirk into his thigh. The sharp pain he experienced warded off sleep for a time, but eventually he felt his eyes closing once more. Resolved to outwit the spell which had proved too much for the retainers, he twisted the knife in his thigh, and thus increased the pain and kept his loyal watch, while blood continually dripped upon the oil-paper.

While Ito Soda watched he saw the sliding doors drawn open and a beautiful woman creep softly into the apartment. With a smile she noticed the sleeping retainers, and was about to approach the Prince when she observed Ito Soda. After she had spoken curtly to him she approached the Prince and inquired how he fared, but the Prince was too ill to make a reply. Ito Soda watched every movement, and believed she tried to bewitch the Prince, but she was always frustrated in her evil purpose by the dauntless eyes of Ito Soda, and at last she was compelled to retire.

In the morning the retainers awoke, and were filled with shame when they learnt how Ito Soda had kept his vigil. The councillors loudly praised the young soldier for his loyalty and enterprise, and he was commanded to keep watch again that night. He did so, and once more the false O Toyo entered the sick-room, and, as on the previous night, she was compelled to retreat without being able to cast her spell over the Prince.

It was discovered that immediately the faithful Soda had kept guard the Prince was able to obtain peaceful slumber, and, moreover, that he began to get better, for the false O Toyo, having been frustrated on two occasions, now kept away altogether, and the guard was not troubled with mysterious drowsiness. Soda, impressed by these strange circumstances, went to one of the councillors and informed him that the so-called O Toyo was a goblin of some kind.

That night Soda planned to go to the creature's room and try to kill her, arranging that in case she should escape there should be eight retainers outside waiting to capture her and despatch her immediately.

At the appointed hour Soda went to the creature's apartment, pretending that he bore a message from the Prince.

"What is your message?" inquired the woman.

"Kindly read this letter," replied Soda, and with these words he drew his dirk and tried to kill her.

The false O Toyo seized a halberd and endeavoured to strike her adversary. Blow followed blow, but at last perceiving that flight would serve her better than battle she threw away her weapon, and in a moment the lovely maiden turned into a cat and sprang on to the roof. The eight men waiting outside in case of emergency shot at the animal, but the creature succeeded in eluding them.

The cat made all speed for the mountains, and caused trouble among the people who lived in the vicinity, but was finally killed during a hunt ordered by the Prince Hizen. The Prince became well again, and Ito Soda received the honour and reward he so richly deserved.

Yorimasa

A LONG TIME AGO a certain Emperor became seriously ill. He was unable to sleep at night owing to a most horrible and unaccountable noise he heard proceeding from the roof of the palace, called the Purple Hall of the North Star. A number of his courtiers decided to lie in wait for this strange nocturnal visitor. As soon as the sun set they noticed that a dark cloud crept from the eastern horizon, and alighted on the roof of the august palace. Those who waited in the imperial bed-chamber heard extraordinary scratching sounds, as if what had at first appeared to be a cloud had suddenly changed into a beast with gigantic and powerful claws.

Night after night this terrible visitant came, and night after night the Emperor grew worse. He at last became so ill that it was obvious to all those in attendance upon him that unless something could be done to destroy this monster the Emperor would certainly die.

At last it was decided that Yorimasa was the one knight in the kingdom valiant enough to relieve his Majesty of these terrible hauntings. Yorimasa accordingly made elaborate preparations for the fray. He took his best bow and steel-headed arrows, donned his armour, over which he wore a hunting-dress, and a ceremonial cap instead of his usual helmet.

At sunset he lay in concealment outside the palace. While he thus waited thunder crashed overhead, lightning blazed in the sky, and the wind shrieked like a pack of wild demons. But Yorimasa was a brave man, and the fury of the elements in no way daunted him. When midnight came he saw a black cloud rush through the sky and rest upon the roof of the palace. At the north-east corner it stopped. Once more the lightning flashed in the sky, and this time he saw the gleaming eyes of a large animal. Noting the exact position of this strange monster, he pulled at his bow till it became as round as the full moon. In another moment his steel-headed arrow hit its mark. There was an awful roar of anger, and then a heavy thud as the huge monster rolled from the palace roof to the ground.

Yorimasa and his retainer ran forward and despatched the fearful creature they saw before them. This evil monster of the night was as large as a horse. It had the head of an ape, and the body and claws were like those of a tiger, with a serpent's tail, wings of a bird, and the scales of a dragon.

It was no wonder that the Emperor gave orders that the skin of this monster should be kept for all time as a curiosity in the Imperial treasure-house. From the very moment the creature died the Emperor's health rapidly improved, and Yorimasa was rewarded for his services by being presented with a sword called Shishi-wo, which means "the King of Lions." He was also promoted at Court, and finally married the Lady Ayame, the most beautiful of ladies-in-waiting at the Imperial Court.

Beauty and the Beast

ONCE UPON A TIME, in a very far-off country, there lived a merchant who had been so fortunate in all his undertakings that he was enormously rich. As he had, however, six sons and six daughters, he found that his money was not too much to let them all have everything they fancied, as they were accustomed to do.

But one day a most unexpected misfortune befell them. Their house caught fire and was speedily burnt to the ground, with all the splendid furniture, the books, pictures, gold, silver, and precious goods it contained; and this was only the beginning of their troubles. Their father, who had until this moment prospered in all ways, suddenly lost every ship he had upon the sea, either by dint of pirates, shipwreck, or fire. Then he heard that his clerks in distant countries, whom he trusted entirely, had proved unfaithful; and at last from great wealth he fell into the direst poverty.

All that he had left was a little house in a desolate place at least a hundred leagues from the town in which he had lived, and to this he was forced to retreat with his children, who were in despair at the idea of leading such a different life. Indeed, the daughters at first hoped that their friends, who had been so numerous while they were rich, would insist on their staying in their houses now they no longer possessed one. But they soon found that they were left alone, and that their former friends even attributed their misfortunes to their own extravagance, and showed no intention of offering them any help. So nothing was left for them but to take their departure to the cottage, which stood in the midst of a dark forest, and seemed to be the most dismal place upon the face of the earth. As they were too poor to have any servants, the girls had to work hard, like peasants, and the sons, for their part, cultivated the fields to earn their living. Roughly clothed, and living in the simplest way, the girls regretted unceasingly the luxuries and amusements of their former life; only the youngest tried to be brave and cheerful. She had been as sad as anyone when misfortune overtook her father, but, soon recovering her natural gaiety, she set to work to make the best of things, to amuse her father and brothers as well as she could, and to try to persuade her sisters to join her in dancing and singing. But they would do nothing of the sort, and, because she was not as doleful as themselves, they declared that this miserable life was all she was fit for. But she was really far prettier and cleverer than they were; indeed, she was so lovely that she was always called Beauty. After two years, when they were all beginning to get used to their new life, something happened to disturb their tranquillity. Their father received the news that one of his ships, which he had believed to be lost, had come safely into port with a rich cargo. All the sons and daughters at once thought that their poverty was at an end, and wanted to set out directly for the town; but their father, who was more prudent, begged them to wait a little, and, though it was harvest time, and he could ill be spared, determined to go himself first, to make inquiries. Only the youngest daughter had any doubt but that they would soon again be as rich as they were before, or at least rich enough to live comfortably in some town where they would find amusement and gay companions once more. So they all loaded their father with commissions for jewels and dresses which it would have taken a fortune to buy; only Beauty, feeling sure that it was of no use, did not ask for anything. Her father, noticing her silence, said: "And what shall I bring for you, Beauty?"

"The only thing I wish for is to see you come home safely," she answered.

But this only vexed her sisters, who fancied she was blaming them for having asked for such costly things. Her father, however, was pleased, but as he thought that at her age she certainly ought to like pretty presents, he told her to choose something.

"Well, dear father," she said, "as you insist upon it, I beg that you will bring me a rose. I have not seen one since we came here, and I love them so much."

So the merchant set out and reached the town as quickly as possible, but only to find that his former companions, believing him to be dead, had divided between them the goods which the ship had brought; and after six months of trouble and expense he found himself as poor as when he started, having been able to recover only just enough to pay the cost of his journey. To make matters worse, he was obliged to leave the town in the most terrible weather, so that by the time he was within a few leagues of his home he was almost exhausted with cold and fatigue. Though he knew it would take some hours to get through the forest, he was so anxious to be at his journey's end that he resolved to go on; but night overtook him, and the deep snow and bitter frost made it impossible for his horse to carry him any further. Not a house was to be seen; the only shelter he could get was the hollow trunk of a great tree, and there he crouched all the night which seemed to him the longest he had ever known. In spite of his weariness the howling of the wolves kept him awake, and even when at last the day broke he was not much better off, for the falling snow had covered up every path, and he did not know which way to turn.

At length he made out some sort of track, and though at the beginning it was so rough and slippery that he fell down more than once, it presently became easier, and led him into an avenue of trees which ended in a splendid castle. It seemed to the merchant very strange that no snow had fallen in the avenue, which was entirely composed of orange trees, covered with flowers and fruit. When he reached the first court of the castle he saw before him a flight of agate steps, and went up them, and passed through several splendidly furnished rooms. The pleasant warmth of the air revived him, and he felt very hungry; but there seemed to be nobody in all this vast and splendid palace whom he could ask to give him something to eat. Deep silence reigned everywhere, and at last, tired of roaming through empty rooms and galleries, he stopped in a room smaller than the rest, where a clear fire was burning and a couch was drawn up closely to it. Thinking that this must be prepared for someone who was expected, he sat down to wait till he should come, and very soon fell into a sweet sleep.

When his extreme hunger wakened him after several hours, he was still alone; but a little table, upon which was a good dinner, had been drawn up close to him, and, as he had eaten nothing for twenty-four hours, he lost no time in beginning his meal, hoping that he might soon have an opportunity of thanking his considerate entertainer, whoever it might be. But no one appeared, and even after another long sleep, from which he awoke completely refreshed, there was no sign of anybody, though a fresh meal of dainty cakes and fruit was prepared upon the little table at his elbow. Being naturally timid, the silence began to terrify him, and he resolved to search once more through all the rooms; but it was of no use. Not even a servant was to be seen; there was no sign of life in the palace! He began to wonder what he should do, and to amuse himself by pretending that all the treasures he saw were his own, and considering how he would divide them among his children. Then he went down into the garden, and though it was winter everywhere else, here the sun shone, and the birds sang, and the flowers bloomed, and the air was soft and sweet. The merchant, in ecstacies with all he saw and heard, said to himself:

"All this must be meant for me. I will go this minute and bring my children to share all these delights."

In spite of being so cold and weary when he reached the castle, he had taken his horse to the stable and fed it. Now he thought he would saddle it for his homeward journey, and he turned down the path which led to the stable. This path had a hedge of roses on each side of it, and the merchant thought he had never seen or smelt such exquisite flowers. They reminded him of his promise to Beauty, and he stopped and had just gathered one to take to her when he was startled by a strange noise behind him. Turning round, he saw a frightful Beast, which seemed to be very angry and said, in a terrible voice:

"Who told you that you might gather my roses? Was it not enough that I allowed you to be in my palace and was kind to you? This is the way you show your gratitude, by stealing my flowers! But your insolence shall not go unpunished." The merchant, terrified by these furious words, dropped the fatal rose, and, throwing himself on his knees, cried: "Pardon me, noble sir. I am truly grateful to you for your hospitality, which was so magnificent that I could not imagine that you would be offended by my taking such a little thing as a rose." But the Beast's anger was not lessened by this speech.

"You are very ready with excuses and flattery," he cried; "but that will not save you from the death you deserve."

"Alas!" thought the merchant, "if my daughter could only know what danger her rose has brought me into!"

And in despair he began to tell the Beast all his misfortunes, and the reason of his journey, not forgetting to mention Beauty's request.

"A king's ransom would hardly have procured all that my other daughters asked." he said: "but I thought that I might at least take Beauty her rose. I beg you to forgive me, for you see I meant no harm."

The Beast considered for a moment, and then he said, in a less furious tone:

"I will forgive you on one condition – that is, that you will give me one of your daughters."

"Ah!" cried the merchant, "if I were cruel enough to buy my own life at the expense of one of my children's, what excuse could I invent to bring her here?"

"No excuse would be necessary," answered the Beast. "If she comes at all she must come willingly. On no other condition will I have her. See if any one of them is courageous enough, and loves you well enough to come and save your life. You seem to be an honest man, so I will trust you to go home. I give you a month to see if either of your daughters will come back with you and stay here, to let you go free. If neither of them is willing, you must come alone, after bidding them good-by for ever, for then you will belong to me. And do not imagine that you can hide from me, for if you fail to keep your word I will come and fetch you!" added the Beast grimly.

The merchant accepted this proposal, though he did not really think any of his daughters could be persuaded to come. He promised to return at the time appointed, and then, anxious to escape from the presence of the Beast, he asked permission to set off at once. But the Beast answered that he could not go until next day.

"Then you will find a horse ready for you," he said. "Now go and eat your supper, and await my orders."

The poor merchant, more dead than alive, went back to his room, where the most delicious supper was already served on the little table which was drawn up before a blazing fire. But he was too terrified to eat, and only tasted a few of the dishes, for fear the Beast should be angry if he did not obey his orders. When he had finished he heard a great noise in the next room, which he knew meant that the Beast was coming. As he could do nothing to escape his visit, the only thing that remained was to seem as little afraid as possible; so when the Beast appeared and asked roughly if he had supped well, the merchant answered humbly that he had, thanks to his host's kindness. Then the Beast warned him to remember their agreement, and to prepare his daughter exactly for what she had to expect.

"Do not get up to-morrow," he added, "until you see the sun and hear a golden bell ring. Then you will find your breakfast waiting for you here, and the horse you are to ride will be ready in the courtyard. He will also bring you back again when you come with your daughter a month hence. Farewell. Take a rose to Beauty, and remember your promise!"

The merchant was only too glad when the Beast went away, and though he could not sleep for sadness, he lay down until the sun rose. Then, after a hasty breakfast, he went to gather Beauty's rose, and mounted his horse, which carried him off so swiftly that in an instant he had lost sight of the palace, and he was still wrapped in gloomy thoughts when it stopped before the door of the cottage.

His sons and daughters, who had been very uneasy at his long absence, rushed to meet him, eager to know the result of his journey, which, seeing him mounted upon a splendid horse and wrapped in a rich mantle, they supposed to be favourable. He hid the truth from them at first, only saying sadly to Beauty as he gave her the rose:

"Here is what you asked me to bring you; you little know what it has cost."

But this excited their curiosity so greatly that presently he told them his adventures from beginning to end, and then they were all very unhappy. The girls lamented loudly over their lost hopes, and the sons declared that their father should not return to this terrible castle, and began to make plans for killing the Beast if it should come to fetch him. But he reminded them that he had promised to go back. Then the girls were very angry with Beauty, and said it was all her fault, and that if she had asked for something sensible this would never have happened, and complained bitterly that they should have to suffer for her folly.

Poor Beauty, much distressed, said to them:

"I have, indeed, caused this misfortune, but I assure you I did it innocently. Who could have guessed that to ask for a rose in the middle of summer would cause so much misery? But as I did the mischief it is only just that I should suffer for it. I will therefore go back with my father to keep his promise."

At first nobody would hear of this arrangement, and her father and brothers, who loved her dearly, declared that nothing should make them let her go; but Beauty was firm. As the time drew near she divided all her little possessions between her sisters, and said good-by to everything she loved, and when the fatal day came she encouraged and cheered her father as they mounted together the horse which had brought him back. It seemed to fly rather than gallop, but so smoothly that Beauty was not frightened; indeed, she would have enjoyed the journey if she had not feared what might happen to her at the end of it. Her father still tried to persuade her to go back, but in vain. While they were talking the night fell, and then, to their great surprise, wonderful coloured lights began to shine in all directions, and splendid fireworks blazed out before them; all the forest was illuminated by them, and even felt pleasantly warm, though it had been bitterly cold before. This lasted until they reached the avenue of orange trees, where were statues holding flaming torches, and when they got nearer to the palace they saw that it was illuminated from the roof to the ground, and music sounded softly from the courtyard. "The Beast must be very hungry," said Beauty, trying to laugh, "if he makes all this rejoicing over the arrival of his prey."

But, in spite of her anxiety, she could not help admiring all the wonderful things she saw.

The horse stopped at the foot of the flight of steps leading to the terrace, and when they had dismounted her father led her to the little room he had been in before, where they found a splendid fire burning, and the table daintily spread with a delicious supper.

The merchant knew that this was meant for them, and Beauty, who was rather less frightened now that she had passed through so many rooms and seen nothing of the Beast, was quite willing to begin, for her long ride had made her very hungry. But they had hardly finished their meal when the noise of the Beast's footsteps was heard approaching, and Beauty clung to her father in terror, which became all the greater when she saw how frightened he was. But when the Beast really appeared, though she trembled at the sight of him, she made a great effort to hide her terror, and saluted him respectfully.

This evidently pleased the Beast. After looking at her he said, in a tone that might have struck terror into the boldest heart, though he did not seem to be angry:

"Good-evening, old man. Good-evening, Beauty."

The merchant was too terrified to reply, but Beauty answered sweetly: "Good-evening, Beast."

"Have you come willingly?" asked the Beast. "Will you be content to stay here when your father goes away?"

Beauty answered bravely that she was quite prepared to stay.

"I am pleased with you," said the Beast. "As you have come of your own accord, you may stay. As for you, old man," he added, turning to the merchant, "at sunrise to-morrow you will take your departure. When the bell rings get up quickly and eat your breakfast, and you will find the same horse waiting to take you home; but remember that you must never expect to see my palace again."

Then turning to Beauty, he said:

"Take your father into the next room, and help him to choose everything you think your brothers and sisters would like to have. You will find two travelling-trunks there; fill them as full as you can. It is only just that you should send them something very precious as a remembrance of yourself."

Then he went away, after saying, "Good-by, Beauty; good-by, old man;" and though Beauty was beginning to think with great dismay of her father's departure, she was afraid to disobey the Beast's orders; and they went into the next room, which had shelves and cupboards all round it. They were greatly surprised at the riches it contained. There were splendid dresses fit for a queen, with all the ornaments that were to be worn with them; and when Beauty opened the cupboards she was quite dazzled by the gorgeous jewels that lay in heaps upon every shelf. After choosing a vast quantity, which she divided between her sisters – for she had made a heap of the wonderful dresses for each of them – she opened the last chest, which was full of gold.

"I think, father," she said, "that, as the gold will be more useful to you, we had better take out the other things again, and fill the trunks with it." So they did this; but the more they put in the more room there seemed to be, and at last they put back all the jewels and dresses they had taken out, and Beauty even added as many more of the jewels as she could carry at once; and then the trunks were not too full, but they were so heavy that an elephant could not have carried them!

"The Beast was mocking us," cried the merchant; "he must have pretended to give us all these things, knowing that I could not carry them away."

"Let us wait and see," answered Beauty. "I cannot believe that he meant to deceive us. All we can do is to fasten them up and leave them ready."

So they did this and returned to the little room, where, to their astonishment, they found breakfast ready. The merchant ate his with a good appetite, as the Beast's generosity made him believe that he might perhaps venture to come back soon and see Beauty. But she felt sure that her father was leaving her for ever, so she was very sad when the bell rang sharply for the second time, and warned them that the time had come for them to part. They went down into the courtyard, where two horses were waiting, one loaded with the two trunks, the other for him to ride. They were pawing the ground in their impatience to start, and the merchant was forced to bid Beauty a hasty farewell; and as soon as he was mounted he went off at such a pace that she lost sight of him in an instant. Then Beauty began to cry, and wandered sadly back to her own room. But she soon found that she was very sleepy, and as she had nothing better to do she lay down and instantly fell asleep. And then she dreamed that she was walking by a brook bordered with trees, and lamenting her sad fate, when a young prince, handsomer than anyone she had ever seen, and with a voice that went straight to her heart, came and said to her, "Ah, Beauty! you are not so unfortunate as you suppose. Here you will be rewarded for all you have suffered elsewhere. Your every wish shall be gratified. Only try to find me out, no matter how I may be disguised, as I love you dearly, and in making me happy you will find your own happiness. Be as true-hearted as you are beautiful, and we shall have nothing left to wish for."

"What can I do, Prince, to make you happy?" said Beauty.

"Only be grateful," he answered, "and do not trust too much to your eyes. And, above all, do not desert me until you have saved me from my cruel misery."

After this she thought she found herself in a room with a stately and beautiful lady, who said to her:

"Dear Beauty, try not to regret all you have left behind you, for you are destined to a better fate. Only do not let yourself be deceived by appearances."

Beauty found her dreams so interesting that she was in no hurry to awake, but presently the clock roused her by calling her name softly twelve times, and then she got up and found her dressing-table set out with everything she could possibly want; and when her toilet was finished she found dinner was waiting in the room next to hers. But dinner does not take very long when you are all by yourself, and very soon she sat down cosily in the corner of a sofa, and began to think about the charming Prince she had seen in her dream.

"He said I could make him happy," said Beauty to herself.

"It seems, then, that this horrible Beast keeps him a prisoner. How can I set him free? I wonder why they both told me not to trust to appearances? I don't understand it. But, after all, it was only a dream, so why should I trouble myself about it? I had better go and find something to do to amuse myself."

So she got up and began to explore some of the many rooms of the palace.

The first she entered was lined with mirrors, and Beauty saw herself reflected on every side, and thought she had never seen such a charming room. Then a bracelet which was hanging from a chandelier caught her eye, and on taking it down she was greatly surprised to find that it held a portrait of her unknown admirer, just as she had seen him in her dream. With great delight she slipped the bracelet on her arm, and went on into a gallery of pictures, where she soon found a portrait of the same handsome Prince, as large as life, and so well painted that as she studied it he seemed to smile kindly at her. Tearing herself away from the portrait at last, she passed through into a room which contained every musical instrument under the sun, and here she amused herself for a long while in trying some of them, and singing until she was tired. The next room was a library, and she saw everything she had ever wanted to read, as well as everything she had read, and it seemed to her that a whole lifetime would not be enough to even read the names of the books, there were so many. By this time it was growing dusk, and wax candles in diamond and ruby candlesticks were beginning to light themselves in every room.

Beauty found her supper served just at the time she preferred to have it, but she did not see anyone or hear a sound, and, though her father had warned her that she would be alone, she began to find it rather dull.

But presently she heard the Beast coming, and wondered tremblingly if he meant to eat her up now.

However, as he did not seem at all ferocious, and only said gruffly:

"Good-evening, Beauty," she answered cheerfully and managed to conceal her terror. Then the Beast asked her how she had been amusing herself, and she told him all the rooms she had seen.

Then he asked if she thought she could be happy in his palace; and Beauty answered that everything was so beautiful that she would be very hard to please if she could not be happy. And after about an hour's talk Beauty began to think that the Beast was not nearly so terrible as she had supposed at first. Then he got up to leave her, and said in his gruff voice:

"Do you love me, Beauty? Will you marry me?"

"Oh! what shall I say?" cried Beauty, for she was afraid to make the Beast angry by refusing.

"Say 'yes' or 'no' without fear," he replied.

"Oh! no, Beast," said Beauty hastily.

"Since you will not, good-night, Beauty," he said.

And she answered, "Good-night, Beast," very glad to find that her refusal had not provoked him. And after he was gone she was very soon in bed and asleep, and dreaming of her unknown Prince. She thought he came and said to her:

"Ah, Beauty! why are you so unkind to me? I fear I am fated to be unhappy for many a long day still."

And then her dreams changed, but the charming Prince figured in them all; and when morning came her first thought was to look at the portrait, and see if it was really like him, and she found that it certainly was.

This morning she decided to amuse herself in the garden, for the sun shone, and all the fountains were playing; but she was astonished to find that every place was familiar to her, and presently she came to the brook where the myrtle trees were growing where she had first met the Prince in her dream, and that made her think more than ever that he must be kept a prisoner by the Beast. When she was tired she went back to the palace, and found a new room full of materials for every kind of work – ribbons to make into bows, and silks to work into flowers. Then there was an aviary full of rare birds, which were so tame that they flew to Beauty as soon as they saw her, and perched upon her shoulders and her head.

"Pretty little creatures," she said, "how I wish that your cage was nearer to my room, that I might often hear you sing!"

So saying she opened a door, and found, to her delight, that it led into her own room, though she had thought it was quite the other side of the palace.

There were more birds in a room farther on, parrots and cockatoos that could talk, and they greeted Beauty by name; indeed, she found them so entertaining that she took one or two back to her room, and they talked to her while she was at supper; after which the Beast paid her his usual visit, and asked her the same questions as before, and then with a gruff "good-night" he took his departure, and Beauty went to bed to dream of her mysterious Prince. The days passed swiftly in different amusements, and after a while Beauty found out another strange thing in the palace, which often pleased her when she was tired of being alone. There was one room which she had not noticed particularly; it was empty, except that under each of the windows stood a very comfortable chair; and the first time she had looked out of the window it had seemed to her that a black curtain prevented her from seeing anything outside. But the second time she went into the room, happening to be tired, she sat down in one of the chairs, when instantly the curtain was rolled aside, and a most amusing pantomime was acted before her; there were dances, and coloured lights, and music, and pretty dresses, and it was all so gay that Beauty was in ecstacies. After that she tried the other seven windows in turn, and there was some new and surprising entertainment to be seen from each of them, so that Beauty never could feel lonely any more. Every evening after supper the Beast came to see her, and always before saying good-night asked her in his terrible voice:

"Beauty, will you marry me?"

And it seemed to Beauty, now she understood him better, that when she said, "No, Beast," he went away quite sad. But her happy dreams of the handsome young Prince soon made her forget the poor Beast, and the only thing that at all disturbed her was to be constantly told to distrust appearances, to let her heart guide her, and not her eyes, and many other equally perplexing things, which, consider as she would, she could not understand.

So everything went on for a long time, until at last, happy as she was, Beauty began to long for the sight of her father and her brothers and sisters; and one night, seeing her look very sad, the Beast asked her what was the matter. Beauty had quite ceased to be afraid of him. Now she knew that he was really gentle in spite of his ferocious looks and his dreadful voice. So she answered that she was longing to see her home once more. Upon hearing this the Beast seemed sadly distressed, and cried miserably.

"Ah! Beauty, have you the heart to desert an unhappy Beast like this? What more do you want to make you happy? Is it because you hate me that you want to escape?"

"No, dear Beast," answered Beauty softly, "I do not hate you, and I should be very sorry never to see you any more, but I long to see my father again. Only let me go for two months, and I promise to come back to you and stay for the rest of my life."

The Beast, who had been sighing dolefully while she spoke, now replied:

"I cannot refuse you anything you ask, even though it should cost me my life. Take the four boxes you will find in the room next to your own, and fill them with everything you wish to take with you. But remember your promise and come back when the two months are over, or you may have cause to repent it, for if you do not come in good time you will find your faithful Beast dead. You will not need any chariot to bring you back. Only say good-by to all your brothers and sisters the night before you come away, and when you have gone to bed turn this ring round upon your finger and say firmly: 'I wish to go back to my palace and see my Beast again.' Good-night, Beauty. Fear nothing, sleep peacefully, and before long you shall see your father once more."

As soon as Beauty was alone she hastened to fill the boxes with all the rare and precious things she saw about her, and only when she was tired of heaping things into them did they seem to be full.

Then she went to bed, but could hardly sleep for joy. And when at last she did begin to dream of her beloved Prince she was grieved to see him stretched upon a grassy bank, sad and weary, and hardly like himself.

"What is the matter?" she cried.

He looked at her reproachfully, and said:

"How can you ask me, cruel one? Are you not leaving me to my death perhaps?"

"Ah! don't be so sorrowful," cried Beauty; "I am only going to assure my father that I am safe and happy. I have promised the Beast faithfully that I will come back, and he would die of grief if I did not keep my word!"

"What would that matter to you?" said the Prince "Surely you would not care?"

"Indeed, I should be ungrateful if I did not care for such a kind Beast," cried Beauty indignantly. "I would die to save him from pain. I assure you it is not his fault that he is so ugly."

Just then a strange sound woke her – someone was speaking not very far away; and opening her eyes she found herself in a room she had never seen before, which was certainly not nearly so splendid as those she was used to in the Beast's palace. Where could she be? She got up and dressed hastily, and then saw that the boxes she had packed the night before were all in the room. While she was wondering by what magic the Beast had transported them and herself to this strange place she suddenly heard her father's voice, and rushed out and greeted him joyfully. Her brothers and sisters were all astonished at her appearance, as they had never expected to see her again, and there was no end to the questions they asked her. She had also much to hear about what had happened to them while she was away, and of her father's journey home. But when they heard that she had only come to be with them for a short time, and then must go back to the Beast's palace for ever, they lamented loudly. Then Beauty asked her father what he thought could be the meaning of her strange dreams, and why the Prince constantly begged her not to trust to appearances. After much consideration, he answered: "You tell me yourself that the Beast, frightful as he is, loves you dearly, and deserves your love and gratitude for his gentleness and kindness; I think the Prince must mean you to understand that you ought to reward him by doing as he wishes you to, in spite of his ugliness."

Beauty could not help seeing that this seemed very probable; still, when she thought of her dear Prince who was so handsome, she did not feel at all inclined to marry the Beast. At any rate, for two months she need not decide, but could enjoy herself with her sisters. But though they were rich now, and lived in town again, and had plenty of acquaintances, Beauty found that nothing amused her very much; and she often thought of the palace, where she was so happy, especially as at home she never once dreamed of her dear Prince, and she felt quite sad without him.

Then her sisters seemed to have got quite used to being without her, and even found her rather in the way, so she would not have been sorry when the two months were over but for her father and brothers, who begged her to stay, and seemed so grieved at the thought of her departure that she had not the courage to say good-by to them. Every day when she got up she meant to say it at night, and when night came she put it off again, until at last she had a dismal dream which helped her to make up her mind. She thought she was wandering in a lonely path in the palace gardens, when she heard groans which seemed to come from some bushes hiding the entrance of a cave, and running quickly to see what could be the matter, she found the Beast stretched out upon his side, apparently dying. He reproached her faintly with being the cause of his distress, and at the same moment a stately lady appeared, and said very gravely:

"Ah! Beauty, you are only just in time to save his life. See what happens when people do not keep their promises! If you had delayed one day more, you would have found him dead."

Beauty was so terrified by this dream that the next morning she announced her intention of going back at once, and that very night she said good-by to her father and all her brothers and sisters, and as soon as she was in bed she turned her ring round upon her finger, and said firmly, "I wish to go back to my palace and see my Beast again," as she had been told to do.

Then she fell asleep instantly, and only woke up to hear the clock saying "Beauty, Beauty" twelve times in its musical voice, which told her at once that she was really in the palace once more. Everything was just as before, and her birds were so glad to see her! But Beauty thought she had never known such a long day, for she was so anxious to see the Beast again that she felt as if suppertime would never come.

But when it did come and no Beast appeared she was really frightened; so, after listening and waiting for a long time, she ran down into the garden to search for him. Up and down the paths and avenues ran poor Beauty, calling him in vain, for no one answered, and not a trace of him could she find; until at last, quite tired, she stopped for a minute's rest, and saw that she was standing opposite the shady path she had seen in her dream. She rushed down it, and, sure enough, there was the cave, and in it lay the Beast – asleep, as Beauty thought. Quite glad to have found him, she ran up and stroked his head, but, to her horror, he did not move or open his eyes.

"Oh! he is dead; and it is all my fault," said Beauty, crying bitterly.

But then, looking at him again, she fancied he still breathed, and, hastily fetching some water from the nearest fountain, she sprinkled it over his face, and, to her great delight, he began to revive.

"Oh! Beast, how you frightened me!" she cried. "I never knew how much I loved you until just now, when I feared I was too late to save your life."

"Can you really love such an ugly creature as I am?" said the Beast faintly. "Ah! Beauty, you only came just in time. I was dying because I thought you had forgotten your promise. But go back now and rest, I shall see you again by and by."

Beauty, who had half expected that he would be angry with her, was reassured by his gentle voice, and went back to the palace, where supper was awaiting her; and afterward the Beast came in as usual, and talked about the time she had spent with her father, asking if she had enjoyed herself, and if they had all been very glad to see her.

Beauty answered politely, and quite enjoyed telling him all that had happened to her. And when at last the time came for him to go, and he asked, as he had so often asked before, "Beauty, will you marry me?"

She answered softly, "Yes, dear Beast."

As she spoke a blaze of light sprang up before the windows of the palace; fireworks crackled and guns banged, and across the avenue of orange trees, in letters all made of fire-flies, was written: 'Long live the Prince and his Bride.'

Turning to ask the Beast what it could all mean, Beauty found that he had disappeared, and in his place stood her long-loved Prince! At the same moment the wheels of a chariot were heard upon the terrace, and two ladies entered the room. One of them Beauty recognized as the stately lady she had seen in her dreams; the other was also so grand and queenly that Beauty hardly knew which to greet first.

But the one she already knew said to her companion:

"Well, Queen, this is Beauty, who has had the courage to rescue your son from the terrible enchantment. They love one another, and only your consent to their marriage is wanting to make them perfectly happy."

"I consent with all my heart," cried the Queen. "How can I ever thank you enough, charming girl, for having restored my dear son to his natural form?"

And then she tenderly embraced Beauty and the Prince, who had meanwhile been greeting the Fairy and receiving her congratulations.

"Now," said the Fairy to Beauty, "I suppose you would like me to send for all your brothers and sisters to dance at your wedding?"

And so she did, and the marriage was celebrated the very next day with the utmost splendour, and Beauty and the Prince lived happily ever after.

The Unicorn

A BELIEF IN THE UNICORN, like that in the dragon, appears to have obtained among both Eastern and Western authors, at a very early period. In this case, however, it has survived the revulsion from a fatuous confidence in the fables and concocted specimens of the Middle Ages, and even now the existence or non-existence of this remarkable animal remains a debateable question.

Until within a late period occasional correspondents of the South African journals continued to assert its existence, basing their communications on the reports of hunters from the interior, while but a few hundred years since travellers spoke of actually seeing it or of passing through countries in which its existence was absolutely affirmed to them. Horns, generally those of the narwhal, but occasionally of one species of rhinoceros, were brought home and deposited in museums as those of the veritable unicorn, or sold, under the same pretext, for large sums, on account of their reputed valuable medicinal properties. The animal is variously described as resembling a horse or some kind of deer; this description may possibly refer to some animal of a type intermediate to them, now almost, if not quite, extinct. In some instances it is supposed that a species of rhinoceros is indicated.

There has been much discussion as to the identity of the animal referred to in many passages of the Bible, the Hebrew name of which, *Reem*, has been translated 'unicorn.' Mr. W. Smith considers that a species of rhinoceros could not have been indicated, as it is spoken of in one passage as a sacrificial animal, whereas the ceremonial ritual of the Jews forbade the use of any animal not possessing the double qualifications of chewing the cud and being cloven-footed. The qualities attributed to it are great strength, an indomitable disposition, fierce nature, and an active and playful disposition when young. He considers that the passage, Deut. xxxiii. 17, should be rendered "his horns are like the horns of a unicorn," and not, as it is given, "horns of unicorns;" and is of opinion that some species of wild ox is intended.

Among profane Western authors we first find the unicorn referred to by Ctesias, who describes it as having one horn, a cubit long. Herodotus also mentions it in the passage, "For the eastern side of Libya, where the wanderers dwell, is low and sandy, as far as the river Triton; but westward of that, the land of the husbandmen is very hilly and abounds with forests and wild beasts, for this is the tract in which the huge serpents are found, and the lions, the elephants, the bears, the aspicks, and the horned asses;" and again, "Among the wanderers are none of these, but quite other animals, as antelopes, &c. &c., and asses, not of the horned sort, but of a kind which does not need to drink."

Aristotle mentions two unicorn animals. "There are only a few [animals] that have a solid hoof and one horn, as the Indian ass and the oryx."

Pliny tells us that the Orsæan Indians hunt down a very fierce animal called the monoceros, which has the head of the stag, the feet of the elephant, and the tail of the boar, while the rest of the body is like that of the horse. It makes a deep lowing noise, and has a single black horn, projecting from the middle of its forehead, and two cubits in length. This animal, it is said, cannot be taken alive. In speaking of the Indian ass, he says, "the Indian ass is only a one-horned animal;" and of the oryx of Africa, "the oryx is both one-horned and cloven-footed."

Ælian transfers the locality back again from Africa to Asia, and it may be presumed, in the following quotation, that he indicates the country north of the Himalaya, Tibet, and Tartary, which still has the reputation of being one of the homes of the unicorn.

"They say that there are mountains in the innermost regions of India inaccessible to men, and full of wild beasts; where those creatures which with us are domesticated, such as sheep, dogs, goats, and cattle, range about at their own free will, free from any charge by a shepherd or herdsman.

"Both historians, and the more learned of the Indians, among whom the Brahmins may be specified, declare that there is a countless number of these beasts. Among them they enumerate the unicorn, which they call cartazonon, and say that it reaches the size of a horse of mature age, possesses a mane and reddish yellow hair, and that it excels in swiftness through the excellence of its feet and of its whole body. Like the elephant, it has inarticulate feet, and it has a boar's tail; one black horn projects between the eyebrows, not awkwardly, but with a certain natural twist, and terminating in a sharp point.

"It has, of all animals, the harshest and most contentious voice. It is said to be gentle to other beasts approaching it, but to fight with its fellows. Not only are the males at variance in natural contention amongst themselves, but they also fight with the females, and carry their combats to the length of killing the conquered; for not only are their bodies generally indued with great strength, but also they are armed with an invincible horn. It frequents desert regions and wanders alone and solitary. In the breeding season it is of gentle demeanour towards the female, and they feed together; when this has passed and the female has become gravid, it again becomes fierce and wanders alone.

"They say that the young, while still of tender age, are carried to the King of the Prasians for exhibition of their strength, and exposed in combats on festivals; for no one remembers them to have been captured of mature age."

Cæsar records the reputed existence in his day, within the bounds of the great Hercynian Forest, of a bull, shaped like a stag, with one horn projecting from the middle of its forehead and between the ears.

Cosmas, surnamed Indicopleustes, a merchant of Alexandria, who lived in the sixth century, and made a voyage to India, and subsequently wrote works on cosmography, gives a figure of the unicorn, not, as he says, from actual sight of it, but reproduced from four figures of it in brass contained in the palace of the King of Ethiopia. He states, from report, that "it is impossible to take this ferocious beast alive; and that all its strength lies in its horn. When it finds itself pursued and in danger of capture, it throws itself from a precipice, and turns so aptly in falling, that it receives all the shock upon the horn, and so escapes safe and sound." It is noteworthy that this mode of escape is attributed, at the present day, to both the musk ox and the Ovis Ammon.

Marco Polo may or may not indicate a rhinoceros [in a passage that mentions "beaucoup d'éléphants et de licornes et d'autres bêtes sauvages" ("many elephants and unicorns and other wild beasts").]

But no such inference can be attached to the descriptions of the Ethiopian unicorn by Leo and Ludolphus.

The first says:

"The unicorn is found in the mountains of high Ethiopia. It is of an ash colour and resembles a colt of two years old, excepting that it has the head of a goat, and in the middle of its forehead a horn three feet long, which is smooth and white like ivory, and has yellow streaks running along from top to bottom.

"This horn is an antidote against poison, and it is reported that other animals delay drinking till it has soaked its horn in the water to purify it. This animal is so nimble that it can neither be killed nor taken. But it casts its horn like a stag, and the hunters find it in the deserts. But the truth of this is called in question by some authors."

Ludolphus says:

"Here is also another beast, called arucharis, with one horn, fierce and strong, of which unicorn several have been seen feeding in the woods."

Coming down to later days we find the unicorn described by Lewes Vertomannus – he who, having visited, among other places, the site of the legend of St. George and the Dragon, and undergone a variety of adventures, visits, in the course of them, the temple of Mecca, and, as follows, gives a description "of the unicorns of the Temple of Mecha, which are not seen in any other place."

"On the other part of the temple are parks or places enclosed, where are seen two unicorns, named of the Greeks monocerotæ, and are there showed to the people for a miracle, and not without good reason, for the seldomness and strange nature. The one of them, which is much higher than the other, yet not much unlike to a colt of thirty months of age; in the forehead groweth only one horn, in manner right foorth, of the length of three cubits. The other is much younger, of the age of one year, and like a young colt; the horn of this is of the length of four handfulls.

"This beast is of the colour of a horse of weesell colour, and hath the head like a hart, but no long neck, a thynne mane hanging only on the one side. Their leggs are thin and slender like a fawn or hind. The hoofs of the fore-feet are divided in two, much like the feet of a goat. The outer part of the hinder feet is very full of hair.

"This beast doubtless seemeth wild and fierce, yet tempereth that fierceness with a certain comeliness.

"These unicorns one gave to the Sultan of Mecha as a most precious and rare gift. They were sent him out of Ethiope by a king of that country who desired by that present to gratify the Sultan of Mecha."

Visiting the interior of Arabia from Aden, and afterwards starting for Persia, Vertomannus was driven back by a contrary wind to Zeila (in Africa), which he describes as being an important city with much merchandise – when again he says, "I saw there also certain kyne, having only one horn in the middle of the forehead, as hath the unicorn, and about a span in length, but the horn bendeth backwards. They are of bright shining red colour."

In an account of the travels of Johann Grueber, Jesuit (about 1661), contained in Astley's collection of voyages, we find: –

"Sining is a great and populous city, built at the vast wall of China, through the gate of which the merchants from India enter Katay or China. There are stairs to go a-top of the wall, and many travel on it from the gate at Sining to the next at Soochew, which is eighteen days' journey, having a delightful prospect all the way, from the wall, of the innumerable habitations on one side, and the various wild beasts which range the desert on the other side.

"Besides wild bulls, here are tigers, lions, elephants, rhinoceroses, and monoceroses, which are a kind of horned asses.

"Thus the merchants view the beasts free from danger, especially from that part of the wall which, running southward, approaches Quang-si, Yunnan, and Tibet; for at certain times of the year they betake themselves to the Yellow River, and parts near the wall which abound with thickets, in order to get pasture and seek their prey."

Father Jerome Lobo, a Portuguese Jesuit, who embarked for Abyssinia in the year 1622, states that: –

"In the province of Agaus has been seen the unicorn; that beast so much talked of and so little known. The prodigious swiftness with which the creature runs from one wood into another has given me no opportunity of examining it particularly; yet I have had so near a sight of it as to be able to give some description of it.

"The shape is the same with that of a beautiful horse, exact and nicely proportioned, of a bay colour, with a black tail, which in some provinces is long, in others very short; some have long manes hanging to the ground. They are so timorous that they never feed but surrounded with other beasts that defend them.

"Deer and other defenceless animals often herd about the elephant, which, contenting himself with roots and leaves, preserves the beasts that place themselves, as it were, under his protection, from the others that would devour them."

There is a somewhat doubtful story contained in the *Narrative of a Journey from St. Petersburg, in Russia, to Peking, in China*, in 1719, to the effect that between Tobolsky and Tomski: –

"Our baggage having waited at Tara till our arrival, we left that place on the 18th, and next came to a large Russian village sixty versts from Tara, and the last inhabited by Russians till you pass the Baraba and come to the river Oby ... One of these hunters told me the following story, which was confirmed by several of his neighbours, that in the year 1713, in the month of March, being out a-hunting, he discovered the track of a stag, which he pursued. At overtaking the animal he was somewhat startled on observing it had only one horn, stuck in the middle of its forehead. Being near this village, he drove it home, and showed it, to the great admiration of the spectators. He afterwards killed it, and ate the flesh, and sold the horn to a comb-maker in the town of Tara, for ten alteens, about fifteen pence sterling.

"I inquired carefully about the shape and size of this unicorn, as I shall call it, and was told that it exactly resembled a stag.

"The horn was of a brownish colour, about one archæon or twenty-eight inches long, and twisted from the root till within a finger's length of the tip, where it was divided, like a fork, into two points, very sharp."

One of the most trustworthy of observers, the Abbé Huc, speaks very positively on the subject of the unicorn. He says: "The unicorn really exists in Thibet ... We had for a long time a small Mongol Treatise on Natural History, for the use of children, in which a unicorn formed one of the pictorial illustrations … The Chinese Itinerary says, on the subject of the lake you see before your arrival at Atzder (going from east to west), 'The unicorn, a very curious animal, is found in the vicinity of this lake, which is forty *li* long.'"

The unicorn is known in Thibet by the name of *serou*; in Mongolia, by that of *kere*; while in a Tibetan manuscript examined by the late Major Lattre, it is called the one-horned *tsopo*.

Mr. Hazlitt, in his notes appended to the statement by Huc as to the unicorn, states that Mr. Hodgson, of Nepaul, sent to Calcutta the skin and horn of a unicorn that died in the menagerie of the Rajah of Nepaul.

It was described as being very fierce, and abundant in the plains of Tingri, in the southern part of the Thibetan province of Tsang, watered by the Arroun; it assembled round salt beds. The form is graceful, colour reddish, two tufts of hair project from the exterior of each nostril, and there is much down round the hair and mouth. The hair is rough and seems hollow. Doctor Able designated it *Antelope Hodgsonii.*

Baron von Müller described, through the medium of M. Antoine d'Abbadie, a unicorn animal which he had received when at Melpes in Kordofan: –

"I met, on the 17th of April 1848, a man who was in the habit of selling to me specimens of animals. One day he asked me if I wished also for an *a'nasa*, which he described thus: 'It is the size of a small donkey, has a thick body and thin bones, coarse hair, and tail like a boar. It has a long horn on its forehead, and lets it hang when alone, but erects it immediately on seeing an enemy. It is a formidable weapon, but I do not know its exact length. The *a'nasa* is found not far from here (Melpes), towards the south-southwest. I have seen it often in the wild grounds, where the negroes kill it, and carry it home to make shields from its skin.' N.B. – This man was well acquainted with the rhinoceros, which he distinguished, under the name of *fetit*, from the *a'nasa*.

"On June the 14th I was at Kursi, also in Kordofan, and met there a slave merchant who was not acquainted with my first informer, and gave me spontaneously the same description of the *a'nasa*, adding that he had killed and eaten one long ago, and that its flesh was well flavoured."

This creature is mentioned by Rupell, under the name of *Nillekma* or *Arase*, as indigenous to Kordofan, and, by Cavassi, as known in Congo under that of *Abada*.

Mr. Freeman, in the *South African Christian Recorder* (vol. i.), gives the native account of an animal not uncommon in Makooa, and called the *Ndzoodzoo*, described as being about the size of a horse, extremely fleet and strong, with a single horn from two feet to two and a half feet in length, projecting from its forehead, which is said to be flexible when the animal is asleep, and capable of being curled up at pleasure, but becoming stiff and hard under the excitement of rage. It is extremely fierce, and invariably attacks a man when it discerns him. The female is without a horn.

Our latest information as to this species comes from Prejevalski, who, speaking of it as the orongo, says that it has elegant black horns standing vertically above the head; the back is dun-coloured; the middle of the breast, stomach, and rump, white; seen at a distance it appears white; it is very numerous in Northern Tibet. He adds: "Another prevalent superstition is that the orongo has only one horn growing vertically from the centre of the head. In Kansu and Kokonor we were told that unicorns were rare, one or two in a thousand. The Mongols in Tsaidan deny it, but say it may be so in south-west Tibet."

Turning to the Chinese classics and books of antiquity, we find references, sometimes vague and mythical, sometimes exact, to several distinct unicorn animals. These may be enumerated as: –

1. The Ki-Lin, represented in Japan by the Kirin.
2. The King.
3. The Kioh Twan.

4. The Poh.
5. The Hiai Chai.
6. The Too Jon Sheu.

Besides these there are clear descriptions of the rhinoceros, which cannot in any way be confounded with the above. The only one of these popularly familiar is the Ki-Lin, the history of which is interwoven with that of remote ages. The first mention of it is made in the Bamboo Books – only in that part, however, of them which is apparently a commentary, note, or subsequent addition, though some authorities hold it to be a portion of the actual text. The work states that, during the reign of Hwang-Ti (B.C. 2697), Ki-Lins appeared in the parks.

Their appearance was generally supposed to signalise the reign of an upright monarch, and Confucius considered that the appearance of one during his epoch was a bad omen, as it did not harmonise with the troubled state of the times. The name Ki-Lin is a generic or dual word, composed of those of the Ki and the Lin, the respective male and female of the creature.

This peculiar species of word formation is adopted in other instances in reference to birds and animals; thus we have the male Fung and the female Hwang united in the Fung Hwang, or so-called Chinese phœnix, and the Yuen and Yang in the Yuen Yang, or mandarin duck.

Sometimes the word Lin alone is used with the same generic meaning.

The *'Rh Ya*, in the original text, defines the Lin as having a Kiun's body (the Kiun is a kind of muntjack or deer), an ox's tail, and one horn. The commentary states that the tip of the horn is fleshy, and that the King Yang chapter of the *Spring and Autumn Annals* of Confucius defines it as a horned Kiun.

The preface to the *Shi Shu* quotes Li Sian to the effect that the Lin is an auspicious and perfect beast.

Sun Yen says it is a spiritual beast. The *Shwoh Wan* says the Lin is the female of the K'i and the K'i is a beast endowed with goodness, possessing a Kiun's body, an ox's tail, and one horn. According to the *Shwoh Wan*, the Lin may be considered as a large female deer. Now the *Shu King* considers that many of these beasts are comprised under the Ki-Lin, only the characters, though retaining the sound, have become altered in form.

Chen Nau calls it Lin-che-chi and Man Chw'en says that the Lin is truthful, and reducible to rule.

The *Li Yuen* says: "If the unicorn can once be tamed, then the other beasts will not show terror."

Ta Tai, in the *Li Ki*, quoting the *Yih [King]*, says there are 360 kinds of hairy creatures, and the Ki-Lin is the chief of them.

The *Li Ki*, commenting on the *King Fang I Chw'en*, says: "The Lin has a Kiun's body, an ox's tail, a horse's hoof, and is of five colours. It is twelve feet high."

Again, in commenting on Fuh Kien's *Ho Chwen*, it says: "The Lin springs from the earth's central regions. It is a beast of superior integrity, is attached to its mother, and reducible to rule. The Shu King, quoting Luh Li, says the Lin has a Kiun's body, an ox's tail, a horse's feet, and a yellow colour, round hoofs, and one horn; the tip of the horn is erect and fleshy.

"Its call in the middle part thereof is like a monastery bell. Its pace is regular; it rambles only on selected grounds and after it has examined the locality. It will not live in herds, or be accompanied in its movements. It cannot be beguiled into pitfalls, or captured in snares. When the monarch is virtuous, this beast appears."

At present there are Lin existing on the frontiers of Ping Cheu. Even the large or small Lin are always like deer, so that this species is not the auspicious Ying Lin; although Tsz Ma Siang Su, in his odes on the shooting of the Mi and trapping Lin, says that it is.

The top of the horn being fleshy is a characteristic of the Lin, and Mao Chw'en says that the Lin's horn is an emblem of goodness. Ching Tsien says that the horn has a fleshy termination, indicating the peaceful character of the beast, and that it has no use for it.

The *Book of Rites*, quoting the *Kwang Ya*, says that on account of its elegant style it takes place, *par excellence*, among the large-horned beasts; the existing edition of the Kwang Ya omits this.

The *Kung Yang Chw'en* says the Kiun also has horns.

Kung Ssun Tsz, in the annals of the fourteenth year of the Duke Ngai (State of Lu), says that the Kiun has fleshy horns.

Kwoh, in his preface, proves the Lin to have a Kiun's body.

The *'Rh Ya* gives the drawing of a unicorn animal called the Ki; but no reference to the horn is given in the text, which simply describes it as a large Kiun with a yak's tail and dog's feet.

The Ki is not defined in the *'Rh Ya*, and the only information I have as to it is derived from Williams' dictionary, where it is stated to be "a fabulous auspicious animal, which appears when sages are born; the male of the Chinese unicorn. It is drawn like a piebald scaly horse, with one horn and a cow's tail, and may have had a living original in some extinct equine animal." But there is a very full account of an animal called the King. It is not impossible that it is identical with the King which, in the usual brief style of the original text of the *'Rh Ya*, is epitomised as a large Biao (a kind of stag), with an ox's tail and one horn; and the several commentaries on it are as follows: –

"In the time of the Emperor Wu, of the Han dynasty, during the worship of heaven and earth at the solstices at Yung, there was captured a unicorn beast like a Piao; it was at that time designated the Lin; it was, however, a Piao related to the Chang (a kind of deer)."

The Shwoh Wan says: "The King is a large stag with an ox's tail and one horn." It may be a large form of the Piao. The Wang Hwu Analects say that the Piao is an object of the chase, and that it is as swift as a stag.

Kwan Tsz, in the Ti Yuen volume, says that as there are Mi and Piao and many species of deer, so also the Piao is a species of deer.

The 'Shi Ki,' in the book *Fung Shen*, says that during the worship at the solstices at Yung, there was captured a one-horned beast like a Piao, and that the local authorities assert that as His Majesty was making reverential invocations on the country altar to the Supreme Being, he was recompensed for the sacrifice by a beast which was a unicorn.

Wu Chao's preface to the *Loh Yiu* says: "The body is like that of a muntjack, and it has one horn;" while the Spring and Autumn (Annals) allude to this animal in speaking of the horned Kiun.

The inhabitants of Ch'u say the Kiun is a Piao. Kwoh, in his preface, says that the capture made in the time of Wu, of the Han dynasty, was actually a Piao, as demonstrated by the Han books. The Chung Kiun narrative states that in Shang Yung was captured a white Lin bearing one horn, of which the tip was fleshy. At the present day nothing has been heard of a Piao with a fleshy tip, therefore these must be different beasts.

Kwoh also says that the Piao is identical with the Chang, and the Chang with the Kiun. This corresponds with what Wei Chao So had already stated, that the people of Ch'u assert that the Kiun is a Piao, and that the Piao is certainly a kind of deer.

Its meat is eminently savoury.

Luh Ki says that of all four-footed creatures, the Piao is the most excellent.

Yeu Shi states in the *Kiao Sz* annals ('Sacrifices to Heaven and Earth'), that the Piao is a kind of deer. Its body exactly resembles that of the Chang.

Finally, the explanatory prefaces of many classical works, when commenting on the *'Rh Ya*, say that the Piao is identical with the Chang and of a black colour; and they confirm Kwoh's opinion, although the *'Rh Ya* forgets to allude to the three characters denoting the black colour.

It was probably some unicorn animal which is referred to in the General History of China, called the *Tong Kien Kang Mu* (*vide* Père de Mailla's translation), as having been presented to the Emperor Yung Loh of the Ming dynasty, in A.D. 1415, by envoys from Bengal. De Mailla says it was called a Ki-Lin by the Chinese out of flattery.

Again, the same History says that in the succeeding year the kingdom of Malin sent as tribute a Ki-Lin similar to that from Bengal.

The Ki-Rin, a Japanese version of the Ki-Lin, is simply borrowed from Chinese sources. It is figured in the illustrated edition of the great Japanese Encyclopedia *Kasira gaki zou vo Sin mou dzu wi tai sei*, and represented, as in the Chinese drawings, as covered with scales; but it must be noted that nothing in any of the texts of either country warrants this furniture of the body.

The same encyclopedia figures another unicorn beast under the name of the Kai Tsi, and describes it as being an animal of foreign countries, resembling a lion, and having a single horn. It is also called the Sin You or divine sheep. It is able to distinguish between right and wrong. When Kau You exercised criminal jurisdiction, he handed over those whose crime was doubtful to the Kai Tsu, and it is said that this animal destroyed the guilty and spared the innocent.

This is described in the Chinese work *Yuen Kien Léi Han*, under the name of the Hiai Chai, and similar powers of discrimination are there attributed to it.

A synonym for it was the Chiai Tung. It states that, according to the *Si Yang Y Shu*, a one-horned spiritual lamb was born in the Ping Shen district, and in the twenty-first year of Kai Yuen. The horn was fleshy, and the top of the head covered with white hair. The second chapter on the same subject says that, in ancient times, if parties were at law, the judge brought this animal out, and it would gore at the guilty one.

The Kioh Twan is yet another unicorn animal described in the *Yuen Kien Léi Han*, which is said to have the appearance of a deer with the tail of a horse, but to be of a greenish colour, with one horn above the nose, and to be capable of traversing eighteen thousand li in one day.

The *Li Kau Sing Sha Shao* says that the Emperor Yuen Ti Su sent his ambassadors to the western part of India, who procured animals several tens of feet in height, unicorn, like the rhinoceros. The rumour went that these were inauspicious for the Emperor, and they were immediately returned.

The Poh

The *Shan Hai King* describes an animal as existing among the plains of Mongolia, having the appearance of a horse, with a white body, black tail, one horn, teeth and claws like a tiger, which howls like the roll of a drum, devours tigers and leopards, and is capable of being used instead of soldiers; it is called Poh.

The *'Rh Ya* describes the same animal as like a horse, with saw teeth, existing on tigers and leopards.

The 'History of the North' says that in the Kingdom of Peh Chi a magistrate named Chung Wa held office, who was very equitable in his rule. His district was invaded by some ferocious animals. Suddenly six of the Poh came and killed and devoured them as a reward for his good rule.

The Sung History says that a man named Leu Chang, an ambassador, arrived at a district called Shen Su, where the mountains contained a strange animal, in appearance like a horse, but capable of eating tigers and leopards. The people were unacquainted with it, and asked Leu Chang what it was, who said it was called the Poh, and referred them to the *Shan Hai King* for a description of it.

Among other remarkable and interesting drawings which have come down from antiquity in the *San Li T'u*, or illustrated edition of the three (ceremonial) rituals, are some representing the various targets used by officials of different ranks in the military examinations, in which the arrows had to be lodged by shooting upwards from a distance. These are fashioned in the form of animals, one realising the idea of the sphynx, and two representing unicorn animals, called respectively the Lu – which, according to some, is like an ass with one horn, but, according to others, differing from a donkey in having a cleft hoof – and the Sz, which is said to be like an ox with one horn.

The Too Jon Shen is the name of an animal with a lion-like body and head, cloven hoofs, and a blunt short horn projecting from the centre of the forehead. Two pairs of these form a portion of the avenue of stone figures of animals leading up to the Ming tombs, about eighty miles north of Pekin. I have not found it described in any book.

A writer in the *China Review* endeavours to prove that the Ki-Lin is a (From the Ming Tombs.) reminiscence of the giraffe, which he supposes may once have spread over Asia, and, in addition to various passages included among those which I have quoted above, adduces one from the *Wu Tsah Tsu*, which states that, "In the period Yung Loh of the Ming dynasty (1403-1425) a Ki-Lin was caught, and a painter was ordered to make a sketch and hand it up to the high magistrates. According to the picture, the body was perfectly shaped like that of a deer, *but the neck was very long, perhaps three or four feet*." I must admit that I cannot agree with him in his conclusions. Harris has given much better arguments in favour of the unicorn being merely a species of oryx. He appears to me, however, to speak too absolutely, to make his facts too pliant, and to base his main belief on the untenable theory that the myth, tradition, or theory is based on the profile drawing of an oryx, exhibiting one horn only. We might just as soon expect people to start stories of two-legged cows or horses, or one-legged races of men, if so slender a basis for forging a species were sufficient. What the zoological status of the unicorn may be I am not prepared to show, but I find it impossible to believe that a creature whose existence has been affirmed by so many authors, at so many different dates, and from so many different countries, can be, as mythologists demand, merely the symbol of a myth. There is a possible solution, which does not appear to have struck previous writers on the subject, viz., that the unicorn may be merely a hybrid produced occasionally and at more or less rare intervals.

By accepting this view we could explain the extraordinary combinations of character assigned to it, and the discrepancy which exists between the qualities of courage and gentleness ascribed to it by Western and Chinese authors. A valuable chapter remains to be written by naturalists and progressionists on the limits within which hybridization exists in a state of nature among the higher animals; its prevalence among the lower and among plants is, of course, well known. A cross between some equine and cervine species might readily result in a unicorn offspring, and either the courageous qualities of the sire or the gentleness of the dam might preponderate, according to the relations of the species in each of the instances.

As an alternative, we may speculate on the unicorn being a generic name for several distinct species of (probably) now extinct animals; missing links between the three families, the Equidæ, Cervidæ, and Bovidæ; creatures which were the contemporaries of prehistoric man, and which, before they finally expired, attracted the attention of his descendants, during early historic times, by the rare appearance of a few surviving individuals.

The supernatural qualities ascribed to these by various nations must be considered merely the embroidery of fancy, designed to enrich and adorn an article esteemed rare and valuable.

Creatures from the Depths

Introduction

'I SEEM', SAID SIR ISAAC NEWTON, 'to have been only like a boy playing on the seashore, and diverting myself in now and then finding a smoother pebble or a prettier shell than ordinary, whilst the great ocean of truth lay all undiscovered before me.' In the centuries since this observation, his successor-scientists have made extraordinary progress in finding out about the world beneath the waves. Even so, its farthest, deepest reaches remain substantially unexplored, its ecology and geography only scantly understood.

And that is just by the experts. For the rest of us the sea is still as mysterious as it ever was. Not only that: in the vast blankness we see stretching away from us as we gaze out over its ruffled surface, it emblematizes the mysteriousness of our existence as a whole. We may paddle in its shallows, even venture into deeper waters here and there – but there are always dark unfathomable depths we will never know. The dancing waves that buoy us up so amiably as we splash around would just as soon drown us, we cannot quite forget: the sea exemplifies the final indifference of our universe. Hence its mythic function as a source of all manner of menace to the human world – reflected in all the weird and frightening creatures it sends ashore. But the sea also serves as our guarantee that other lives, other possibilities do exist 'out there', beyond the limits of our everyday. So we relish our stories of friendly fish, benevolent monsters and beautiful mermaids; tales of devotion, loyalty and love.

The Kraken

NEVER, WITHIN THE HISTORY OF MANKIND, does there appear to have been a time when dwellers by the sea did not believe in some awful and gigantic monsters inhabiting that unknown and vague immensity.

Whether we turn to Genesis to find great sea-monsters first of created sentient beings, or ransack the voluminous records of ancient civilisations, the result is the same. What a picture is that of the Hindu sage in the Fish Avatar of Krishna, finding himself and his eight companions alone in their ark upon the infinite sea, being visited by the god as an indescribably huge serpent extending a million leagues, shining like the sun, and with one stupendous horn, sky-piercing.

In the brief compass of this chapter I do not propose to *réchauffer* any sea-serpent stories, ancient or modern. More especially because my subject is the Kraken, and while I hold most firmly that the gigantic mollusc which can alone be given that title is the *fons et origo* of all true sea-serpent stories, it is with facts relating to the former that I have alone to deal. As might have been expected, all stories of sea-monsters have a strong family likeness, showing pretty conclusively their common derivation, with such differences as the locality and personality of the narrative must be held accountable for. But among sea-folk, as among all people leading lives in close contact with the elemental forces of Nature, legends persist with marvellous vitality, and so the story of the Kraken is to be found wherever men go down to the sea in ships, and do business in great waters.

Substantially the story is: that long low-lying banks have been discovered by vessels, which have moored thereto, only to find the supposed land developing wondrous peculiarities. Amid tremendous turmoil of seething waters, arms innumerable, like a nest of mighty serpents, arose from the deep, followed at last by a horrible head, of a bigness and diabolical appearance unspeakably appalling. Fascinated by the terrible eyes that, large as shields, glared upon them, the awe-stricken seamen beheld some of the far-reaching tentacles, covered with multitudes of mouths, embracing their vessel, while others searched her alow and aloft, culling the trembling men from the rigging like ripe fruit, and conveying them forthwith into an abysmal mouth where they vanished for ever.

Such a story, especially when embellished by professional story-tellers, has of course met with well-merited scepticism, but sight has been largely lost of the fact that from very early times much independent testimony has been borne to the existence of immense molluscæ in many waters, sufficiently huge and horrific to have furnished a substantial basis for any number of hair-raising yarns. And having myself for some years been engaged in the sperm whale fishery, all over the globe, I now venture to bear the testimony of another eyewitness to the truth of many Kraken legends, however much they may have been, and are now, doubted.

To eager students of marine natural history, nothing can well be stranger than the manner in which, with two or three honourable exceptions, the sperm whale fishers of the world have 'sinned their mercies.' To them as to no other class of sea-farers have been vouchsafed not glimpses merely, but consecutive months and years of the closest intimacy with the secret things of old ocean, embracing almost the whole navigable globe. And when, unpressed for time, they have leisurely entered those slumbrous latitudes so anxiously avoided by the hurried, worried merchantman, how utterly have they neglected their marvellous opportunities of observation of the wonders there revealed. It may not be generally known that during long-persisting calms the sea surface changes its character. From limpid blue it becomes greasy and pale, from that health-laden odour to which the gratified nostrils dilate, and the satisfied lungs expand, there is a gruesome change to an unwholesome stench of stagnation and decaying things, such as the genius of Coleridge depicted when he sang:

> *"The very deep did rot; O Christ!*
> *That ever this should be!*
> *Yea, slimy things did crawl with legs*
> *Upon the slimy sea."*

Strangest of all the strange visitors to the upper world at such times is the gigantic squid, or cuttle-fish. Of all the Myriad species of mollusca this monster may fairly claim chief place, and neither in ancient or modern times have any excited more interest than he. Gazing with childlike fear upon his awe-inspiring and uncanny bulk, the ancients have done their best to transmit their impressions to posterity. Aristotle writes voluminously upon the subject, as he did about most things, but his cuttles are such as are known to most of us. Pliny leaves on record much concerning the Sepiadæ which is evidently accurate in the main, mentioning especially one monster slain on the coast of Spain which was in the habit of robbing the salt-fish warehouses. Pliny caused the great head to be sent to Lucullus, and states that it filled a cask of fifteen amphoræ. Its arms were thirty feet long, so thick that a man could hardly embrace them at their bases, and provided with suckers, or acetabula, as large as basins holding four or five gallons. But those who have leisure and inclination may pursue the subject in the works of Ælian, Paulinus (who describes the monster as a gigantic crab), Bartholinus, Athanasius Kircher, Athenæus, Olaus Magnus, and others. Pontoppidan, Bishop of Bergen, in his *Natural History of Norway*, has done more than any other ancient or modern writer to discredit reports, essentially truthful, by the outrageous fabrications he tells by way of embellishment of the facts which he received. Least trustworthy of all, he has been in this connection most quoted of all, but here he shall be mentioned only to hold his inventions up to the scorn they so richly deserve.

The gigantic squid is, unlike most of the cephalopoda, a decapod, not an octopod, since it possesses, in addition to the eight branchiæ with which all the family are provided, two tentacula of double their length, having acetabula only in a small cluster at their ends. This fact was noticed by Athanasius Kircher, who describes a large animal seen in the Sicilian seas which had *ten* rays, or branches, and a body equal in size to that of a whale; which, seeing how wide is the range in size among whales, is certainly not over-definite. Coming down to much later days, we find Denys de Montfort *facile princeps* in his descriptions of the Kraken. Unfortunately, his reputation for truthfulness is but so-so, and he is reported to have expressed great delight at the ease with which he could gull credulous people. Still the best of his stories may be quoted, remembering that, as far as his description of the monster is concerned, he does not appear to have exaggerated at all.

He records how he became acquainted with a master mariner of excellent repute, who had made many voyages to the Indies for the Gothenburg Company, by name Jean Magnus Dens. To this worthy, sailing his ship along the African coast, there fell a stark calm, the which he, even as do prudent shipmasters to-day, turned to good account by having his men scrape and cleanse the outside of the vessel, they being suspended near the water by stages for that purpose. While thus engaged, suddenly there arose from the blue placidity beneath a most "awful monstrous," cuttle-fish, which threw its arms over the stage, and seizing two of the men, drew them below the surface. Another man, who was climbing on board, was also seized, but after a fearful struggle his shipmates succeeded in rescuing him. That same night he died in raving madness. The mollusc's arms were stated to be at the base of the bigness of a fore-yard (*vergue d'un mât de misaine*), while the suckers were as large as ladles (*cueillier à pot*).

One who should have done better – Dr. Shaw, in his lectures – calmly makes of that "fore-yard" a "mizen-mast," and of the "ladles" "pot-lids," which may have been loose translation, even as the scraping "gratter" is funnily rendered "raking," as if the ship's bottom were a hayfield, but looks uncommonly like editorial expansion, which the story really does not require.

Another story narrated by Denys de Montfort relates how a vessel was attacked by a huge "poulp," which endeavoured to drag down vessel and all; but the crew, assisted by their patron, St. Thomas, succeeded in severing so many of the monster's arms from his body that he was fain to depart, and leave them in peace. In gratitude for their marvellous deliverance they caused an *ex voto* picture to be painted of the terrible scene, and hung in their parish church, for a testimony to the mighty power of the saint.

In the *Phil. Trans.* of the Royal Society, Dr. Schewediawer tells of a sperm whale being hooked which had in its mouth a tentaculum of the Sepia Octopodia, twenty-seven feet long. This was not its entire length, for one end was partly digested, so that when *in situ* it must have been a great deal longer. When we consider, says the learned doctor, the enormous bulk of the animal to which the tentaculum here spoken of belonged, we shall cease to wonder at the common saying of sailors that the cuttle-fish is the largest in the ocean.

In Figuier's *Ocean World* he quotes largely from Michelet, that great authority on the Mollusca, giving at length the latter's highly poetical description of the vast family of "murderous suckers," as he terms the cephalopoda.

In the same work, too, will be found a most matter-of-fact description and illustration of the meeting of the French corvette *Alecton* with an immense calamary between Tenerife and Madeira. This account was furnished by Lieutenant Bayer to the Académie des Sciences, and is evidently a sober record of fact. The monster's body was hauled alongside, and an attempt was made to secure it by means of a hawser passed round it, but of course, as soon as any strain was put upon the rope, it drew completely through the soft gelatinous carcass, severing it in two. The length of this creature's body was 50 feet. But M. Figuier is not satisfied; he says that even this account must be taken *cum grano salis*, so unwilling is he to believe in a monster that would evidently settle the great Kraken and sea-serpent question once for all.

Even Dr. Solander and Mr. Banks, after finding a cuttle six feet long floating upon the sea near Cape Horn, which was quite beyond all their previous experience, could not bring themselves to believe in the existence of any larger. So at the beginning of this century, while people had largely consented to accept the sea-serpent, they would have none of the Kraken or anything which might reasonably explain the persistence of evidence about him. But had these scientific sceptics only taken the trouble to interview the crews of the South Sea whalers, that sailed in such a goodly fleet from our ports during the first half of the century, they must have been convinced that, so far from the Kraken being a myth, he is one of the most substantial of facts, unless, indeed, they believed that all whalemen were in a conspiracy to deceive them on that point.

Any thoughtful observer who has ever seen a school of sperm whales, numbering several hundreds, and understood, from the configuration of their jaws, that they must of necessity feed upon large creatures, can never after feel difficulty in believing that, in order to supply the enormous demand for food made by these whales, their prey must be imposing in size and abundant in quantity.

On my first meeting with the cachalot, on terms of mutual destruction, I knew nothing of his habits, and cared less. But seeing him, when wounded, vomiting huge masses of white substance, my curiosity was aroused, and when I saw that these masses were parts of a mighty creature almost identical in structure with the small squid so often picked up on deck, where it falls in its frantic efforts to escape from dolphins (*Coryphœna*), albacore, or bonito, my amazement was great. Some of these fragments were truly heroic in size.

Surgeon Beale, in his book on the sperm whale, only credits the cachalot with being able to swallow a man, but with all the respect due to so great a writer, I am bound to say that such masses as I have seen ejected from the stomach of the dying whale could only have entered a throat to which a man was as a pill is to us. We can, however, only speak of what we have seen, and perhaps Dr. Beale had never seen such large pieces ejected.

In an article in *Nature* of June 4, 1896, I have described an encounter which I witnessed between a gigantic squid and a sperm whale, in the Straits of Malacca, which, as far as I am concerned, has settled conclusively the Kraken and sea-serpent question for me. This terrific combat took place under the full glare of a tropical moon, upon the surface of a perfectly calm sea, within a mile of the ship. Every detail of the struggle was clearly visible through a splendid glass, and is indelibly graven upon my mind. It was indeed a battle of giants – perhaps all the more solemnly impressive from being waged in perfect silence. The contrast between the livid whiteness of the mollusc's body and the massive blackness of the whale – the convulsive writhing of the tremendous arms, as, like a Medusa's head magnified a thousand times, they wound and gripped about the columnar head of the great mammal – made a picture unequalled in all the animal world for intense interest. The immense eyes, at least a foot in diameter, glared out of the dead white of the head, inky black, appalling in their fixity of gaze. Could we have seen more nearly, and in daylight, we should have also found that the sea was turned from its normal blue into a dusky brown by the discharge of the great cephalopod's reservoir of sepia, which in such a creature must have been a tank of considerable capacity. Each of those far-reaching arms were of course furnished with innumerable sucking discs, most of them a foot in diameter, and, in addition to the adhering apparatus, provided with a series of claws set round the inner edges of the suckers, large as those of a grizzly bear. Besides the eight arms, there were the two tentacula, double the length of the arms, or over sixty feet long – in fact, about the length of the animal's body, and quite worthy of being taken for a pair of sea-serpents by themselves. But the whale apparently took no heed of the Titanic struggles of this enormous mollusc. He was busy wielding his mighty jaws, not in mastication, but in tearing asunder the soft flesh into convenient lumps for being swallowed. All around were numerous smaller whales or sharks, joining in the plentiful feast, like jackals round a lion. Every fisherman worth his salt knows how well all fish that swim in the sea love the sapid flesh of the cephalopoda, making it the finest bait known, and in truth it is, and always has been, a succulent dainty, where known, for mankind as well. But it is evident from the scanty number of times that the gigantic cuttle-fish has been reported, that his habitat is well beneath the surface, yet not so far down but that he may be easily reached by the whale, and also find food for his own vast bulk. Probably they prey upon one another. From what we know of the habits of those members of the family who live in accessible waters, it is evident that nothing comes amiss to them in the way of fish or flesh, dead or alive.

The Prince of Monaco, who is a devotee of marine natural history, was fortunate enough to witness some bay whalers at Terceira early this year catching a sperm whale. He and his scientific assistants were alike amazed at seeing the contents of the whale's stomach ejected before death, but their amazement became hysterical delight when they found that the ejecta consisted of portions of huge cuttle-fish, as yet unknown to scientific classification. The species was promptly named after the Prince, *Lepidoteuthis Grimaldii*, and a paper prepared and read before the Académie des Sciences at Paris. So profoundly impressed was the Prince with what he had seen, that he at once determined to convert his yacht into a whaler, in order to become better acquainted with these wonderful creatures, so long known to the obtuse and careless whale-fishers. One interesting circumstance noted by the Prince was the number of circular impressions made upon the tough and stubborn substance of the whale's head, hard as hippopotamus hide, showing the tremendous power exerted by the mollusc as well as his inability to do the whale any harm.

But were I to describe in detail the numerous occasions upon which I have seen, not certainly the entire mollusc, but such enormous portions of their bodies as would justify estimating them as fully as large as the whales feeding upon them, it would become merely tedious repetition.

As I write, comes the news that an immense squid has just been found stranded on the west coast of Ireland, having arms thirty feet in length, a formidable monster indeed.

In conclusion, it may be interesting to know that these molluscs progress, while undisturbed, literally on their heads, with all the eight arms which surround the head acting as feet as well as hands to convey food to the ever-gaping mouth; but when moving quickly, as in flight, or to attack, they eject a stream of water from an aperture in the neck, which drives them backwards at great speed, all the arms being close together. Close to this aperture is the intestinal opening, a strange position truly. Strangest, perhaps, of all is the manner in which some species grow, at certain seasons, an additional tentacle, which, when complete, becomes detached and floats away. In process of time it finds a female, to which it clings, and which it at once impregnates. It then falls off, and perishes. It is probable that the animal kingdom, in all its vast range, presents no stranger method than this of the propagation of species.

Demons of the Sea

"COME OUT ON DECK and have a look, Darky!" Jepson cried, rushing into the half deck. "The Old Man says there's been a submarine earthquake, and the sea's all bubbling and muddy!"

Obeying the summons of Jepson's excited tone, I followed him out. It was as he had said; the everlasting blue of the ocean was mottled with splotches of a muddy hue, and at times a large bubble would appear, to burst with a loud 'pop.' Aft, the skipper and the three mates could be seen on the poop, peering at the sea through their glasses. As I gazed out over the gently heaving water, far off to windward something was hove up into the evening air. It appeared to be a mass of seaweed, but fell back into the water with a sullen plunge as though it were something more substantial. Immediately after this strange occurrence, the sun set with tropical swiftness, and in the brief afterglow things assumed a strange unreality.

The crew were all below, no one but the mate and the helmsman remaining on the poop. Away forward, on the topgallant forecastle head the dim figure of the man on lookout could be seen, leaning against the forestay. No sound was heard save the occasional jingle of a chain sheet, of the flog of the steering gear as a small swell passed under our counter. Presently the mate's voice broke the silence, and, looking up, I saw that the Old Man had come on deck, and was talking with him. From the few stray words that could be overheard, I knew they were talking of the strange happenings of the day.

Shortly after sunset, the wind, which had been fresh during the day, died down, and with its passing the air grew oppressively hot. Not long after two bells, the mate sung out for me, and ordered me to fill a bucket from overside and bring it to him. When I had carried out his instructions, he placed a thermometer in the bucket.

"Just as I thought," he muttered, removing the instrument and showing it to the skipper; "ninety-nine degrees. Why, the sea's hot enough to make tea with!"

"Hope it doesn't get any hotter," growled the latter; "if it does, we shall all be boiled alive."

At a sign from the mate, I emptied the bucket and replaced it in the rack, after which I resumed my former position by the rail. The Old Man and the mate walked the poop side by side. The air grew hotter as the hours passed and after a long period of silence broken only by the occasional 'pop' of a bursting gas bubble, the moon arose. It shed but a feeble light, however, as a heavy mist had arisen from the sea, and through this, the moonbeams struggled weakly. The mist, we decided, was due to the excessive heat of the sea water; it was a very wet mist, and we were soon soaked to the skin. Slowly the interminable night wore on, and the sun arose, looking dim and ghostly through the mist that rolled and billowed about the ship. From time to time we took the temperature of the sea, although we found but a slight increase therein. No work was done, and a feeling as of something impending pervaded the ship.

The fog horn was kept going constantly, as the lookout peered through the wreathing mists. The captain walked the poop in company with the mates, and once the third mate spoke and pointed out into the clouds of fog. All eyes followed his gesture; we saw what was apparently a black line, which seemed to cut the whiteness of the billows. It reminded us of nothing so much as an enormous cobra standing on its tail. As we looked it vanished. The grouped mates were evidently puzzled; there seemed to be a difference of opinion among them. Presently as they argued, I heard the second mate's voice:

"That's all rot," he said. "I've seen things in fog before, but they've always turned out to be imaginary."

The third shook his head and made some reply I could not overhear, but no further comment was made. Going below that afternoon, I got a short sleep, and on coming on deck at eight bells, I found that the steam still held us; if anything, it seemed to be thicker than ever. Hansard, who had been taking the temperatures during my watch below, informed me that the sea was three degrees hotter, and that the Old Man was getting into a rare old state. At three bells I went forward to have a look over the bows, and a chin with Stevenson, whose lookout it was. On gaining the forecastle head, I went to the side and looked down into the water. Stevenson came over and stood beside me.

"Rum go, this," he grumbled.

He stood by my side for a time in silence; we seemed to be hypnotized by the gleaming surface of the sea. Suddenly out of the depths, right before us, there arose a monstrous black face. It was like a frightful caricature of a human countenance. For a moment we gazed petrified; my blood seemed to suddenly turn to ice water; I was unable to move. With a mighty effort of will, I regained my self-control and, grasping Stevenson's arm, I found I could do no more than croak, my powers of speech seemed gone. "Look!" I gasped. "Look!"

Stevenson continued to stare into the sea, like a man turned to stone. He seemed to stoop further over, as if to examine the thing more closely. "Lord," he exclaimed, "it must be the devil himself!"

As though the sound of his voice had broken a spell, the thing disappeared. My companion looked at me, while I rubbed my eyes, thinking that I had been asleep, and that the awful vision had been a frightful nightmare. One look at my friend, however, disabused me of any such thought. His face wore a puzzled expression.

"Better go aft and tell the Old Man," he faltered.

I nodded and left the forecastle head, making my way aft like one in a trance. The skipper and the mate were standing at the break of the poop, and running up the ladder I told them what we had seen.

"Bosh!" sneered the Old Man. "You've been looking at your own ugly reflection in the water."

Nevertheless, in spite of his ridicule, he questioned me closely. Finally he ordered the mate forward to see it he could see anything. The latter, however, returned in a few moments, to report that nothing unusual could be seen. Four bells were struck, and we were relieved for tea. Coming on deck afterward, I found the men clustered together forward. The sole topic of conversation with them was the thing that Stevenson and I had seen.

"I suppose, Darky, it couldn't have been a reflection by any chance, could it?" one of the older men asked.

"Ask Stevenson," I replied as I made my way aft.

At eight bells, my watch came on deck again, to find that nothing further had developed. But, about an hour before midnight, the mate, thinking to have a smoke, sent me to his room for a box of matches with which to light his pipe. It took me no time to clatter down the brass-treaded ladder, and back to the poop, where I handed him the desired article. Taking the box, he removed a match and struck it on the heel of his boot. As he did so, far out in the night a muffled screaming arose. Then came a clamor as of hoarse braying, like an ass but considerably deeper, and with a horribly suggestive human note running through it.

"Good God! Did you hear that, Darky?" asked the mate in awed tones.

"Yes, sir," I replied, listening – and scarcely noticing his question – for a repetition of the strange sounds. Suddenly the frightful bellowing broke out afresh. The mate's pipe fell to the deck with a clatter.

"Run for'ard!" he cried. "Quick, now, and see if you can see anything."

With my heart in my mouth, and pulses pounding madly I raced forward. The watch were all up on the forecastle head, clustered around the lookout. Each man was talking and gesticulating wildly. They became silent, and turned questioning glances toward me as I shouldered my way among them.

"Have you seen anything?" I cried.

Before I could receive an answer, a repetition of the horrid sounds broke out again, profaning the night with their horror. They seemed to have definite direction now, in spite of the fog that enveloped us. Undoubtedly, too, they were nearer. Pausing a moment to make sure of their bearing, I hastened aft and reported to the mate. I told him that nothing could be seen, but that the sounds apparently came from right ahead of us. On hearing this he ordered the man at the wheel to let the ship's head come off a couple of points. A moment later a shrill screaming tore its way through the night, followed by the hoarse braying sounds once more.

"It's close on the starboard bow!" exclaimed the mate, as he beckoned the helmsman to let her head come off a little more. Then, singing out for the watch, he ran forward, slacking the lee braces on the way. When he had the yards trimmed to his satisfaction on the new course, he returned to the poop and hung far out over the rail listening intently. Moments passed that seemed like hours, yet the silence remained unbroken. Suddenly the sounds began again, and so close that it seemed as though they must be right aboard of us. At this time I noticed a strange booming note mingled with the brays. And once or twice there came a sound that can only be described as a sort of 'gug, gug.' Then would come a wheezy whistling, for all the world like an asthmatic person breathing.

All this while the moon shone wanly through the steam, which seemed to me to be somewhat thinner. Once the mate gripped me by the shoulder as the noises rose and fell again. They now seemed to be coming from a point broad on our beam. Every eye on the ship was straining into the mist, but with no result. Suddenly one of the men cried out, as something long and black slid past us into the fog astern. From it there rose four indistinct and ghostly towers, which resolved themselves into spars and ropes, and sails.

"A ship! It's a ship!" we cried excitedly. I turned to Mr. Gray; he, too, had seen something, and was staring aft into the wake. So ghostlike, unreal, and fleeting had been our glimpse of the stranger, that we were not sure that we had seen an honest, material ship, but thought that we had been vouchsafed a vision of some phantom vessel like the Flying Dutchman. Our sails gave a sudden flap, the clew irons flogging the bulwarks with hollow thumps. The mate glanced aloft.

"Wind's dropping," he growled savagely. "We shall never get out of this infernal place at this gait!"

Gradually the wind fell until it was a flat calm. No sound broke the deathlike silence save the rapid patter of the reef points, as she gently rose and fell on the light swell. Hours passed, and the watch was relieved and I then went below. At seven bells we were called again, and as I went along the deck to the galley, I noticed that the fog seemed thinner, and the air cooler. When eight bells were struck I relieved Hansard at coiling down the ropes. From him I learned that the steam had begun to clear about four bells, and that the temperature of the sea had fallen ten degrees.

In spite of the thinning mist, it was not until about a half an hour later that we were able to get a glimpse of the surrounding sea. It was still mottled with dark patches, but the bubbling and popping had ceased. As much of the surface of the ocean as could be seen had a peculiarly desolate aspect. Occasionally a wisp of steam would float up from the nearer sea, and roll undulatingly across its silent surface, until lost in the vagueness that still held the hidden horizon. Here and there columns of steam rose up in pillars, which gave me the impression that the sea was hot in patches. Crossing to the starboard side and looking over, I found that conditions there were similar to those to port. The desolate aspect of the sea filled me with an idea of chilliness, although the air was quite warm and muggy. From the break of the poop the mate called to me to get his glasses.

When I had done this, he took them from me and walked to the taffrail. Here he stood for some moments polishing them with his handkerchief. After a moment he raised them to his eyes, and peered long and intently into the mist astern. I stood for some time staring at the point on which the mate had focused his glasses. Presently something shadowy grew upon my vision. Steadily watching it, I distinctly saw the outlines of a ship take form in the fog.

"See!" I cried, but even as I spoke, a lifting wraith of mist disclosed to view a great four-masted bark lying becalmed with all sails set, within a few hundred yards of our stern. As though a curtain had been raised, and then allowed to fall, the fog once more settled down, hiding the strange bark from our sight. The mate was all excitement, striding with quick, jerky steps, up and down the poop, stopping every few moments to peer through his glasses at the point where the four-master had disappeared in the fog. Gradually, as the mists dispersed again, the vessel could be seen more plainly, and it was then that we got an inkling of the cause of the dreadful noises during the night.

For some time the mate watched her silently, and as he watched the conviction grew upon me that in spite of the mist, I could detect some sort of movement on board of her. After some time had passed, the doubt became a certainty, and I could also see a sort of splashing in the water alongside of her. Suddenly the mate put his glasses on top of the wheel box and told me to bring him the speaking trumpet. Running to the companionway, I secured the trumpet and was back at his side.

The mate raised it to his lips, and taking a deep breath, sent a hail across the water that should have awakened the dead. We waited tensely for a reply. A moment later a deep, hollow mutter came from the bark; higher and louder it swelled, until we realized that we were listening to the same sounds we had heard the night before. The mate stood aghast at this answer to his hail; in a voice barely more than a hushed whisper, he bade me call the Old Man. Attracted by the mate's hail and its unearthly reply, the watch had all come aft and were clustered in the mizzen rigging in order to see better.

After calling the captain, I returned to the poop, where I found the second and third mates talking with the chief. All were engaged in trying to pierce the clouds of mist that half hid our strange consort and to arrive at some explanation of the strange phenomena of the past few hours. A moment later the captain appeared carrying his telescope. The mate gave him a brief account of the state of affairs and handed him the trumpet. Giving me the telescope to hold, the captain hailed the shadowy bark. Breathlessly we all listened, when again, in answer to the Old Man's hail, the frightful sounds rose on the still morning air. The skipper lowered the trumpet and stood with an expression of astonished horror on his face.

"Lord!" he exclaimed. "What an ungodly row!"

At this, the third, who had been gazing through his binoculars, broke the silence.

"Look," he ejaculated. "There's a breeze coming up astern." At his words the captain looked up quickly, and we all watched the ruffling water.

"That packet yonder is bringing the breeze with her," said the skipper. "She'll be alongside in half an hour!"

Some moments passed, and the bank of fog had come to within a hundred yards of our taffrail. The strange vessel could be distinctly seen just inside the fringe of the driving mist wreaths. After a short puff, the wind died completely, but as we stared with hypnotic fascination, the water astern of the stranger ruffled again with a fresh catspaw. Seemingly with the flapping of her sails, she drew slowly up to us. As the leaden seconds passed, the big four-master approached us steadily. The light air had now reached us, and with a lazy lift of our sails, we, too, began to forge slowly through that weird sea. The bark was now within fifty yards of our stern, and she was steadily drawing nearer, seeming to be able to outfoot us with ease. As she came on she luffed sharply, and came up into the wind with her weather leeches shaking.

I looked toward her poop, thinking to discern the figure of the man at the wheel, but the mist coiled around her quarter, and objects on the after end of her became indistinguishable. With a rattle of chain sheets on her iron yards, she filled away again. We meanwhile had gone ahead, but it was soon evident that she was the better sailor, for she came up to us hand over fist. The wind rapidly freshened and the mist began to drift away before it, so that each moment her spars and cordage became more plainly visible. The skipper and the mates were watching her intently when an almost simultaneous exclamation of fear broke from them.

"My God!"

And well they might show signs of fear, for crawling about the bark's deck were the most horrible creatures I had ever seen. In spite of their unearthly strangeness there was something vaguely familiar about them. Then it came to me that the face that Stevenson and I had seen during he night belonged to one of them. Their bodies had something of the shape of a seal's, but of a dead, unhealthy white. The lower part of the body ended in a sort of double-curved tail on which they appeared to be able to shuffle about. In place of arms, they had two long, snaky feelers, at the ends of which were two very humanlike hands, which were equipped with talons instead of nails. Fearsome indeed were these parodies of human beings!

Their faces, which, like their tentacles, were black, were the most grotesquely human things about them, and the upper jaw closed into the lower, after the manner of the jaws of an octopus. I have seen men among certain tribes of natives who had faces uncommonly like theirs, but yet no native I had ever seen could have given me the extraordinary feeling of horror and revulsion I experienced toward these brutal-looking creatures.

"What devilish beasts!" burst out the captain in disgust.

With this remark he turned to the mates, and as he did so, the expressions on their faces told me that they had all realized what the presence of these bestial-looking brutes meant. If, as was doubtless the case, these creatures had boarded the bark and destroyed her crew, what would prevent them from doing the same with us? We were a smaller ship and had a smaller crew, and the more I thought of it the less I liked it.

We could now see the name on the bark's bow with the naked eye. It read *Scottish Heath*, while on her boats we could see the name bracketed with Glasgow, showing that she hailed from that port. It was a remarkable coincidence that she should have a slant from just the quarter in which yards were trimmed, as before we saw her she must have been drifting around with everything 'aback.' But now in this light air she was able to run along beside us with no one at her helm. But steering herself she was, and although at times she yawed wildly, she never got herself aback. As we gazed at her we noticed a sudden movement on board of her, and several of the creatures slid into the water.

"See! See! They've spotted us. They're coming for us!" cried the mate wildly.

It was only too true, scores of them were sliding into the sea, letting themselves down by means of their long tentacles. On they came, slipping by scores and hundreds into the water, and swimming toward us in droves. The ship was making about three knots, otherwise they would have caught us in a very few minutes. But they persevered, gaining slowly but surely, and drawing nearer and nearer. The long, tentacle-like arms rose out of the sea in hundreds, and the foremost ones were already within a score of yards of the ship before the Old Man bethought himself to shout to the mates to fetch up the half dozen cutlasses that comprised the ship's armoury. Then, turning to me, he ordered me to go down to his cabin and bring up the two revolvers out of the top drawer of the chart table, also a box of cartridges that was there.

When I returned with the weapons he loaded them and handed one to the mate. Meanwhile the pursuing creatures were coming steadily nearer, and soon half a dozen of the leaders were directly under our counter. Immediately the captain leaned over the rail and emptied his pistol into them, but without any apparent effect. He must have realized how puny and ineffectual his efforts were, for he did not reload his weapon.

Some dozens of the brutes had reached us, and as they did so, their tentacles rose into the air and caught our rail. I heard the third mate scream suddenly, and turning, I saw him dragged quickly to the rail, with a tentacle wrapped completely around him. Snatching a cutlass, the second mate hacked off the tentacle where it joined the body. A gout of blood splashed into the third mate's face, and he fell to the deck. A dozen more of those arms rose and wavered in the air, but they now seemed some yards astern of us. A rapidly widening patch of clear water appeared between us and the foremost of our pursuers, and we raised a wild shout of joy. The cause was soon apparent; for a fine fair wind had sprung up, and with the increase in its force, the *Scottish Heath* had got herself aback, while we were rapidly leaving the monsters behind us. The third mate rose to his feet with a dazed look, and as he did so something fell to the deck. I picked it up and found that it was the severed portion of the tentacle of the third's late adversary. With a grimace of disgust I tossed it into the sea, as I needed no reminder of that awful experience.

Three weeks later we anchored in San Francisco. There the captain made a full report of the affair to the authorities, with the result that a gunboat was despatched to investigate. Six weeks later she returned to report that she had been unable to find any signs, either of the ship herself or of the fearful creatures that had attacked her. And since then nothing, as far as I know, has ever been heard of the four-masted bark *Scottish Heath*, last seen by us in the possession of creatures that may rightly be called demons of the sea.

Whether she still floats, occupied by her hellish crew, or whether some storm has sent her to her last resting place beneath the waves is surely a matter of conjecture. Perchance on some dark, fog-bound night, a ship in that wilderness of waters may hear cries and sounds beyond those of the wailing of the winds. Then let them look to it, for it may be that the demons of the sea are near them.

The Sea Raiders

I

UNTIL THE EXTRAORDINARY AFFAIR at Sidmouth, the peculiar species *Haploteuthis ferox* was known to science only generically, on the strength of a half-digested tentacle obtained near the Azores, and a decaying body pecked by birds and nibbled by fish, found early in 1896 by Mr. Jennings, near Land's End.

In no department of zoological science, indeed, are we quite so much in the dark as with regard to the deep-sea cephalopods. A mere accident, for instance, it was that led to the Prince of Monaco's discovery of nearly a dozen new forms in the summer of 1895, a discovery in which the before-mentioned tentacle was included. It chanced that a cachalot was killed off Terceira by some sperm whalers, and in its last struggles charged almost to the Prince's yacht, missed it, rolled under, and died within twenty yards of his rudder. And in its agony it threw up a number of large objects, which the Prince, dimly perceiving they were strange and important, was, by a happy expedient, able to secure before they sank. He set his screws in motion, and kept them circling in the vortices thus created until a boat could be lowered. And these specimens were whole cephalopods and fragments of cephalopods, some of gigantic proportions, and almost all of them unknown to science!

It would seem, indeed, that these large and agile creatures, living in the middle depths of the sea, must, to a large extent, for ever remain unknown to us, since under water they are too nimble for nets, and it is only by such rare unlooked-for accidents that specimens can be obtained. In the case of *Haploteuthis ferox*, for instance, we are still altogether ignorant of its habitat, as ignorant as we are of the breeding-ground of the herring or the sea-ways of the salmon. And zoologists are altogether at a loss to account for its sudden appearance on our coast. Possibly it was the stress of a hunger migration that drove it hither out of the deep. But it will be, perhaps, better to avoid necessarily inconclusive discussion, and to proceed at once with our narrative.

The first human being to set eyes upon a living *Haploteuthis* – the first human being to survive, that is, for there can be little doubt now that the wave of bathing fatalities and boating accidents that travelled along the coast of Cornwall and Devon in early May was due to this cause – was a retired tea-dealer of the name of Fison, who was stopping at a Sidmouth boarding-house. It was in the afternoon, and he was walking along the cliff path between Sidmouth and Ladram Bay. The cliffs in this direction are very high, but down the red face of them in one place a kind of ladder staircase has been made. He was near this when his attention was attracted by what at first he thought to be a cluster of birds struggling over a fragment of food that caught the sunlight, and glistened pinkish-white. The tide was right out, and this object was not only far below him, but remote across a broad waste of rock reefs covered with dark seaweed and interspersed with silvery shining tidal pools. And he was, moreover, dazzled by the brightness of the further water.

In a minute, regarding this again, he perceived that his judgment was in fault, for over this struggle circled a number of birds, jackdaws and gulls for the most part, the latter gleaming blindingly when the sunlight smote their wings, and they seemed minute in comparison with it. And his curiosity was, perhaps, aroused all the more strongly because of his first insufficient explanations.

As he had nothing better to do than amuse himself, he decided to make this object, whatever it was, the goal of his afternoon walk, instead of Ladram Bay, conceiving it might perhaps be a great fish of some sort, stranded by some chance, and flapping about in its distress. And so he hurried down the long steep ladder, stopping at intervals of thirty feet or so to take breath and scan the mysterious movement.

At the foot of the cliff he was, of course, nearer his object than he had been; but, on the other hand, it now came up against the incandescent sky, beneath the sun, so as to seem dark and indistinct. Whatever was pinkish of it was now hidden by a skerry of weedy boulders. But he perceived that it was made up of seven rounded bodies, distinct or connected, and that the birds kept up a constant croaking and screaming, but seemed afraid to approach it too closely.

Mr. Fison, torn by curiosity, began picking his way across the wave-worn rocks, and, finding the wet seaweed that covered them thickly rendered them extremely slippery, he stopped, removed his shoes and socks, and coiled his trousers above his knees. His object was, of course, merely to avoid stumbling into the rocky pools about him, and perhaps he was rather glad, as all men are, of an excuse to resume, even for a moment, the sensations of his boyhood. At any rate, it is to this, no doubt, that he owes his life.

He approached his mark with all the assurance which the absolute security of this country against all forms of animal life gives its inhabitants. The round bodies moved to and fro, but it was only when he surmounted the skerry of boulders I have mentioned that he realised the horrible nature of the discovery. It came upon him with some suddenness.

The rounded bodies fell apart as he came into sight over the ridge, and displayed the pinkish object to be the partially devoured body of a human being, but whether of a man or woman he was unable to say. And the rounded bodies were new and ghastly-looking creatures, in shape somewhat resembling an octopus, and with huge and very long and flexible tentacles, coiled copiously on the ground. The skin had a glistening texture, unpleasant to see, like shiny leather. The downward bend of the tentacle-surrounded mouth, the curious excrescence at the bend, the tentacles, and the large intelligent eyes, gave the creatures a grotesque suggestion of a face. They were the size of a fair-sized swine about the body, and the tentacles seemed to him to be many feet in length. There were, he thinks, seven or eight at least of the creatures. Twenty yards beyond them, amid the surf of the now returning tide, two others were emerging from the sea.

Their bodies lay flatly on the rocks, and their eyes regarded him with evil interest; but it does not appear that Mr. Fison was afraid, or that he realised that he was in any danger. Possibly his confidence is to be ascribed to the limpness of their attitudes. But he was horrified, of course, and intensely excited and indignant at such revolting creatures preying upon human flesh. He thought they had chanced upon a drowned body. He shouted to them, with the idea of driving them off, and, finding they did not budge, cast about him, picked up a big rounded lump of rock, and flung it at one.

And then, slowly uncoiling their tentacles, they all began moving towards him – creeping at first deliberately, and making a soft purring sound to each other.

In a moment Mr. Fison realised that he was in danger. He shouted again, threw both his boots, and started off, with a leap, forthwith. Twenty yards off he stopped and faced about, judging them slow, and behold! the tentacles of their leader were already pouring over the rocky ridge on which he had just been standing!

At that he shouted again, but this time not threatening, but a cry of dismay, and began jumping, striding, slipping, wading across the uneven expanse between him and the beach. The tall red cliffs seemed suddenly at a vast distance, and he saw, as though they were creatures in another world, two minute workmen engaged in the repair of the ladder-way, and little suspecting the race for life that was beginning below them. At one time he could hear the creatures splashing in the pools not a dozen feet behind him, and once he slipped and almost fell.

They chased him to the very foot of the cliffs, and desisted only when he had been joined by the workmen at the foot of the ladder-way up the cliff. All three of the men pelted them with stones for a time, and then hurried to the cliff top and along the path towards Sidmouth, to secure assistance and a boat, and to rescue the desecrated body from the clutches of these abominable creatures.

II

And, as if he had not already been in sufficient peril that day, Mr. Fison went with the boat to point out the exact spot of his adventure.

As the tide was down, it required a considerable detour to reach the spot, and when at last they came off the ladder-way, the mangled body had disappeared. The water was now running in, submerging first one slab of slimy rock and then another, and the four men in the boat – the workmen, that is, the boatman, and Mr. Fison – now turned their attention from the bearings off shore to the water beneath the keel.

At first they could see little below them, save a dark jungle of laminaria, with an occasional darting fish. Their minds were set on adventure, and they expressed their disappointment freely. But presently they saw one of the monsters swimming through the water seaward, with a curious rolling motion that suggested to Mr. Fison the spinning roll of a captive balloon. Almost immediately after, the waving streamers of laminaria were extraordinarily perturbed, parted for a moment, and three of these beasts became darkly visible, struggling for what was probably some fragment of the drowned man. In a moment the copious olive-green ribbons had poured again over this writhing group.

At that all four men, greatly excited, began beating the water with oars and shouting, and immediately they saw a tumultuous movement among the weeds. They desisted to see more clearly, and as soon as the water was smooth, they saw, as it seemed to them, the whole sea bottom among the weeds set with eyes.

"Ugly swine!" cried one of the men. "Why, there's dozens!"

And forthwith the things began to rise through the water about them. Mr. Fison has since described to the writer this startling eruption out of the waving laminaria meadows. To him it seemed to occupy a considerable time, but it is probable that really it was an affair of a few seconds only. For a time nothing but eyes, and then he speaks of tentacles streaming out and parting the weed fronds this way and that. Then these things, growing larger, until at last the bottom was hidden by their intercoiling forms, and the tips of tentacles rose darkly here and there into the air above the swell of the waters.

One came up boldly to the side of the boat, and, clinging to this with three of its sucker-set tentacles, threw four others over the gunwale, as if with an intention either of oversetting the boat or of clambering into it. Mr. Fison at once caught up the boathook, and, jabbing furiously at the soft tentacles, forced it to desist. He was struck in the back and almost pitched overboard by the boatman, who was using his oar to resist a similar attack on the other side of the boat. But the tentacles on either side at once relaxed their hold at this, slid out of sight, and splashed into the water.

"We'd better get out of this," said Mr. Fison, who was trembling violently. He went to the tiller, while the boatman and one of the workmen seated themselves and began rowing. The other workman stood up in the fore part of the boat, with the boathook, ready to strike any more tentacles that might appear. Nothing else seems to have been said. Mr. Fison had expressed the common feeling beyond amendment. In a hushed, scared mood, with faces white and drawn, they set about escaping from the position into which they had so recklessly blundered.

But the oars had scarcely dropped into the water before dark, tapering, serpentine ropes had bound them, and were about the rudder; and creeping up the sides of the boat with a looping motion came the suckers again. The men gripped their oars and pulled, but it was like trying to move a boat in a floating raft of weeds. "Help here!" cried the boatman, and Mr. Fison and the second workman rushed to help lug at the oar.

Then the man with the boathook – his name was Ewan, or Ewen – sprang up with a curse, and began striking downward over the side, as far as he could reach, at the bank of tentacles that now clustered along the boat's bottom. And, at the same time, the two rowers stood up to get a better purchase for the recovery of their oars. The boatman handed his to Mr. Fison, who lugged desperately, and, meanwhile, the boatman opened a big clasp-knife, and, leaning over the side of the boat, began hacking at the spiring arms upon the oar shaft.

Mr. Fison, staggering with the quivering rocking of the boat, his teeth set, his breath coming short, and the veins starting on his hands as he pulled at his oar, suddenly cast his eyes seaward. And there, not fifty yards off, across the long rollers of the incoming tide, was a large boat standing in towards them, with three women and a little child in it. A boatman was rowing, and a little man in a pinkribboned straw hat and whites stood in the stern, hailing them. For a moment, of course, Mr. Fison thought of help, and then he thought of the child. He abandoned his oar forthwith, threw up his arms in a frantic gesture, and screamed to the party in the boat to keep away "for God's sake!" It says much for the modesty and courage of Mr. Fison that he does not seem to be aware that there was any quality of heroism in his action at this juncture. The oar he had abandoned was at once drawn under, and presently reappeared floating about twenty yards away.

At the same moment Mr. Fison felt the boat under him lurch violently, and a hoarse scream, a prolonged cry of terror from Hill, the boatman, caused him to forget the party of excursionists altogether. He turned, and saw Hill crouching by the forward rowlock, his face convulsed with terror, and his right arm over the side and drawn tightly down. He gave now a succession of short, sharp cries, "Oh! oh! oh! – oh!" Mr. Fison believes that he must have been hacking at the tentacles below the waterline, and have been grasped by them, but, of course, it is quite impossible to say now certainly what had happened. The boat was heeling over, so that the gunwale was within ten inches of the water, and both Ewan and the other labourer were striking down into the water, with oar and boathook, on either side of Hill's arm. Mr. Fison instinctively placed himself to counterpoise them.

Then Hill, who was a burly, powerful man, made a strenuous effort, and rose almost to a standing position. He lifted his arm, indeed, clean out of the water. Hanging to it was a complicated tangle of brown ropes; and the eyes of one of the brutes that had hold of him, glaring straight and resolute, showed momentarily above the surface. The boat heeled more and more, and the green-brown water came pouring in a cascade over the side. Then Hill slipped and fell with his ribs across the side, and his arm and the mass of tentacles about it splashed back into the water. He rolled over; his boot kicked Mr. Fison's knee as that gentleman rushed forward to seize him, and in another moment fresh tentacles had whipped about his waist and neck, and after a brief, convulsive struggle, in which the boat was nearly capsized, Hill was lugged overboard. The boat righted with a violent jerk that all but sent Mr. Fison over the other side, and hid the struggle in the water from his eyes.

He stood staggering to recover his balance for a moment, and as he did so, he became aware that the struggle and the inflowing tide had carried them close upon the weedy rocks again. Not four yards off a table of rock still rose in rhythmic movements above the in-wash of the tide. In a moment Mr. Fison seized the oar from Ewan, gave one vigorous stroke, then, dropping it, ran to the bows and leapt. He felt his feet slide over the rock, and, by a frantic effort, leapt again towards a further mass. He stumbled over this, came to his knees, and rose again.

"Look out!" cried someone, and a large drab body struck him. He was knocked flat into a tidal pool by one of the workmen, and as he went down he heard smothered, choking cries, that he believed at the time came from Hill. Then he found himself marvelling at the shrillness and variety of Hill's voice. Someone jumped over him, and a curving rush of foamy water poured over him, and passed. He scrambled to his feet dripping, and, without looking seaward, ran as fast as his terror would let him shoreward. Before him, over the flat space of scattered rocks, stumbled the two workmen – one a dozen yards in front of the other.

He looked over his shoulder at last, and, seeing that he was not pursued, faced about. He was astonished. From the moment of the rising of the cephalopods out of the water, he had been acting too swiftly to fully comprehend his actions. Now it seemed to him as if he had suddenly jumped out of an evil dream.

For there were the sky, cloudless and blazing with the afternoon sun, the sea weltering under its pitiless brightness, the soft creamy foam of the breaking water, and the low, long, dark ridges of rock. The righted boat floated, rising and falling gently on the swell about a dozen yards from shore. Hill and the monsters, all the stress and tumult of that fierce fight for life, had vanished as though they had never been.

Mr. Fison's heart was beating violently; he was throbbing to the finger-tips, and his breath came deep.

There was something missing. For some seconds he could not think clearly enough what this might be. Sun, sky, sea, rocks – what was it? Then he remembered the boatload of excursionists. It had vanished. He wondered whether he had imagined it. He turned, and saw the two workmen standing side by side under the projecting masses of the tall pink cliffs. He hesitated whether he should make one last attempt to save the man Hill. His physical excitement seemed to desert him suddenly, and leave him aimless and helpless. He turned shoreward, stumbling and wading towards his two companions.

He looked back again, and there were now two boats floating, and the one farthest out at sea pitched clumsily, bottom upward.

III

So it was *Haploteuthis ferox* made its appearance upon the Devonshire coast. So far, this has been its most serious aggression. Mr. Fison's account, taken together with the wave of boating and bathing casualties to which I have already alluded, and the absence of fish from the Cornish coasts that year, points clearly to a shoal of these voracious deep-sea monsters prowling slowly along the sub-tidal coastline. Hunger migration has, I know, been suggested as the force that drove them hither; but, for my own part, I prefer to believe the alternative theory of Hemsley. Hemsley holds that a pack or shoal of these creatures may have become enamoured of human flesh by the accident of a foundered ship sinking among them, and have wandered in search of it out of their accustomed zone; first waylaying and following ships, and so coming to our shores in the wake of the Atlantic traffic. But to discuss Hemsley's cogent and admirably-stated arguments would be out of place here.

It would seem that the appetites of the shoal were satisfied by the catch of eleven people – for so far as can be ascertained, there were ten people in the second boat, and certainly these creatures gave no further signs of their presence off Sidmouth that day. The coast between Seaton and Budleigh Salterton was patrolled all that evening and night by four Preventive Service boats, the men in which were armed with harpoons and cutlasses, and as the evening advanced, a number of more or less similarly equipped expeditions, organised by private individuals, joined them. Mr. Fison took no part in any of these expeditions.

About midnight excited hails were heard from a boat about a couple of miles out at sea to the southeast of Sidmouth, and a lantern was seen waving in a strange manner to and fro and up and down. The nearer boats at once hurried towards the alarm. The venturesome occupants of the boat, a seaman, a curate, and two schoolboys, had actually seen the monsters passing under their boat. The creatures, it seems, like most deep-sea organisms, were phosphorescent, and they had been floating, five fathoms deep or so, like creatures of moonshine through the blackness of the water, their tentacles retracted and as if asleep, rolling over and over, and moving slowly in a wedge-like formation towards the south-east.

These people told their story in gesticulated fragments, as first one boat drew alongside and then another. At last there was a little fleet of eight or nine boats collected together, and from them a tumult, like the chatter of a marketplace, rose into the stillness of the night. There was little or no disposition to pursue the shoal, the people had neither weapons nor experience for such a dubious chase, and presently – even with a certain relief, it may be – the boats turned shoreward.

And now to tell what is perhaps the most astonishing fact in this whole astonishing raid. We have not the slightest knowledge of the subsequent movements of the shoal, although the whole south-west coast was now alert for it. But it may, perhaps, be significant that a cachalot was stranded off Sark on June 3. Two weeks and three days after this Sidmouth affair, a living *Haploteuthis* came ashore on Calais sands. It was alive, because several witnesses saw its tentacles moving in a convulsive way. But it is probable that it was dying. A gentleman named Pouchet obtained a rifle and shot it.

That was the last appearance of a living *Haploteuthis*. No others were seen on the French coast. On the 15th of June a dead body, almost complete, was washed ashore near Torquay, and a few days later a boat from the Marine Biological station, engaged in dredging off Plymouth, picked up a rotting specimen, slashed deeply with a cutlass wound. How the former specimen had come by its death it is impossible to say. And on the last day of June, Mr. Egbert Caine, an artist, bathing near Newlyn, threw up his arms, shrieked, and was drawn under. A friend bathing with him made no attempt to save him, but swam at once for the shore. This is the last fact to tell of this extraordinary raid from the deeper sea. Whether it is really the last of these horrible creatures it is, as yet, premature to say. But it is believed, and certainly it is to be hoped, that they have returned now, and returned for good, to the sunless depths of the middle seas, out of which they have so strangely and so mysteriously arisen.

The Seal-Killer's Adventure

THERE WAS ONCE UPON A TIME a man who lived upon the northern coasts, not far from 'Taigh Jan Crot Callow' (John-o'-Groat's House), and he gained his livelihood by catching and killing fish, of all sizes and denominations. He had a particular liking for the killing of those wonderful beasts, half dog half fish, called 'Roane,' or seals, no doubt because he got a long price for their skins, which are not less curious than they are valuable. The truth is, that the most of these animals are neither dogs nor cods, but downright fairies, as this narration will show; and, indeed, it is easy for any man to convince himself of the fact by a simple examination of his *tobacco-spluichdan*, for the dead skins of those beings are never the same for four-and-twenty hours together. Sometimes the *spluichdan* will erect its bristles almost perpendicularly, while, at other times, it reclines them even down; one time it resembles a bristly sow, at another time a *sleekit cat*; and what dead skin, except itself, could perform such cantrips? Now, it happened one day, as this notable fisher had returned from the prosecution of his calling, that he was called upon by a man who seemed a great stranger, and who said he had been despatched for him by a person who wished to contract for a quantity of seal-skins, and that the fisher must accompany him (the stranger) immediately to see the person who wished to contract for the skins, as it was necessary that he should be served that evening. Happy in the prospect of making a good bargain, and never suspecting any duplicity, he instantly complied. They both mounted a steed belonging to the stranger, and took the road with such velocity that, although the direction of the wind was towards their backs, yet the fleetness of their movement made it appear as if it had been in their faces. On reaching a stupendous precipice which overhung the sea, his guide told him they had now reached their destination.

"Where is the person you spoke of!" inquired the astonished seal-killer.

"You shall see that presently," replied the guide. With that they immediately alighted, and, without allowing the seal-killer much time to indulge the frightful suspicions that began to pervade his mind, the stranger seized him with irresistible force, and plunged headlong with him into the sea. After sinking down, down, nobody knows how far, they at length reached a door, which, being open, led them into a range of apartments, filled with inhabitants – not people, but seals, who could nevertheless speak and feel like human folk; and how much was the seal-killer surprised to find that he himself had been unconsciously transformed into the like image. If it were not so, he would probably have died from the want of breath. The nature of the poor fisher's thoughts may be more easily conceived than described. Looking at the nature of the quarters into which he had landed, all hopes of escape from them appeared wholly chimerical, whilst the degree of comfort, and length of life which the barren scene promised him were far from being flattering. The 'Roane,' who all seemed in very low spirits, appeared to feel for him, and endeavoured to soothe the distress which he evinced by the amplest assurances of personal safety. Involved in sad meditation on his evil fate, he was quickly roused from his stupor by his guide's producing a huge gully or joctaleg, the object of which he supposed was to put an end to all his earthly cares. Forlorn as was his situation, however, he did not wish to be killed; and, apprehending instant destruction, he fell down, and earnestly implored for mercy. The poor generous animals did not mean him any harm, however much his former conduct deserved it, and he was accordingly desired to pacify himself, and cease his cries.

"Did you ever see that knife before?" said the stranger to the fisher.

The latter instantly recognized his own knife, which he had that day stuck into a seal, and with which it had escaped, and acknowledged it was formerly his own, for what would be the use of denying it?

"Well," rejoined the guide, "the apparent seal which made away with it is my father, who has lain dangerously ill ever since, and no means can stay his fleeting breath without your aid. I have been obliged to resort to the artifice I have practised to bring you hither, and I trust that my filial duty to my father will readily excuse me."

Having said this, he led into another apartment the trembling seal-killer, who expected every minute to be punished for his own ill-treatment of the father. There he found the identical seal with which he had had the encounter in the morning, suffering most grievously from a tremendous cut in its hind-quarter. The seal-killer was then desired, with his hand, to cicatrise the wound, upon doing which it immediately healed, and the seal arose from its bed in perfect health. Upon this the scene changed from mourning to rejoicing – all was mirth and glee. Very different, however, were the feelings of the unfortunate seal-catcher, who expected no doubt to be metamorphosed into a seal for the remainder of his life. However, his late guide accosting him, said –

"Now, sir, you are at liberty to return to your wife and family, to whom I am about to conduct you; but it is on this express condition, to which you must bind yourself by a solemn oath, viz. that you will never maim or kill a seal in all your lifetime hereafter."

To this condition, hard as it was, he joyfully acceded; and the oath being administered in all due form, he bade his new acquaintance most heartily and sincerely a long farewell. Taking hold of his guide, they issued from the place and swam up, till they regained the surface of the sea, and, landing at the said stupendous pinnacle, they found their former steed ready for a second canter. The guide breathed upon the fisher, and they became like men. They mounted their horse, and fleet as had been their course towards the precipice, their return from it was doubly swift; and the honest seal-killer was laid down at his own door-cheek, where his guide made him such a present as would have almost reconciled him to another similar expedition, such as rendered his loss of profession, in so far as regarded the seals, a far less intolerable hardship than he had at first considered it.

The Wonderful Tune

MAURICE CONNOR was the king, and that's no small word, of all the pipers in Munster. He could play jig and planxty without end, and Ollistrum's March, and the Eagle's Whistle, and the Hen's Concert, and odd tunes of every sort and kind. But he knew one, far more surprising than the rest, which had in it the power to set everything dead or alive dancing.

In what way he learned it is beyond my knowledge, for he was mighty cautious about telling how he came by so wonderful a tune. At the very first note of that tune, the brogues began shaking upon the feet of all who heard it – old or young it mattered not – just as if their brogues had the ague; then the feet began going – going – going from under them, and at last up and away with them, dancing like mad! – Whisking here, there, and every where, like a straw in a storm – there was no halting while the music lasted!

Not a fair, nor a wedding, nor a patron in the seven parishes round, was counted worth the speaking of without "blind Maurice and his pipes." His mother, poor woman, used to lead him about from one place to another, just like a dog.

Down through Iveragh – a place that ought to be proud of itself, for 'tis Daniel O'Connell's country – Maurice Connor and his mother were taking their rounds. Beyond all other places Iveragh is the place for stormy coast and steep mountains: as proper a spot it is as any in Ireland to get yourself drowned, or your neck broken on the land, should you prefer that. But, notwithstanding, in Ballinskellig bay there is a neat bit of ground, well fitted for diversion, and down from it towards the water, is a clean smooth piece of strand – the dead image of a calm summer's sea on a moonlight night, with just the curl of the small waves upon it.

Here it was that Maurice's music had brought from all parts a great gathering of the young men and the young women – *O the darlints!* – for 'twas not every day the strand of Trafraska was stirred up by the voice of a bagpipe. The dance began; and as pretty a rinkafadda it was as ever was danced. "Brave music," said every body, "and well done," when Maurice stopped.

"More power to your elbow, Maurice, and a fair wind in the bellows," cried Paddy Dorman, a hump-backed dancing-master, who was there to keep order. "'Tis a pity," said he, "if we'd let the piper run dry after such music; 'twould be a disgrace to Iveragh, that didn't come on it since the week of the three Sundays." So, as well became him, for he was always a decent man, says he: "Did you drink, piper?"

"I will, sir," says Maurice, answering the question on the safe side, for you never yet knew piper or schoolmaster who refused his drink.

"What will you drink, Maurice?" says Paddy.

"I'm no ways particular," says Maurice; "I drink anything, and give God thanks, barring *raw* water; but if 'tis all the same to you, mister Dorman, maybe you wouldn't lend me the loan of a glass of whiskey."

"I've no glass, Maurice," said Paddy; "I've only the bottle."

"Let that be no hindrance," answered Maurice; "my mouth just holds a glass to the drop; often I've tried it, sure."

So Paddy Dorman trusted him with the bottle – more fool was he; and, to his cost, he found that though Maurice's mouth might not hold more than the glass at one time, yet, owing to the hole in his throat, it took many a filling.

"That was no bad whisky neither," says Maurice, handing back the empty bottle.

"By the holy frost, then!" says Paddy, "'tis but *cowld* comfort there's in that bottle now; and 'tis your word we must take for the strength of the whisky, for you've left us no sample to judge by": and to be sure Maurice had not.

Now I need not tell any gentleman or lady with common understanding, that if he or she was to drink an honest bottle of whiskey at one pull, it is not at all the same thing as drinking a bottle of water; and in the whole course of my life, I never knew more than five men who could do so without being overtaken by the liquor. Of these Maurice Connor was not one, though he had a stiff head enough of his own – he was fairly tipsy. Don't think I blame him for it; 'tis often a good man's case; but true is the word that says, "when liquor's in, sense is out"; and puff, at a breath, before you could say "Lord save us!" out he blasted his wonderful tune.

'Twas really then beyond all belief or telling the dancing Maurice himself could not keep quiet; staggering now on one leg, now on the other, and rolling about like a ship in a cross sea, trying to humour the tune. There was his mother too, moving her old bones as light as the youngest girl of them all; but her dancing, no, nor the dancing of all the rest, is not worthy the speaking about to the work that was going on down on the strand. Every inch of it covered with all manner of fish jumping and plunging about to the music, and every moment more and more would tumble in out of the water, charmed by the wonderful tune. Crabs of monstrous size spun round and round on one claw with the nimbleness of a dancing-master, and twirled and tossed their other claws about like limbs that did not belong to them. It was a sight surprising to behold. But perhaps you may have heard of father Florence Conry, a Franciscan Friar, and a great Irish poet; *bolg an dana*, as they used to call him – a wallet of poems. If you have not he was as pleasant a man as one would wish to drink with of a hot summer's day; and he has rhymed out all about the dancing fishes so neatly, that it would be a thousand pities not to give you his verses; so here's my hand at an upset of them into English:

The big seals in motion,
Like waves of the ocean,
Or gouty feet prancing,
Came heading the gay fish,
Crabs, lobsters, and cray fish,
Determined on dancing.
The sweet sounds they follow'd,
The gasping cod swallow'd;
'Twas wonderful, really!
And turbot and flounder,
'Mid fish that were rounder,
Just caper'd as gaily.
John-dories came tripping;
Dull hake, by their skipping
To frisk it seem'd given;
Bright mackerel went springing,
Like small rainbows winging
Their flight up to heaven.
The whiting and haddock
Left salt-water paddock,
This dance to be put in:
Where skate with flat faces
Edged out some odd plaices;
But soles kept their footing.
Sprats and herrings in powers
Of silvery showers
All number out-number'd;
And great ling so lengthy
Were there in such plenty,
The shore was encumber'd.
The scollop and oyster
Their two shells did roister,
Like castanets fitting;
While limpets moved clearly,

And rocks very nearly
With laughter were splitting.

Never was such an ullabulloo in this world, before or since; 'twas as if heaven and earth were coming together; and all out of Maurice Connor's wonderful tune!

In the height of all these doings, what should there be dancing among the outlandish set of fishes but a beautiful young woman – as beautiful as the dawn of day! She had a cocked hat upon her head; from under it her long green hair – just the colour of the sea – fell down behind, without hinderance to her dancing. Her teeth were like rows of pearl; her lips for all the world looked like red coral; and she had an elegant gown, as white as the foam of the wave, with little rows of purple and red sea-weeds settled out upon it; for you never yet saw a lady, under the water or over the water, who had not a good notion of dressing herself out.

Up she danced at last to Maurice, who was flinging his feet from under him as fast as hops – for nothing in this world could keep still while that tune of his was going on – and says she to him, chaunting it out with a voice as sweet as honey –

"I'm a lady of honour
Who live in the sea;
Come down, Maurice Connor,
And be married to me.

"Silver plates and gold dishes
You shall have, and shall be
The king of the fishes,
When you're married to me."

Drink was strong in Maurice's head, and out he chaunted in return for her great civility. It is not every lady, maybe, that would be after making such an offer to a blind piper; therefore 'twas only right in him to give her as good as she gave herself – so says Maurice,

"I'm obliged to you, madam:
Off a gold dish or plate,
If a king, and I had 'em,
I could dine in great state.

"With your own father's daughter
I'd be sure to agree;
But to drink the salt water
Wouldn't do so with me!"

The lady looked at him quite amazed, and swinging her head from side to side like a great scholar, "Well," says she, "Maurice, if you're not a poet, where is poetry to be found?"

In this way they kept on at it, framing high compliments; one answering the other, and their feet going with the music as fast as their tongues. All the fish kept dancing too: Maurice heard the clatter, and was afraid to stop playing lest it might be displeasing to the fish, and not knowing what so many of them may take it into their heads to do to him if they got vexed.

Well, the lady with the green hair kept on coaxing of Maurice with soft speeches, till at last she overpersuaded him to promise to marry her, and be king over the fishes, great and small. Maurice was well fitted to be their king, if they wanted one that could make them dance; and he surely would drink, barring the salt water, with any fish of them all.

When Maurice's mother saw him, with that unnatural thing in the form of a green-haired lady as his guide, and he and she dancing down together so lovingly to the water's edge through the thick of the fishes, she called out after him to stop and come back. "Oh then," says she, "as if I was not widow enough before, there he is going away from me to be married to that scaly woman. And who knows but 'tis grandmother I may be to a hake or a cod – Lord help and pity me, but 'tis a mighty unnatural thing! – and maybe 'tis boiling and eating my own grandchild I'll be, with a bit of salt butter, and I not knowing it! – Oh Maurice, Maurice, if there's any love or nature left in you, come back to your own *ould* mother, who reared you like a decent Christian!"

Then the poor woman began to cry and ullagoane so finely that it would do anyone good to hear her.

Maurice was not long getting to the rim of the water; there he kept playing and dancing on as if nothing was the matter, and a great thundering wave coming in towards him ready to swallow him up alive; but as he could not see it, he did not fear it. His mother it was who saw it plainly through the big tears that were rolling down her cheeks; and though she saw it, and her heart was aching as much as ever mother's heart ached for a son, she kept dancing, dancing, all the time for the bare life of her. Certain it was she could not help it, for Maurice never stopped playing that wonderful tune of his.

He only turned the bothered ear to the sound of his mother's voice, fearing it might put him out in his steps, and all the answer he made back was –

"Whisht with you, mother – sure I'm going to be king over the fishes down in the sea, and for a token of luck, and a sign that I am alive and well, I'll send you in, every twelvemonth on this day, a piece of burned wood to Trafraska." Maurice had not the power to say a word more, for the strange lady with the green hair, seeing the wave just upon them, covered him up with herself in a thing like a cloak with a big hood to it, and the wave curling over twice as high as their heads, burst upon the strand, with a rush and a roar that might be heard as far as Cape Clear.

That day twelvemonth the piece of burned wood came ashore in Trafraska. It was a queer thing for Maurice to think of sending all the way from the bottom of the sea. A gown or a pair of shoes would have been something like a present for his poor mother; but he had said it, and he kept his word. The bit of burned wood regularly came ashore on the appointed day for as good, ay, and better than a hundred years. The day is now forgotten, and may be that is the reason why people say how Maurice Connor has stopped sending the luck-token to his mother. Poor woman, she did not live to get as much as one of them; for what through the loss of Maurice, and the fear of eating her own grandchildren, she died in three weeks after the dance – some say it was the fatigue that killed her, but whichever it was, Mrs. Connor was decently buried with her own people.

Seafaring men have often heard off the coast of Kerry, on a still night, the sound of music coming up from the water; and some, who have had good ears, could plainly distinguish Maurice Connor's voice singing these words to his pipes:

"Beautiful shore, with thy spreading strand,
Thy crystal water, and diamond sand;
Never would I have parted from thee
But for the sake of my fair ladie."

The Lady of Gollerus

ON THE SHORE of Smerwick harbour, one fine summer's morning, just at daybreak, stood Dick Fitzgerald 'shoghing the dudeen', which may be translated, smoking his pipe. The sun was gradually rising behind the lofty Brandon, the dark sea was getting green in the light, and the mists clearing away out of the valleys went rolling and curling like the smoke from the corner of Dick's mouth.

"'Tis just the pattern of a pretty morning," said Dick, taking the pipe from between his lips, and looking towards the distant ocean, which lay as still and tranquil as a tomb of polished marble. "Well, to be sure," continued he, after a pause, "'tis mighty lonesome to be talking to one's self by way of company, and not to have another soul to answer one – nothing but the child of one's own voice, the echo! I know this, that if I had the luck, or may be the misfortune," said Dick, with a melancholy smile, "to have the woman, it would not be this way with me! And what in the wide world is a man without a wife? He's no more surely than a bottle without a drop of drink in it, or dancing without music, or the left leg of a scissors, or a fishing-line without a hook, or any other matter that is no ways complete. Is it not so?" said Dick Fitzgerald, casting his eyes towards a rock upon the strand, which, though it could not speak, stood up as firm and looked as bold as ever Kerry witness did.

But what was his astonishment at beholding, just at the foot of that rock, a beautiful young creature combing her hair, which was of a sea-green colour; and now the salt water shining on it appeared, in the morning light, like melted butter upon cabbage.

Dick guessed at once that she was a Merrow, although he had never seen one before, for he spied the *cohuleen driuth*, or little enchanted cap, which the sea people use for diving down into the ocean, lying upon the strand near her; and he had heard that, if once he could possess himself of the cap she would lose the power of going away into the water: so he seized it with all speed, and she, hearing the noise, turned her head about as natural as any Christian.

When the Merrow saw that her little diving-cap was gone, the salt tears – doubly salt, no doubt, from her – came trickling down her cheeks, and she began a low mournful cry with just the tender voice of a new-born infant. Dick, although he knew well enough what she was crying for, determined to keep the *cohuleen driuth*, let her cry never so much, to see what luck would come out of it. Yet he could not help pitying her; and when the dumb thing looked up in his face, with her cheeks all moist with tears, 'twas enough to make anyone feel, let alone Dick, who had ever and always, like most of his countrymen, a mighty tender heart of his own.

"Don't cry, my darling," said Dick Fitzgerald; but the Merrow, like any bold child, only cried the more for that.

Dick sat himself down by her side, and took hold of her hand by way of comforting her. 'Twas in no particular an ugly hand, only there was a small web between the fingers, as there is in a duck's foot; but 'twas as thin and as white as the skin between egg and shell.

"What's your name, my darling?" says Dick, thinking to make her conversant with him; but he got no answer; and he was certain sure now, either that she could not speak, or did not understand him: he therefore squeezed her hand in his, as the only way he had of talking to her.

It's the universal language; and there's not a woman in the world, be she fish or lady, that does not understand it.

The Merrow did not seem much displeased at this mode of conversation; and making an end of her whining all at once, "Man," says she, looking up in Dick Fitzgerald's face; "man, will you eat me?"

"By all the red petticoats and check aprons between Dingle and Tralee," cried Dick, jumping up in amazement, "I'd as soon eat myself, my jewel! Is it I eat you, my pet? Now, 'twas some ugly ill-looking thief of a fish put that notion into your own pretty head, with the nice green hair down upon it, that is so cleanly combed out this morning!"

"Man," said the Merrow, "what will you do with me if you won't eat me?"

Dick's thoughts were running on a wife: he saw, at the first glimpse, that she was handsome; but since she spoke, and spoke too like any real woman, he was fairly in love with her. 'Twas the neat way she called him man that settled the matter entirely.

"Fish," says Dick, trying to speak to her after her own short fashion; "fish," says he, "here's my word, fresh and fasting, for you this blessed morning, that I'll make you Mistress Fitzgerald before all the world, and that's what I'll do."

"Never say the word twice," says she; "I'm ready and willing to be yours, Mister Fitzgerald; but stop, if you please, till I twist up my hair." It was some time before she had settled it entirely to her liking; for she guessed, I suppose, that she was going among strangers, where she would be looked at. When that was done, the Merrow put the comb in her pocket, and then bent down her head and whispered some words to the water that was close to the foot of the rock.

Dick saw the murmur of the words upon the top of the sea, going out towards the wide ocean, just like a breath of wind rippling along, and, says he, in the greatest wonder, "Is it speaking you are, my darling, to the salt water?"

"It's nothing else," says she, quite carelessly; "I'm just sending word home to my father not to be waiting breakfast for me; just to keep him from being uneasy in his mind."

"And who's your father, my duck?" said Dick.

"What!" said the Merrow, "did you never hear of my father? He's the king of the waves to be sure!"

"And yourself, then, is a real king's daughter?" said Dick, opening his two eyes to take a full and true survey of his wife that was to be. "Oh, I'm nothing else but a made man with you, and a king your father; to be sure he has all the money that's down at the bottom of the sea!"

"Money," repeated the Merrow, "what's money?"

"'Tis no bad thing to have when one wants it," replied Dick; "and maybe now the fishes have the understanding to bring up whatever you bid them?"

"Oh yes," said the Merrow, "they bring me what I want."

"To speak the truth then," said Dick, "'tis a straw bed I have at home before you, and that, I'm thinking, is no ways fitting for a king's daughter; so if 'twould not be displeasing to you, just to mention a nice feather bed, with a pair of new blankets – but what am I talking about? Maybe you have not such things as beds down under the water?"

"By all means," said she, "Mr. Fitzgerald – plenty of beds at your service. I've fourteen oyster-beds of my own, not to mention one just planting for the rearing of young ones."

"You have?" says Dick, scratching his head and looking a little puzzled. "'Tis a feather bed I was speaking of; but, clearly, yours is the very cut of a decent plan to have bed and supper so handy to each other, that a person when they'd have the one need never ask for the other."

However, bed or no bed, money or no money, Dick Fitzgerald determined to marry the Merrow, and the Merrow had given her consent. Away they went, therefore, across the strand, from Gollerus to Ballinrunnig, where Father Fitzgibbon happened to be that morning.

"There are two words to this bargain, Dick Fitzgerald," said his Reverence, looking mighty glum. "And is it a fishy woman you'd marry? The Lord preserve us! Send the scaly creature home to her own people; that's my advice to you, wherever she came from."

Dick had the *cohuleen driuth* in his hand, and was about to give it back to the Merrow, who looked covetously at it, but he thought for a moment, and then says he, "Please your Reverence, she's a king's daughter."

"If she was the daughter of fifty kings," said Father Fitzgibbon, "I tell you, you can't marry her, she being a fish."

"Please your Reverence," said Dick again, in an undertone, "she is as mild and as beautiful as the moon."

"If she was as mild and as beautiful as the sun, moon, and stars, all put together, I tell you, Dick Fitzgerald," said the Priest, stamping his right foot, "you can't marry her, she being a fish."

"But she has all the gold that's down in the sea only for the asking, and I'm a made man if I marry her; and," said Dick, looking up slily, "I can make it worth anyone's while to do the job."

"Oh! That alters the case entirely," replied the Priest; "why there's some reason now in what you say: why didn't you tell me this before? Marry her by all means, if she was ten times a fish. Money, you know, is not to be refused in these bad times, and I may as well have the hansel of it as another, that maybe would not take half the pains in counselling you that I have done."

So Father Fitzgibbon married Dick Fitzgerald to the Merrow, and like any loving couple, they returned to Gollerus well pleased with each other. Everything prospered with Dick – he was at the sunny side of the world; the Merrow made the best of wives, and they lived together in the greatest contentment.

It was wonderful to see, considering where she had been brought up, how she would busy herself about the house, and how well she nursed the children; for, at the end of three years there were as many young Fitzgeralds – two boys and a girl.

In short, Dick was a happy man, and so he might have been to the end of his days if he had only had the sense to take care of what he had got; many another man, however, beside Dick, has not had wit enough to do that.

One day, when Dick was obliged to go to Tralee, he left the wife minding the children at home after him, and thinking she had plenty to do without disturbing his fishing-tackle.

Dick was no sooner gone than Mrs. Fitzgerald set about cleaning up the house, and chancing to pull down a fishing-net, what should she find behind it in a hole in the wall but her own *cohuleen driuth*. She took it out and looked at it, and then she thought of her father the king, and her mother the queen, and her brothers and sisters, and she felt a longing to go back to them.

She sat down on a little stool and thought over the happy days she had spent under the sea; then she looked at her children, and thought on the love and affection of poor Dick, and how it would break his heart to lose her. "But," says she, "he won't lose me entirely, for I'll come back to him again, and who can blame me for going to see my father and my mother after being so long away from them?"

She got up and went towards the door, but came back again to look once more at the child that was sleeping in the cradle. She kissed it gently, and as she kissed it a tear trembled for an instant in her eye and then fell on its rosy cheek. She wiped away the tear, and turning to the eldest little girl, told her to take good care of her brothers, and to be a good child herself until she came back. The Merrow then went down to the strand. The sea was lying calm and smooth, just heaving and glittering in the sun, and she thought she heard a faint sweet singing, inviting her to come down. All her old ideas and feelings came flooding over her mind, Dick and her children were at the instant forgotten, and placing the *cohuleen driuth* on her head she plunged in.

Dick came home in the evening, and missing his wife he asked Kathleen, his little girl, what had become of her mother, but she could not tell him. He then inquired of the neighbours, and he learned that she was seen going towards the strand with a strange-looking thing like a cocked hat in her hand. He returned to his cabin to search for the *cohuleen driuth*. It was gone, and the truth now flashed upon him.

Year after year did Dick Fitzgerald wait expecting the return of his wife, but he never saw her more. Dick never married again, always thinking that the Merrow would sooner or later return to him, and nothing could ever persuade him but that her father the king kept her below by main force; "for," said Dick, "she surely would not of herself give up her husband and her children."

While she was with him she was so good a wife in every respect that to this day she is spoken of in the tradition of the country as the pattern for one, under the name of The Lady of Gollerus.

Finn Blood

IN SVARTFJORD, north of Senje, dwelt a lad called Eilert. His neighbours were seafaring Finns, and among their children was a pale little girl, remarkable for her long black hair and her large eyes. They dwelt behind the crag on the other side of the promontory, and fished for a livelihood, as also did Eilert's parents; wherefore there was no particular goodwill between the families, for the nearest fishing ground was but a small one, and each would have liked to have rowed there alone.

Nevertheless, though his parents didn't like it at all, and even forbade it, Eilert used to sneak regularly down to the Finns. There they had always strange tales to tell, and he heard wondrous things about the recesses of the mountains, where the original home of the Finns was, and where, in the olden time, dwelt the Finn Kings, who were masters among the magicians. There, too, he heard tell of all that was beneath the sea, where the Mermen and the Draugs hold sway. The latter are gloomy evil powers, and many a time his blood stood still in his veins as he sat and listened. They told him that the Draug usually showed himself on the strand in the moonlight on those spots which were covered with sea-wrack; that he had a bunch of seaweed instead of a head, but shaped so peculiarly that whoever came across him absolutely couldn't help gazing into his pale and horrible face. They themselves had seen him many a time, and once they had driven him, thwart by thwart, out of the boat where he had sat one morning, and turned the oars upside down. When Eilert hastened homewards in the darkness round the headland, along the strand, over heaps of seaweed, he dare scarcely look around him, and many a time the sweat absolutely streamed from his forehead.

In proportion as hostility increased among the old people, they had a good deal of fault to find with one another, and Eilert heard no end of evil things spoken about the Finns at home. Now it was this, and now it was that. They didn't even row like honest folk, for, after the Finnish fashion, they took high and swift strokes, as if they were womenkind, and they all talked together, and made a noise while they rowed, instead of being 'silent in the boat.' But what impressed Eilert most of all was the fact that, in the Finnwoman's family, they practised sorcery and idolatry, or so folks said. He also heard tell of something beyond all question, and that was the shame of having Finn blood in one's veins, which also was the reason why the Finns were not as good as other honest folk, so that the magistrates gave them their own distinct burial-ground in the churchyard, and their own separate 'Finn-pens' in church. Eilert had seen this with his own eyes in the church at Berg.

All this made him very angry, for he could not help liking the Finn folks down yonder, and especially little Zilla. They two were always together: she knew such a lot about the Merman. Henceforth his conscience always plagued him when he played with her; and whenever she stared at him with her large black eyes while she told him tales, he used to begin to feel a little bit afraid, for at such times he reflected that she and her people belonged to the Damned, and that was why they knew so much about such things. But, on the other hand, the thought of it made him so bitterly angry, especially on her account. She, too, was frequently taken aback by his odd behaviour towards her, which she couldn't understand at all; and then, as was her wont, she would begin laughing at and teasing him by making him run after her, while she went and hid herself.

One day he found her sitting on a boulder by the sea-shore. She had in her lap an eider duck which had been shot, and could only have died quite recently, for it was still warm, and she wept bitterly over it. It was, she sobbed, the same bird which made its nest every year beneath the shelter of their outhouse – she knew it quite well, and she showed him a red-coloured feather in its white breast. It had been struck dead by a single shot, and only a single red drop had come out of it; it had tried to reach its nest, but had died on its way on the strand. She wept as if her heart would break, and dried her face with her hair in impetuous Finnish fashion. Eilert laughed at her as boys will, but he overdid it, and was very pale the whole time. He dared not tell her that that very day he had taken a random shot with his father's gun from behind the headland at a bird a long way off which was swimming ashore.

One autumn Eilert's father was downright desperate. Day after day on the fishing grounds his lines caught next to nothing, while he was forced to look on and see the Finn pull up one rich catch after another. He was sure, too, that he had noticed malicious gestures over in the Finn's boat. After that his whole house nourished a double bitterness against them; and when they talked it over in the evening, it was agreed, as a thing beyond all question, that Finnish sorcery had something to do with it. Against this there was only one remedy, and that was to rub corpse-mould on the lines; but one must beware of doing so, lest one should thereby offend the dead, and expose oneself to their vengeance, while the sea-folk would gain power over one at the same time.

Eilert bothered his head a good deal over all this; it almost seemed to him as if he had had a share in the deed, because he was on such a good footing with the Finn folks.

On the following Sunday both he and the Finn folks were at Berg church, and he secretly abstracted a handful of mould from one of the Finn graves, and put it in his pocket. The same evening, when they came home, he strewed the mould over his father's lines unobserved. And, oddly enough, the very next time his father cast his lines, as many fish were caught as in the good old times. But after this Eilert's anxiety became indescribable. He was especially cautious while they were working of an evening round the fireside, and it was dark in the distant corners of the room. He sat there with a piece of steel in his pocket. To beg 'forgiveness' of the dead is the only helpful means against the consequences of such deeds as his, otherwise one will be dragged off at night, by an invisible hand, to the churchyard, though one were lashed fast to the bed by a ship's hawser.

When Eilert, on the following 'Preaching Sunday,' went to church, he took very good care to go to the grave, and beg forgiveness of the dead.

As Eilert grew older, he got to understand that the Finn folks must, after all, be pretty much the same sort of people as his own folks at home; but, on the other hand, another thought was now uppermost in his mind, the thought, namely, that the Finns must be of an inferior stock, with a taint of disgrace about them. Nevertheless, he could not very well do without Zilla's society, and they were very much together as before, especially at the time of their confirmation.

But when Eilert became a man, and mixed more with the people of the parish, he began to fancy that this old companionship lowered him somewhat in the eyes of his neighbours. There was nobody who did not believe as a matter of course that there was something shameful about Finn blood, and he, therefore, always tried to avoid her in company.

The girl understood it all well enough, for latterly she took care to keep out of his way. Nevertheless, one day she came, as had been her wont from childhood, down to their house, and begged for leave to go in their boat when they rowed to church next day. There were lots of strangers present from the village, and so Eilert, lest folks should think that he and she were engaged, answered mockingly, so that every one could hear him, "that church-cleansing was perhaps a very good thing for Finnish sorcery," but she must find some one else to ferry her across.

After that she never spoke to him at all, but Eilert was anything but happy in consequence.

Now it happened one winter that Eilert was out all alone fishing for Greenland shark. A shark suddenly bit. The boat was small, and the fish was very big; but Eilert would not give in, and the end of the business was that his boat capsized.

All night long he lay on the top of it in the mist and a cruel sea. As now he sat there almost fainting for drowsiness, and dimly conscious that the end was not far off, and the sooner it came the better, he suddenly saw a man in seaman's clothes sitting astride the other end of the boat's bottom, and glaring savagely at him with a pair of dull reddish eyes. He was so heavy that the boat's bottom began to slowly sink down at end where he sat. Then he suddenly vanished, but it seemed to Eilert as if the sea-fog lifted a bit; the sea had all at once grown quite calm (at least, there was now only a gentle swell); and right in front of him lay a little low grey island, towards which the boat was slowly drifting.

The skerry was wet, as if the sea had only recently been flowing over it, and on it he saw a pale girl with such lovely eyes. She wore a green kirtle, and round her body a broad silver girdle with figures upon it, such as the Finns use. Her bodice was of tar-brown skin, and beneath her stay-laces, which seemed to be of green sea-grass, was a foam-white chemise, like the feathery breast of a sea-bird.

When the boat came drifting on to the island, she came down to him and said, as if she knew him quite well, "So you're come at last, Eilert; I've been waiting for you so long!"

It seemed to Eilert as if an icy cold shudder ran through his body when he took the hand which helped him ashore; but it was only for the moment, and he forgot it instantly.

In the midst of the island there was an opening with a brazen flight of steps leading down to a splendid cabin. Whilst he stood there thinking things over a bit, he saw two heavy dog-fish swimming close by – they were, at least, twelve to fourteen ells long.

As they descended, the dog-fish sank down too, each on one side of the brazen steps. Oddly enough, it looked as if the island was transparent. When the girl perceived that he was frightened, she told him that they were only two of her father's bodyguard, and shortly afterwards they disappeared. She then said that she wanted to take him to her father, who was waiting for them. She added that, if he didn't find the old gentleman precisely as handsome as he might expect, he had, nevertheless, no need to be frightened, nor was he to be astonished too much at what he saw.

He now perceived that he was under water, but, for all that, there was no sign of moisture. He was on a white sandy bottom, covered with chalk-white, red, blue, and silvery-bright shells. He saw meadows of sea-grass, mountains thick with woods of bushy seaweed and sea-wrack, and the fishes darted about on every side just as the birds swarm about the rocks that sea-fowl haunt.

As they two were thus walking along together she explained many things to him. High up he saw something which looked like a black cloud with a white lining, and beneath it moved backwards and forwards a shape resembling one of the dog-fish.

"What you see there is a vessel," said she; "there's nasty weather up there now, and beneath the boat goes he who was sitting along with you on the bottom of the boat just now. If it is wrecked, it will belong to us, and then you will not be able to speak to father to-day." As she said this there was a wild rapacious gleam in her eyes, but it was gone again immediately.

And, in point of fact, it was no easy matter to make out the meaning of her eyes. As a rule, they were unfathomably dark with the lustre of a night-billow through which the sea-fire sparkles; but, occasionally, when she laughed, they took a bright sea-green glitter, as when the sun shines deep down into the sea.

Now and again they passed by a boat or a vessel half buried in the sand, out and in of the cabin doors and windows of which fishes swam to and fro. Close by the wrecks wandered human shapes which seemed to consist of nothing but blue smoke. His conductress explained to him that these were the spirits of drowned men who had not had Christian burial – one must beware of them, for dead ones of this sort are malignant. They always know when one of their own race is about to be wrecked, and at such times they howl the death-warning of the Draug through the wintry nights.

Then they went further on their way right across a deep dark valley. In the rocky walls above him he saw a row of four-cornered white doors, from which a sort of glimmer, as from the northern lights, shot downwards through the darkness. This valley stretched in a north-eastwardly direction right under Finmark, she said, and inside the white doors dwelt the old Finn Kings who had perished on the sea. Then she went and opened the nearest of these doors – here, down in the salt ocean, was the last of the kings, who had capsized in the very breeze that he himself had conjured forth, but could not afterwards quell. There, on a block of stone, sat a wrinkled yellow Finn with running eyes and a polished dark-red crown. His large head rocked backwards and forwards on his withered neck, as if it were in the swirl of an ocean current. Beside him, on the same block, sat a still more shrivelled and yellow little woman, who also had a crown on, and her garments were covered with all sorts of coloured stones; she was stirring up a brew with a stick. If she only had fire beneath it, the girl told Eilert, she and her husband would very soon have dominion again over the salt sea, for the thing she was stirring about was magic stuff.

In the middle of a plain, which opened right before them at a turn of the road, stood a few houses together like a little town, and, a little further on, Eilert saw a church turned upside down, looking, with its long pointed tower, as if it were mirrored in the water. The girl explained to him that her father dwelt in these houses, and the church was one of the seven that stood in his realm, which extended all over Helgoland and Finmark. No service was held in them yet, but it would be held when the drowned bishop, who sat outside in a brown study, could only hit upon the name of the Lord that was to be served, and then all the Draugs would go to church. The bishop, she said, had been sitting and pondering the matter over these eight hundred years, so he would no doubt very soon get to the bottom of it. A hundred years ago the bishop had advised them to send up one of the Draugs to Rödö church to find out all about it; but every time the word he wanted was mentioned he couldn't catch the sound of it. In the mountain 'Kunnan' King Olaf had hung a church-bell of pure gold, and it is guarded by the first priest who ever came to Nordland, who stands there in a white chasuble.

On the day the priest rings the bell, Kunnan will become a big stone church, to which all Nordland, both above and below the sea, will resort. But time flies, and therefore all who come down here below are asked by the bishop if they can tell him that name.

At this Eilert felt very queer indeed, and he felt queerer still when he began reflecting and found, to his horror, that he also had forgotten that name.

While he stood there in thought, the girl looked at him so anxiously. It was almost as if she wanted to help him to find it and couldn't, and with that she all at once grew deadly pale.

The Draug's house, to which they now came, was built of boat's keels and large pieces of wreckage, in the interstices of which grew all sorts of sea-grass and slimy green stuff. Three monstrously heavy green posts, covered with shell-fish, formed the entrance, and the door consisted of planks which had sunk to the bottom and were full of clincher-nails. In the middle of it, like a knocker, was a heavy rusty iron mooring-ring, with the worn-away stump of a ship's hawser hanging to it. When they came up to it, a large black arm stretched out and opened the door.

They were now in a vaulted chamber, with fine shell-sand on the floor. In the corners lay all sorts of ropes, yarn, and boating-gear, and among them casks and barrels and various ship's inventories. On a heap of yarn, covered by an old red-patched sail, Eilert saw the Draug, a broad-shouldered, strongly built fellow, with a glazed hat shoved back on to the top of his head, with dark-red tangled hair and beard, small tearful dog-fish eyes, and a broad mouth, round which there lay for the moment a good-natured seaman's grin. The shape of his head reminded one somewhat of the big sort of seal which is called Klakkekal – his skin about the neck looked dark and shaggy, and the tops of his fingers grew together. He sat there with turned-down sea-boots on, and his thick grey woollen stockings reached right up to his thigh. He wore besides, plain freize clothes with bright glass buttons on his waistcoat. His spacious skin jacket was open, and round his neck he had a cheap red woollen scarf.

When Eilert came up, he made as if he would rise, and said good naturedly, "Good day, Eilert – you've certainly had a hard time of it to-day! Now you can sit down, if you like, and take a little grub. You want it, I'm sure;" and with that he squirted out a jet of tobacco juice like the spouting of a whale. With one foot, which for that special purpose all at once grew extraordinarily long, he fished out of a corner, in true Nordland style, the skull of a whale to serve as a chair for Eilert, and shoved forward with his hand a long ship's drawer full of first-rate fare. There was boiled groats with sirup, cured fish, oatcakes with butter, a large stack of flatcakes, and a multitude of the best hotel dishes besides.

The Merman bade him fall to and eat his fill, and ordered his daughter to bring out the last keg of Thronhjem aqua vitæ. "Of that sort the last is always the best," said he. When she came with it, Eilert thought he knew it again: it was his father's, and he himself, only a couple of days before, had bought the brandy from the wholesale dealer at Kvæford; but he didn't say anything about that now. The quid of tobacco, too, which the Draug turned somewhat impatiently in his mouth before he drank, also seemed to him wonderfully like the lead on his own line. At first it seemed to him as if he didn't quite know how to manage with the keg – his mouth was so sore; but afterwards things went along smoothly enough.

So they sat for some time pretty silently, and drank glass after glass, till Eilert began to think that they had had quite enough. So, when it came to his turn again, he said no, he would rather not; whereupon the Merman put the keg to his own mouth and drained it to the very dregs. Then he stretched his long arm up to the shelf, and took down another. He was now in a better humour, and began to talk of all sorts of things. But every time he laughed, Eilert felt queer, for the Draug's mouth gaped ominously wide, and showed a greenish pointed row of teeth, with a long interval between each tooth, so that they resembled a row of boat stakes.

The Merman drained keg after keg, and with every keg he grew more communicative. With an air as if he were thinking in his own mind of something very funny, he looked at Eilert for a while and blinked his eyes. Eilert didn't like his expression at all, for it seemed to him to say: "Now, my lad, whom I have fished up so nicely, look out for a change!" But instead of that he said, "You had a rough time of it last night, Eilert, my boy, but it wouldn't have gone so hard with you if you hadn't streaked the lines with corpse-mould, and refused to take my daughter to church" – here he suddenly broke off, as if he had said too much, and to prevent himself from completing the sentence, he put the brandy-keg to his mouth once more. But the same instant Eilert caught his glance, and it was so full of deadly hatred that it sent a shiver right down his back.

When, after a long, long draught, he again took the keg from his mouth, the Merman was again in a good humour, and told tale after tale. He stretched himself more and more heavily out on the sail, and laughed and grinned complacently at his own narrations, the humour of which was always a wreck or a drowning. From time to time Eilert felt the breath of his laughter, and it was like a cold blast. If folks would only give up their boats, he said, he had no very great desire for the crews. It was driftwood and ship-timber that he was after, and he really couldn't get on without them. When his stock ran out, boat or ship he must have, and surely nobody could blame him for it either.

With that he put the keg down empty, and became somewhat more gloomy again. He began to talk about what bad times they were for him and her. It was not as it used to be, he said. He stared blankly before him for a time, as if buried in deep thought. Then he stretched himself out backwards at full length, with feet extending right across the floor, and gasped so dreadfully that his upper and lower jaws resembled two boats' keels facing each other. Then he dozed right off with his neck turned towards the sail.

Then the girl again stood by Eilert's side, and bade him follow her.

They now went the same way back, and again ascended up to the skerry. Then she confided to him that the reason why her father had been so bitter against him was because he had mocked her with the taunt about church-cleansing when she had wanted to go to church – the name the folks down below wanted to know might, the Merman thought, be treasured up in Eilert's memory; but during their conversation on their way down to her father, she had perceived that he also had forgotten it. And now he must look to his life.

It would be a good deal later on in the day before the old fellow would begin inquiring about him. Till then he, Eilert, must sleep so as to have sufficient strength for his flight – she would watch over him.

The girl flung her long dark hair about him like a curtain, and it seemed to him that he knew those eyes so well. He felt as if his cheek were resting against the breast of a white sea-bird, it was so warm and sleep-giving – a single reddish feather in the middle of it recalled a dark memory. Gradually he sank off into a doze, and heard her singing a lullaby, which reminded him of the swell of the billows when it ripples up and down along the beach on a fine sunny day. It was all about how they had once been playmates together, and how later on he would have nothing to say to her. Of all she sang, however, he could only recollect the last words, which were these –

> "Oh, thousands of times have we played on the shore,
> And caught little fishes – dost mind it no more?
> We raced with the surf as it rolled at our feet,
> And the lurking old Merman we always did cheat.

"Yes, much shalt thou think of at my lullaby,
Whilst the billows do rock and the breezes do sigh.
Who sits now and weeps o'er thy cheeks? It is she
Who gave thee her soul, and whose soul lived in thee.

"But once as an eider-duck homeward I came
Thou didst lie 'neath a rock, with thy rifle didst aim;
In my breast thou didst strike me; the blood thou dost see
Is the mark that I bear, oh! beloved one, of thee."

Then it seemed to Eilert as if she sat and wept over him, and that, from time to time, a drop like a splash of sea-water fell upon his cheek. He felt now that he loved her so dearly.

The next moment he again became uneasy. He fancied that right up to the skerry came a whale, which said that he, Eilert, must now make haste; and when he stood on its back he stuck the shaft of an oar down its nostril, to prevent it from shooting beneath the sea again. He perceived that in this way the whale could be steered accordingly as he turned the oar to the right or left; and now they coasted the whole land of Finmark at such a rate that the huge mountain islands shot by them like little rocks. Behind him he saw the Draug in his half-boat, and he was going so swiftly that the foam stood mid-mast high. Shortly afterwards he was again lying on the skerry, and the lass smiled so blithely; she bent over him and said, "It is I, Eilert."

With that he awoke, and saw that the sunbeams were running over the wet skerry, and the Mermaid was still sitting by his side. But presently the whole thing changed before his eyes. It was the sun shining through the window-panes, on a bed in the Finn's hut, and by his side sat the Finn girl supporting his back, for they thought he was about to die. He had lain there delirious for six weeks, ever since the Finn had rescued him after capsizing, and this was his first moment of consciousness.

After that it seemed to him that he had never heard anything so absurd and presumptuous as the twaddle that would fix a stigma of shame or contempt on Finn blood, and the same spring he and the Finn girl Zilla were betrothed, and in the autumn they were married.

There were Finns in the bridal procession, and perhaps many said a little more about that than they need have done; but every one at the wedding agreed that the fiddler, who was also a Finn, was the best fiddler in the whole parish, and the bride the prettiest girl.

Hilda's Mermaid

LITTLE HILDA'S FATHER was a sailor and went away on long voyages. Hilda lived in a little cottage on the shore and used to spin and knit while her father was away, for her mother was dead and she had to be the housekeeper. Some days she would go out in her boat and fish, for Hilda was fond of the water. She was born and had always lived on the shore. When the water was very calm Hilda would look down into the blue depths and try to see a mermaid. She was very anxious to see one, she had heard her father tell such wonderful stories about them – how they sang, and combed their beautiful long hair.

One night when the wind was blowing and the rain was beating hard upon her window Hilda could hear the horn warning the sailors off the rocks. Hilda lighted her father's big lantern and ran down to the shore and hung it on the mast of a wreck which lay there, so the sailors would not run their ships upon it. Little Hilda was not afraid, for she had seen many such storms. When she returned to her cottage she found the door was unlatched, but thought the wind had blown it open. When she entered she found a little girl with beautiful hair sitting on the floor. She was a little frightened at first, for the girl wore a green dress and it was wound around her body in the strangest manner.

"I saw your light," said the child, "and came in. The wind blew me far up on shore. I should not have come up on a night like this, but a big wave looked so tempting I thought I would jump on it and have a nice ride, but it was nearer the shore than I thought it, and it landed me right near your door."

"Oh, my!" How Hilda's heart beat, for she knew this child must be a mermaid. Then she saw what she had thought a green dress was really her body and tail curled up on the floor, and it was beautiful as the lamp fell upon it and made it glisten.

"Will you have some of my supper?" asked Hilda, for she wanted to be hospitable, although she had not the least idea what mermaids ate.

"Thank you," answered the mermaid. "I am not very hungry, but if you could give me a seaweed sandwich I should like it."

Poor Hilda did not know what to do, but she went to the closet and brought out some bread, which she spread with nice fresh butter, and filled a glass with milk. She told her she was sorry, but she did not have any seaweed sandwiches, but she hoped she would like what she had prepared. The little mermaid ate it and Hilda was pleased.

"Do you live here all the time?" she asked Hilda. "I should think you would be very warm and want to be in the water part of the time."

Hilda told her she could not live in the water as she did, because her body was not like hers.

"Oh, I am so sorry!" replied the mermaid. "I hoped you would visit me some time; we have such good times, my sisters and I, under the sea."

"Tell me about your home," said Hilda.

"Come and sit beside me and I will," she replied.

Hilda sat upon the floor by her side. The mermaid felt of Hilda's clothes and thought it must be a bother to have so many clothes.

"How can you swim?" she asked.

Hilda told her she put on a bathing-suit, but the mermaid thought that a nuisance.

"I will tell you about our house first," she began. "Our father, Neptune, lives in a beautiful castle at the bottom of the sea. It is built of mother-of-pearl. All around the castle grow beautiful green things, and it has fine white sand around it also. All my sisters live there, and we are always glad to get home after we have been at the top of the ocean, it is so nice and cool in our home. The wind never blows there and the rain does not reach us."

"You do not mind being wet by the rain, do you?" asked Hilda.

"Oh no!" said the mermaid, "but the rain hurts us. It falls in little sharp points and feels like pebbles."

"How do you know how pebbles feel?" Hilda asked.

"Oh, sometimes the nereids come and bother us; they throw pebbles and stir up the water so we cannot see."

"Who are the nereids?" asked Hilda.

"They are the sea-nymphs; but we make the dogfish drive them away. We are sirens, and they are very jealous of us because we are more beautiful than they," said the mermaid.

Hilda thought she was rather conceited, but the little mermaid seemed to be quite unconscious she had conveyed that impression.

"How do you find your way home after you have been at the top of the ocean?" asked Hilda.

"Oh, when Father Neptune counts us and finds any missing he sends a whale to spout; sometimes he sends more than one, and we know where to dive when we see that."

"What do you eat besides seaweed sandwiches?" asked Hilda.

"Fish eggs, and very little fish," answered the mermaid. "When we have a party we have cake."

Hilda opened her eyes. "Where do you get cake?" she asked.

"We make it. We grind coral into flour and mix it with fish eggs; then we put it in a shell and send a mermaid to the top of the ocean with it and she holds it in the sun until it bakes. We go to the Gulf Stream and gather grapes and we have sea-foam and lemonade to drink."

"Lemonade?" said Hilda. "Where do you get your lemons?"

"Why, the sea-lemon!" replied the mermaid; "that is a small mussel-fish the colour of a lemon."

"What do you do at your parties – you cannot dance?" said Hilda.

"We swim to the music, circle around and dive and glide."

"But the music – where do you get musicians?" Hilda continued.

"We have plenty of music," replied the mermaid. "The sea-elephant trumpets for us; then there is the pipefish, the swordfish runs the scales of the sea-adder with his sword, the sea-shells blob, and altogether we have splendid music. But it is late, and we must not talk any more."

So the little mermaid curled herself up and soon they were asleep.

The sun shining in the window awakened Hilda next morning and she looked about her. The mermaid was not there, but Hilda was sure it had not been a dream, for she found pieces of seaweed on the floor, and every time she goes out in her boat she looks for her friend, and when the whales spout she knows they are telling the mermaids to come home.

The Huldrefish

IT WAS SUCH AN ODD TROUT that Nona hauled in at the end of his fishing-line. Large and fat, red spotted and shiny, it sprawled and squirmed, with its dirty yellow belly above the water, to wriggle off the hook. And when he got it into the boat, and took it off the hook, he saw that it had only two small slits where the eyes should have been.

It must be a huldrefish, thought one of the boatmen, for rumour had it that that lake was one of those which had a double bottom.

But Nona didn't trouble his head very much about what sort of a fish it was, so long as it was a big one. He was ravenously hungry, and bawled to them to row as rapidly as possible ashore so as to get it cooked.

He had been sitting the whole afternoon with empty lines out in the mountain lake there; but as for the trout, it was only an hour ago since it had been steering its way through the water with its rudder of a tail, and allowed itself to be fooled by a hook, and already it lay cooked red there on the dish.

But now Nona recollected about the strange eyes, and felt for them, and pricked away at its head with his fork. There was nothing but slits outside, and yet there was a sort of hard eyeball inside. The head was strangely shaped, and looked very peculiar in many respects.

He was vexed that he had not examined it more closely before it was cooked; it was not so easy now to make out what it really was. It had tasted first-rate, however, and that was something.

But at night there was, as it were, a gleam of bright water before his eyes, and he lay half asleep, thinking of the odd fish he had pulled up.

He was in his boat again, he thought, and it seemed to him as if his hands felt the fish wriggling and sprawling for its life, and shooting its snout backwards and forwards to get off the hook.

All at once it grew so heavy and strong that it drew the boat after it by the line.

It went along at a frightful speed, while the lake gradually diminished, as it were, and dried up.

There was an irresistible sucking of the water in the direction the fish went, which was towards a hole at the bottom of the lake like a funnel, and right into this hole went the boat.

It glided for a long time in a sort of twilight along a subterranean river, which dashed and splashed about him. The air that met him was, at first, chilly and cellar-like; gradually, however, it grew milder and milder, and warmer and warmer.

The stream now flowed along calmly and quietly, and broadened out continually till it fell into a large lake.

Beyond the borders of this lake, but only half visible in the gloom, stretched swamps and morasses, where he heard sounds as of huge beasts wading and trampling. Serpent like they rose and writhed with a crashing and splashing and snorting amidst the tepid mud and mire.

By the phosphorescent gleams he saw various fishes close to his boat, but all of them lacked eyes.

And he caught glimpses of the outlines of gigantic sea-serpents stretching far away into the darkness. He now understood that it was from down here that they pop up their heads off the coast in the dog days when the sea is warm.

The lindworm, with its flat head and duck's beak, darted after fish, and crept up to the surface of the earth through the slimy ways of mire and marsh.

Through the warm and choking gloom there came, from time to time, a cooling chilling blast from the cold curves and winds of the slimy and slippery greenish lichworm, which bores its way through the earth and eats away the coffins that are rotting in the churchyards.

Horrible shapeless monsters, with streaming manes, such as are said to sometimes appear in mountain tarns, writhed and wallowed and seized their prey in the fens and marshes.

And he caught glimpses of all sorts of humanlike creatures, such as fishermen and sailors meet and marvel at on the sea, and landsmen see outside the elfin mounds.

And, besides, that there was a soft whizzing and an endless hovering and swarming of beings, whose shapes were nevertheless invisible to the eye of man.

Then the boat glided into miry pulpy water, where her course tended downwards, and where the earth-vault above darkened as it sank lower and lower.

All at once a blinding strip of light shot down from a bright blue slit high, high, above him.

A stuffy vapour stood round about him. The water was as yellow and turbid as that which comes out of steam boilers.

And he called to mind the peculiar tepid undrinkable water which bubbles up by the side of artesian wells. It was quite hot. Up there they were boring down to a world of warm watercourses and liquid strata beneath the earth's crust.

Heat as from an oven rose up from the huge abysses and dizzying clefts, whilst mighty steaming waterfalls roared and shook the ground.

All at once he felt as if his body were breaking loose, freeing itself, and rising in the air. He had a feeling of infinite lightness, of a wondrous capability for floating in higher atmospheres and recovering equilibrium.

And, before he knew how it was, he found himself up on the earth again.

The Little Mermaid

FAR OUT IN the ocean, where the water is as blue as the prettiest cornflower, and as clear as crystal, it is very, very deep; so deep, indeed, that no cable could fathom it: many church steeples, piled one upon another, would not reach from the ground beneath to the surface of the water above. There dwell the Sea King and his subjects. We must not imagine that there is nothing at the bottom of the sea but bare yellow sand. No, indeed; the most singular flowers and plants grow there; the leaves and stems of which are so pliant, that the slightest agitation of the water causes them to stir as if they had life. Fishes, both large and small, glide between the branches, as birds fly among the trees here upon land. In the deepest spot of all, stands the castle of the Sea King. Its walls are built of coral, and the long, gothic windows are of the clearest amber. The roof is formed of shells, that open and close as the water flows over them. Their appearance is very beautiful, for in each lies a glittering pearl, which would be fit for the diadem of a queen.

The Sea King had been a widower for many years, and his aged mother kept house for him. She was a very wise woman, and exceedingly proud of her high birth; on that account she wore twelve oysters on her tail; while others, also of high rank, were only allowed to wear six. She was, however, deserving of very great praise, especially for her care of the little sea-princesses, her grand-daughters. They were six beautiful children; but the youngest was the prettiest of them all; her skin was as clear and delicate as a rose-leaf, and her eyes as blue as the deepest sea; but, like all the others, she had no feet, and her body ended in a fish's tail. All day long they played in the great halls of the castle, or among the living flowers that grew out of the walls. The large amber windows were open, and the fish swam in, just as the swallows fly into our houses when we open the windows, excepting that the fishes swam up to the princesses, ate out of their hands, and allowed themselves to be stroked. Outside the castle there was a beautiful garden, in which grew bright red and dark blue flowers, and blossoms like flames of fire; the fruit glittered like gold, and the leaves and stems waved to and fro continually. The earth itself was the finest sand, but blue as the flame of burning sulphur. Over everything lay a peculiar blue radiance, as if it were surrounded by the air from above, through which the blue sky shone, instead of the dark depths of the sea. In calm weather the sun could be seen, looking like a purple flower, with the light streaming from the calyx. Each of the young princesses had a little plot of ground in the garden, where she might dig and plant as she pleased. One arranged her flower-bed into the form of a whale; another thought it better to make hers like the figure of a little mermaid; but that of the youngest was round like the sun, and contained flowers as red as his rays at sunset. She was a strange child, quiet and thoughtful; and while her sisters would be delighted with the wonderful things which they obtained from the wrecks of vessels, she cared for nothing but her pretty red flowers, like the sun, excepting a beautiful marble statue. It was the representation of a handsome boy, carved out of pure white stone, which had fallen to the bottom of the sea from a wreck. She planted by the statue a rose-coloured weeping willow. It grew splendidly, and very soon hung its fresh branches over the statue, almost down to the blue sands. The shadow had a violet tint, and waved to and fro like the branches; it seemed as if the crown of the tree and the root were at play, and trying to kiss each other. Nothing gave her so much pleasure as to hear about the world above the sea. She made her old grandmother tell her all she knew of the ships and of the towns, the people and the animals. To her it seemed most wonderful and beautiful to hear that the flowers of the land should have fragrance, and not those below the sea; that the trees of the forest should be green; and that the fishes among the trees could sing so sweetly, that it was quite a pleasure to hear them. Her grandmother called the little birds fishes, or she would not have understood her; for she had never seen birds.

"When you have reached your fifteenth year," said the grand-mother, "you will have permission to rise up out of the sea, to sit on the rocks in the moonlight, while the great ships are sailing by; and then you will see both forests and towns."

In the following year, one of the sisters would be fifteen: but as each was a year younger than the other, the youngest would have to wait five years before her turn came to rise up from the bottom of the ocean, and see the earth as we do. However, each promised to tell the others what she saw on her first visit, and what she thought the most beautiful; for their grandmother could not tell them enough; there were so many things on which they wanted information. None of them longed so much for her turn to come as the youngest, she who had the longest time to wait, and who was so quiet and thoughtful. Many nights she stood by the open window, looking up through the dark blue water, and watching the fish as they splashed about with their fins and tails. She could see the moon and stars shining faintly; but through the water they looked larger than they do to our eyes. When something like a black cloud passed between her and them, she knew that it was either a whale swimming over her head, or a ship full of human beings, who never imagined that a pretty little mermaid was standing beneath them, holding out her white hands towards the keel of their ship.

As soon as the eldest was fifteen, she was allowed to rise to the surface of the ocean. When she came back, she had hundreds of things to talk about; but the most beautiful, she said, was to lie in the moonlight, on a sandbank, in the quiet sea, near the coast, and to gaze on a large town nearby, where the lights were twinkling like hundreds of stars; to listen to the sounds of the music, the noise of carriages, and the voices of human beings, and then to hear the merry bells peal out from the church steeples; and because she could not go near to all those wonderful things, she longed for them more than ever. Oh, did not the youngest sister listen eagerly to all these descriptions? and afterwards, when she stood at the open window looking up through the dark blue water, she thought of the great city, with all its bustle and noise, and even fancied she could hear the sound of the church bells, down in the depths of the sea.

In another year the second sister received permission to rise to the surface of the water, and to swim about where she pleased. She rose just as the sun was setting, and this, she said, was the most beautiful sight of all. The whole sky looked like gold, while violet and rose-coloured clouds, which she could not describe, floated over her; and, still more rapidly than the clouds, flew a large flock of wild swans towards the setting sun, looking like a long white veil across the sea. She also swam towards the sun; but it sunk into the waves, and the rosy tints faded from the clouds and from the sea.

The third sister's turn followed; she was the boldest of them all, and she swam up a broad river that emptied itself into the sea. On the banks she saw green hills covered with beautiful vines; palaces and castles peeped out from amid the proud trees of the forest; she heard the birds singing, and the rays of the sun were so powerful that she was obliged often to dive down under the water to cool her burning face. In a narrow creek she found a whole troop of little human children, quite naked, and sporting about in the water; she wanted to play with them, but they fled in a great fright; and then a little black animal came to the water; it was a dog, but she did not know that, for she had never before seen one. This animal barked at her so terribly that she became frightened, and rushed back to the open sea. But she said she should never forget the beautiful forest, the green hills, and the pretty little children who could swim in the water, although they had not fish's tails.

The fourth sister was more timid; she remained in the midst of the sea, but she said it was quite as beautiful there as nearer the land. She could see for so many miles around her, and the sky above looked like a bell of glass. She had seen the ships, but at such a great distance that they looked like sea-gulls. The dolphins sported in the waves, and the great whales spouted water from their nostrils till it seemed as if a hundred fountains were playing in every direction.

The fifth sister's birthday occurred in the winter; so when her turn came, she saw what the others had not seen the first time they went up. The sea looked quite green, and large icebergs were floating about, each like a pearl, she said, but larger and loftier than the churches built by men. They were of the most singular shapes, and glittered like diamonds. She had seated herself upon one of the largest, and let the wind play with her long hair, and she remarked that all the ships sailed by rapidly, and steered as far away as they could from the iceberg, as if they were afraid of it. Towards evening, as the sun went down, dark clouds covered the sky, the thunder rolled and the lightning flashed, and the red light glowed on the icebergs as they rocked and tossed on the heaving sea. On all the ships the sails were reefed with fear and trembling, while she sat calmly on the floating iceberg, watching the blue lightning, as it darted its forked flashes into the sea.

When first the sisters had permission to rise to the surface, they were each delighted with the new and beautiful sights they saw; but now, as grown-up girls, they could go when they pleased, and they had become indifferent about it. They wished themselves back again in the water, and after a month had passed they said it was much more beautiful down below, and pleasanter to be at home. Yet often, in the evening hours, the five sisters would twine their arms round each other, and rise to the surface, in a row. They had more beautiful voices than any human being could have; and before the approach of a storm, and when they expected a ship would be lost, they swam before the vessel, and sang sweetly of the delights to be found in the depths of the sea, and begging the sailors not to fear if they sank to the bottom. But the sailors could not understand the song, they took it for the howling of the storm. And these things were never to be beautiful for them; for if the ship sank, the men were drowned, and their dead bodies alone reached the palace of the Sea King.

When the sisters rose, arm-in-arm, through the water in this way, their youngest sister would stand quite alone, looking after them, ready to cry, only that the mermaids have no tears, and therefore they suffer more. "Oh, were I but fifteen years old," said she: "I know that I shall love the world up there, and all the people who live in it."

At last she reached her fifteenth year. "Well, now, you are grown up," said the old dowager, her grandmother; "so you must let me adorn you like your other sisters;" and she placed a wreath of white lilies in her hair, and every flower leaf was half a pearl. Then the old lady ordered eight great oysters to attach themselves to the tail of the princess to show her high rank.

"But they hurt me so," said the little mermaid.

"Pride must suffer pain," replied the old lady. Oh, how gladly she would have shaken off all this grandeur, and laid aside the heavy wreath! The red flowers in her own garden would have suited her much better, but she could not help herself: so she said, "Farewell," and rose as lightly as a bubble to the surface of the water. The sun had just set as she raised her head above the waves; but the clouds were tinted with crimson and gold, and through the glimmering twilight beamed the evening star in all its beauty. The sea was calm, and the air mild and fresh. A large ship, with three masts, lay becalmed on the water, with only one sail set; for not a breeze stirred, and the sailors sat idle on deck or amongst the rigging. There was music and song on board; and, as darkness came on, a hundred coloured lanterns were lighted, as if the flags of all nations waved in the air. The little mermaid swam close to the cabin windows; and now and then, as the waves lifted her up, she could look in through clear glass window-panes, and see a number of well-dressed people within. Among them was a young prince, the most beautiful of all, with large black eyes; he was sixteen years of age, and his birthday was being kept with much rejoicing. The sailors were dancing on deck, but when the prince came out of the cabin, more than a hundred rockets rose in the air, making it as bright as day. The little mermaid was so startled that she dived under water; and when she again stretched out her head, it appeared as if all the stars of heaven were falling around her, she had never seen such fireworks before. Great suns spurted fire about, splendid fireflies flew into the blue air, and everything was reflected in the clear, calm sea beneath. The ship itself was so brightly illuminated that all the people, and even the smallest rope, could be distinctly and plainly seen. And how handsome the young prince looked, as he pressed the hands of all present and smiled at them, while the music resounded through the clear night air.

It was very late; yet the little mermaid could not take her eyes from the ship, or from the beautiful prince. The coloured lanterns had been extinguished, no more rockets rose in the air, and the cannon had ceased firing; but the sea became restless, and a moaning, grumbling sound could be heard beneath the waves: still the little mermaid remained by the cabin window, rocking up and down on the water, which enabled her to look in. After a while, the sails were quickly unfurled, and the noble ship continued her passage; but soon the waves rose higher, heavy clouds darkened the sky, and lightning appeared in the distance. A dreadful storm was approaching; once more the sails were reefed, and the great ship pursued her flying course over the raging sea. The waves rose mountains high, as if they would have overtopped the mast; but the ship dived like a swan between them, and then rose again on their lofty, foaming crests. To the little mermaid this appeared pleasant sport; not so to the sailors. At length the ship groaned and creaked; the thick planks gave way under the lashing of the sea as it broke over the deck; the mainmast snapped asunder like a reed; the ship lay over on her side; and the water rushed in. The little mermaid now perceived that the crew were in danger; even she herself was obliged to be careful to avoid the beams and planks of the wreck which lay scattered on the water. At one moment it was so pitch dark that she could not see a single object, but a flash of lightning revealed the whole scene; she could see every one who had been on board excepting the prince; when the ship parted, she had seen him sink into the deep waves, and she was glad, for she thought he would now be with her; and then she remembered that human beings could not live in the water, so that when he got down to her father's palace he would be quite dead. But he must not die. So she swam about among the beams and planks which strewed the surface of the sea, forgetting that they could crush her to pieces. Then she dived deeply under the dark waters, rising and falling with the waves, till at length she managed to reach the young prince, who was fast losing the power of swimming in that stormy sea. His limbs were failing him, his beautiful eyes were closed, and he would have died had not the little mermaid come to his assistance. She held his head above the water, and let the waves drift them where they would.

In the morning the storm had ceased; but of the ship not a single fragment could be seen. The sun rose up red and glowing from the water, and its beams brought back the hue of health to the prince's cheeks; but his eyes remained closed. The mermaid kissed his high, smooth forehead, and stroked back his wet hair; he seemed to her like the marble statue in her little garden, and she kissed him again, and wished that he might live. Presently they came in sight of land; she saw lofty blue mountains, on which the white snow rested as if a flock of swans were lying upon them. Near the coast were beautiful green forests, and close by stood a large building, whether a church or a convent she could not tell. Orange and citron trees grew in the garden, and before the door stood lofty palms. The sea here formed a little bay, in which the water was quite still, but very deep; so she swam with the handsome prince to the beach, which was covered with fine, white sand, and there she laid him in the warm sunshine, taking care to raise his head higher than his body. Then bells sounded in the large white building, and a number of young girls came into the garden. The little mermaid swam out farther from the shore and placed herself between some high rocks that rose out of the water; then she covered her head and neck with the foam of the sea so that her little face might not be seen, and watched to see what would become of the poor prince. She did not wait long before she saw a young girl approach the spot where he lay. She seemed frightened at first, but only for a moment; then she fetched a number of people, and the mermaid saw that the prince came to life again, and smiled upon those who stood round him. But to her he sent no smile; he knew not that she had saved him. This made her very unhappy, and when he was led away into the great building, she dived down sorrowfully into the water, and returned to her father's castle. She had always been silent and thoughtful, and now she was more so than ever. Her sisters asked her what she had seen during her first visit to the surface of the water; but she would tell them nothing. Many an evening and morning did she rise to the place where she had left the prince. She saw the fruits in the garden ripen till they were gathered, the snow on the tops of the mountains melt away; but she never saw the prince, and therefore she returned home, always more sorrowful than before. It was her only comfort to sit in her own little garden, and fling her arm round the beautiful marble statue which was like the prince; but she gave up tending her flowers, and they grew in wild confusion over the paths, twining their long leaves and stems round the branches of the trees, so that the whole place became dark and gloomy. At length she could bear it no longer, and told one of her sisters all about it. Then the others heard the secret, and very soon it became known to two mermaids whose intimate friend happened to know who the prince was. She had also seen the festival on board ship, and she told them where the prince came from, and where his palace stood.

"Come, little sister," said the other princesses; then they entwined their arms and rose up in a long row to the surface of the water, close by the spot where they knew the prince's palace stood. It was built of bright yellow shining stone, with long flights of marble steps, one of which reached quite down to the sea. Splendid gilded cupolas rose over the roof, and between the pillars that surrounded the whole building stood life-like statues of marble. Through the clear crystal of the lofty windows could be seen noble rooms, with costly silk curtains and hangings of tapestry; while the walls were covered with beautiful paintings which were a pleasure to look at. In the centre of the largest saloon a fountain threw its sparkling jets high up into the glass cupola of the ceiling, through which the sun shone down upon the water and upon the beautiful plants growing round the basin of the fountain. Now that she knew where he lived, she spent many an evening and many a night on the water near the palace. She would swim much nearer the shore than any of the others ventured to do; indeed once she went quite up the narrow channel under the marble balcony, which threw a broad shadow on the water. Here she would sit and watch the young prince, who thought himself quite alone in the bright moonlight. She saw him many times of an evening sailing in a pleasant boat, with music playing and flags waving. She peeped out from among the green rushes, and if the wind caught her long silvery-white veil, those who saw it believed it to be a swan, spreading out its wings. On many a night, too, when the fishermen, with their torches, were out at sea, she heard them relate so many good things about the doings of the young prince, that she was glad she had saved his life when he had been tossed about half-dead on the waves. And she remembered that his head had rested on her bosom, and how heartily she had kissed him; but he knew nothing of all this, and could not even dream of her. She grew more and more fond of human beings, and wished more and more to be able to wander about with those whose world seemed to be so much larger than her own. They could fly over the sea in ships, and mount the high hills which were far above the clouds; and the lands they possessed, their woods and their fields, stretched far away beyond the reach of her sight. There was so much that she wished to know, and her sisters were unable to answer all her questions. Then she applied to her old grandmother, who knew all about the upper world, which she very rightly called the lands above the sea.

"If human beings are not drowned," asked the little mermaid, "can they live forever? do they never die as we do here in the sea?"

"Yes," replied the old lady, "they must also die, and their term of life is even shorter than ours. We sometimes live to three hundred years, but when we cease to exist here we only become the foam on the surface of the water, and we have not even a grave down here of those we love. We have not immortal souls, we shall never live again; but, like the green sea-weed, when once it has been cut off, we can never flourish more. Human beings, on the contrary, have a soul which lives forever, lives after the body has been turned to dust. It rises up through the clear, pure air beyond the glittering stars. As we rise out of the water, and behold all the land of the earth, so do they rise to unknown and glorious regions which we shall never see."

"Why have not we an immortal soul?" asked the little mermaid mournfully; "I would give gladly all the hundreds of years that I have to live, to be a human being only for one day, and to have the hope of knowing the happiness of that glorious world above the stars."

"You must not think of that," said the old woman; "we feel ourselves to be much happier and much better off than human beings."

"So I shall die," said the little mermaid, "and as the foam of the sea I shall be driven about never again to hear the music of the waves, or to see the pretty flowers nor the red sun. Is there anything I can do to win an immortal soul?"

"No," said the old woman, "unless a man were to love you so much that you were more to him than his father or mother; and if all his thoughts and all his love were fixed upon you, and the priest placed his right hand in yours, and he promised to be true to you here and hereafter, then his soul would glide into your body and you would obtain a share in the future happiness of mankind. He would give a soul to you and retain his own as well; but this can never happen. Your fish's tail, which amongst us is considered so beautiful, is thought on earth to be quite ugly; they do not know any better, and they think it necessary to have two stout props, which they call legs, in order to be handsome."

Then the little mermaid sighed, and looked sorrowfully at her fish's tail. "Let us be happy," said the old lady, "and dart and spring about during the three hundred years that we have to live, which is really quite long enough; after that we can rest ourselves all the better. This evening we are going to have a court ball."

It is one of those splendid sights which we can never see on earth. The walls and the ceiling of the large ball-room were of thick, but transparent crystal. May hundreds of colossal shells, some of a deep red, others of a grass green, stood on each side in rows, with blue fire in them, which lighted up the whole saloon, and shone through the walls, so that the sea was also illuminated. Innumerable fishes, great and small, swam past the crystal walls; on some of them the scales glowed with a purple brilliancy, and on others they shone like silver and gold. Through the halls flowed a broad stream, and in it danced the mermen and the mermaids to the music of their own sweet singing. No one on earth has such a lovely voice as theirs. The little mermaid sang more sweetly than them all. The whole court applauded her with hands and tails; and for a moment her heart felt quite gay, for she knew she had the loveliest voice of any on earth or in the sea. But she soon thought again of the world above her, for she could not forget the charming prince, nor her sorrow that she had not an immortal soul like his; therefore she crept away silently out of her father's palace, and while everything within was gladness and song, she sat in her own little garden sorrowful and alone. Then she heard the bugle sounding through the water, and thought – "He is certainly sailing above, he on whom my wishes depend, and in whose hands I should like to place the happiness of my life. I will venture all for him, and to win an immortal soul, while my sisters are dancing in my father's palace, I will go to the sea witch, of whom I have always been so much afraid, but she can give me counsel and help."

And then the little mermaid went out from her garden, and took the road to the foaming whirlpools, behind which the sorceress lived. She had never been that way before: neither flowers nor grass grew there; nothing but bare, grey, sandy ground stretched out to the whirlpool, where the water, like foaming mill-wheels, whirled round everything that it seized, and cast it into the fathomless deep. Through the midst of these crushing whirlpools the little mermaid was obliged to pass, to reach the dominions of the sea witch; and also for a long distance the only road lay right across a quantity of warm, bubbling mire, called by the witch her turfmoor. Beyond this stood her house, in the centre of a strange forest, in which all the trees and flowers were polypi, half animals and half plants; they looked like serpents with a hundred heads growing out of the ground. The branches were long slimy arms, with fingers like flexible worms, moving limb after limb from the root to the top. All that could be reached in the sea they seized upon, and held fast, so that it never escaped from their clutches. The little mermaid was so alarmed at what she saw, that she stood still, and her heart beat with fear, and she was very nearly turning back; but she thought of the prince, and of the human soul for which she longed, and her courage returned. She fastened her long flowing hair round her head, so that the polypi might not seize hold of it. She laid her hands together across her bosom, and then she darted forward as a fish shoots through the water, between the supple arms and fingers of the ugly polypi, which were stretched out on each side of her. She saw that each held in its grasp something it had seized with its numerous little arms, as if they were iron bands. The white skeletons of human beings who had perished at sea, and had sunk down into the deep waters, skeletons of land animals, oars, rudders, and chests of ships were lying tightly grasped by their clinging arms; even a little mermaid, whom they had caught and strangled; and this seemed the most shocking of all to the little princess.

She now came to a space of marshy ground in the wood, where large, fat water-snakes were rolling in the mire, and showing their ugly, drab-coloured bodies. In the midst of this spot stood a house, built with the bones of shipwrecked human beings. There sat the sea witch, allowing a toad to eat from her mouth, just as people sometimes feed a canary with a piece of sugar. She called the ugly water-snakes her little chickens, and allowed them to crawl all over her bosom.

"I know what you want," said the sea witch; "it is very stupid of you, but you shall have your way, and it will bring you to sorrow, my pretty princess. You want to get rid of your fish's tail, and to have two supports instead of it, like human beings on earth, so that the young prince may fall in love with you, and that you may have an immortal soul." And then the witch laughed so loud and disgustingly, that the toad and the snakes fell to the ground, and lay there wriggling about. "You are but just in time," said the witch; "for after sunrise to-morrow I should not be able to help you till the end of another year. I will prepare a draught for you, with which you must swim to land tomorrow before sunrise, and sit down on the shore and drink it. Your tail will then disappear, and shrink up into what mankind calls legs, and you will feel great pain, as if a sword were passing through you. But all who see you will say that you are the prettiest little human being they ever saw. You will still have the same floating gracefulness of movement, and no dancer will ever tread so lightly; but at every step you take it will feel as if you were treading upon sharp knives, and that the blood must flow. If you will bear all this, I will help you."

"Yes, I will," said the little princess in a trembling voice, as she thought of the prince and the immortal soul.

"But think again," said the witch; "for when once your shape has become like a human being, you can no more be a mermaid. You will never return through the water to your sisters, or to your father's palace again; and if you do not win the love of the prince, so that he is willing to forget his father and mother for your sake, and to love you with his whole soul, and allow the priest to join your hands that you may be man and wife, then you will never have an immortal soul. The first morning after he marries another your heart will break, and you will become foam on the crest of the waves."

"I will do it," said the little mermaid, and she became pale as death.

"But I must be paid also," said the witch, "and it is not a trifle that I ask. You have the sweetest voice of any who dwell here in the depths of the sea, and you believe that you will be able to charm the prince with it also, but this voice you must give to me; the best thing you possess will I have for the price of my draught. My own blood must be mixed with it, that it may be as sharp as a two-edged sword."

"But if you take away my voice," said the little mermaid, "what is left for me?"

"Your beautiful form, your graceful walk, and your expressive eyes; surely with these you can enchain a man's heart. Well, have you lost your courage? Put out your little tongue that I may cut it off as my payment; then you shall have the powerful draught."

"It shall be," said the little mermaid.

Then the witch placed her cauldron on the fire, to prepare the magic draught.

"Cleanliness is a good thing," said she, scouring the vessel with snakes, which she had tied together in a large knot; then she pricked herself in the breast, and let the black blood drop into it. The steam that rose formed itself into such horrible shapes that no one could look at them without fear. Every moment the witch threw something else into the vessel, and when it began to boil, the sound was like the weeping of a crocodile. When at last the magic draught was ready, it looked like the clearest water. "There it is for you," said the witch. Then she cut off the mermaid's tongue, so that she became dumb, and would never again speak or sing. "If the polypi should seize hold of you as you return through the wood," said the witch, "throw over them a few drops of the potion, and their fingers will be torn into a thousand pieces." But the little mermaid had no occasion to do this, for the polypi sprang back in terror when they caught sight of the glittering draught, which shone in her hand like a twinkling star.

So she passed quickly through the wood and the marsh, and between the rushing whirlpools. She saw that in her father's palace the torches in the ballroom were extinguished, and all within asleep; but she did not venture to go in to them, for now she was dumb and going to leave them forever, she felt as if her heart would break. She stole into the garden, took a flower from the flower-beds of each of her sisters, kissed her hand a thousand times towards the palace, and then rose up through the dark blue waters. The sun had not risen when she came in sight of the prince's palace, and approached the beautiful marble steps, but the moon shone clear and bright. Then the little mermaid drank the magic draught, and it seemed as if a two-edged sword went through her delicate body: she fell into a swoon, and lay like one dead. When the sun arose and shone over the sea, she recovered, and felt a sharp pain; but just before her stood the handsome young prince. He fixed his coal-black eyes upon her so earnestly that she cast down her own, and then became aware that her fish's tail was gone, and that she had as pretty a pair of white legs and tiny feet as any little maiden could have; but she had no clothes, so she wrapped herself in her long, thick hair. The prince asked her who she was, and where she came from, and she looked at him mildly and sorrowfully with her deep blue eyes; but she could not speak. Every step she took was as the witch had said it would be, she felt as if treading upon the points of needles or sharp knives; but she bore it willingly, and stepped as lightly by the prince's side as a soap-bubble, so that he and all who saw her wondered at her graceful-swaying movements. She was very soon arrayed in costly robes of silk and muslin, and was the most beautiful creature in the palace; but she was dumb, and could neither speak nor sing.

Beautiful female slaves, dressed in silk and gold, stepped forward and sang before the prince and his royal parents: one sang better than all the others, and the prince clapped his hands and smiled at her. This was great sorrow to the little mermaid; she knew how much more sweetly she herself could sing once, and she thought, "Oh if he could only know that! I have given away my voice forever, to be with him."

The slaves next performed some pretty fairy-like dances, to the sound of beautiful music. Then the little mermaid raised her lovely white arms, stood on the tips of her toes, and glided over the floor, and danced as no one yet had been able to dance. At each moment her beauty became more revealed, and her expressive eyes appealed more directly to the heart than the songs of the slaves. Every one was enchanted, especially the prince, who called her his little foundling; and she danced again quite readily, to please him, though each time her foot touched the floor it seemed as if she trod on sharp knives.

The prince said she should remain with him always, and she received permission to sleep at his door, on a velvet cushion. He had a page's dress made for her, that she might accompany him on horseback. They rode together through the sweet-scented woods, where the green boughs touched their shoulders, and the little birds sang among the fresh leaves. She climbed with the prince to the tops of high mountains; and although her tender feet bled so that even her steps were marked, she only laughed, and followed him till they could see the clouds beneath them looking like a flock of birds travelling to distant lands. While at the prince's palace, and when all the household were asleep, she would go and sit on the broad marble steps; for it eased her burning feet to bathe them in the cold sea-water; and then she thought of all those below in the deep.

Once during the night her sisters came up arm-in-arm, singing sorrowfully, as they floated on the water. She beckoned to them, and then they recognized her, and told her how she had grieved them. After that, they came to the same place every night; and once she saw in the distance her old grandmother, who had not been to the surface of the sea for many years, and the old Sea King, her father, with his crown on his head. They stretched out their hands towards her, but they did not venture so near the land as her sisters did.

As the days passed, she loved the prince more fondly, and he loved her as he would love a little child, but it never came into his head to make her his wife; yet, unless he married her, she could not receive an immortal soul; and, on the morning after his marriage with another, she would dissolve into the foam of the sea.

"Do you not love me the best of them all?" the eyes of the little mermaid seemed to say, when he took her in his arms, and kissed her fair forehead.

"Yes, you are dear to me," said the prince; "for you have the best heart, and you are the most devoted to me; you are like a young maiden whom I once saw, but whom I shall never meet again. I was in a ship that was wrecked, and the waves cast me ashore near a holy temple, where several young maidens performed the service. The youngest of them found me on the shore, and saved my life. I saw her but twice, and she is the only one in the world whom I could love; but you are like her, and you have almost driven her image out of my mind. She belongs to the holy temple, and my good fortune has sent you to me instead of her; and we will never part."

"Ah, he knows not that it was I who saved his life," thought the little mermaid. "I carried him over the sea to the wood where the temple stands: I sat beneath the foam, and watched till the human beings came to help him. I saw the pretty maiden that he loves better than he loves me;" and the mermaid sighed deeply, but she could not shed tears. "He says the maiden belongs to the holy temple, therefore she will never return to the world. They will meet no more: while I am by his side, and see him every day. I will take care of him, and love him, and give up my life for his sake."

Very soon it was said that the prince must marry, and that the beautiful daughter of a neighbouring king would be his wife, for a fine ship was being fitted out. Although the prince gave out that he merely intended to pay a visit to the king, it was generally supposed that he really went to see his daughter. A great company were to go with him. The little mermaid smiled, and shook her head. She knew the prince's thoughts better than any of the others.

"I must travel," he had said to her; "I must see this beautiful princess; my parents desire it; but they will not oblige me to bring her home as my bride. I cannot love her; she is not like the beautiful maiden in the temple, whom you resemble. If I were forced to choose a bride, I would rather choose you, my dumb foundling, with those expressive eyes." And then he kissed her rosy mouth, played with her long waving hair, and laid his head on her heart, while she dreamed of human happiness and an immortal soul. "You are not afraid of the sea, my dumb child," said he, as they stood on the deck of the noble ship which was to carry them to the country of the neighbouring king. And then he told her of storm and of calm, of strange fishes in the deep beneath them, and of what the divers had seen there; and she smiled at his descriptions, for she knew better than any one what wonders were at the bottom of the sea.

In the moonlight, when all on board were asleep, excepting the man at the helm, who was steering, she sat on the deck, gazing down through the clear water. She thought she could distinguish her father's castle, and upon it her aged grandmother, with the silver crown on her head, looking through the rushing tide at the keel of the vessel. Then her sisters came up on the waves, and gazed at her mournfully, wringing their white hands. She beckoned to them, and smiled, and wanted to tell them how happy and well off she was; but the cabin-boy approached, and when her sisters dived down he thought it was only the foam of the sea which he saw.

The next morning the ship sailed into the harbour of a beautiful town belonging to the king whom the prince was going to visit. The church bells were ringing, and from the high towers sounded a flourish of trumpets; and soldiers, with flying colours and glittering bayonets, lined the rocks through which they passed. Every day was a festival; balls and entertainments followed one another.

But the princess had not yet appeared. People said that she was being brought up and educated in a religious house, where she was learning every royal virtue. At last she came. Then the little mermaid, who was very anxious to see whether she was really beautiful, was obliged to acknowledge that she had never seen a more perfect vision of beauty. Her skin was delicately fair, and beneath her long dark eye-lashes her laughing blue eyes shone with truth and purity.

"It was you," said the prince, "who saved my life when I lay dead on the beach," and he folded his blushing bride in his arms. "Oh, I am too happy," said he to the little mermaid; "my fondest hopes are all fulfilled. You will rejoice at my happiness; for your devotion to me is great and sincere."

The little mermaid kissed his hand, and felt as if her heart were already broken. His wedding morning would bring death to her, and she would change into the foam of the sea. All the church bells rung, and the heralds rode about the town proclaiming the betrothal. Perfumed oil was burning in costly silver lamps on every altar. The priests waved the censers, while the bride and bridegroom joined their hands and received the blessing of the bishop. The little mermaid, dressed in silk and gold, held up the bride's train; but her ears heard nothing of the festive music, and her eyes saw not the holy ceremony; she thought of the night of death which was coming to her, and of all she had lost in the world. On the same evening the bride and bridegroom went on board ship; cannons were roaring, flags waving, and in the centre of the ship a costly tent of purple and gold had been erected. It contained elegant couches, for the reception of the bridal pair during the night. The ship, with swelling sails and a favourable wind, glided away smoothly and lightly over the calm sea. When it grew dark a number of coloured lamps were lit, and the sailors danced merrily on the deck. The little mermaid could not help thinking of her first rising out of the sea, when she had seen similar festivities and joys; and she joined in the dance, poised herself in the air as a swallow when he pursues his prey, and all present cheered her with wonder. She had never danced so elegantly before. Her tender feet felt as if cut with sharp knives, but she cared not for it; a sharper pang had pierced through her heart. She knew this was the last evening she should ever see the prince, for whom she had forsaken her kindred and her home; she had given up her beautiful voice, and suffered unheard-of pain daily for him, while he knew nothing of it. This was the last evening that she would breathe the same air with him, or gaze on the starry sky and the deep sea; an eternal night, without a thought or a dream, awaited her: she had no soul and now she could never win one. All was joy and gayety on board ship till long after midnight; she laughed and danced with the rest, while the thoughts of death were in her heart. The prince kissed his beautiful bride, while she played with his raven hair, till they went arm-in-arm to rest in the splendid tent. Then all became still on board the ship; the helmsman, alone awake, stood at the helm. The little mermaid leaned her white arms on the edge of the vessel, and looked towards the east for the first blush of morning, for that first ray of dawn that would bring her death. She saw her sisters rising out of the flood: they were as pale as herself; but their long beautiful hair waved no more in the wind, and had been cut off.

"We have given our hair to the witch," said they, "to obtain help for you, that you may not die to-night. She has given us a knife: here it is, see it is very sharp. Before the sun rises you must plunge it into the heart of the prince; when the warm blood falls upon your feet they will grow together again, and form into a fish's tail, and you will be once more a mermaid, and return to us to live out your three hundred years before you die and change into the salt sea foam. Haste, then; he or you must die before sunrise. Our old grandmother moans so for you, that her white hair is falling off from sorrow, as ours fell under the witch's scissors. Kill the prince and come back; hasten: do you not see the first red streaks in the sky? In a few minutes the sun will rise, and you must die." And then they sighed deeply and mournfully, and sank down beneath the waves.

The little mermaid drew back the crimson curtain of the tent, and beheld the fair bride with her head resting on the prince's breast. She bent down and kissed his fair brow, then looked at the sky on which the rosy dawn grew brighter and brighter; then she glanced at the sharp knife, and again fixed her eyes on the prince, who whispered the name of his bride in his dreams. She was in his thoughts, and the knife trembled in the hand of the little mermaid: then she flung it far away from her into the waves; the water turned red where it fell, and the drops that spurted up looked like blood. She cast one more lingering, half-fainting glance at the prince, and then threw herself from the ship into the sea, and thought her body was dissolving into foam. The sun rose above the waves, and his warm rays fell on the cold foam of the little mermaid, who did not feel as if she were dying. She saw the bright sun, and all around her floated hundreds of transparent beautiful beings; she could see through them the white sails of the ship, and the red clouds in the sky; their speech was melodious, but too ethereal to be heard by mortal ears, as they were also unseen by mortal eyes. The little mermaid perceived that she had a body like theirs, and that she continued to rise higher and higher out of the foam. "Where am I?" asked she, and her voice sounded ethereal, as the voice of those who were with her; no earthly music could imitate it.

"Among the daughters of the air," answered one of them. "A mermaid has not an immortal soul, nor can she obtain one unless she wins the love of a human being. On the power of another hangs her eternal destiny. But the daughters of the air, although they do not possess an immortal soul, can, by their good deeds, procure one for themselves. We fly to warm countries, and cool the sultry air that destroys mankind with the pestilence. We carry the perfume of the flowers to spread health and restoration. After we have striven for three hundred years to all the good in our power, we receive an immortal soul and take part in the happiness of mankind. You, poor little mermaid, have tried with your whole heart to do as we are doing; you have suffered and endured and raised yourself to the spirit-world by your good deeds; and now, by striving for three hundred years in the same way, you may obtain an immortal soul."

The little mermaid lifted her glorified eyes towards the sun, and felt them, for the first time, filling with tears. On the ship, in which she had left the prince, there were life and noise; she saw him and his beautiful bride searching for her; sorrowfully they gazed at the pearly foam, as if they knew she had thrown herself into the waves. Unseen she kissed the forehead of the bride, and fanned the prince, and then mounted with the other children of the air to a rosy cloud that floated through the aether.

"After three hundred years, thus shall we float into the kingdom of heaven," said she. "And we may even get there sooner," whispered one of her companions. "Unseen we can enter the houses of men, where there are children, and for every day on which we find a good child, who is the joy of his parents and deserves their love, our time of probation is shortened. The child does not know, when we fly through the room, that we smile with joy at his good conduct, for we can count one year less of our three hundred years. But when we see a naughty or a wicked child, we shed tears of sorrow, and for every tear a day is added to our time of trial!"

The Serpent of the Sea

IN THE TIMES OF OUR FOREFATHERS, under Thunder Mountain was a village called K'iákime ('Home of the Eagles'). It is now in ruins; the roofs are gone, the ladders have decayed, the hearths grown cold. But when it was all still perfect, and, as it were, new, there lived in this village a maiden, the daughter of the priest-chief. She was beautiful, but possessed of this peculiarity of character: There was a sacred spring of water at the foot of the terrace whereon stood the town. We now call it the Pool of the Apaches; but then it was sacred to Kólowissi (the Serpent of the Sea).

Now, at this spring the girl displayed her peculiarity, which was that of a passion for neatness and cleanliness of person and clothing. She could not endure the slightest speck or particle of dust or dirt upon her clothes or person, and so she spent most of her time in washing all the things she used and in bathing herself in the waters of this spring.

Now, these waters, being sacred to the Serpent of the Sea, should not have been defiled in this way. As might have been expected, Kólowissi became troubled and angry at the sacrilege committed in the sacred waters by the maiden, and he said: "Why does this maiden defile the sacred waters of my spring with the dirt of her apparel and the dun of her person? I must see to this." So he devised a plan by which to prevent the sacrilege and to punish its author.

When the maiden came again to the spring, what should she behold but a beautiful little child seated amidst the waters, splashing them, cooing and smiling. It was the Sea Serpent, wearing the semblance of a child – for a god may assume any form at its pleasure, you know. There sat the child, laughing and playing in the water. The girl looked around in all directions – north, south, east, and west – but could see no one, nor any traces of persons who might have brought hither the beautiful little child. She said to herself: "I wonder whose child this may be! It would seem to be that of some unkind and cruel mother, who has deserted it and left it here to perish. And the poor little child does not yet know that it is left all alone. Poor little thing! I will take it in my arms and care for it."

The maiden then talked softly to the young child, and took it in her arms, and hastened with it up the hill to her house, and, climbing up the ladder, carried the child in her arms into the room where she slept.

Her peculiarity of character, her dislike of all dirt or dust, led her to dwell apart from the rest of her family, in a room by herself above all of the other apartments.

She was so pleased with the child that when she had got him into her room she sat down on the floor and played with him, laughing at his pranks and smiling into his face; and he answered her in baby fashion with cooings and smiles of his own, so that her heart became very happy and loving. So it happened that thus was she engaged for a long while and utterly unmindful of the lapse of time.

Meanwhile, the younger sisters had prepared the meal, and were awaiting the return of the elder sister.

"Where, I wonder, can she be?" one of them asked.

"She is probably down at the spring," said the old father; "she is bathing and washing her clothes, as usual, of course! Run down and call her."

But the younger sister, on going, could find no trace of her at the spring. So she climbed the ladder to the private room of this elder sister, and there found her, as has been told, playing with the little child. She hastened back to inform her father of what she had seen. But the old man sat silent and thoughtful. He knew that the waters of the spring were sacred. When the rest of the family were excited, and ran to behold the pretty prodigy, he cried out, therefore: "Come back! come back! Why do you make fools of yourselves? Do you suppose any mother would leave her own child in the waters of this or any other spring? There is something more of meaning than seems in all this."

When they again went and called the maiden to come down to the meal spread for her, she could not be induced to leave the child.

"See! it is as you might expect," said the father. "A woman will not leave a child on any inducement; how much less her own."

The child at length grew sleepy. The maiden placed it on a bed, and, growing sleepy herself, at length lay by its side and fell asleep. Her sleep was genuine, but the sleep of the child was feigned.

The child became elongated by degrees, as it were, fulfilling some horrible dream, and soon appeared as an enormous Serpent that coiled itself round and round the room until it was full of scaly, gleaming circles. Then, placing its head near the head of the maiden, the great Serpent surrounded her with its coils, taking finally its own tail in its mouth.

The night passed, and in the morning when the breakfast was prepared, and yet the maiden did not descend, and the younger sisters became impatient at the delay, the old man said: "Now that she has the child to play with, she will care little for aught else. That is enough to occupy the entire attention of any woman."

But the little sister ran up to the room and called. Receiving no answer, she tried to open the door; she could not move it, because the Serpent's coils filled the room and pressed against it. She pushed the door with all her might, but it could not be moved. She again and again called her sister's name, but no response came. Beginning now to be frightened, she ran to the skyhole over the room in which she had left the others and cried out for help. They hastily joined her – all save the old father – and together were able to press the door sufficiently to get a glimpse of the great scales and folds of the Serpent. Then the women all ran screaming to the old father. The old man, priest and sage as he was, quieted them with these words: "I expected as much as this from the first report which you gave me. It was impossible, as I then said, that a woman should be so foolish as to leave her child playing even near the waters of the spring. But it is not impossible, it seems, that one should be so foolish as to take into her arms a child found as this one was."

Thereupon he walked out of the house, deliberately and thoughtful, angry in his mind against his eldest daughter. Ascending to her room, he pushed against the door and called to the Serpent of the Sea: "Oh, Kólowissi! It is I, who speak to thee, O Serpent of the Sea I, thy priest. Let, I pray thee, let my child come to me again, and I will make atonement for her errors. Release her, though she has been so foolish, for she is thine, absolutely thine. But let her return once more to us that we may make atonement to thee more amply." So prayed the priest to the Serpent of the Sea.

When he had done this the great Serpent loosened his coils, and as he did so the whole building shook violently, and all the villagers became aware of the event, and trembled with fear.

The maiden at once awoke and cried piteously to her father for help.

"Come and release me, oh, my father! Come and release me!" she cried.

As the coils loosened she found herself able to rise. No sooner had she done this than the great Serpent bent the folds of his large coils nearest the doorway upward so that they formed an arch. Under this, filled with terror, the girl passed. She was almost stunned with the dread din of the monster's scales rasping past one another with a noise like the sound of flints trodden under the feet of a rapid runner, and once away from the writhing mass of coils, the poor maiden ran like a frightened deer out of the doorway, down the ladder and into the room below, casting herself on the breast of her mother.

But the priest still remained praying to the Serpent; and he ended his prayer as he had begun it, saying: "It shall be even as I have said; she shall be thine!"

He then went away and called the two warrior priest-chiefs of the town, and these called together all the other priests in sacred council. Then they performed the solemn ceremonies of the sacred rites – preparing plumes, prayer-wands, and offerings of treasure.

After four days of labour, these things they arranged and consecrated to the Serpent of the Sea. On that morning the old priest called his daughter and told her she must make ready to take these sacrifices and yield them up, even with herself – most precious of them all – to the great Serpent of the Sea; that she must yield up also all thoughts of her people and home forever, and go hence to the house of the great Serpent of the Sea, even in the Waters of the World. "For it seems," said he, "to have been your desire to do thus, as manifested by your actions. You used even the sacred water for profane purposes; now this that I have told you is inevitable. Come; the time when you must prepare yourself to depart is near at hand."

She went forth from the home of her childhood with sad cries, clinging to the neck of her mother and shivering with terror. In the plaza, amidst the lamentations of all the people, they dressed her in her sacred cotton robes of ceremonial, embroidered elaborately, and adorned her with earrings, bracelets, beads – many beautiful, precious things. They painted her cheeks with red spots as if for a dance; they made a road of sacred meal toward the Door of the Serpent of the Sea – a distant spring in our land known to this day as the Doorway to the Serpent of the Sea – four steps toward this spring did they mark in sacred terraces on the ground at the western way of the plaza. And when they had finished the sacred road, the old priest, who never shed one tear, although all the villagers wept sore – for the maiden was very beautiful – instructed his daughter to go forth on the terraced road, and, standing there, call the Serpent to come to her.

Then the door opened, and the Serpent descended from the high room where he was coiled, and, without using ladders, let his head and breast down to the ground in great undulations. He placed his head on the shoulder of the maiden, and the word was given – the word: "It is time" – and the maiden slowly started toward the west, cowering beneath her burden; but whenever she staggered with fear and weariness and was like to wander from the way, the Serpent gently pushed her onward and straightened her course.

Thus they went toward the river trail and in it, on and over the Mountain of the Red Paint; yet still the Serpent was not all uncoiled from the maiden's room in the house, but continued to crawl forth until they were past the mountain – when the last of his length came forth. Here he began to draw himself together again and to assume a new shape. So that ere long his serpent form contracted, until, lifting his head from the maiden's shoulder, he stood up, in form a beautiful youth in sacred gala attire! He placed the scales of his serpent form, now small, under his flowing mantle, and called out to the maiden in a hoarse, hissing voice: "Let us speak one to the other. Are you tired, girl?" Yet she never moved her head, but plodded on with her eyes cast down.

"Are you weary, poor maiden?" – then he said in a gentler voice, as he arose erect and fell a little behind her, and wrapped his scales more closely in his blanket – and he was now such a splendid and brave hero, so magnificently dressed! And he repeated, in a still softer voice: "Are you still weary, poor maiden?"

At first she dared not look around, though the voice, so changed, sounded so far behind her and thrilled her wonderfully with its kindness. Yet she still felt the weight on her shoulder, the weight of that dreaded Serpent's head; for you know after one has carried a heavy burden on his shoulder or back, if it be removed he does not at once know that it is taken away; it seems still to oppress and pain him. So it was with her; but at length she turned around a little and saw a young man – a brave and handsome young man.

"May I walk by your side?" said he, catching her eye. "Why do you not speak with me?"

"I am filled with fear and sadness and shame," said she.

"Why?" asked he. "What do you fear?"

"Because I came with a fearful creature forth from my home, and he rested his head upon my shoulder, and even now I feel his presence there," said she, lifting her hand to the place where his head had rested, even still fearing that it might be there."

"But I came all the way with you," said he, "and I saw no such creature as you describe."

Upon this she stopped and turned back and looked again at him, and said: "You came all the way? I wonder where this fearful being has gone!"

He smiled, and replied: "I know where he has gone."

"Ah, youth and friend, will he now leave me in peace," said she, "and let me return to the home of my people?"

"No," replied he, "because he thinks very much of you."

"Why not? Where is he?"

"He is here," said the youth, smiling, and laying his hand on his own heart. "I am he."

"You are he?" cried the maiden. Then she looked at him again, and would not believe him.

"Yea, my maiden, I am he!" said he. And he drew forth from under his flowing mantle the shrivelled serpent scales, and showed them as proofs of his word. It was wonderful and beautiful to the maiden to see that he was thus, a gentle being; and she looked at him long.

Then he said: "Yes, I am he. I love you, my maiden! Will you not haply come forth and dwell with me? Yes, you will go with me, and dwell with me, and I will dwell with you, and I will love you. I dwell not now, but ever, in all the Waters of the World, and in each particular water. In all and each you will dwell with me forever, and we will love each other."

Behold! As they journeyed on, the maiden quite forgot that she had been sad; she forgot her old home, and followed and descended with him into the Doorway of the Serpent of the Sea and dwelt with him ever after.

It was thus in the days of the ancients. Therefore the ancients, no less than ourselves, avoided using springs, except for the drinking of their water; for to this day we hold the flowing springs the most precious things on earth, and therefore use them not for any profane purposes whatsoever.

The Talking Fish

LONG, LONG BEFORE your great-grandfather was born there lived in the village of Everlasting Happiness two men called Li and Sing. Now, these two men were close friends, living together in the same house. Before settling down in the village of Everlasting Happiness they had ruled as high officials for more than twenty years. They had often treated the people very harshly, so that everybody, old and young, disliked and hated them. And yet, by robbing the wealthy merchants and by cheating the poor, these two evil companions had become rich, and it was in order to spend their ill-gotten gains in idle amusements that they sought out the village of Everlasting Happiness. "For here," said they, "we can surely find that joy which has been denied us in every other place. Here we shall no longer be scorned by men and reviled by women."

Consequently these two men bought for themselves the finest house in the village, furnished it in the most elegant manner, and decorated the walls with scrolls filled with wise sayings and pictures by famous artists. Outside there were lovely gardens filled with flowers and birds, and oh, ever so many trees with queer twisted branches growing in the shape of tigers and other wild animals.

Whenever they felt lonely Li and Sing invited rich people of the neighbourhood to come and dine with them, and after they had eaten, sometimes they would go out upon the little lake in the centre of their estate, rowing in an awkward flat-bottomed boat that had been built by the village carpenter.

One day, on such an occasion, when the sun had been beating down fiercely upon the clean-shaven heads of all those on the little barge, for you must know this was long before the day when hats were worn – at least, in the village of Everlasting Happiness – Mr. Li was suddenly seized with a giddy feeling, which rapidly grew worse and worse until he was in a burning fever.

"Snake's blood mixed with powdered deer-horn is the thing for him," said the wise-looking doctor who was called in, peering at Li carefully through his huge glasses, "Be sure," he continued, addressing Li's personal attendant, and, at the same time, snapping his long finger-nails nervously, "be sure, above all, not to leave him alone, for he is in danger of going raving mad at any moment, and I cannot say what he may do if he is not looked after carefully. A man in his condition has no more sense than a baby."

Now, although these words of the doctor's really made Mr. Li angry, he was too ill to reply, for all this time his head had been growing hotter and hotter, until at last a feverish sleep overtook him. No sooner had he closed his eyes than his faithful servant, half-famished, rushed out of the room to join his fellows at their mid-day meal.

Li awoke with a start. He had slept only ten minutes. "Water, water," he moaned, "bathe my head with cold water. I am half dead with pain!" But there was no reply, for the attendant was dining happily with his fellows.

"Air, air," groaned Mr. Li, tugging at the collar of his silk shirt. "I'm dying for water. I'm starving for air. This blazing heat will kill me. It is hotter than the Fire god himself ever dreamed of making it. Wang, Wang!" clapping his hands feebly and calling to his servant, "air and water, air and water!"

But still no Wang.

At last, with the strength that is said to come from despair, Mr. Li arose from his couch and staggered toward the doorway. Out he went into the paved courtyard, and then, after only a moment's hesitation, made his way across it into a narrow passage that led into the lake garden.

"What do they care for a man when he is sick?" he muttered. "My good friend Sing is doubtless even now enjoying his afternoon nap, with a servant standing by to fan him, and a block of ice near his head to cool the air. What does he care if I die of a raging fever? Doubtless he expects to inherit all my money. And my servants! That rascal Wang has been with me these ten years, living on me and growing lazier every season! What does he care if I pass away? Doubtless he is certain that Sing's servants will think of something for him to do, and he will have even less work than he has now. Water, water! I shall die if I don't soon find a place to soak myself!"

So saying, he arrived at the bank of a little brook that flowed in through a water gate at one side of the garden and emptied itself into the big fish-pond. Flinging himself down by a little stream Li bathed his hands and wrists in the cool water. How delightful! If only it were deep enough to cover his whole body, how gladly would he cast himself in and enjoy the bliss of its refreshing embrace!

For a long time he lay on the ground, rejoicing at his escape from the doctor's clutches. Then, as the fever began to rise again, he sprang up with a determined cry, "What am I waiting for? I will do it. There's no one to prevent me, and it will do me a world of good. I will cast myself head first into the fish-pond. It is not deep enough near the shore to drown me if I should be too weak to swim, and I am sure it will restore me to strength and health."

He hastened along the little stream, almost running in his eagerness to reach the deeper water of the pond. He was like some small Tom Brown who had escaped from the watchful eye of the master and run out to play in a forbidden spot.

Hark! Was that a servant calling? Had Wang discovered the absence of his employer? Would he sound the alarm, and would the whole place soon be alive with men searching for the fever-stricken patient?

With one last sigh of satisfaction Li flung himself, clothes and all, into the quiet waters of the fish-pond. Now Li had been brought up in Fukien province on the seashore, and was a skilful swimmer. He dived and splashed to his heart's content, then floated on the surface. "It takes me back to my boyhood," he cried, "why, oh why, is it not the fashion to swim? I'd love to live in the water all the time and yet some of my countrymen are even more afraid than a cat of getting their feet wet. As for me, I'd give anything to stay here for ever."

"You would, eh?" chuckled a hoarse voice just under him, and then there was a sort of wheezing sound, followed by a loud burst of laughter. Mr. Li jumped as if an arrow had struck him, but when he noticed the fat, ugly monster below, his fear turned into anger. "Look here, what do you mean by giving a fellow such a start! Don't you know what the Classics say about such rudeness?"

The giant fish laughed all the louder. "What time do you suppose I have for Classics? You make me laugh till I cry!"

"But you must answer my question," cried Mr. Li, more and more persistently, forgetting for the moment that he was not trying some poor culprit for a petty crime. "Why did you laugh? Speak out at once, fellow!"

"Well, since you are such a saucy piece," roared the other, "I will tell you. It was because you awkward creatures, who call yourselves men, the most highly civilized beings in the world, always think you understand a thing fully when you have only just found out how to do it."

"You are talking about the island dwarfs, the Japanese," interrupted Mr. Li, "We Chinese seldom undertake to do anything new."

"Just hear the man!" chuckled the fish. "Now, fancy your wishing to stay in the water for ever! What do you know about water? Why you're not even provided with the proper equipment for swimming. What would you do if you really lived here always?"

"What am I doing now?" spluttered Mr. Li, so angry that he sucked in a mouthful of water before he knew it.

"Floundering," retorted the other.

"Don't you see me swimming? Are those big eyes of yours made of glass?"

"Yes, I see you all right," guffawed the fish, "that's just it! I see you too well. Why you tumble about as awkwardly as a water buffalo wallowing in a mud puddle!"

Now, as Mr. Li had always considered himself an expert in water sports, he was, by this time, speechless with rage, and all he could do was to paddle feebly round and round with strokes just strong enough to keep himself from sinking.

"Then, too," continued the fish, more and more calm as the other lost his temper, "you have a very poor arrangement for breathing. If I am not mistaken, at the bottom of this pond you would find yourself worse off than I should be at the top of a palm tree. What would you do to keep yourself from starving? Do you think it would be convenient if you had to flop yourself out on to the land every time you wanted a bite to eat? And yet, being a man, I doubt seriously if you would be content to take the proper food for fishes. You have hardly a single feature that would make you contented if you were to join an under-water school. Look at your clothes, too, water-soaked and heavy. Do you think them suitable to protect you from cold and sickness? Nature forgot to give you any scales. Now I'm going to tell you a joke, so you must be sure to laugh. Fishes are like grocery shops – always judged by their scales. As you haven't a sign of a scale, how will people judge you? See the point, eh? Nature gave you a skin, but forgot the outer covering, except, perhaps at the ends of your fingers and your toes You surely see by this time why I consider your idea ridiculous?"

Sure enough, in spite of his recent severe attack of fever, Mr. Li had really cooled completely off. He had never understood before what great disadvantages there were connected with being a man. Why not make use of this chance acquaintance, find out from him how to get rid of that miserable possession he had called his manhood, and gain the delights that only a fish can have? "Then, are you indeed contented with your lot?" he asked finally. "Are there not moments when you would prefer to be a man?"

"I, a man!" thundered the other, lashing the water with his tail. "How dare you suggest such a disgraceful change! Can it be that you do not know my rank? Why, my fellow, you behold in me a favourite nephew of the king!"

"Then, may it please your lordship," said Mr. Li, softly, "I should be exceedingly grateful if you would speak a kind word for me to your master. Do you think it possible that he could change me in some manner into a fish and accept me as a subject?"

"Of course!" replied the other, "all things are possible to the king. Know you not that my sovereign is a loyal descendant of the great water dragon, and, as such, can never die, but lives on and on and on, for ever and ever and ever, like the ruling house of Japan?"

"Oh, oh!" gasped Mr. Li, "even the Son of Heaven, our most worshipful emperor, cannot boast of such long years. Yes, I would give my fortune to be a follower of your imperial master."

"Then follow me," laughed the other, starting off at a rate that made the water hiss and boil for ten feet around him.

Mr. Li struggled vainly to keep up. If he had thought himself a good swimmer, he now saw his mistake and every bit of remaining pride was torn to tatters. "Please wait a moment," he cried out politely, "I beg of you to remember that I am only a man!"

"Pardon me," replied the other, "it was stupid of me to forget, especially as I had just been talking about it."

Soon they reached a sheltered inlet at the farther side of the pond. There Mr. Li saw a gigantic carp idly floating about in a shallow pool, and then lazily flirting his huge tail or fluttering his fins proudly from side to side. Attendant courtiers darted hither and thither, ready to do the master's slightest bidding. One of them, splendidly attired in royal scarlet, announced, with a downward flip of the head, the approach of the King's nephew who was leading Mr. Li to an audience with his Majesty.

"Whom have you here, my lad?" began the ruler, as his nephew, hesitating for words to explain his strange request, moved his fins nervously backwards and forwards. "Strange company, it seems to me, you are keeping these days."

"Only a poor man, most royal sir," replied the other, "who beseeches your Highness to grant him your gracious favour."

> *"When man asks favour of a fish,*
> *'Tis hard to penetrate his wish –*
> *He often seeks a lordly dish*
> *To serve upon his table,"*

repeated the king, smiling. "And yet, nephew, you think this fellow is really peaceably inclined and is not coming among us as a spy?"

Before his friend could answer, Mr. Li had cast himself upon his knees in the shallow water, before the noble carp, and bowed thrice, until his face was daubed with mud from the bottom of the pool. "Indeed, your Majesty, I am only a poor mortal who seeks your kindly grace. If you would but consent to receive me into your school of fishes. I would for ever be your ardent admirer and your lowly slave."

"In sooth, the fellow talks as if in earnest," remarked the king, after a moment's reflection, "and though the request is, perhaps, the strangest to which I have ever listened, I really see no reason why I should not turn a fishly ear. But, have the goodness first to cease your bowing. You are stirring up enough mud to plaster the royal palace of a shark."

Poor Li, blushing at the monarch's reproof, waited patiently for the answer to his request.

"Very well, so be it," cried the king impulsively, "your wish is granted. Sir Trout," turning to one of his courtiers, "bring hither a fish-skin of proper size for this ambitious fellow."

No sooner said than done. The fish-skin was slipped over Mr. Li's head, and his whole body was soon tucked snugly away in the scaly coat. Only his arms remained uncovered. In the twinkling of an eye Li felt sharp pains shoot through every part of his body. His arms began to shrivel up and his hands changed little by little until they made an excellent pair of fins, just as good as those of the king himself. As for his legs and feet, they suddenly began to stick together until, wriggle as he would, Li could not separate them. "Ah, ha!" thought he, "my kicking days are over, for my toes are now turned into a first-class tail."

"Not so fast," laughed the king, as Li, after thanking the royal personage profusely, started out to try his new fins; "not so fast, my friend. Before you depart, perhaps I'd better give you a little friendly advice, else your new powers are likely to land you on the hook of some lucky fisherman, and you will find yourself served up as a prize of the pond."

"I will gladly listen to your lordly counsel, for the words of the Most High to his lowly slave are like pearls before sea slugs. However, as I was once a man myself I think I understand the simple tricks they use to catch us fish, and I am therefore in position to avoid trouble."

"Don't be so sure about it. 'A hungry carp often falls into danger,' as one of our sages so wisely remarked. There are two cautions I would impress upon you. One is, never, never, eat a dangling worm; no matter how tempting it looks there are sure to be horrible hooks inside. Secondly, always swim like lightning if you see a net, but in the opposite direction. Now, I will have you served your first meal out of the royal pantry, but after that, you must hunt for yourself, like every other self-respecting citizen of the watery world."

After Li had been fed with several slugs, followed by a juicy worm for dessert, and after again thanking the king and the king's nephew for their kindness, he started forth to test his tail and fins. It was no easy matter, at first, to move them properly. A single flirt of the tail, no more vigorous than those he had been used to giving with his legs, would send him whirling round and round in the water, for all the world like a living top; and when he wriggled his fins, ever so slightly, as he thought, he found himself sprawling on his back in a most ridiculous fashion for a dignified member of fishkind. It took several hours of constant practice to get the proper stroke, and then he found he could move about without being conscious of any effort. It was the easiest thing he had ever done in his life; and oh! the water was so cool and delightful! "Would that I might enjoy that endless life the poets write of!" he murmured blissfully.

Many hours passed by until at last Li was compelled to admit that, although he was not tired, he was certainly hungry. How to get something to eat? Oh! why had he not asked the friendly nephew a few simple questions? How easily his lordship might have told him the way to get a good breakfast! But alas! without such advice, it would be a whale's task to accomplish it. Hither and thither he swam, into the deep still water, and along the muddy shore; down, down to the pebbly bottom – always looking, looking for a tempting worm. He dived into the weeds and rushes, poked his nose among the lily pads. All for nothing! No fly or worm of any kind to gladden his eager eyes! Another hour passed slowly away, and all the time his hunger was growing greater and greater. Would the fish god, the mighty dragon, not grant him even one little morsel to satisfy his aching stomach, especially since, now that he was a fish, he had no way of tightening up his belt, as hungry soldiers do when they are on a forced march?

Just as Li was beginning to think he could not wriggle his tail an instant longer, and that soon, very soon, he would feel himself slipping, slipping, slipping down to the bottom of the pond to die – at that very moment, chancing to look up, he saw, oh joy! a delicious red worm dangling a few inches above his nose. The sight gave new strength to his weary fins and tail. Another minute, and he would have had the delicate morsel in his mouth, when alas! he chanced to recall the advice given him the day before by great King Carp. "No matter how tempting it looks, there are sure to be horrible hooks inside." For an instant Li hesitated. The worm floated a trifle nearer to his half-open mouth. How tempting! After all, what was a hook to a fish when he was dying? Why be a coward? Perhaps this worm was an exception to the rule, or perhaps, perhaps any thing – really a fish in such a plight as Mr. Li could not be expected to follow advice – even the advice of a real KING.

Pop! He had it in his mouth. Oh, soft morsel, worthy of a king's desire! Now he could laugh at words of wisdom, and eat whatever came before his eye. But ugh! What was that strange feeling that – Ouch! it was the fatal hook!

With one frantic jerk, and a hundred twists and turns, poor Li sought to pull away from the cruel barb that stuck so fast in the roof of his mouth. It was now too late to wish he had kept away from temptation. Better far to have starved at the bottom of the cool pond than to be jerked out by some miserable fisherman to the light and sunshine of the busy world. Nearer and nearer he approached the surface. The more he struggled the sharper grew the cruel barb. Then, with one final splash, he found himself dangling in mid-air, swinging helplessly at the end of a long line. With a chunk he fell into a flat-bottomed boat, directly on top of several smaller fish.

"Ah, a carp!" shouted a well-known voice gleefully; "the biggest fish I've caught these three moons. What good luck!"

It was the voice of old Chang, the fisherman, who had been supplying Mr. Li's table ever since that official's arrival in the village of Everlasting Happiness. Only a word of explanation, and he, Li, would be free once more to swim about where he willed. And then there should be no more barbs for him. An escaped fish fears the hook.

"I say, Chang," he began, gasping for breath, "really now, you must chuck me overboard at once, for, don't you see, I am Mr. Li, your old master. Come, hurry up about it. I'll excuse you this time for your mistake, for, of course, you had no way of knowing. Quick!"

But Chang, with a savage jerk, pulled the hook from Li's mouth, and looked idly towards the pile of glistening fish, gloating over his catch, and wondering how much money he could demand for it. He had heard nothing of Mr. Li's remarks, for Chang had been deaf since childhood.

"Quick, quick, I am dying for air," moaned poor Li, and then, with a groan, he remembered the fisherman's affliction.

By this time they had arrived at the shore, and Li, in company with his fellow victims, found himself suddenly thrown into a wicker basket. Oh, the horrors of that journey on land! Only a tiny bit of water remained in the closely-woven thing. It was all he could do to breathe.

Joy of joys! At the door of his own house he saw his good friend Sing just coming out. "Hey, Sing," he shouted, at the top of his voice, "help, help! This son of a turtle wants to murder me.

He has me in here with these fish, and doesn't seem to know that I am Li, his master. Kindly order him to take me to the lake and throw me in, for it's cool there and I like the water life much better than that on land."

Li paused to hear Sing's reply, but there came not a single word.

"I beg your honour to have a look at my catch," said old Chang to Sing. "Here is the finest fish of the season. I have brought him here so that you and my honoured master, Mr. Li, may have a treat. Carp is his favourite delicacy."

"Very kind of you, my good Chang, I'm sure, but I fear poor Mr. Li will not eat fish for some time. He has a bad attack of fever."

"There's where you're wrong," shouted Li, from his basket, flopping about with all his might, to attract attention, "I'm going to die of a chill. Can't you recognize your old friend? Help me out of this trouble and you may have all my money for your pains."

"Hey, what's that!" questioned Sing, attracted, as usual, by the word money. "Shades of Confucius! It sounds as if the carp were talking."

"What, a talking fish," laughed Chang. "Why, master, I've lived nigh on to sixty year, and such a fish has never come under my sight. There are talking birds and talking beasts for that matter; but talking fish, who ever heard of such a wonder? No, I think your ears must have deceived you, but this carp will surely cause talk when I get him into the kitchen. I'm sure the cook has never seen his like. Oh, master! I hope you will be hungry when you sit down to this fish. What a pity Mr. Li couldn't help you to devour it!"

"Help to devour myself, eh?" grumbled poor Li, now almost dead for lack of water. "You must take me for a cannibal, or some other sort of savage."

Old Chang had now gone round the house to the servants' quarters, and, after calling out the cook, held up poor Li by the tail for the chef to inspect.

With a mighty jerk Li tore himself away and fell at the feet of his faithful cook. "Save me, save me!" he cried out in despair; "this miserable Chang is deaf and doesn't know that I am Mr. Li, his master. My fish voice is not strong enough for his hearing. Only take me back to the pond and set me free. You shall have a pension for life, wear good clothes and eat good food, all the rest of your days. Only hear me and obey! Listen, my dear cook, listen!"

"The thing seems to be talking," muttered the cook, "but such wonders cannot be. Only ignorant old women or foreigners would believe that a fish could talk." And seizing his former master by the tail, he swung him on to a table, picked up a knife, and began to whet it on a stone.

"Oh, oh!" screamed Li, "you will stick a knife into me! You will scrape off my beautiful shiny scales! You will whack off my lovely new fins! You will murder your old master!"

"Well, you won't talk much longer," growled the cook, "I'll show you a trick or two with the blade."

So saying, with a gigantic thrust, he plunged the knife deep into the body of the trembling victim.

With a shrill cry of horror and despair, Mr. Li awoke from the deep sleep into which he had fallen. His fever was gone, but he found himself trembling with fear at thought of the terrible death that had come to him in dreamland.

"Thanks be to Buddha, I am not a fish!" he cried out joyfully; "and now I shall be well enough to enjoy the feast to which Mr. Sing has bidden guests for tomorrow. But alas, now that I can eat the old fisherman's prize carp, it has changed back into myself.

"If only the good of our dreams came true,
I shouldn't mind dreaming the whole day through."

The Bronze Buddha of Kamakura and the Whale

THE GREAT BRONZE BUDDHA of Kamakura, or the Daibutsu, is undoubtedly one of the most remarkable sights in Japan. In its sitting posture, it is fifty feet high, ninety-seven feet in circumference, the length of its face eight feet, and as for its thumbs they are three feet round. It is probably the tallest piece of bronze in the world. Such an enormous image naturally created a considerable sensation in the days when Kamakura was a flourishing city, laid out by the great General Yoritomo. The roads in and about the city were densely packed with pilgrims, anxious to gaze upon the latest marvel, and all agreed that this bronze image was the biggest thing in the world.

Now it may be that certain sailors who had seen this marvel chatted about it as they plied their nets. Whether this was so or not, a mighty whale, who lived in the Northern Sea, happened to hear about the Bronze Buddha of Kamakura, and as he regarded himself as being far bigger than anything on land, the idea of a possible rival did not meet with his approval. He deemed it impossible that little men could construct anything that could vie with his enormous bulk, and laughed heartily at the very absurdity of such a conception.

His laughter, however, did not last long. He was inordinately jealous, and when he heard about the numerous pilgrimages to Kamakura and the incessant praise evoked from those who had seen the image he grew exceedingly angry, lashed the sea into foam, and blew down his nose with so much violence that the other creatures of the deep gave him a very wide berth. His loneliness only aggravated his trouble, and he was unable to eat or sleep, and in consequence grew thin. He at last decided to chat the matter over with a kindly shark.

The shark answered the whale's heated questions with quiet solicitude, and consented to go to the Southern Sea in order that he might take the measurement of the image, and bring back the result of his labour to his agitated friend.

The shark set off upon his journey, until he came to the shore, where he could see the image towering above him, about half a mile inland. As he could not walk on dry land he was about to renounce his quest, when he had the good fortune to discover a rat enjoying a scamper along a junk. He explained his mission to the rat, and requested that much-flattered little creature to take the measurement of the Bronze Buddha.

So the rat climbed down the junk, swam ashore, and entered the dark temple where the Great Buddha stood. At first he was so overcome by the magnificence he saw about him that he was uncertain as to how to proceed in carrying out the shark's request. He eventually decided to walk round the image, counting his footsteps as he went. He discovered after he had performed this task that he had walked exactly five thousand paces, and on his return to the junk he told the shark the measurement of the base of the Bronze Buddha.

The shark, with profuse thanks to the rat, returned to the Northern Sea, and informed the whale that the reports concerning the size of this exasperating image were only too true.

'A little knowledge is a dangerous thing' evidently applies equally well to whales, for the whale of this legend, after receiving the information, grew more furious than ever. As in a story familiar to English children, he put on magic boots in order to travel on land as well as he had always done in the sea.

The whale reached the Kamakura temple at night. He discovered that the priests had gone to bed, and were apparently fast asleep. He knocked at the door. Instead of the dismal murmur of a half-awake priest he heard the Lord Buddha say, in a voice that rang like the sound of a great bell: "Come in!"

"I cannot," replied the whale, "because I am too big. Will you please come out and see me?"

When Buddha found out who his visitor was, and what he wanted at so unearthly an hour, he condescendingly stepped down from his pedestal and came outside the temple. There was utter amazement on both sides. Had the whale possessed knees they would assuredly have knocked together. He knocked his head on the ground instead. For his part, Buddha was surprised to find a creature of such gigantic proportions.

We can imagine the consternation of the chief priest when he found that the pedestal did not bear the image of his Master. Hearing a strange conversation going on outside the temple, he went out to see what was taking place. The much-frightened priest was invited to join in the discussion, and was requested to take the measurement of the image and the whale, and accordingly began to measure with his rosary. During this proceeding the image and the whale awaited the result with bated breath. When the measurements had been taken the whale was found to be two inches longer and taller than the image.

The whale went back to the Northern Sea more utterly vain than ever, while the image returned to its temple and sat down again, and there it has remained to this day, none the worse, perhaps, for finding that it was not quite so big as it imagined. Dealers in dry goods and dealers in wood and iron agreed from that day to this to differ as to what was a foot – and the difference was a matter of two inches.

The Gratitude of the Samébito

THERE WAS A MAN named Tawaraya Tōtarō, who lived in the Province of Ōmi. His house was situated on the shore of Lake Biwa, not far from the famous temple called Ishiyamadera. He had some property, and lived in comfort; but at the age of twenty-nine he was still unmarried. His greatest ambition was to marry a very beautiful woman; and he had not been able to find a girl to his liking.

One day, as he was passing over the Long Bridge of Séta, he saw a strange being crouching close to the parapet. The body of this being resembled the body of a man, but was black as ink; its face was like the face of a demon; its eyes were green as emeralds; and its beard was like the beard of a dragon. Tōtarō was at first very much startled. But the green eyes looked at him so gently that after a moment's hesitation he ventured to question the creature. Then it answered him, saying: "I am a Samébito – a Shark-Man of the sea; and until a short time ago I was in the service of the Eight Great Dragon-Kings [Hachi-Dai-Ryū-Ō] as a subordinate officer in the Dragon-Palace [Ryūgū]. But because of a small fault which I committed, I was dismissed from the Dragon-Palace, and also banished from the Sea. Since then I have been wandering about here – unable to get any food, or even a place to lie down. If you can feel any pity for me, do, I beseech you, help me to find a shelter, and let me have something to eat!"

This petition was uttered in so plaintive a tone, and in so humble a manner, that Tōtarō's heart was touched. "Come with me," he said. "There is in my garden a large and deep pond where you may live as long as you wish; and I will give you plenty to eat."

The Samébito followed Tōtarō home, and appeared to be much pleased with the pond.

Thereafter, for nearly half a year, this strange guest dwelt in the pond, and was every day supplied by Tōtarō with such food as sea-creatures like.

Now, in the seventh month of the same year, there was a female pilgrimage (nyonin-mōdé) to the great Buddhist temple called Miidera, in the neighbouring town of Ōtsu; and Tōtarō went to Ōtsu to attend the festival. Among the multitude of women and young girls there assembled, he observed a person of extraordinary beauty. She seemed about sixteen years old; her face was fair and pure as snow; and the loveliness of her lips assured the beholder that their every utterance would sound 'as sweet as the voice of a nightingale singing upon a plum-tree.' Tōtarō fell in love with her at sight. When she left the temple he followed her at a respectful distance, and discovered that she and her mother were staying for a few days at a certain house in the neighbouring village of Séta. By questioning some of the village folk, he was able also to learn that her name was Tamana; that she was unmarried; and that her family appeared to be unwilling that she should marry a man of ordinary rank – for they demanded as a betrothal-gift a casket containing ten thousand jewels.

Tōtarō returned home very much dismayed by this information. The more that he thought about the strange betrothal-gift demanded by the girl's parents, the more he felt that he could never expect to obtain her for his wife. Even supposing that there were as many as ten thousand jewels in the whole country, only a great prince could hope to procure them.

But not even for a single hour could Tōtarō banish from his mind the memory of that beautiful being. It haunted him so that he could neither eat nor sleep; and it seemed to become more and more vivid as the days went by. And at last he became ill – so ill that he could not lift his head from the pillow. Then he sent for a doctor.

The doctor, after having made a careful examination, uttered an exclamation of surprise. "Almost any kind of sickness," he said, "can be cured by proper medical treatment, except the sickness of love. Your ailment is evidently love-sickness. There is no cure for it. In ancient times Rōya-Ō Hakuyo died of that sickness; and you must prepare yourself to die as he died." So saying, the doctor went away, without even giving any medicine to Tōtarō. About this time the Shark-Man that was living in the garden-pond heard of his master's sickness, and came into the house to wait upon Tōtarō. And he tended him with the utmost affection both by day and by night. But he did not know either the cause or the serious nature of the sickness until nearly a week later, when Tōtarō, thinking himself about to die, uttered these words of farewell: –

"I suppose that I have had the pleasure of caring for you thus long, because of some relation that grew up between us in a former state of existence. But now I am very sick indeed, and every day my sickness becomes worse; and my life is like the morning dew which passes away before the setting of the sun. For your sake, therefore, I am troubled in mind. Your existence has depended upon my care; and I fear that there will be no one to care for you and to feed you when I am dead... My poor friend!... Alas! our hopes and our wishes are always disappointed in this unhappy world!"

No sooner had Tōtarō spoken these words than the Samébito uttered a strange wild cry of pain, and began to weep bitterly. And as he wept, great tears of blood streamed from his green eyes and rolled down his black cheeks and dripped upon the floor. And, falling, they were blood; but, having fallen, they became hard and bright and beautiful – became jewels of inestimable price, rubies splendid as crimson fire. For when men of the sea weep, their tears become precious stones.

Then Tōtarō, beholding this marvel, was so amazed and overjoyed that his strength returned to him. He sprang from his bed, and began to pick up and to count the tears of the Shark-Man, crying out the while: "My sickness is cured! I shall live! I shall live!"

Therewith, the Shark-Man, greatly astonished, ceased to weep, and asked Tōtarō to explain this wonderful cure; and Tōtarō told him about the young person seen at Miidera, and about the extraordinary marriage-gift demanded by her family. "As I felt sure," added Tōtarō, "that I should never be able to get ten thousand jewels, I supposed that my suit would be hopeless. Then I became very unhappy, and at last fell sick. But now, because of your generous weeping, I have many precious stones; and I think that I shall be able to marry that girl. Only – there are not yet quite enough stones; and I beg that you will be good enough to weep a little more, so as to make up the full number required."

But at this request the Samébito shook his head, and answered in a tone of surprise and of reproach: –

"Do you think that I am like a harlot – able to weep whenever I wish? Oh, no! Harlots shed tears in order to deceive men; but creatures of the sea cannot weep without feeling real sorrow. I wept for you because of the true grief that I felt in my heart at the thought that you were going to die. But now I cannot weep for you, because you have told me that your sickness is cured."

"Then what am I to do?" plaintively asked Tōtarō. "Unless I can get ten thousand jewels, I cannot marry the girl!"

The Samébito remained for a little while silent, as if thinking. Then he said: –

"Listen! To-day I cannot possibly weep any more. But to-morrow let us go together to the Long Bridge of Séta, taking with us some wine and some fish. We can rest for a time on the bridge; and while we are drinking the wine and eating the fish, I shall gaze in the direction of the Dragon-Palace, and try, by thinking of the happy days that I spent there, to make myself feel homesick – so that I can weep."

Tōtarō joyfully assented.

Next morning the two, taking plenty of wine and fish with them, went to the Séta bridge, and rested there, and feasted. After having drunk a great deal of wine, the Samébito began to gaze in the direction of the Dragon-Kingdom, and to think about the past. And gradually, under the softening influence of the wine, the memory of happier days filled his heart with sorrow, and the pain of homesickness came upon him, so that he could weep profusely. And the great red tears that he shed fell upon the bridge in a shower of rubies; and Tōtarō gathered them as they fell, and put them into a casket, and counted them until he had counted the full number of ten thousand. Then he uttered a shout of joy.

Almost in the same moment, from far away over the lake, a delightful sound of music was heard; and there appeared in the offing, slowly rising from the waters, like some fabric of cloud, a palace of the colour of the setting sun.

At once the Samébito sprang upon the parapet of the bridge, and looked, and laughed for joy. Then, turning to Tōtarō, he said: –

"There must have been a general amnesty proclaimed in the Dragon-Realm; the Kings are calling me. So now I must bid you farewell.

I am happy to have had one chance of befriending you in return for your goodness to me."

With these words he leaped from the bridge; and no man ever saw him again. But Tōtarō presented the casket of red jewels to the parents of Tamana, and so obtained her in marriage.

The Good Sea Monster

ON AN ISLAND OF ROCKS out in the ocean lived a sea monster. His head was large, and when he opened his mouth it looked like a cave.

It had been said that he was so huge that he could swallow a ship, and that on stormy nights he sat on the rocks and the flashing of his eyes could be seen for miles around.

The sailors spoke of him with fear and trembling, but, as you can see, the sea monster had really been a friend to them, showing them the rock in the storm by flashing his eyes; but because he looked so hideous all who beheld him thought he must be a cruel monster.

One night there was a terrible storm, and the monster went out into the ocean to see if any ship was wrecked in the night, and, if possible, help any one that was floating about.

He found one little boy floating about on a plank. His name was Ko-Ko, and when he saw the monster he was afraid, but when Ko-Ko saw that the monster did not attempt to harm him he climbed on the monster's back and he took him to the rocky island. Then the monster went back into the sea and Ko-Ko wondered if he were to be left alone. But after a while the monster returned and opened his mouth very wide.

Ko-Ko ran when he saw the huge mouth, for he thought the monster intended to swallow him, but as he did not follow him Ko-Ko went back.

The monster opened his mouth again, and Ko-Ko asked, "Do you want me to go inside?" and the monster nodded his head.

"It must be for my own good," said Ko-Ko, "for he could easily swallow me if he wished, without waiting for me to walk in."

So Ko-Ko walked into the big mouth and down a dark passage, but what the monster wanted him to do he could not think. He could see very faintly now, and after a while he saw a stove, a chair, and a table. "I will take these out," said Ko-Ko, "for I am sure I can use them."

He took them to a cave on the island, and when he returned the monster was gone; but he soon returned, and again he opened his mouth.

Ko-Ko walked in this time without waiting, and he found boxes and barrels of food, which he stored away in the cave. When Ko-Ko had removed everything the monster lay down and went to sleep.

Ko-Ko cooked his dinner and then he awoke the monster and said, "Dinner is ready," but the monster shook his head and plunged into the ocean. He soon returned with his mouth full of fish. Then Ko-Ko knew that the monster had brought all the things from the sunken ship for him, and he began to wish that the monster could talk, for he no longer feared him.

"I wish you could talk," he said.

"I can," the monster replied. "No one ever wished it before. An old witch changed me into a monster and put me on this island, where no one could reach me, and the only way I can be restored to my original form is for some one to wish it."

"I wish it," said Ko-Ko.

"You have had your wish," said the monster, "and I can talk; but for me to become a man some one else must wish it."

The monster and Ko-Ko lived for a long time on the island. He took Ko-Ko for long rides on his back, and when the waves were too high and Ko-Ko was afraid the monster would open his mouth and Ko-Ko would crawl inside and be brought back safe to the island.

One night, after a storm, Ko-Ko saw something floating on the water, and he jumped on the monster's back and they swam out to it.

It proved to be a little girl, about Ko-Ko's age, who had been on one of the wrecked vessels, and they brought her to the island.

At first she was afraid of the monster, but when she learned that he had saved Ko-Ko as well as her and brought them all their food she became as fond of him as Ko-Ko was.

"I wish he were a man," she said one day, as she sat on his back with Ko-Ko, ready for a sail. Splash went both children into the water, and there in place of the monster was an old man. He caught the children in his arms and brought them to the shore.

"But what will we do for food, now that you are a man?" asked Ko-Ko.

"We shall want for nothing now," replied the old man. "I am a sea-god and can do many things, now that I have my own form again. We will change this island into a beautiful garden, and when the little girl and you are grown up and married you shall have a castle, and all the sea-gods and nymphs will care for you. You will never want for anything again.

"I will take you out on the ocean on the backs of my dolphins."

Ko-Ko and the little girl lived on the enchanted island, and all the things that the old sea-god promised came true.

The Giant Crab

ONCE UPON A TIME there was a lake in the mountains, and in that lake lived a huge Crab. I daresay you have often seen crabs boiled, and put on a dish for you to eat; and perhaps at the seaside you have watched them sidling away at the bottom of a pool. Sometimes a boy or girl bathing in the sea gets a nip from a crab, and then there is squeaking and squealing. But our Crab was much larger than these; he was the largest Crab ever heard of; he was bigger than a dining-room table, and his claws were as big as an armchair. Fancy what it must be to have a nip from such claws as those!

Well, this huge Crab lived all alone in the lake. Now the different animals that lived in the wild mountains used to come to that lake to drink; deer and antelopes, foxes and wolves, lions and tigers and elephants. And whenever they came into the water to drink, the great Crab was on the watch; and one of them at least never went up out of the water again. The Crab used to nip it with one of his huge claws and pull it under, and then the poor beast was drowned, and made a fine dinner for the big Crab.

This went on for a long time, and the Crab grew bigger and bigger every day, fattening on the animals that came there to drink. So at last all the animals were afraid to go near that lake. This was a pity, because there was very little water in the mountains, and the creatures did not know what to do when they were thirsty.

At last a great Elephant made up his mind to put an end to the Crab and his doings. So he and his wife agreed that they would lead a herd of elephants there to drink, and while the other elephants were drinking, they would look out for the Crab.

They did as they arranged. When the herd of elephants got to the lake, these two went in first, and kept farthest out in the water, watching for the Crab; and the others drank, and trumpeted, and washed themselves close inshore.

Soon they had had enough, and began to go out of the water; and then, sure enough, the Elephant felt a tremendous nip on the leg. The Crab had crawled up under the water and got him fast. He nodded to his wife, who bravely stayed by his side; and then she began:

"Dear Mr. Crab!" she said, "please let my husband go!"

The Crab poked his eyes out of the water. You know a crab's eyes grow on a kind of little stalk; and this Crab was so big, that his eyes looked like two thick tree-trunks, with a cannon-ball on the top of each. Now this Crab was a great flirt, or rather he used to be a great flirt, but lately he had nobody to flirt with, because he had eaten up all the creatures that came near him. And Mrs. Elephant was a beautiful elephant, with a shiny brown skin, and elegant flapping ears, and a curly trunk, and two white tusks that twinkled when she smiled. So when the big Crab saw this beautiful elephant, he thought he would like to have a kiss; and he said in a wheedling tone:

"Dear little Elephant! Will you give me a kiss?"

Then Mrs. Elephant pretended to be very pleased, and put her head on one side, and flapped her tail; and she looked so sweet and so tempting, that the Crab let go the other elephant, and began to crawl slowly towards her, waving his eyes about as he went.

All this while Mr. Elephant had been in great pain from the nip of the Crab's claw, but he had said nothing, for he was a very brave Elephant. But he did not mean to let his wife come to any harm; not he! It was all part of their trick. And as soon as he felt his leg free, he trumpeted loud and long, and jumped right upon the Crab's back!

Crack, crack! went the Crab's shell; for, big as he was, an elephant was too heavy for him to carry. Crack, crack, crack! The Elephant jumped up and down on his back, and in a very short time the Crab was crushed to mincemeat.

What rejoicing there was among the animals when they saw the Crab crushed to death! From far and near they came, and passed a vote of thanks to the Elephant and his wife, and made them King and Queen of all the animals in the mountains.

As for the Crab, there was nothing left of him but his claws, which were so hard that nothing could even crack them; so they were left in the pool. And in the autumn there came a great flood, and carried the claws down into the river; and the river carried them hundreds of miles away, to a great city; where the King's sons found them, and made out of them two immense drums, which they always beat when they go to war; and the very sound of these drums is enough to frighten the enemy away.

Kind William and the Water Sprite

THERE ONCE LIVED a poor weaver, whose wife died a few years after their marriage. He was now alone in the world except for their child, who was a very quick and industrious little lad, and, moreover, of such an obliging disposition that he gained the nickname of Kind William.

On his seventh birthday his father gave him a little net with a long handle, and with this Kind William betook himself to a shallow part of the river to fish. After wandering on for some time, he found a quiet pool dammed in by stones, and here he dipped for the minnows that darted about in the clear brown water. At the first and second casts he caught nothing, but with the third he landed no less than twenty-one little fishes, and such minnows he had never seen, for as they leaped and struggled in the net they shone with alternate tints of green and gold.

He was gazing at them with wonder and delight, when a voice behind him cried, in piteous tones –

"Oh, my little sisters! Oh, my little sisters!"

Kind William turned round, and saw, sitting on a rock that stood out of the stream, a young girl weeping bitterly. She had a very pretty face, and abundant yellow hair of marvellous length, and of such uncommon brightness that even in the shade it shone like gold. She was dressed in grass green, and from her knees downwards she was hidden by the clumps of fern and rushes that grew by the stream.

"What ails you, my little lass?" said Kind William.

But the maid only wept more bitterly, and wringing her hands, repeated, "Oh, my little sisters! Oh, my little sisters!" presently adding in the same tone, "The little fishes! Oh, the little fishes!"

"Dry your eyes, and I will give you half of them," said the good-natured child; "and if you have no net you shall fish with me this afternoon."

But at this proposal the maid's sobs redoubled, and she prayed and begged with frantic eagerness that he would throw the fish back into the river. For some time Kind William would not consent to throw away his prize, but at last he yielded to her excessive grief, and emptied the net into the pool, where the glittering fishes were soon lost to sight under the sand and pebbles.

The girl now laughed and clapped her hands.

"This good deed you shall never rue, Kind William," said she, "and even now it shall repay you threefold. How many fish did you catch?"

"Twenty-one," said Kind William, not without regret in his tone.

The maid at once began to pull hairs out of her head, and did not stop till she had counted sixty-three, and laid them together in her fingers. She then began to wind the lock up into a curl, and it took far longer to wind than the sixty-three hairs had taken to pull. How long her hair really was Kind William never could tell, for after it reached her knees he lost sight of it among the fern; but he began to suspect that she was no true village maid, but a water sprite, and he heartily wished himself safe at home.

"Now," said she, when the lock was wound, "will you promise me three things?"

"If I can do so without sin," said Kind William.

"First," she continued, holding out the lock of hair, "will you keep this carefully, and never give it away? It will be for your own good."

"One never gives away gifts," said Kind William, "I promise that."

"The second thing is to spare what you have spared. Fish up the river and down the river at your will, but swear never to cast net in this pool again."

"One should not do kindness by halves," said Kind William. "I promise that also."

"Thirdly, you must never tell what you have now seen and heard till thrice seven years have passed. And now come hither, my child, and give me your little finger, that I may see if you can keep a secret."

But by this time Kind William's hairs were standing on end, and he gave the last promise more from fear than from any other motive, and seized his net to go.

"No hurry, no hurry," said the maiden (and the words sounded like the rippling of a brook over pebbles). Then bending towards him, with a strange smile, she added, "You are afraid that I shall pinch too hard, my pretty boy. Well, give me a farewell kiss before you go."

"I kiss none but the miller's lass," said Kind William, sturdily; for she was his little sweetheart. Besides, he was afraid that the water witch would enchant him and draw him down. At his answer she laughed till the echoes rang, but Kind William shuddered to hear that the echoes seemed to come from the river instead of from the hills; and they rang in his ears like a distant torrent leaping over rocks.

"Then listen to my song," said the water sprite. With which she drew some of her golden hairs over her arm, and tuning them as if they had been the strings of a harp, she began to sing:

"Warp of woollen and woof of gold:
When seven and seven and seven are told."

But when Kind William heard that the river was running with the cadence of the tune, he could bear it no longer, and took to his heels. When he had run a few yards he heard a splash, as if a salmon had jumped, and on looking back he found that the yellow-haired maiden was gone.

Kind William was trustworthy as well as obliging, and he kept his word. He said nothing of his adventure. He put the yellow lock into an old china teapot that had stood untouched on the mantelpiece for years. And fishing up the river and down the river he never again cast net into the haunted pool. And in course of time the whole affair passed from his mind.

Fourteen years went by, and Kind William was Kind William still. He was as obliging as ever, and still loved the miller's daughter, who, for her part, had not forgotten her old playmate. But the miller's memory was not so good, for the fourteen years had been prosperous ones with him, and he was rich, whereas they had only brought bad trade and poverty to the weaver and his son. So the lovers were not allowed even to speak to each other.

One evening Kind William wandered by the river-side lamenting his hard fate. It was his twenty-first birthday, and he might not even receive the good wishes of the day from his old playmate. It was just growing dusk, a time when prudent bodies hurry home from the neighbourhood of fairy rings, sprite-haunted streams, and the like, and Kind William was beginning to quicken his pace, when a voice from behind him sang:

"Warp of woollen and woof of gold:
When seven and seven and seven are told."

Kind William felt sure that he had heard this before, though he could not recall when or where; but suspecting that it was no mortal voice that sang, he hurried home without looking behind him. Before he reached the house he remembered all, and also that on this very day his promise of secrecy expired.

Meanwhile the old weaver had been sadly preparing the loom to weave a small stock of yarn, which he had received in payment for some work. He had set up the warp, and was about to fill the shuttle, when his son came in and told the story, and repeated the water sprite's song.

"Where is the lock of hair, my son?" asked the old man.

"In the teapot still, if you have not touched it," said Kind William; "but the dust of fourteen years must have destroyed all gloss and colour."

On searching the teapot, however, the lock of hair was found to be as bright as ever, and it lay in the weaver's hand like a coil of gold.

"It is the song that puzzles me," said Kind William. "Seven, and seven, and seven make twenty-one. Now that is just my age."

"There is your warp of woollen, if that is anything," added the weaver, gazing at the loom with a melancholy air.

"And this is golden enough," laughed Kind William, pointing to the curl. "Come, father, let us see how far one hair will go on the shuttle." And suiting the action to the word, he began to wind. He wound the shuttle full, and then sat down to the loom and began to throw.

The result was a fabric of such beauty that the Weavers shouted with amazement, and one single hair served for the woof of the whole piece.

Before long there was not a town dame or a fine country lady but must needs have a dress of the new stuff, and before the sixty-three hairs were used up, the fortunes of the weaver and his son were made.

About this time the miller's memory became clearer, and he was often heard to speak of an old boy-and-girl love between his dear daughter and the wealthy manufacturer of the golden cloth. Within a year and a day Kind William married his sweetheart, and as money sticks to money, in the end he added the old miller's riches to his own.

Moreover there is every reason to believe that he and his wife lived happily to the end of their days.

And what became of the water sprite?

That you must ask somebody else, for I do not know.

DRAGONS & SERPENTS

Introduction

FOR THE ANCIENTS, the heraldic historian John Vinycomb tells us, the dragon was 'the embodiment of malignant and destructive power', possessing 'attributes of the most terrible kind'. Yet he was also struck by its ubiquity: the dragon seems to have sprung up spontaneously as a mythological figure across the entire world, from Wales to China, from Canada to Japan.

We discuss it alongside the serpent here because, in East Asia especially, the idea of the dragon seems to have grown out of that of the real-life snake. Especially the water-snake – for again, in Eastern Asia, this monster was identified more with water than (as in the West) with fire. Eastern dragons, then, were associated with fertility and plenty, so –dreadful as they undoubtedly were – they could have positive aspects in a way that Western snakes never could.

In the Judaeo-Christian tradition, of course, the serpent was notorious as the instrument through which the Devil managed to tempt the first humans. The Bible's Book of Genesis describes how the snake enticed Adam and Eve in the Garden of Eden, prompting their 'Original Sin', and so their Fall. From that time forth, the snake would sidle sinisterly through the world, creeping on its belly and hissing lies with its forked tongue. It had become an agent of evil and the sworn enemy of humankind. As the stories here show, the dragon may just about always be a monster, but it can vary widely in character and form.

The Dragon

THE DRAGON is the most interesting and most frequently seen of all chimerical figures, and it is a remarkable fact that such a creature appears at an early period of the world's history to have been known in the East and in countries widely separated. Long anterior to the dawn of civilisation in the West of Europe, even in far-off China and Japan in the extreme East of Asia we find the dragon delineated in very much the same form in which it appears in our national heraldry.

The ancients conceived it as the embodiment of malignant and destructive power, and with attributes of the most terrible kind. Classic story makes us acquainted with many dreadful monsters of the dragon kind, to which reference will afterwards be more particularly made.

It is often argued that the monsters of tradition are but the personification of solar influences, storms, the desert wind, the great deeps, rivers inundating their banks, or other violent phenomena of nature, and so, no doubt, they are, and have been; but the strange fact remains that the same draconic form with slight modifications constantly appears as the type of the thing most dreaded, and instead of melting into an abstraction and dying out of view, it has remained from age to age, in form, distinctly a ferocious flying reptile, until in the opinion of many the tradition has been justified by prosaic science. It is surprising to find that the popular conception of the dragon – founded on tradition, passed on through hundreds of generations – not only retains its identity, but bears a startling resemblance to the original antediluvian saurians, whose fossil remains now come to light through geological research, almost proving the marvellous power of tradition and the veracity of those who passed it on.

Mr. Moncure Conway (*Demonology, or Devil Lore*) says: "The opinion has steadily gained that the conventional dragon is the traditional form of some huge saurian. It has been suggested that some of those extinct saurians may have been contemporaneous with the earliest men, and that traditions of conflicts with them, transmitted orally and pictorially, have resulted in preserving their forms in fable proximately."

"Among the geological specimens in the British Museum," says Hugh Miller, "the visitor sees shapes that more than rival in strangeness the great dragons and griffins of mediæval legends; enormous jaws, bristling with pointed teeth, gape horrid, in stone, under staring eye-sockets a foot in diameter; and necks that half equal in length the entire body of a boa-constrictor. And here we see a winged dragon that, armed with sharp teeth and strong claws, has careered through the air on leathern wings like those of a bat." We are also told in the sacred Scriptures by Moses of "fiery serpents," and by Isaiah of "a fiery flying serpent." Other monsters – dragons, cockatrices, and some of whose form we have no conception – are also mentioned. Euripides describes a dragon or snake breathing forth fire and slaughter, and rowing its way with its wings. It is evident that such a creature may at one time have existed. Looking at the widespread belief in dragons, there seems little doubt that the semi-myth of to-day is the traditional successor of a really once-existent animal, whose huge size, snake-like appearance, and possibly dangerous powers of offence made him so terrible that the earlier races of mankind adopted him unanimously as the most fearful embodiment of animal ferocity to be found.

One of the latest acquisitions in the Natural History Museum, South Kensington, is the skeleton of that enormous creature the long-limbed dinosaur (*Diplodicus Carnegii*), recently discovered in

America, eighty-nine feet in length from the head to the tip of the tail, the huge bulky framework of the monster measuring eleven feet in height at the shoulder. The enormous length of its neck and tail, with relatively small head, would indicate it to be an amphibious inhabitant of the waters, feeding on the vegetation growing in its depths.

Mr. Moncure Conway, in his remarkable work, *Demonology, or Devil Lore*, describes all intermediate stages between demon and devil under the head of dragon. This he believes to be the only fabulous form which accurately describes all the transitions. Throughout all the representations of the dragon one feature is common, and that is the idealized serpent. The dragon possesses all the properties of the demon along with that of harmfulness, but differs from the devil in not having the desire of doing evil. The dragon in mythology is the combination of every bad feature in nature, all of which is combined into one horrible whole. "The modern conventional dragon," says Mr. Conway, "is a terrible monster. His body is partially green, with memories of the sea and of slime, and partly brown or dark, with lingering shadows of storm-clouds. The lightning flames still in his red eyes, and flashes from his fire-breathing mouth.

The thunderbolt of Jove, the spear of Woden, are in the barbed point of his tail. His huge wings – bat-like and spiked – sum up all the mysteries of extinct harpies and vampires. Spine of crocodile is on his neck, tail of the serpent and all the jagged ridges of rocks and sharp thorns of jungles bristle round him, while the ice of glaciers and brassy glitter of sunstrokes are in his scales. He is ideal of all that is hard, destructive, perilous, loathsome, horrible in nature; every detail of him has been seen through and vanquished by man, here or there; but in selection and combination they rise again as principles, and conspire to form one great generalization of the forms of pain, the sum of every creature's worst."

"The External Forms of Dragons are greatly dependent on the nature of the country in which they originate. In the far north, where exist the legends of the swan and pigeon, maidens and vampires, exists the swan-shaped dragon. As demons of excessive heat principally existed in the south, so in the north the great enemy of man was excessive cold. In the northern countries is found also the serpent element, but as serpents are there frequently harmless, this feature does not enter much into their composition. The Cuttlefish is supposed to have helped in the formation of the Hydra, which in its turn assisted in forming the dragon of the Apocalypse. Assyrian ideas also seem to have assisted in the pictorial impersonations of the hydra. This many-headed monster is a representation of a torrent, which being cut off in one direction breaks out in another. The conflicts of Hercules with the hydra are repeated in those of the Assyrian Bel with Trinant (the deep), and also in the contentions of St. Michael with the dragon. The old dragon myths left in Europe were frequently utilized by the Christians. Other saints besides St. Michael were invested with the feats of Hercules; St. Margaret, St. Andrew, and many others are pictured as trampling dragons under their feet. The Egyptian dragon is based on the crocodile, and this form being received into Christian symbolism did greatly away with other pagan monsters. The hideousness of the crocodile and the alligator could easily be exaggerated so as to suit the most horrible contortions of the human imagination. Amongst the most terrible dragons is Typhon, the impersonation of all the terrors of nature. Son of Tartarus, father of the harpies and of the winds, he lives in the African deserts; from thence fled in fear, to escape his terrible breath, all the gods and goddesses. He is coiled in the whirlwind, and his many heads are symbolical of the tempest, the scrive, the hurricane, and the tornado."

Under the head of The Colonial Dragon Mr. Conway has embodied all the horrors and difficulties with which the early colonists would be beset. Amongst these he places the Gorgon and the Chimera. The most widely spread of all is the last named, and from it is supposed that all Christian and British dragons are descended. The Christian myth of St. George and the Dragon is but a variation of Bellerophon and the Chimera, in which the last has given place to the dragon and the pagan hero to St. George.

"In ancient families there are usually traditions of some far-distant ancestor having slain a desperate monster. It is always the colonial dragon that has been borrowed by poets and romancers. The Dragon killed by Guy of Warwick is but another variation of the chimera. There is again the Sockburn Worm, slain by Sir John Conyers for the devouring of the people of the neighbourhood; the well-known tradition of the Lambton Worm is in reality a modification of the Aryan Dragon of the Storm Cloud; smaller than a man's hand he swells out to prodigious dimensions."

A favourite subject for Chinese and Japanese painting and sculpture is a dragon very much of the same type, and a monstrous representation of a dragon in the form of a huge Saurian still forms the central object at Japanese festivals.

Among the Chinese the dragon is the representation of sovereignty, and is the imperial emblem borne upon banners, and otherwise displayed as the national ensign. To the people of that vast country it represents everything powerful and imposing; and it plays an important part in many religious ceremonies and observances. Dr. S. Wells Williams, the eminent sinalogue, describes the fabulous monster of Chinese imagination in the following passage: "There are three dragons – the *lung* in the sky, the *li* in the sea, and the *kiau* in the marshes. The first is the only *authentic* species according to the Chinese; it has the head of a camel, the horns of a deer, eyes of a rabbit, ears of a cow, neck of a snake, belly of a frog, scales of a carp, claws of a hawk, and palm of a tiger. On each side of the mouth are whiskers, and its beard contains a bright pearl; the breath is sometimes changed into water and sometimes into fire, and its voice is like the jingling of copper pans. The dragon of the sea occasionally ascends to heaven in waterspouts, and is the ruler of all oceanic phenomena." The fishermen and sailors before venturing away from land or returning to port, burn joss-sticks and beat gongs to ward off the evil influences of the dragon, and it is worshipped in a variety of ways. According to a fable current in China, the Celestial Emperor Hoang-ti was carried up to heaven, along with seventy other persons, by a great dragon; those who were only able to catch at his moustaches were shaken off and thrown on the ground. It is still the custom when an emperor dies to say that the dragon has ascended to heaven. An eclipse the simple Celestials believe to be caused by a great dragon that seeks to devour the sun or moon. A great noise is made by firing guns, beating drums, and the rattling and jangling of pairs of discordant instruments to frighten the monster away. A frequent subject of their artists is the dreadful dragon sprawling through masses of curling clouds in the act of grasping at or swallowing the great luminary, a subject which no doubt bears a deeper meaning than we see, and one intimately connected with their mythology.

In some of their splendid festivals the worship of the dragon is celebrated with great excitement and furore. On the Canton river a boat of immense length formed like a dragon in many wondrous folds, rowed by fifty or more natives, with wild music and dancing, and accompanied by a crowd of junks; the unfurling of sails and the streaming of flags from the masts, the beating of drums, the noise and smoke from the firing of guns, all exhibit the fondness of a people for the pleasures of a national holiday.

Dragon's Teeth – Cadmus slew the dragon that guarded the well of Ares, and sowed some of the teeth, from which sprang up the armed men who all killed each other except five, who were the ancestors of the Thebans. Those teeth which Cadmus did not sow, came to the possession of Ætes, King of Colchis; and one of the tasks he enjoined on Jason was to sow these teeth and slay the armed warriors that rose therefrom. The frequent allusion to the classic term *dragon's teeth* refers to subjects of civil strife; whatever rouses citizens to rise in arms.

The mythical dragon has left the lasting impress of his name in various ways in our language and literature, as in the art of nearly every country.

☊ *Dragon's Head and* ☋ *Dragon's Tail* – In astronomy *Nodes* are the opposite points in which the orbit of a planet, or of a moon, crosses the ecliptic. The ascending node marked by the character (☊), termed the *Dragon's head*, is where the planet or moon ascends from the south to the north side of the ecliptic, and the descending node indicated by the character (☋) the Dragon's tail is where it passes from the north to the south side.

Draco, a constellation in the northern hemisphere, representing the monster that watched the golden apples in the garden of the Hesperides, slain by Hercules, and set as a constellation in the heavens.

Draco volens, a meteor sometimes visible in marshy countries – *Ignus fatuus*, or will-o'-the-wisp.

Draco volens, or flying dragon, a curious class of saurian reptiles peculiar to the East Indies, having membranous attachments to their limbs, which give them the appearance of flying as they leap from tree to tree.

Dragon's blood, a vegetable balsam of a dark red colour brought from India, Africa, and South America. So called from its resemblance to dried and hardened masses of blood.

Medea and the Golden Fleece

AT COLCHIS JASON MET MEDEA, the daughter of King Aeëtes and a priestess of Hecate, who had all the ambiguous powers of sorcery and magic that that position bestowed. Medea quickly fell in love with Jason, the intensity of her feeling heightened by a love charm which the goddesses Hera and Aphrodite gave to Jason. When presented to Medea, it made her helpless against falling for him. King Aeëtes himself was less taken with the young hero – a prophecy had foretold him that Jason would engineer the fall of his reign. Thus when Jason explained the purpose of his quest – to retrieve the Golden Fleece – Aeëtes saw the means by which to defy his fate. He gave Jason two challenges to claim the fleece, both of which had the certain expectation of death. Despite the difficulty of the tasks, Jason accepted them.

The first challenge was a clash of man and beast. Jason was to sow a field with dragon teeth, the plough to be pulled by two bronze-hoofed oxen with brutal temperaments and fire-breathing jaws. Few men would have survived such an encounter, but Jason dominated the creatures with his muscle and indomitable attitude, and scattered the dragon's teeth into the ground. Yet no sooner had the teeth sunk into the turned soil, than they transformed into fully armed warriors, intent on killing Jason. With the clear thinking born only in those already familiar with death, Jason crouched down behind his shield, hiding from the earth-born opponents. He threw a huge boulder, itself heavier than four normal men could handle, into the midst of the warriors, who in their surprise turned upon one another and fought to the death. Jason added the cut of his own blade, until all opponents were dead and the first challenge had been fulfilled.

Now came the second challenge – to take the fleece itself from beneath the dragon. Jason and Medea crept into the sacred grove at night. Yet no amount of stealth could avoid the unresting eyes of the dragon, who started to uncoil himself from his slumber with a resonating, chilling hiss that awoke people for miles around. The creature fixed the two in his gaze, its muscles tensing, and Jason drew his sword, ready to fight to an almost certain death. Medea stepped forward, however, and armed with nothing more than a sleep-inducing potion that she cast under the creature's nose, she overcame the dragon. Steadily the creature softened, drifting back into sleep under the power of the charm. Seizing the moment, Jason rushed around the dragon and took the Golden Fleece from the oak.

Jason and Medea were momentarily stunned by the magnificence of the fleece, radiating a shimmering light on the ground around their feet. But there was little time for contemplation. Jason was fully aware of Aeëtes' threatening purpose towards him, and he moved in haste back to the Argo. Medea, in the thrall of love, went with him accompanied by her little brother Apsyrtus.

Here Medea's madness began to reveal itself, in the most unnatural way. Aeëtes was quickly informed of the Argonauts' escape, and set off in pursuit with his naval forces. Medea, breaking all bonds of sibling tenderness, murdered her brother and cut his body into pieces, strewing the bloody parts along the River Phasis, down which Aeëtes was following. The king, overcome by shock, grief and tenderness, stopped to retrieve the parts, giving Medea chance to make good her escape with Jason. Through this unsettling act, the Argo made open waters and began the long journey back to home.

The Cockatrice, or Basilisk

THIS ANIMAL WAS CALLED the king of the serpents. In confirmation of his royalty, he was said to be endowed with a crest, or comb upon the head, constituting a crown. He was supposed to be produced from the egg of a cock hatched under toads or serpents. There were several species of this animal. One species burned up whatever they approached; a second were a kind of wandering Medusa's heads, and their look caused an instant horror which was immediately followed by death. In Shakespeare's play of *Richard the Third*, Lady Anne, in answer to Richard's compliment on her eyes, says "Would they were basilisk's, to strike thee dead!"

The basilisks were called kings of serpents because all other serpents and snakes, behaving like good subjects, and wisely not wishing to be burned up or struck dead, fled the moment they heard the distant hiss of their king, although they might be in full feed upon the most delicious prey, leaving the sole enjoyment of the banquet to the royal monster.

The Roman naturalist Pliny thus describes him. "He does not impel his body, like other serpents, by a multiplied flexion, but advances lofty and upright. He kills the shrubs, not only by contact, but by breathing on them, and splits the rocks, such power of evil is there in him." It was formerly believed that if killed by a spear from on horseback the power of the poison conducted through the weapon killed not only the rider, but the horse also. To this Lucan alludes in these lines:

> "What though the Moor the basilisk hath slain,
> And pinned him lifeless to the sandy plain,
> Up through the spear the subtle venom flies,
> The hand imbibes it, and the victor dies."

Such a prodigy was not likely to be passed over in the legends of the saints. Accordingly we find it recorded that a certain holy man, going to a fountain in the desert, suddenly beheld a basilisk. He immediately raised his eyes to heaven, and with a pious appeal to the Deity laid the monster dead at his feet.

These wonderful powers of the basilisk are attested by a host of learned persons, such as Galen, Avicenna, Scaliger, and others. Occasionally one would demur to some part of the tale while he admitted the rest. Jonston, a learned physician, sagely remarks, "I would scarcely believe that it kills with its look, for who could have seen it and lived to tell the story?" The worthy sage was not aware that those who went to hunt the basilisk of this sort took with them a mirror, which reflected back the deadly glare upon its author, and by a kind of poetical justice slew the basilisk with his own weapon.

But what was to attack this terrible and unapproachable monster? There is an old saying that "everything has its enemy" – and the cockatrice quailed before the weasel. The basilisk might look daggers, the weasel cared not, but advanced boldly to the conflict. When bitten, the weasel retired for a moment to eat some rue, which was the only plant the basilisks could not wither, returned with renewed strength and soundness to the charge, and never left the enemy till he was stretched dead on the plain. The monster, too, as if conscious of the irregular way in which he came into the world, was supposed to have a great antipathy to a cock; and well he might, for as soon as he heard the cock crow he expired.

The basilisk was of some use after death. Thus we read that its carcass was suspended in the temple of Apollo, and in private houses, as a sovereign remedy against spiders, and that it was also hung up in the temple of Diana, for which reason no swallow ever dared enter the sacred place.

The reader will, we apprehend, by this time have had enough of absurdities, but still we can imagine his anxiety to know what a cockatrice was like. The following is from Aldrovandus, a celebrated naturalist of the sixteenth century, whose work on natural history, in thirteen folio volumes, contains with much that is valuable a large proportion of fables and inutilities. In particular he is so ample on the subject of the cock and the bull that from his practice, all rambling, gossiping tales of doubtful credibility are called cock and bull stories.

Shelley, in his 'Ode to Naples,' full of the enthusiasm excited by the intelligence of the proclamation of a Constitutional Government at Naples, in 1820, thus uses an allusion to the basilisk:

> *What though Cimmerian Anarchs dare blaspheme*
> *Freedom and thee? thy shield is as a mirror*
> *To make their blind slaves see, and with fierce gleam*
> *To turn his hungry sword upon the wearer;*
> *A new Actaeon's error*
> *Shall theirs have been – devoured by their own hounds!*
> *Be thou like the imperial Basilisk*
> *Killing thy foe with unapparent wounds!*
> *Gaze on oppression, till at that dread risk*
> *Aghast she pass from the Earth's disk,*
> *Fear not, but gaze – for freemen mightier grow,*
> *And slaves more feeble, gazing on their foe;*
> *If Hope and Truth and Justice may avail,*
> *Thou shalt be great – All hail!*

The Seven-Headed Serpent

ONCE UPON A TIME there was a king who determined to take a long voyage. He assembled his fleet and all the seamen, and set out. They went straight on night and day, until they came to an island which was covered with large trees, and under every tree lay a lion. As soon as the King had landed his men, the lions all rose up together and tried to devour them. After a long battle they managed to overcome the wild beasts, but the greater number of the men were killed. Those who remained alive now went on through the forest and found on the other side of it a beautiful garden, in which all the plants of the world flourished together. There were also in the garden three springs: the first flowed with silver, the second with gold, and the third with pearls. The men unbuckled their knapsacks and filled them with those precious things. In the middle of the garden they found a large lake, and when they reached the edge of it the Lake began to speak, and said to them, "What men are you, and what brings you here? Are you come to visit our king?" But they were too much frightened to answer.

Then the Lake said, "You do well to be afraid, for it is at your peril that you are come hither. Our king, who has seven heads, is now asleep, but in a few minutes he will wake up and come to me to take his bath! Woe to anyone who meets him in the garden, for it is impossible to escape from him. This is what you must do if you wish to save your lives. Take off your clothes and spread them on the path which leads from here to the castle. The King will then glide over something soft, which he likes very much, and he will be so pleased with that that he will not devour you. He will give you some punishment, but then he will let you go."

The men did as the Lake advised them, and waited for a time. At noon the earth began to quake, and opened in many places, and out of the openings appeared lions, tigers, and other wild beasts, which surrounded the castle, and thousands and thousands of beasts came out of the castle following their king, the Seven-headed Serpent. The Serpent glided over the clothes which were spread for him, came to the Lake, and asked it who had strewed those soft things on the path? The Lake answered that it had been done by people who had come to do him homage. The King commanded that the men should be brought before him. They came humbly on their knees, and in a few words told him their story. Then he spoke to them with a mighty and terrible voice, and said, "Because you have dared to come here, I lay upon you the punishment. Every year you must bring me from among your people twelve youths and twelve maidens, that I may devour them. If you do not do this, I will destroy your whole nation."

Then he desired one of his beasts to show the men the way out of the garden, and dismissed them. They then left the island and went back to their own country, where they related what had happened to them. Soon the time came round when the King of the Beasts would expect the youths and maidens to be brought to him. The King therefore issued a proclamation inviting twelve youths and twelve maidens to offer themselves up to save their country; and immediately many young people, far more than enough, hastened to do so. A new ship was built, and set with black sails, and in it the youths and maidens who were appointed for the King of the Beasts embarked and set out for his country. When they arrived there they went at once to the Lake, and this time the lions did not stir, nor did the springs flow, and neither did the Lake speak. So they waited then, and it was not long before the earth quaked even more terribly than the first time.

The Seven-headed Serpent came without his train of beasts, saw his prey waiting for him, and devoured it in one mouthful. Then the ship's crew returned home, and the same thing happened yearly until many years had passed.

Now the King of this unhappy country was growing old, and so was the Queen, and they had no children. One day the Queen was sitting at the window weeping bitterly because she was childless, and knew that the crown would therefore pass to strangers after the King's death. Suddenly a little old woman appeared before her, holding an apple in her hand, and said, "Why do you weep, my Queen, and what makes you so unhappy?"

"Alas, good mother," answered the Queen, "I am unhappy because I have no children."

"Is that what vexes you?" said the old woman. "Listen to me. I am a nun from the Spinning Convent and my mother when she died left me this apple. Whoever eats this apple shall have a child."

The Queen gave money to the old woman, and bought the apple from her. Then she peeled it, ate it, and threw the rind out of the window, and it so happened that a mare that was running loose in the court below ate up the rind. After a time the Queen had a little boy, and the mare also had a male foal. The boy and the foal grew up together and loved each other like brothers. In course of time the King died, and so did the Queen, and their son, who was now nineteen years old, was left alone. One day, when he and his horse were talking together, the Horse said to him, "Listen to me, for I love you and wish for your good and that of the country. If you go on every year sending twelve youths and twelve maidens to the King of the Beasts, your country will very soon be ruined. Mount upon my back: I will take you to a woman who can direct you how to kill the Seven-headed Serpent."

Then the youth mounted his horse, who carried him far away to a mountain which was hollow, for in its side was a great underground cavern. In the cavern sat an old woman spinning. This was the cloister of the nuns, and the old woman was the Abbess. They all spent their time in spinning, and that is why the convent has this name. All round the walls of the cavern there were beds cut out of the solid rock, upon which the nuns slept, and in the middle a light was burning. It was the duty of the nuns to watch the light in turns, that it might never go out, and if anyone of them let it go out the others put her to death.

As soon as the King's son saw the old Abbess spinning he threw himself at her feet and entreated her to tell him how he could kill the Seven-headed Serpent.

She made the youth rise, embraced him, and said, "Know, my son, that it is I who sent the nun to your mother and caused you to be born, and with you the horse, with whose help you will be able to free the world from the monster. I will tell you what you have to do. Load your horse with cotton, and go by a secret passage which I will show you, which is hidden from the wild beasts, to the Serpent's palace. You will find the King asleep upon his bed, which is all hung round with bells, and over his bed you will see a sword hanging. With this sword only it is possible to kill the Serpent, because even if its blade breaks a new one will grow again for every head the monster has. Thus you will be able to cut off all his seven heads. And this you must also do in order to deceive the King: you must slip into his bed-chamber very softly, and stop up all the bells which are round his bed with cotton. Then take down the sword gently, and quickly give the monster a blow on his tail with it. This will make him waken up, and if he catches sight of you he will seize you. But you must quickly cut off his first head, and then wait till the next one comes up. Then strike it off also, and so go on till you have cut off all his seven heads."

The old Abbess then gave the Prince her blessing, and he set out upon his enterprise, arrived at the Serpent's castle by following the secret passage which she had shown him, and by carefully attending to all her directions he happily succeeded in killing the monster. As soon as the wild beasts heard of their king's death, they all hastened to the castle, but the youth had long since mounted his horse and was already far out of their reach. They pursued him as fast as they could, but they found it impossible to overtake him, and he reached home in safety. Thus he freed his country from this terrible oppression.

Sigurd

ONCE, IN THE HALL OF THE VOLSUNGS, the great line of warriors who are celebrated in the great Scandinavian epic, the Volsung saga, a wedding took place. This was the wedding of Signy, who was to marry the king of Gothland, called Siggeir. Signy was the twin sister of Sigmund, who supported her marriage along with everyone in the kingdom. In the hall of the Volsungs was an unusual sight – built into the hall itself was a huge living oak tree whose branches supported the roof. This oak tree was called Branstock, and it brought good luck to the Volsungs, who tended it carefully.

On this day, the day of the wedding feast, there were great festivities underway. Great platters of food groaned on tables, and mead was passed around in horns as the joyful crowd toasted the health of the new couple. Suddenly there was silence, for in the midst of the crowd appeared a stranger with a wide-brimmed hat. He had only one eye, and his feet were bare and dirtied from his travels. In his hand he carried a spectacular sword, which glinted and shone in the light as if it were made of pure gold. He walked purposefully towards Branstock, and plunged the sword into the trunk of the tree without murmuring a word.

Then he turned, and addressed the crowd:

"Whosoever draws this sword from the tree will have it as a gift from me. Whosoever has as his own my sword will have victory in every battle he fights." With that the stranger left the room, and there was silence. There was no doubt in any one of their minds that the great Odin had been amongst them.

Each of the men in the group stood up, longing for a chance to pull out the sword. Every great Viking warrior took his turn, while the others chattered excitedly. But one by one they pulled, and tugged and yanked at that sword until there was only one man left amongst them – the small, fair young Sigmund. He stood and walked towards the sword, the room growing silent. Each of King Volsung's nine sons had failed as had the king himself. No one doubted that this young man would do so as well.

Sigmund laid his hands on the hilt of the sword and with a mighty pull, brought it from the trunk of the tree with ease.

This sword became Sigmund's property and as he grew older, he used it often, becoming the greatest Viking warrior that ever was. And then the day came when Sigmund had reached the final years of his life. He lay dying on a field, the last of the Volsung line, and as he spoke his final words, his beloved wife Hiordis bathed his face and wept over her dear husband.

"I have met with Odin once again," he whispered to Hiordis. "I know it was he because my sword could not match the mighty spear he carried. He has come to bring me to Valhalla, and dear one I am ready to go."

He held out a weary hand and brushed away Hiordis's tears. "Fear not, little one," he said quietly, "for in your womb you carry my son, and he will be the greatest warrior ever known – greater still than any Volsung. He will take my sword, and he shall reign supreme." And then Sigmund died, as the Valkyrs led him gently to his peace.

Hiordis went on to marry the son of the King of Denmark, a man called Alf, who did not know that the child she carried belonged to Sigmund. When she gave birth there were great festivities, and the boy who was born was called Sigurd.

It is here that this story joins another, for once, just three or four years before Sigurd became a youth, and an apprentice to a smithy, Odin, Hoenir and Loki were walking in Midgard when they came across a burbling stream, rich with salmon and other fine fish. As they prepared to catch one for their meal, they were startled by the movement of an otter, who was just wakening at the side of the stream. Quickly Loki grabbed the otter and killed it, and a fire was quickly built while the otter was skinned. The men dined greedily, and with the pelt of the otter over their backs, they made their way towards a cabin, which was just peeking from between the trees. They knocked at the door and were startled to be met by an angry man who was summoning his thralls to help him tie up the three strangers.

Odin stepped forward. "Do you not know that passers-by are to be treated with kindness, and given a bed for the night? Do you not know that Odin has decreed this?" Odin was in his customary disguise and the angry stranger had no idea who he was dealing with.

The stranger, whose name was Kreidmar, scowled at Odin and said, "Not when they have murdered my son."

Kreidmar's son had been a form-shifter, and had just finished a fine meal of salmon, which he had caught in the shape of an otter. He had been murdered before he could become a man again.

Loki and Odin apologized profusely, and offered to do anything in their power to repay Kreidmar.

"There is only one thing you can do," said Kreidmar, "and that is to fill my son's otter pelt with gold, and then cover every hair on its back until I cannot see it at all."

The three men agreed, and set out at once for a waterfall where they knew that a dwarf by the name of Andvari lived as a sharp-toothed pike and guarded a magnificent treasure of gold and jewels. With characteristic cunning, Loki managed to divert the fish, and as Andvari was changed back into a dwarf, to retrieve the treasure.

Loki and Odin gathered together the splendid gold broaches, rings, necklaces and ornaments, and as they made to leave, they saw something glinting from the pocket of the trembling dwarf.

"What's that?" said Loki, ever quick of eye.

"Oh, this…" said Andvari, "…this you cannot have. This ring has a curse on it. Whoever owns it once it leaves my care will have nothing but disaster."

Loki had little fear curses and enchantment, for he could rival the best with his own, and he snatched the ring from the dwarf and the three men made their way back to the cabin. There they stuffed the pelt of Kreidmar's son, and then covered the body with more gold. Finally they were finished.

Kreidmar came to inspect. "Ha!" he cried at once. "I see a whisker still uncovered. You have failed in your task and I will kill you all."

Loki stepped forward and bent down on his knee. "Please sir," he said graciously. "I have this one ring here which will cover the hair, but it holds an evil curse and I do not wish it upon you or your family."

"Give me the ring," snarled Kreidmar, "and all of you – be off!"

The three travellers continued on their way and soon forgot about Kreidmar and his son, but just moments after they left, the curse began to take effect. Kreidmar had two more sons, one called Fafnir, who also changed shape, and another called Regin. Regin was away, working as a blacksmith in Denmark, and he had as his pupil none other than Sigurd, son of Sigmund. Fafnir, however, lived at home, and on the very day that the curse fell upon his father, Fafnir took on a peculiar glint in his eye and began to covet the treasure that filled his brother's pelt.

A few days later, he murdered his father, and changing shape, he became a monstrous dragon, hiding himself away in a cave and guarding his magnificent treasure.

Now Regin, far away from the treasure had, as part of the curse, begun to covet it himself, and he began to hatch a plan to have it returned. He assessed the young Sigurd, who was working with him, and noticing his bravery and his amazing skill with arms, he decided to approach him to see if he would fight the dragon.

"Sigurd," he said slyly, "I notice that you have come of an age that you may want to practise some of your great father's skills. There is a dragon I know of, one who guards a treasure. Perhaps you would like to test those skills?"

Now Sigurd was just young enough to be tempted by the idea of fighting a dragon for treasure, and he went off into the forest the following day to find a horse. As he walked through the trees, where the horses ran free, he met an elderly man, one with just one eye, who suggested that Sigurd test the horses before he made his selection. And so together Sigurd and the old man sent the horses into a nearby river. All of the horses swam easily to the other side, and then galloped off into the distance. Only one horse returned – a lustrous grey stallion with a powerful body and fine, intelligent eyes.

"Take that horse," said the old man. "He is a descendant of Odin's own horse, Sleipnir, and he will care for you in times of trouble."

With that the old man disappeared, leaving Sigurd in no doubt as to who he had just seen. Turning to the horse, he stroked it and was rewarded by a happy snort. "I'll call you Grani," he said to the horse, "and together we shall kill a dragon."

Sigurd returned to Regin to tell him of his new horse, and to request that the blacksmith make him a great sword with which to kill the dragon. Regin began working, toiling over the hot forge until a sword was brought forth, gleaming. Sigurd lifted it into his hands, and then laid a heavy blow on the anvil. The sword broke into thousands of tiny pieces, and Regin looked at Sigurd in surprise. Back he went to the forge once again, and another sword was made, this one stronger and with a gleam that was even brighter than the first. Again, Sigurd lifted the sword and brought it down on the anvil, and again, it shattered into tiny pieces.

Regin shook his head, and began work on a third. "Go home, Sigurd, I will have another for you to try tomorrow."

Sigurd was puzzled by the course of events, and a seed of doubt had entered his mind about the ambitions of his tutor. Regin seemed very keen to have the dragon slain, and Sigurd wondered why. He approached his mother and explained the whole story to her.

Hiordis said, "My son there is a secret of which you are not aware. You are not the son of the man you think your father. You are the son of King Sigmund, and just before he died, he presented me with the pieces of this sword, which you may have forged to protect you. This sword will slay your dragon, if that is what you wish, and this same sword will protect you from whatever Regin has in store for you."

The following day, Sigurd returned to the smithy with the sword, and it was placed in the fire by Regin. Suddenly there was a flash of bright light and the sword emerged of its own accord, glittering in the firelight like a crystal. Sigurd reached for the sword and brought it down on the anvil. At once the anvil split in two and the gleam was reflected in the eyes of Regin. He could think of nothing now but the treasure, and so it was that the two gentlemen set off.

When they reached the cave of the dragon, Regin said to Sigurd, "Go on now, Boy, and slay the dragon. There will be treasure for us both. Whatever you do, don't let his blood touch you for you will burn for certain."

Sigurd set off in the direction of the dragon, and as he approached, the stranger from the woods appeared to him once again.

"Sigurd, what Regin tells you is wrong. Bathe in the blood of the dragon, for it will make you invincible. Approach him from the back for if you go this way you will surely be burned." With that the one-eyed man disappeared.

Sigurd did as he was bid, and he struck the great dragon from behind, slaying him at once. He cut a hole in the dragon's neck, and stripping off his clothes, he bathed in the dragon's blood until every part of his body was covered except for a tiny spot between his shoulderblades where a piece of heather had rested.

Gathering up the treasure, he returned to Regin who was delighted to hear of the spoils. "Do me one more favour, Sigurd," he asked, "cut out the heart of the dragon so that I may eat it, and a part of my brother may live on in me."

Sigurd returned to the dragon and did as he was asked. As he roasted the heart over a fire, a drop of the blood fell on to his hand, where it burned and began to smoke. Suddenly he began to hear voices. Looking around he saw no people, but the voices persisted. And it was at that moment that Sigurd realized that he could hear the birds speaking to one another, and they were discussing him! Sigurd listened while they spoke of Regin's treachery and how foolish he was to have trusted him. And when Sigurd looked up, there was Regin, ready to strike him down. With his mighty sword, Sigurd beheaded the blacksmith with one swing.

And so it as that Sigurd gathered up the treasure. As he put the same cursed ring in his pocket, he heard the birds say, "He must not take the cursed ring. Does the great Sigurd not know what will happen if he does?"

But shrugging their words aside, Sigurd made off for home. As he travelled, he saw in the distance a fine castle, surrounded by white light. He coaxed Grani up and over the light, and he landed on the marble flagstones of the castle courtyard. Dismounting, Sigurd laid down his sword and entered the castle. There, in the main hallway, lay a knight in shining armour. Sigurd quietly reached towards the knights helmet, and lifted it gently off, curious to see what great warrior lay there in state. But to his great surprise, a tumble of hair fell out from beneath the helmet and there lay an exquisite girl. He prodded her, and as if by magic her armour disappeared, and her eyes opened.

When this girl caught eyes with Sigurd there came between them a feeling that happens most infrequently; it was a love with such intensity that Sigurd knew at once that she was a part of him, and he her. He slipped his hand into his pocket and withdrew the ring, slipping it on her finger. Some say this girl was called Brunhilde, and that she was the daughter of Odin. Other say she was born of Sigurd's need, and therefore was, in truth, a part of himself. Whoever she was, she became a part of Sigurd's life, and a part of the curse that he had just placed on her slender finger. But that, and the other tales of Sigurd and his adventures, is another story.

The Great Red Dragon of Wales

EVERY OLD COUNTRY that has won fame in history and built up a civilization of its own, has a national flower. Besides this, some living creature, bird, or beast, or, it may be, a fish is on its flag. In places of honour, it stands as the emblem of the nation; that is, of the people, apart from the land they live on. Besides flag and symbol, it has a motto. That of Wales is: 'Awake: It is light.'

Now because the glorious stories of Wales, Scotland and Ireland have been nearly lost in that of mighty England, men have at times, almost forgotten about the leek, the thistle, and the shamrock, which stand for the other three divisions of the British Isles.

Yet each of these peoples has a history as noble as that of which the rose and the lion are the emblems. Each has also its patron saint and civilizer. So we have Saint George, Saint David, Saint Andrew, and Saint Patrick, all of them white-souled heroes. On the union flag, or standard of the United Kingdom, we see their three crosses.

The lion of England, the harp of Ireland, the thistle of Scotland, and the Red Dragon of Wales represent the four peoples in the British Isles, each with its own speech, traditions, and emblems; yet all in unity and in loyalty, none excelling the Welsh, whose symbol is the Red Dragon. In classic phrase, we talk of Albion, Scotia, Cymry, and Hibernia.

But why red? Almost all the other dragons in the world are white, or yellow, green or purple, blue, or pink. Why a fiery red colour like that of Mars?

Borne on the banners of the Welsh archers, who in old days won the battles of Crecy and Agincourt, and now seen on the crests on the town halls and city flags, in heraldry, and in art, the red dragon is as rampant, as when King Arthur sat with His Knights at the Round Table.

The Red Dragon has four three-toed claws, a long, barbed tongue, and tail ending like an arrow head. With its wide wings unfolded, it guards those ancient liberties, which neither Saxon, nor Norman, nor German, nor kings on the throne, whether foolish or wise, have ever been able to take away. No people on earth combine so handsomely loyal freedom and the larger patriotism, or hold in purer loyalty to the union of hearts and hands in the British Empire, which the sovereign represents, as do the Welsh.

The Welsh are the oldest of the British peoples. They preserve the language of the Druids, bards, and chiefs, of primeval ages which go back and far beyond any royal line in Europe, while most of their fairy tales are pre-ancient and beyond the dating.

Why the Cymric dragon is red, is thus told, from times beyond human record.

It was in those early days, after the Romans in the south had left the island, and the Cymric king, Vortigern, was hard pressed by the Picts and Scots of the north. To his aid, he invited over from beyond the North Sea, or German Ocean, the tribes called the Long Knives, or Saxons, to help him.

But once on the big island, these friends became enemies and would not go back. They wanted to possess all Britain.

Vortigern thought this was treachery. Knowing that the Long Knives would soon attack him, he called his twelve wise men together for their advice. With one voice, they advised him to retreat westward behind the mountains into Cymry. There he must build a strong fortress and there defy his enemies.

So the Saxons, who were Germans, thought they had driven the Cymry beyond the western borders of the country which was later called England, and into what they named the foreign or Welsh parts. Centuries afterwards, this land received the name of Wales.

People in Europe spoke of Galatians, Wallachians, Belgians, Walloons, Alsatians, and others as 'Welsh.' They called the new fruit imported from Asia walnuts, but the names 'Wales' and 'Welsh' were unheard of until after the fifth century.

The place chosen for the fortified city of the Cymry was among the mountains. From all over his realm, the King sent for masons and carpenters and collected the materials for building. Then, a solemn invocation was made to the gods by the Druid priests. These grand looking old men were robed in white, with long, snowy beards falling over their breasts, and they had milk-white oxen drawing their chariot. With a silver knife they cut the mistletoe from the tree-branch, hailing it as a sign of favour from God. Then with harp, music and song they dedicated the spot as a stronghold of the Cymric nation.

Then the King set the diggers to work. He promised a rich reward to those men of the pick and shovel who should dig the fastest and throw up the most dirt, so that the masons could, at the earliest moment, begin their part of the work.

But it all turned out differently from what the king expected. Some dragon, or powerful being underground, must have been offended by this invasion of his domain; for, the next morning, they saw that everything in the form of stone, timber, iron or tools, had disappeared during the night. It looked as if an earthquake had swallowed them all up.

Both king and seers, priests and bards, were greatly puzzled at this. However, not being able to account for it, and the Saxons likely to march on them at any time, the sovereign set the diggers at work and again collected more wood and stone.

This time, even the women helped, not only to cook the food, but to drag the logs and stones. They were even ready to cut off their beautiful long hair to make ropes, if necessary.

But in the morning, all had again disappeared, as if swept by a tempest. The ground was bare. Nevertheless, all hands began again, for all hearts were united.

For the third time, the work proceeded. Yet when the sun rose next morning, there was not even a trace of either material or labour.

What was the matter? Had some dragon swallowed everything up?

Vortigern again summoned his twelve wise men, to meet in council, and to inquire concerning the cause of the marvel and to decide what was to be done.

After long deliberation, while all the workmen and people outside waited for their verdict, the wise men agreed upon a remedy.

Now in ancient times, it was a custom, all over the world, notably in China and Japan and among our ancestors, that when a new castle or bridge was to be built, they sacrificed a human being. This was done either by walling up the victim while alive, or by mixing his or her blood with the cement used in the walls. Often it was a virgin or a little child thus chosen by lot and made to die, the one for the many.

The idea was not only to ward off the anger of the spirits of the air, or to appease the dragons under ground, but also to make the workmen do their best work faithfully, so that the foundation should be sure and the edifice withstand the storm, the wind, and the earthquake shocks.

So, nobody was surprised, or raised his eyebrows, or shook his head, or pursed up his lips, when the king announced that what the wise men declared, must be done and that quickly. Nevertheless, many a mother hugged her darling more closely to her bosom, and fathers feared for their sons or daughters, lest one of these, their own, should be chosen as the victim to be slain.

King Vortigern had the long horn blown for perfect silence, and then he spoke:

"A child must be found who was born without a father. He must be brought here and be solemnly put to death. Then his blood will be sprinkled on the ground and the citadel will be built securely."

Within an hour, swift runners were seen bounding over the Cymric hills. They were dispatched in search of a boy without a father, and a large reward was promised to the young man who found what was wanted. So into every part of the Cymric land, the searchers went.

One messenger noticed some boys playing ball. Two of them were quarreling. Coming near, he heard one say to the other:

"Oh, you boy without a father, nothing good will ever happen to you."

"This must be the one looked for," said the royal messenger to himself. So he went up to the boy, who had been thus twitted and spoke to him thus:

"Don't mind what he says." Then he prophesied great things, if he would go along with him. The boy was only too glad to go, and the next day the lad was brought before King Vortigern.

The workmen and their wives and children, numbering thousands, had assembled for the solemn ceremony of dedicating the ground by shedding the boy's blood. In strained attention the people held their breath.

The boy asked the king:

"Why have your servants brought me to this place?"

Then the sovereign told him the reason, and the boy asked:

"Who instructed you to do this?"

"My wise men told me so to do, and even the sovereign of the land obeys his wise councillors."

"Order them to come to me, Your Majesty," pleaded the boy.

When the wise men appeared, the boy, in respectful manner, inquired of them thus:

"How was the secret of my life revealed to you? Please speak freely and declare who it was that discovered me to you."

Turning to the king, the boy added:

"Pardon my boldness, Your Majesty. I shall soon reveal the whole matter to you, but I wish first to question your advisers. I want them to tell you what is the real cause, and reveal, if they can, what is hidden here underneath the ground."

But the wise men were confounded. They could not tell and they fully confessed their ignorance.

The boy then said:

"There is a pool of water down below. Please order your men to dig for it."

At once the spades were plied by strong hands, and in a few minutes the workmen saw their faces reflected, as in a looking glass. There was a pool of clear water there.

Turning to the wise men, the boy asked before all:

"Now tell me, what is in the pool?"

As ignorant as before, and now thoroughly ashamed, the wise men were silent.

"Your Majesty, I can tell you, even if these men cannot. There are two vases in the pool."

Two brave men leaped down into the pool. They felt around and brought up two vases, as the boy had said.

Again, the lad put a question to the wise men:

"What is in these vases?"

Once more, those who professed to know the secrets of the world, even to the demanding of the life of a human being, held their tongues.

"There is a tent in them," said the boy. "Separate them, and you will find it so."

By the king's command, a soldier thrust in his hand and found a folded tent.

Again, while all wondered, the boy was in command of the situation. Everything seemed so reasonable, that all were prompt and alert to serve him.

"What a splendid chief and general, he would make, to lead us against our enemies, the 'Long Knives!'" whispered one soldier to another.

"What is in the tent?" asked the boy of the wise men.

Not one of the twelve knew what to say, and there was an almost painful silence.

"I will tell you, Your Majesty, and all here, what is in this tent. There are two serpents, one white and one red. Unfold the tent."

With such a leader, no soldier was afraid, nor did a single person in the crowd draw back? Two stalwart fellows stepped forward to open the tent.

But now, a few of the men and many of the women shrank back while those that had babies, or little folks, snatched up their children, fearing lest the poisonous snakes might wriggle towards them.

The two serpents were coiled up and asleep, but they soon showed signs of waking, and their fiery, lidless eyes glared at the people.

"Now, Your Majesty, and all here, be you the witnesses of what will happen. Let the King and wise men look in the tent."

At this moment, the serpents stretched themselves out at full length, while all fell back, giving them a wide circle to struggle in.

Then they reared their heads. With their glittering eyes flashing fire, they began to struggle with each other. The white one rose up first, threw the red one into the middle of the arena, and then pursued him to the edge of the round space.

Three times did the white serpent gain the victory over the red one.

But while the white serpent seemed to be gloating over the other for a final onset, the red one, gathering strength, erected its head and struck at the other.

The struggle went on for several minutes, but in the end the red serpent overcame the white, driving it first out of the circle, then from the tent, and into the pool, where it disappeared, while the victorious red one moved into the tent again.

When the tent flap was opened for all to see, nothing was visible except a red dragon; for the victorious serpent had turned into this great creature which combined in one new form the body and the powers of bird, beast, reptile and fish. It had wings to fly, the strongest animal strength, and could crawl, swim, and live in either water or air, or on the earth. In its body was the sum total of all life.

Then, in the presence of all the assembly, the youth turned to the wise men to explain the meaning of what had happened. But not a word did they speak. In fact, their faces were full of shame before the great crowd.

"Now, Your Majesty, let me reveal to you the meaning of this mystery."

"Speak on," said the King, gratefully.

"This pool is the emblem of the world, and the tent is that of your kingdom. The two serpents are two dragons. The white serpent is the dragon of the Saxons, who now occupy several of the provinces and districts of Britain and from sea to sea. But when they invade our soil our people will finally drive them back and hold fast forever their beloved Cymric land. But you must choose another site, on which to erect your castle."

After this, whenever a castle was to be built no more human victims were doomed to death. All the twelve men, who had wanted to keep up the old cruel custom, were treated as deceivers of the people. By the King's orders, they were all put to death and buried before all the crowd.

To-day, like so many who keep alive old and worn-out notions by means of deception and falsehood, these men are remembered only by the Twelve Mounds, which rise on the surface of the field hard by.

As for the boy, he became a great magician, or, as we in our age would call him, a man of science and wisdom, named Merlin. He lived long on the mountain, but when he went away with a friend, he placed all his treasures in a golden cauldron and hid them in a cave. He rolled a great stone over its mouth. Then with sod and earth he covered it all over so as to hide it from view. His purpose was to leave this, his wealth, for a leader, who, in some future generation, would use it for the benefit of his country, when most needed.

This special person will be a youth with yellow hair and blue eyes. When he comes to Denas, a bell will ring to invite him into the cave. The moment his foot is over the place, the stone of entrance will open of its own accord. Anyone else will be considered an intruder and it will not be possible for him to carry away the treasure.

The Two Brothers

THERE WERE ONCE UPON A TIME two brothers, one rich and the other poor. The rich one was a goldsmith and evil-hearted. The poor one supported himself by making brooms, and was good and honourable. The poor one had two children, who were twin brothers and as like each other as two drops of water. The two boys went backwards and forwards to the rich house, and often got some of the scraps to eat.

It happened once when the poor man was going into the forest to fetch brush-wood, that he saw a bird which was quite golden and more beautiful than any he had ever chanced to meet with.

He picked up a small stone, threw it at him, and was lucky enough to hit him, but one golden feather only fell down, and the bird flew away. The man took the feather and carried it to his brother, who looked at it and said, "It is pure gold!" and gave him a great deal of money for it.

Next day the man climbed into a birch-tree, and was about to cut off a couple of branches when the same bird flew out, and when the man searched he found a nest, and an egg lay inside it, which was of gold. He took the egg home with him, and carried it to his brother, who again said, "It is pure gold," and gave him what it was worth.

At last the goldsmith said, "I should indeed like to have the bird itself."

The poor man went into the forest for the third time, and again saw the golden bird sitting on the tree, so he took a stone and brought it down and carried it to his brother, who gave him a great heap of gold for it. "Now I can get on," thought he, and went contentedly home.

The goldsmith was crafty and cunning, and knew very well what kind of a bird it was. He called his wife and said, "Roast me the gold bird, and take care that none of it is lost. I have a fancy to eat it all myself." The bird, however, was no common one, but of so wondrous a kind that whosoever ate its heart and liver found every morning a piece of gold beneath his pillow. The woman made the bird ready, put it on the spit, and let it roast.

Now it happened that while it was at the fire, and the woman was forced to go out of the kitchen on account of some other work, the two children of the poor broom-maker ran in, stood by the spit and turned it round once or twice. And as at that very moment two little bits of the bird fell down into the dripping-tin, one of the boys said, "We will eat these two little bits; I am so hungry, and no one will ever miss them."

Then the two ate the pieces, but the woman came into the kitchen and saw that they were eating something and said, "What have ye been eating?"

"Two little morsels which fell out of the bird," answered they.

"That must have been the heart and the liver," said the woman, quite frightened, and in order that her husband might not miss them and be angry, she quickly killed a young cock, took out his heart and liver, and put them beside the golden bird. When it was ready, she carried it to the goldsmith, who consumed it all alone, and left none of it.

Next morning, however, when he felt beneath his pillow, and expected to bring out the piece of gold, no more gold pieces were there than there had always been.

The two children did not know what a piece of good-fortune had fallen to their lot. Next morning when they arose, something fell rattling to the ground, and when they picked it up there were two gold pieces! They took them to their father, who was astonished and said, "How can that have happened?"

When next morning they again found two, and so on daily, he went to his brother and told him the strange story. The goldsmith at once knew how it had come to pass, and that the children had eaten the heart and liver of the golden bird, and in order to revenge himself, and because he was envious and hard-hearted, he said to the father, "Thy children are in league with the Evil One, do not take the gold, and do not suffer them to stay any longer in thy house, for he has them in his power, and may ruin thee likewise."

The father feared the Evil One, and painful as it was to him, he nevertheless led the twins forth into the forest, and with a sad heart left them there.

And now the two children ran about the forest, and sought the way home again, but could not find it, and only lost themselves more and more. At length they met with a huntsman, who asked, "To whom do you children belong?"

"We are the poor broom-maker's boys," they replied, and they told him that their father would not keep them any longer in the house because a piece of gold lay every morning under their pillows.

"Come," said the huntsman, "that is nothing so very bad, if at the same time you keep honest, and are not idle."

As the good man liked the children, and had none of his own, he took them home with him and said, "I will be your father, and bring you up till you are big."

They learnt huntsmanship from him, and the piece of gold which each of them found when he awoke was kept for them by him in case they should need it in the future.

When they were grown up, their foster-father one day took them into the forest with him, and said, "Today shall you make your trial shot, so that I may release you from your apprenticeship, and make you huntsmen."

They went with him to lie in wait and stayed there a long time, but no game appeared. The huntsman, however, looked above him and saw a covey of wild geese flying in the form of a triangle, and said to one of them, "Shoot me down one from each corner."

He did it, and thus accomplished his trial shot. Soon after another covey came flying by in the form of the figure two, and the huntsman bade the other also bring down one from each corner, and his trial shot was likewise successful.

"Now," said the foster-father, "I pronounce you out of your apprenticeship; you are skilled huntsmen."

Thereupon the two brothers went forth together into the forest, and took counsel with each other and planned something. And in the evening when they had sat down to supper, they said to their foster-father, "We will not touch food, or take one mouthful, until you have granted us a request."

Said he, "What, then, is your request?"

They replied, "We have now finished learning, and we must prove ourselves in the world, so allow us to go away and travel."

Then spake the old man joyfully, "You talk like brave huntsmen, that which you desire has been my wish; go forth, all will go well with you."

Thereupon they ate and drank joyously together.

When the appointed day came, their foster-father presented each of them with a good gun and a dog, and let each of them take as many of his saved-up gold pieces as he chose. Then he accompanied them a part of the way, and when taking leave, he gave them a bright knife, and said, "If ever you separate, stick this knife into a tree at the place where you part, and when one of you goes back, he will be able to see how his absent brother is faring, for the side of the knife which is turned in the direction by which he went will rust if he dies, but will remain bright as long as he is alive."

The two brothers went still farther onwards, and came to a forest which was so large that it was impossible for them to get out of it in one day. So they passed the night in it, and ate what they had put in their hunting-pouches, but they walked all the second day likewise, and still did not get out.

As they had nothing to eat, one of them said, "We must shoot something for ourselves or we shall suffer from hunger," and loaded his gun, and looked about him. And when an old hare came running up towards them, he laid his gun on his shoulder, but the hare cried:

> *"Dear huntsman, do but let me live,*
> *Two little ones to thee I'll give."*

and sprang instantly into the thicket, and brought two young ones. But the little creatures played so merrily, and were so pretty, that the huntsmen could not find it in their hearts to kill them. They therefore kept them with them, and the little hares followed on foot. Soon after this, a fox crept past; they were just going to shoot it, but the fox cried:

> *"Dear hunstman, do but let me live,*
> *Two little ones I'll also give."*

He, too, brought two little foxes, and the huntsmen did not like to kill them either, but gave them to the hares for company, and they followed behind. It was not long before a wolf strode out of the thicket; the huntsmen made ready to shoot him, but the wolf cried:

> *"Dear huntsman, do but let me live,*
> *Two little ones I'll likewise give."*

The huntsmen put the two wolves beside the other animals, and they followed behind them. Then a bear came who wanted to trot about a little longer, and cried:

"Dear huntsman, do but let me live,
Two little ones I, too, will give."

The two young bears were added to the others, and there were already eight of them. At length who came? A lion came, and tossed his mane. But the huntsmen did not let themselves be frightened and aimed at him likewise, but the lion also said,

"Dear huntsman, do but let me live,
Two little ones I, too, will give."

And he brought his little ones to them, and now the huntsmen had two lions, two bears, two wolves, two foxes, and two hares, who followed them and served them.

In the meantime their hunger was not appeased by this, and they said to the foxes, "Hark ye, cunning fellows, provide us with something to eat. You are crafty and deep."

They replied, "Not far from here lies a village, from which we have already brought many a fowl; we will show you the way there."

So they went into the village, bought themselves something to eat, had some food given to their beasts, and then travelled onwards. The foxes, however, knew their way very well about the district and where the poultry-yards were, and were able to guide the huntsmen.

Now they travelled about for a while, but could find no situations where they could remain together, so they said, "There is nothing else for it, we must part." They divided the animals, so that each of them had a lion, a bear, a wolf, a fox, and a hare, then they took leave of each other, promised to love each other like brothers till their death, and stuck the knife which their foster-father had given them, into a tree, after which one went east, and the other went west.

The younger, however, arrived with his beasts in a town which was all hung with black crape. He went into an inn, and asked the host if he could accommodate his animals. The innkeeper gave him a stable, where there was a hole in the wall, and the hare crept out and fetched himself the head of a cabbage, and the fox fetched himself a hen, and when he had devoured that got the cock as well, but the wolf, the bear, and the lion could not get out because they were too big. Then the innkeeper let them be taken to a place where a cow was just then lying on the grass, that they might eat till they were satisfied. And when the huntsman had taken care of his animals, he asked the innkeeper why the town was thus hung with black crape?

Said the host, "Because our King's only daughter is to die tomorrow."

The huntsman inquired if she was "sick unto death?"

"No," answered the host, "she is vigorous and healthy, nevertheless she must die!"

"How is that?" asked the huntsman. "There is a high hill without the town, whereon dwells a dragon who every year must have a pure virgin, or he lays the whole country waste, and now all the maidens have already been given to him, and there is no longer anyone left but the King's daughter, yet there is no mercy for her; she must be given up to him, and that is to be done tomorrow."

Said the huntsman, "Why is the dragon not killed?"

"Ah," replied the host, "so many knights have tried it, but it has cost all of them their lives. The King has promised that he who conquers the dragon shall have his daughter to wife, and shall likewise govern the kingdom after his own death."

The huntsman said nothing more to this, but next morning took his animals, and with them ascended the dragon's hill. A little church stood at the top of it, and on the altar three full cups were standing, with the inscription, 'Whosoever empties the cups will become the strongest man on earth, and will be able to wield the sword which is buried before the threshold of the door.'

The huntsman did not drink, but went out and sought for the sword in the ground, but was unable to move it from its place. Then he went in and emptied the cups, and now he was strong enough to take up the sword, and his hand could quite easily wield it. When the hour came when the maiden was to be delivered over to the dragon, the King, the marshal, and courtiers accompanied her. From afar she saw the huntsman on the dragon's hill, and thought it was the dragon standing there waiting for her, and did not want to go up to him, but at last, because otherwise the whole town would have been destroyed, she was forced to go the miserable journey. The King and courtiers returned home full of grief; the King's marshal, however, was to stand still, and see all from a distance.

When the King's daughter got to the top of the hill, it was not the dragon which stood there, but the young huntsman, who comforted her, and said he would save her, led her into the church, and locked her in. It was not long before the seven-headed dragon came thither with loud roaring.

When he perceived the huntsman, he was astonished and said, "What business hast thou here on the hill?"

The huntsman answered, "I want to fight with thee."

Said the dragon, "Many knights have left their lives here, I shall soon have made an end of thee too," and he breathed fire out of seven jaws.

The fire was to have lighted the dry grass, and the huntsman was to have been suffocated in the heat and smoke, but the animals came running up and trampled out the fire. Then the dragon rushed upon the huntsman, but he swung his sword until it sang through the air, and struck off three of his heads. Then the dragon grew right furious, and rose up in the air, and spat out flames of fire over the huntsman, and was about to plunge down on him, but the huntsman once more drew out his sword, and again cut off three of his heads.

The monster became faint and sank down, nevertheless it was just able to rush upon the huntsman, but he with his last strength smote its tail off, and as he could fight no longer, called up his animals who tore it in pieces. When the struggle was ended, the huntsman unlocked the church, and found the King's daughter lying on the floor, as she had lost her senses with anguish and terror during the contest. He carried her out, and when she came to herself once more, and opened her eyes, he showed her the dragon all cut to pieces, and told her that she was now delivered.

She rejoiced and said, "Now thou wilt be my dearest husband, for my father has promised me to him who kills the dragon."

Thereupon she took off her necklace of coral, and divided it amongst the animals in order to reward them, and the lion received the golden clasp. Her pocket-handkerchief, however, on which was her name, she gave to the huntsman, who went and cut the tongues out of the dragon's seven heads, wrapped them in the handkerchief, and preserved them carefully.

That done, as he was so faint and weary with the fire and the battle, he said to the maiden, "We are both faint and weary, we will sleep awhile."

Then she said, "yes," and they lay down on the ground, and the huntsman said to the lion, "Thou shalt keep watch, that no one surprises us in our sleep," and both fell asleep.

The lion lay down beside them to watch, but he also was so weary with the fight, that he called to the bear and said, "Lie down near me, I must sleep a little: if anything comes, waken me."

Then the bear lay down beside him, but he also was tired, and called the wolf and said, "Lie down by me, I must sleep a little, but if anything comes, waken me."

Then the wolf lay down by him, but he was tired likewise, and called the fox and said, "Lie down by me, I must sleep a little; if anything comes, waken me."

Then the fox lay down beside him, but he too was weary, and called the hare and said, "Lie down near me, I must sleep a little, and if anything should come, waken me."

Then the hare sat down by him, but the poor hare was tired too, and had no one whom he could call there to keep watch, and fell asleep. And now the King's daughter, the huntsman, the lion, the bear, the wolf, the fox, and the hare, were all sleeping a sound sleep.

The marshal, however, who was to look on from a distance, took courage when he did not see the dragon flying away with the maiden, and finding that all the hill had become quiet, ascended it. There lay the dragon hacked and hewn to pieces on the ground, and not far from it were the King's daughter and a huntsman with his animals, and all of them were sunk in a sound sleep. And as he was wicked and godless he took his sword, cut off the huntsman's head, and seized the maiden in his arms, and carried her down the hill.

Then she awoke and was terrified, but the marshal said, "Thou art in my hands, thou shalt say that it was I who killed the dragon."

"I cannot do that," she replied, "for it was a huntsman with his animals who did it."

Then he drew his sword, and threatened to kill her if she did not obey him, and so compelled her that she promised it. Then he took her to the King, who did not know how to contain himself for joy when he once more looked on his dear child in life, whom he had believed to have been torn to pieces by the monster.

The marshal said to him, "I have killed the dragon, and delivered the maiden and the whole kingdom as well, therefore I demand her as my wife, as was promised."

The King said to the maiden, "Is what he says true?"

"Ah, yes," she answered, "it must indeed be true, but I will not consent to have the wedding celebrated until after a year and a day," for she thought in that time she should hear something of her dear huntsman.

The animals, however, were still lying sleeping beside their dead master on the dragon's hill, and there came a great humble-bee and lighted on the hare's nose, but the hare wiped it off with his paw, and went on sleeping. The humble-bee came a second time, but the hare again rubbed it off and slept on. Then it came for the third time, and stung his nose so that he awoke.

As soon as the hare was awake, he roused the fox, and the fox, the wolf, and the wolf the bear, and the bear the lion. And when the lion awoke and saw that the maiden was gone, and his master was dead, he began to roar frightfully and cried, "Who has done that? Bear, why didst thou not waken me?" The bear asked the wolf, "Why didst thou not waken me?" and the wolf the fox, "Why didst thou not waken me?" and the fox the hare, "Why didst thou not waken me?" The poor hare alone did not know what answer to make, and the blame rested with him.

Then they were just going to fall upon him, but he entreated them and said, "Kill me not, I will bring our master to life again. I know a mountain on which a root grows which, when placed in the mouth of anyone, cures him of all illness and every wound. But the mountain lies two hundred hours journey from here."

The lion said, "In four-and-twenty hours must thou have run thither and have come back, and have brought the root with thee."

Then the hare sprang away, and in four-and-twenty hours he was back, and brought the root with him. The lion put the huntsman's head on again, and the hare placed the root in his mouth, and immediately everything united together again, and his heart beat, and life came back.

Then the huntsman awoke, and was alarmed when he did not see the maiden, and thought, "She must have gone away whilst I was sleeping, in order to get rid of me."

The lion in his great haste had put his master's head on the wrong way round, but the huntsman did not observe it because of his melancholy thoughts about the King's daughter. But at noon, when he was going to eat something, he saw that his head was turned backwards and could not understand it, and asked the animals what had happened to him in his sleep.

Then the lion told him that they, too, had all fallen asleep from weariness, and on awaking, had found him dead with his head cut off, that the hare had brought the life-giving root, and that he, in his haste, had laid hold of the head the wrong way, but that he would repair his mistake.

Then he tore the huntsman's head off again, turned it round, and the hare healed it with the root.

The huntsman, however, was sad at heart, and travelled about the world, and made his animals dance before people. It came to pass that precisely at the end of one year he came back to the same town where he had delivered the King's daughter from the dragon, and this time the town was gaily hung with red cloth.

Then he said to the host, "What does this mean? Last year the town was all hung with black crape, what means the red cloth today?"

The host answered, "Last year our King's daughter was to have been delivered over to the dragon, but the marshal fought with it and killed it, and so tomorrow their wedding is to be solemnized, and that is why the town was then hung with black crape for mourning, and is today covered with red cloth for joy!"

Next day when the wedding was to take place, the huntsman said at midday to the inn-keeper, "Do you believe, sir host, that I while with you here today shall eat bread from the King's own table?"

"Nay," said the host, "I would bet a hundred pieces of gold that that will not come true."

The huntsman accepted the wager, and set against it a purse with just the same number of gold pieces.

Then he called the hare and said, "Go, my dear runner, and fetch me some of the bread which the King is eating."

Now the little hare was the lowest of the animals, and could not transfer this order to any of the others, but had to get on his legs himself.

"Alas!" thought he, "if I bound through the streets thus alone, the butchers' dogs will all be after me."

It happened as he expected, and the dogs came after him and wanted to make holes in his good skin. But he sprang away – have you have never seen one running? – and sheltered himself in a sentry-box without the soldier being aware of it. Then the dogs came and wanted to have him out, but the soldier did not understand a jest, and struck them with the butt-end of his gun, till they ran away yelling and howling.

As soon as the hare saw that the way was clear, he ran into the palace and straight to the King's daughter, sat down under her chair, and scratched at her foot.

Then she said, "Wilt thou get away?" and thought it was her dog.

The hare scratched her foot for the second time, and she again said, "Wilt thou get away?" and thought it was her dog.

But the hare did not let itself be turned from its purpose, and scratched her for the third time.

Then she peeped down, and knew the hare by its collar. She took him on her lap, carried him into her chamber, and said, "Dear Hare, what dost thou want?"

He answered, "My master, who killed the dragon, is here, and has sent me to ask for a loaf of bread like that which the King eats."

Then she was full of joy and had the baker summoned, and ordered him to bring a loaf such as was eaten by the King.

The little hare said, "But the baker must likewise carry it thither for me, that the butchers' dogs may do no harm to me."

The baker carried if for him as far as the door of the inn, and then the hare got on his hind legs, took the loaf in his front paws, and carried it to his master.

Then said the huntsman, "Behold, sir host, the hundred pieces of gold are mine."

The host was astonished, but the huntsman went on to say, "Yes, sir host, I have the bread, but now I will likewise have some of the King's roast meat."

The host said, "I should indeed like to see that," but he would make no more wagers.

The huntsman called the fox and said, "My little fox, go and fetch me some roast meat, such as the King eats."

The red fox knew the bye-ways better, and went by holes and corners without any dog seeing him, seated himself under the chair of the King's daughter, and scratched her foot.

Then she looked down and recognized the fox by its collar, took him into her chamber with her and said, "Dear fox, what dost thou want?"

He answered, "My master, who killed the dragon, is here, and has sent me. I am to ask for some roast meat such as the King is eating."

Then she made the cook come, who was obliged to prepare a roast joint, the same as was eaten by the King, and to carry it for the fox as far as the door. Then the fox took the dish, waved away with his tail the flies which had settled on the meat, and then carried it to his master.

"Behold, sir host," said the huntsman, "bread and meat are here but now I will also have proper vegetables with it, such as are eaten by the King."

Then he called the wolf, and said, "Dear Wolf, go thither and fetch me vegetables such as the King eats."

Then the wolf went straight to the palace, as he feared no one, and when he got to the King's daughter's chamber, he twitched at the back of her dress, so that she was forced to look round.

She recognized him by his collar, and took him into her chamber with her, and said, "Dear Wolf, what dost thou want?"

He answered, "My master, who killed the dragon, is here, I am to ask for some vegetables, such as the King eats."

Then she made the cook come, and he had to make ready a dish of vegetables, such as the King ate, and had to carry it for the wolf as far as the door, and then the wolf took the dish from him, and carried it to his master.

"Behold, sir host," said the huntsman, "now I have bread and meat and vegetables, but I will also have some pastry to eat like that which the King eats."

He called the bear, and said, "Dear Bear, thou art fond of licking anything sweet; go and bring me some confectionery, such as the King eats."

Then the bear trotted to the palace, and everyone got out of his way, but when he went to the guard, they presented their muskets, and would not let him go into the royal palace. But he got up on his hind legs, and gave them a few boxes on the ears, right and left, with his paws, so that the whole watch broke up, and then he went straight to the King's daughter, placed himself behind her, and growled a little.

Then she looked behind her, knew the bear, and bade him go into her room with her, and said, "Dear Bear, what dost thou want?"

He answered, "My master, who killed the dragon, is here, and I am to ask for some confectionery, such as the King eats."

Then she summoned her confectioner, who had to bake confectionery such as the King ate, and carry it to the door for the bear; then the bear first licked up the comfits which had rolled down, and then he stood upright, took the dish, and carried it to his master.

"Behold, sir host," said the huntsman, "now I have bread, meat, vegetables and confectionery, but I will drink wine also, and such as the King drinks."

He called his lion to him and said, "Dear Lion, thou thyself likest to drink till thou art intoxicated, go and fetch me some wine, such as is drunk by the King." Then the lion strode through the streets, and the people fled from him, and when he came to the watch, they wanted to bar the way against him, but he did but roar once, and they all ran away. Then the lion went to the royal apartment, and knocked at the door with his tail.

Then the King's daughter came forth, and was almost afraid of the lion, but she knew him by the golden clasp of her necklace, and bade him go with her into her chamber, and said, "Dear Lion, what wilt thou have?"

He answered, "My master, who killed the dragon, is here, and I am to ask for some wine such as is drunk by the King."

Then she bade the cup-bearer be called, who was to give the lion some wine like that which was drunk by the King.

The lion said, "I will go with him, and see that I get the right wine."

Then he went down with the cup-bearer, and when they were below, the cup-bearer wanted to draw him some of the common wine that was drunk by the King's servants, but the lion said, "Stop, I will taste the wine first," and he drew half a measure, and swallowed it down at one draught.

"No," said he, "that is not right."

The cup-bearer looked at him askance, but went on, and was about to give him some out of another barrel which was for the King's marshal.

The lion said, "Stop, let me taste the wine first," and drew half a measure and drank it.

"That is better, but still not right," said he.

Then the cup-bearer grew angry and said, "How can a stupid animal like you understand wine?"

But the lion gave him a blow behind the ears, which made him fall down by no means gently, and when he had got up again, he conducted the lion quite silently into a little cellar apart, where the King's wine lay, from which no one ever drank. The lion first drew half a measure and tried the wine, and then he said that may possibly be the right sort, and bade the cup-bearer fill six bottles of it. And now they went upstairs again, but when the lion came out of the cellar into the open air, he reeled here and there, and was rather drunk, and the cup-bearer was forced to carry the wine as far as the door for him, and then the lion took the handle of the basket in his mouth, and took it to his master.

The huntsman said, "Behold, sir host, here have I bread, meat, vegetables, confectionery and wine such as the King has, and now I will dine with my animals," and he sat down and ate and drank, and gave the hare, the fox, the wolf, the bear, and the lion also to eat and to drink, and was joyful, for he saw that the King's daughter still loved him. And when he had finished his dinner, he said, "Sir host, now have I eaten and drunk, as the King eats and drinks, and now I will go to the King's court and marry the King's daughter."

Said the host, "How can that be, when she already has a betrothed husband, and when the wedding is to be solemnized today?" Then the huntsman drew forth the handkerchief which the King's daughter had given him on the dragon's hill, and in which were folded the monster's seven tongues, and said, "That which I hold in my hand shall help me to do it." Then the innkeeper looked at the handkerchief, and said, "Whatever I believe, I do not believe that, and I am willing to stake my house and courtyard on it."

The huntsman, however, took a bag with a thousand gold pieces, put it on the table, and said, "I stake that on it."

Now the King said to his daughter, at the royal table, "What did all the wild animals want, which have been coming to thee, and going in and out of my palace?"

She replied, "I may not tell you, but send and have the master of these animals brought, and you will do well." The King sent a servant to the inn, and invited the stranger, and the servant came just as the huntsman had laid his wager with the innkeeper.

Then said he, "Behold, sir host, now the King sends his servant and invites me, but I do not go in this way." And he said to the servant, "I request the Lord King to send me royal clothing, and a carriage with six horses, and servants to attend me."

When the King heard the answer, he said to his daughter, "What shall I do?"

She said, "Cause him to be fetched as he desires to be, and you will do well."

Then the King sent royal apparel, a carriage with six horses, and servants to wait on him. When the huntsman saw them coming, he said, "Behold, sir host, now I am fetched as I desired to be," and he put on the royal garments, took the handkerchief with the dragon's tongues with him, and drove off to the King.

When the King saw him coming, he said to his daughter, "How shall I receive him?"

She answered, "Go to meet him and you will do well."

Then the King went to meet him and led him in, and his animals followed. The King gave him a seat near himself and his daughter, and the marshal, as bridegroom, sat on the other side, but no longer knew the huntsman. And now at this very moment, the seven heads of the dragon were brought in as a spectacle, and the King said, "The seven heads were cut off the dragon by the marshal, wherefore today I give him my daughter to wife."

The the huntsman stood up, opened the seven mouths, and said, "Where are the seven tongues of the dragon?"

Then was the marshal terrified, and grew pale and knew not what answer he should make, and at length in his anguish he said, "Dragons have no tongues."

The huntsman said, "Liars ought to have none, but the dragon's tongues are the tokens of the victor," and he unfolded the handkerchief, and there lay all seven inside it. And he put each tongue in the mouth to which it belonged, and it fitted exactly.

Then he took the handkerchief on which the name of the princess was embroidered, and showed it to the maiden, and asked to whom she had given it, and she replied, "To him who killed the dragon."

And then he called his animals, and took the collar off each of them and the golden clasp from the lion, and showed them to the maiden and asked to whom they belonged.

She answered, "The necklace and golden clasp were mine, but I divided them among the animals who helped to conquer the dragon."

Then spake the huntsman, "When I, tired with the fight, was resting and sleeping, the marshal came and cut off my head. Then he carried away the King's daughter, and gave out that it was he who had killed the dragon, but that he lied I prove with the tongues, the handkerchief, and the necklace." And then he related how his animals had healed him by means of a wonderful root, and how he had travelled about with them for one year, and had at length again come there and had learnt the treachery of the marshal by the inn-keeper's story.

Then the King asked his daughter, "Is it true that this man killed the dragon?"

And she answered, "Yes, it is true. Now can I reveal the wicked deed of the marshal, as it has come to light without my connivance, for he wrung from me a promise to be silent. For this reason, however, did I make the condition that the marriage should not be solemnized for a year and a day."

Then the King bade twelve councillors be summoned who were to pronounce judgment on the marshal, and they sentenced him to be torn to pieces by four bulls. The marshal was therefore executed, but the King gave his daughter to the huntsman, and named him his viceroy over the whole kingdom. The wedding was celebrated with great joy, and the young King caused his father and his foster-father to be brought, and loaded them with treasures.

Neither did he forget the inn-keeper, but sent for him and said, "Behold, sir host, I have married the King's daughter, and your house and yard are mine."

The host said, "Yes, according to justice it is so."

But the young King said, "It shall be done according to mercy," and told him that he should keep his house and yard, and gave him the thousand pieces of gold as well.

And now the young King and Queen were thoroughly happy, and lived in gladness together. He often went out hunting because it was a delight to him, and the faithful animals had to accompany him. In the neighbourhood, however, there was a forest of which it was reported that it was haunted, and that whosoever did but enter it did not easily get out again. The young King, however, had a great inclination to hunt in it, and let the old King have no peace until he allowed him to do so. So he rode forth with a great following, and when he came to the forest, he saw a snow-white hart and said to his people, "Wait here until I return, I want to chase that beautiful creature," and he rode into the forest after it, followed only by his animals.

The attendants halted and waited until evening, but he did not return, so they rode home, and told the young Queen that the young King had followed a white hart into the enchanted forest, and had not come back again. Then she was in the greatest concern about him.

He, however, had still continued to ride on and on after the beautiful wild animal, and had never been able to overtake it; when he thought he was near enough to aim, he instantly saw it bound away into the far distance, and at length it vanished altogether. And now he perceived that he had penetrated deep into the forest, and blew his horn but he received no answer, for his attendants could not hear it. And as night, too, was falling, he saw that he could not get home that day, so he dismounted from his horse, lighted himself a fire near a tree, and resolved to spend the night by it.

While he was sitting by the fire, and his animals also were lying down beside him, it seemed to him that he heard a human voice. He looked round, but could perceive nothing.

Soon afterwards, he again heard a groan as if from above, and then he looked up, and saw an old woman sitting in the tree, who wailed unceasingly, "Oh, oh, oh, how cold I am!"

Said he, "Come down, and warm thyself if thou art cold."

But she said, "No, thy animals will bite me."

He answered, "They will do thee no harm, old mother, do come down."

She, however, was a witch, and said, "I will throw down a wand from the tree, and if thou strikest them on the back with it, they will do me no harm."

Then she threw him a small wand, and he struck them with it, and instantly they lay still and were turned into stone. And when the witch was safe from the animals, she leapt down and touched him also with a wand, and changed him to stone. Thereupon she laughed, and dragged him and the animals into a vault, where many more such stones already lay.

As, however, the young King did not come back at all, the Queen's anguish and care grew constantly greater. And it so happened that at this very time the other brother who had turned to the east when they separated, came into the kingdom. He had sought a situation, and had found none, and had then travelled about here and there, and had made his animals dance. Then it came into his mind that he would just go and look at the knife that they had thrust in the trunk of a tree at their parting, that he might learn how his brother was.

When he got there his brother's side of the knife was half rusted, and half bright. Then he was alarmed and thought, "A great misfortune must have befallen my brother, but perhaps I can still save him, for half the knife is still bright."

He and his animals travelled towards the west, and when he entered the gate of the town, the guard came to meet him, and asked if he was to announce him to his consort the young Queen, who had for a couple of days been in the greatest sorrow about his staying away, and was afraid he had been killed in the enchanted forest? The sentries, indeed, thought no otherwise than that he was the young King himself, for he looked so like him, and had wild animals running behind him. Then he saw that they were speaking of his brother, and thought, "It will be better if I pass myself off for him, and then I can rescue him more easily."

So he allowed himself to be escorted into the castle by the guard, and was received with the greatest joy. The young Queen indeed thought that he was her husband, and asked him why he had stayed away so long. He answered, "I had lost myself in a forest, and could not find my way out again any sooner."

At night he was taken to the royal bed, but he laid a two-edged sword between him and the young Queen; she did not know what that could mean, but did not venture to ask.

He remained in the palace a couple of days, and in the meantime inquired into everything which related to the enchanted forest, and at last he said, "I must hunt there once more."

The King and the young Queen wanted to persuade him not to do it, but he stood out against them, and went forth with a larger following. When he had got into the forest, it fared with him as with his brother; he saw a white hart and said to his people, "Stay here, and wait until I return, I want to chase the lovely wild beast," and then he rode into the forest and his animals ran after him.

But he could not overtake the hart, and got so deep into the forest that he was forced to pass the night there.

And when he had lighted a fire, he heard someone wailing above him, "Oh, oh, oh, how cold I am!"

Then he looked up, and the self-same witch was sitting in the tree.

Said he, "If thou art cold, come down, little old mother, and warm thyself."

She answered, "No, thy animals will bite me."

But he said, "They will not hurt thee."

Then she cried, "I will throw down a wand to thee, and if thou smitest them with it they will do me no harm." When the huntsman heard that, he had no confidence in the old woman, and said, "I will not strike my animals. Come down, or I will fetch thee."

Then she cried, "What dost thou want? Thou shalt not touch me."

But he replied, "If thou dost not come, I will shoot thee."

Said she, "Shoot away, I do not fear thy bullets!"

Then he aimed, and fired at her, but the witch was proof against all leaden bullets, and laughed, and yelled and cried, "Thou shalt not hit me."

The huntsman knew what to do, tore three silver buttons off his coat, and loaded his gun with them, for against them her arts were useless, and when he fired she fell down at once with a scream. Then he set his foot on her and said, "Old witch, if thou dost not instantly confess where my brother is, I will seize thee with both my hands and throw thee into the fire."

She was in a great fright, begged for mercy and said, "He and his animals lie in a vault, turned to stone."

Then he compelled her to go thither with him, threatened her, and said, "Old sea-cat, now shalt thou make my brother and all the human beings lying here, alive again, or thou shalt go into the fire!"

She took a wand and touched the stones, and then his brother with his animals came to life again, and many others, merchants, artisans, and shepherds, arose, thanked him for their deliverance, and went to their homes.

But when the twin brothers saw each other again, they kissed each other and rejoiced with all their hearts. Then they seized the witch, bound her and laid her on the fire, and when she was burnt the forest opened of its own accord, and was light and clear, and the King's palace could be seen at about the distance of a three hours walk.

Thereupon the two brothers went home together, and on the way told each other their histories. And when the youngest said that he was ruler of the whole country in the King's stead, the other observed, "That I remarked very well, for when I came to the town, and was taken for thee, all royal honours were paid me; the young Queen looked on me as her husband, and I had to eat at her side, and sleep in thy bed."

When the other heard that, he became so jealous and angry that he drew his sword, and struck off his brother's head. But when he saw him lying there dead, and saw his red blood flowing, he repented most violently: "My brother delivered me," cried he, "and I have killed him for it," and he bewailed him aloud.

Then his hare came and offered to go and bring some of the root of life, and bounded away and brought it while yet there was time, and the dead man was brought to life again, and knew nothing about the wound.

After this they journeyed onwards, and the youngest said, "Thou lookest like me, hast royal apparel on as I have, and the animals follow thee as they do me; we will go in by opposite gates, and arrive at the same time from the two sides in the aged King's presence."

So they separated, and at the same time came the watchmen from the one door and from the other, and announced that the young King and the animals had returned from the chase.

The King said, "It is not possible, the gates lie quite a mile apart."

In the meantime, however, the two brothers entered the courtyard of the palace from opposite sides, and both mounted the steps.

Then the King said to the daughter, "Say which is thy husband. Each of them looks exactly like the other, I cannot tell."

Then she was in great distress, and could not tell; but at last she remembered the necklace which she had given to the animals, and she sought for and found her little golden clasp on the lion, and she cried in her delight, "He who is followed by this lion is my true husband."

Then the young King laughed and said, "Yes, he is the right one," and they sat down together to table, and ate and drank, and were merry.

Thatt night when the young King went to bed, his wife said, "Why hast thou for these last nights always laid a two-edged sword in our bed? I thought thou hadst a wish to kill me." Then he knew how true his brother had been.

The Treasure of the Dragon

AN OLD SAILOR brought to my town the news of having seen, in a very distant island, a terrible dragon which guarded an immense treasure. Half of the body of this guardian was a fish, the other half a lion; it moreover had such powerful wings that it could rise to an extraordinary height. Air, water, or land were his elements, and when any ships came near to the coast they were soon attacked by that ever vigilant monster.

Many expeditions were made, but all succumbed to the talons of that invincible animal; moreover, the treasure was so splendid that it excited the envy of adventurers from all parts of the earth.

Among the innumerable precious stones which with thousands of gold bars formed those riches, there was a statue of natural size made out of a single diamond, and which was worth such a fabulous sum that all the treasures of the earth would not suffice to buy it.

The fear of the dragon did not lessen the enthusiasm of the lads of my town; on the contrary, it was a further stimulus to their bravery and daring, and so, in little less than a month, an expedition was formed of the bravest and most ambitious.

They set out on the 15th of September on a bark named the *Temeraire* – a handsome brigantine, the swiftest that ever glided over the waves. After fourteen days' sailing they found themselves at about a league from the island where the treasure and the dragon were. Behold what happened!

The members of the expedition met in council in order to take their measures, and agreed as follows: to launch some boats in order to land in three or four places at the same time; to carry a great quantity of ammunition so as to be able to fire upon the dragon; and, lastly, to divide the treasure in equal parts and to distribute it among the expeditionaries. There was only one vote against, that of a cabin boy, a youth of eighteen, who opposed the dividing of the party, believing it better to wait for the dragon on board the ship, and from there to fight it with cannons.

"If you are afraid, stay behind," they all said to him, and nobody paid any attention to the cabin boy's scheme.

As nobody trusted his companions, all embarked in the bunches, fearful of being cheated if they did not witness the division of the treasure, leaving on board only the cabin boy and the pilot, a very experienced old sailor who had not uttered any opinion at the meeting. The launches being full and the crews armed, they left the ship and rowed near to the coast.

Pascual, for so the cabin boy was named, prepared the bow-gun, loading it up to the mouth, and also seized a strong sharp spear. Then he sat down in the bows, and from there, with a telescope, watched the progress of his companions. The latter were about a hundred yards from the coast when a tremendous roar was heard; he saw the dragon fly up into the air and fall upon one of the launches. Several gunshots were heard, and soon the launch disappeared under the water. The bullets glanced off the skin of the terrible animal, which threw itself in turn upon the other launches and sank them.

Its work of extermination finished, the dragon returned to the island, shaking its wings, reddened by the blood of its victims.

The pilot, terrified, wished to go back to his country, but Pascual prevented it, and directed him to go at full sail towards the island.

The pilot gave way to the solicitations of the cabin boy, who now no longer thought of the treasure but of avenging the death of his companions.

They had arrived at some hundred fathoms from the coast when they saw the dragon, which was advancing towards them. Pascual rapidly aimed the small cannon, but the ball struck on some rocks, and the dragon, more irritated than ever, threw himself upon the brigantine. It described a couple of circles in the air like an eagle choosing its prey, and at length threw itself upon Pascual, who, mounted on a round house, valiantly waited for it.

Such was the violence of the attack that the dragon, on attempting to break the spear with which the heroic boy greeted it, sent it quite through one of its claws, and so great was the pain that it made a horrible outcry and rose up in the air full of terrible frenzy. The spear remained fixed in the claw, and to it hung Pascual, who, by his weight, increased the woes of the dragon. In vain the latter tried to get rid of that singular guest; all its efforts were useless, Pascual bestrode his spear like an enthusiastic gymnast. Then becoming furious, it threw itself into the sea in order to try to drown him. Pascual swam like a fish and dived like a seal; so his enemy was not able to liberate itself from him. Being now desperate, it went to the island, dragging the cabin boy with it; the latter had hardly touched *terra firma* when, using the spear as a lever, he gave it a turn with all his might, twisting the wounded claw in such a way that the pain deprived the monster of its strength and consciousness. Giving a cry it fell to the ground defenceless. Pascual then got out his jack-knife and looked with care for the joints between the formidable scales which served the dragon as armour. There he thrust it in many times, with the aid of a stone which he used in place of a hammer.

The dragon was now dead, and Pascual thought of his companions and went down to the shore to seek them. His search was useless, for he did not even find a trace of them. He looked towards the spot where he had left the brigantine, and that had also disappeared; doubtless the old pilot was afraid and had gone away with the ship.

Then our hero decided to seek the treasure, but in vain he went over the island in all directions: he found not the least sign of it. Then he returned to the spot where he had seen the dragon lying when they had approached the island, and he saw that there was an enormous stone which no doubt covered the entrance of the grotto where the treasure was to be found. He applied the spear to the joints and succeeded in moving it, and after some effort he brought into view a winding staircase, down which he hurriedly went. The first room to which the staircase gave access had its walls covered with rubies, the second with emeralds, and the third with pearls and diamonds. In the centre stood the magnificent statue made out of a single diamond, and which represented a very beautiful princess. Pascual was astounded at such extraordinary beauty, and burst into an exclamation of admiration.

Presently he noticed the pedestal of the statue, on which might be read:

'In a stone lies the disenchantment.'

Then the cabin boy looked at all the projections of the room, and pressing one of them heard a creak, and instantaneously, as the scenes in a fairy comedy are changed, the grotto disappeared; each precious stone was changed into a human being, and the beautiful princess, again turned to flesh and blood, came slowly down from her pedestal, and, giving her hand to the valiant lad, offered to reward his bravery by giving him all the riches of her kingdom, and with them her heart. Among the disenchanted beings were all his companions of the expedition, who embraced Pascual, and, what was very strange, did not envy him, recognising that his triumph was deserved. All the destroyed boats appeared on the coast, and in them they embarked, each one going to his own country and the cabin boy to that of the princess.

Pascual is now no longer Pascual, but His Highness Prince Pascual I., a very good man, according to what his subjects say.

Vasilica the Brave

ONCE UPON A TIME, in a certain town there dwelt a gipsy blacksmith, who was the best iron worker in the whole empire.

This gipsy had a son as fair and handsome as a Roumanian fawn, and as strong and as brave as a young lion. He played with the sledge hammer as if it were a toy; twisted the great anvil between his fingers, and broke across his knee a thick iron bar as though it were a reed.

The life of a working blacksmith, however, was not to his taste, athletic sports, and playing at soldiers with his young comrades pleased him better, pretending that he was a great Captain, and strutting about in a coloured paper helmet. He liked racing and wrestling, and running about in the open air all day long – to quarrel, and to come off victorious. As I have already said, he was very strong, stronger than the strongest man. He did not know the meaning of fear, and was calm and cool in the greatest peril; he laughed at ill the frightful tales of dragons and evil spirits recounted by the old women of the neighbourhood.

So he was called Vasilica the Brave.

His father, seeing that he was not diligent at learning, either his own trade, or any other, thought it best that he should become a soldier. But the boy did not wish to be placed under the command of others, for with his strength he could overcome them all.

Seeing that his father was always urging him to take to some business, and now that he was grown to manhood, the time had arrived for him to gain his livelihood, he made a small bundle of his clothes, and left home without telling anyone where he was going to, or without having come to any conclusion himself on that point.

II

As he went along the highway, his bundle on a stick slung over his shoulder, he heard in the distance the neighing and shrieking of a horse, enough to make his hair stand on end.

Another in his place would have turned back; he, on the contrary, threw his bundle on the grass, and ran quickly in the direction from whence the sound came, and before he could say "God help me," he reached a large field in the middle of which a terrible scene met his view. A large and awful dragon was twisting itself round a beautiful horse, squeezing the very life out of its body, beating it with its wings, and biting it with its ferocious mouth, until the poor animal was covered with blood.

The horse, though strong and brave, had only his teeth and hoofs to defend himself with, so that the dragon, having so great an advantage, would soon have finished the strife.

When the horse saw Vasilica appear, he called to him, "quick! quick! come here and save me, I shall be of much use to you in the world."

Then the dragon, said, "mind your own affairs, youngster, if you do not wish to be ground to powder."

Vasilica had no weapon, but hearing the dragon calling to him with so much assurance, fearlessly rushed towards him, careless of his tail, which beat the ground like a thousand whips, seized him by the head from behind, jerked it once upwards, twisted it to the right and to the left, and the dragon's head remained in his hands. The wings of the terrible animal became as powerless as those of a wet turkey, its tail no longer beat the ground, and its body fell in a heap below.

The horse, freed from the terrible grip, shook himself, throwing the foam in all directions, and going up to Vasilica said, "master, I thank thee; be thou my master until death."

III

Now we find Vasilica with the horse, and such a horse! After having caught his bundle, he mounted quickly, and scratched his ear in hesitation, not knowing what direction to take.

"Where are we going, master?" said the horse, seeing his indecision.

"I scarcely know!" said Vasilica, looking in various directions.

"Where are you going?" again said the horse.

"Where I shall be able to do brave deeds, don't you know that I am the renowned Vasilica?" said he with pride.

"Vasilica the brave! Oh, I have heard mention of this name with fear, and if what you say is true, go where I will take you, and you will find what you seek."

"What sayest thou?"

"I say that if thou art really the renowned Vasilica, then thou must do a brave and good deed, that is, to rescue my mistress and her three sisters from three fearful dragons, that have held them in their power for so many years."

"Are these dragons formidable?" asked Vasilica.

"Indeed, yes," replied the horse, "no man has yet dared to approach one of them in strength or in power."

"Let me only encounter them; I have a lance in readiness for them," said Vasilica.

"Don't boast, master, for you do not know with whom you have to do, my first master was not to be despised, but nevertheless, he was eaten alive by the weakest of these dragons; had the other taken him in hand, who is the strongest in the world, then what would have become of him?"

"Who was your master?" asked Vasilica.

"He was the son of a powerful emperor, who fell in love with the daughter of a neighbouring emperor, and when he went to ask her in marriage, the father replied, 'first of all you must rescue the two other sisters from the power of the dragons, and when you have done this, I will give you my daughter to wife.' My master joyfully agreed to this proposal, and made his preparations to depart. But during the night, the dragons came and carried off also his intended bride, which only increased his eagerness to depart. The emperor's son was brave, but imprudent, and lily advice was useless, for he would not listen to me, and so in consequence fell all easy prey to those monsters, who took his life without the slightest remorse. Since then I have been without a master, wandering about, searching for some brave personage of renown, to revenge the death of my master, and to rescue those three unhappy Princesses from life-long captivity. Many years have passed since I began my search, and I have been unable to find any one who dared to put his strength in opposition to that of the dragons. To-day, passing by here, I encountered the hideous monster, who nearly cut the thread of my life, and would have done so had it not been for your valiant and powerful arm."

"Pray tell me, where do these dragons live?" said Vasilica.

"You must traverse nine kingdoms, and cross nine seas; but have no anxiety on that account, for I am a flying horse, and can go like the wind, and gallop as quick as thought. I can transform myself to any shape I please, and have also the same power over others; come with me, rescue these unfortunate sisters from captivity, I am sure you will vanquish these terrible dragons, and become possessed of their boundless treasures, for I have heard them often say, 'if ever Vasilica the brave crosses our path, our power is at an end.'"

"Let us go," said Vasilica, with pride; the horse spread his wings, and they disappeared from sight.

IV

After having gone some distance through the clouds, the horse and rider descended in a green field, studded with numberless flowers, in the centre of which stood a castle, all in copper, and which glistened quite dazzling in the sun.

"This is the palace of the biggest dragon," said the horse "go, knock at the gate, and it will be opened by the eldest Princess. Enter without fear, for the dragon is absent, and when he returns, you will know of it, for he will fling his club six miles before him, which club will enter the castle alone, and hang itself up on its own nail in the wall. If you wish to acquaint him with your presence, take up the club, fling it back, and go forwards and meet him."

Vasilica listened attentively, dismounted by the side of the wall, left the horse there to feed, and went straight to the Gate of the Palace, where he knocked three times.

The eldest Princess was walking alone in the court of the palace without attendants, and when she heard the knocking at the gate, she opened it in person.

Since she had been spirited away by the dragon, her eyes had not rested on a human creature, for the palace was situated in an uninhabited country.

Seeing Vasilica, she uttered a cry of surprise, and stood like a statue.

"Good day, Princess!" said Vasilica.

"Thank you! brave knight," stammered she.

"What wind has blown you here?"

"A favourable wind," said he, "the wind of freedom."

"May God hear you! but I cannot believe it," said she, with a sigh.

"Will you allow me, lady, a little rest and shelter?" asked Vasilica, entering the court.

"With very good will," said she, "only you must enter quickly, or the dragon will find you here." Leave that to me, lady, I am a match for him."

So she sheltered her guest, and offered him all that she had of the best, according to the old Roumanian traditions of hospitality, without asking who he was, from whence he came, or whither he was going.

After he seemed refreshed, she began to question him of the world in general. While Vasilica was recounting to her what had happened lately, they suddenly heard a tremendous bellowing, followed by a trembling of the ground which shook the castle to its foundations. On hearing this, the Princess became pale as death, and cried, "Woe is me! Where shall I hide you – for the dragon is coming?" "Have no anxiety on my account, for we are safe," answered Vasilica. At that same moment, the gate was flung open, and the dragon's club was thrown in; with a whistling noise it sprung on to a table, and from thence hung itself on a nail.

Vasilica seeing this, seized the club from the nail, and turning it round in a circle three times, flung it beyond the gate twice the distance which it had originally come. The dragon coming along at a rapid pace towards the palace, hearing the roar of his club, stopped and exclaimed to himself, "What can this mean?" Hardly had he finished this exclamation, before his club clove through the air and fell at his feet, and penetrated the earth for a yard deep.

"My club!" cried the dragon, unearthing his weapon with great difficulty. "Who has dared to lay hands on this, and to throw it with all its weight, such a tremendous distance? Only Vasilica the Brave is capable of such an act."

"You have guessed well, monster," answered a voice close by, "Vasilica stands before you! I bow with humility in your presence."

"Ha! it is you," cried the dragon, grinding his teeth; "it is well you have come, for how long have I not thirsted for your blood? Tell me quickly what method of combat do you prefer? Wrestling, or the sword thrust?"

"Wrestling is better, because it is more equal," said Vasilica.

"Good, so be it," cried the dragon, dashing towards him so as to crush him with the weight of his body; but he had found his match at last though his size was gigantic, while Vasilica appeared slight, but sinewy and well knit. When he closed with the dragon, and flung his arms round him, it was with a grip of iron, and his muscles stood out like the tendons of a bull. The dragon flung himself to the right, but Vasilica twisting to the left nearly overthrew him.

The first struggle did not prove victorious to either, for they were both strong and brave.

They fought hand to hand, three hours, without relaxation; their feet had entered the ground up to their knees; perspiration was pouring from them, as from a fountain; the blood was trickling from their wounds, but neither would yield. Towards sunset, Vasilica concentrated all his force, and with one mighty push overthrew the dragon, thrust his dagger into his throat, and, finally, beheaded him, flinging the body into the moat. Dragging the head along with him to the palace, at the feet of the Emperor's daughter, he cried, "Princess, behold! Thou art a widow; but thou art free from the demon who kept thee enslaved."

"May God repay you tenfold," replied the Princess, weeping for joy.

V

Finding herself delivered from the dragon, sunshine returned to the face of the Princess, and she set before her deliverer the best food she had; and entertained him for a week to restore himself, and recruit his strength.

At the end of this time, our hero took leave of the Princess, and mounting his horse flew off into the air. On descending, he saw glittering in the rays of the sun, a palace in pure silver.

"Here," says the horse, "is the residence of the second dragon, and he is more powerful than the one whose head you cut off; and yet he is less formidable than the third dragon. Go to his palace without fear, acquit yourself as you did with the first."

Vasilica departed, and knocking at the gate, it was opened by the second Princess, who remained equally astonished as her eldest sister had been. She received him with joy, and entertained him hospitably. While at the table the club of the second dragon entered, jumped from the table to the hook in the wall; the performance being accompanied by even a louder noise than on the previous occasion.

The Princess became pale, and trembled with fright; but Vasilica, with the greatest coolness, took the club from its resting place, and sent it back with two-fold force.

He set off at once to meet the dragon, who, seeing his club whirling through the air, and burying itself at his feet, in the ground, for a depth of two feet, in his turn became pale and said: "Only Vasilica the Brave, can have done this, and if he has reached so far as here, then surely my eldest brother is dead."

"You are correct in your calculations," said Vasilica, appearing on the scene, "be quick and prepare yourself for battle, I am thirsting to drink your blood, as I drank that of your brother."

"Don't be too sure about that," cried the dragon furiously, "shall we wrestle or fight with swords?"

"Wrestling is more equal," said Vasilica.

They fought for four long hours, and strove one against the other with so much force, that they sank into the ground up to their waists. Rivers of perspiration ran from them, but neither one nor the other would yield.

Towards night-fall, Vasilica, by a superhuman effort, gave the dragon a grip, and threw him heavily down, he made great efforts to rise, but the well-tempered dagger of Vasilica, entered his throat in an instant, and his life-blood welled out and stained the whole field.

Seeing that the dragon did not move, Vasilica cut off his head, and hid the trunk under a bridge.

On entering the palace he was received with great joy by the Princess, and remained her guest for two weeks.

VI

After taking leave of the Princess, Vasilica again mounted his horse, and they flew away into space. On descending towards the earth a third time, a shining golden palace met their view. When they were near it, the horse said to its master, "up to this time we have done our best, and we have come out victorious; but now you must be very cautious, for this is the most terrible of all the dragons, and the strongest creature that ever lived."

"So far I have told you to go forward and conquer, but now I say, reflect, while there is yet time."

"Vasilica does not fly from danger," answered he with pride; "if I turn back, the youngest Princess, who was the intended bride of your first master, and for whom he sacrificed his life, will remain in captivity; how then can you tell me to flee?"

"Do as you like!" said the horse, "only I repeat, reflect! and be careful; I also will try and help you, put faith in me, and with God's blessing, we will be victorious." With this conversation, they arrived in front of the palace, Vasilica dismounted, knocked at the gate, and entered as he had previously done, being received by the youngest daughter of the Emperor.

When at table, the third dragon announced himself by his club; Vasilica seized it, before it had time to place itself on the nail, and threw it out twice as quickly as it came in.

The dragon was approaching the bridge when he saw his club pelting along, and burying itself in the ground at his feet.

"This is the work of Vasilica the Brave," cried the dragon, foaming at the mouth; "he has killed my two brothers, and now I intend to kill him."

"Get to work, then," said Vasilica, obstructing his path.

"Well!" cried the dragon, how shall we fight? by wrestling, or by the sword?"

"Wrestling, as with the others," said Vasilica.

They closed at once, and now it was a fearful trial of strength, and they fought from noon to eventide. They had kicked up the earth until it reached their throats; Perspiration poured from them like a foaming cascade; blood spurted from their veins like water from a pump, and yet neither was victorious.

Fighting in this way, the dragon suddenly jumped from the hole in which he found himself, on to the bridge, and changed himself into a flaming red dragon, with a mouth quite two yards wide, and a seven forked tail. Hardly had this taken place, than Vasilica, by the aid of his horse, took the form of a green dragon, just as formidable as his adversary.

Dashing at each other with open mouths and tails erect, they met in the centre of the bridge, and they began to bite each other, to beat with their wings, and to lash with their tails. This unparalleled combat lasted till midnight: from their bodies oozed streams of black blood, from their eyes shot sparks of fire, from their nostrils sulphur, and from their mouths tongues of flame.

The red dragon became only a wheel of fire, and rolled quickly into the green dragon, so as to cut him in twain.

At the same moment, the green dragon was also a green wheel of flaming fire, and beat into the red wheel with unheard of force.

After this strife had lasted more than two hours, the red wheel demanded respite, seeing that its axle from the rapid motion, had taken fire; but the green wheel would not consent, although sparks of fare were perceptible in its axle also. At this moment, high up in the air above their heads, appeared a vulture.

"Vulture, dear vulture," cried the red wheel, "go down to the river, dip your wings in water, and come and wet my axle, then I will give you a dead body to feed on."

"Vulture, dear vulture," cried the green wheel, "go down to the river, dip your wings in water, and come and wet my axle, and then I will give you three dead bodies to feed on."

The vulture went to the river, clipped his wings, and wetted the axle of the green wheel. Instantaneously its force was redoubled, and it attacked its enemy with renewed power.

The red wheel was one sheet of livid fire, and exploded with a deafening noise.

The green wheel became once more Vasilica, who, dagger in hand, struck the red wheel, which also took its original shape, poured out streams of blood, and fell lifeless.

Vasilica, seeing the monster stretched on the bridge stiff and dead, cut off its head, and kicking the carcass towards the vulture, cried, "there, eat this, and afterwards the other two dragons, which I have left near the drawbridges of their palaces."

"I do not need them," answered the vulture, who speedily changed himself into the faithful horse.

"How is this?" cried Vasilica. "You, my deliverer?" as he saw his beloved horse by his side.

"Yes, Master," said the horse, "I have kept my promise; I changed you into a dragon, and into a wheel of fire, when you needed it, and I have given you all the help in my power."

"You have repaid your debt," said Vasilica, "for you have saved my life, and now we are quits. Let us go and set. at liberty the youngest Princess, and then we will return home."

"He! he! we haven't yet time to go back."

"Why?" asked Vasilica. "We have yet more to do," said the horse; "we have conquered the dragons, but their mother yet remains, and she is more formidable than they."

"Come along," said Vasilica, impetuously, "let us go and vanquish her also."

"Not so fast, my master, we must rest awhile, for we have striven hard, and we have yet much to do."

"Lot us go to the palace, then," said Vasilica.

The youngest princess, on learning that she was free from captivity, clapped her hands with joy, and entertained her deliverer and his valiant horse for three weeks, with the best that the castle afforded.

VII

After three weeks had elapsed, the horse called his master aside one day, and said to him: "Master, we have had great trouble before we got free from those three monsters, and as yet we have not gained much; for the Princesses for whom we have fought, are even yet in great danger, until we have overcome the artful mother of the dragons."

"Let us set off at once," said Vasilica, vaulting into the saddle.

"It is easy to say 'Go,' but it is rather difficult to attain, for this she-dragon cannot be fought by wrestling, or by the sword, but must be combatted with her own weapons of cunning and deceit;

and she is as deceitful as she is wicked. She will meet you with a kiss, and stab you from behind. If we can entrap her youngest daughter, we may then well say that we have got the upper hand. She has three daughters, all very lovely, but the youngest is perfection. If by fair means or foul, we can entice this young creature away, then the old one is in our power."

"If it be only a question of turning the head of a pretty girl, leave me alone for that, for I am a proficient in the art," said Vasilica, swelling with pride.

"He! he! master," it is not all plain sailing; the girl, perhaps, you maybe able to charm; but the old one has a keen scent, and directly she smells who you are, it is finished with us."

"Come along, and we'll see what happens."

They flew along, over vale, mountain, and forest, until a golden palace, put together with large diamond nails, came in sight. The dragoness had not yet received news of the death of her three sons; had she done so, the earth would have quaked at their approach.

In the beautiful garden, at the back of the palace, she was taking the air with her daughters, when her youngest daughter heard, near to her, the purring of a cat; on looking down, there was a beautiful little white kitten at her feet, playing and rubbing itself against the bottom of her robe.

"Ah! mother," said she, "see what a pretty kitten;" at the same time taking it up in her hands. Her mother not hearing her, she kept the kitten in her arms, entered a kiosque near, and seating herself on a low divan, took it on her lap and began patting and caressing it. The kitten rolled on its back, purring, and tapping her hands with its soft paws, and while playing, her 'kerchief slipped off her neck.

All at once the mother enters, and sniffing to the right and to the left, exclaimed: "There's the smell of man's flesh here, from the other world!"

"A man," said the girl, astonished, "what do you mean?" and went on playing with the kitten. "There is no one here, I assure you."

"No one has come? You are stupid my child, it is a pity that you are my daughter. Throw a handkerchief round your neck, for it is not decent to sit there without one."

"But where do you see even the shadow of a man, mother?"

"Where? What is that on your lap?"

"Don't you see? It is a kitten."

"Kitten, kitten," said the mother, "but his eyes sparkle like those of a brave man; put on your 'kerchief, and you, kitten, take back your own shape, and come to table, for my house is open to all well meaning travellers. If you don't obey me, I will tear you in a thousand pieces."

The kitten, to whom this was addressed, went on with his play, taking no more notice than an actual kitten would.

This indifference, enraged the dragoness.

"Youngster!" she exclaimed, "if you don't take your original shape, I will fling you into the pond in the garden, which is very deep, and as cold as ice."

Still the kitten remained impassive, so she seized it by the nape of the neck, and carried it to the edge of the pond, again repeating her command. The kitten for reply began to play with a morsel of ribbon hanging from her dress.

"Let him alone, mother! Don't fling him into the pond! Don't you see it is a kitten, like all kittens? If he had been a man, he would have been afraid, and would have obeyed you."

"Don't speak! for you don't know what you say," said the dragoness, and seizing the kitten, she was about to throw it into the water.

The girl cried entreatingly that her kitten might not be drowned; the kitten, seeing its peril, stuck its claws into the dragoness, and scratched her so severely, that she flung it away from her in disgust.

"You are rightly punished," said her daughter, "now are you convinced that it is a kitten?"

"Kitten! kitten! but his eyes are man's eyes," cried the mother, in uncontrollable rage.

"Be so good as to let my kitten alone, for it is the only plaything I have ever had," said the girl, going after it, and holding it to her bosom.

But the dragoness was not easily deceived, and seizing her daughter by the hand, dragged her indoors, entered the kitchen, opened the door of the oven, and taking the kitten from her daughter said, "now sir, if you won't change yourself into a man, I will throw you into the hot oven."

The kitten's only reply was to play with a lighted ember, and burning itself, began to mew with pain, and jumped through the window.

The girl pursued it, hoping to catch and caress it, but the kitten was already over the wall and on the road beyond; the young girl hurried through the gate to catch it, so that it might not escape into the wood.

She was too late, for it was already in the wood, and forgetting the danger incurred, she set off in pursuit.

The kitten enticed the maiden slowly along, but as soon as she tried to catch it, it slipped through her fingers, and glided gently forwards, so that before she was aware of it, she found herself in the middle of a dense forest.

Then the kitten suddenly transformed himself into Vasilica the Brave, seized the maiden in his arms, sprang with her on to his faithful horse, and journeyed many hours, until he reached his native city.

Who can recount the rejoicings of his parents, the joy of his comrades, the happiness, and the wealth of the young couple? Vasilica, in every palace which he visited, had received gifts of precious stones, so that his leather girdle was as full of diamonds and sapphires, as is his native country now of his valiant descendants.

The Prince and the Dragon

ONCE UPON A TIME there lived an emperor who had three sons. They were all fine young men, and fond of hunting, and scarcely a day passed without one or other of them going out to look for game.

One morning the eldest of the three princes mounted his horse and set out for a neighbouring forest, where wild animals of all sorts were to be found. He had not long left the castle, when a hare sprang out of a thicket and dashed across the road in front. The young man gave chase at once, and pursued it over hill and dale, till at last the hare took refuge in a mill which was standing by the side of a river. The prince followed and entered the mill, but stopped in terror by the door, for, instead of a hare, before him stood a dragon, breathing fire and flame. At this fearful sight the prince turned to fly, but a fiery tongue coiled round his waist, and drew him into the dragon's mouth, and he was seen no more.

A week passed away, and when the prince never came back everyone in the town began to grow uneasy. At last his next brother told the emperor that he likewise would go out to hunt, and that perhaps he would find some clue as to his brother's disappearance. But hardly had the castle gates closed on the prince than the hare sprang out of the bushes as before, and led the huntsman up hill and down dale, till they reached the mill. Into this the hare flew with the prince at his heels, when, lo! instead of the hare, there stood a dragon breathing fire and flame; and out shot a fiery tongue which coiled round the prince's waist, and lifted him straight into the dragon's mouth, and he was seen no more.

Days went by, and the emperor waited and waited for the sons who never came, and could not sleep at night for wondering where they were and what had become of them. His youngest son wished to go in search of his brothers, but for long the emperor refused to listen to him, lest he should lose him also. But the prince prayed so hard for leave to make the search, and promised so often that he would be very cautious and careful, that at length the emperor gave him permission, and ordered the best horse in the stables to be saddled for him.

Full of hope the young prince started on his way, but no sooner was he outside the city walls than a hare sprang out of the bushes and ran before him, till they reached the mill. As before, the animal dashed in through the open door, but this time he was not followed by the prince. Wiser than his brothers, the young man turned away, saying to himself: "There are as good hares in the forest as any that have come out of it, and when I have caught them, I can come back and look for you."

For many hours he rode up and down the mountain, but saw nothing, and at last, tired of waiting, he went back to the mill. Here he found an old woman sitting, whom he greeted pleasantly.

"Good morning to you, little mother," he said; and the old woman answered: "Good morning, my son."

"Tell me, little mother," went on the prince, "where shall I find my hare?"

"My son," replied the old woman, "that was no hare, but a dragon who has led many men hither, and then has eaten them all." At these words the prince's heart grew heavy, and he cried, "Then my brothers must have come here, and have been eaten by the dragon!"

"You have guessed right," answered the old woman; "and I can give you no better counsel than to go home at once, before the same fate overtakes you."

"Will you not come with me out of this dreadful place?" said the young man.

"He took me prisoner, too," answered she, "and I cannot shake off his chains."

"Then listen to me," cried the prince. "When the dragon comes back, ask him where he always goes when he leaves here, and what makes him so strong; and when you have coaxed the secret from him, tell me the next time I come."

So the prince went home, and the old woman remained in the mill, and as soon as the dragon returned she said to him:

"Where have you been all this time – you must have travelled far?"

"Yes, little mother, I have indeed travelled far." answered he. Then the old woman began to flatter him, and to praise his cleverness; and when she thought she had got him into a good temper, she said: "I have wondered so often where you get your strength from; I do wish you would tell me. I would stoop and kiss the place out of pure love!" The dragon laughed at this, and answered:

"In the hearthstone yonder lies the secret of my strength."

Then the old woman jumped up and kissed the hearth; whereat the dragon laughed the more, and said:

"You foolish creature! I was only jesting. It is not in the hearthstone, but in that tall tree that lies the secret of my strength." Then the old woman jumped up again and put her arms round the tree, and kissed it heartily. Loudly laughed the dragon when he saw what she was doing.

"Old fool," he cried, as soon as he could speak, "did you really believe that my strength came from that tree?"

"Where is it then?" asked the old woman, rather crossly, for she did not like being made fun of.

"My strength," replied the dragon, "lies far away; so far that you could never reach it. Far, far from here is a kingdom, and by its capital city is a lake, and in the lake is a dragon, and inside the dragon is a wild boar, and inside the wild boar is a pigeon, and inside the pigeon a sparrow, and inside the sparrow is my strength." And when the old woman heard this, she thought it was no use flattering him any longer, for never, never, could she take his strength from him.

The following morning, when the dragon had left the mill, the prince came back, and the old woman told him all that the creature had said. He listened in silence, and then returned to the castle, where he put on a suit of shepherd's clothes, and taking a staff in his hand, he went forth to seek a place as tender of sheep.

For some time he wandered from village to village and from town to town, till he came at length to a large city in a distant kingdom, surrounded on three sides by a great lake, which happened to be the very lake in which the dragon lived. As was his custom, he stopped everybody whom he met in the streets that looked likely to want a shepherd and begged them to engage him, but they all seemed to have shepherds of their own, or else not to need any. The prince was beginning to lose heart, when a man who had overheard his question turned round and said that he had better go and ask the emperor, as he was in search of some one to see after his flocks.

"Will you take care of my sheep?" said the emperor, when the young man knelt before him.

"Most willingly, your Majesty," answered the young man, and he listened obediently while the emperor told him what he was to do.

"Outside the city walls," went on the emperor, "you will find a large lake, and by its banks lie the richest meadows in my kingdom. When you are leading out your flocks to pasture, they will all run straight to these meadows, and none that have gone there have ever been known to come back. Take heed, therefore, my son, not to suffer your sheep to go where they will, but drive them to any spot that you think best."

With a low bow the prince thanked the emperor for his warning, and promised to do his best to keep the sheep safe. Then he left the palace and went to the market-place, where he bought two greyhounds, a hawk, and a set of pipes; after that he took the sheep out to pasture. The instant the animals caught sight of the lake lying before them, they trotted off as fast as their legs would go to the green meadows lying round it. The prince did not try to stop them; he only placed his hawk on the branch of a tree, laid his pipes on the grass, and bade the greyhounds sit still; then, rolling up his sleeves and trousers, he waded into the water crying as he did so: "Dragon! dragon! if you are not a coward, come out and fight with me!" And a voice answered from the depths of the lake:

"I am waiting for you, O prince;" and the next minute the dragon reared himself out of the water, huge and horrible to see. The prince sprang upon him and they grappled with each other and fought together till the sun was high, and it was noonday. Then the dragon gasped:

"O prince, let me dip my burning head once into the lake, and I will hurl you up to the top of the sky." But the prince answered, "Oh, ho! my good dragon, do not crow too soon! If the emperor's daughter were only here, and would kiss me on the forehead, I would throw you up higher still!" And suddenly the dragon's hold loosened, and he fell back into the lake.

As soon as it was evening, the prince washed away all signs of the fight, took his hawk upon his shoulder, and his pipes under his arm, and with his greyhounds in front and his flock following after him he set out for the city. As they all passed through the streets the people stared in wonder, for never before had any flock returned from the lake.

The next morning he rose early, and led his sheep down the road to the lake. This time, however, the emperor sent two men on horseback to ride behind him, with orders to watch the prince all day long. The horsemen kept the prince and his sheep in sight, without being seen themselves. As soon as they beheld the sheep running towards the meadows, they turned aside up a steep hill, which overhung the lake. When the shepherd reached the place he laid, as before, his pipes on the grass and bade the greyhounds sit beside them, while the hawk he perched on the branch of the tree. Then he rolled up his trousers and his sleeves, and waded into the water crying:

"Dragon! dragon! if you are not a coward, come out and fight with me!" And the dragon answered:

"I am waiting for you, O prince," and the next minute he reared himself out of the water, huge and horrible to see. Again they clasped each other tight round the body and fought till it was noon, and when the sun was at its hottest, the dragon gasped:

"O prince, let me dip my burning head once in the lake, and I will hurl you up to the top of the sky." But the prince answered:

"Oh, ho! my good dragon, do not crow too soon! If the emperor's daughter were only here, and would kiss me on the forehead, I would throw you up higher still!" And suddenly the dragon's hold loosened, and he fell back into the lake.

As soon as it was evening the prince again collected his sheep, and playing on his pipes he marched before them into the city. When he passed through the gates all the people came out of their houses to stare in wonder, for never before had any flock returned from the lake.

Meanwhile the two horsemen had ridden quickly back, and told the emperor all that they had seen and heard. The emperor listened eagerly to their tale, then called his daughter to him and repeated it to her.

"To-morrow," he said, when he had finished, "you shall go with the shepherd to the lake, and then you shall kiss him on the forehead as he wishes."

But when the princess heard these words, she burst into tears, and sobbed out:

"Will you really send me, your only child, to that dreadful place, from which most likely I shall never come back?"

"Fear nothing, my little daughter, all will be well. Many shepherds have gone to that lake and none have ever returned; but this one has in these two days fought twice with the dragon and has escaped without a wound. So I hope to-morrow he will kill the dragon altogether, and deliver this land from the monster who has slain so many of our bravest men."

Scarcely had the sun begun to peep over the hills next morning, when the princess stood by the shepherd's side, ready to go to the lake. The shepherd was brimming over with joy, but the princess only wept bitterly. "Dry your tears, I implore you," said he. "If you will just do what I ask you, and when the time comes, run and kiss my forehead, you have nothing to fear."

Merrily the shepherd blew on his pipes as he marched at the head of his flock, only stopping every now and then to say to the weeping girl at his side:

"Do not cry so, Heart of Gold; trust me and fear nothing." And so they reached the lake.

In an instant the sheep were scattered all over the meadows, and the prince placed his hawk on the tree, and his pipes on the grass, while he bade his greyhounds lie beside them. Then he rolled up his trousers and his sleeves, and waded into the water, calling:

"Dragon! dragon! if you are not a coward, come forth, and let us have one more fight together." And the dragon answered: "I am waiting for you, O prince;" and the next minute he reared himself out of the water, huge and horrible to see. Swiftly he drew near to the bank, and the prince sprang to meet him, and they grasped each other round the body and fought till it was noon. And when the sun was at its hottest, the dragon cried:

"O prince, let me dip my burning head in the lake, and I will hurl you to the top of the sky." But the prince answered:

"Oh, ho! my good dragon, do not crow too soon! If the emperor's daughter were only here, and she would kiss my forehead, I would throw you higher still."

Hardly had he spoken, when the princess, who had been listening, ran up and kissed him on the forehead. Then the prince swung the dragon straight up into the clouds, and when he touched the earth again, he broke into a thousand pieces. Out of the pieces there sprang a wild boar and galloped away, but the prince called his hounds to give chase, and they caught the boar and tore it to bits. Out of the pieces there sprang a hare, and in a moment the greyhounds were after it, and they caught it and killed it; and out of the hare there came a pigeon. Quickly the prince let loose his hawk, which soared straight into the air, then swooped upon the bird and brought it to his master. The prince cut open its body and found the sparrow inside, as the old woman had said.

"Now," cried the prince, holding the sparrow in his hand, "now you shall tell me where I can find my brothers."

"Do not hurt me," answered the sparrow, "and I will tell you with all my heart. Behind your father's castle stands a mill, and in the mill are three slender twigs. Cut off these twigs and strike their roots with them, and the iron door of a cellar will open. In the cellar you will find as many people, young and old, women and children, as would fill a kingdom, and among them are your brothers."

By this time twilight had fallen, so the prince washed himself in the lake, took the hawk on his shoulder and the pipes under his arm, and with his greyhounds before him and his flock behind him, marched gaily into the town, the princess following them all, still trembling with fright. And so they passed through the streets, thronged with a wondering crowd, till they reached the castle.

Unknown to anyone, the emperor had stolen out on horseback, and had hidden himself on the hill, where he could see all that happened. When all was over, and the power of the dragon was broken for ever, he rode quickly back to the castle, and was ready to receive the prince with open arms, and to promise him his daughter to wife. The wedding took place with great splendour, and for a whole week the town was hung with coloured lamps, and tables were spread in the hall of the castle for all who chose to come and eat. And when the feast was over, the prince told the emperor and the people who he really was, and at this everyone rejoiced still more, and preparations were made for the prince and princess to return to their own kingdom, for the prince was impatient to set free his brothers.

The first thing he did when he reached his native country was to hasten to the mill, where he found the three twigs as the sparrow had told him. The moment that he struck the root the iron door flew open, and from the cellar a countless multitude of men and women streamed forth. He bade them go one by one wheresoever they would, while he himself waited by the door till his brothers passed through. How delighted they were to meet again, and to hear all that the prince had done to deliver them from their enchantment. And they went home with him and served him all the days of their lives, for they said that he only who had proved himself brave and faithful was fit to be king.

The Boy and the Dragon

ONCE, LONG AGO, before the white man came to Canada, a boy was living with his parents in a village near the ocean. As he had no brothers or sisters, he was often lonely, and he longed for adventure and companionship. At last he decided to set out to seek his fortune elsewhere. He was just on the point of leaving his home when it was noised abroad one day that there had come into the land a great dragon, who was doing great havoc and damage wherever he went. The country was in great terror, for the dragon carried off women and children and devoured them one by one. And what was still more mystifying, he had power to take on human form, and often he changed himself into a man of pleasing shape and manner and came among the people to carry out his cruel designs before they knew that he was near. The Chief of the tribe called for volunteers to meet the dragon-man, but none of his warriors responded. They were strong and mighty in combat with men, but it was a different matter to encounter a dragon.

When the youth heard this dreadful story and saw the terror of his people, he said, "Here is my chance to do a great deed," for somehow he felt that he had more than human power. So he said good-bye to his parents and set out on his adventure. He travelled all day inland through the forest, until at evening he came to a high hill in the centre of an open space. He said, "I will climb this hill, and perhaps I can see all the country round about me." So he went slowly to the top. As he stood there, looking over the country which he could see for many miles around, a man suddenly appeared beside him. He was a very pleasant fellow, and they talked together for some time. The boy was on his guard, but he thought, "Surely this man with the good looks cannot be the dragon," and he laughed at his suspicions and put them from his mind.

The stranger said, "Where are you going?" And the boy answered, "I am going far away. I am seeking adventure in the forest for it is very lonely down by the sea." But he did not tell him of his real errand. "You may stay with me to-night," said the new-comer. "I have a very comfortable lodge not far from here, and I will give you food." The boy was very hungry and tired, and he went along with the man to his lodge. When they reached the house the boy was surprised to see a great heap of bleached bones lying before the door. But he showed no fear nor did he comment on the horrible sight. Inside the lodge sat a very old and bent woman, tending a pot. She was stirring it with a big stick, and the boy saw that it contained meat stew. When she placed the stew before them, the boy said he would rather have corn, for he feared to taste the meat. The old woman fried some corn for him, and he had a good meal.

After they had eaten, the man went out to gather wood for the fire, and the boy sat talking to the old woman. And she said to him, "You are very young and beautiful and innocent – the most handsome I have yet seen in this place. And because of that, I will take pity on you and warn you of your danger. The man whom you met in the forest and whom you supped with to-night is none other than the dragon-man of whom you have often heard. He cannot be killed in ordinary combat, and it would be folly for you to try. To-morrow he will kill you if you are still here. Take these moccasins that I will give you, and in the morning when you get up put them on your feet. With one step you will reach by their power the hill you see in the distance. Give this piece of birch bark with the picture on it to a man you will meet there, and he will tell you what next to do. But remember that no matter how far you go, the dragon-man will overtake you in the evening." The youth took the moccasins and the birch bark bearing the mystic sign and hid them under his coat, and said, "I will do as you advise." But the woman said, "There is one more condition. You must kill me in the morning before you go, and put this robe over my body. Then the dragon-man's spell over me will be broken, and when he leaves me, I will rouse myself with my power back to life."

The youth went to sleep, and the dragon-man slept all night beside him so as not to let him escape. The next morning, when the dragon-man was out to get water from the stream some distance away, the boy at once carried out the old woman's orders of the night before. First of all he killed the old woman with a blow and covered her body with a bright cloak, for he knew that when the dragon-man would leave the place she would soon rise again. Then he put the magic moccasins on his feet and with one great step he reached the distant hill. Here, sure enough, he met an old man. He gave him the piece of birch bark bearing the mystic sign. The man looked at it closely and smiled and said, "So it is you I was told to wait for. That is well, for you are indeed a comely youth." The man gave him another pair of moccasins in exchange for those he was wearing, and another piece of birch bark bearing another inscription. He pointed to a hill that rose blue in the distance and said, "With one step you will reach that hill. Give this bark to a man you will meet there, and all will be well."

The boy put the moccasins on his feet, and with one step he reached the distant hill. There he met another old man, to whom he gave the birch bark. This man gave him another pair of moccasins and a large maple leaf bearing a strange symbol, and told him to go to another spot, where he would receive final instructions. He did as he was told, and here he met a very old man, who said, "Down yonder there is a stream. Go towards it and walk straight into it, as if you were on dry ground. But do not look at the water. Take this piece of birch bark bearing these magic figures, and it will change you into whatever you wish, and it will keep you from harm." The boy took the bark and did as he was told, and soon found himself on the opposite bank of the stream. He followed the stream for some distance, and at evening he came to a lake. As he was looking about for a warm place to pass the night, he suddenly came upon the dragon-man, now in the form of a monster dragon, hiding behind the trees. The old woman's words had come true, for his enemy had overtaken him before nightfall, as she had said. There was no time to lose, so the boy waved his magic bark, and at once he became a little fish with red fins, moving slowly in the lake.

When the dragon-man saw the little fish, he cried, "Little fish of the red fins, have you seen the youth I am looking for?"

"No, sir," said the little fish, "I have seen no one; I have been asleep. But if he passes this way I will tell you," and he moved rapidly out into the lake.

The dragon-man moved down along the bank of the lake, while the youth watched him from the water. He met a Toad in the path, and said, "Little Toad, have you seen the youth I am looking for? If he passed this way you would surely have seen him."

"I am minding my own business," answered the Toad, and he hopped away into the moss. Then the dragon-man saw a very large fish with his head above water, looking for flies, and he said, "Have you seen the boy I am looking for?"

"Yes," said the fish, "you have just been talking to him," and he laughed to himself and disappeared. The dragon-man went back and searched everywhere for Toad, but he could not find him. As he looked he came upon a musk-rat running along by the stream, and he said angrily, "Have you seen the person I am looking for?"

"No," said the rat. "I think you are he," said the dragon-man. Then the musk-rat began to cry bitterly and said, "No, no; the boy you are looking for passed by just now, and he stepped on the roof of my house and broke it in." The dragon-man was deceived again. He went on and soon came upon old Turtle splashing around in the mud. "You are very old and wise," he said, hoping to flatter him, "you have surely seen the person I am looking for."

"Yes," said Turtle, "he is farther down the stream. Go across the river and you will find him. But beware, for if you do not know him when you see him, he will surely kill you." Turtle knew well that the dragon-man would now meet his fate.

The dragon-man followed the lake till he came to the river. For greater caution, so that he might be less easily seen, he changed himself to a Snake. Then he attempted to cross the stream. But the youth, still in the form of a fish and still using the power of his magic bark with the mystic sign, was swimming round and round in a circle in the middle of the river. A rapid whirlpool arose where he swam, but it was not visible on the surface. As the Snake approached it, he saw nothing but clear water. He failed to recognize his enemy, and as Turtle had told him, he swam into the whirlpool before he was aware of it, and was quickly drawn to the bottom, where he was drowned.

The youth fished him up and cut off his head. Then he changed back to his own form. He went to the dragon-man's lodge to see how the old woman had fared, but she had gone with her bright robe, and the lodge was empty. Then the youth went back to his home and reported what he had done. And he received many rich gifts from the Chief for his brave deed, and the land was never troubled again by dragons. But from that time the snake family was hated because its shape had concealed the dragon-man, and to this day an Indian will not let a snake escape with his life if he meets one of them in his path. For they still are mindful of the adventure of their ancestor in the old days, and they are suspicious of the evil power the snake family secretly possess.

The Dragon After His Winter Sleep

ONCE THERE WAS a scholar who was reading in the upper story of his house. It was a rainy, cloudy day and the weather was gloomy. Suddenly he saw a little thing which shone like a fire-fly. It crawled upon the table, and wherever it went it left traces of burns, curved like the tracks of a rainworm. Gradually it wound itself about the scholar's book and the book, too, grew black. Then it occurred to him that it might be a dragon. So he carried it out of doors on the book. There he stood for quite some time; but it sat uncurled, without moving in the least.

Then the scholar said: "It shall not be said of me that I was lacking in respect." With these words he carried back the book and once more laid it on the table. Then he put on his robes of ceremony, made a deep bow and escorted the dragon out on it again.

No sooner had he left the door, than he noticed that the dragon raised his head and stretched himself. Then he flew up from the book with a hissing sound, like a radiant streak. Once more he turned around toward the scholar, and his head had already grown to the size of a barrel, while his body must have been a full fathom in length. He gave one more snaky twist, and then there was a terrible crash of thunder and the dragon went sailing through the air.

The scholar then returned and looked to see which way the little creature had come. And he could follow his tracks hither and thither, to his chest of books.

The Dragon's Pearl

MANY HUNDREDS OF YEARS AGO a mother and her son lived together by the banks of the Min river in the province of Shu, which we now call Sichuan. They were extremely poor, and the young boy had to look after his mother, who was very old and very ill. Although he worked long hours cutting and selling grass for animal food; he barely made enough to support them both, and was always afraid that ruin lay just around the next corner.

One summer, as the earth grew brown through lack of rain, and the supply of good grass became even more sparse than usual, the young boy was forced to journey farther and farther from home to make any living at all; higher and higher into the mountains he went in search of pasture. Then one day, tired and thirsty, the boy was just about to set out empty-handed on the long homeward journey, when he came across a patch of the most verdant, tall grass he had ever seen, waving in the breeze, and giving off a pleasing scent of Spring. The boy was so delighted that he cut down the whole patch, and joyfully carried it down the mountain to his village. He sold the grass for more than he often earned in a week, and for once he and his sick mother were able to eat a good meal of fish and rice.

The next day the boy returned to the same area, hoping to find a similar patch of grass nearby, but to his complete amazement, the very spot which he had harvested the day before had grown again fully, as green and luscious as before. Once again, he cut down the whole patch and returned home. This happened day after day, and the boy and his mother were delighted by the upturn in their fortunes. The only disadvantage was the distance the boy had to travel every day, a long, hazardous journey into the mountains, and it occurred to him that if this was a magic patch of grass, it should grow equally well in his village as it did in the mountains.

The very next day he made several journeys to the mountains, and dug up the patch, grass, roots, soil and all, and carried it back to a spot just near his house, where he carefully re-laid the plot of earth. As he was doing so, he found to his wonder and delight, hidden in the roots of the grass, the largest, most beautiful pearl he had ever seen. He rushed to show it to his mother, and even with her failing sight, she realized that it must be of enormous value. They decided to keep it safely hidden until the boy could go to the city to sell it in the market there. The old woman hid it at the bottom of their large rice jar, which contained just enough to cover the stone, and the boy went back to re-laying the magic grass patch.

The next day he rushed out of bed to go and harvest his crop, only to find that, far from luxuriant pasture he had expected, the grass on the patch was withered, brown, and obviously dying. The boy wept for his folly in moving the earth and destroying its magic, and went inside to confess his failure to his mother. As he was going into the house, he heard his mother cry out, and rushing to her, found her standing in amazement over the rice jar. It was full to the brim with rice, and on the top of the jar lay the pearl, glinting in the morning sun. Then they knew that this must be a magic pearl. They placed it in their virtually empty money box, and sure enough, the next morning, they discovered that it too was absolutely full, the pearl sitting on top of the golden pile like a jewel on top of a crown.

Mother and son used their magic pearl wisely, and became quite wealthy; naturally in a small village this fortune did not go unremarked, and the neighbours who had been kind to the mother and son in their times of hardship now found themselves handsomely repaid, and those in need found ready relief for their distress.

However, the villagers were curious as to the source of this new wealth, and it did not take long for the story of the fabulous pearl to become known. One day the boy found himself surrounded by people demanding to see the stone. Foolishly he took it from its hiding place and showed it to the assembled throng. Some of the crowd grew threatening, jostling and pushing, and asking why the boy should be allowed to keep such a lucky find. The son saw that the situation was about to turn ugly, and without thinking, he put the pearl into his mouth to keep it safe. But in the uproar he accidentally swallowed it with a loud gulp.

Immediately, the boy felt as if he was on fire, his throat and then his stomach was consumed with a heat so intense he did not know how to endure it. He ran to his house and threw the contents of the water bucket down his throat, but it had no impact on the searing pain; he dashed to the well, and pulled up bucket after bucket of water, but to no avail. Although he drank gallon after gallon he was still burning up, and in a frenzy of despair he threw himself down on the banks of the Min and began to lap up the river as fast as he could, until eventually he had drunk it absolutely dry. As the last drop of the mighty river disappeared down his throat, there was a huge crack of thunder, and a violent storm erupted. The earth shook, lightning flashed across the sky, rain lashed down from the heavens, and the terrified villagers all fell to the ground in fear. Still the boy was shaking like a leaf, and his frightened mother grabbed hold of his legs, which suddenly started to grow. Horns sprouted on his forehead, scales appeared in place of his skin, and his eyes grew wider, and seemed to spit fire. Racked by convulsions the boy grew bigger and bigger. The horrified mother saw that he was turning into a dragon before her very eyes, and understood that the pearl must have belonged to the dragon guardian of the river. For every water dragon has a magic pearl which is its most treasured possession.

The river was now filling up with all the rain, and the dragon-boy started to slither towards it, his weeping mother still clinging to his scaly legs. With a powerful jerk, he managed to shake her free, but even as he headed for the torrent, he could still hear her despairing cries. Each time she called out, he turned his huge body to look at her, each writhing motion throwing up mud-banks at the side of the river, until, with a last anguished roar, he slid beneath the waves for the last time and disappeared for ever. And to this day the mud banks on the Min river are called the 'Looking Back at Mother' banks, in memory of the dragon-boy and his magic pearl.

My Lord Bag of Rice

ONE DAY THE GREAT HIDESATO came to a bridge that spanned the beautiful Lake Biwa. He was about to cross it when he noticed a great serpent-dragon fast asleep obstructing his progress. Hidesato, without a moment's hesitation, climbed over the monster and proceeded on his way.

He had not gone far when he heard someone calling to him. He looked back and saw that in the place of the dragon a man stood bowing to him with much ceremony. He was a strange-looking fellow with a dragon-shaped crown resting upon his red hair.

"I am the Dragon King of Lake Biwa," explained the red-haired man. "A moment ago I took the form of a horrible monster in the hope of finding a mortal who would not be afraid of me. You, my lord, showed no fear, and I rejoice exceedingly. A great centipede comes down from yonder mountain, enters my palace, and destroys my children and grandchildren. One by one they have become food for this dread creature, and I fear soon that unless something can be done to slay this centipede I myself shall become a victim. I have waited long for a brave mortal. All men who have hitherto seen me in my dragon-shape have run away. You are a brave man, and I beg that you will kill my bitter enemy."

Hidesato, who always welcomed an adventure, the more so when it was a perilous one, readily consented to see what he could do for the Dragon King.

When Hidesato reached the Dragon King's palace he found it to be a very magnificent building indeed, scarcely less beautiful than the Sea King's palace itself. He was feasted with crystallised lotus leaves and flowers, and ate the delicacies spread before him with choice ebony chopsticks. While he feasted ten little goldfish danced, and just behind the goldfish ten carp made sweet music on the *koto* and *samisen*. Hidesato was just thinking how excellently he had been entertained, and how particularly good was the wine, when they all heard an awful noise like a dozen thunderclaps roaring together.

Hidesato and the Dragon King hastily rose and ran to the balcony. They saw that Mount Mikami was scarcely recognisable, for it was covered from top to bottom with the great coils of the centipede. In its head glowed two balls of fire, and its hundred feet were like a long winding chain of lanterns.

Hidesato fitted an arrow to his bowstring and pulled it back with all his might. The arrow sped forth into the night and struck the centipede in the middle of the head, but glanced off immediately without inflicting any wound. Again Hidesato sent an arrow whirling into the air, and again it struck the monster and fell harmlessly to the ground. Hidesato had only one arrow left. Suddenly remembering the magical effect of human saliva, he put the remaining arrow-head into his mouth for a moment, and then hastily adjusted it to his bow and took careful aim.

The last arrow struck its mark and pierced the centipede's brain. The creature stopped moving; the light in its eyes and legs darkened and then went out, and Lake Biwa, with its palace beneath, was shrouded in awful darkness. Thunder rolled, lightning flashed, and it seemed for the moment that the Dragon King's palace would topple to the ground.

The next day, however, all sign of storm had vanished. The sky was clear. The sun shone brightly. In the sparkling blue lake lay the body of the great centipede.

The Dragon King and those about him were overjoyed when they knew that their dread enemy had been destroyed. Hidesato was again feasted, even more royally than before. When he finally departed he did so with a retinue of fishes suddenly converted into men. The Dragon King bestowed upon our hero five precious gifts – two bells, a bag of rice, a roll of silk, and a cooking-pot.

The Dragon King accompanied Hidesato as far as the bridge, and then he reluctantly allowed the hero and the procession of servants carrying the presents to proceed on their way.

When Hidesato reached his home the Dragon King's servants put down the presents and suddenly disappeared.

The presents were no ordinary gifts. The rice-bag was inexhaustible, there was no end to the roll of silk, and the cooking-pot would cook without fire of any kind. Only the bells were without magical properties, and these were presented to a temple in the vicinity. Hidesato grew rich, and his fame spread far and wide. People now no longer called him Hidesato, but Tawara Toda, or 'My Lord Bag of Rice.'

Human Serpents

SINCE THE BEGINNING OF THE WORLD the serpent has been regarded as the most mystic of reptiles. He was called "more subtil than any beast of the field," from the day on which he spoke to Eve and said that if she ate of the fruit of the Tree of Life, her eyes should be opened and she should surely not die, and he has been endowed with human powers again and again, worshipped as a god in every part of the world and depicted in ancient art as possessed of human form and attributes. In Aztec paintings the mother of the human race is always represented in conversation with a serpent who is erect. This is the serpent, "who once spoke with a human voice."

Mythology has numberless legends which tell of human or semi-human serpents. The ancient kings of Thebes and Delphi claimed kingship with the snake, and Cadmus and his wife Harmonia, quitting Thebes, went to reign over a tribe of Eel-men in Illyria and became transformed into snakes, just as now Kaffir kings are said to turn into boa-constrictors or other deadly serpents, and some other African tribes believe that their dead chiefs become crocodiles.

Cecrops, the first king of Athens, was supposed to have been half-serpent and half-man, and Cychreus, after slaying a snake which ravaged the island of Salamis, appeared in the form of his victim.

When Minerva contended with Neptune for the city of Athens, she created the olive which became sacred to her, and she planted it on the Acropolis and placed it in the charge of the serpent-god, Erechthonios, who is represented as half-serpent, half-man, the lower extremities being serpentine.

The story of Alexander's birth, as told by Plutarch, is one of the most curious of the man-serpent traditions. Olympias, his mother, kept tame snakes in the house and one of them was said to have been found in her bed, and was thought to be the real father of Alexander the Great. Lucian adopts this view of Alexander's parentage.

The worship of serpent-gods is found amongst many nations. The Chinese god Foki, for instance, is said to have had the form of a man, terminating in the tail of a snake. The same belief in serpent-gods exists among the primitive Turanian tribes. The Accadians made the serpent one of the principal attributes, and one of the forms of Hea, and we find a very important allusion to a mythological serpent in the words from an Accadian dithyramb uttered by a god, perhaps by Hea: –

Like the enormous serpent with seven heads, the weapon with seven heads I hold it.
Like the serpent which beats the waves of the sea attacking the enemy in front,
Devastator in the shock of battle, extending his power over heaven and earth, the weapon
with (seven) heads (I hold it).

The story of Crishna is very similar to that of Hercules in Grecian mythology, the serpent forming a prominent feature in both. Crishna conquers a dragon, into which the Assoor Aghe had transformed himself to swallow him up. He defeats also Kalli Naga (the black or evil spirit with a thousand heads) who, placing himself in the bed of the river Jumna, poisoned the stream, so that all the companions of Crishna and his cattle, who tasted of it, perished. He overcame Kalli Naga, without arms, and in the form of a child. The serpent twisted himself about the body of Crishna, but the god tore off his heads, one after the other, and trampled them under his feet. Before he had completely destroyed Kalli Naga, the wife and children of the monster (serpents also) came and besought him to release their relative. Crishna took pity on them, and releasing Kalli Naga, said to him, "Begone quickly into the abyss: this place is not proper for thee since I have engaged with thee, thy name shall remain through all the period of time and devatars and men shall henceforth remember thee without dismay." So the serpent with his wife and children went into the abyss, and the water which had been affected by his poison became pure and wholesome.

Crishna also destroyed the serpent-king of Egypt and his army of snakes.

Lamia was an evil spirit having the semblance of a serpent, with the head, or at least the mouth, of a beautiful woman, whose whole figure the demon assumed for the purpose of securing the love of some man whom, it was supposed, she desired to tear to pieces and devour. Lycius is said to have fallen in love with one of these spirits, but was delivered by his master, Apollonius, who, "by some probable conjectures," found her out to be a serpent, a lamia.

Keats made use of this idea in his poem, 'Lamia.' Later the word was used to mean a witch or enchantress. Melusina was another beautiful serpent-woman who disappeared from her husband's presence every Saturday, and turned into a human fish or serpent.

A modern version of the legend of Melusina is found in Wales. To assume the shape of a snake, witches prepared special charms, and sometimes a ban was placed upon enemies by which they turned into snakes for a time.

A young farmer in Anglesea went to South Wales and there he met a handsome girl whose eyes were "sometimes blue, sometimes grey, and sometimes like emeralds," but they always sparkled and glittered. He fell in love with her at first sight, and she agreed to become his wife if he would allow her to disappear twice a year for a fortnight without questioning her as to where she went. To this arrangement the young husband agreed.

For some years he did not trouble himself about his wife's absence, but his mother began nagging at him, saying that he ought to find out where she went and what she did. Taking his mother's advice, he disguised himself and followed his wife to a lonely part of a forest not far from their home. Hiding himself behind a huge rock, he noticed from this point of vantage that his wife took off her girdle and threw it down in the deep grass near a dark pool. Then she vanished, and the next moment he saw a large and handsome snake glide through the grass, just where she had been standing. He chased the reptile, but the snake disappeared into a hole near the pool. The husband went home and waited patiently for his wife's return, and when she came, he requested her to tell him where she had been. This she refused to do, and when he asked her what she did with her girdle, she blushed painfully.

The next time when she was intending to go away, he seized and hid the girdle, and thus deferred her departure. She was taken ill, and he, hoping to rid her of a baneful charm, threw the girdle in the fire. Then his wife writhed in agony, and when the girdle was burnt up she died. The neighbours called her the Snake-Woman of the South on account of this strange story of her doings.

A shoemaker in the Vale of Taff married a widow for her money and, as love seemed lacking on both sides, it was not long before serious quarrels occurred between the couple. Although it was said that hard blows were struck on both sides, the neighbours remarked that it was strange the shoemaker's wife appeared amongst them without a trace of a bruise on her person. At night loud cries and deep groans arose from the shoemaker's dwelling, and a certain gentleman of an inquisitive turn of mind decided to discover what took place and hid himself in a loft over the kitchen, to spy on the couple. Whatever he may have learnt during the proceedings, he said nothing, and a report was spread that he had been "paid to hold his tongue and not divulge the family secret." At last, however, his discretion failed him, and anger against the shoemaker, with whom he fell into a dispute, made him reveal what he knew. He said that as soon as angry words passed between husband and wife, the latter "assumed from the shoulders upwards, the shape of a snake, and deliberately and maliciously sucked her partner's blood and pierced him with her venomous fangs."

No marks were found on the husband's body, but he grew ever thinner and weaker, and after ailing for many months he died. The doctor who tended him in his last illness declared that he had died from the poisonous sting of a serpent. After this verdict the spy was given the credit of his story, which, however, had a gruesome sequel. He and the doctor were found lying helpless in the churchyard one morning. When roused from what seemed a fatal slumber, they said they had been invited by the shoemaker's widow to drink with her in memory of her late dear second husband. Then she sprang upon them in the shape of a snake and stung them severely. They had only strength enough left to crawl to the churchyard, where they would probably have died from torpor had not the neighbours roused them. The widow was never seen again, but a snake constantly appeared in the neighbourhood and could not be killed by any means, so that it earned the name of 'the old snake-woman.'

Oliver Wendell Holmes, who was interested in the subject of prenatal influences, depicted the heroine of his well-known novel, *Elsie Venner*, as a girl who had received the taint of a serpent before birth, from a snakebite suffered by her mother. Elsie's friend, Helen Darley, knew the secret of the fascination which looked out of the cold, glittering eyes. She knew the significance of the strange repulsion which she felt in her own intimate consciousness underlying the inexplicable attraction which drew her towards the young girl in spite of her repugnance.

When Elsie was taken ill her doctor said that she had lived a double being, as it were, the consequence of the blight which fell upon her in the dim period before consciousness.

Elsie Venner is an American story, but India, where the snake is even more familiar, is the home of many human-serpent stories, and legends of serpent descent.

Near Jait in the Mathura district is a tank with the broken statue of a hooded serpent on it. Once upon a time a Raja married a princess from a distant country and, after a short stay there, decided to take his wife home, but she refused to go until he had declared his lineage. The Raja told her she would regret her curiosity, but she persisted. Finally he took her to the river and there warned her again. She would not take heed and he entreated her not to be alarmed at whatever she saw, adding that if she did she would lose him. Saying this, he began slowly to descend into the water, all the time trying to dissuade her from her purpose, till it became too late and the water rose to his neck. Then, after a last attempt to induce her to give up her curiosity, he dived and reappeared in the form of a Naga (serpent). Raising his hood over the water he said, "This is my lineage! I am a Nagbansi."

His wife could not suppress an exclamation of grief, on which the Naga was turned into stone, where he lies to this day.

A member of the family of Buddha fell in love with the daughter of a serpent-king. He was married to her and presently became the sovereign of the country. His wife had obtained possession of a human body, but a nine-headed snake occasionally appeared at the back of her neck. While she slept one night her husband chopped the serpent in two at a single blow, and this caused her to become blind.

Another curious legend is told of a Buddha priest who had become a serpent because he had killed the tree Elapatra, and he then resided in a beautiful lake near Taxila. In the days of Hiuen-Tsiang, when the people of the country wanted fine weather or rain they went to the spring accompanied by a priest, and, "snapping their fingers, invoked the serpent," and immediately obtained their wishes.

The snake tribe is common enough in the Punjaub. Snake families go through many ceremonies, saying that in olden days the serpent was a great king. If they find a dead snake they put clothes on it and give it a regular funeral. The snake changes its form every hundred years, when it becomes either a man or a bull. Snake-charmers have the power of recognising these transformed snakes, and follow them stealthily until they return to their holes and then ask them where treasure is hidden. This they will do on consideration of a drop of blood from the little finger of a first-born son.

Among fairy tales the favourite story is that of a human being who dons a snake-skin, and when it is burnt he resumes human form. The snake-bridegroom is an exceedingly popular version of this idea.

There was once a poor woman, who had never borne a child and she prayed to God that she might be blessed with one, even though she were to bring forth a snake. And God heard her prayer, and in due course she gave birth to a snake. Directly the reptile saw the light of day it slipped down from her lap into the grass and disappeared. Now the poor woman mourned constantly for the snake, because after God had heard and granted her prayer, it grieved her that the being whom she had conceived should have vanished without leaving a trace as to its whereabouts. Twenty years passed, and then the snake returned and said to its mother, "I am the serpent to which you gave birth, and which fled from you into the grass, and I have come back, mother, so that you may demand the king's daughter for me in marriage."

At first the mother rejoiced at the sight of her son, but soon she grew mournful because she did not know how she dare to demand the hand of the king's daughter for a serpent, especially as she was very poor. But the serpent said, "Go along, mother, and do what I ask; even if the king won't give his daughter, he can't cut your head off for the mere asking. But whatever he says to you do not look back until you get home again."

The mother allowed herself to be persuaded and went to the king. At first the servants would not let her into the palace, but she went on asking until they admitted her. When she entered the king's presence she said to him, "Most gracious Majesty, there is your sword and here is my head. Strike if you must, but let me tell you first that for a long time I was childless and then I prayed to God to bless me, even though I were to bring forth a serpent, and He blessed me and I brought forth a serpent. As soon as it saw the light it vanished into the grass and after twenty years it has returned to me and has sent me here to ask for the hand of your daughter in marriage."

The king burst into laughter and said, "I will give my daughter to your son if he builds me a bridge of pearls and precious stones from my palace to his house."

Then the mother turned to go home, and never looked back, and when she left the palace a bridge of pearls and diamonds arose all the way behind her till she reached her own house. When the mother told the serpent what the king had said, the serpent remarked to her, "Go again and see whether the king will give me his daughter, but whatever he answers don't look round as you come back."

This time the king told the mother that if her son could give his daughter a better palace than his own, he should have her for a wife. The mother went back without looking behind her, and found that her house had changed into a palace, and everything in it was three times as good as in the king's palace. All the furniture was made of pure gold.

Then the serpent asked his mother to go back to the palace and fetch the king's daughter, and this time the king told the princess she must marry the serpent. There was a splendid wedding, and in due course the young wife found she was to become a mother. Then her friends grew inquisitive, saying, "If you are living with a serpent how can you hope to have a child?" At first she would not answer, but when her mother-in-law insisted on putting the same question, she replied, "Mother, your son is not really a serpent, but a young man, so handsome that there is none other like him. Every evening he strips off his snake-skin and in the morning he enters it again."

When the serpent's mother heard this she rejoiced greatly, and longed to see her son after he had stripped off his snake-skin.

Presently the two conspirators arranged that when the young man had gone to bed, they should burn the discarded skin, and while his mother put it in the oven, his wife was to pour cold water on her husband lest he should be destroyed by the heat. No sooner had he laid himself down to sleep, than they carried out their plan, but the smell of the burning skin made him cry out, "What have you done? May God punish you. Where can I go in the condition I now am?" But the women comforted him and said it was better for him to live among ordinary mortals than in the snake form, and before long the king resigned his throne in his favour, and all turned out happily.

A very similar story is told of a queen who also gives birth to a serpent. She is allowed to nurse and fondle her offspring in the usual fashion, but for twenty-two years it does not speak and its first utterance is to demand from its parents a wife.

When the parents remark that no nice girl would care to marry a serpent, he tells them not to look in too high a class for a mate.

In this case the father does the wooing, but the mother evokes the truth about her son. When she learns about the snake-skin, she makes the young wife help to burn it, and tragedy results. The husband curses his wife, saying that she will not see him again until she has worn through iron shoes, and that she shall not give birth to her child until he embraces her once more by putting his right arm round her. Then he vanishes for three years, and all that time she is unable to bear her child, so she decides to seek her husband. She travels through the world and comes to the house of the Sun's mother, and when the Sun comes indoors she inquires whether he has seen her husband. But the Sun can do nothing for her but to send her to the Moon. The same disappointment awaits her there, and the Moon sends her to the Winds. After many striking adventures she finds her husband, makes him undo his curse, and gives birth to a son who has golden locks and golden hands.

In another story of serpent-marriage a woman stands in doubt because she cannot cross a river. A serpent comes out of the river and says, "What will you give me if I carry you across?" The woman, having no other possessions, promises to give her coming child; if it is a girl as a wife, if a boy as a 'name friend.' In after years she has to fulfil her promise and, taking her daughter to the bank of the river, she sees the snake draw her beneath the water. In the course of time the girl bears her husband four snake sons.

An Ainu girl gave birth to a snake as the result of the sun's rays shining on her while she slept, and the snake turned into a child.

The Dyaks and Silakans will not kill the cobra because in remote ages a female ancestor brought forth twins, a boy and a cobra. The cobra went to the forest, but told the mother to warn her children that if they were ever bitten by cobras they must stay in the same place for a whole day and that then the venom would take no effect. The boy then met his cobra brother in the jungle one day and cut off his tail, so that now all cobras have a blunted tail.

In folk-tales the serpent frequently mates with a woman. A curious Basuto story concerns a girl called Senkepeng, who was deserted by her friends and taken home by an old woman, who said she would make a nice wife for her son. Her son turned out to be a serpent, whom no one had ever seen outside his hut, but he had married all the girls of the tribe in succession with fatal results to them, because he ate all the food. Every morning the girl was awakened by a blow of the serpent's tail and was then ordered to go and prepare his food. At last she grew tired of this treatment and resolved to run away. Her serpent-husband pursued her, but she sang a charm or incantation and this delayed his progress and gave her a chance of continuing her flight. Whenever the serpent came up to her she repeated her song.

At last she reached her father's village and told her story, and people were ready to defend her against her pursuer. As soon as the serpent came in sight Senkepeng sang her charm, and the people attacked the serpent and slew it. Presently the serpent's mother arrived and burnt the mutilated corpse, wrapping the ashes in a skin which she threw into a pond. Walking three times round the pond, without speaking a word, she caused her son to come to life again, and he came out of the pond as a human being, and Senkepeng welcomed him as her husband. In another variant the serpent's ashes are put in a vase of clay, which is given to Senkepeng. Afterwards she uncovers the vase and a man steps out from it.

The first Dindje Indian had two wives, one of whom would have nothing to say to him. She used to disappear during the day, and he followed her to find out her secret. He saw her go into a marsh where she met a serpent. When she returned to the hut she had several children, but hid them from her husband under a cover. The man discovered the hiding-place, and there found horrible little men-serpents, which he killed. Thereupon the woman left him and he never saw her again.

In a Bengal story a mighty serpent, after slaughtering a whole family except one beautiful daughter, carries her off to his watery tank, from which she is rescued by a prince. In Russia it is believed that mortal maidens are carried off by serpents.

The Indians are very superstitious. Otto Stoll, author of *Suggestion und Hypnotismus*, showed a friendly Cakchiquel Indian one of his hairs under the microscope. The Indian asked to have it back that he might preserve it, saying that if it were lost, it would turn into a snake, and he would then have to suffer great trouble through snakes all his life. When Dr. Stoll appeared to be sceptical, he told him that he had often seen the long hairs which native women combed out and let fall into the river, become transformed into serpents as they fell. This is a widespread belief, and in an early Mexican dictionary by Molina, in 1571, the word 'tzoncoatl' is translated, 'the snake which is formed out of horse's hair which fell into the water.'

The white snake especially may sometimes be a lovely transformed maiden, as appears from the story of a cowboy who makes a friend of a white snake which comes to play with him and twines about his legs. One evening in midsummer he beholds a fair maiden, who says she is the daughter of an Eastern king and has been forced to spend her life through enchantment in the form of a white snake, with permission to resume human shape on midsummer night every quarter of a century. The cowboy is the first human being who has not shrunk from her when she appears in reptile form. She tells him that she will come again, and will wind herself three times round his body and give him three kisses. If he should shrink from her then she will have to remain a snake for ever. When she appears, the youth stands firm while the reptile caresses him and, lo and behold, there is a crash and a flash and he finds himself in a magnificent palace, with a beautiful girl beside him who becomes his wife.

The Russians have a story of some girls bathing, when a snake comes out of the water and sits upon the clothes of the prettiest one, saying he will not move till she promises to marry him. She agrees, and that very night an army of snakes seize her and carry her beneath the water, where they become men and women. She stays for some years with her husband, and is then allowed to go home and visit her mother. The latter, discovering the husband's name, goes to the water and calls upon him. When he comes to the surface she chops off his head with an axe. Probably the snake-bride has been told by her husband not to mention his name for fear of his death, the name being taboo.

In a Zuni legend the daughter of a chief bathes in a pool sacred to Kolowissa, the serpent of the sea. Kolowissa in anger appears to the maiden in the form of a child, whom she takes to her home. There the child changes into an enormous serpent, who induces her to go away with him, and when she does so he transforms himself again into a handsome youth.

Incredulous that such happiness can befall her, she expresses her doubts to the young man, but he then shows her his shrivelled snake-skin as proof that he is the god of the waters and that he loves her well enough to make her his wife.

A beautiful girl in New Guinea was beloved by a chief of a strange tribe, and he was so fearful of entering her father's territory that he asked a sorcerer for a charm which would enable him to change into a snake the moment he crossed the boundary of his own country. In this form he entered the girl's hut, and on seeing the reptile she began to scream. Her father, however, was more astute and saw the serpent was really a man, so he bade his daughter to go to him, as he must be a great chief to be thus able to transform himself. She obeyed his command, and as the serpent went slowly, her father advised her to burn his tail with a hot banana leaf to make him hurry. This she also did, but at the boundary the snake vanished and presently a handsome young man came up to her and told her he was the serpent, showing certain burns on his feet and legs in proof of the statement.

In France the serpent with a jewel in its head is called *vouivre*, which is the same as our basilisk or dragon. The *vouivre* is a reptile from a yard to two yards long, having only one eye in its head, which shines like a jewel and is called the carbuncle. This jewel is regarded as of inestimable value, and those who can obtain one of these treasures become enormously rich. Many of the legends deal with the robbery of this jewel from the serpent, a crime which is frequently punishable by death or madness.

The French have several variants of the story of St. George and the Dragon. At the castle of Vaugrenans, for instance, there lived a lovely lady whose beauty had led her far astray from the path of virtue. She was changed into a basilisk and terrorized the country by her misdeeds. Her son George was a handsome knight, whose natural piety led him to live a life of good deeds. George decided that he must set his country free from the depredations of the monster reptile, which never ceased to prey upon the neighbourhood and he did battle with it as once the archangel, St. Michael, had combated the dragon. George killed the serpent and his horse trampled what remained of it beneath its hoofs.

George was very sad, however, in spite of his victory, and he asked St. Michael, who had witnessed the struggle, what was the punishment for one who had slain his own mother.

"He ought to be burnt," replied St. Michael, "and his ashes strewn to the winds."

So George had to suffer the penalty of being burnt and his ashes were scattered to the winds. So far the story bears a marked resemblance to the family story of the Lambton worm, but the French tale has a curious sequel. The ashes fell in one heap instead of scattering to the wind, and a young girl who was passing gathered them up. Near by she found an apple of Paradise, which she ate. In due course she gave birth to a son, and when the infant was baptized, it cried in a loud tone of voice, "I am called George and I have been born on this earth for the second time." Later he was made a saint.

The Roman genius, which accompanies every man through life as his protector, frequently took the shape of a serpent.

In many lands, by eating a snake, wisdom is acquired, or the language of animals mastered, and generally a particular snake is mentioned by name. Thus with Arabs and Swahilis it is the king of snakes: among Swedish, Danish, Celtic or Slavonic peoples it is a white snake or the fabulous basilisk with a crown on its head, which resembles the jewel-headed serpent of Eastern lore.

In the country of Râma there stood a brick *stupa* or tower, about a hundred feet high, in the time of Hiuen-Tsiang. The *stupa* constantly emitted rays of glory, and by the side of it was a Naga tank. The Naga frequently changed his appearance into that of a man, and, as such, encircled the tower in the practice of religion, that is, he turned religiously with his right hand towards the tower.

In New Guinea it is believed that a witch is possessed by spirits which can be expelled in the form of snakes. Among the Ainus, madness is explained as possession by snakes. The Zulus believe that an ancestor who wishes to approach a kraal takes serpent shape. In Madagascar different species of snakes are the abode for different classes, one for common people, one for chiefs, and one for women, and in certain parts of Europe it is solemnly believed that people may assume serpent-form during sleep.

The fact that the serpent-stories of the nature here collected, are so numerous seems to point to a definite occult connection between the highest living organism, man, who is represented by a vertical line, and the reptile, the serpent, represented by the horizontal line, the two together forming the right angle.

Prince Lindworm

ONCE UPON A TIME, there was a fine young King who was married to the loveliest of Queens. They were exceedingly happy, all but for one thing – they had no children. And this often made them both sad, because the Queen wanted a dear little child to play with, and the King wanted an heir to the kingdom.

One day the Queen went out for a walk by herself, and she met an ugly old woman. The old woman was just like a witch, but she was a nice kind of witch, not the cantankerous sort. She said, "Why do you look so doleful, pretty lady?"

"It's no use my telling you," answered the Queen, "nobody in the world can help me."

"Oh, you never know," said the old woman. "Just you let me hear what your trouble is, and maybe I can put things right."

"My dear woman, how can you?" said the Queen, and she told her, "The King and I have no children, that's why I am so distressed."

"Well, you needn't be," said the old witch. "I can set that right in a twinkling, if only you will do exactly as I tell you. Listen. Tonight, at sunset, take a little drinking-cup with two ears" (that is, handles), "and put it bottom upwards on the ground in the northwest corner of your garden. Then go and lift it up tomorrow morning at sunrise, and you will find two roses underneath it, one red and one white. If you eat the red rose, a little boy will be born to you; if you eat the white rose, a little girl will be sent. But, whatever you do, you mustn't eat both the roses, or you'll be sorry – that I warn you! Only one – remember that!"

"Thank you a thousand times," said the Queen, "this is good news indeed!" And she wanted to give the old woman her gold ring; but the old woman wouldn't take it.

So the Queen went home and did as she had been told, and next morning at sunrise she stole out into the garden and lifted up the little drinking-cup. She was surprised, for indeed she had hardly expected to see anything. But there were the two roses underneath it, one red and one white. And now she was dreadfully puzzled, for she did not know which to choose. "If I choose the red one," she thought, "and I have a little boy, he may grow up and go to the wars and get killed. But if I choose the white one, and have a little girl, she will stay at home awhile with us, but later on she will get married and go away and leave us. So, whichever it is, we may be left with no child after all."

However, at last she decided on the white rose, and she ate it. And it tasted so sweet, that she took and ate the red one too, without ever remembering the old woman's solemn warning.

Some time after this, the King went away to the wars, and while he was still away, the Queen became the mother of twins. One was a lovely baby boy, and the other was a Lindworm, or serpent. She was terribly frightened when she saw the Lindworm, but he wriggled away out of the room, and nobody seemed to have seen him but herself, so that she thought it must have been a dream. The baby Prince was so beautiful and so healthy, the Queen was full of joy, and likewise, as you may suppose, was the King when he came home and found his son and heir. Not a word was said by anyone about the Lindworm – only the Queen thought about it now and then.

Many days and years passed by, and the baby grew up into a handsome young Prince, and it was time that he got married. The King sent him off to visit foreign kingdoms, in the Royal coach, with six white horses, to look for a Princess grand enough to be his wife. But at the very first crossroads, the way was stopped by an enormous Lindworm, enough to frighten the bravest. He lay in the middle of the road with a great wide open mouth, and cried, "A bride for me before a bride for you!" Then the Prince made the coach turn round and try another road, but it was all no use. For, at the first cross-ways, there lay the Lindworm again, crying out, "A bride for me before a bride for you!" So the Prince had to turn back home again to the castle, and give up his visits to the foreign kingdoms. And his mother, the Queen, had to confess that what the Lindworm said was true. For he was really the eldest of her twins, and so he ought to have a wedding first.

There seemed nothing for it but to find a bride for the Lindworm, if his younger brother, the Prince, were to be married at all. So the King wrote to a distant country, and asked for a Princess to marry his son (but, of course, he didn't say which son), and presently a Princess arrived. But she wasn't allowed to see her bridegroom until he stood by her side in the great hall and was married to her, and then, of course, it was too late for her to say she wouldn't have him. But next morning the Princess had disappeared. The Lindworm lay sleeping all alone, and it was quite plain that he had eaten her.

A little while after, the Prince decided that he might now go journeying again in search of a Princess. And off he drove in the Royal chariot with the six white horses. But at the first cross-ways, there lay the Lindworm, crying with his great wide open mouth, "A bride for me before a bride for you!" So the carriage tried another road, and the same thing happened, and they had to turn back again this time, just as formerly. And the King wrote to several foreign countries, to know if anyone would marry his son. At last another Princess arrived, this time from a very far distant land. And, of course, she was not allowed to see her future husband before the wedding took place – and then, lo and behold! it was the Lindworm who stood at her side. And next morning the Princess had disappeared, and the Lindworm lay sleeping all alone; and it was quite clear that he had eaten her.

By and by the Prince started on his quest for the third time, and at the first crossroads there lay the Lindworm with his great wide open mouth, demanding a bride as before. And the Prince went straight back to the castle, and told the King: "You must find another bride for my elder brother."

"I don't know where I am to find her," said the King, "I have already made enemies of two great Kings who sent their daughters here as brides, and I have no notion how I can obtain a third lady. People are beginning to say strange things, and I am sure no Princess will dare to come."

Now, down in a little cottage near a wood, there lived the King's shepherd, an old man with his only daughter. And the King came one day and said to him, "Will you give me your daughter to marry my son the Lindworm? And I will make you rich for the rest of your life."

"No, sire," said the shepherd, "that I cannot do. She is my only child, and I want her to take care of me when I am old. Besides, if the Lindworm would not spare two beautiful Princesses, he won't spare her either. He will just gobble her up, and she is much too good for such a fate."

But the King wouldn't take 'no' for an answer, and at last the old man had to give in.

Well, when the old shepherd told his daughter that she was to be Prince Lindworm's bride, she was utterly in despair. She went out into the woods, crying and wringing her hands and bewailing her hard fate. And while she wandered to and fro, an old witch-woman suddenly appeared out of a big hollow oak tree, and asked her, "Why do you look so doleful, pretty lass?" The shepherd-girl said, "It's no use my telling you, for nobody in the world can help me."

"Oh, you never know," said the old woman. "Just you let me hear what your trouble is, and maybe I can put things right."

"Ah, how can you?" said the girl, "For I am to be married to the King's eldest son, who is a Lindworm. He has already married two beautiful Princesses, and devoured them, and he will eat me too! No wonder I am distressed."

"Well, you needn't be," said the witch-woman. "All that can be set right in a twinkling, if only you will do exactly as I tell you." So the girl said she would. "Listen, then," said the old woman. "After the marriage ceremony is over, and when it is time for you to retire to rest, you must ask to be dressed in ten snow-white shifts. And you must then ask for a tub full of lye," (that is, washing water prepared with wood-ashes) "and a tub full of fresh milk, and as many whips as a boy can carry in his arms – and have all these brought into your bed-chamber. Then, when the Lindworm tells you to shed a shift, you do bid him slough a skin. And when all his skins are off, you must dip the whips in the lye and whip him; next, you must wash him in the fresh milk; and, lastly, you must take him and hold him in your arms, if it's only for one moment."

"The last is the worst notion – ugh!" said the shepherd's daughter, and she shuddered at the thought of holding the cold, slimy, scaly Lindworm.

"Do just as I have said, and all will go well," said the old woman. Then she disappeared again in the oak tree.

When the wedding-day arrived, the girl was fetched in the Royal chariot with the six white horses, and taken to the castle to be decked as a bride. And she asked for ten snow-white shifts to be brought her, and the tub of lye, and the tub of milk, and as many whips as a boy could carry in his arms. The ladies and courtiers in the castle thought, of course, that this was some bit of peasant superstition, all rubbish and nonsense. But the King said, "Let her have whatever she asks for." She was then arrayed in the most wonderful robes, and looked the loveliest of brides. She was led to the hall where the wedding ceremony was to take place, and she saw the Lindworm for the first time as he came in and stood by her side. So they were married, and a great wedding-feast was held, a banquet fit for the son of a king.

When the feast was over, the bridegroom and bride were conducted to their apartment, with music, and torches, and a great procession. As soon as the door was shut, the Lindworm turned to her and said, "Fair maiden, shed a shift!" The shepherd's daughter answered him, "Prince Lindworm, slough a skin!"

"No one has ever dared tell me to do that before!" said he.

"But I command you to do it now!" said she. Then he began to moan and wriggle, and in a few minutes a long snake-skin lay upon the floor beside him. The girl drew off her first shift, and spread it on top of the skin.

The Lindworm said again to her, "Fair maiden, shed a shift."

The shepherd's daughter answered him, "Prince Lindworm, slough a skin."

"No one has ever dared tell me to do that before," said he.

"But I command you to do it now," said she. Then with groans and moans he cast off the second skin, and she covered it with her second shift. The Lindworm said for the third time, "Fair maiden, shed a shift." The shepherd's daughter answered him again, "Prince Lindworm, slough a skin."

"No one has ever dared tell me to do that before," said he, and his little eyes rolled furiously. But the girl was not afraid, and once more she commanded him to do as she bade.

And so this went on until nine Lindworm skins were lying on the floor, each of them covered with a snow-white shift. And there was nothing left of the Lindworm but a huge thick mass, most horrible to see. Then the girl seized the whips, dipped them in the lye, and whipped him as hard as ever she could. Next, she bathed him all over in the fresh milk. Lastly, she dragged him on to the bed and put her arms round him. And she fell fast asleep that very moment.

Next morning very early, the King and the courtiers came and peeped in through the keyhole. They wanted to know what had become of the girl, but none of them dared enter the room. However, in the end, growing bolder, they opened the door a tiny bit. And there they saw the girl, all fresh and rosy, and beside her lay no Lindworm, but the handsomest prince that anyone could wish to see.

The King ran out and fetched the Queen, and after that there were such rejoicings in the castle as never were known before or since. The wedding took place all over again, much finer than the first, with festivals and banquets and merrymakings for days and weeks. No bride was ever so beloved by a King and Queen as this peasant maid from the shepherd's cottage. There was no end to their love and their kindness towards her, because, by her sense and her calmness and her courage, she had saved their son, Prince Lindworm.

Batcha and the Dragon

ONCE UPON A TIME there was a shepherd who was called Batcha. During the summer he pastured his flocks high up on the mountain where he had a little hut and a sheepfold.

One day in autumn while he was lying on the ground, idly blowing his pipes, he chanced to look down the mountain slope. There he saw a most amazing sight. A great army of snakes, hundreds and hundreds in number, was slowly crawling to a rocky cliff not far from where he was lying.

When they reached the cliff, every serpent bit off a leaf from a plant that was growing there. They then touched the cliff with the leaves and the rock opened. One by one they crawled inside. When the last one had disappeared, the rock closed.

Batcha blinked his eyes in bewilderment.

"What can this mean?" he asked himself. "Where are they gone? I think I'll have to climb up there myself and see what that plant is. I wonder will the rock open for me?"

He whistled to Dunay, his dog, and left him in charge of the sheep. Then he made his way over to the cliff and examined the mysterious plant. It was something he had never seen before.

He picked a leaf and touched the cliff in the same place where the serpents had touched it. Instantly the rock opened.

Batcha stepped inside. He found himself in a huge cavern the walls of which glittered with gold and silver and precious stones. A golden table stood in the centre and upon it a monster serpent, a very king of serpents, lay coiled up fast asleep. The other serpents, hundreds and hundreds of them, lay on the ground around the table. They also were fast asleep. As Batcha walked about, not one of them stirred.

Batcha sauntered here and there examining the walls and the golden table and the sleeping serpents. When he had seen everything he thought to himself:

"It's very strange and interesting and all that, but now it's time for me to get back to my sheep."

It's easy to say: "Now I'm going," but when Batcha tried to go he found he couldn't, for the rock had closed. So there he was locked in with the serpents.

He was a philosophical fellow and so, after puzzling a moment, he shrugged his shoulders and said:

"Well, if I can't get out I suppose I'll have to stay here for the night."

With that he drew his cape about him, lay down, and was soon fast asleep.

He was awakened by a rustling murmur. Thinking that he was in his own hut, he sat up and rubbed his eyes. Then he saw the glittering walls of the cavern and remembered his adventure.

The old king serpent still lay on the golden table but no longer asleep. A movement like a slow wave was rippling his great coils. All the other serpents on the ground were facing the golden table and with darting tongues were hissing:

"Is it time? Is it time?"

The old king serpent slowly lifted his head and with a deep murmurous hiss said:

"Yes, it is time."

He stretched out his long body, slipped off the golden table, and glided away to the wall of the cavern. All the smaller serpents wriggled after him.

Batcha followed them, thinking to himself:

"I'll go out the way they go."

The old king serpent touched the wall with his tongue and the rock opened. Then he glided aside and the serpents crawled out, one by one. When the last one was out, Batcha tried to follow, but the rock swung shut in his face, again locking him in.

The old king serpent hissed at him in a deep breathy voice:

"Hah, you miserable man creature, you can't get out! You're here and here you stay!"

"But I can't stay here," Batcha said. "What can I do in here? I can't sleep forever! You must let me out! I have sheep at pasture and a scolding wife at home in the valley. She'll have a thing or two to say if I'm late in getting back!"

Batcha pleaded and argued until at last the old serpent said:

"Very well, I'll let you out, but not until you have made me a triple oath that you won't tell anyone how you came in."

Batcha agreed to this. Three times he swore a mighty oath not to tell anyone how he had entered the cavern.

"I warn you," the old serpent said, as he opened the wall, "if you break this oath a terrible fate will overtake you!"

Without another word Batcha hurried through the opening.

Once outside he looked about him in surprise. Everything seemed changed. It was autumn when he had followed the serpents into the cavern. Now it was spring!

"What has happened?" he cried in fright. "Oh, what an unfortunate fellow I am! Have I slept through the winter? Where are my sheep? And my wife – what will she say?"

With trembling knees he made his way to his hut. His wife was busy inside. He could see her through the open door. He didn't know what to say to her at first, so he slipped into the sheepfold and hid himself while he tried to think out some likely story.

While he was crouching there, he saw a finely dressed gentleman come to the door of the hut and ask his wife where her husband was.

The woman burst into tears and explained to the stranger that one day in the previous autumn her husband had taken out his sheep as usual and had never come back.

"Dunay, the dog," she said, "drove home the sheep and from that day to this nothing has ever been heard of my poor husband. I suppose a wolf devoured him, or the witches caught him and tore him to pieces and scattered him over the mountain. And here I am left, a poor forsaken widow! Oh dear, oh dear, oh dear!"

Her grief was so great that Batcha leaped out of the sheepfold to comfort her.

"There, there, dear wife, don't cry! Here I am, alive and well! No wolf ate me, no witches caught me. I've been asleep in the sheepfold – that's all. I must have slept all winter long!"

At sight and sound of her husband, the woman stopped crying. Her grief changed to surprise, then to fury.

"You wretch!" she cried. "You lazy, good-for-nothing loafer! A nice kind of shepherd you are to desert your sheep and yourself to idle away the winter sleeping like a serpent! That's a fine story, isn't it, and I suppose you think me fool enough to believe it! Oh, you – you sheep's tick, where have you been and what have you been doing?"

She flew at Batcha with both hands and there's no telling what she would have done to him if the stranger hadn't interfered.

"There, there," he said, "no use getting excited! Of course he hasn't been sleeping here in the sheepfold all winter. The question is, where has he been? Here is some money for you. Take it and go along home to your cottage in the valley. Leave Batcha to me and I promise you I'll get the truth out of him."

The woman abused her husband some more and then, pocketing the money, went off.

As soon as she was gone, the stranger changed into a horrible looking creature with a third eye in the middle of his forehead.

"Good heavens!" Batcha gasped in fright. "He's the wizard of the mountain! Now what's going to happen to me!"

Batcha had often heard terrifying stories of the wizard, how he could himself take any form he wished and how he could turn a man into a ram.

"Aha!" the wizard laughed. "I see you know me! Now then, no more lies! Tell me: where have you been all winter long?"

At first Batcha remembered his triple oath to the old king serpent and he feared to break it. But when the wizard thundered out the same question a second time and a third time, and grew bigger and more horrible looking each time he spoke, Batcha forgot his oath and confessed everything.

"Now come with me," the wizard said. "Show me the cliff. Show me the magic plant."

What could Batcha do but obey? He led the wizard to the cliff and picked a leaf of the magic plant.

"Open the rock," the wizard commanded.

Batcha laid the leaf against the cliff and instantly the rock opened.

"Go inside!" the wizard ordered.

But Batcha's trembling legs refused to move.

The wizard took out a book and began mumbling an incantation. Suddenly the earth trembled, the sky thundered, and with a great hissing whistling sound a monster dragon flew out of the cavern. It was the old king serpent whose seven years were up and who was now become a flying dragon. From his huge mouth he breathed out fire and smoke. With his long tail he swished right and left among the forest trees and these snapped and broke like little twigs.

The wizard, still mumbling from his book, handed Batcha a bridle.

"Throw this around his neck!" he commanded.

Batcha took the bridle but was too terrified to act. The wizard spoke again and Batcha made one uncertain step in the dragon's direction. He lifted his arm to throw the bridle over the dragon's head, when the dragon suddenly turned on him, swooped under him, and before Batcha knew what was happening he found himself on the dragon's back and he felt himself being lifted up, up, up, above the tops of the forest trees, above the very mountains themselves.

For a moment the sky was so dark that only the fire, spurting from the dragon's eyes and mouth, lighted them on their way.

The dragon lashed this way and that in fury, he belched forth great floods of boiling water, he hissed, he roared, until Batcha, clinging to his back, was half dead with fright.

Then gradually his anger cooled. He ceased belching forth boiling water, he stopped breathing fire, his hisses grew less terrifying.

"Thank God!" Batcha gasped. "Perhaps now he'll sink to earth and let me go."

But the dragon was not yet finished with punishing Batcha for breaking his oath. He rose still higher until the mountains of the earth looked like tiny ant-hills, still up until even these had disappeared. On, on they went, whizzing through the stars of heaven.

At last the dragon stopped flying and hung motionless in the firmament. To Batcha this was even more terrifying than moving.

"What shall I do? What shall I do?" he wept in agony. "If I jump down to earth I'll kill myself and I can't fly on up to heaven! Oh, dragon, have mercy on me! Fly back to earth and let me go and I swear before God that never again until death will I offend you!"

Batcha's pleading would have moved a stone to pity but the dragon, with an angry shake of his tail, only hardened his heart.

Suddenly Batcha heard the sweet voice of the skylark that was mounting to heaven.

"Skylark!" he called. "Dear skylark, bird that God loves, help me, for I am in great trouble! Fly up to heaven and tell God Almighty that Batcha, the shepherd, is hung in midair on a dragon's back. Tell Him that Batcha praises Him forever and begs Him to deliver him."

The skylark carried this message to heaven and God Almighty, pitying the poor shepherd, took some birch leaves and wrote on them in letters of gold. He put them in the skylark's bill and told the skylark to drop them on the dragon's head.

So the skylark returned from heaven and, hovering over Batcha, dropped the birch leaves on the dragon's head.

The dragon instantly sank to earth, so fast that Batcha lost consciousness.

When he came to himself he was sitting before his own hut. He looked about him. The dragon's cliff had disappeared. Otherwise everything was the same.

It was late afternoon and Dunay, the dog, was driving home the sheep. There was a woman coming up the mountain path.

Batcha heaved a great sigh.

"Thank God I'm back!" he said to himself. "How fine it is to hear Dunay's bark! And here comes my wife, God bless her! She'll scold me, I know, but even if she does, how glad I am to see her!"

The Story of the Shipwrecked Traveller

PREFIXED TO THE NARRATIVE of the shipwrecked traveller is the following: "A certain servant of wise understanding has said, Let your heart be of good cheer, Oh prince. Verily we have arrived at [our] homes. The mallet has been grasped, and the anchor-post has been driven into the ground, and the bow of the boat has grounded on the bank. Thanksgivings have been offered up to God, and every man has embraced his neighbour. Our sailors have returned in peace and safety, and our fighting men have lost none of their comrades, even though we travelled to the uttermost parts of Uauat (Nubia), and through the country of Senmut (Northern Nubia). Verily we have arrived in peace, and we have reached our own land [again]. Hearken, Oh prince, to me, even though I be a poor man. Wash yourself, and let water run over your fingers. I would that you should be ready to return an answer to the man who addresses you, and to speak to the King [from] your heart, and assuredly you must give your answer promptly and without hesitation. The mouth of a man delivers him, and his words provide a covering for [his] face. Act you according to the promptings of your heart, and when you have spoken [you will have made him] be at rest."

The shipwrecked traveller then narrates his experiences in the following words: I will now speak and give you a description of the things that [once] happened to me myself [when] I was journeying to the copper mines of the king. I went down into the sea in a ship that was one hundred and fifty cubits in length, and forty cubits in breadth, and it was manned by one hundred and fifty sailors who were chosen from among the best sailors of Egypt. They had looked upon the sky, they had looked upon the land, and their hearts were more understanding than the hearts of lions. Now although they were able to say beforehand when a tempest was coming, and could tell when a squall was going to rise before it broke upon them, a storm actually overtook us when we were still on the sea. Before we could make the land the wind blew with redoubled violence, and it drove before it upon us a wave that was eight cubits [high]. A plank was driven towards me by it, and I seized it; and as for the ship, those who were therein perished, and not one of them escaped.

Then a wave of the sea bore me along and cast me up upon an island, and I passed three days there by myself, with none but mine own heart for a companion; I laid me down and slept in a hollow in a thicket, and I hugged the shade. And I lifted up my legs (i.e. I walked about), so that I might find out what to put in my mouth, and I found there figs and grapes, and all kinds of fine large berries; and there were there gourds, and melons, and pumpkins as large as barrels, and there were also there fish and water-fowl. There was no [food] of any sort or kind that did not grow in this island. And when I had eaten all I could eat, I laid the remainder of the food upon the ground, for it was too much for me [to carry] in my arms. I then dug a hole in the ground and made a fire, and I prepared pieces of wood and a burnt-offering for the gods.

And I heard a sound [as of] thunder, which I thought to be [caused by] a wave of the sea, and the trees rocked and the earth quaked, and I covered my face. And I found [that the sound was caused by] a serpent that was coming towards me. It was thirty cubits in length, and its beard was more than two cubits in length, and its body was covered with [scales of] gold, and the two ridges over its eyes were of pure lapis-lazuli (i.e. they were blue); and it coiled its whole length up before me. And it opened its mouth to me, now I was lying flat on my stomach in front of it, and it said to me, "Who has brought you here? Who has brought you here, Oh miserable one? Who has brought you here? If you do not immediately declare to me who has brought you to this island, I will make you know what it is to be burnt with fire, and you will become a thing that is invisible. You speak to me, but I cannot hear what you say; I am before you, do you not know me?" Then the serpent took me in its mouth, and carried me off to the place where it was wont to rest, and it set me down there, having done me no harm whatsoever; I was sound and whole, and it had not carried away any portion of my body. And it opened its mouth to me whilst I was lying flat on my stomach, and it said to me, "Who has brought you here? Who has brought you here, Oh miserable one? Who has brought you here to this island of the sea, the two sides of which are in the waves?"

Then I made answer to the serpent, my two hands being folded humbly before it, and I said to it, "I am one who was travelling to the mines on a mission of the king in a ship that was one hundred and fifty cubits long, and fifty cubits in breadth, and it was manned by a crew of one hundred and fifty men, who were chosen from among the best sailors of Egypt. They had looked upon the sky, they had looked upon the earth, and their hearts were more understanding than the hearts of lions. They were able to say beforehand when a tempest was coming, and to tell when a squall was about to rise before it broke. The heart of every man among them was wiser than that of his neighbour, and the arm of each was stronger than that of his neighbour; there was not one weak man among them. Nevertheless it blew a gale of wind whilst we were still on the sea and before we could make the land. A gale rose, which continued to increase in violence, and with it there came upon [us] a wave eight cubits [high]. A plank of wood was driven towards me by this wave, and I seized it; and as for the ship, those who were therein perished and not one of them escaped alive [except] myself. And now behold me by your side! It was a wave of the sea that brought me to this island."

And the serpent said to me, "Have no fear, have no fear, Oh little one, and let not your face be sad, now that you have arrived at the place where I am. Verily, God has spared your life, and you have been brought to this island where there is food. There is no kind of food that is not here, and it is filled with good things of every kind. Verily, you shall pass month after month on this island, until you have come to the end of four months, and then a ship shall come, and there shall be therein sailors who are acquaintances of thine, and you shall go with them to your country, and you shall die in your native town." [And the serpent continued,] "What a joyful thing it is for the man who has experienced evil fortunes, and has passed safely through them, to declare them! I will now describe to you some of the things that have happened to me on this island. I used to live here with my brethren, and with my children who dwelt among them; now my children and my brethren together numbered seventy-five. I do not make mention of a little maiden who had been brought to me by fate. And a star fell [from heaven], and these (i.e. his children, and his brethren, and the maiden) came into the fire which fell with it. I myself was not with those who were burnt in the fire, and I was not in their midst, but I [well-nigh] died [of grief] for them. And I found a place wherein I buried them all together. Now, if you are strong, and your heart flourishes, you shall fill both your arms (i.e. embrace) with your children, and you shall kiss your wife, and you shall see your own house, which is the most beautiful thing of all, and you shall reach your country, and you shall live therein again together with your brethren, and dwell therein."

Then I cast myself down flat upon my stomach, and I pressed the ground before the serpent with my forehead, saying, "I will describe your power to the King, and I will make him understand your greatness. I will cause to be brought to you the unguent and spices called aba, and hekenu, and inteneb, and khasait, and the incense that is offered up in the temples, whereby every god is propitiated. I will relate [to him] the things that have happened to me, and declare the things that have been seen by me through your power, and praise and thanksgiving shall be made to you in my city in the presence of all the nobles of the country. I will slaughter bulls for you, and will offer them up as burnt-offerings, and I will pluck feathered fowl in your [honour]. And I will cause to come to you boats laden with all the most costly products of the land of Egypt, even according to what is done for a god who is beloved by men and women in a land far away, whom they know not." Then the serpent smiled at me, and the things which I had said to it were regarded by it in its heart as nonsense, for it said to me, "You have not a very great store of myrrh [in Egypt], and all that you have is incense. Behold, I am the Prince of Punt, and the myrrh which is therein belongs to me. And as for the heken which you have said you will cause to be brought to me, is it not one of the chief [products] of this island? And behold, it shall come to pass that when you have once departed from this place, you shall never more see this island, for it shall disappear into the waves."

And in due course, even as the serpent had predicted, a ship arrived, and I climbed up to the top of a high tree, and I recognized those who were in it. Then I went to announce the matter to the serpent, but I found that it had knowledge thereof already. And the serpent said to me, "A safe [journey], a safe [journey], Oh little one, to your house. You shall see your children [again]. I beseech you that my name may be held in fair repute in your city, for verily this is the thing which I desire of you."

Then I threw myself flat upon my stomach, and my two hands were folded humbly before the serpent. And the serpent gave me a [ship-] load of things, namely, myrrh, heken, inteneb, khasait, thsheps and shaas spices, eye-paint (antimony), skins of panthers, great balls of incense, tusks of elephants, greyhounds, apes, monkeys, and beautiful and costly products of all sorts and kinds. And when I had loaded these things into the ship, and had thrown myself flat upon my stomach in order to give thanks to it for the same, it spoke to me, saying, "Verily you shall travel to [your] country in two months, and you shall fill both your arms with your children, and you shall renew your youth in your coffin." Then I went down to the place on the sea-shore where the ship was, and I hailed the bowmen who were in the ship, and I spoke words of thanksgiving to the lord of this island, and those who were in the ship did the same. Then we set sail, and we journeyed on and returned to the country of the King, and we arrived there at the end of two months, according to all that the serpent had said. And I entered into the presence of the King, and I took with me for him the offerings which I had brought out of the island. And the King praised me and thanked me in the presence of the nobles of all his country, and he appointed me to be one of his bodyguard, and I received my wages along with those who were his [regular] servants.

Cast you your glance then upon me [Oh Prince], now that I have set my feet on my native land once more, having seen and experienced what I have seen and experienced. Listen to me, for verily it is a good thing to listen to men. And the Prince said to me, "Make not yourself out to be perfect, my friend! Does a man give water to a fowl at daybreak which he is going to kill during the day?"

Here ends [The Story of the Shipwrecked Traveller], which has been written from the beginning to the end thereof according to the text that has been found written in an [ancient] book. It has been written (i.e. copied) by Ameni-Amen-aa, a scribe with skilful fingers. Life, strength, and health be to him!

SUPERNATURAL BEASTS & BEINGS

Introduction

WEREWOLVES BELONG both to the human realm and the animal kingdom. In doing so, in defiance of all scientific law and logical consistency, they also straddle the natural and supernatural realms. So it is with the Changeling too, a fairy infant substituted for a mortal child: he or she inhabits several existential planes at once.

The metaphysics of it all can be bewildering. The 'Kildare Pooka', once a human, now a shapeshifting spirit (we see him as an ass), works out his punishment for laziness by helping with the household's work. Only until he is offered recompense, however. Once the Pooka has earned their gratitude, he's gone – ironically leaving those who have thanked him high and dry.

The Chinese Ape Sun Wu Kung becomes such a clever sorcerer that he can walk on the air and change his shape at will. Powerful as he is, however, the Buddha will put him in his place. His story is said to be an allegory, with the resourceful ape reflecting the ever-adaptable human heart; his acceptance of the Buddha's reprimand, the humility by which it might be saved.

The 'supernatural beasts' in this section come in myriad forms, their stories offering many different moral lessons. What these tales have in common – their colour and ebullience apart – is the wit and subtlety with which they highlight human situations, raising intriguing questions about human relationships and human life.

The Werewolf in Myth and Legend

AN EXTRAORDINARY STORY about a werewolf comes from Ansbach in 1685:

The supposed incarnation of a dead burgomaster of that town was said to be ravishing the neighbouring country in the form of a wolf, devouring cattle as well as women and children. At last the ferocious beast was caught and slaughtered, and its carcass was encased in a suit of flesh-coloured cere-cloth, while its head and face were adorned with a chestnut-coloured wig and long white beard, after the animal's snout had been cut off and a mask resembling the dead burgomaster's features had been substituted. This effigy was hanged, its skin stuffed and put in a museum, where it was pointed out as a proof of the actual existence of werewolves. This incident appears to prove that the belief in werewolves had been shaken at that date, but it has never been finally eradicated, and it is only natural that a theme which has had such world-wide credence should occur again and again in mythology and literature. It is dealt with in the story of the festival of the god Zeus, which was held every nine years on the Wolf mountain in Arcadia. During the banquet a man, having tasted of a flowing bowl in which human and animal flesh were mixed, was turned into a wolf and remained a wolf nine years. If he had abstained from eating human flesh in the interval he became once more a man. The tradition appears to have originated in the existence of a society of cannibal wolf-worshippers, a member of which perhaps represented the sacred animal for nine years in succession.

This compares in some degree with the practices of the Human Leopard Society, which is of comparatively recent origin.

Lycaon, the King of Arcadia and father of Callisto, was turned into a wolf because he offered human sacrifices to Jupiter, or, in the version given by Ovid, because he tried to murder Jupiter, who was his guest. Others believe that Lycaon is the Constellation of the Wolf, and that in him were the united qualities of wolf, king, and constellation.

Pliny points out that the origin of transformation into wolves was due to Evanthes, a Greek author of good repute, who tells the story of Antheus, the Arcadian, a member of whose family is chosen by lot and then taken to a certain lake in the district, across which he swims and is changed into a wolf for a space of nine years. So, too, Demæntus, during a sacrifice of human victims, tasted the entrails of a boy who had been slaughtered, upon which he turned into a wolf, but ten years later he was victorious in the pugilistic contests at the Olympic games.

The following quaint story is taken from Petronius, being told by one Niceros, at a banquet given by Trimalchio.

"It happened that my master was gone to Capua to dispose of some second-hand goods. I took the opportunity and persuaded our guest to walk with me to our fifth milestone. He was a valiant soldier, and a sort of a grim water-drinking Pluto. About cock-crow, when the moon was shining as bright as midday, we came amongst the monuments. My friend began addressing himself to the stars, but I was rather in a mood to sing or count them; and when I turned to look at him, lo! he had already stripped himself and laid his clothes near him. My heart was in my nostrils, and I stood like a dead man; but he made a mark round his clothes and on a sudden became a wolf. Do not think I jest, I would not lie for any man's estate. But to return to what I am saying. When he became a wolf he began howling and fled into the woods. At first I hardly knew where I was, and afterwards, when I went to take up his clothes, they were turned into stone. Who then was more like to die from fear than I? Yet I drew my sword, and cutting the air right and left came thus to my sweetheart's house. When I entered the courtyard I was like to breathe my last, perspiration poured from my neck, and my eyes were dim. My Melissa met me to ask where I had been so late, and said, 'Had you only come sooner you might have helped us, for a wolf came to the farm and worried our cattle; but he had not the best of the joke, for all he escaped, as our servant ran a lance through his neck.' When I heard this I could not doubt what had happened, and as the day dawned I ran home as fast as a robbed innkeeper. When I came to the spot where the clothes had been turned into stone I could find nothing except blood. But when I got home I found my friend, the soldier, in bed, bleeding at the neck like an ox, and a doctor dressing his wound. I then knew he was a turnskin; nor would I ever have broken bread with him again, no not if you had killed me."

The expression turnskin or turncoat is a translation of the Latin *versipelles*, a term used to describe a werewolf.

Another story in which the human being suffers from the wound inflicted on the werewolf concerns a fine lady of Saintonge, who used to wander at night in the forests in the shape of a wolf. One day she caught her paw in a trap set by the hunters. This put an end to her nocturnal wanderings, and afterwards she had to keep a glove on the hand that had been trapped, to conceal the mutilation of two of her fingers.

Eliphas Levi, the occultist, has endeavoured to explain this sympathetic condition between the man and his animal presentment.

"We must speak here of lycanthropy, or the nocturnal transformation of men into wolves, histories so well substantiated that sceptical science has had recourse to furious maniacs, and to masquerading as animals for explanations. But such hypotheses are puerile and explain nothing. Let us seek elsewhere the solution of the mystery, and establish – First, that no person has been killed by a werewolf except by suffocation, without effusion of blood and without wounds. Second, that werewolves, though tracked, hunted, and even maimed, have never been killed on the spot. Third, that persons suspected of these transformations have always been found at home, after the pursuit of the werewolf, more or less wounded, sometimes dying, but invariably in their natural form....

"We have spoken of the sidereal body, which is the mediator between the soul and the material organism. This body remains awake very often while the other is asleep, and by thought transports itself through all space which universal magnetism opens to it. It thus lengthens, without breaking, the sympathetic chain attaching it to the heart and brain, and that is why there is danger in waking up dreaming persons with a start, for the shock may sever the chain at a blow and cause instantaneous death. The form of our sidereal body is conformable to the habitual condition of our thoughts, and in the long run it is bound to modify the features of the material organism. Let us now be bold enough to assert that the werewolf is nothing more than the sidereal body of a man whose savage and sanguinary instincts are represented by the wolf, who, whilst his phantom is wandering abroad, sleeps painfully in his bed, and dreams that he is a veritable wolf. What renders the werewolf visible is the almost somnambulistic over-excitement caused by the fear of those who see it, or their disposition, more particularly among simple country-folk, to place themselves in direct communication with the astral light which is the common medium of dreams and visions. The blows inflicted on the werewolf really wound the sleeper by the odic and sympathetic conjestion of the astral light and by the correspondence of the immaterial with the material body...."

This peculiarity of the wound dealt to the werewolf being reproduced in the human being is emphasized by an incident which occurred about 1588 in a tiny village situated in the mountains of Auvergne. A gentleman was gazing one evening from the windows of his castle when he saw a hunter he knew passing on his way to the chase. Calling to him, he begged that on his return he would report what luck he had had. The hunter after pursuing his way was attacked by a large wolf. He fired off his gun without hitting the animal. Then he struck at it with his hunting knife, severing one of the paws, which he picked up and put in his knapsack. The wounded wolf ran quickly into the forest. When the hunter reached the castle he told his friend of his strange fight with a wolf, and to emphasise his story opened his knapsack, in which to his horror and surprise he saw, not a wolf's paw as he had expected, but the hand of a woman which had a gold ring on one of the fingers.

The owner recognized the ring as belonging to his wife, and hastening into the kitchen to question her he found her with one arm hidden beneath the folds of a shawl. He drew it aside and saw she had lost her hand. Then she confessed that it was she who, in the form of a wolf, had attacked the hunter. She was arrested and burnt to death soon afterwards at Ryon.

In another variation of the werewolf story, the human being retains a material object acquired by his animal replica and is freed thereby from his obsession.

A man, who from his childhood had been a werewolf, when returning one night with his wife from a merrymaking, observed that the hour was at hand when the transformation usually took place. Giving the reins to his wife, he got out of the cart and said, "If anyone comes to thee, strike at it with thy apron." Then he went away and a few minutes later the poor woman was attacked by a wolf. Remembering what her husband had told her, she struck at it with her apron, and the animal tore out a piece and ran off. Presently the man himself returned holding in his mouth the torn fragment of the apron. Then his wife cried out in terror, "Good Lord, man! Why, thou art a werewolf!"

"Thank thee, mother!" replied he, "but now I am free!" and after this incident he kept human form until the day of his death.

In 'William of Palermo,' the old romance known as 'William and the Werewolf,' translated from the French at the command of Sir Humphrey de Bohun about A.D. 1350, the werewolf appears as a sort of a guardian angel. The brother of the King Apulia, envious of the heir-apparent, bribes two women to murder the king's son. While the boy William is at play a werewolf runs off with him, swims across the Straits of Messina, and carries him into a forest near Rome, where it takes care of him and provides him with food. The werewolf in reality is Alphonso, heir to the Spanish throne, who has been transformed by his stepmother Queen Braunde, who desires her own son Braundinis to wear the crown of Spain.

The werewolf embraces the king's son
With his fore-feet,
And so familiar with him
Is the king's son, that all pleases him,
Whatever the beast does for him.

While the werewolf seeks provender, a cowherd finds William and takes him to his hut, where the Emperor meets him when out hunting. Placing him behind him on his horse he takes him to Rome and gives him in charge of his daughter Melior, to be her page.

William and Melior fall in love with one another, and to avoid the Emperor's wrath devise an escape, disguised in the skins of white bears, helped by Melior's friend Alexandrine. When Melior asks whether she makes a bold bear, Alexandrine answers, "Yes, Madame, you are a grisly ghost enough, and look ferocious." Together the lovers wander out of the garden on all fours and making their way to the forest hide in a den. Meanwhile the werewolf has followed William's fortunes, and finding the wanderers in need, he sets on a harmless passer-by who carries provisions, and seizing bread and boiled beef out of his bag, lays it before the lovers, then runs off and, attacking another traveller, secures two flagons of wine.

Being pursued, the lovers escape to Palermo, led always by the werewolf, Alphonso, half-brother to Braundinis, who was destined by Melior's father to become his son-in-law. William does battle with the proposed suitor and, still helped by the werewolf, whose symbol is painted on his shield, overcomes his rival, takes the King and Queen of Spain prisoner and refuses to let them go until Queen Braunde promises to transform the rightful heir from a wolf back into a human being. "Unless she disenchants you, she shall be burnt," he says forcibly. Braunde takes her stepson, the wolf, into a private chamber, draws forth a magic ring with a stone in it that is proof against all witchcraft and binds it with a red silk thread round the wolf's neck. Then she takes a book out of a casket and reads in it a long time till he turns into a man. The werewolf is delighted, but apologizes to his stepmother for having no clothes on, and she commands him to choose who shall fetch his clothes. He answers that he will take his attire and the order of knighthood from the worthiest man alive, William of Palermo. William, being called, enters the chamber, where he sees a man who is an utter stranger and is only satisfied when he hears Alphonso's explanation, "I am the werewolf who saved you from many perils." William and Melior are married, all ends happily and William becomes Emperor of Rome.

The Bretons give the name of Bisclavaret to the werewolf, or wer-fox, which throws itself upon the hunter's horse and terrorizes it. The same thing is called Garwal by the Normans. Bisclavaret is supposed to be a wizard, and if in olden times an unknown lady offered food to the hunters at the moment the animal appeared she was thought to be a witch.

Marie de France in her 'Lay of the Bisclavaret' used the idea of a werewolf, and again in this case the animal has no savage instincts except against his enemies, a faithless wife and her perfidious lover.

A gallant knight of Brittany, a favourite with the king, weds a fair lady whom he loves tenderly. Only one cloud darkens the wife's horizon. Her husband leaves her invariably three days a week and she does not know where he goes. One day she has the temerity to ask him, and he warns her that the information may be dangerous, but when she pleads with him he says:

"Learn then that I become a werewolf during my absence. I go into the forest, hide in the thickets and seek my prey."

"But, my dear, tell me whether you take off your clothes," says the wife, "or whether you keep them on?"

"I am naked when the transformation occurs, Madame."

"And where do you leave your clothes?"

"I must not tell you, because if I were seen when I take them off I should remain a werewolf for the rest of my life. I can only recover human form at the moment I put them on again. After that you will not be surprised if I say no more." But she urges him to tell her, and finally he says that he hides his clothes under a bush near an old stone cross in the corner of a chapel, and there he puts them on when he wishes to resume his original shape.

Frightened by his awful story the wife decides to live with him no more and immediately sends for a young man who is in love with her, tells him the story and enjoins him to go and take away her husband's clothes. Thus she betrays her husband, the werewolf, who does not return and is given up for dead, and some time after she marries her false lover.

About a year later the king goes on a hunting expedition in the forest. There he comes across the werewolf, and the hounds immediately take up the scent and give chase the whole day long. Wounded by the hunters and wearied nigh unto death, the wolf seizes the bridle of the king's horse and licks his majesty's foot. The king, in great fear, calls his companions to look at the extraordinary wild beast that is capable of this humble action. He refuses to allow the wolf to be slaughtered and takes it back, in his train, to the castle. There the wolf lives in great comfort like a domestic pet and harms no one.

Presently a great function is held at the court and the werewolf's former wife comes there with her new husband. The moment the wolf sets eyes on him he springs at his throat, and would surely have killed him had not the king beaten him off with a whip. For the rest of the gentleman's visit the wolf is kept under strict discipline.

Some time afterwards, the king, accompanied by his faithful wolf, pays a visit to the lady, and the animal springs at her ferociously and bites off her nose. Then the courtiers say that the matter must be inquired into, for the wolf only turns savage when in the presence of this lady and her new husband. The king decides to have the couple arrested and the lady has to confess what happened, saying she thinks the werewolf must be her transformed husband. After hearing her story the king orders the werewolf's clothes to be placed where he can get them privately, and after waiting outside the room in which the metamorphosis is to take place, for some time, he enters and finds the former knight, his old friend whom he thought dead, lying quietly asleep. He restores all his honours and has his faithless wife chased out of the kingdom in company with her false lover. All their daughters are born without noses as a punishment for the wicked fraud practised on the werewolf.

Olaus Magnus declares that although the inhabitants of Prussia, Livonia, and Lithuania suffer considerably from the depredations of wolves as far as their cattle are concerned, their losses are not so serious in this quarter as those they suffer at the hands of werewolves.

On Christmas Eve multitudes of werewolves gather at a certain spot and band together to attack human beings and animals. They besiege isolated houses, break in the doors and devour every living thing. They burst into the beer-cellars and there empty the casks, thus proving their human tastes. A ruined castle near Courland appears to have been their favourite meeting-place, where thousands congregate in order to test their agility. If any of them fail to bound over the castle wall they are slain by the others, as they are considered in that case to be incompetent for the work in hand.

It is believed that a messenger in the person of a lame youth is sent round the neighbourhood to call these followers of the devil to a general conclave. Those who are reluctant to attend the meeting are beaten with iron scourges. When the gathering is assembled the human forms vanish and the whole multitude become wolves. The troops follow the leader, "firmly convinced in their imagination that they are transformed into wolves." The sorcery lasts for twelve days, and at the expiration of this period the human forms are resumed.

Referring further to these Courland werewolves, it is said of them that Satan holds them in his net in three ways. Firstly they execute certain depredations, such as mangling cattle, in their human shapes, but in such a state of hallucination that they believe themselves to be wolves and are regarded as such by others in a like predicament. Though not true werewolves they hunt in packs. Secondly they leave their bodies lying asleep and send forth their imagination in a dream that they believe they have injured the cattle, but that it is the devil who does what is suggested to them by their thoughts, and thirdly that the evil one induces real wolves to do the horrid deeds, but impresses the scene so vividly on the mind of the sleeper that he considers himself to be guilty of the act.

The following stories exemplify these conditions. The first is told of a man who when starting on a journey saw a wolf attacking one of his sheep. He fired and it fled wounded into the thicket. On his return he was told that he had fired at one of his tenants, called Mickel.

Mickel's wife, when questioned, said that her husband had been sowing rye and had asked her how he could get some meat for a feast. She said on no account was he to steal from the master's flock as it was well guarded by dogs. Mickel ignored her advice and had attacked the sheep. He came home limping badly and in a passion had fallen upon his own horse and had torn its throat. It seemed as though he were bewitched or in a trance.

In 1684 a curious incident occurred to a man who had gone hunting in a forest. At dusk a pack of wolves had rushed towards him, and as he levelled his gun with the intention of aiming at the leader a voice arose from their midst, saying, "Don't fire, sir, for no good will come of it." Then the phantom pack rushed onwards and he saw it no more.

The third story is about a man-wolf who was accused of sorcery of the most flagrant kind. Finding a difficulty in getting evidence against the criminal, the judge sent a peasant to his cell who was charged with the unpleasant task of forcing a confession. The prisoner was told that he might avenge himself upon another peasant to whom he owed a grudge, by destroying his cow secretly, and if possible when in the shape of a wolf himself. After much persuasion the supposed werewolf undertook to carry out the suggested plan. The next morning the cow in question was found to be fearfully mangled, but the strange part of the story is this, that although witnesses were set to watch the man in his cell, they swore unanimously that he had never left it and had passed the whole of the night in deep sleep, only at one time making slight movements of his head, his hands and his feet.

Just as the man who thinks he changes into a wolf suffers from lycanthropy, so the one who believes he changes into a dog is suffering from kynanthropy, and those who change into kine from boanthropy. Every part of the world chooses a special animal as being the most suitable for disguise, and naturally enough the animal is one which is common to the district. Thus we find the tiger chosen for India and Asia, the bear for Northern Europe, the lion, leopard, and hyæna for Africa, the jaguar for South America, and so forth.

Many superstitions surround the tiger. Besides being the abode of the soul of a dead man it may be the temporary or even the permanent form of a living human being. In India it is said that a certain root brings about the metamorphosis and that another root is used for the antidote. In Central Java powers of transformation are believed to be hereditary, no shame is attached to it, and the wer-tiger is looked upon as a friendly animal, and if his friends call upon him by name he behaves like a domestic pet and is believed to guard the fields. In the Malay Peninsula faith in the genuine wer-tiger persists, and it is thought there also that the soul of a dead wizard enters the animal's body. During the process of transformation the corpse is laid in the forest, and beside it a supply of rice and water is placed, sufficient for seven days, in which time transmigration, resulting from a compact made by the pawang's ancestors, is complete. A ceremony is also gone through by the son of a pawang who wishes to succeed his father in tiger's form.

A wer-tiger belief exists in India, and the Garrows think the mania is produced by a special drug which is laid on the forehead. First the wer-tiger pulls the earrings out of his ears and then wanders forth alone, shunning the company of his fellow-man. The disease lasts about fourteen days, and patients are said to have glaring red eyes, their hair dishevelled and bristled, and a peculiar convulsive manner of moving the head. When taken by fits of this kind they are believed to go forth in the night to ride on the backs of tigers.

Another form of the belief is the wizard in the shape of a tiger, and the Thana tradition is that mediums are possessed by a tiger spirit. The Binuas of Johore think that every *pawang* has an immortal tiger spirit.

The belief that lion form is assumed by wizards is found near the Luapula and on the Zambezi, where a certain drink is supposed to effect the transformation. Among the Tumbukas people smear themselves with white clay, which gives them a certain power of metempsychosis. Not only can men take lions' shape but lions can change into men.

The Werewolf Trials

IN POITOU the peasants have a curious expression, *"courir la galipote,"* which means to turn into a werewolf or other human-animal by night and chase prey through the woods. The galipote is the familiar or imp which the sorcerer has the power to send forth.

In the dark ages sorcerers capable of this accomplishment were dealt with according to the law, and hundreds were sent to trial for practising black arts, being condemned, in most instances, to be burnt alive or broken on the wheel. One of the most notorious historical cases was that of Pierre Bourgot, who served the devil for two years and was tried by the Inquisitor-General Boin.

Johannus Wierius gives in full the confession of Bourgot, otherwise called Great Peter, and of Michael Verding. The prisoners, who were accused of wicked practices in December, 1521, believed they had been transformed into wolves.

About nineteen years before Pierre's arrest at Pouligny a dreadful storm occurred which scattered the flock of sheep of which he was shepherd, and while he went far afield to search for them he met three black horsemen, one of whom said to him, "Where are you going, my friend? You appear to be in trouble."

Pierre told him that he was seeking his sheep, and the horseman bade him take courage, saying that if he would only have faith, his master would protect the straying sheep and see that no harm came to them.

Pierre thanked him and promised to meet him again in the same place a few days later. Soon afterwards he found the stray sheep.

The black horseman, at their second meeting, told Pierre that he served the devil, and Pierre agreed to do likewise if he promised him protection for his flock. Then the devil's servant made him renounce God, the Virgin Mary, and all the saints of Paradise, his baptism and the tenets of Christianity. Pierre swore that he would do so, and kissed the horseman's left hand, which was as black as ink and felt stone-cold. Then he knelt down and took an oath of allegiance to the devil, and the horseman forbade him thenceforth to repeat the Apostles' creed.

For two years Pierre remained in the service of the evil one, and during that time he never entered a church until mass was over, or at least until after the holy water had been sprinkled.

Meanwhile his flock was kept in perfect safety, and this sense of security made him so indifferent about the devil that he began to go to church again and to say the creed. This went on for eight or nine years, when he was told by one Michael Verding that he must once more render obedience to the evil one, his master. In return for his homage Pierre was told that he would receive a sum of money.

Michael led him one evening to a clearing in the woods at Chastel Charlon, where many strangers were dancing. Each performer held in his hand a green torch which emitted a blue flame. Michael told Pierre to bestir himself and that then he would receive payment, so Pierre threw off his clothes and Michael smeared his body with an ointment which he carried. Pierre believed that he had been transformed into a wolf, and was horrified to find that he had four paws and a thick pelt. He found himself able to run with the speed of the wind. Michael had also made use of the salve and had become equally agile. After an hour or two they resumed human shape, their respective masters giving them another salve for this purpose. After this experience Pierre complained that he felt utterly weary, and his master told him that was of no consequence and that he would be speedily restored to his usual state of health.

Pierre was often transformed into a werewolf after this first attempt, and on one occasion he fell upon a boy of seven with the intention of killing and eating him, but the child screamed so loudly that he beat a hasty retreat to the spot where his clothes lay in a heap, rubbed himself hurriedly with the ointment and resumed human form to escape capture. Another time Michael and he killed an old woman who was gathering peas, and one day whilst in the shape of wolves they devoured the whole of a little girl except for one arm, and Michael said her flesh tasted excellent, although it apparently gave Pierre indigestion. They confessed also to strangling a young woman, whose blood they drank.

Among other disgusting crimes, Pierre murdered a girl of eight in a garden by cracking her neck between his jaws, and he killed a goat near to the farm of one Master Pierre Lerugen, first by setting on it with his teeth and then by gashing its throat with a knife. The latter operation leads to the belief that he had resumed his ordinary shape at the time.

A peculiar point worth noticing about the case of Michael and Pierre was that the former was able to transform himself at any moment with his clothes on, while the latter had to strip and rub in ointment to achieve the same result. At the time of his confession Pierre declared that he could not recollect where the wolf's fur went to when he became human again.

He also deposed that an ash-coloured powder was given to him, which he rubbed upon his arms and left hand and thus caused the death of every animal he touched. Here there would seem to be some discrepancy, for he declared that in many instances he strangled, bit, or wounded his victims!

Garinet gives a good account of the important trial in 1573 of Gilles Garnier, who was arrested for having devoured several children whilst in the form of a werewolf.

The prisoner was accused of seizing a young girl aged ten or twelve in a vineyard near Dôle, of killing her and dragging her into a wood, and of tearing the flesh from her bones with his teeth and claws. He found this food so palatable that he carried some of it away with him and offered to share it with his wife. A week after the feast of All Saints he captured another young girl near the village of La Pouppé, and was about to slay and devour her when someone hastened to her rescue and he took flight.

A week later, being still in the form of a wolf, he had killed and eaten a boy at a spot between Gredisans and Menoté, about a league from Dôle. He was accused also of being in the shape of a man when he caught another boy of twelve or thirteen years of age and carried him into the wood to strangle him, and, "in spite of the fact that it was Friday," he would have devoured his flesh had he not been interrupted by the approach of some strangers, who were too late, however, to save the boy's life. Garnier, having admitted all the charges against him, the judge pronounced the following sentence: –

"The condemned man is to be dragged to the place of execution and there burnt alive and his body reduced to ashes."

The account of the trial, which took place on the 18th day of January, 1573, was accompanied by a letter from Daniel d'Ange to the Dean of the Church of Sens which contained the following passage: –

"Gilles Garnier, lycophile, as I may call him, lived the life of a hermit, but has since taken a wife, and having no means of support for his family fell into the way, as is natural to defiant and desperate people of rude habits, of wandering into the woods and wild places. In this state he was met by a phantom in the shape of a man, who told him that he could perform miracles, among other things declaring that he would teach him how to change at will into a wolf, lion, or leopard, and because the wolf is more familiar in this country than the other kinds of wild beasts he chose to disguise himself in that shape, which he did, using a salve with which he rubbed himself for this purpose, as he has since confessed before dying, after recognising the evil of his ways."

The affair made such a stir in the neighbourhood, and the dread of werewolves had risen to such a pitch, that it was found necessary to ask the help of the populace in suppressing the nuisance. A legal decree was issued which empowered the people at Dôle to "assemble with javelins, pikes, arquebuses, and clubs to hunt and pursue the werewolf, and to take, bind, and kill it without incurring the usual fine or penalty for indulging in the chase without permission."

Boguet is the authority who cites the following cases of lycanthropy:

A boy called Benedict, aged about fifteen, one day climbed a tree to gather some fruit, when he saw a wolf attacking his little sister, who was playing at the foot of the tree.

The boy climbed down quickly, and the animal, which was tailless, let go of the little girl and turned upon her brother, who defended himself with a knife. According to the boy's account, the wolf tore the knife out of his hand and struck at his throat. A neighbour ran to the rescue and carried the boy home, where he died a few days after from the wound. Whilst he lay dying he declared that the wolf which had injured him had fore-paws shaped like human hands, but that its hind feet were covered with fur.

After inquiry it was proved that a young and demented girl called Perrenette Gandillon believed herself to be a wolf and had done this horrible deed. She was caught by the populace and torn limb from limb. This case occurred in the Jura mountains in 1598.

Soon afterwards Perrenette's brother Pierre was accused of being a werewolf, and confessed that he had been to the witches' Sabbath in this form. His son George had also been anointed with salve and had killed goats whilst he was in animal shape. Antoinette, his sister, was accused of sorcery and of intercourse with the devil, who appeared to her in the form of a black goat. Several members of the Gandillon family were arrested, and in prison Pierre and George conducted themselves as though they were possessed, walking on all fours and howling like wild beasts.

Not long after the Gandillon family had been disposed of, one Jeanne Perrin gave evidence that she was walking near a wood with her friend Clauda Gaillard, who disappeared suddenly behind a bush, and that the next moment there came forth a tailless wolf which frightened her so much that she made the sign of the cross and ran away. She was sure that the hind legs of the wolf were like human limbs. When Clauda saw her again she assured Jeanne that the wolf had not meant to do her harm, and from this it was thought that Clauda had taken the shape of the wolf.

One of the best known of the werewolf trials concerns Jacques Rollet, the man-wolf of Caude, who was accused of having devoured a little boy.

He was tried and condemned in Angers in 1598. Rollet came from the parish of Maumusson, near to Nantes, and he carried on his practices in a desolate spot near Caude, where some villagers one day found the corpse of a boy of about fifteen, mangled and blood-bespattered. As they approached the body three wolves bounded into the forest and were lost to sight, but the men gave chase, and following in the animals' tracks, came suddenly upon a half-naked human being, with long hair and beard, his hands covered with blood and his teeth chattering with fear. On his claw-like nails they found shreds of human flesh.

This miserable specimen of man-animal was hauled up before the judge, and under examination he inquired of one of the witnesses whether he remembered shooting at three wolves. The witness said he remembered the incident perfectly. Rollet confessed that he was one of the wolves and that he was able to transform himself by means of a salve. The other wolves were his companions, Jean and Julian, who knew the same means of acquiring animal shape. All the particulars he gave as to the murder were accurate, and he confessed to having killed and eaten women, lawyers, attorneys, and bailiffs, though the last-named he found tough and tasteless. In other respects his evidence was confused, and he was judged to be of weak intellect, and though condemned to death was sent finally to a madhouse, where he was sentenced to two years' detention.

There was an epidemic of lycanthropy throughout this year, and on the 4th of December a tailor of Châlons was burnt in Paris for having decoyed children into his shop, a cask full of human bones being discovered in the cellar. For the space of a few years no notorious werewolf trials appear to have taken place, but the year 1603 was almost as prolific in this respect as 1598.

Information came before the criminal court at Roche Chalais that a wild beast was ravaging the district, that it appeared to be a wolf, and that it had attacked a young girl called Margaret Poiret in full daylight.

A youth of thirteen or fourteen in the service of Peter Combaut deposed to the fact that he had thrown himself upon the said Margaret, whilst transformed into a wolf, and that he would have devoured her had she not defended herself stoutly with a stick. He also confessed to having eaten two or three little girls.

Evidence was given on May 29th, 1603, by three witnesses, one of whom was Margaret herself. She said she had been accustomed to mind cattle in the company of the boy, Jean Grenier, and that he had often frightened her by telling her horrible tales about being able to change into a wolf whenever he wished, and that he had killed many dogs and sucked their blood, but that he preferred to devour young children. He said he had recently killed a child, and after eating part of her flesh had thrown the rest to a companion wolf.

Margaret described the beast which had attacked her as stouter and shorter than a real wolf, with a smaller head, a short tail, and reddish hide. After she struck at it, the animal drew back and sat down on its haunches like a dog, at a distance of about twelve paces. Its look was so ferocious that she ran away at once.

The third witness was Jeanne Gaboriaut, who was eighteen years old. She gave evidence that one day, when she was tending cattle in company with other girls, Jean Grenier came up and asked which was the most beautiful shepherdess amongst them. Jeanne asked him why he wanted to know. He said because he wished to marry the prettiest, and if it was Jeanne he would choose her.

Jeanne said, "Who is your father?" and he told her that he was the son of a priest.

Then she replied that he was too dark in appearance for her taste, and when he answered he had been like that for a long time, she asked him whether he had turned black from cold or whether he had been burnt black.

He said the cause was a wolf's skin he was wearing, which had been given to him by one Pierre Labourant, and when he wore it he could turn into a wolf at will or any other animal he preferred, and he went on with details similar to those he had disclosed to Margaret Poiret.

It was proved, however, that Grenier was not the son of a priest, but of a labourer, Pierre Grenier, and that he lived in the parish of St. Antoine de Pizan.

When questioned as to his crimes, he confessed to the assault upon Margaret Poiret as described by her, and also that he had entered a house in the guise of a wolf, and finding no one there but a babe in its cradle he seized it by the throat and carried it behind a hedge in the garden, where he ate as much of the body as he could and threw the remainder to another wolf.

At St. Antoine de Pizan he attacked a girl in a black dress who was tending sheep, and he killed and devoured her, a strange point being that her dress was not torn, as happens in the case when real wolves make the assault.

When questioned as to how he managed to turn into a wolf, he said that a neighbour, called Pierre la Tilhaire, had introduced him in the forest to the Lord thereof, who had given wolf-skins to both, as well as a salve for anointing themselves. When asked where he kept the skins and the pot of ointment he replied that they were in the hands of the Lord of the Forest, from whom he could obtain them whenever he wished.

He declared that he had changed into a wolf and gone coursing four times with his companion Pierre la Tilhaire, but they had killed no one. The best time for the hunt was an hour or two a day when the moon was on the wane, but he also went out at night on some occasions.

When asked whether his father knew of these proceedings, he replied in the affirmative, and declared that his father had rubbed him three times with the ointment and helped him into the wolf's skin.

The inquiry into Jean Grenier's case was a very lengthy one and was adjourned several times, but eventually he was sentenced to imprisonment for life at Bordeaux on September 6th, 1603, his youth and want of mental development being pleaded in extenuation of the crimes of infanticide he had undoubtedly committed. The president of the Court declared that lycanthropy was a form of hallucination and was not in itself a punishable crime. Jean's father was acquitted of complicity, and allowed to leave the court without a stain on his character, and Jean was sent to a monastery.

In 1610, after Jean had been at the Monastery of the Cordeliers in Bordeaux for seven years, De Lancre, who relates his story, went to see him. He was then about twenty years of age and of diminutive stature. His black eyes were haggard and deep-set, and he refused to look anyone straight in the face. His teeth were long, sharp, and protruding, his nails were also long and black, and his mind was a mere blank.

He told De Lancre, not without pride, that he had been a werewolf, but that he had given up the practice. When he first arrived at the monastery he had preferred to go on all fours, eating such food as he found on the ground. He confessed that he still craved for raw human flesh, especially the flesh of little girls, and he hoped it would not be long before he had another opportunity of tasting it. He had been visited twice during his confinement by the Lord of the Forest, as he called the mysterious person who had given him the wolf-skin, but that both times he had made the sign of the cross and his visitor had departed in haste.

In other respects his tale was identical with the experiences he had related before the court.

De Lancre thought that the name Grenier or Garnier was a fatal name in connection with werewolves.

Evidence was given as to the times, places, and number of murders, and many of the facts were proved incontestably.

Jean's evidence as to the part his father had played in his misdeeds was hazy. He said that on one occasion his father had accompanied him, also wearing a wolf-skin, and that together they had killed a young girl dressed in white, and that they had devoured her flesh, the month being May of 1601.

He also added curious details regarding the Lord of the Forest, who had forbidden him to bite the thumbnail of his left hand, which was thicker and longer than the others, and that if he lost sight of it while in the form of a wolf he would quickly recover his human shape.

When confronted with his father Jean altered some of the details of his story, and it was agreed that long imprisonment and extended cross-examination had worn out his already feeble intellect.

It is worth pointing out that in the cases of Rollet, the tailor of Châlons, and the Gandillon family, the prisoners were accused of murder and cannibalism, but not of association with wolves, and that in the trial of Garnier evidence was given as to the depredations of the wolf rather than of the accused. There was doubtless a difficulty in proving the identity of the perpetrator of the murders.

A new era in these trials begins with that of Jean Grenier, for from that time onward medical men became more enlightened, and the belief spread that lycanthropy was a mental malady, with cannibalistic tendencies which had developed under diseased conditions.

In his *Dæmonologie*, 1597, a reply to Reginald Scott's *Discoverie of Witchcraft*, James I of England declared that werewolves were victims of a delusion induced by a state of melancholia, and about the same period wolves became practically extinct in England, and only harmless creatures such as the cat, hare, and weasel were left for the sorcerer to change into with any possibility of a safe and natural disguise.

For many years afterwards the confessions of witches, who were executed for their crimes, bore striking resemblance to those made by werewolves, and many strange facts which were published at these trials have never been, and may never be, satisfactorily explained on a purely materialistic basis.

The Werewolf

IN THE REIGN OF EGBERT THE SAXON there dwelt in Britain a maiden named Yseult, who was beloved of all, both for her goodness and for her beauty. But, though many a youth came wooing her, she loved Harold only, and to him she plighted her troth.

Among the other youth of whom Yseult was beloved was Alfred, and he was sore angered that Yseult showed favour to Harold, so that one day Alfred said to Harold: "Is it right that old Siegfried should come from his grave and have Yseult to wife?" Then added he, "Prithee, good sir, why do you turn so white when I speak your grandsire's name?"

Then Harold asked, "What know you of Siegfried that you taunt me? What memory of him should vex me now?"

"We know and we know," retorted Alfred. "There are some tales told us by our grandmas we have not forgot."

So ever after that Alfred's words and Alfred's bitter smile haunted Harold by day and night.

Harold's grandsire, Siegfried the Teuton, had been a man of cruel violence. The legend said that a curse rested upon him, and that at certain times he was possessed of an evil spirit that wreaked its fury on mankind. But Siegfried had been dead full many years, and there was naught to mind the world of him save the legend and a cunning-wrought spear which he had from Brunehilde, the witch. This spear was such a weapon that it never lost its brightness, nor had its point been blunted. It hung in Harold's chamber, and it was the marvel among weapons of that time.

Yseult knew that Alfred loved her, but she did not know of the bitter words which Alfred had spoken to Harold. Her love for Harold was perfect in its trust and gentleness. But Alfred had hit the truth: the curse of old Siegfried was upon Harold – slumbering a century, it had awakened in the blood of the grandson, and Harold knew the curse that was upon him, and it was this that seemed to stand between him and Yseult. But love is stronger than all else, and Harold loved.

Harold did not tell Yseult of the curse that was upon him, for he feared that she would not love him if she knew. Whensoever he felt the fire of the curse burning in his veins he would say to her, "To-morrow I hunt the wild boar in the uttermost forest," or, "Next week I go stag-stalking among the distant northern hills." Even so it was that he ever made good excuse for his absence, and Yseult thought no evil things, for she was trustful; ay, though he went many times away and was long gone, Yseult suspected no wrong. So none beheld Harold when the curse was upon him in its violence.

Alfred alone bethought himself of evil things. "'T is passing strange," quoth he, "that ever and anon this gallant lover should quit our company and betake himself whither none knoweth. In sooth 't will be well to have an eye on old Siegfried's grandson."

Harold knew that Alfred watched him zealously, and he was tormented by a constant fear that Alfred would discover the curse that was on him; but what gave him greater anguish was the fear that mayhap at some moment when he was in Yseult's presence, the curse would seize upon him and cause him to do great evil unto her, whereby she would be destroyed or her love for him would be undone forever. So Harold lived in terror, feeling that his love was hopeless, yet knowing not how to combat it.

Now, it befell in those times that the country round about was ravaged of a werewolf, a creature that was feared by all men howe'er so valorous. This werewolf was by day a man, but by night a wolf given to ravage and to slaughter, and having a charmed life against which no human agency availed aught. Wheresoever he went he attacked and devoured mankind, spreading terror and desolation round about, and the dream-readers said that the earth would not be freed from the werewolf until some man offered himself a voluntary sacrifice to the monster's rage.

Now, although Harold was known far and wide as a mighty huntsman, he had never set forth to hunt the werewolf, and, strange enow, the werewolf never ravaged the domain while Harold was therein. Whereat Alfred marvelled much, and oftentimes he said: "Our Harold is a wondrous huntsman. Who is like unto him in stalking the timid doe and in crippling the fleeing boar? But how passing well doth he time his absence from the haunts of the werewolf. Such valor beseemeth our young Siegfried."

Which being brought to Harold his heart flamed with anger, but he made no answer, lest he should betray the truth he feared.

It happened so about that time that Yseult said to Harold, "Wilt thou go with me to-morrow even to the feast in the sacred grove?"

"That can I not do," answered Harold. "I am privily summoned hence to Normandy upon a mission of which I shall some time tell thee. And I pray thee, on thy love for me, go not to the feast in the sacred grove without me."

"What say'st thou?" cried Yseult. "Shall I not go to the feast of Ste. Aelfreda? My father would be sore displeased were I not there with the other maidens. 'T were greatest pity that I should despite his love thus."

"But do not, I beseech thee," Harold implored. "Go not to the feast of Ste. Aelfreda in the sacred grove! And thou would thus love me, go not – see, thou my life, on my two knees I ask it!"

"How pale thou art," said Yseult, "and trembling."

"Go not to the sacred grove upon the morrow night," he begged.

Yseult marvelled at his acts and at his speech. Then, for the first time, she thought him to be jealous – whereat she secretly rejoiced (being a woman).

"Ah," quoth she, "thou dost doubt my love," but when she saw a look of pain come on his face she added – as if she repented of the words she had spoken – "or dost thou fear the werewolf?"

Then Harold answered, fixing his eyes on hers, "Thou hast said it; it is the werewolf that I fear."

"Why dost thou look at me so strangely, Harold?" cried Yseult. "By the cruel light in thine eyes one might almost take thee to be the werewolf!"

"Come hither, sit beside me," said Harold tremblingly, "and I will tell thee why I fear to have thee go to the feast of Ste. Aelfreda to-morrow evening. Hear what I dreamed last night. I dreamed I was the werewolf – do not shudder, dear love, for 't was only a dream.

"A grizzled old man stood at my bedside and strove to pluck my soul from my bosom.

"'What would'st thou?' I cried.

"'Thy soul is mine,' he said, 'thou shalt live out my curse. Give me thy soul – hold back thy hands – give me thy soul, I say.'

"'Thy curse shall not be upon me,' I cried. 'What have I done that thy curse should rest upon me? Thou shalt not have my soul.'

"'For my offence shalt thou suffer, and in my curse thou shalt endure hell – it is so decreed.'

"So spake the old man, and he strove with me, and he prevailed against me, and he plucked my soul from my bosom, and he said, 'Go, search and kill' – and – and lo, I was a wolf upon the moor.

"The dry grass crackled beneath my tread. The darkness of the night was heavy and it oppressed me. Strange horrors tortured my soul, and it groaned and groaned, gaoled in that wolfish body. The wind whispered to me; with its myriad voices it spake to me and said, 'Go, search and kill.' And above these voices sounded the hideous laughter of an old man. I fled the moor – whither I knew not, nor knew I what motive lashed me on.

"I came to a river and I plunged in. A burning thirst consumed me, and I lapped the waters of the river – they were waves of flame, and they flashed around me and hissed, and what they said was, 'Go, search and kill,' and I heard the old man's laughter again.

"A forest lay before me with its gloomy thickets and its sombre shadows – with its ravens, its vampires, its serpents, its reptiles, and all its hideous brood of night. I darted among its thorns and crouched amid the leaves, the nettles, and the brambles. The owls hooted at me and the thorns pierced my flesh. 'Go, search and kill,' said everything. The hares sprang from my pathway; the other beasts ran bellowing away; every form of life shrieked in my ears – the curse was on me – I was the werewolf.

"On, on I went with the fleetness of the wind, and my soul groaned in its wolfish prison, and the winds and the waters and the trees bade me, 'Go, search and kill, thou accursed brute; go, search and kill.'

"Nowhere was there pity for the wolf; what mercy, thus, should I, the werewolf, show? The curse was on me and it filled me with a hunger and a thirst for blood. Skulking on my way within myself I cried, 'Let me have blood, oh, let me have human blood, that this wrath may be appeased, that this curse may be removed.'

"At last I came to the sacred grove. Sombre loomed the poplars, the oaks frowned upon me. Before me stood an old man – 'twas he, grizzled and taunting, whose curse I bore. He feared me not. All other living things fled before me, but the old man feared me not. A maiden stood beside him. She did not see me, for she was blind.

"'Kill, kill,' cried the old man, and he pointed at the girl beside him.

"Hell raged within me – the curse impelled me – I sprang at her throat. I heard the old man's laughter once more, and then – then I awoke, trembling, cold, horrified."

Scarce was this dream told when Alfred strode that way.

"Now, by'r Lady," quoth he, "I bethink me never to have seen a sorrier twain."

Then Yseult told him of Harold's going away and how that Harold had besought her not to venture to the feast of Ste. Aelfreda in the sacred grove.

"These fears are childish," cried Alfred boastfully. "And thou sufferest me, sweet lady, I will bear thee company to the feast, and a score of my lusty yeomen with their good yew-bows and honest spears, they shall attend me. There be no werewolf, I trow, will chance about with us."

Whereat Yseult laughed merrily, and Harold said: "'T is well; thou shalt go to the sacred grove, and may my love and Heaven's grace forefend all evil."

Then Harold went to his abode, and he fetched old Siegfried's spear back unto Yseult, and he gave it into her two hands, saying, "Take this spear with thee to the feast to-morrow night. It is old Siegfried's spear, possessing mighty virtue and marvellous."

And Harold took Yseult to his heart and blessed her, and he kissed her upon her brow and upon her lips, saying, "Farewell, oh, my beloved. How wilt thou love me when thou know'st my sacrifice. Farewell, farewell forever, oh, alder-liefest mine."

So Harold went his way, and Yseult was lost in wonderment.

On the morrow night came Yseult to the sacred grove wherein the feast was spread, and she bore old Siegfried's spear with her in her girdle. Alfred attended her, and a score of lusty yeomen were with him. In the grove there was great merriment, and with singing and dancing and games withal did the honest folk celebrate the feast of the fair Ste. Aelfreda.

But suddenly a mighty tumult arose, and there were cries of "The werewolf!" "The werewolf!" Terror seized upon all – stout hearts were frozen with fear. Out from the further forest rushed the werewolf, wood wroth, bellowing hoarsely, gnashing his fangs and tossing hither and thither the yellow foam from his snapping jaws. He sought Yseult straight, as if an evil power drew him to the spot where she stood. But Yseult was not afeared; like a marble statue she stood and saw the werewolf's coming. The yeomen, dropping their torches and casting aside their bows, had fled; Alfred alone abided there to do the monster battle.

At the approaching wolf he hurled his heavy lance, but as it struck the werewolf's bristling back the weapon was all to-shivered.

Then the werewolf, fixing his eyes upon Yseult, skulked for a moment in the shadow of the yews and thinking then of Harold's words, Yseult plucked old Siegfried's spear from her girdle, raised it on high, and with the strength of despair sent it hurtling through the air.

The werewolf saw the shining weapon, and a cry burst from his gaping throat – a cry of human agony. And Yseult saw in the werewolf's eyes the eyes of some one she had seen and known, but 't was for an instant only, and then the eyes were no longer human, but wolfish in their ferocity. A supernatural force seemed to speed the spear in its flight. With fearful precision the weapon smote home and buried itself by half its length in the werewolf's shaggy breast just above the heart, and then, with a monstrous sigh – as if he yielded up his life without regret – the werewolf fell dead in the shadow of the yews.

Then, ah, then in very truth there was great joy, and loud were the acclaims, while, beautiful in her trembling pallor, Yseult was led unto her home, where the people set about to give great feast to do her homage, for the werewolf was dead, and she it was that had slain him.

But Yseult cried out: "Go, search for Harold – go, bring him to me. Nor eat, nor sleep till he be found."

"Good my lady," quoth Alfred, "how can that be, since he hath betaken himself to Normandy?"

"I care not where he be," she cried. "My heart stands still until I look into his eyes again."

"Surely he hath not gone to Normandy," outspake Hubert. "This very eventide I saw him enter his abode."

They hastened thither – a vast company. His chamber door was barred.

"Harold, Harold, come forth!" they cried, as they beat upon the door, but no answer came to their calls and knockings. Afeared, they battered down the door, and when it fell they saw that Harold lay upon his bed.

"He sleeps," said one. "See, he holds a portrait in his hand – and it is her portrait. How fair he is and how tranquilly he sleeps."

But no, Harold was not asleep. His face was calm and beautiful, as if he dreamed of his beloved, but his raiment was red with the blood that streamed from a wound in his breast – a gaping, ghastly spear wound just above his heart.

The Werewolf

ONCE UPON A TIME there was a king, who reigned over a great kingdom. He had a queen, but only a single daughter, a girl. In consequence the little girl was the apple of her parents' eyes; they loved her above everything else in the world, and their dearest thought was the pleasure they would take in her when she was older. But the unexpected often happens; for before the king's daughter began to grow up, the queen her mother fell ill and died. It is not hard to imagine the grief that reigned, not alone in the royal castle, but throughout the land; for the queen had been beloved of all. The king grieved so that he would not marry again, and his one joy was the little princess.

A long time passed, and with each succeeding day the king's daughter grew taller and more beautiful, and her father granted her every wish. Now there were a number of women who had nothing to do but wait on the princess and carry out her commands. Among them was a woman who had formerly married and had two daughters. She had an engaging appearance, a smooth tongue and a winning way of talking, and she was as soft and pliable as silk; but at heart she was full of machinations and falseness. Now when the queen died, she at once began to plan how she might marry the king, so that her daughters might be kept like royal princesses. With this end in view, she drew the young princess to her, paid her the most fulsome compliments on everything she said and did, and was forever bringing the conversation around to how happy she would be were the king to take another wife. There was much said on this head, early and late, and before very long the princess came to believe that the woman knew all there was to know about everything. So she asked her what sort of a woman the king ought to choose for a wife. The woman answered as sweet as honey: "It is not my affair to give advice in this matter; yet he should choose for queen some one who is kind to the little princess. For one thing I know, and that is, were I fortunate enough to be chosen, my one thought would be to do all I could for the little princess, and if she wished to wash her hands, one of my daughters would have to hold the wash-bowl and the other hand her the towel." This and much more she told the king's daughter, and the princess believed it, as children will.

From that day forward the princess gave her father no peace, and begged him again and again to marry the good court lady. Yet he did not want to marry her. But the king's daughter gave him no rest; but urged him again and again, as the false court lady had persuaded her to do. Finally, one day, when she again brought up the matter, the king cried: "I can see you will end by having your own way about this, even though it be entirely against my will. But I will do so only on one condition."

"What is the condition?" asked the princess.

"If I marry again," said the king, "it is only because of your ceaseless pleading. Therefore you must promise that, if in the future you are not satisfied with your step-mother or your step-sisters, not a single lament or complaint on your part reaches my ears." This she promised the king, and it was agreed that he should marry the court lady and make her queen of the whole country.

As time passed on, the king's daughter had grown to be the most beautiful maiden to be found far and wide; the queen's daughters, on the other hand, were homely, evil of disposition, and no one knew any good of them. Hence it was not surprising that many youths came from East and West to sue for the princess's hand; but that none of them took any interest in the queen's daughters. This made the step-mother very angry; but she concealed her rage, and was as sweet and friendly as ever. Among the wooers was a king's son from another country. He was young and brave, and since he loved the princess dearly, she accepted his proposal and they plighted their troth. The queen observed this with an angry eye, for it would have pleased her had the prince chosen one of her own daughters. She therefore made up her mind that the young pair should never be happy together, and from that time on thought only of how she might part them from each other.

An opportunity soon offered itself. News came that the enemy had entered the land, and the king was compelled to go to war. Now the princess began to find out the kind of step-mother she had. For no sooner had the king departed than the queen showed her true nature, and was just as harsh and unkind as she formerly had pretended to be friendly and obliging. Not a day went by without her scolding and threatening the princess; and the queen's daughters were every bit as malicious as their mother. But the king's son, the lover of the princess, found himself in even worse position. He had gone hunting one day, had lost his way, and could not find his people. Then the queen used her black arts and turned him into a werewolf, to wander through the forest for the remainder of his life in that shape. When evening came and there was no sign of the prince, his people returned home, and one can imagine what sorrow they caused when the princess learned how the hunt had ended. She grieved, wept day and night, and was not to be consoled. But the queen laughed at her grief, and her heart was filled with joy to think that all had turned out exactly as she wished.

Now it chanced one day, as the king's daughter was sitting alone in her room, that she thought she would go herself into the forest where the prince had disappeared. She went to her step-mother and begged permission to go out into the forest, in order to forget her surpassing grief. The queen did not want to grant her request, for she always preferred saying no to yes. But the princess begged her so winningly that at last she was unable to say no, and she ordered one of her daughters to go along with her and watch her. That caused a great deal of discussion, for neither of the step-daughters wanted to go with her; each made all sorts of excuses, and asked what pleasures were there in going with the king's daughter, who did nothing but cry. But the queen had the last word in the end, and ordered that one of her daughters must accompany the princess, even though it be against her will. So the girls wandered out of the castle into the forest. The king's daughter walked among the trees, and listened to the song of the birds, and thought of her lover, for whom she longed, and who was now no longer there. And the queen's daughter followed her, vexed, in her malice, with the king's daughter and her sorrow.

After they had walked a while, they came to a little hut, lying deep in the dark forest. By then the king's daughter was very thirsty, and wanted to go into the little hut with her step-sister, in order to get a drink of water. But the queen's daughter was much annoyed and said: "Is it not enough for me to be running around here in the wilderness with you? Now you even want me, who am a princess, to enter that wretched little hut. No, I will not step a foot over the threshold! If you want to go in, why go in alone!"

The king's daughter lost no time; but did as her step-sister advised, and stepped into the little hut. When she entered she saw an old woman sitting there on a bench, so enfeebled by age that her head shook. The princess spoke to her in her usual friendly way: "Good evening, motherkin. May I ask you for a drink of water?"

"You are heartily welcome to it," said the old woman. "Who may you be, that step beneath my lowly roof and greet me in so winning a way?" The king's daughter told her who she was, and that she had gone out to relieve her heart, in order to forget her great grief.

"And what may your great grief be?" asked the old woman.

"No doubt it is my fate to grieve," said the princess, "and I can never be happy again. I have lost my only love, and God alone knows whether I shall ever see him again." And she also told her why it was, and the tears ran down her cheeks in streams, so that any one would have felt sorry for her. When she had ended the old woman said: "You did well in confiding your sorrow to me. I have lived long and may be able to give you a bit of good advice. When you leave here you will see a lily growing from the ground. This lily is not like other lilies, however, but has many strange virtues. Run quickly over to it, and pick it. If you can do that then you need not worry, for then one will appear who will tell you what to do." Then they parted and the king's daughter thanked her and went her way; while the old woman sat on the bench and wagged her head. But the queen's daughter had been standing without the hut the entire time, vexing herself, and grumbling because the king's daughter had taken so long.

So when the latter stepped out, she had to listen to all sorts of abuse from her step-sister, as was to be expected. Yet she paid no attention to her, and thought only of how she might find the flower of which the old woman had spoken. They went through the forest, and suddenly she saw a beautiful white lily growing in their very path. She was much pleased and ran up at once to pick it; but that very moment it disappeared and reappeared somewhat further away.

The king's daughter was now filled with eagerness, no longer listened to her step-sister's calls, and kept right on running; yet each time when she stooped to pick the lily, it suddenly disappeared and reappeared somewhat further away. Thus it went for some time, and the princess was drawn further and further into the deep forest. But the lily continued to stand, and disappear and move further away, and each time the flower seemed larger and more beautiful than before. At length the princess came to a high hill, and as she looked toward its summit, there stood the lily high on the naked rock, glittering as white and radiant as the brightest star. The king's daughter now began to climb the hill, and in her eagerness she paid no attention to stones nor steepness. And when at last she reached the summit of the hill, lo and behold! the lily no longer evaded her grasp; but remained where it was, and the princess stooped and picked it and hid it in her bosom, and so heartfelt was her happiness that she forgot her step-sisters and everything else in the world.

For a long time she did not tire of looking at the beautiful flower. Then she suddenly began to wonder what her step-mother would say when she came home after having remained out so long. And she looked around, in order to find the way back to the castle. But as she looked around, behold, the sun had set and no more than a little strip of daylight rested on the summit of the hill. Below her lay the forest, so dark and shadowed that she had no faith in her ability to find the homeward path. And now she grew very sad, for she could think of nothing better to do than to spend the night on the hill-top. She seated herself on the rock, put her hand to her cheek, cried, and thought of her unkind step-mother and step-sisters, and of all the harsh words she would have to endure when she returned. And she thought of her father, the king, who was away at war, and of the love of her heart, whom she would never see again; and she grieved so bitterly that she did not even know she wept. Night came and darkness, and the stars rose, and still the princess sat in the same spot and wept. And while she sat there, lost in her thoughts, she heard a voice say: "Good evening, lovely maiden! Why do you sit here so sad and lonely?"

She stood up hastily, and felt much embarrassed, which was not surprising. When she looked around there was nothing to be seen but a tiny old man, who nodded to her and seemed to be very humble. She answered: "Yes, it is no doubt my fate to grieve, and never be happy again. I have lost my dearest love, and now I have lost my way in the forest, and am afraid of being devoured by wild beasts."

"As to that," said the old man, "you need have no fear. If you will do exactly as I say, I will help you." This made the princess happy; for she felt that all the rest of the world had abandoned her. Then the old man drew out flint and steel and said: "Lovely maiden, you must first build a fire." She did as he told her, gathered moss, brush and dry sticks, struck sparks and lit such a fire on the hill-top that the flame blazed up to the skies. That done the old man said: "Go on a bit and you will find a kettle of tar, and bring the kettle to me." This the king's daughter did. The old man continued: "Now put the kettle on the fire." And the princess did that as well. When the tar began to boil, the old man said: "Now throw your white lily into the kettle." The princess thought this a harsh command, and earnestly begged to be allowed to keep the lily. But the old man said: "Did you not promise to obey my every command? Do as I tell you or you will regret it." The king's daughter turned away her eyes, and threw the lily into the boiling tar; but it was altogether against her will, so fond had she grown of the beautiful flower.

The moment she did so a hollow roar, like that of some wild beast, sounded from the forest. It came nearer, and turned into such a terrible howling that all the surrounding hills reëchoed it. Finally there was a cracking and breaking among the trees, the bushes were thrust aside, and the princess saw a great grey wolf come running out of the forest and straight up the hill. She was much frightened and would gladly have run away, had she been able. But the old man said: "Make haste, run to the edge of the hill and the moment the wolf comes along, upset the kettle on him!" The princess was terrified, and hardly knew what she was about; yet she did as the old man said, took the kettle, ran to the edge of the hill, and poured its contents over the wolf just as he was about to run up. And then a strange thing happened: no sooner had she done so, than the wolf was transformed, cast off his thick grey pelt, and in place of the horrible wild beast, there stood a handsome young man, looking up to the hill. And when the king's daughter collected herself and looked at him, she saw that it was really and truly her lover, who had been turned into a werewolf.

It is easy to imagine how the princess felt. She opened her arms, and could neither ask questions nor reply to them, so moved and delighted was she. But the prince ran hastily up the hill, embraced her tenderly, and thanked her for delivering him. Nor did he forget the little old man, but thanked him with many civil expressions for his powerful aid. Then they sat down together on the hill-top, and had a pleasant talk. The prince told how he had been turned into a wolf, and of all he had suffered while running about in the forest; and the princess told of her grief, and the many tears she had shed while he had been gone. So they sat the whole night through, and never noticed it until the stars grew pale and it was light enough to see. When the sun rose, they saw that a broad path led from the hill-top straight to the royal castle; for they had a view of the whole surrounding country from the hill-top. Then the old man said: "Lovely maiden, turn around! Do you see anything out yonder?"

"Yes," said the princess, "I see a horseman on a foaming horse, riding as fast as he can."

Then the old man said: "He is a messenger sent on ahead by the king your father. And your father with all his army is following him." That pleased the princess above all things, and she wanted to descend the hill at once to meet her father. But the old man detained her and said: "Wait a while, it is too early yet. Let us wait and see how everything turns out."

Time passed and the sun was shining brightly, and its rays fell straight on the royal castle down below. Then the old man said: "Lovely maiden, turn around! Do you see anything down below?"

"Yes," replied the princess, "I see a number of people coming out of my father's castle, and some are going along the road, and others into the forest."

The old man said: "Those are your step-mother's servants. She has sent some to meet the king and welcome him; but she has sent others to the forest to look for you." At these words the princess grew uneasy, and wished to go down to the queen's servants. But the old man withheld her and said: "Wait a while, and let us first see how everything turns out."

More time passed, and the king's daughter was still looking down the road from which the king would appear, when the old man said: "Lovely maiden, turn around! Do you see anything down below?"

"Yes," answered the princess, "there is a great commotion in my father's castle, and they are hanging it with black." The old man said: "That is your step-mother and her people. They will assure your father that you are dead."

Then the king's daughter felt bitter anguish, and she implored from the depths of her heart: "Let me go, let me go, so that I may spare my father this anguish!" But the old man detained her and said: "No, wait, it is still too early. Let us first see how everything turns out."

Again time passed, the sun lay high above the fields, and the warm air blew over meadow and forest. The royal maid and youth still sat on the hill-top with the old man, where we had left them. Then they saw a little cloud rise against the horizon, far away in the distance, and the little cloud grew larger and larger, and came nearer and nearer along the road, and as it moved one could see it was agleam with weapons, and nodding helmets, and waving flags, one could hear the rattle of swords, and the neighing of horses, and finally recognize the banner of the king. It is not hard to imagine how pleased the king's daughter was, and how she insisted on going down and greeting her father. But the old man held her back and said: "Lovely maiden, turn around! Do you see anything happening at the castle?"

"Yes," answered the princess, "I can see my step-mother and step-sisters coming out, dressed in mourning, holding white 'kerchiefs to their faces, and weeping bitterly." The old man answered: "Now they are pretending to weep because of your death. Wait just a little while longer. We have not yet seen how everything will turn out."

After a time the old man said again: "Lovely maiden, turn around! Do you see anything down below?"

"Yes," said the princess, "I see people bringing a black coffin – now my father is having it opened. Look, the queen and her daughters are down on their knees, and my father is threatening them with his sword!" Then the old man said: "Your father wished to see your body, and so your evil step-mother had to confess the truth."

When the princess heard that she said earnestly: "Let me go, let me go, so that I may comfort my father in his great sorrow!" But the old man held her back and said: "Take my advice and stay here a little while longer. We have not yet seen how everything will turn out."

Again time went by, and the king's daughter and the prince and the old man were still sitting on the hill-top. Then the old man said: "Lovely maiden, turn around! Do you see anything down below?"

"Yes," answered the princess, "I see my father and my step-sisters and my step-mother with all their following moving this way." The old man said: "Now they have started out to look for you. Go down and bring up the wolf's pelt in the gorge." The king's daughter did as he told her. The old man continued: "Now stand at the edge of the hill." And the princess did that, too. Now one could see the queen and her daughters coming along the way, and stopping just below the hill. Then the old man said: "Now throw down the wolf's pelt!" The princess obeyed him, and threw down the wolf's pelt according to his command. It fell directly on the evil queen and her daughters. And then a most wonderful thing happened: no sooner had the pelt touched the three evil women than they immediately changed shape, and turning into three horrible werewolves, they ran away as fast as they could into the forest, howling dreadfully.

No more had this happened than the king himself arrived at the foot of the hill with his whole retinue. When he looked up and recognized the princess, he could not at first believe his eyes; but stood motionless, thinking her a vision. Then the old man cried: "Lovely maiden, now hasten, run down and make your father happy!" There was no need to tell the princess twice. She took her lover by the hand and they ran down the hill. When they came to the king, the princess ran on ahead, fell on her father's neck, and wept with joy. And the young prince wept as well, and the king himself wept; and their meeting was a pleasant sight for every one. There was great joy and many embraces, and the princess told of her evil step-mother and step-sisters and of her lover, and all that she had suffered, and of the old man who had helped them in such a wonderful way. But when the king turned around to thank the old man he had completely vanished, and from that day on no one could say who he had been or what had become of him.

The king and his whole retinue now returned to the castle, where the king had a splendid banquet prepared, to which he invited all the able and distinguished people throughout the kingdom, and bestowed his daughter on the young prince. And the wedding was celebrated with gladness and music and amusements of every kind for many days. I was there, too, and when I rode through the forest I met a wolf with two young wolves, and they showed me their teeth and seemed very angry. And I was told they were none other than the evil step-mother and her two daughters.

The Metal Pig

IN THE CITY of Florence, not far from the Piazza del Granduca, runs a little street called Porta Rosa. In this street, just in front of the market-place where vegetables are sold, stands a pig, made of brass and curiously formed. The bright color has been changed by age to dark green; but clear, fresh water pours from the snout, which shines as if it had been polished, and so indeed it has, for hundreds of poor people and children seize it in their hands as they place their mouths close to the mouth of the animal, to drink. It is quite a picture to see a half-naked boy clasping the well-formed creature by the head, as he presses his rosy lips against its jaws. Every one who visits

Florence can very quickly find the place; he has only to ask the first beggar he meets for the Metal Pig, and he will be told where it is.

It was late on a winter evening; the mountains were covered with snow, but the moon shone brightly, and moonlight in Italy is like a dull winter's day in the north; indeed it is better, for clear air seems to raise us above the earth, while in the north a cold, gray, leaden sky appears to press us down to earth, even as the cold damp earth shall one day press on us in the grave. In the garden of the grand duke's palace, under the roof of one of the wings, where a thousand roses bloom in winter, a little ragged boy had been sitting the whole day long; a boy, who might serve as a type of Italy, lovely and smiling, and yet still suffering. He was hungry and thirsty, yet no one gave him anything; and when it became dark, and they were about to close the gardens, the porter turned him out. He stood a long time musing on the bridge which crosses the Arno, and looking at the glittering stars, reflected in the water which flowed between him and the elegant marble bridge Della Trinità. He then walked away towards the Metal Pig, half knelt down, clasped it with his arms, and then put his mouth to the shining snout and drank deep draughts of the fresh water. Close by, lay a few salad-leaves and two chestnuts, which were to serve for his supper. No one was in the street but himself; it belonged only to him, so he boldly seated himself on the pig's back, leaned forward so that his curly head could rest on the head of the animal, and, before he was aware, he fell asleep.

It was midnight. The Metal Pig raised himself gently, and the boy heard him say quite distinctly, "Hold tight, little boy, for I am going to run;" and away he started for a most wonderful ride. First, they arrived at the Piazza del Granduca, and the metal horse which bears the duke's statue, neighed aloud. The painted coats-of-arms on the old council-house shone like transparent pictures, and Michael Angelo's David tossed his sling; it was as if everything had life. The metallic groups of figures, among which were Perseus and the Rape of the Sabines, looked like living persons, and cries of terror sounded from them all across the noble square. By the Palazzo degli Uffizi, in the arcade, where the nobility assemble for the carnival, the Metal Pig stopped. "Hold fast," said the animal; "hold fast, for I am going up stairs."

The little boy said not a word; he was half pleased and half afraid. They entered a long gallery, where the boy had been before. The walls were resplendent with paintings; here stood statues and busts, all in a clear light as if it were day. But the grandest appeared when the door of a side room opened; the little boy could remember what beautiful things he had seen there, but to-night everything shone in its brightest colors. Here stood the figure of a beautiful woman, as beautifully sculptured as possible by one of the great masters. Her graceful limbs appeared to move; dolphins sprang at her feet, and immortality shone from her eyes. The world called her the Venus de' Medici. By her side were statues, in which the spirit of life breathed in stone; figures of men, one of whom whetted his sword, and was named the Grinder; wrestling gladiators formed another group, the sword had been sharpened for them, and they strove for the goddess of beauty. The boy was dazzled by so much glitter; for the walls were gleaming with bright colors, all appeared living reality.

As they passed from hall to hall, beauty everywhere showed itself; and as the Metal Pig went step by step from one picture to the other, the little boy could see it all plainly. One glory eclipsed another; yet there was one picture that fixed itself on the little boy's memory, more especially because of the happy children it represented, for these the little boy had seen in daylight. Many pass this picture by with indifference, and yet it contains a treasure of poetic feeling; it represents Christ descending into Hades. They are not the lost whom the spectator sees, but the heathen of olden times. The Florentine, Angiolo Bronzino, painted this picture; most beautiful is the expression on the face of the two children, who appear to have full confidence that they shall reach heaven at last. They are embracing each other, and one little one stretches out his hand towards another who stands below him, and points to himself, as if he were saying, "I am going to heaven." The older people stand as if uncertain, yet hopeful, and they bow in humble adoration to the Lord Jesus. On this picture the boy's eyes rested longer than on any other: the Metal Pig stood still before it. A low sigh was heard. Did it come from the picture or from the animal? The boy raised his hands towards the smiling children, and then the Pig ran off with him through the open vestibule.

"Thank you, thank you, you beautiful animal," said the little boy, caressing the Metal Pig as it ran down the steps.

"Thanks to yourself also," replied the Metal Pig; "I have helped you and you have helped me, for it is only when I have an innocent child on my back that I receive the power to run. Yes; as you see, I can even venture under the rays of the lamp, in front of the picture of the Madonna, but I may not enter the church; still from without, and while you are upon my back, I may look in through the open door. Do not get down yet, for if you do, then I shall be lifeless, as you have seen me in the Porta Rosa."

"I will stay with you, my dear creature," said the little boy. So then they went on at a rapid pace through the streets of Florence, till they came to the square before the church of Santa Croce. The folding-doors flew open, and light streamed from the altar through the church into the deserted square. A wonderful blaze of light streamed from one of the monuments in the left-side aisle, and a thousand moving stars seemed to form a glory round it; even the coat-of-arms on the tomb-stone shone, and a red ladder on a blue field gleamed like fire. It was the grave of Galileo. The monument is unadorned, but the red ladder is an emblem of art, signifying that the way to glory leads up a shining ladder, on which the prophets of mind rise to heaven, like Elias of old. In the right aisle of the church every statue on the richly carved sarcophagi seemed endowed with life. Here stood Michael Angelo; there Dante, with the laurel wreath round his brow; Alfieri and Machiavelli; for here side by side rest the great men – the pride of Italy. The church itself is very beautiful, even more beautiful than the marble cathedral at Florence, though not so large. It seemed as if the carved vestments stirred, and as if the marble figures they covered raised their heads higher, to gaze upon the brightly colored glowing altar where the white-robed boys swung the golden censers, amid music and song, while the strong fragrance of incense filled the church, and streamed forth into the square. The boy stretched forth his hands towards the light, and at the same moment the Metal Pig started again so rapidly that he was obliged to cling tightly to him. The wind whistled in his ears, he heard the church door creak on its hinges as it closed, and it seemed to him as if he had lost his senses – then a cold shudder passed over him, and he awoke.

It was morning; the Metal Pig stood in its old place on the Porta Rosa, and the boy found he had slipped nearly off its back. Fear and trembling came upon him as he thought of his mother; she had sent him out the day before to get some money, he had not done so, and now he was hungry and thirsty. Once more he clasped the neck of his metal horse, kissed its nose, and nodded farewell to it. Then he wandered away into one of the narrowest streets, where there was scarcely room for a loaded donkey to pass. A great iron-bound door stood ajar; he passed through, and climbed up a brick staircase, with dirty walls and a rope for a balustrade, till he came to an open gallery hung with rags. From here a flight of steps led down to a court, where from a well water was drawn up by iron rollers to the different stories of the house, and where the water-buckets hung side by side. Sometimes the roller and the bucket danced in the air, splashing the water all over the court. Another broken-down staircase led from the gallery, and two Russian sailors running down it almost upset the poor boy. They were coming from their nightly carousal. A woman not very young, with an unpleasant face and a quantity of black hair, followed them. "What have you brought home?" she asked. when she saw the boy.

"Don't be angry," he pleaded; "I received nothing, I have nothing at all;" and he seized his mother's dress and would have kissed it. Then they went into a little room. I need not describe it, but only say that there stood in it an earthen pot with handles, made for holding fire, which in Italy is called a marito. This pot she took in her lap, warmed her fingers, and pushed the boy with her elbow.

"Certainly you must have some money," she said. The boy began to cry, and then she struck him with her foot till he cried out louder.

"Will you be quiet? or I'll break your screaming head;" and she swung about the fire-pot which she held in her hand, while the boy crouched to the earth and screamed.

Then a neighbor came in, and she had also a marito under her arm. "Felicita," she said, "what are you doing to the child?"

"The child is mine," she answered; "I can murder him if I like, and you too, Giannina." And then she swung about the fire-pot. The other woman lifted up hers to defend herself, and the two pots clashed together so violently that they were dashed to pieces, and fire and ashes flew about the room. The boy rushed out at the sight, sped across the courtyard, and fled from the house. The poor child ran till he was quite out of breath; at last he stopped at the church, the doors of which were opened to him the night before, and went in. Here everything was bright, and the boy knelt down by the first tomb on his right, the grave of Michael Angelo, and sobbed as if his heart would break. People came and went, mass was performed, but no one noticed the boy, excepting an elderly citizen, who stood still and looked at him for a moment, and then went away like the rest. Hunger and thirst overpowered the child, and he became quite faint and ill. At last he crept into a corner behind the marble monuments, and went to sleep. Towards evening he was awakened by a pull at his sleeve; he started up, and the same old citizen stood before him.

"Are you ill? where do you live? have you been here all day?" were some of the questions asked by the old man. After hearing his answers, the old man took him home to a small house close by, in a back street. They entered a glovemaker's shop, where a woman sat sewing busily. A little white poodle, so closely shaven that his pink skin could plainly be seen, frisked about the room, and gambolled upon the boy.

"Innocent souls are soon intimate," said the woman, as she caressed both the boy and the dog. These good people gave the child food and drink, and said he should stay with them all night, and that the next day the old man, who was called Giuseppe, would go and speak to his mother. A little homely bed was prepared for him, but to him who had so often slept on the hard stones it was a royal couch, and he slept sweetly and dreamed of the splendid pictures and of the Metal Pig. Giuseppe went out the next morning, and the poor child was not glad to see him go, for he knew that the old man was gone to his mother, and that, perhaps, he would have to go back. He wept at the thought, and then he played with the little, lively dog, and kissed it, while the old woman looked kindly at him to encourage him. And what news did Giuseppe bring back? At first the boy could not hear, for he talked a great deal to his wife, and she nodded and stroked the boy's cheek.

Then she said, "He is a good lad, he shall stay with us, he may become a clever glovemaker, like you. Look what delicate fingers he has got; Madonna intended him for a glovemaker." So the boy stayed with them, and the woman herself taught him to sew; and he ate well, and slept well, and became very merry. But at last he began to tease Bellissima, as the little dog was called. This made the woman angry, and she scolded him and threatened him, which made him very unhappy, and he went and sat in his own room full of sad thoughts. This chamber looked upon the street, in which hung skins to dry, and there were thick iron bars across his window. That night he lay awake, thinking of the Metal Pig; indeed, it was always in his thoughts. Suddenly he fancied he heard feet outside going pit-a-pat. He sprung out of bed and went to the window. Could it be the Metal Pig? But there was nothing to be seen; whatever he had heard had passed already. Next morning, their neighbor, the artist, passed by, carrying a paint-box and a large roll of canvas.

"Help the gentleman to carry his box of colors," said the woman to the boy; and he obeyed instantly, took the box, and followed the painter. They walked on till they reached the picture gallery, and mounted the same staircase up which he had ridden that night on the Metal Pig. He remembered all the statues and pictures, the beautiful marble Venus, and again he looked at the Madonna with the Saviour and St. John. They stopped before the picture by Bronzino, in which Christ is represented as standing in the lower world, with the children smiling before Him, in the sweet expectation of entering heaven; and the poor boy smiled, too, for here was his heaven.

"You may go home now," said the painter, while the boy stood watching him, till he had set up his easel.

"May I see you paint?" asked the boy; "may I see you put the picture on this white canvas?"

"I am not going to paint yet," replied the artist; then he brought out a piece of chalk. His hand moved quickly, and his eye measured the great picture; and though nothing appeared but a faint line, the figure of the Saviour was as clearly visible as in the colored picture.

"Why don't you go?" said the painter. Then the boy wandered home silently, and seated himself on the table, and learned to sew gloves. But all day long his thoughts were in the picture gallery; and so he pricked his fingers and was awkward. But he did not tease Bellissima. When evening came, and the house door stood open, he slipped out. It was a bright, beautiful, starlight evening, but rather cold. Away he went through the already-deserted streets, and soon came to the Metal Pig; he stooped down and kissed its shining nose, and then seated himself on its back.

"You happy creature," he said; "how I have longed for you! we must take a ride to-night."

But the Metal Pig lay motionless, while the fresh stream gushed forth from its mouth. The little boy still sat astride on its back, when he felt something pulling at his clothes. He looked down, and there was Bellissima, little smooth-shaven Bellissima, barking as if she would have said, "Here I am too; why are you sitting there?"

A fiery dragon could not have frightened the little boy so much as did the little dog in this place. "Bellissima in the street, and not dressed!" as the old lady called it; "what would be the end of this?"

The dog never went out in winter, unless she was attired in a little lambskin coat which had been made for her; it was fastened round the little dog's neck and body with red ribbons, and was decorated with rosettes and little bells. The dog looked almost like a little kid when she was allowed to go out in winter, and trot after her mistress. And now here she was in the cold, and not dressed. Oh, how would it end? All his fancies were quickly put to flight; yet he kissed the Metal Pig once more, and then took Bellissima in his arms. The poor little thing trembled so with cold, that the boy ran homeward as fast as he could.

"What are you running away with there?" asked two of the police whom he met, and at whom the dog barked. "Where have you stolen that pretty dog?" they asked; and they took it away from him.

"Oh, I have not stolen it; do give it to me back again," cried the boy, despairingly.

"If you have not stolen it, you may say at home that they can send to the watch-house for the dog." Then they told him where the watch-house was, and went away with Bellissima.

Here was a dreadful trouble. The boy did not know whether he had better jump into the Arno, or go home and confess everything. They would certainly kill him, he thought.

"Well, I would gladly be killed," he reasoned; "for then I shall die, and go to heaven:" and so he went home, almost hoping for death.

The door was locked, and he could not reach the knocker. No one was in the street; so he took up a stone, and with it made a tremendous noise at the door.

"Who is there?" asked somebody from within.

"It is I," said he. "Bellissima is gone. Open the door, and then kill me."

Then indeed there was a great panic. Madame was so very fond of Bellissima. She immediately looked at the wall where the dog's dress usually hung; and there was the little lambskin.

"Bellissima in the watch-house!" she cried. "You bad boy! how did you entice her out? Poor little delicate thing, with those rough policemen! and she'll be frozen with cold."

Giuseppe went off at once, while his wife lamented, and the boy wept. Several of the neighbors came in, and amongst them the painter. He took the boy between his knees, and questioned him; and, in broken sentences, he soon heard the whole story, and also about the Metal Pig, and the wonderful ride to the picture-gallery, which was certainly rather incomprehensible. The painter, however, consoled the little fellow, and tried to soften the lady's anger; but she would not be pacified till her husband returned with Bellissima, who had been with the police. Then there was great rejoicing, and the painter caressed the boy, and gave him a number of pictures. Oh, what beautiful pictures these were! – figures with funny heads; and, above all, the Metal Pig was there too. Oh, nothing could be more delightful. By means of a few strokes, it was made to appear on the paper; and even the house that stood behind it had been sketched in. Oh, if he could only draw and paint! He who could do this could conjure all the world before him. The first leisure moment during the next day, the boy got a pencil, and on the back of one of the other drawings he attempted to copy the drawing of the Metal Pig, and he succeeded. Certainly it was rather crooked, rather up and down, one leg thick, and another thin; still it was like the copy, and he was overjoyed at what he had done. The pencil would not go quite as it ought, – he had found that out; but the next day he tried again. A second pig was drawn by the side of the first, and this looked a hundred times better; and the third attempt was so good, that everybody might know what it was meant to represent.

And now the glovemaking went on but slowly. The orders given by the shops in the town were not finished quickly; for the Metal Pig had taught the boy that all objects may be drawn upon paper; and Florence is a picture-book in itself for any one who chooses to turn over its pages. On the Piazza dell Trinita stands a slender pillar, and upon it is the goddess of Justice, blindfolded, with her scales in her hand. She was soon represented on paper, and it was the glovemaker's boy who placed her there. His collection of pictures increased; but as yet they were only copies of lifeless objects, when one day Bellissima came gambolling before him: "Stand still," cried he, "and I will draw you beautifully, to put amongst my collection."

But Bellissima would not stand still, so she must be bound fast in one position. He tied her head and tail; but she barked and jumped, and so pulled and tightened the string, that she was nearly strangled; and just then her mistress walked in.

"You wicked boy! the poor little creature!" was all she could utter.

She pushed the boy from her, thrust him away with her foot, called him a most ungrateful, good-for-nothing, wicked boy, and forbade him to enter the house again. Then she wept, and kissed her little half-strangled Bellissima. At this moment the painter entered the room. In the year 1834 there was an exhibition in the Academy of Arts at Florence. Two pictures, placed side by side, attracted a large number of spectators. The smaller of the two represented a little boy sitting at a table, drawing; before him was a little white poodle, curiously shaven; but as the animal would not stand still, it had been fastened with a string to its head and tail, to keep it in one position.

The truthfulness and life in this picture interested every one. The painter was said to be a young Florentine, who had been found in the streets, when a child, by an old glovemaker, who had brought him up. The boy had taught himself to draw: it was also said that a young artist, now famous, had discovered talent in the child just as he was about to be sent away for having tied up madame's favorite little dog, and using it as a model. The glovemaker's boy had also become a great painter, as the picture proved; but the larger picture by its side was a still greater proof of his talent. It represented a handsome boy, clothed in rags, lying asleep, and leaning against the Metal Pig in the street of the Porta Rosa. All the spectators knew the spot well. The child's arms were round the neck of the Pig, and he was in a deep sleep. The lamp before the picture of the Madonna threw a strong, effective light on the pale, delicate face of the child. It was a beautiful picture. A large gilt frame surrounded it, and on one corner of the frame a laurel wreath had been hung; but a black band, twined unseen among the green leaves, and a streamer of crape, hung down from it; for within the last few days the young artist had – died.

What Was It?

IT IS, I CONFESS, with considerable diffidence that I approached the strange narrative which I am about to relate. The events which I purpose detailing are of so extraordinary a character that I am quite prepared to meet with an unusual amount of incredulity and scorn. I accept all such beforehand. I have, I trust, the literary courage to face unbelief. I have, after mature consideration, resolved to narrate, in as simple and straightforward a manner as I can compass, some facts that passed under my observation, in the month of July last, and which, in the annals of the mysteries of physical science, are wholly unparalleled.

I live at No. — Twenty-sixth Street, in New York. The house is in some respects a curious one. It has enjoyed for the last two years the reputation of being haunted. The house is very spacious. A hall of noble size leads to a large spiral staircase winding through its centre, while the various apartments are of imposing dimensions. It was built some fifteen or twenty years since by Mr. A——, the well-known New York merchant, who five years ago threw the commercial world into convulsions by a stupendous bank fraud. Mr. A——, as every one knows, escaped to Europe, and died not long after, of a broken heart. Almost immediately after the news of his decease reached this country and was verified, the report spread in Twenty-sixth Street that No. — was haunted. Legal measures had dispossessed the widow of its former owner, and it was inhabited merely by a care-taker and his wife, placed there by the house-agent into whose hands it had passed for purposes of renting or sale. These people declared that they were troubled with unnatural noises. Doors were opened without any visible agency. The remnants of furniture scattered through the various rooms were, during the night, piled one upon the other by unknown hands. Invisible feet passed up and down the stairs in broad daylight, accompanied by the rustle of unseen silk dresses, and the gliding of viewless hands along the massive balusters. The care-taker and his wife declared they would live there no longer. The house-agent laughed, dismissed them, and put others in their place. The noises and supernatural manifestations continued. The neighbourhood caught up the story, and the house remained untenanted for three years. Several persons negotiated for it; but, somehow, always before the bargain was closed they heard the unpleasant rumours and declined to treat any further.

It was in this state of things that my landlady, who at that time kept a boarding-house in Bleecker Street, and who wished to move farther up town, conceived the bold idea of renting No. — Twenty-sixth Street. Happening to have in her house rather a plucky and philosophical set of boarders, she laid her scheme before us, stating candidly everything she had heard respecting the ghostly qualities of the establishment to which she wished to remove us. With the exception of two timid persons – a sea-captain and a returned Californian, who immediately gave notice that they would leave – all of Mrs. Moffat's guests declared that they would accompany her in her incursion into the abode of spirits.

Our removal was effected in the month of May, and we were charmed with our new residence.

Of course we had no sooner established ourselves at No. — than we began to expect the ghosts. We absolutely awaited their advent with eagerness. Our dinner conversation was supernatural. I found myself a person of immense importance, it having leaked out that I was tolerably well versed in the history of supernaturalism, and had once written a story the foundation of which was a ghost. If a table or wainscot panel happened to warp when we were assembled in the large drawing-room, there was an instant silence, and every one was prepared for an immediate clanking of chains and a spectral form.

After a month of psychological excitement, it was with the utmost dissatisfaction that we were forced to acknowledge that nothing in the remotest degree approaching the supernatural had manifested itself.

Things were in this state when an incident took place so awful and inexplicable in its character that my reason fairly reels at the bare memory of the occurrence. It was the tenth of July. After dinner was over I repaired, with my friend Dr. Hammond, to the garden to smoke my evening pipe. Independent of certain mental sympathies which existed between the doctor and myself, we were linked together by a vice. We both smoked opium. We knew each other's secret and respected it. We enjoyed together that wonderful expansion of thought, that marvellous intensifying of the perceptive faculties, that boundless feeling of existence when we seem to have points of contact with the whole universe – in short, that unimaginable spiritual bliss, which I would not surrender for a throne, and which I hope you, reader, will never – never taste.

On the evening in question, the tenth of July, the doctor and myself drifted into an unusually metaphysical mood. We lit our large meerschaums, filled with fine Turkish tobacco, in the core of which burned a little black nut of opium, that, like the nut in the fairy tale, held within its narrow limits wonders beyond the reach of kings; we paced to and fro, conversing. A strange perversity dominated the currents of our thoughts. They would not flow through the sun-lit channels into which we strove to divert them. For some unaccountable reason, they constantly diverged into dark and lonesome beds, where a continual gloom brooded. It was in vain that, after our old fashion, we flung ourselves on the shores of the East, and talked of its gay bazaars, of the splendours of the time of Haroun, of harems and golden palaces. Black afreets continually arose from the depths of our talk, and expanded, like the one the fisherman released from the copper vessel, until they blotted everything bright from our vision. Insensibly, we yielded to the occult force that swayed us, and indulged in gloomy speculation. We had talked some time upon the proneness of the human mind to mysticism, and the almost universal love of the terrible, when Hammond suddenly said to me, "What do you consider to be the greatest element of terror?"

The question puzzled me. That many things were terrible, I knew. But it now struck me, for the first time, that there must be one great and ruling embodiment of fear – a King of Terrors, to which all others must succumb. What might it be? To what train of circumstances would it owe its existence?

"I confess, Hammond," I replied to my friend, "I never considered the subject before. That there must be one Something more terrible than any other thing, I feel. I cannot attempt, however, even the most vague definition."

"I am somewhat like you, Harry," he answered. "I feel my capacity to experience a terror greater than anything yet conceived by the human mind – something combining in fearful and unnatural amalgamation hitherto supposed incompatible elements. The calling of the voices in Brockden Brown's novel of *Wieland* is awful; so is the picture of the *Dweller on the Threshold*, in Bulwer's *Zanoni*; but," he added, shaking his head gloomily, "there is something more horrible still than these."

"Look here, Hammond," I rejoined, "let us drop this kind of talk, for Heaven's sake! We shall suffer for it, depend on it."

"I don't know what's the matter with me to-night," he replied, "but my brain is running upon all sorts of weird and awful thoughts. I feel as if I could write a story like Hoffman, to-night, if I were only master of a literary style."

"Well, if we are going to be Hoffmanesque in our talk, I'm off to bed. Opium and nightmares should never be brought together. How sultry it is! Good-night, Hammond."

"Good-night, Harry. Pleasant dreams to you."

"To you, gloomy wretch, afreets, ghouls, and enchanters."

We parted, and each sought his respective chamber. I undressed quickly and got into bed, taking with me, according to my usual custom, a book over which I generally read myself to sleep. I opened the volume as soon as I had laid my head upon the pillow, and instantly flung it to the other side of the room. It was Goudon's *History of Monsters*, – a curious French work, which I had lately imported from Paris, but which, in the state of mind I had then reached, was anything but an agreeable companion. I resolved to go to sleep at once; so, turning down my gas until nothing but a little blue point of light glimmered on the top of the tube, I composed myself to rest.

The room was in total darkness. The atom of gas that still remained alight did not illuminate a distance of three inches round the burner. I desperately drew my arm across my eyes, as if to shut out even the darkness and tried to think of nothing. It was in vain. The confounded themes touched on by Hammond in the garden kept obtruding themselves on my brain. I battled against them. I erected ramparts of would-be blankness of intellect to keep them out. They still crowded upon me. While I was lying still as a corpse, hoping that by a perfect physical inaction I should hasten mental repose, an awful incident occurred. A Something dropped, as it seemed, from the ceiling, plumb upon my chest, and the next instant I felt two bony hands encircling my throat, endeavouring to choke me.

I am no coward, and am possessed of considerable physical strength. The suddenness of the attack, instead of stunning me, strung every nerve to its highest tension. My body acted from instinct, before my brain had time to realize the terrors of my position. In an instant I wound two muscular arms around the creature, and squeezed it, with all the strength of despair, against my chest. In a few seconds the bony hands that had fastened on my throat loosened their hold, and I was free to breathe once more. Then commenced a struggle of awful intensity. Immersed in the most profound darkness, totally ignorant of the nature of the Thing by which I was so suddenly attacked, finding my grasp slipping every moment, by reason, it seemed to me, of the entire nakedness of my assailant, bitten with sharp teeth in the shoulder, neck, and chest, having every moment to protect my throat against a pair of sinewy, agile hands, which my utmost efforts could not confine – these were a combination of circumstances to combat which required all the strength, skill, and courage that I possessed.

At last, after a silent, deadly, exhausting struggle, I got my assailant under by a series of incredible efforts of strength. Once pinned, with my knee on what I made out to be its chest, I knew that I was victor. I rested for a moment to breathe. I heard the creature beneath me panting in the darkness, and felt the violent throbbing of a heart. It was apparently as exhausted as I was; that was one comfort. At this moment I remembered that I usually placed under my pillow, before going to bed, a large yellow silk pocket-handkerchief. I felt for it instantly; it was there. In a few seconds more I had, after a fashion, pinioned the creature's arms.

I now felt tolerably secure. There was nothing more to be done but to turn on the gas, and, having first seen what my midnight assailant was like, arouse the household. I will confess to being actuated by a certain pride in not giving the alarm before; I wished to make the capture alone and unaided.

Never losing my hold for an instant, I slipped from the bed to the floor, dragging my captive with me. I had but a few steps to make to reach the gas-burner; these I made with the greatest caution, holding the creature in a grip like a vice. At last I got within arm's length of the tiny speck of blue light which told me where the gas-burner lay. Quick as lightning I released my grasp with one hand and let on the full flood of light. Then I turned to look at my captive.

I cannot even attempt to give any definition of my sensations the instant after I turned on the gas. I suppose I must have shrieked with terror, for in less than a minute afterward my room was crowded with the inmates of the house. I shudder now as I think of that awful moment. I saw nothing! Yes; I had one arm firmly clasped round a breathing, panting, corporeal shape, my other hand gripped with all its strength a throat as warm, and apparently fleshly, as my own; and yet, with this living substance in my grasp, with its body pressed against my own, and all in the bright glare of a large jet of gas, I absolutely beheld nothing! Not even an outline – a vapour!

I do not, even at this hour, realize the situation in which I found myself. I cannot recall the astounding incident thoroughly. Imagination in vain tries to compass the awful paradox.

It breathed. I felt its warm breath upon my cheek. It struggled fiercely. It had hands. They clutched me. Its skin was smooth, like my own. There it lay, pressed close up against me, solid as stone – and yet utterly invisible!

I wonder that I did not faint or go mad on the instant. Some wonderful instinct must have sustained me; for absolutely, in place of loosening my hold on the terrible Enigma, I seemed to gain an additional strength in my moment of horror, and tightened my grasp with such wonderful force that I felt the creature shivering with agony.

Just then Hammond entered my room at the head of the household. As soon as he beheld my face – which, I suppose, must have been an awful sight to look at – he hastened forward, crying, "Great Heaven, what has happened?"

"Hammond! Hammond!" I cried, "come here. Oh, this is awful! I have been attacked in bed by something or other, which I have hold of; but I can't see it – I can't see it!"

Hammond, doubtless struck by the unfeigned horror expressed in my countenance, made one or two steps forward with an anxious yet puzzled expression. A very audible titter burst from the remainder of my visitors. This suppressed laughter made me furious. To laugh at a human being in my position! It was the worst species of cruelty. Now, I can understand why the appearance of a man struggling violently, as it would seem, with an airy nothing, and calling for assistance against a vision, should have appeared ludicrous. Then, so great was my rage against the mocking crowd that had I the power I would have stricken them dead where they stood.

"Hammond! Hammond!" I cried again, despairingly, "for God's sake come to me. I can hold the – the thing but a short while longer. It is overpowering me. Help me! Help me!"

"Harry," whispered Hammond, approaching me, "you have been smoking too much opium."

"I swear to you, Hammond, that this is no vision," I answered, in the same low tone. "Don't you see how it shakes my whole frame with its struggles? If you don't believe me convince yourself. Feel it – touch it."

Hammond advanced and laid his hand in the spot I indicated. A wild cry of horror burst from him. He had felt it!

In a moment he had discovered somewhere in my room a long piece of cord, and was the next instant winding it and knotting it about the body of the unseen being that I clasped in my arms.

"Harry," he said, in a hoarse, agitated voice, for, though he preserved his presence of mind, he was deeply moved, "Harry, it's all safe now. You may let go, old fellow, if you're tired. The Thing can't move."

I was utterly exhausted, and I gladly loosed my hold.

Hammond stood holding the ends of the cord, that bound the Invisible, twisted round his hand, while before him, self-supporting as it were, he beheld a rope laced and interlaced, and stretching tightly around a vacant space. I never saw a man look so thoroughly stricken with awe. Nevertheless his face expressed all the courage and determination which I knew him to possess. His lips, although white, were set firmly, and one could perceive at a glance that, although stricken with fear, he was not daunted.

The confusion that ensued among the guests of the house who were witnesses of this extraordinary scene between Hammond and myself – who beheld the pantomime of binding this struggling Something – who beheld me almost sinking from physical exhaustion when my task of jailer was over – the confusion and terror that took possession of the bystanders, when they saw all this, was beyond description. The weaker ones fled from the apartment. The few who remained clustered near the door and could not be induced to approach Hammond and his Charge. Still incredulity broke out through their terror. They had not the courage to satisfy themselves, and yet they doubted. It was in vain that I begged of some of the men to come near and convince themselves by touch of the existence in that room of a living being which was invisible. They were incredulous, but did not dare to undeceive themselves. How could a solid, living, breathing body be invisible, they asked. My reply was this. I gave a sign to Hammond, and both of us – conquering our fearful repugnance to touch the invisible creature – lifted it from the ground, manacled as it was, and took it to my bed. Its weight was about that of a boy of fourteen.

"Now, my friends," I said, as Hammond and myself held the creature suspended over the bed, "I can give you self-evident proof that here is a solid, ponderable body, which, nevertheless, you cannot see. Be good enough to watch the surface of the bed attentively."

I was astonished at my own courage in treating this strange event so calmly; but I had recovered from my first terror, and felt a sort of scientific pride in the affair, which dominated every other feeling.

The eyes of the bystanders were immediately fixed on my bed. At a given signal Hammond and I let the creature fall. There was the dull sound of a heavy body alighting on a soft mass. The timbers of the bed creaked. A deep impression marked itself distinctly on the pillow, and on the bed itself. The crowd who witnessed this gave a low cry, and rushed from the room. Hammond and I were left alone with our Mystery.

We remained silent for some time, listening to the low irregular breathing of the creature on the bed and watching the rustle of the bed-clothes as it impotently struggled to free itself from confinement. Then Hammond spoke.

"Harry, this is awful."

"Ay, awful."

"But not unaccountable."

"Not unaccountable! What do you mean? Such a thing has never occurred since the birth of the world. I know not what to think, Hammond. God grant that I am not mad and that this is not an insane fantasy!"

"Let us reason a little, Harry. Here is a solid body which we touch but which we cannot see. The fact is so unusual that it strikes us with terror. Is there no parallel, though, for such a phenomenon? Take a piece of pure glass. It is tangible and transparent. A certain chemical coarseness is all that prevents its being so entirely transparent as to be totally invisible. It is not theoretically impossible, mind you, to make a glass which shall not reflect a single ray of light – a glass so pure and homogeneous in its atoms that the rays from the sun will pass through it as they do through the air, refracted but not reflected. We do not see the air, and yet we feel it."

"That's all very well, Hammond, but these are inanimate substances. Glass does not breathe, air does not breathe. This thing has a heart that palpitates – a will that moves it – lungs that play, and inspire and respire."

"You forget the phenomena of which we have so often heard of late," answered the doctor gravely. "At the meetings called 'spirit circles,' invisible hands have been thrust into the hands of those persons round the table – warm, fleshly hands that seemed to pulsate with mortal life."

"What? Do you think, then, that this thing is—"

"I don't know what it is," was the solemn reply; "but please the gods I will, with your assistance, thoroughly investigate it."

We watched together, smoking many pipes, all night long, by the bedside of the unearthly being that tossed and panted until it was apparently wearied out. Then we learned by the low, regular breathing that it slept.

The next morning the house was all astir. The boarders congregated on the landing outside my room, and Hammond and myself were lions. We had to answer a thousand questions as to the state of our extraordinary prisoner, for as yet not one person in the house except ourselves could be induced to set foot in the apartment.

The creature was awake. This was evidenced by the convulsive manner in which the bed-clothes were moved in its efforts to escape. There was something truly terrible in beholding, as it were, those second-hand indications of the terrible writhings and agonized struggles for liberty which themselves were invisible.

Hammond and myself had racked our brains during the long night to discover some means by which we might realize the shape and general appearance of the Enigma. As well as we could make out by passing our hands over the creature's form, its outlines and lineaments were human. There was a mouth; a round, smooth head without hair; a nose, which, however, was little elevated above the cheeks; and its hands and feet felt like those of a boy. At first we thought of placing the being on a smooth surface and tracing its outlines with chalk, as shoemakers trace the outline of the foot. This plan was given up as being of no value. Such an outline would give not the slightest idea of its conformation.

A happy thought struck me. We would take a cast of it in plaster-of-Paris. This would give us the solid figure, and satisfy all our wishes. But how to do it. The movements of the creature would disturb the setting of the plastic covering, and distort the mould. Another thought. Why not give it chloroform? It had respiratory organs – that was evident by its breathing. Once reduced to a state of insensibility, we could do with it what we would. Doctor X—— was sent for; and after the worthy physician had recovered from the first shock of amazement, he proceeded to administer the chloroform. In three minutes afterward we were enabled to remove the fetters from the creature's body, and a modeller was busily engaged in covering the invisible form with the moist clay. In five minutes more we had a mould, and before evening a rough fac-simile of the

Mystery. It was shaped like a man – distorted, uncouth, and horrible, but still a man. It was small, not over four feet and some inches in height, and its limbs revealed a muscular development that was unparalleled. Its face surpassed in hideousness anything I had ever seen. Gustave Doré, or Callot, or Tony Johannot, never conceived anything so horrible. There is a face in one of the latter's illustrations to *Un Voyage où il vous plaira*, which somewhat approaches the countenance of this creature, but does not equal it. It was the physiognomy of what I should fancy a ghoul might be. It looked as if it was capable of feeding on human flesh.

Having satisfied our curiosity, and bound every one in the house to secrecy, it became a question what was to be done with our Enigma? It was impossible that we should keep such a horror in our house; it was equally impossible that such an awful being should be let loose upon the world. I confess that I would have gladly voted for the creature's destruction. But who would shoulder the responsibility? Who would undertake the execution of this horrible semblance to a human being? Day after day this question was deliberated gravely. The boarders all left the house. Mrs. Moffat was in despair, and threatened Hammond and myself with all sorts of legal penalties if we did not remove the Horror. Our answer was, "We will go if you like, but we decline taking this creature with us. Remove it yourself if you please. It appeared in your house. On you the responsibility rests." To this there was, of course, no answer. Mrs. Moffat could not obtain for love or money a person who would even approach the Mystery.

At last it died. Hammond and I found it cold and stiff one morning in the bed. The heart had ceased to beat, the lungs to inspire. We hastened to bury it in the garden. It was a strange funeral, the dropping of that viewless corpse into the damp hole. The cast of its form I gave to Doctor X——, who keeps it in his museum in Tenth Street.

As I am on the eve of a long journey from which I may not return, I have drawn up this narrative of an event the most singular that has ever come to my knowledge.

A Dead Wife Among the Fairies

THERE ONCE WAS A MAN who lived with a wife he loved. They had been married for many years, and they made their home in a lighthouse, on the rocky coast by the sea. The waves threw up a spray but never dampened them, for they were sealed tight in their little world inside that lighthouse, and they lived happily there together, needing little else but the other. And so they lived, working together and talking all the day, lighting their beacon in the mists and fogs which fell over the sea like a woollen blanket.

Then one day, the good wife died, and she was buried in the hillside, under the rocks. And on those rocks the man sat each day, never lighting his beacon when the mists and fogs fell over the sea, staring instead at the rock which marked her grave, which marked the end of his life too. And so it was that he became a little mad, and went to see a witch, a fairy midwife who practised the magic of the earth and who could tell him how to get her back, his wife that he loved so well.

He saw her in her cottage, over the hill and across the brae, and she shook her head, and warned him to leave the dead with the fairies, for after death there can be no real life on earth, where the light would turn into dust any mortal who tried to return. But for the poor widowed man there could be no real life either, and so he begged the fairy witch to tell him her secrets and at last she did.

He was to go, she said, to a cave at the brae of Versabreck, on the night of a full moon, and he should take with him a black cat, and a Bible, and a thick wooden staff. There he must cry for his wife, and read to her from the psalms, and when he heard her voice once more, he must throw in the black cat and wait quietly for her to appear. Now the fairy folk would never let a mortal who had died pass back to his own land, so they would rally round her, and fight to keep her in their dust-webbed cave, which led to the Land of Light. The staff was to beat them with, for they could be sent back into their cave by the force of his will.

The moon waned and then it waxed again, and soon the night of the full moon arrived. The man was shivering with the fear of seeing his wife once more, yet he longed to touch her body, to feel her warmth, to hear her tender voice, so he steeled his quivering nerves and set off for the cave at the brae of Versabreck, and under his arm he held a black cat, and a Bible and a thick wooden staff. There he cried for his wife, and he read to her from the psalms, and when he heard her voice once more, he threw in the black cat and waited quietly for her to appear.

Now the fairy folk fought for their mortal princess, and struggled to keep her in their dust-webbed cave, which led to the Land of Light, but he beat them with his staff, and sent them back into their cave by the force of his will.

And there was his wife, paler to be sure, and nothing more than skin and bones, but she smiled her same familiar smile, and although her body held no warmth and she smelled rather sour, he held her to him once again and heard her tender voice. And together they walked to their lighthouse home, snug in a warm embrace, and they lit their beacon in the mists and fogs which fell over the sea like a woollen blanket. When day broke, his wife was safe in the fairy cave again, for light would turn to dust any mortal who tried to return from the dead. And so her husband would watch carefully as the moon waned and then waxed, when they could meet again.

The Fairies and the Blacksmith

THERE ONCE WAS A BLACKSMITH by the name of Alasdair MacEachern, and he lived in a cottage on the Isle of Islay with his son Neil. They lived alone for the blacksmith's poor wife had breathed no more than once or twice when Neil was born to them, but Alasdair MacEachern, or Alasdair of the Strong Arm, as he came to be known, found great comfort in his son and they lived contentedly, with familiar habits and routines that brought them much happiness.

Neil was a slim youth, with unruly hair and eyes that shone with dreams. He was quiet, but easy, and his slight, pale frame gave him the countenance of one weaker than he was. When Neil was but a child the neighbours of Alasdair MacEachern had warned the blacksmith of the fairies who lived just over the knoll, the fairies who would find one so slight and dreamy a perfect prize for their Land of Light. And so it was that each night Alasdair MacEachern hung above the door to his cottage a branch of rowan, a charm against the fairies who might come to steal away his son.

They lived many years this way, until the day came when Alasdair MacEachern had to travel some distance, sleeping the night away from his cottage and his son. Before he left, he warned his son about the rowan branch, and Neil agreed to put it in its place above the door that night. Neil loved the green grass of the hills, and to breathe in the crisp, sunlit air of the banks of the streams that trickled through their land, but he loved more his life with his father and his work on the forge. He had no wish for a life of dancing and eternal merriment in the Land of Light.

And so it was that Neil wished his father a fond farewell, swept the cottage, tended to the goats and to the chickens, and made himself a feast of cornbread and oatcakes, and goat's cheese and milk, and took himself to the soft green grass of the hills, and walked there by the sunlit banks of the streams until dark fell upon him. And then Neil returned to his cottage next to the forge, and he swept the crumbs from his pockets, and tended to the goats and to the chickens, and laid himself in his tiny box-bed in the corner of the room, by the roaring hearth, and fell fast asleep. Not once had the thought of the branch of rowan crept across his sleepy mind.

It was late in the afternoon when Alasdair of the Strong Arm returned to his cottage, and he found the hearth quite cold, and the floor unswept, and the goats and the chickens untended. His son was there, for he answered his father's call, but there was no movement from his box-bed in the corner and Alasdair crossed the room with great concern.

"I am ill, Father," said a small, weak voice, and there laid the body of Neil, yellowed and shrunk, hardly denting his meagre mattress.

"But how ... how could, in just one day ..." Alasdair stared with shock at his son, for he smelled old, of decay, and his skin was like charred paper, folded and crisp and creased. But it was his son, no doubt, for the shape and the face were the same. And Neil laid like this for days on end, changing little, but eating steadily, his appetite strange and fathomless. And it was because of this strange illness that Alasdair MacEachern paid a visit to a wiseman, who came at once to the bedside of Neil, for he was a boy well regarded by his neighbours.

The wiseman looked only once at Neil, and drew the unhappy blacksmith outside the cottage. He asked many questions and then he was quiet. When he finally spoke his words were measured, and his tone quite fearful. The blood of Alasdair MacEachern ran cold.

"This is not your son Neil," said the man of knowledge. "He has been carried off by the Little People and they have left a changeling in his place."

"Alas, then, what can I do?" The great blacksmith was visibly trembling now, for Neil was as central to his life as the fiery heat of the forge itself. And then the wiseman spoke, and he told Alasdair MacEachern how to proceed.

"You must first be sure that is a changeling lying in the bed of Neil, and you must go back to the cottage and collect as many egg shells as you can, filling them with water and carrying them as if they weighed more than ten tons of iron and bricks. And then, arrange them round the side of the fire where the changeling can see you. His words will give him away."

So Alasdair MacEachern gathered together the shells of twenty eggs and did as he was bidden, and soon a thin voice called out from his son's bed, "In all of my eight hundred years I have never seen such a sight." And with a hoot and a cackle, the changeling sank back into the bed.

Alasdair returned to the wiseman and confirmed what had taken place. The old man nodded his head.

"It is indeed a changeling and he must be disposed of, before you can bring back your son. You must follow these steps: light a large, hot fire in the centre of the cottage, where it can be easily seen by the changeling. And then, when he asks you 'What's the use of that,' you must grab him by the shirtfront, and thrust him deep into the fire. Then he'll fly through the roof of the cottage."

Alasdair of the Strong Arm did as requested, certain now that that wizened, strange creature was not his son, and as the fire began to roar, the voice called out, reedy and slim, "What's the use of that?" at which the brave blacksmith seized the body that lay in Neil's bed and placed it firmly in the flames. There was a terrible scream, and the changeling flew straight through the roof, a sour yellow smoke all that remained of him.

And so Alasdair MacEachern cleared away the traces of the fire, and returned once more to the man of knowledge, for it was time to find his son, and he could delay no longer.

The wiseman bade him go to fetch three things: a Bible, a sword, and a crowing cock. He was to follow the stream that trickled through their land to the grassy green knoll where the fairies danced and played eternally. On the night of the next full moon, that hill would open, and it was through this door that Alasdair must go to seek his son.

It was many days before the moon had waned, and then waxed again, but it stood, a gleaming beacon in the sky at last, and Alasdair MacEachern collected together his sword and his Bible and his crowing cock and set out for the green knoll where the fairies danced. And as the moon rose high in the sky, and lit the shadowy land, a door burst open in the hill, spilling out laughter and song and a bright light that blazed like the fire in the hearth of the blacksmith's cottage. And it was into that light and sound that the courageous Alasdair MacEachern stepped, firmly thrusting his sword into the frame of the door to stop it closing, for no fairy can touch the sword of a mortal man.

There, at a steaming forge, stood his son, as small and as wild-looking as the little folk themselves. He worked silently, absorbed in his labours, and started only when he heard the voice of his father.

"Release my son from this enchantment," shouted Alasdair MacEachern, holding the Bible high in the air, for fairies have no power over mortals who hold the good Lord's book, and they stood back now, cross and foiled.

"Return him to me, to his own land," bawled the blacksmith, but the fairies began to smirk, and they slowly crept around him in a circle, taunting him, poking at him with blades of honed green grass. They began to dance, a slow and wiry gyration, moving to a weird song that tugged at the mind of the blacksmith, that threatened to overcome him. He struggled to stay upright, and as he stabbed his arms out in front of him, he dropped his cock, who woke with a howl and gave one mighty crow that sent the little fairies shrieking from the doorway to the other side, sent them howling away from the cock and the blacksmith and his son, who they pushed now towards him, sending them all slipping towards the threshold of their world. For daylight was the curfew of the fairies, and it was with true fear that the crow of the red-combed cock was heard, for little people may never see the light of day per chance they turn at once to stone.

They struggled now, prodding the mortals from their world, and begging in an awkward chant for Alasdair MacEachern to release his dirk from their door. And as he drew it from the threshold, and stood once more in the land of mortals with his son, a small and crafty fairy thrust his face from the hillside, and called out a curse that fell upon the son of the hapless blacksmith like the mist of a foggy night.

"May your son not speak until the day he breaks the curse." The head popped back, and the fairy was gone, never to be seen again.

And so it was that Alasdair MacEachern and his son Neil went to live again in their familiar, cosy cottage next to the forge, and took up their work, their habits and their routines in place once more. Neil's tongue was frozen by the curse of the fairies, but his manner was unchanged, and this father and his son lived contentedly, for speech is not always necessary to those who live simply, with things and people to which they have grown accustomed.

One day, a year and a week from the fairy's fateful full moon, Alasdair set his son the task of forging the new claymore for the Chief of his clan. As his silent son held the metal to the fire, he started, and looked for one instant as wild as he had in the Land of the Light, for suddenly Neil had remembered, and in that flash of memory he recalled the intricate forging of the fairies' swords, how he'd learned to temper the blades of their glowing weapons with words of wisdom and charms, with magic and spells as well as with fire. Now he leapt into action, and worked with a ferocity and speed that set his father, Alasdair of the Strong Arm, reeling with shock and with fear.

And then the motion stopped, and holding up a sword that gleamed like the light of the full moon, he said quietly, "There is a sword that will never fail the man who grasps it by the hilt."

From that time onwards Neil spoke again, for unwittingly he had removed the curse of the fairies by fashioning a fairy sword to sever a fairy spell. Never again did he remember his days in the fairy kingdom, never again could he forge a fairy sword, but the Chief of his clan never lost a battle from that day, and the sword remained the greatest of his possessions.

Neil and his father, Alasdair MacEachern, returned to their cottage, the finest blacksmiths in all the land, their forge casting a glow that could be seen from hills all round, almost as far as the Land of Light, where the fairies kick up their heels in fury at the thought of that blacksmith and his clever son.

Wee Johnnie in the Cradle

THERE ONCE WAS A MAN and his wife who lived on a farm on the edge of a wood where fairies were known to lay their small hats. They were a young man and wife and they had not been married long before a child was born to them, a child they called Johnnie. Now wee Johnnie was an unhappy baby, and from the beginning he cried so loudly that the birds ceased their flight over the farmer's cottage, and the creatures of the woodland kept a surly distance. The man's wife longed for the days when she could tend the fields with her husband, and chat to him of things which those who are newly wed have to chat of, and to go to market, where they would share a dram and have a carry-on like they had in the days before wee Johnnie was born.

But Johnnie was there now, and their cosy cottage became messy and damp, and some days the hearth was not lit because the man and his wife were so intent on silencing the squalling boy, and some days they could not even look one another in the eye, so unhappy and disillusioned they had become.

And then, perchance, a kindly neighbour, a tailor by trade, took pity on the man and his wife, who grew ever thinner and ever more hostile as the cries of wee Johnnie grew wilder and lustier as he grew larger and stronger.

"I'll take yer bairn and ye can take yer wife to market," he said to the farmer one day, and the man and his wife eagerly agreed and set off for the day.

They had not been gone longer than a minute or two, when the kindly tailor, who had placed himself beside the fire and was bracing himself for an afternoon of wailing, was startled from his reverie by a deep voice.

"Fetch me a glass o' that whiskey, there, in the press," it said. And the tailor looked about him in amazement, the room empty but for the wee Johnnie in the cradle who was mercifully silent.

"I said to ye, fetch me a glass," and up from the cradle of wee Johnnie popped wee Johnnie's head, and from the mouth on that head came that deep and bossy voice.

The tailor rose and did as he was bidden, and when the baby had drained the glass, and then another, and let out a belch that was very unbabyish indeed, he said to the wee bairn, "You aren't Johnnie, are ye, ye are a fairy without a doubt."

"And if I am," said the fairy changeling, "what will ye say to them, me mam and da?"

"I, I dunna know," said the tailor carefully, settling himself back into his chair to watch the fairy more carefully.

"Get me some pipes," said Johnnie the fairy, "I like a bit of music with me drink."

"I haven't any ... and I dunna play," said the tailor, crossing himself and moving further from the loathsome baby.

"Fetch me a straw then," he replied. And when the tailor complied, the fairy Johnnie played a song which was so exquisite, so effortlessly beautiful that the tailor was quite calmed. Never before had he heard music so haunting, and he would remember that melody until his dying day, although he could never repeat it himself or pass it on. But he was broken from his reverie, for wee Johnnie was speaking.

"Me mam and da, when will they be back?" he whispered.

The tailor looked startled, for the day had been pulled from under him, and it was time indeed for the farmer and his wife to return. He looked anxiously from the window and as they drew up he heard wee Johnnie begin to howl with all the vigour of a slaughtered beast, and he watched as a deep frown furrowed the brow of the farmer's wife, and a dull shadow cast itself across the face of her husband.

He must tell them, for the cruel fairy was manipulating them, taunting them with his tortuous cries. And their own wee bairn was somewhere lost to them.

He pulled the farmer aside as his wife went to tend to the wailing bairn, and told him of the fairy. A bemused look crossed his face and he struggled to keep his composure. "My wife, she'll not believe it," he said finally.

But the tailor had a plan. He told the farmer to pretend to leave for market the following day, and he, the tailor, would step in to look after the bairn once again. But the farmer and his wife were not really to leave, they should hide themselves outside the cottage walls and watch when the wee Johnnie thought them gone.

And so it happened that the next day the man and his wife set out for market again, but drove their horses only round the grassy bend, returning stealthily to look through the windows of their cottage. And there was wee Johnnie, sipping on a glass of their best whiskey, puffing idly on a straw pipe that played a song which was so exquisite, so effortlessly beautiful that they were quite calmed. Never before had they heard music so haunting, and they would remember that melody until their dying day, although they could never repeat it.

But when they heard that wee Johnnie's coarse voice demanding more drink, they were snapped from their reverie, and they flew into the cottage and thrust the changeling intruder on the burning griddle which the tailor had prepared for that purpose.

And the scream that ensued was not that of their own baby, and the puff of sickening smoke which burst from the fairy as he disappeared renewed their determination.

And then there was silence, an empty peace that caused the man and his wife to look at one another in dismay, for what had they done to cause their baby to be stolen from them, and where was their own wee Johnnie now?

Then a gurgle burst forth, and there was a movement in the corner of the room where the tiny cradle lay. They rushed to its side, and there lay Johnnie, brought back from his fairy confinement, smiling and waving tiny fat arms, with cheeks like pink buttons, and a smile so merry that the cottage of the man and his wife was warmed once again.

The tailor left them then, a grin on his face as he whistled to himself a tune which was so exquisite, so effortlessly beautiful that he was quite calmed.

The Kildare Pooka

MR. H— R—, when he was alive, used to live a good deal in Dublin, and he was once a great while out of the country on account of the 'ninety-eight' business. But the servants kept on in the big house at Rath— all the same as if the family was at home. Well, they used to be frightened out of their lives after going to their beds with the banging of the kitchen-door, and the clattering of fire-irons, and the pots and plates and dishes. One evening they sat up ever so long, keeping one another in heart with telling stories about ghosts and fetches, and that when – what would you have of it? – the little scullery boy that used to be sleeping over the horses, and could not get room at the fire, crept into the hot hearth, and when he got tired listening to the stories, sorra fear him, but he fell dead asleep.

Well and good, after they were all gone and the kitchen fire raked up, he was woke with the noise of the kitchen door opening, and the trampling of an ass on the kitchen floor. He peeped out, and what should he see but a big ass, sure enough, sitting on his curabingo and yawning before the fire. After a little he looked about him, and began scratching his ears as if he was quite tired, and says he, "I may as well begin first as last." The poor boy's teeth began to chatter in his head, for says he, "Now he's goin' to ate me"; but the fellow with the long ears and tail on him had something else to do. He stirred the fire, and then he brought in a pail of water from the pump, and filled a big pot that he put on the fire before he went out. He then put in his hand – foot, I mean – into the hot hearth, and pulled out the little boy. He let a roar out of him with the fright, but the pooka only looked at him, and thrust out his lower lip to show how little he valued him, and then he pitched him into his pew again.

Well, he then lay down before the fire till he heard the boil coming on the water, and maybe there wasn't a plate, or a dish, or a spoon on the dresser that he didn't fetch and put into the pot, and wash and dry the whole bilin' of 'em as well as e'er a kitchen-maid from that to Dublin town. He then put all of them up on their places on the shelves; and if he didn't give a good sweepin' to the kitchen, leave it till again. Then he comes and sits foment the boy, let down one of his ears, and cocked up the other, and gave a grin. The poor fellow strove to roar out, but not a dheeg 'ud come out of his throat. The last thing the pooka done was to rake up the fire, and walk out, giving such a slap o' the door, that the boy thought the house couldn't help tumbling down.

Well, to be sure if there wasn't a hullabullo next morning when the poor fellow told his story! They could talk of nothing else the whole day. One said one thing, another said another, but a fat, lazy scullery girl said the wittiest thing of all. "Musha!" says she, "if the pooka does be cleaning up everything that way when we are asleep, what should we be slaving ourselves for doing his work?"

"*Shu gu dheine*," says another; "them's the wisest words you ever said, Kauth; it's meeself won't contradict you."

So said, so done. Not a bit of a plate or dish saw a drop of water that evening, and not a besom was laid on the floor, and everyone went to bed soon after sundown. Next morning everything was as fine as fine in the kitchen, and the lord mayor might eat his dinner off the flags. It was great ease to the lazy servants, you may depend, and everything went on well till a foolhardy gag of a boy said he would stay up one night and have a chat with the pooka.

He was a little daunted when the door was thrown open and the ass marched up to the fire.

"An then, sir," says he, at last, picking up courage, "if it isn't taking a liberty, might I ax who you are, and why you are so kind as to do half of the day's work for the girls every night?"

"No liberty at all," says the pooka, says he: "I'll tell you, and welcome. I was a servant in the time of Squire R.'s father, and was the laziest rogue that ever was clothed and fed, and done nothing for it. When my time came for the other world, this is the punishment was laid on me – to come here and do all this labour every night, and then go out in the cold. It isn't so bad in the fine weather; but if you only knew what it is to stand with your head between your legs, facing the storm, from midnight to sunrise, on a bleak winter night."

"And could we do anything for your comfort, my poor fellow?" says the boy.

"Musha, I don't know," says the pooka; "but I think a good quilted frieze coat would help to keep the life in me them long nights."

"Why then, in troth, we'd be the ungratefullest of people if we didn't feel for you."

To make a long story short, the next night but two the boy was there again; and if he didn't delight the poor pooka, holding up a fine warm coat before him, it's no mather! Betune the pooka and the man, his legs was got into the four arms of it, and it was buttoned down the breast and the belly, and he was so pleazed he walked up to the glass to see how he looked. "Well," says he, "it's a long lane that has no turning. I am much obliged to you and your fellow-servants. You have made me happy at last. Good-night to you."

So he was walking out, but the other cried, "Och! Sure your going too soon. What about the washing and sweeping?"

"Ah, you may tell the girls that they must now get their turn. My punishment was to last till I was thought worthy of a reward for the way I done my duty. You'll see me no more." And no more they did, and right sorry they were for having been in such a hurry to reward the ungrateful pooka.

The Rabbi's Bogey-Man

RABBI LION, of the ancient city of Prague, sat in his study in the Ghetto looking very troubled. Through the window he could see the River Moldau with the narrow streets of the Jewish quarter clustered around the cemetery, which still stands to-day, and where is to be seen this famous plan's tomb. Beyond the Ghetto rose the towers and spires of the city, but just at that moment it was not the cruelty of the people to the Jews that occupied the rabbi's thoughts. He was unable to find a servant, even one to attend the fire on the Sabbath for him.

The truth was that the people were a little afraid of the rabbi. He was a very learned man, wise and studious, and a scientist; and because he did wonderful things people called him a magician. His experiments in chemistry frightened them. Late at nights they saw little spurts of blue and red flame shine from his window, and they said that demons and witches came at his beck and call. So nobody would enter his service.

"If, as they declare, I am truly a magician," he said to himself, "why should I not make for myself a servant, one that will tend the fire for me on the Sabbath?"

He set to work on his novel idea and in a few weeks had completed his mechanical creature, a woman. She looked like a big, strong, labouring woman, and the rabbi was greatly pleased with his handiwork.

"Now to endow it with life," he said.

Carefully, in the silence of his mysterious study at midnight, he wrote out the Unpronounceable Sacred Name of God on a piece of parchment. Then he rolled it up and placed it in the mouth of the creature.

Immediately it sprang up and began to move like a living thing. It rolled its eyes, waved its arms, and nearly walked through the window. In alarm, Rabbi Lion snatched the parchment from its mouth and the creature fell helpless to the floor.

"I must be careful," said the rabbi. "It is a wonderful machine with its many springs and screws and levers, and will be most useful to me as soon as I learn to control it properly."

All the people marvelled when they saw the rabbi's machine-woman running errands and doing many duties, controlled only by his thoughts. She could do everything but speak, and Rabbi Lion discovered that he must take the Name from her mouth before he went to sleep. Otherwise, she might have done mischief.

One cold Sabbath afternoon, the rabbi was preaching in the synagogue and the little children stood outside his house looking at the machine-woman seated by the window. When they rolled their eyes she did, and at last they shouted: "Come and play with us."

She promptly jumped through the window and stood among the boys and girls.

"We are cold," said one. "Canst thou make a fire for us?"

The creature was made to obey orders, so she at once collected sticks and lit a fire in the street. Then, with the children, she danced round the blaze in great glee. She piled on all the sticks and old barrels she could find, and soon the fire spread and caught a house. The children ran away in fear while the fire blazed so furiously that the whole town became alarmed. Before the flames could be extinguished, a number of houses had been burned down and much damage done. The creature could not be found, and only when the parchment with the Name, which could not burn, was discovered amid the ashes, was it known that she had been destroyed in the conflagration.

The Council of the city was indignant when it learned of the strange occurrence, and Rabbi Lion was summoned to appear before King Rudolf.

"What is this I hear," asked his majesty. "Is it not a sin to make a living creature?"

"It had no life but that which the Sacred Name gave it," replied the rabbi.

"I understand it not," said the king. "Thou wilt be imprisoned and must make another creature, so that I may see it for myself. If it is as thou sayest, thy life shall be spared. If not – if, in truth, thou profanest God's sacred law and makest a living thing, thou shalt die and all thy people shall be expelled from this city."

Rabbi Lion at once set to work, and this time made a man, much bigger than the woman that had been burned.

"As your majesty sees," said the rabbi, when his task was completed, "it is but a creature of wood and glue with springs at the joints. Now observe," and he put the Sacred Name in its mouth.

Slowly the creature rose to its feet and saluted the monarch who was so delighted that he cried: "Give him to me, rabbi."

"That cannot be," said Rabbi Lion, solemnly. "The Sacred Name must not pass from my possession. Otherwise the creature may do great damage again. This time I shall take care and will not use the man on the Sabbath."

The king saw the wisdom of this and set the rabbi at liberty and allowed him to take the creature to his house. The Jews looked on in wonderment when they saw the creature walking along the street by the side of Rabbi Lion, but the children ran away in fear, crying: "The bogey-man."

The rabbi exercised caution with his bogey-man this time, and every Friday, just before Sabbath commenced, he took the name from its mouth so as to render it powerless.

It became more wonderful every day, and one evening it startled the rabbi from a doze by beginning to speak.

"I want to be a soldier," it said, "and fight for the king. I belong to the king. You made me for him."

"Silence," cried Rabbi Lion, and it had to obey. "I like not this," said the rabbi to himself. "This monster must not become my master, or it may destroy me and perhaps all the Jews."

He could not help but wonder whether the king was right and that it must be a sin to create a man. The creature not only spoke, but grew surly and disobedient, and yet the rabbi hesitated to break it up, for it was most useful to him. It did all his cooking, washing and cleaning, and three servants could not have performed the work so neatly and quickly.

One Friday afternoon when the rabbi was preparing to go to the synagogue, he heard a loud noise in the street.

"Come quickly," the people shouted at his door. "Your bogey-man is trying to get into the synagogue."

Rabbi Lion rushed out in a state of alarm. The monster had slipped from the house and was battering down the door of the synagogue.

"What art thou doing?" demanded the rabbi, sternly.

"Trying to get into the synagogue to destroy the scrolls of the Holy Law," answered the monster. "Then wilt thou have no power over me, and I shall make a great army of bogey-men who shall fight for the king and kill all the Jews."

"I will kill thee first," exclaimed Rabbi Lion, and springing forward he snatched the parchment with the Name so quickly from the creature's mouth that it collapsed at his feet a mass of broken springs and pieces of wood and glue.

For many years afterward these pieces were shown to visitors in the attic of the synagogue when the story was told of the rabbi's bogey-man.

Invoker of the Beast

I

IT WAS QUIET AND TRANQUIL, and neither joyous nor sad. There was an electric light in the room. The walls seemed impregnable. The window was overhung by heavy, dark-green draperies, even denser in tone than the green of the wall-paper. Both doors – the large one at the side, and the small one in the depth of the alcove that faced the window – were securely bolted. And there, behind them, reigned darkness and desolation in the broad corridor as well as in the spacious and cold reception-room, where melancholy plants yearned for their native soil.

Gurov was lying on the divan. A book was in his hands. He often paused in his reading. He meditated and mused during these pauses, and it was always about the same thing. Always about them.

They hovered near him. This he had noticed long ago. They were hiding. Their manner; was importunate. They rustled very quietly. For a long time they remained invisible to the eye. But one day, when Gurov awoke rather tired; sad and pale, and languidly turned on the electric light to dissipate the greyish gloom of an early winter morning – he espied one of them suddenly.

Small, grey, shifty and nimble, he flashed by, and in the twinkling of an eye disappeared.

And thereafter, in the morning, or in the evening, Gurov grew used to seeing these small, shifty, house sprites run past him. This time he did not doubt that they would appear.

To begin with he felt a slight headache, afterwards a sudden flash of heat, then of cold. Then, out of the corner, there emerged the long, slender Fever with her ugly, yellow face and her bony dry hands; she lay down at his side, and embraced him, and fell to kissing him and to laughing. And these rapid kisses of the affectionate and cunning Fever, and these slow approaches of the slight headache were agreeable.

Feebleness spread itself over, the whole body, and lassitude also. This too was agreeable. It made him feel as though all the turmoil of life had receded into the distance. And people also became far away, unimportant, even unnecessary. He preferred to be with these quiet ones, these house sprites.

Gurov had not been out for some days. He had locked himself in at home. He did not permit any one to come to him. He was alone. He thought about them. He awaited them.

II

This tedious waiting was cut short in a strange and unexpected manner. He heard the slamming of a distant door, and presently he became aware of the sound of unhurried footfalls which came from the direction of the reception-room, just behind the door of his room. Some one was approaching with a sure and nimble step.

Gurov turned his head toward the door. A gust of cold entered the room. Before him stood a boy, most strange and wild in aspect. He was dressed in linen draperies, half-nude, barefoot, smooth-skinned, sun-tanned, with black tangled hair and dark, burning eyes. An amazingly perfect, handsome face; handsome to a degree which made it terrible to gaze upon its beauty. And it portrayed neither good nor evil.

Gurov was not astonished. A masterful mood took hold of him. He could hear the house sprites scampering away to conceal themselves.

The boy began to speak.

"Aristomarchon! Perhaps you have forgotten your promise? Is this the way of valiant men? You left me when I was in mortal danger, you had made me a promise, which it is evident you did not intend to keep. I have sought for you such a long time! And here I have found you, living at your ease, and in luxury."

Gurov fixed a perplexed gaze upon the half-nude, handsome lad; and turgid memories awoke in his soul. Something long since submerged arose in dim outlines and tormented his memory, which struggled to find a solution to the strange apparition; a solution, moreover, which seemed so near and so intimate.

And what of the invincibility of his walls? Something had happened round him, some mysterious transformation had taken place. But Gurov, engulfed in his vain exertions to recall something very near to him and yet slipping away in the tenacious embrace of ancient memory, had not yet succeeded in grasping the nature of the change that he felt had taken place. He turned to the wonderful boy.

"Tell me, gracious boy, simply and clearly, without unnecessary reproaches, what had I promised you, and when had I left you in a time of mortal danger? I swear to you, by all the holies, that my conscience could never have permitted me such a mean action as you reproach me with."

The boy shook his head. In a sonorous voice, suggestive of the melodious outpouring of a stringed instrument, he said: "Aristomarchon, you always have been a man skilful with words, and not less skilful in matters requiring daring and prudence. If I have said that you left me in a moment of mortal danger I did not intend it as a reproach, and I do not understand why you speak of your conscience. Our projected affair was difficult and dangerous, but who can hear us now; before whom, with your craftily arranged words and your dissembling ignorance of what happened this morning at sunrise, can you deny that you had given me a promise?"

The electric light grew dim. The ceiling seemed to darken and to recede into height. There was a smell of grass; its forgotten name, once, long ago, suggested something gentle and joyous. A breeze blew. Gurov raised himself, and asked: "What sort of an affair had we two contrived? Gracious boy, I deny nothing. Only I don't know what you are speaking of. I don't remember."

Gurov felt as though the boy were looking at him, yet not directly. He felt also vaguely conscious of another presence no less unfamiliar and alien than that of this curious stranger, and it seemed to him that the unfamiliar form of this other presence coincided with his own form. An ancient soul, as it were, had taken possession of Gurov and enveloped him in the long-lost freshness of its vernal attributes.

It was growing darker, and there was increasing purity and coolness in the air. There rose up in his soul the joy and ease of pristine existence. The stars glowed brilliantly in the dark sky. The boy spoke.

"We had undertaken to kill the Beast. I tell you this under the multitudinous gaze of the all-seeing sky. Perhaps you were frightened. That's quite likely too! We had planned a great, terrible affair, that our names might be honoured by future generations."

Soft, tranquil, and monotonous was the sound of a stream which purled its way in the nocturnal silence. The stream was invisible, but its nearness was soothing and refreshing. They stood under the broad shelter of a tree and continued the conversation begun at some other time.

Gurov asked: "Why do you say that I had left you in a moment of mortal danger? Who am I that I should be frightened and run away?"

The boy burst into a laugh. His mirth had the sound of music, and as it passed into speech his voice still quavered with sweet, melodious laughter.

"Aristomarchon, how cleverly you feign to have forgotten all! I don't understand what makes you do this, and with such a mastery that you bring reproaches against yourself which I have not even dreamt of. You had left me in a moment of mortal danger because it had to be, and you could not have helped me otherwise than by forsaking me at the moment. You will surely not remain stubborn in your denial when I remind you of the words of the Oracle?"

Gurov suddenly remembered. A brilliant light, as it were, unexpectedly illumined the dark domain of things forgotten. And in wild ecstasy, in a loud and joyous voice, he exclaimed: "One shall kill the Beast!"

The boy laughed. And Aristomarchon asked: "Did you kill the Beast, Timarides?"

"With what?" exclaimed Timarides. "However strong my hands are, I was not one who could kill the Beast with a blow of the fist. We, Aristomarchon, had not been prudent and we were unarmed. We were playing in the sand by the stream. The Beast came upon us suddenly and he laid his paw upon me. It was for me to offer up my life as a sweet sacrifice to glory and to a noble cause; it was for you to execute our plan. And while he was tormenting my defenceless and unresisting body, you, fleet-footed Aristomarchon, could have run for your lance, and killed the now blood-intoxicated Beast. But the Beast did not accept my sacrifice. I lay under him, quiescent and still, gazing into his bloodshot eyes. He held his heavy paw on my shoulder, his breath came in hot, uneven gasps, and he sent out low snarls. Afterwards, he put out his huge, hot tongue and licked my face; then he left me."

"Where is he now?" asked Aristomarchon.

In a voice strangely tranquil and strangely sonorous in the quiet arrested stillness of the humid air, Timarides replied: "He followed me. I do not know how long I have been wandering until I found you. He followed me. I led him on by the smell of my blood. I do not know why he has not touched me until now. But here I have enticed him to you. You had better get the weapon which you had hidden so carefully and kill the Beast, while I in my turn will leave you in the moment of mortal danger, eye to eye with the enraged creature. Here's luck to you, Aristomarchon!"

As soon as he uttered these words Timarides, started, to run. For a short time his cloak was visible in the darkness, a glimmering patch of white. And then he disappeared. In the same instant the air resounded with the savage bellowing of the Beast, and his ponderous tread became audible. Pushing aside the growth of shrubs there emerged from the darkness the huge, monstrous head of the Beast, flashing a livid fire out of its two enormous, flaming eyes. And in the dark silence of nocturnal trees the towering ferocious shape of the Beast loomed ominously as it approached Aristomarchon.

Terror filled Aristomarchon's heart.

"Where is the lance?" was the thought that quickly flashed across his brain.

And in that instant, feeling the fresh night breeze on his face, Aristomarchon realized that he was running from the Beast. His ponderous springs and his spasmodic roars resounded closer and closer behind him. And as the Beast came up with him a loud cry rent the silence of the night. The cry came from Aristomarchon, who, recalling then some ancient and terrible words, pronounced loudly the incantation of the walls.

And thus enchanted the walls erected themselves around him....

III

Enchanted, the walls stood firm and were lit up. A dreary light was cast upon them by the dismal electric lamp. Gurov was in his usual surroundings.

Again came the nimble Fever and kissed him with her yellow, dry lips, and caressed him with her dry, bony hands, which exhaled heat and cold. The same thin volume, with its white pages, lay on the little table beside the divan where, as before, Gurov rested in the caressing embrace of the affectionate Fever, who showered upon him her rapid kisses. And again there stood beside him, laughing and rustling, the tiny house sprites.

Gurov said loudly and indifferently: "The incantation of the walls!"

Then he paused. But in what consisted this incantation? He had forgotten the words. Or had they never existed at all?

The little, shifty, grey demons danced round the slender volume with its ghostly white pages, and kept on repeating with their rustling voices: "Our walls are strong. We are in the walls. We have nothing to fear from the outside."

In their midst stood one of them, a tiny object like themselves, yet different from the rest. He was all black. His mantle fell from his shoulders in folds of smoke and flame. His eyes flashed like lightning. Terror and joy alternated quickly.

Gurov spoke: "Who are you?"

The black demon answered: "I am the Invoker of the Beast. In one of your long-past existences you left the lacerated body of Timarides on the banks of a forest stream. The Beast had satiated himself on the beautiful body of your friend; he had gorged himself on the flesh that might have partaken of the fullness of earthly happiness; a creature of superhuman perfection had perished in order to gratify for a moment the appetite of the ravenous and ever insatiable Beast. And the blood, the wonderful blood, the sacred wine of happiness and joy, the wine of superhuman bliss – what had been the fate of this wonderful blood? Alas! The thirsty, ceaselessly thirsty Beast drank of it to gratify his momentary desire, and is thirsty anew. You had left the body of Timarides, mutilated by the Beast, on the banks of the forest stream; you forgot the promise you had given your valorous friend, and even the words of the ancient Oracle had not banished fear from your heart. And do you think that you are safe, that the Beast will not find you?"

There was austerity in the sound of his voice. While he was speaking the house sprites gradually ceased their dance; the little, grey house sprites stopped to listen to the Invoker of the Beast.

Gurov then said in reply: "I am not worried about the Beast! I have pronounced eternal enchantment upon my walls and the Beast shall never penetrate hither, into my enclosure."

The little grey ones were overjoyed, their voices tinkled with merriment and laughter; having gathered round, hand in hand, in a circle, they were on the point of bursting forth once more into dance, when the voice of the Invoker of the Beast rang out again, sharp and austere.

"But I am here. I am here because I have found you. I am here because the incantation of the walls is dead. I am here because Timarides is waiting and importuning me. Do you hear the gentle laugh of the brave, trusting lad? Do you hear the terrible bellowing of the Beast?"

From behind the wall, approaching nearer, could be heard the fearsome bellowing of the Beast.

"The Beast is bellowing behind the wall, the invincible wall!" exclaimed Gurov in terror. "My walls are enchanted for ever, and impregnable against foes."

Then spoke the black demon, and there was an imperious ring in his voice: "I tell you, man, the incantation of the walls is dead. And if you think you can save yourself by pronouncing the incantation of the walls, why then don't you utter the words?"

A cold shiver passed down Gurov's spine. The incantation! He had forgotten the words of the ancient spell. And what mattered it? Was not the ancient incantation dead – dead?

Everything about him confirmed with irrefutable evidence the death of the ancient incantation of the walls – because the walls, and the light and the shade which fell upon them, seemed dead and wavering. The Invoker of the Beast spoke terrible words. And Gurov's mind was now in a whirl, now in pain, and the affectionate Fever did not cease to torment him with her passionate kisses. Terrible words resounded, almost deadening his senses – while the Invoker of the Beast grew larger and larger, and hot fumes breathed from him, and grim terror. His eyes ejected fire, and when at last he grew so tall as to screen off the electric light, his black cloak suddenly fell from his shoulders. And Gurov recognized him – it was the boy Timarides.

"Will you kill the Beast?" asked Timarides in a sonorous voice. "I have enticed him, I have led him to you, I have destroyed the incantation of the walls. The cowardly gift of inimical gods, the incantation of the walls, had turned into naught my sacrifice, and had saved you from your action. But the ancient incantation of the walls is dead – be quick, then, to take hold of your sword and kill the Beast. I have been a boy – I have become the Invoker of the Beast. He had drunk of my blood, and now he thirsts anew; he had partaken also of my flesh, and he is hungry again, the insatiable, pitiless Beast. I have called him to you, and you, in fulfilment of your promise, may kill the Beast. Or die yourself."

He vanished. A terrible bellowing shook the walls. A gust of icy moisture blew across to Gurov.

The wall facing the spot where Gurov lay opened, and the huge, ferocious and monstrous Beast entered. Bellowing savagely, he approached Gurov and laid his ponderous paw upon his breast. Straight into his heart plunged the pitiless claws. A terrible pain shot through his whole body. Shifting his blood-red eyes the Beast inclined his head toward Gurov and, crumbling the bones of his victim with his teeth, began to devour his yet-palpitating heart.

The Ogre Courting

IN DAYS WHEN OGRES were still the terror of certain districts, there was one who had long kept a whole neighbourhood in fear without any one daring to dispute his tyranny.

By thefts and exactions, by heavy ransoms from merchants too old and tough to be eaten, in one way and another, the Ogre had become very rich; and although those who knew could tell of huge cellars full of gold and jewels, and yards and barns groaning with the weight of stolen goods, the richer he grew the more anxious and covetous he became. Moreover, day by day, he added to his stores; for though (like most ogres) he was as stupid as he was strong, no one had ever been found, by force or fraud, to get the better of him.

What he took from the people was not their heaviest grievance. Even to be killed and eaten by him was not the chance they thought of most. A man can die but once; and if he is a sailor, a shark may eat him, which is not so much better than being devoured by an ogre. No, that was not the worst. The worst was this – he would keep getting married. And as he liked little wives, all the short women lived in fear and dread. And as his wives always died very soon, he was constantly courting fresh ones.

Some said he ate his wives; some said he tormented, and others, that he only worked them to death. Everybody knew it was not a desirable match, and yet there was not a father who dare refuse his daughter if she were asked for. The Ogre only cared for two things in a woman – he liked her to be little, and a good housewife.

Now it was when the Ogre had just lost his twenty-fourth wife (within the memory of man) that these two qualities were eminently united in the person of the smallest and most notable woman of the district, the daughter of a certain poor farmer. He was so poor that he could not afford properly to dower his daughter, who had in consequence remained single beyond her first youth. Everybody felt sure that Managing Molly must now be married to the Ogre. The tall girls stretched themselves till they looked like maypoles, and said, "Poor thing!" The slatterns gossiped from house to house, the heels of their shoes clacking as they went, and cried that this was what came of being too thrifty.

And sure enough, in due time, the giant widower came to the farmer as he was in the field looking over his crops, and proposed for Molly there and then. The farmer was so much put out that he did not know what he said in reply, either when he was saying it, or afterwards, when his friends asked about it. But he remembered that the Ogre had invited himself to sup at the farm that day week.

Managing Molly did not distress herself at the news.

"Do what I bid you, and say as I say," said she to her father, "and if the Ogre does not change his mind, at any rate you shall not come empty-handed out of the business."

By his daughter's desire the farmer now procured a large number of hares, and a barrel of white wine, which expenses completely emptied his slender stocking, and on the day of the Ogre's visit, she made a delicious and savoury stew with the hares in the biggest pickling tub, and the wine-barrel was set on a bench near the table.

When the Ogre came, Molly served up the stew, and the Ogre sat down to sup, his head just touching the kitchen rafters. The stew was perfect, and there was plenty of it. For what Molly and her father ate was hardly to be counted in the tubful. The Ogre was very much pleased, and said politely:

"I'm afraid, my dear, that you have been put to great trouble and expense on my account, I have a large appetite, and like to sup well."

"Don't mention it, sir," said Molly. "The fewer rats the more corn. How do you cook them?"

"Not one of all the extravagant hussies I have had as wives ever cooked them at all," said the Ogre; and he thought to himself, "Such a stew out of rats! What frugality! What a housewife!"

When he broached the wine, he was no less pleased, for it was of the best.

"This, at any rate, must have cost you a great deal, neighbour," said he, drinking the farmer's health as Molly left the room.

"I don't know that rotten apples could be better used," said the farmer; "but I leave all that to Molly. Do you brew at home?"

"We give our rotten apples to the pigs," growled the Ogre. "But things will be better ordered when she is my wife."

The Ogre was now in great haste to conclude the match, and asked what dowry the farmer would give his daughter.

"I should never dream of giving a dowry with Molly," said the farmer, boldly. "Whoever gets her, gets dowry enough. On the contrary, I shall expect a good round sum from the man who deprives me of her. Our wealthiest farmer is just widowed, and therefore sure to be in a hurry for marriage. He has an eye to the main chance, and would not grudge to pay well for such a wife, I'll warrant."

"I'm no churl myself," said the Ogre, who was anxious to secure his thrifty bride at any price; and he named a large sum of money, thinking, "We shall live on rats henceforward, and the beef and mutton will soon cover the dowry."

"Double that, and we'll see," said the farmer, stoutly.

But the Ogre became angry, and cried; "What are you thinking of, man? Who is to hinder my carrying your lass off, without 'with your leave' or 'by your leave,' dowry or none?"

"How little you know her!" said the farmer. "She is so firm that she would be cut to pieces sooner than give you any benefit of her thrift, unless you dealt fairly in the matter."

"Well, well," said the Ogre, "let us meet each other." And he named a sum larger than he at first proposed, and less than the farmer had asked. This the farmer agreed to, as it was enough to make him prosperous for life.

"Bring it in a sack to-morrow morning," said he to the Ogre, "and then you can speak to Molly; she's gone to bed now."

The next morning, accordingly, the Ogre appeared, carrying the dowry in a sack, and Molly came to meet him.

"There are two things," said she, "I would ask of any lover of mine: a new farmhouse, built as I should direct, with a view to economy; and a feather-bed of fresh goose feathers, filled when the old woman plucks her geese. If I don't sleep well, I cannot work well."

"That is better than asking for finery," thought the Ogre; "and after all the house will be my own." So, to save the expense of labour, he built it himself, and worked hard, day after day, under Molly's orders, till winter came. Then it was finished.

"Now for the feather-bed," said Molly. "I'll sew up the ticking, and when the old woman plucks her geese, I'll let you know."

When it snows, they say the old woman up yonder is plucking her geese, and so at the first snowstorm Molly sent for the Ogre.

"Now you see the feathers falling," said she, "so fill the bed."

"How am I to catch them?" cried the Ogre.

"Stupid! don't you see them lying there in a heap?" cried Molly; "get a shovel, and set to work."

The Ogre accordingly carried in shovelfuls of snow to the bed, but as it melted as fast as he put it in, his labour never seemed done. Towards night the room got so cold that the snow would not melt, and now the bed was soon filled.

Molly hastily covered it with sheets and blankets, and said: "Pray rest here to-night, and tell me if the bed is not comfort itself. To-morrow we will be married."

So the tired Ogre lay down on the bed he had filled, but, do what he would, he could not get warm.

"The sheets must be damp," said he, and in the morning he woke with such horrible pains in his bones that he could hardly move, and half the bed had melted away. "It's no use," he groaned, "she's a very managing woman, but to sleep on such a bed would be the death of me." And he went off home as quickly as he could, before Managing Molly could call upon him to be married; for she was so managing that he was more than half afraid of her already.

When Molly found that he had gone, she sent the farmer after him.

"What does he want?" cried the Ogre, when they told him the farmer was at the door.

"He says the bride is waiting for you," was the reply.

"Tell him I'm too ill to be married," said the Ogre.

But the messenger soon returned:

"He says she wants to know what you will give her to make up for the disappointment."

"She's got the dowry, and the farm, and the feather-bed," groaned the Ogre; "what more does she want?"

But again the messenger returned:

"She says you've pressed the feather-bed flat, and she wants some more goose feathers."

"There are geese enough in the yard," yelled the Ogre, "Let him drive them home; and if he has another word to say, put him down to roast."

The farmer, who overheard this order, lost no time in taking his leave, and as he passed through the yard he drove home as fine a flock of geese as you will see on a common.

It is said that the Ogre never recovered from the effects of sleeping on the old woman's goose feathers, and was less powerful than before.

As for Managing Molly, being now well dowered, she had no lack of offers of marriage, and was soon mated to her mind.

The Flying Ogre

THERE ONCE LIVED in Sianfu an old Buddhist monk, who loved to wander in lonely places. In the course of his wanderings he once came to the Kuku-Nor, and there he saw a tree which was a thousand feet high and many cords in breadth. It was hollow inside and one could see the sky shining down into it from above.

When he had gone on a few miles, he saw in the distance a girl in a red coat, barefoot, and with unbound hair, who was running as fast as the wind. In a moment she stood before him.

"Take pity on me and save my life!" said she to him.

When the monk asked her what was the trouble, she replied: "A man is pursuing me. If you will tell him you have not seen me, I will be grateful to you all my life long!"

With that she ran up to the hollow tree and crawled into it.

When the monk had gone a little further, he met one who rode an armoured steed. He wore a garment of gold, a bow was slung across his shoulders, and a sword hung at his side. His horse ran with the speed of lightning, and covered a couple of miles with every step. Whether it ran in the air or on the ground, its speed was the same.

"Have you seen the girl in the red coat?" asked the stranger. And when the monk replied that he had seen nothing, the other continued: "Bonze, you should not lie! This girl is not a human being, but a flying ogre. Of flying ogres there are thousands of varieties, who bring ruin to people everywhere. I have already slain a countless number of them, and have pretty well done away with them. But this one is the worst of all. Last night the Lord of the Heavens gave me a triple command, and that is the reason I have hurried down from the skies. There are eight thousand of us under way in all directions to catch this monster. If you do not tell the truth, monk, then you are sinning against heaven itself!"

Upon that the monk did not dare deceive him, but pointed to the hollow tree. The messenger of the skies dismounted, stepped into the tree and looked about him. Then he once more mounted his horse, which carried him up the hollow trunk and out at the end of the tree. The monk looked up and could see a small, red flame come out of the tree-top. It was followed by the messenger of the skies. Both rose up to the clouds and disappeared. After a time there fell a rain of blood. The ogre had probably been hit by an arrow or captured.

Afterward the monk told the tale to the scholar who wrote it down.

The Ape Sun Wu King

FAR, FAR AWAY to the east, in the midst of the Great Sea there is an island called the Mountain of Flowers and Fruits. And on this mountain there is a high rock. Now this rock, from the very beginning of the world, had absorbed all the hidden seed power of heaven and earth and sun and moon, which endowed it with supernatural creative gifts. One day the rock burst, and out came an egg of stone. And out of this stone egg a stone ape was hatched by magic power. When he broke the shell he bowed to all sides. Then he gradually learned to walk and to leap, and two streams of golden radiance broke from his eyes which shot up to the highest of the castles of heaven, so that the Lord of the Heavens was frightened. So he sent out the two gods, Thousandmile-Eye and Fine-Ear, to find out what had happened. The two gods came back and reported: "The rays shine from the eyes of the stone ape who was hatched out of the egg which came from the magic rock. There is no reason for uneasiness."

Little by little the ape grew up, ran and leaped about, drank from the springs in the valleys, ate the flowers and fruits, and time went by in unconstrained play.

One day, during the summer, when he was seeking coolness, together with the other apes on the island, they went to the valley to bathe. There they saw a waterfall which plunged down a high cliff. Said the apes to each other: "Whoever can force his way through the waterfall, without suffering injury, shall be our king." The stone ape at once leaped into the air with joy and cried: "I will pass through!" Then he closed his eyes, bent down low and leaped through the roar and foam of the waters. When he opened his eyes once more he saw an iron bridge, which was shut off from the outer world by the waterfall as though by a curtain.

At its entrance stood a tablet of stone on which were graven the words: "This is the heavenly cave behind the water-curtain on the Blessed Island of Flowers and Fruits." Filled with joy, the stone ape leaped out again through the waterfall and told the other apes what he had found. They received the news with great content, and begged the stone ape to take them there. So the tribe of apes leaped through the water on the iron bridge, and then crowded into the cave castle where they found a hearth with a profusion of pots, cups and platters. But all were made of stone. Then the apes paid homage to the stone ape as their king, and he was given the name of Handsome King of the Apes. He appointed long-tailed, ring-tailed and other monkeys to be his officials and counsellors, servants and retainers, and they led a blissful life on the mountain, sleeping by night in their cave castle, keeping away from birds and beasts, and their king enjoyed untroubled happiness. In this way some three hundred years went by.

One day, when the King of the Apes sat with his subjects at a merry meal, he suddenly began to weep. Frightened, the apes asked him why he so suddenly grew sad amid all his bliss. Said the King: "It is true that we are not subject to the law and rule of man, that birds and beasts do not dare attack us, yet little by little we grow old and weak, and some day the hour will strike when Death, the Ancient, will drag us off! Then we are gone in a moment, and can no longer dwell upon earth!" When the apes heard these words, they hid their faces and sobbed. But an old ape, whose arms were connected in such a way that he could add the length of one to that of the other, stepped forth from the ranks. In a loud tone of voice he said: "That you have hit upon this thought, O King, shows the desire to search for truth has awakened you! Among all living creatures, there are but three kinds who are exempt from Death's power: the Buddhas, the blessed spirits and the gods. Whoever attains one of these three grades escapes the rod of re-birth, and lives as long as the Heavens themselves."

The King of the Apes said: "Where do these three kinds of beings live?" And the old ape replied: "They live in caves and on holy mountains in the great world of mortals." The King was pleased when he heard this, and told his apes that he was going to seek out gods and sainted spirits in order to learn the road to immortality from them. The apes dragged up peaches and other fruits and sweet wine to celebrate the parting banquet, and all made merry together.

On the following morning the Handsome King of the Apes rose very early, built him a raft of old pine trees and took a bamboo staff for a pole. Then he climbed on the raft, quite alone, and poled his way through the Great Sea. Wind and waves were favourable and he reached Asia. There he went ashore. On the strand he met a fisherman. He at once stepped up to him, knocked him down, tore off his clothes and put them on himself. Then he wandered around and visited all famous spots, went into the market-places, the densely populated cities, learned how to conduct himself properly, and how to speak and act like a well-bred human being. Yet his heart was set on learning the teaching of the Buddhas, the blessed spirits and the holy gods. But the people of the country in which he was were only concerned with honours and wealth. Not one of them seemed to care for life. Thus he went about until nine years had passed by unnoticed. Then he came to the strand of the Western Sea and it occurred to him: "No doubt there are gods and saints on the other side of the sea!" So he built another raft, floated it over the Western Sea and reached the land of the west. There he let his raft drift, and went ashore. After he had searched for many days, he suddenly saw a high mountain with deep, quiet valleys. As the Ape King went toward it, he heard a man singing in the woods, and the song sounded like one the blessed spirits might sing. So he hastily entered the wood to see who might be singing. There he met a wood-chopper at work. The Ape King bowed to him and said: "Venerable, divine master, I fall down and worship at your feet!"

Said the wood-chopper: "I am only a workman; why do you call me divine master?"

"Then, if you are no blessed god, how comes it you sing that divine song?" The wood-chopper laughed and said: "You are at home in music. The song I was singing was really taught me by a saint."

"If you are acquainted with a saint," said the Ape King, "he surely cannot live far from here. I beg of you to show me the way to his dwelling."

The wood-chopper replied: "It is not far from here. This mountain is known as the Mountain of the Heart. In it is a cave where dwells a saint who is called 'The Discerner.' The number of his disciples who have attained blessedness is countless. He still has some thirty to forty disciples gathered about him. You need only follow this path which leads to the south, and you cannot miss his dwelling." The Ape King thanked the wood-chopper and, sure enough, he came to the cave which the latter had described to him. The gate was locked and he did not venture to knock. So he leaped up into a pine tree, picked pine-cones and devoured the seed.

Before long one of the saint's disciples came and opened the door and said: "What sort of a beast is it that is making such a noise?" The Ape King leaped down from his tree, bowed, and said: "I have come in search of truth. I did not venture to knock." Then the disciple had to laugh and said: "Our master was seated lost in meditation, when he told me to lead in the seeker after truth who stood without the gate, and here you really are. Well, you may come along with me!" The Ape King smoothed his clothes, put his hat on straight, and stepped in. A long passage led past magnificent buildings and quiet hidden huts to the place where the master was sitting upright on a seat of white marble. At his right and left stood his disciples, ready to serve him. The Ape King flung himself down on the ground and greeted the master humbly. In answer to his questions he told him how he had found his way to him. And when he was asked his name, he said: "I have no name. I am the ape who came out of the stone." So the master said: "Then I will give you a name. I name you Sun Wu Kung." The Ape King thanked him, full of joy, and thereafter he was called Sun Wu Kung. The master ordered his oldest disciple to instruct Sun Wu Kung in sweeping and cleaning, in going in and out, in good manners, how to labour in the field and how to water the gardens. In the course of time he learned to write, to burn incense and read the sutras. And in this way some six or seven years went by.

One day the master ascended the seat from which he taught, and began to speak regarding the great truth. Sun Wu Kung understood the hidden meaning of his words, and commenced to jerk about and dance in his joy. The master reproved him: "Sun Wu Kung, you have still not laid aside your wild nature! What do you mean by carrying on in such an unfitting manner?" Sun Wu Kung bowed and answered: "I was listening attentively to you when the meaning of your words was disclosed to my heart, and without thinking I began to dance for joy. I was not giving way to my wild nature." Said the master: "If your spirit has really awakened, then I will announce the great truth to you. But there are three hundred and sixty ways by means of which one may reach this truth. Which way shall I teach you?" Said Sun Wu Kung: "Whichever you will, O Master!" Then the Master asked: "Shall I teach you the way of magic?" Said Sun Wu Kung: "What does magic teach one?" The Master replied: "It teaches one to raise up spirits, to question oracles, and to foretell fortune and misfortune."

"Can one secure eternal life by means of it?" inquired Sun Wu Kung.

"No," was the answer.

"Then I will not learn it."

"Shall I teach you the sciences?"

"What are the sciences?"

"They are the nine schools of the three faiths. You learn how to read the holy books, pronounce incantations, commune with the gods, and call the saints to you."

"Can one gain eternal life by means of them?"

"No."

"Then I will not learn them."

"The way of repose is a very good way."

"What is the way of repose?"

"It teaches how to live without nourishment, how to remain quiescent in silent purity, and sit lost in meditation."

"Can one gain eternal life in this way?"

"No."

"Then I will not learn it."

"The way of deeds is also a good way."

"What does that teach?"

"It teaches one to equalize the vital powers, to practise bodily exercise, to prepare the elixir of life and to hold one's breath."

"Will it give one eternal life?"

"Not so."

"Then I will not learn it! I will not learn it!"

Thereupon the Master pretended to be angry, leaped down from his stand, took his cane and scolded: "What an ape! This he will not learn, and that he will not learn! What are you waiting to learn, then?" With that he gave him three blows across the head, retired to his inner chamber, and closed the great door after him.

The disciples were greatly excited, and overwhelmed Sun Wu Kung with reproaches. Yet the latter paid no attention to them, but smiled quietly to himself, for he had understood the riddle which the Master had given him to solve. And in his heart he thought: "His striking me over the head three times meant that I was to be ready at the third watch of the night. His withdrawing to his inner chamber and closing the great door after him, meant that I was to go in to him by the back door, and that he would make clear the great truth to me in secret." Accordingly he waited until evening, and made a pretense of lying down to sleep with the other disciples. But when the third watch of the night had come he rose softly and crept to the back door. Sure enough it stood ajar. He slipped in and stepped before the Master's bed. The Master was sleeping with his face turned toward the wall, and the ape did not venture to wake him, but knelt down in front of the bed. After a time the Master turned around and hummed a stanza to himself:

"A hard, hard grind,Truth's lesson to expound.One talks oneself deaf, dumb and blind,Unless the right man's found."

Then Sun Wu Kung replied: "I am waiting here reverentially!"

The Master flung on his clothes, sat up in bed and said harshly: "Accursed ape! Why are you not asleep? What are you doing here?"

Sun Wu Kung answered: "Yet you pointed out to me yesterday that I was to come to you at the third watch of the night, by the back door, in order to be instructed in the truth. Therefore I have ventured to come. If you will teach me in the fulness of your grace, I will be eternally grateful to you."

Thought the Master to himself: "There is real intelligence in this ape's head, to have made him understand me so well." Then he replied: "Sun Wu Kung, it shall be granted you! I will speak freely with you. Come quite close to me, and then I will show you the way to eternal life."

With that he murmured into his ear a divine, magical incantation to further the concentration of his vital powers, and explained the hidden knowledge word for word. Sun Wu Kung listened to him eagerly, and in a short time had learned it by heart. Then he thanked his teacher, went out again and lay down to sleep. From that time forward he practised the right mode of breathing, kept guard over his soul and spirit, and tamed the natural instincts of his heart. And while he did so three more years passed by. Then the task was completed.

One day the Master said to him: "Three great dangers still threaten you. Everyone who wishes to accomplish something out of the ordinary is exposed to them, for he is pursued by the envy of demons and spirits. And only those who can overcome these three great dangers live as long as the heavens."

Then Sun Wu Kung was frightened and asked: "Is there any means of protection against these dangers?"

Then the Master again murmured a secret incantation into his ear, by means of which he gained the power to transform himself seventy-two times.

And when no more than a few days had passed Sun Wu Kung had learned the art.

One day the Master was walking before the cave in the company of his disciples. He called Sun Wu Kung up to him and asked: "What progress have you made with your art? Can you fly already?"

"Yes, indeed," said the ape.

"Then let me see you do so."

The ape leaped into the air to a distance of five or six feet from the ground. Clouds formed beneath his feet, and he was able to walk on them for several hundred yards. Then he was forced to drop down to earth again.

The Master said with a smile: "I call that crawling around on the clouds, not floating on them, as do the gods and saints who fly over the whole world in a single day. I will teach you the magic incantation for turning somersaults on the clouds. If you turn one of those somersaults you advance eighteen thousand miles at a clip."

Sun Wu Kung thanked him, full of joy, and from that time on he was able to move without limitation of space in any direction.

One day Sun Wu Kung was sitting together with the other disciples under the pine-tree by the gate, discussing the secrets of their teachings. Finally they asked him to show them some of his transforming arts. Sun Wu Kung could not keep his secret to himself, and agreed to do so.

With a smile he said: "Just set me a task! What do you wish me to change myself into?"

They said: "Turn yourself into a pine-tree."

So Sun Wu Kung murmured a magic incantation, turned around – and there stood a pine-tree before their very eyes. At this they all broke out into a horse-laugh. The Master heard the noise and came out of the gate, dragging his cane behind him.

"Why are you making such a noise?" he called out to them harshly.

Said they: "Sun Wu Kung has turned himself into a pine-tree, and this made us laugh."

"Sun Wu Kung, come here!" said the Master. "Now just tell me what tricks you are up to? Why do you have to turn yourself into a pine-tree? All the work you have done means nothing more to you than a chance to make magic for your companions to wonder at. That shows that your heart is not yet under control."

Humbly Sun Wu Kung begged his forgiveness.

But the Master said: "I bear you no ill will, but you must go away."

With tears in his eyes Sun Wu Kung asked him: "But where shall I go?"

"You must go back again whence you came," said the Master. And when Sun Wu Kung sadly bade him farewell, he threatened him: "Your savage nature is sure to bring down evil upon you some time. You must tell no one that you are my pupil. If you so much as breathe a word about it, I will fetch your soul and lock it up in the nethermost hell, so that you cannot escape for a thousand eternities."

Sun Wu Kung replied: "I will not say a word! I will not say a word!"

Then he once more thanked him for all the kindness shown him, turned a somersault and climbed up to the clouds.

Within the hour he had passed the seas, and saw the Mountain of Flowers and Fruits lying before him. Then he felt happy and at home again, let his cloud sink down to earth and cried: "Here I am back again, children!" And at once, from the valley, from behind the rocks, out of the grass and from amid the trees came his apes. They came running up by thousands, surrounded and greeted him, and inquired as to his adventures. Sun Wu Kung said: "I have now found the way to eternal life, and need fear Death the Ancient no longer." Then all the apes were overjoyed, and competed with each other in bringing flowers and fruits, peaches and wine, to welcome him. And again they honoured Sun Wu Kung as the Handsome Ape King.

Sun Wu Kung now gathered the apes about him and questioned them as to how they had fared during his absence.

Said they: "It is well that you have come back again, great king! Not long ago a devil came here who wanted to take possession of our cave by force. We fought with him, but he dragged away many of your children and will probably soon return."

Sun Wu Kung grew very angry and said: "What sort of a devil is this who dares be so impudent?"

The apes answered: "He is the Devil-King of Chaos. He lives in the north, who knows how many miles away. We only saw him come and go amid clouds and mist."

Sun Wu Kung said: "Wait, and I will see to him!" With that he turned a somersault and disappeared without a trace.

In the furthest north rises a high mountain, upon whose slope is a cave above which is the inscription: 'The Cave of the Kidneys.' Before the door little devils were dancing. Sun Wu Kung called harshly to them: "Tell your Devil-King quickly that he had better give me my children back again!" The little devils were frightened, and delivered the message in the cave. Then the Devil-King reached for his sword and came out. But he was so large and broad that he could not even see Sun Wu Kung. He was clad from head to foot in black armour, and his face was as black as the bottom of a kettle. Sun Wu Kung shouted at him: "Accursed devil, where are your eyes, that you cannot see the venerable Sun?" Then the devil looked to the ground and saw a stone ape standing before him, bare-headed, dressed in red, with a yellow girdle and black boots. So the Devil-King laughed and said: "You are not even four feet high, less than thirty years of age, and weaponless, and yet you venture to make such a commotion." Said Sun Wu Kung: "I am not too small for you; and I can make myself large at will. You scorn me because I am without a weapon, but my two fists can thresh to the very skies." With that he stooped, clenched his fists and began to give the devil a beating.

The devil was large and clumsy, but Sun Wu Kung leaped about nimbly. He struck him between the ribs and between the wind and his blows fell ever more fast and furious. In his despair the devil raised his great knife and aimed a blow at Sun Wu Kung's head. But the latter avoided the blow, and fell back on his magic powers of transformation. He pulled out a hair, put it in his mouth, chewed it, spat it out into the air and said: "Transform yourself!" And at once it turned into many hundreds of little apes who began to attack the devil. Sun Wu Kung, be it said, had eighty-four thousand hairs on his body, every single one of which he could transform. The little apes with their sharp eyes, leaped around with the greatest rapidity. They surrounded the Devil-King on all sides, tore at his clothes, and pulled at his legs, until he finally measured his length on the ground. Then Sun Wu Kung stepped up, tore his knife from his hand, and put an end to him. After that he entered the cave and released his captive children, the apes. The transformed hairs he drew to him again, and making a fire, he burned the evil cave to the ground. Then he gathered up those he had released, and flew back with them like a storm-wind to his cavern on the Mountain of Flowers and Fruits, joyfully greeted by all the apes.

After Sun Wu Kung had obtained possession of the Devil-King's great knife, he exercised his apes every day. They had wooden swords and lances of bamboo, and played their martial music on reed pipes. He had them build a camp so that they would be prepared for all dangers. Suddenly the thought came to Sun Wu Kung: "If we go on this way, perhaps we may incite some human or animal king to fight with us, and then we would not be able to withstand him with our wooden swords and bamboo lances!" And to his apes he said: "What should be done?" Four baboons stepped forward and said: "In the capital city of the Aulai empire there are warriors without number. And there coppersmiths and steelsmiths are also to be found. How would it be if we were to buy steel and iron and have those smiths weld weapons for us?"

A somersault and Sun Wu Kung was standing before the city moat. Said he to himself: "To first buy the weapons would take a great deal of time. I would rather make magic and take some." So he blew on the ground. Then a tremendous storm-wind arose which drove sand and stones before it, and caused all the soldiers in the city to run away in terror. Then Sun Wu Kung went to the armoury, pulled out one of his hairs, turned it into thousands of little apes, cleared out the whole supply of weapons, and flew back home on a cloud.

Then he gathered his people about him and counted them. In all they numbered seventy-seven thousand. They held the whole mountain in terror, and all the magic beasts and spirit princes who dwelt on it. And these came forth from seventy-two caves and honoured Sun Wu Kung as their head.

One day the Ape King said: "Now you all have weapons; but this knife which I took from the Devil-King is too light, and no longer suits me. What should be done?"

Then the four baboons stepped forward and said: "In view of your spirit powers, O king, you will find no weapon fit for your use on all the earth! Is it possible for you to walk through the water?"

The Ape King answered: "All the elements are subject to me and there is no place where I cannot go."

Then the baboons said: "The water at our cave here flows into the Great Sea, to the castle of the Dragon-King of the Eastern Sea. If your magic power makes it possible, you could go to the Dragon-King and let him give you a weapon."

This suited the Ape King. He leaped on the iron bridge and murmured an incantation. Then he flung himself into the waves, which parted before him and ran on till he came to the palace of water-crystal. There he met a Triton who asked who he was. He mentioned his name and said: "I am the Dragon-King's nearest neighbour, and have come to visit him." The Triton took the message to the castle, and the Dragon-King of the Eastern Sea came out hastily to receive him. He bade him be seated and served him with tea.

Sun Wu Kung said: "I have learned the hidden knowledge and gained the powers of immortality. I have drilled my apes in the art of warfare in order to protect our mountain; but I have no weapon I can use, and have therefore come to you to borrow one."

The Dragon-King now had General Flounder bring him a great spear. But Sun Wu Kung was not satisfied with it. Then he ordered Field-Marshal Eel to fetch in a nine-tined fork, which weighed three thousand six hundred pounds. But Sun Wu Kung balanced it in his hand and said: "Too light! Too light! Too light!"

Then the Dragon-King was frightened, and had the heaviest weapon in his armoury brought in. It weighed seven thousand two hundred pounds. But this was still too light for Sun Wu Kung. The Dragon-King assured him that he had nothing heavier, but Sun Wu Kung would not give in and said: "Just look around!"

Finally the Dragon-Queen and her daughter came out, and said to the Dragon-King: "This saint is an unpleasant customer with whom to deal. The great iron bar is still lying here in our sea; and not so long ago it shone with a red glow, which is probably a sign it is time for it to be taken away."

Said the Dragon-King: "But that is the rod which the Great Yu used when he ordered the waters, and determined the depth of the seas and rivers. It cannot be taken away."

The Dragon-Queen replied: "Just let him see it! What he then does with it is no concern of ours."

So the Dragon-King led Sun Wu Kung to the measuring rod. The golden radiance that came from it could be seen some distance off. It was an enormous iron bar, with golden clamps on either side.

Sun Wu Kung raised it with the exertion of all his strength, and then said: "It is too heavy, and ought to be somewhat shorter and thinner!"

No sooner had he said this than the iron rod grew less. He tried it again, and then he noticed that it grew larger or smaller at command. It could be made to shrink to the size of a pin. Sun Wu Kung was overjoyed and beat about in the sea with the rod, which he had let grow large again, till the waves spurted mountain-high and the dragon-castle rocked on its foundations. The Dragon-King trembled with fright, and all his tortoises, fishes and crabs drew in their heads.

Sun Wu Kung laughed, and said: "Many thanks for the handsome present!" Then he continued: "Now I have a weapon, it is true, but as yet I have no armour. Rather than hunt up two or three other households, I think you will be willing to provide me with a suit of mail."

The Dragon-King told him that he had no armour to give him.

Then the ape said: "I will not leave until you have obtained one for me." And once more he began to swing his rod.

"Do not harm me!" said the terrified Dragon-King, "I will ask my brothers."

And he had them beat the iron drum and strike the golden gong, and in a moment's time all the Dragon-King's brothers came from all the other seas. The Dragon-King talked to them in private and said: "This is a terrible fellow, and we must not rouse his anger! First he took the rod with the golden clamps from me, and now he also insists on having a suit of armour. The best thing to do would be to satisfy him at once, and complain of him to the Lord of the Heavens later."

So the brothers brought a magic suit of golden mail, magic boots and a magic helmet.

Then Sun Wu Kung thanked them and returned to his cave. Radiantly he greeted his children, who had come to meet him, and showed them the rod with the golden clamps. They all crowded up and wished to pick it up from the ground, if only a single time; but it was just as though a dragon-fly had attempted to overthrow a stone column, or an ant were trying to carry a great mountain. It would not move a hair's breadth. Then the apes opened their mouths and stuck out their tongues, and said: "Father, how is it possible for you to carry that heavy thing?" So he told them the secret of the rod and showed them its effects. Then he set his empire in order, and appointed the four baboons field-marshals; and the seven beast-spirits, the ox-spirit, the dragon-spirit, the bird-spirit, the lion-spirit and the rest also joined him.

One day he took a nap after dinner. Before he did so he had let the bar shrink, and had stuck it in his ear. While he was sleeping he saw two men come along in his dream, who had a card on which was written 'Sun Wu Kung.' They would not allow him to resist, but fettered him and led his spirit away. And when they reached a great city the Ape King gradually came to himself. Over the city gate he saw a tablet of iron on which was engraved in large letters: 'The Nether World.'

Then all was suddenly clear to him and he said: "Why, this must be the dwelling-place of Death! But I have long since escaped from his power, and how dare he have me dragged here!" The more he reflected the wilder he grew. He drew out the golden rod from his ear, swung it and let it grow large. Then he crushed the two constables to mush, burst his fetters, and rolled his bar before him into the city. The ten Princes of the Dead were frightened, bowed before him and asked: "Who are you?"

Sun Wu Kung answered: "If you do not know me then why did you send for me and have me dragged to this place? I am the heaven-born saint Sun Wu Kung of the Mountain of Flowers and Fruits. And now, who are you? Tell me your names quickly or I will strike you!"

The ten Princes of the Dead humbly gave him their names.

Sun Wu Kung said: "I, the Venerable Sun, have gained the power of eternal life! You have nothing to say to me! Quick, let me have the Book of Life!"

They did not dare defy him, and had the scribe bring in the book. Sun Wu Kung opened it. Under the head of 'Apes,' No. 1350, he read: "Sun Wu Kung, the heaven-born stone ape. His years shall be three hundred and twenty-four. Then he shall die without illness."

Sun Wu Kung took the brush from the table and struck out the whole ape family from the Book of Life, threw the book down and said: "Now we are even! From this day on I will suffer no impertinences from you!"

With that he cleared a way for himself out of the Nether World by means of his rod, and the ten Princes of the Dead did not venture to stay him, but only complained of him afterward to the Lord of the Heavens.

When Sun Wu Kung had left the city he slipped and fell to the ground. This caused him to wake, and he noticed he had been dreaming. He called his four baboons to him and said: "Splendid, splendid! I was dragged to Death's castle and I caused considerable uproar there. I had them give me the Book of Life, and I struck out the mortal hour of all the apes!" And after that time the apes on the mountain no longer died, because their names had been stricken out in the Nether World.

But the Lord of the Heavens sat in his castle, and had all his servants assembled about him. And a saint stepped forward and presented the complaint of the Dragon-King of the Eastern Sea. And another stepped forward and presented the complaint of the ten Princes of the Dead. The Lord of the Heavens glanced through the two memorials. Both told of the wild, unmannerly conduct of Sun Wu Kung. So the Lord of the Heavens ordered a god to descend to earth and take him prisoner. The Evening Star came forward, however, and said: "This ape was born of the purest powers of heaven and earth and sun and moon. He has gained the hidden knowledge and has become an immortal. Recall, O Lord, your great love for all that which has life, and forgive him his sin! Issue an order that he be called up to the heavens, and be given a charge here, so that he may come to his senses. Then, if he again oversteps your commands, let him be punished without mercy." The Lord of the Heavens was agreeable, had the order issued, and told the Evening Star to take it to Sun Wu Kung. The Evening Star mounted a coloured cloud and descended on the Mountain of Flowers and Fruits.

He greeted Sun Wu Kung and said to him: "The Lord had heard of your actions and meant to punish you. I am the Evening Star of the Western Skies, and I spoke for you. Therefore he has commissioned me to take you to the skies, so that you may be given a charge there."

Sun Wu Kung was overjoyed and answered: "I had just been thinking I ought to pay Heaven a visit some time, and sure enough, Old Star, here you have come to fetch me!"

Then he had his four baboons come and said to them impressively: "See that you take good care of our mountain! I am going up to the heavens to look around there a little!"

Then he mounted a cloud together with the Evening Star and floated up. But he kept turning his somersaults, and advanced so quickly that the Evening Star on his cloud was left behind. Before he knew it he had reached the Southern Gate of Heaven and was about to step carelessly through. The gate-keeper did not wish to let him enter, but he did not let this stop him. In the midst of their dispute the Evening Star came up and explained matters, and then he was allowed to enter the heavenly gate. When he came to the castle of the Lord of the Heavens, he stood upright before it, without bowing his head.

The Lord of the Heavens asked: "Then this hairy face with the pointed lips is Sun Wu Kung?"

He replied: "Yes, I am the Venerable Sun!"

All the servants of the Lord of the Heavens were shocked and said: "This wild ape does not even bow, and goes so far as to call himself the Venerable Sun. His crime deserves a thousand deaths!"

But the Lord said: "He has come up from the earth below, and is not as yet used to our rules. We will forgive him."

Then he gave orders that a charge be found for him. The marshal of the heavenly court reported: "There is no charge vacant anywhere, but an official is needed in the heavenly stables." Thereupon the Lord made him stablemaster of the heavenly steeds. Then the servants of the Lord of the Heavens told him he should give thanks for the grace bestowed on him. Sun Wu Kung called out aloud: "Thanks to command!" took possession of his certificate of appointment, and went to the stables in order to enter upon his new office.

Sun Wu Kung attended to his duties with great zeal. The heavenly steeds grew sleek and fat, and the stables were filled with young foals. Before he knew it half a month had gone by. Then his heavenly friends prepared a banquet for him.

While they were at table Sun Wu Kung asked accidentally: "Stablemaster? What sort of a title is that?"

"Why, that is an official title," was the reply.

"What rank has this office?"

"It has no rank at all," was the answer.

"Ah," said the ape, "is it so high that it outranks all other dignities?"

"No, it is not high, it is not high at all," answered his friends. "It is not even set down in the official roster, but is quite a subordinate position. All you have to do is to attend to the steeds. If you see to it that they grow fat, you get a good mark; but if they grow thin or ill, or fall down, your punishment will be right at hand."

Then the Ape King grew angry: "What, they treat me, the Venerable Sun, in such a shameful way!" and he started up. "On my mountain I was a king, I was a father! What need was there for him to lure me into his heaven to feed horses? I'll do it no longer! I'll do it no longer!"

Hola, and he had already overturned the table, drawn the rod with the golden clamps from his ear, let it grow large and beat a way out for himself to the Southern gate of Heaven. And no one dared stop him.

Already he was back in his island mountain and his people surrounded him and said: "You have been gone for more than ten years, great king! How is it you do not return to us until now?"

The Ape King said: "I did not spend more than about ten days in Heaven. This Lord of the Heavens does not know how to treat his people. He made me his stablemaster, and I had to feed his horses. I am so ashamed that I am ready to die. But I did not put up with it, and now I am here once more!"

His apes eagerly prepared a banquet to comfort him. While they sat at table two horned devil-kings came and brought him a yellow imperial robe as a present. Filled with joy he slipped into it, and appointed the two devil-kings leaders of the vanguard. They thanked him and began to flatter him: "With your power and wisdom, great king, why should you have to serve the Lord of the Heavens? To call you the Great Saint who is Heaven's Equal would be quite in order."

The ape was pleased with this speech and said: "Good, good!" Then he ordered his four baboons to have a flag made quickly, on which was to be inscribed: 'The Great Saint Who Is Heaven's Equal.' And from that time on he had himself called by that title.

When the Lord of the Heavens learned of the flight of the ape, he ordered Li Dsing, the pagoda-bearing god, and his third son, Notscha, to take the Ape King prisoner. They sallied forth at the head of a heavenly warrior host, laid out a camp before his cave, and sent a brave warrior to challenge him to single combat. But he was easily beaten by Sun Wu Kung and obliged to flee, and Sun Wu Kung even shouted after him, laughing: "What a bag of wind! And he calls himself a heavenly warrior! I'll not slay you. Run along quickly and send me a better man!"

When Notscha saw this he himself hurried up to do battle.

Said Sun Wu Kung to him: "To whom do you belong, little one? You must not play around here, for something might happen to you!"

But Notscha cried out in a loud voice: "Accursed ape! I am Prince Notscha, and have been ordered to take you prisoner!" And with that he swung his sword in the direction of Sun Wu Kung.

"Very well," said the latter, "I will stand here and never move."

Then Notscha grew very angry, and turned into a three-headed god with six arms, in which he held six different weapons. Thus he rushed on to the attack.

Sun Wu Kung laughed. "The little fellow knows the trick of it! But easy, wait a bit! I will change shape, too!"

And he also turned himself into a figure with three heads and with six arms, and swung three gold-clamp rods. And thus they began to fight. Their blows rained down with such rapidity that it seemed as though thousands of weapons were flying through the air. After thirty rounds the combat had not yet been decided. Then Sun Wu Kung hit upon an idea. He secretly pulled out one of his hairs, turned it into his own shape, and let it continue the fight with Notscha. He himself, however, slipped behind Notscha, and gave him such a blow on the left arm with his rod that his knees gave way beneath him with pain, and he had to withdraw in defeat.

So Notscha told his father Li Dsing: "This devil-ape is altogether too powerful! I cannot get the better of him!" There was nothing left to do but to return to the Heavens and admit their overthrow. The Lord of the Heavens bowed his head, and tried to think of some other hero whom he might send out.

Then the Evening Star once more came forward and said: "This ape is so strong and so courageous, that probably not one of us here is a match for him. He revolted because the office of stablemaster appeared too lowly for him. The best thing would be to temper justice with mercy, let him have his way, and appoint him Great Saint Who Is Heaven's Equal. It will only be necessary to give him the empty title, without combining a charge with it, and then the matter would be settled."

The Lord of the Heavens was satisfied with this suggestion, and once more sent the Evening Star to summon the new saint. When Sun Wu Kung heard that he had arrived, he said: "The old Evening Star is a good fellow!" and he had his army draw up in line to give him a festive reception. He himself donned his robes of ceremony and politely went out to meet him.

Then the Evening Star told him what had taken place in the Heavens, and that he had his appointment as Great Saint Who Is Heaven's Equal with him.

Thereupon the Great Saint laughed and said: "You also spoke in my behalf before, Old Star! And now you have again taken my part. Many thanks! Many thanks!"

Then when they appeared together in the presence of the Lord of the Heavens the latter said: "The rank of Great Saint Who Is Heaven's Equal is very high. But now you must not cut any further capers."

The Great Saint expressed his thanks, and the Lord of the Heavens ordered two skilled architects to build a castle for him east of the peach-garden of the Queen-Mother of the West. And he was led into it with all possible honours.

Now the Saint was in his element. He had all that heart could wish for, and was untroubled by any work. He took his ease, walked about in the Heavens as he chose, and paid visits to the gods. The Three Pure Ones and the Four Rulers he treated with some little respect; but the planetary gods and the lords of the twenty-eight houses of the moon, and of the twelve zodiac signs, and the other stars he addressed familiarly with a "Hey, you!" Thus he idled day by day, without occupation among the clouds of the Heavens. On one occasion one of the wise said to the Lord of the Heavens: "The holy Sun is idle while day follows day. It is to be feared that some mischievous thoughts may occur to him, and it might be better to give him some charge."

So the Lord of the Heavens summoned the Great Saint and said to him: "The life-giving peaches in the garden of the Queen-Mother will soon be ripe. I give you the charge of watching over them. Do your duty conscientiously!"

This pleased the Saint and he expressed his thanks. Then he went to the garden, where the caretakers and gardeners received him on their knees.

He asked them: "How many trees in all are there in the garden?"

"Three thousand six hundred," replied the gardener. "There are twelve-hundred trees in the foremost row. They have red blossoms and bear small fruit, which ripens every three thousand years. Whoever eats it grows bright and healthy. The twelve hundred trees in the middle row have double blossoms and bear sweet fruit, which ripens every six thousand years. Whoever eats of it is able to float in the rose-dawn without aging. The twelve hundred trees in the last row bear red-striped fruit with small pits. They ripen every nine thousand years. Whoever eats their fruit lives eternally, as long as the Heavens themselves, and remains untouched for thousands of eons."

The Saint heard all this with pleasure. He checked up the lists and from that time on appeared every day or so to see to things. The greater part of the peaches in the last row were already ripe. When he came to the garden, he would on each occasion send away the caretakers and gardeners under some pretext, leap up into the trees, and gorge himself to his heart's content with the peaches.

At that time the Queen-Mother of the West was preparing the great peach banquet to which she was accustomed to invite all the gods of the Heavens. She sent out the fairies in their garments of seven colours with baskets, that they might pick the peaches. The caretaker said to them: "The garden has now been entrusted to the guardianship of the Great Saint Who is Heaven's Equal, so you will first have to announce yourselves to him." With that he led the seven fairies into the garden. There they looked everywhere for the Great Saint, but could not find him. So the fairies said: "We have our orders and must not be late. We will begin picking the peaches in the meantime!" So they picked several baskets full from the foremost row. In the second row the peaches were already scarcer. And in the last row there hung only a single half-ripe peach. They bent down the bough and picked it, and then allowed it to fly up again.

Now it happened that the Great Saint, who had turned himself into a peach-worm, had just been taking his noon-day nap on this bough. When he was so rudely awakened, he appeared in his true form, seized his rod and was about to strike the fairies.

But the fairies said: "We have been sent here by the Queen-Mother. Do not be angry, Great Saint!"

Said the Great Saint: "And who are all those whom the Queen-Mother has invited?"

They answered: "All the gods and saints in the Heavens, on the earth and under the earth."

"Has she also invited me?" said the Saint.

"Not that we know of," said the fairies.

Then the Saint grew angry, murmured a magic incantation and said: "Stay! Stay! Stay!"

With that the seven fairies were banned to the spot. The Saint then took a cloud and sailed away on it to the palace of the Queen-Mother.

On the way he met the Bare-Foot God and asked him: "Where are you going?"

"To the peach banquet," was the answer.

Then the Saint lied to him, saying: "I have been commanded by the Lord of the Heavens to tell all the gods and saints that they are first to come to the Hall of Purity, in order to practise the rites, and then go together to the Queen-Mother."

Then the Great Saint changed himself into the semblance of the Bare-Foot God and sailed to the palace of the Queen-Mother. There he let his cloud sink down and entered quite unconcerned. The meal was ready, yet none of the gods had as yet appeared. Suddenly the Great Saint caught the aroma of wine, and saw well-nigh a hundred barrels of the precious nectar standing in a room to one side. His mouth watered. He tore a few hairs out and turned them into sleep-worms. These worms crept into the nostrils of the cup-bearers so that they all fell asleep. Thereupon he enjoyed the delicious viands to the full, opened the barrels and drank until he was nearly stupefied. Then he said to himself: "This whole affair is beginning to make me feel creepy. I had better go home first of all and sleep a bit." And he stumbled out of the garden with uncertain steps. Sure enough, he missed his way, and came to the dwelling of Laotzse. There he regained consciousness. He arranged his clothing and went in. There was no one to be seen in the place, for at the moment Laotzse was at the God of Light's abode, talking to him, and with him were all his servants, listening. Since he found no one at home the Great Saint went as far as the inner chamber, where Laotzse was in the habit of brewing the elixir of life. Beside the stove stood five gourd containers full of the pills of life which had already been rolled. Said the Great Saint: "I had long since intended to prepare a couple of these pills. So it suits me very well to find them here." He poured out the contents of the gourds, and ate up all the pills of life. Since he had now had enough to eat and drink he thought to himself: "Bad, bad! The mischief I have done cannot well be repaired. If they catch me my life will be in danger. I think I had better go down to earth again and remain a king!" With that he made himself invisible, went out at the Western Gate of Heaven, and returned to the Mountain of Flowers and Fruits, where he told his people who received him the story of his adventures.

When he spoke of the wine-nectar of the peach garden, his apes said: "Can't you go back once more and steal a few bottles of the wine, so that we too may taste of it and gain eternal life?"

The Ape King was willing, turned a somersault, crept into the garden unobserved, and picked up four more barrels. Two of them he took under his arms and two he held in his hands. Then he disappeared with them without leaving a trace and brought them to his cave, where he enjoyed them together with his apes.

In the meantime the seven fairies, whom the Great Saint had banned to the spot, had regained their freedom after a night and a day. They picked up their baskets and told the Queen-Mother what had happened to them. And the cup-bearers, too, came hurrying up and reported the destruction which someone unknown had caused among the eatables and drinkables. The Queen-Mother went to the Lord of the Heavens to complain. Shortly afterward Laotzse also came to him to tell about the theft of the pills of life. And the Bare-Foot God came along and reported that he had been deceived by the Great Saint Who Is Heaven's Equal; and from the Great Saint's palace the servants came running and said that the Saint had disappeared and was nowhere to be found. Then the Lord of the Heavens was frightened, and said: "This whole mess is undoubtedly the work of that devilish ape!"

Now the whole host of Heaven, together with all the star-gods, the time-gods and the mountain-gods was called out in order to catch the ape. Li Dsing once more was its commander-in-chief. He invested the entire mountain, and spread out the sky-net and the earth-net, so that no one could escape. Then he sent his bravest heroes into battle. Courageously the ape withstood all attacks from early morn till sundown. But by that time his most faithful followers had been captured. That was too much for him. He pulled out a hair and turned it into thousands of Ape-Kings, who all hewed about them with golden-clamped iron rods. The heavenly host was vanquished, and the ape withdrew to his cave to rest.

Now it happened that Guan Yin had also gone to the peach banquet in the garden, and had found out what Sun Wu Kung had done. When she went to visit the Lord of the Heavens, Li Dsing was just coming in, to report the great defeat which he had suffered on the Mountain of Flowers and Fruits. Then Guan Yin said to the Lord of the Heavens: "I can recommend a hero to you who will surely get the better of the ape. It is your grandson Yang Oerlang. He has conquered all the beast and bird spirits, and overthrown the elves in the grass and the brush. He knows what has to be done to get the better of such devils."

So Yang Oerlang was brought in, and Li Dsing led him to his camp. Li Dsing asked Yang Oerlang how he would go about getting the better of the ape.

Yang Oerlang laughed and said: "I think I will have to go him one better when it comes to changing shapes. It would be best for you to take away the sky-net so that our combat is not disturbed." Then he requested Li Dsing to post himself in the upper air with the magic spirit mirror in his hand, so that when the ape made himself invisible, he might be found again by means of the mirror. When all this had been arranged, Yang Oerlang went out in front of the cave with his spirits to give battle.

The ape leaped out, and when he saw the powerful hero with the three-tined sword standing before him he asked: "And who may you be?"

The other said: "I am Yang Oerlang, the grandson of the Lord of the Heavens!"

Then the ape laughed and said: "Oh yes, I remember! His daughter ran away with a certain Sir Yang, to whom heaven gave a son. You must be that son!"

Yang Oerlang grew furious, and advanced upon him with his spear. Then a hot battle began. For three hundred rounds they fought without decisive results. Then Yang Oerlang turned himself into a giant with a black face and red hair.

"Not bad," said the ape, "but I can do that too!"

So they continued to fight in that form. But the ape's baboons were much frightened. The beast and planet spirits of Yang Oerlang pressed the apes hard. They slew most of them and the others hid away. When the ape saw this his heart grew uneasy. He drew the magic giant-likeness in again, took his rod and fled. But Yang Oerlang followed hard on his heels. In his urgent need the ape thrust the rod, which he had turned into a needle, into his ear, turned into a sparrow, and flew up into the crest of a tree. Yang Oerlang who was following in his tracks, suddenly lost sight of him. But his keen eyes soon recognized that he had turned himself into a sparrow. So he flung away spear and crossbow, turned himself into a sparrow-hawk, and darted down on the sparrow. But the latter soared high into the air as a cormorant. Yang Oerlang shook his plumage, turned into a great sea-crane, and shot up into the clouds to seize the cormorant. The latter dropped, flew into a valley and dove beneath the waters of a brook in the guise of a fish. When Yang Oerlang reached the edge of the valley, and had lost his trail he said to himself: "This ape has surely turned himself into a fish or a crab! I will change my form as well in order to catch him." So he turned into a fish-hawk and floated above the surface of the water. When the ape in the water caught sight of the fish-hawk, he saw that he was Yang Oerlang. He swiftly swung around and fled, Yang Oerlang in pursuit. When the latter was no further away than the length of a beak, the ape turned, crept ashore as a water-snake and hid in the grass. Yang Oerlang, when he saw the water-snake creep from the water, turned into an eagle and spread his claws to seize the snake. But the water-snake sprang up and turned into the lowest of all birds, a speckled buzzard, and perched on the steep edge of a cliff. When Yang Oerlang saw that the ape had turned himself into so contemptible a creature as a buzzard, he would no longer play the game of changing form with him. He reappeared in his original form, took up his crossbow and shot at the bird. The buzzard slipped and fell down the side of the cliff. At its foot the ape turned himself into the chapel of a field-god. He opened his mouth for a gate, his teeth became the two wings of the door, his tongue the image of the god, and his eyes the windows. His tail was the only thing he did not know what to do with. So he let it stand up stiffly behind him in the shape of a flagpole. When Yang Oerlang reached the foot of the hill he saw the chapel, whose flagpole stood in the rear. Then he laughed and said: "That ape is really a devil of an ape! He wants to lure me into the chapel in order to bite me. But I will not go in. First I will break his windows for him, and then I will stamp down the wings of his door!" When the ape heard this he was much frightened. He made a bound like a tiger, and disappeared without a trace in the air. With a single somersault he reached Yang Oerlang's own temple. There he assumed Yang Oerlang's own form and stepped in. The spirits who were on guard were unable to recognize him. They received him on their knees. So the ape then seated himself on the god's throne, and had the prayers which had come in submitted to him.

When Yang Oerlang no longer saw the ape, he rose in the air to Li Dsing and said: "I was vying with the ape in changing shape. Suddenly I could no longer find him. Take a look in the mirror!" Li Dsing took a look in the magic spirit mirror and then he laughed and said: "The ape has turned himself into your likeness, is sitting in your temple quite at home there, and making mischief."

When Yang Oerlang heard this he took his three-tined spear, and hastened to his temple. The door-spirits were frightened and said: "But father came in only this very minute! How is it that another one comes now?" Yang Oerlang, without paying attention to them, entered the temple and aimed his spear at Sun Wu Kung. The latter resumed his own shape, laughed and said: "Young sir, you must not be angry! The god of this place is now Sun Wu Kung." Without uttering a word Yang Oerlang assailed him. Sun Wu Kung took up his rod and returned the blows. Thus they crowded out of the temple together, fighting, and wrapped in mists and clouds once more gained the Mountain of Flowers and Fruits.

In the meantime Guan Yin was sitting with Laotzse, the Lord of the Heavens and the Queen-Mother in the great hall of Heaven, waiting for news. When none came she said: "I will go with Laotzse to the Southern Gate of Heaven and see how matters stand." And when they saw that the struggle had still not come to an end she said to Laotzse: "How would it be if we helped Yang Oerlang a little? I will shut up Sun Wu Kung in my vase."

But Laotzse said: "Your vase is made of porcelain. Sun Wu Kung could smash it with his iron rod. But I have a circlet of diamonds which can enclose all living creatures. That we can use!" So he flung his circlet through the air from the heavenly gate, and struck Sun Wu Kung on the head with it. Since he had his hands full fighting, the latter could not guard himself against it, and the blow on the forehead caused him to slip. Yet he rose again and tried to escape. But the heavenly hound of Yang Oerlang bit his leg until he fell to the ground. Then Yang Oerlang and his followers came up and tied him with thongs, and thrust a hook through his collar-bone so that he could no longer transform himself. And Laotzse took possession of his diamond circlet again, and returned with Guan Yin to the hall of Heaven. Sun Wu Kung was now brought in in triumph, and was condemned to be beheaded. He was then taken to the place of execution and bound to a post. But all efforts to kill him by means of ax and sword, thunder and lightning were vain. Nothing so much as hurt a hair on his head.

Said Laotzse: "It is not surprising. This ape has eaten the peaches, has drunk the nectar and also swallowed the pills of life. Nothing can harm him. The best thing would be for me to take him along and thrust him into my stove in order to melt the elixir of life out of him again. Then he will fall into dust and ashes."

So Sun Wu Kung's fetters were loosed, and Laotzse took him with him, thrust him into his oven, and ordered the boy to keep up a hot fire.

But along the edge of the oven were graven the signs of the eight elemental forces. And when the ape was thrust into the oven he took refuge beneath the sign of the wind, so that the fire could not injure him; and the smoke only made his eyes smart. He remained in the oven seven times seven days. Then Laotzse had it opened to take a look. As soon as Sun Wu Kung saw the light shine in, he could no longer bear to be shut up, but leaped out and upset the magic oven. The guards and attendants he threw to the ground and Laotzse himself, who tried to seize him, received such a push that he stuck his legs up in the air like an onion turned upside down. Then Sun Wu Kung took his rod out of his ear, and without looking where he struck, hewed everything to bits, so that the star-gods closed their doors and the guardians of the Heavens ran away. He came to the castle of the Lord of the Heavens, and the guardian of the gate with his steel whip was only just in time to hold him back. Then the thirty-six thunder gods were set at him, and surrounded him, though they could not seize him.

The Lord of the Heavens said: "Buddha will know what is to be done. Send for him quickly!"

So Buddha came up out of the west with Ananada and Kashiapa, his disciples. When he saw the turmoil he said: "First of all, let weapons be laid aside and lead out the Saint. I wish to speak with him!" The gods withdrew. Sun Wu Kung snorted and said: "Who are you, who dare to speak to me?" Buddha smiled and replied: "I have come out of the blessed west, Shakiamuni Amitofu. I have heard of the revolt you have raised, and am come to tame you!"

Said Sun Wu Kung: "I am the stone ape who has gained the hidden knowledge. I am master of seventy-two transformations, and will live as long as Heaven itself. What has the Lord of the Heavens accomplished that entitles him to remain eternally on his throne? Let him make way for me, and I will be satisfied!"

Buddha replied with a smile: "You are a beast which has gained magic powers. How can you expect to rule here as Lord of the Heavens? Be it known to you that the Lord of the Heavens has toiled for eons in perfecting his virtues. How many years would you have to pass before you could attain the dignity he has gained? And then I must ask you whether there is anything else you can do, aside from playing your tricks of transformation?"

Said Sun Wu Kung: "I can turn cloud somersaults. Each one carries me eighteen thousand miles ahead. Surely that is enough to entitle me to be the Lord of the Heavens?"

Buddha answered with a smile: "Let us make a wager. If you can so much as leave my hand with one of your somersaults, then I will beg the Lord of the Heavens to make way for you. But if you are not able to leave my hand, then you must yield yourself to my fetters."

Sun Wu Kung suppressed his laughter, for he thought: "This Buddha is a crazy fellow! His hand is not a foot long; how could I help but leap out of it?" So he opened his mouth wide and said: "Agreed!"

Buddha then stretched out his right hand. It resembled a small lotus-leaf. Sun Wu Kung leaped up into it with one bound. Then he said: "Go!" And with that he turned one somersault after another, so that he flew along like a whirlwind. And while he was flying along he saw five tall, reddish columns towering to the skies. Then he thought: "That is the end of the world! Now I will turn back and become Lord of the Heavens. But first I will write down my name to prove that I was there." He pulled out a hair, turned it into a brush, and wrote with great letters on the middle column: 'The Great Saint Who Is Heaven's Equal.' Then he turned his somersaults again until he had reached the place whence he had come. He leaped down from the Buddha's hand laughing and cried: "Now hurry, and see to it that the Lord of the Heavens clears his heavenly castle for me! I have been at the end of the world and have left a sign there!"

Buddha scolded: "Infamous ape! How dare you claim that you have left my hand? Take a look and see whether or not 'The Great Saint Who Is Heaven's Equal,' is written on my middle finger!"

Sun Wu Kung was terribly frightened, for at the first glance he saw that this was the truth. Yet outwardly he pretended that he was not convinced, said he would take another look, and tried to make use of the opportunity to escape. But Buddha covered him with his hand, shoved him out of the gate of Heaven, and formed a mountain of water, fire, wood, earth and metal, which he softly set down on him to hold him fast. A magic incantation pasted on the mountain prevented his escape.

Here he was obliged to lie for hundreds of years, until he finally reformed and was released, in order to help the Monk of the Yangtze-kiang fetch the holy writings from out of the west. He honoured the Monk as his master, and thenceforward was known as the Wanderer. Guan Yin, who had released him, gave the Monk a golden circlet. Sun Wu Kung was induced to put it on, and it at once grew into his flesh so that he could not remove it. And Guan Yin gave the Monk a magic formula by means of which the ring could be tightened, should the ape grow disobedient. But from that time on he was always polite and well-mannered.

The Strange Tale of Doctor Dog

FAR UP IN the mountains of the Province of Hunan in the central part of China, there once lived in a small village a rich gentleman who had only one child. This girl, like the daughter of Kwan-yu in the story of the Great Bell, was the very joy of her father's life.

Now Mr. Min, for that was this gentleman's name, was famous throughout the whole district for his learning, and, as he was also the owner of much property, he spared no effort to teach Honeysuckle the wisdom of the sages, and to give her everything she craved. Of course this was enough to spoil most children, but Honeysuckle was not at all like other children. As sweet as the flower from which she took her name, she listened to her father's slightest command, and obeyed without ever waiting to be told a second time.

Her father often bought kites for her, of every kind and shape. There were fish, birds, butterflies, lizards and huge dragons, one of which had a tail more than thirty feet long. Mr. Min was very skilful in flying these kites for little Honeysuckle, and so naturally did his birds and butterflies circle round and hover about in the air that almost any little western boy would have been deceived and said, "Why, there is a real bird, and not a kite at all!" Then again, he would fasten a queer little instrument to the string, which made a kind of humming noise, as he waved his hand from side to side. "It is the wind singing, Daddy," cried Honeysuckle, clapping her hands with joy; "singing a kite-song to both of us." Sometimes, to teach his little darling a lesson if she had been the least naughty, Mr. Min would fasten queerly twisted scraps of paper, on which were written many Chinese words, to the string of her favourite kite.

"What are you doing, Daddy?" Honeysuckle would ask. "What can those queer-looking papers be?"

"On every piece is written a sin that we have done."

"What is a sin, Daddy?"

"Oh, when Honeysuckle has been naughty; that is a sin!" he answered gently. "Your old nurse is afraid to scold you, and if you are to grow up to be a good woman, Daddy must teach you what is right."

Then Mr. Min would send the kite up high – high over the house-tops, even higher than the tall Pagoda on the hillside. When all his cord was let out, he would pick up two sharp stones, and, handing them to Honeysuckle, would say, "Now, daughter, cut the string, and the wind will carry away the sins that are written down on the scraps of paper."

"But, Daddy, the kite is so pretty. Mayn't we keep our sins a little longer?" she would innocently ask.

"No, child; it is dangerous to hold on to one's sins. Virtue is the foundation of happiness," he would reply sternly, choking back his laughter at her question. "Make haste and cut the cord."

So Honeysuckle, always obedient – at least with her father – would saw the string in two between the sharp stones, and with a childish cry of despair would watch her favourite kite, blown by the wind, sail farther and farther away, until at last, straining her eyes, she could see it sink slowly to the earth in some far-distant meadow.

"Now laugh and be happy," Mr. Min would say, "for your sins are all gone. See that you don't get a new supply of them."

Honeysuckle was also fond of seeing the puppet show, for, you must know, this old-fashioned amusement for children was enjoyed by little folks in China, perhaps three thousand years before your great-grandfather was born. It is even said that the great Emperor, Mu, when he saw these little dancing images for the first time, was greatly enraged at seeing one of them making eyes at his favourite wife. He ordered the showman to be put to death, and it was with difficulty the poor fellow persuaded his Majesty that the dancing puppets were not really alive at all, but only images of cloth and clay.

No wonder then Honeysuckle liked to see the puppets if the Son of Heaven himself had been deceived by their queer antics into thinking them real people of flesh and blood.

But we must hurry on with our story, or some of our readers will be asking, "But where is Dr. Dog? Are you never coming to the hero of this tale?" One day when Honeysuckle was sitting inside a shady pavilion that overlooked a tiny fish-pond, she was suddenly seized with a violent attack of colic. Frantic with pain, she told a servant to summon her father, and then without further ado, she fell over in a faint upon the ground.

When Mr. Min reached his daughter's side, she was still unconscious. After sending for the family physician to come post haste, he got his daughter to bed, but although she recovered from her fainting fit, the extreme pain continued until the poor girl was almost dead from exhaustion.

Now, when the learned doctor arrived and peered at her from under his gigantic spectacles, he could not discover the cause of her trouble. However, like some of our western medical men, he did not confess his ignorance, but proceeded to prescribe a huge dose of boiling water, to be followed a little later by a compound of pulverized deer's horn and dried toadskin.

Poor Honeysuckle lay in agony for three days, all the time growing weaker and weaker from loss of sleep. Every great doctor in the district had been summoned for consultation; two had come from Changsha, the chief city of the province, but all to no avail. It was one of those cases that seem to be beyond the power of even the most learned physicians. In the hope of receiving the great reward offered by the desperate father, these wise men searched from cover to cover in the great Chinese Cyclopedia of Medicine, trying in vain to find a method of treating the unhappy maiden. There was even thought of calling in a certain foreign physician from England, who was in a distant city, and was supposed, on account of some marvellous cures he had brought to pass, to be in direct league with the devil. However, the city magistrate would not allow Mr. Min to call in this outsider, for fear trouble might be stirred up among the people.

Mr. Min sent out a proclamation in every direction, describing his daughter's illness, and offering to bestow on her a handsome dowry and give her in marriage to whoever should be the means of bringing her back to health and happiness. He then sat at her bedside and waited, feeling that he had done all that was in his power. There were many answers to his invitation. Physicians, old and young, came from every part of the Empire to try their skill, and when they had seen poor Honeysuckle and also the huge pile of silver shoes her father offered as a wedding gift, they all fought with might and main for her life; some having been attracted by her great beauty and excellent reputation, others by the tremendous reward.

But, alas for poor Honeysuckle! Not one of all those wise men could cure her! One day, when she was feeling a slight change for the better, she called her father, and, clasping his hand with her tiny one said, "Were it not for your love I would give up this hard fight and pass over into the dark wood; or, as my old grandmother says, fly up into the Western Heavens. For your sake, because I am your only child, and especially because you have no son, I have struggled hard to live, but now I feel that the next attack of that dreadful pain will carry me away. And oh, I do not want to die!"

Here Honeysuckle wept as if her heart would break, and her old father wept too, for the more she suffered the more he loved her.

Just then her face began to turn pale. "It is coming! The pain is coming, father! Very soon I shall be no more. Good-bye, father! Good-bye; good– ." Here her voice broke and a great sob almost broke her father's heart. He turned away from her bedside; he could not bear to see her suffer. He walked outside and sat down on a rustic bench; his head fell upon his bosom, and the great salt tears trickled down his long grey beard.

As Mr. Min sat thus overcome with grief, he was startled at hearing a low whine. Looking up he saw, to his astonishment, a shaggy mountain dog about the size of a Newfoundland. The huge beast looked into the old man's eyes with so intelligent and human an expression, with such a sad and wistful gaze, that the greybeard addressed him, saying, "Why have you come? To cure my daughter?"

The dog replied with three short barks, wagging his tail vigorously and turning toward the half-opened door that led into the room where the girl lay.

By this time, willing to try any chance whatever of reviving his daughter, Mr. Min bade the animal follow him into Honeysuckle's apartment. Placing his forepaws upon the side of her bed, the dog looked long and steadily at the wasted form before him and held his ear intently for a moment over the maiden's heart. Then, with a slight cough he deposited from his mouth into her outstretched hand, a tiny stone. Touching her wrist with his right paw, he motioned to her to swallow the stone.

"Yes, my dear, obey him," counselled her father, as she turned to him inquiringly, "for good Dr. Dog has been sent to your bedside by the mountain fairies, who have heard of your illness and who wish to invite you back to life again."

Without further delay the sick girl, who was by this time almost burned away by the fever, raised her hand to her lips and swallowed the tiny charm. Wonder of wonders! No sooner had it passed her lips than a miracle occurred. The red flush passed away from her face, the pulse resumed its normal beat, the pains departed from her body, and she arose from the bed well and smiling.

Flinging her arms about her father's neck, she cried out in joy, "Oh, I am well again; well and happy; thanks to the medicine of the good physician."

The noble dog barked three times, wild with delight at hearing these tearful words of gratitude, bowed low, and put his nose in Honeysuckle's outstretched hand.

Mr. Min, greatly moved by his daughter's magical recovery, turned to the strange physician, saying, "Noble Sir, were it not for the form you have taken, for some unknown reason, I would willingly give four times the sum in silver that I promised for the cure of the girl, into your possession. As it is, I suppose you have no use for silver, but remember that so long as we live, whatever we have is yours for the asking, and I beg of you to prolong your visit, to make this the home of your old age – in short, remain here for ever as my guest – nay, as a member of my family."

The dog barked thrice, as if in assent. From that day he was treated as an equal by father and daughter. The many servants were commanded to obey his slightest whim, to serve him with the most expensive food on the market, to spare no expense in making him the happiest and best-fed dog in all the world. Day after day he ran at Honeysuckle's side as she gathered flowers in her garden, lay down before her door when she was resting, guarded her Sedan chair when she was carried by servants into the city. In short, they were constant companions; a stranger would have thought they had been friends from childhood.

One day, however, just as they were returning from a journey outside her father's compound, at the very instant when Honeysuckle was alighting from her chair, without a moment's warning, the huge animal dashed past the attendants, seized his beautiful mistress in his mouth, and before anyone could stop him, bore her off to the mountains. By the time the alarm was sounded, darkness had fallen over the valley and as the night was cloudy no trace could be found of the dog and his fair burden.

Once more the frantic father left no stone unturned to save his daughter. Huge rewards were offered, bands of woodmen scoured the mountains high and low, but, alas, no sign of the girl could be found! The unfortunate father gave up the search and began to prepare himself for the grave. There was nothing now left in life that he cared for – nothing but thoughts of his departed daughter. Honeysuckle was gone for ever.

"Alas!" said he, quoting the lines of a famous poet who had fallen into despair:

> *"My whiting hair would make an endless rope,*
> *Yet would not measure all my depth of woe."*

Several long years passed by; years of sorrow for the ageing man, pining for his departed daughter. One beautiful October day he was sitting in the very same pavilion where he had so often sat with his darling. His head was bowed forward on his breast, his forehead was lined with grief. A rustling of leaves attracted his attention. He looked up. Standing directly in front of him was Dr. Dog, and lo, riding on his back, clinging to the animal's shaggy hair, was Honeysuckle, his long-lost daughter; while standing near by were three of the handsomest boys he had ever set eyes upon!

"Ah, my daughter! My darling daughter, where have you been all these years?" cried the delighted father, pressing the girl to his aching breast. "Have you suffered many a cruel pain since you were snatched away so suddenly? Has your life been filled with sorrow?"

"Only at the thought of your grief," she replied, tenderly, stroking his forehead with her slender fingers; "only at the thought of your suffering; only at the thought of how I should like to see you every day and tell you that my husband was kind and good to me. For you must know, dear father, this is no mere animal that stands beside you. This Dr. Dog, who cured me and claimed me as his bride because of your promise, is a great magician. He can change himself at will into a thousand shapes. He chooses to come here in the form of a mountain beast so that no one may penetrate the secret of his distant palace."

"Then he is your husband?" faltered the old man, gazing at the animal with a new expression on his wrinkled face.

"Yes; my kind and noble husband, the father of my three sons, your grandchildren, whom we have brought to pay you a visit."

"And where do you live?"

"In a wonderful cave in the heart of the great mountains; a beautiful cave whose walls and floors are covered with crystals, and encrusted with sparkling gems. The chairs and tables are set with jewels; the rooms are lighted by a thousand glittering diamonds. Oh, it is lovelier than the palace of the Son of Heaven himself! We feed of the flesh of wild deer and mountain goats, and fish from the clearest mountain stream. We drink cold water out of golden goblets, without first boiling it, for it is purity itself. We breathe fragrant air that blows through forests of pine and hemlock. We live only to love each other and our children, and oh, we are so happy! And you, father, you must come back with us to the great mountains and live there with us the rest of your days, which, the gods grant, may be very many."

The old man pressed his daughter once more to his breast and fondled the children, who clambered over him rejoicing at the discovery of a grandfather they had never seen before.

From Dr. Dog and his fair Honeysuckle are sprung, it is said, the well-known race of people called the Yus, who even now inhabit the mountainous regions of the Canton and

Hunan provinces. It is not for this reason, however, that we have told the story here, but because we felt sure every reader would like to learn the secret of the dog that cured a sick girl and won her for his bride.

The Prince and the Ogre's Castle

ONCE UPON A TIME there lived an old King and Queen, who, although they had been married for many years, had no children to brighten their old age or to inherit their kingdom; and in the King's possession, as it happened, were a favourite mare and dog, who also had no offspring. Now both the King and the Queen were very anxious to have children of their own, and also to perpetuate the fine breed represented by the mare and the dog; so the King posted a notice all over his kingdom, offering a very large reward to any Lama or other holy personage who could secure to him and to his horse and dog the birth of children.

In response to this notice many Lamas and recluses presented themselves at the palace, and by means of prayers and religious ceremonies they endeavoured to obtain from the gods what the King and Queen desired; but all their efforts were in vain, and the years passed by without any offspring being born.

Now it chanced that in a neighbouring country there lived a terrible Ogre, who was an export in magic and all the black arts; and it came to his ears that this King had offered a large reward if anyone could secure to him the birth of children for himself, his horse and his dog. So he disguised himself as a holy Lama, and coming up to the palace one day on foot, he asked for an interview with the King. The King, who had almost lost faith in Lamas of any kind, received him courteously, and asked him what he could do to help in the matter.

"Oh, King!" replied the supposed Lama, "I, you must know, am a great recluse, and as the result of many years of solitary meditation, I have become proficient in all the magic arts. I will undertake to secure for you and your horse and dog the birth of offspring as you desire. But I can only do so on one condition, which is as follows: three children will be born to you, three to the horse and three to the dog. They will all be of a miraculous nature, and will grow to their full powers in the course of three years. At the end of three years I will return here, and will claim from you one of each to follow me and serve me and to obey my orders in all matters."

The King gladly agreed to this condition, and asked the Lama how he should proceed in order to secure the desired result. The Lama replied:

"Here, oh King, are nine pills; three of these must be administered to the Queen, three to the horse and three to the dog. In three months' time a child will be born to each, to be followed by two others at intervals of one month."

So saying, he handed the pills to the King and forthwith took his departure. The King accordingly administered the pills as directed, and after three months the Queen gave birth to a boy, the mare to a foal, and the dog to a pup, and these were followed by two others at intervals of one month as the Lama had predicted.

All the young ones grew apace, and at the end of the three years they had all attained to their full growth and powers, and punctually at the conclusion of the third year the Ogre, still disguised as a Lama, returned to the palace to demand his due.

The King and Queen, though reluctant to part with any of their children, resolved to abide by their bargain, and they consulted together as to which of the young Princes should be handed over to the Lama. After some consideration they decided that it would not be advisable to part with the eldest son, as he was heir to the throne, nor with the second, who would have to succeed to the kingdom should any accident or mischance befall his elder brother; so they resolved to send the youngest son, and with him the youngest horse and the youngest dog. These three accordingly were handed over to the Lama, who ordered the Prince to follow him, and started off at once to his own country.

After travelling for some considerable distance they arrived at the top of a high pass, whence the Ogre, pointing down to a great castle standing in the valley below, said to the young Prince:

"That is my house below there; I shall leave you here and you must go on down to the house. When you arrive there you will find a goat tied up near the door of the courtyard, and a bundle of straw lying near by. You pick up the bundle of straw and place it within reach of the goat. Then you must go into the farmyard, where you will find many fowls, and in one corner you will see an earthenware jar full of soaked grain, and you must sprinkle this grain for the fowls to eat. These two tasks I give you to-day, and you are on no account to enter my castle until I rejoin you in the evening."

So saying the Ogre went off in another direction, whilst the young Prince, riding on his horse and followed by his dog, went down to the Ogre's castle. When he reached the gateway he found, as the Ogre had predicted, a goat tied up and a bundle of straw lying in a corner of the courtyard. So he dismounted from his horse, and, picking up the bundle, he carried it near the goat and placed it on the ground. Scarcely had the bundle touched the ground when it became transformed into three great wolves, who, leaping upon the goat, devoured it in an instant, and then fled away to the hills.

The young Prince was very much astonished at seeing this, but being of a courageous spirit he did not allow the incident to frighten him, and proceeded to finish the remainder of his task. So he entered the yard where the poultry were kept, and proceeding to the corner where stood the jar of soaked barley, he took out a handful and scattered it amongst the fowls. As the grain touched the ground it was transformed instantly into three wild cats, who leapt fiercely upon the cocks and hens, and in a few moments, having destroyed them all, fled away into the hills.

The Prince's curiosity was now thoroughly aroused, and he determined, in spite of the Ogre's warning, to enter the house itself, and to discover what sort of place he had come to, so he pushed open the door of the castle and began wandering about all over the house. For some time he found nothing to interest him. The rooms were all well furnished and in good order, but he could find no trace and hear no sound of any living creature.

At last, after having explored the greater part of the building, he suddenly turned a corner in a passage, and saw in front of him a room whose walls were composed entirely of glass. Entering this room he saw in one corner a beautiful lady lying asleep on a couch with a flower behind her ear. The Prince was pleased at finding a human being in this desolate and mysterious castle, and, approaching the lady, he endeavoured to arouse her from her slumber. But all his efforts were in vain; she appeared to be in a sort of trance, and all he could do did not succeed in waking her.

At last in despair he took away the flower which was placed behind her ear, and as he did so she woke and sat up upon her couch, rubbing her eyes. As soon as she perceived the young Prince she was much astonished, and asked him what he was doing in the Ogre's castle. The Prince told her the whole story of his miraculous birth through the magic of the holy Lama, and how he was condemned to serve the Lama as his servant through the agreement which the King his father had made, and how he had carried out the two tasks which the Lama had given him that day.

On hearing this story the lady was very indignant, and spoke to him as follows:

"You must know, oh Prince," said she, "that the person whom you suppose to be a Lama is in reality a fearful and wicked Ogre. The only food of which he partakes is men's hearts, and this house is full of the lifeless bodies of his numerous victims. He, however, is unable to obtain any power over the body of a human being unless that being directly disobeys his orders. Thus it is his practice upon obtaining a fresh servant to set him strange tasks which terrify and repel him. These tasks grow daily more difficult and more odious, until at last one day the servant disobeys his orders, and forthwith his body is at the mercy of the Ogre, who devours the heart and places the lifeless body in a large chamber at the back of this house. The process has evidently begun with you to-day. You have fulfilled all of his tasks without allowing yourself to be terrified by the strange portents which you have observed, but on his return he will no doubt set you further and more disagreeable duties to perform. I, you should know, am a Princess in my own country, and I was handed over to the Ogre by my parents about a year ago in circumstances very similar to your own. But when he had brought me to his castle, instead of destroying me as he does his other victims, he fell in love with me, and I have remained here as his wife ever since. But he is of a very jealous disposition, and never allows me to leave his castle; and for fear I should make my escape during his absence, he invariably, before going out, places an enchanted flower behind my ear which makes me fall into a trance, and I cannot awake until the flower is removed."

The young Prince was very much interested on hearing this story, and he begged the Princess to give him some further information about the Ogre's habits, in order that he might not unawares fall into his power, and might eventually be able to bring about the destruction of the monster.

"It is very difficult," replied the Princess, "for any human being to kill the Ogre, for he is of a supernatural nature, and even if you were to cut off his head he would come to life again at once, unless you could also destroy his 'mascot' – that is to say, the object upon the preservation of which his life in this world depends. Now the Ogre's mascot is very carefully concealed, and its existence and whereabouts are known to no person except myself. I, however, have discovered where it is, and I will reveal the secret to you later, but first I will tell you the method by which you may destroy the Ogre's body. You must know, then, that it is only possible for a human being to strike a mortal blow at the Ogre when his face is turned away. He knows this very well, and will never in any circumstances turn his back upon a man. Similarly, if he can make you turn your back to him he may be able to do you a mischief. When he comes in this evening and finds that you have fulfilled both the tasks he has set you, the first thing he will order you to do will be to walk three times round a great stove which stands in the centre of the kitchen; and if you obey his orders he will follow you from behind and will possibly do you some harm while your back is turned towards him. When he gives you these orders, then, you must not disobey, but you must tell the Ogre that it is so dark in the kitchen that you cannot see your way clearly, and you must ask him to precede you. This he is bound to do, and while he is going round the stove you may perhaps find an opportunity for stabbing him. If, however, you cannot succeed in doing so, and you both pass through this ordeal successfully, he will set you no further task to-night, and I will ascertain from him during the evening what trial he has in store for you to-morrow."

The Prince thanked the young lady for all her good advice, which he promised to follow faithfully in every respect, and she then said to him:

"It is now near the time for the Ogre's return. I will lie down on the couch, and you must place the flower behind my ear just as it was before; and when I fall into a trance you must at once go out into the courtyard and wait the return of the Ogre, and mind you are careful not to let him know that you have been inside the castle."

So saying, the Princess lay down upon her couch, and the young man having placed the flower behind her ear she instantly fell into a deep trance. The Prince then went out into the courtyard and shortly after the Ogre arrived. He had now discarded his lama costume and appeared in his proper form, and riding up to the Prince he asked him in an angry tone whether he had carried out the orders he had received, and on the Prince replying in the affirmative, the Ogre ordered him to come into the kitchen. On entering the kitchen the Ogre pointed to a great stove standing in the centre, and said to the Prince:

"You must now walk three times round that stove."

"It is so dark in here," replied the Prince, "that I cannot see my way at all clearly. Will you please precede me and show me the way?"

The Ogre was very angry at hearing this, but he was unable to refuse, so he started off and ran round the stove three times, the Prince following closely at his heels. But he went so fast that the Prince, although he had his knife ready in his hand, was unable to catch him: and the Ogre, seeing that the Prince was not to be outwitted by this stratagem, went upstairs to his wife, leaving the young man locked up in the kitchen, where he spent the night alone.

Next morning the Ogre started off soon after daylight on his own business, and as soon as he was gone the Prince ran upstairs to the glass room, where he found the lady lying in a trance as before. He took the flower from behind her ear, and she immediately woke up and looked about her.

"Good-morning, Prince," said she. "How did you succeed last night? I hope you followed the instructions which I gave you."

The Prince described to her what had occurred, and she said:

"I have ascertained what the Ogre proposes to do when he returns this evening. He will seat himself in his chair of state in his great hall of audience and will order you to kow-tow to him three times, and if you do so he will seize an opportunity whilst you are lying on your face before him to do you some injury. It will not do, however, absolutely to disobey his orders; but you must explain to him that, being a Prince, you have never had to kow-tow to anybody and do not exactly know how to do it, and you must ask him to show you the proper way to proceed. He cannot refuse your request, and you must take the opportunity of stabbing him or cutting off his head whilst he is lying on his face before you. If you succeed in this come at once to me, and I will show you what else is necessary in order to bring about his complete destruction."

The Prince promised to obey the lady's orders, and after again sending her into a trance by placing the magic flower behind her ear, he returned to the courtyard and awaited the Ogre's return. Just before dusk the Ogre came back and as the Princess had predicted he proceeded at once to the great audience hall, and seated himself on his chair of state.

"Now," said he to the Prince, "you must kow-tow to me three times."

"I am very sorry," answered the Prince, "that I do not know how to do so. Being a Prince myself, I have never had to kow-tow to anybody; but if you will show me the proper manner in which to proceed I will do my best."

This reply made the Ogre very angry, but he was unable to refuse to do as the Prince had asked him. So the Prince took his seat on the Ogre's chair and the Ogre kneeling on the ground before him proceeded to kow-tow three times in the orthodox manner. As the Ogre's face touched the ground the first time the Prince drew his sword; as it touched the ground the second time he raised the sword above his head; and a touched the ground the third and last time the Prince delivered a violent blow, completely severing the Ogre's head from his body. Leaving the body where it lay, the Prince ran up to the glass room as fast as he could, and having awakened the lady from her sleep, he told her what had happened.

"Well done!" said she. "The first part of your task is now accomplished; but as I told you before, it is still necessary to destroy the Ogre's mascot, or he will come to life again in a short time. What you must do now, therefore, is as follows: you must descend into the vaults below the castle, and having traversed nine dark subterranean chambers, you will come to a blank stone wall. You must rap three times on this wall with the hilt of your sword, exclaiming with each rap, 'Open, blank wall;' and as you pronounce these words for the third time the wall will fly asunder, and you will find yourself entering another subterranean chamber. In the centre of this chamber you will see a beautiful boy seated with a goblet of crystal liquid in his hand. This boy is the Ogre's mascot, and upon his existence depends the Ogre's life in this world. You must at once slay the boy, and taking the goblet very carefully in your hand, carry it upstairs to me. But be careful not to spill any of the liquid, as each drop means a man's life."

On receiving these instructions the Prince went down into the vaults at the basement of the castle, and having traversed nine great subterranean chambers, he found his progress stopped by a blank wall. Raising his sword he rapped three times with the hilt on the wall, exclaiming each time as he did so, "Open, blank wall." As he pronounced these words for the third time a grating sound was heard, and with a hollow clang the wall gave way for him.

Advancing a few paces the Prince found himself in a small dungeon, lighted only by the glimmer which issued from a goblet of crystal liquid held in the hand of a beautiful young boy, who was seated in the centre of the chamber. Without a moment's hesitation the Prince thrust his sword through the heart of the boy, and taking the goblet in his hand, he carried it upstairs to the Princess, being very careful on the way not to allow a single drop to be spilt.

When the Princess saw him entering her room with the goblet in his hand she was very much delighted. "Now," said she, "the Ogre is effectually destroyed, and can never more come to life in this world. All that now remains to be done is to restore to life his previous victims."

So saying she ordered the Prince, still carrying the goblet, to follow her, and she proceeded by many winding passages and staircases to a remote part of the great castle. Presently, opening a huge door, she entered a long, low, gloomy chamber, lighted only by a narrow window which looked out over the back part of the castle. When the Prince entered this chamber he was horrified to see that down both sides of it were stretched the bodies of many scores of men, women and children, who lay there fully dressed, but to all appearance quite lifeless.

"These," said the lady, "are the bodies of the Ogre's victims; he has eaten their hearts, but the bodies, as you see, remain unharmed, while the spirit of each one is compressed into a drop of crystal liquor with which that goblet is filled. You must now sprinkle the bodies with the liquid, giving one drop to each."

Accordingly the Prince passed down the rows of lifeless bodies, dropping as he went one drop of the magic liquid on each body; and as the liquor touched the body the life returned, and each person, as if awakened from a long sleep, moved and yawned, and finally sat up and began to talk and walk. In a few moments the transformation was complete, and the Ogre's victims, after thanking the Prince and Princess heartily for their good offices, returned to their own homes. The Prince himself bade farewell to the lady, and leaving her in possession of the Ogre's castle and all its belongings, he himself mounted upon his horse, and with his dog following at his heels, set out in search of further adventures.

The Goblin Spider

SOME TIME AFTER the brave knight Raiko had slain the Goblin of Oeyama, he became seriously ill, and was obliged to keep to his room. At about midnight a little boy always brought him some medicine. This boy was unknown to Raiko, but as he kept so many servants it did not at first awaken suspicion. Raiko grew worse instead of better, and always worse immediately after he had taken the medicine, so he began to think that some supernatural force was the cause of his illness.

At last Raiko asked his head servant if he knew anything about the boy who came to him at midnight. Neither the head servant nor anyone else seemed to know anything about him. By this time Raiko's suspicions were fully awakened, and he determined to go carefully into the matter.

When the small boy came again at midnight, instead of taking the medicine, Raiko threw the cup at his head, and drawing his sword attempted to kill him. A sharp cry of pain rang through the room, but as the boy was flying from the apartment he threw something at Raiko. It spread outward into a huge white sticky web, which clung so tightly to Raiko that he could hardly move. No sooner had he cut the web through with his sword than another enveloped him. Raiko then called for assistance, and his chief retainer met the miscreant in one of the corridors and stopped his further progress with extended sword. The Goblin threw a web over him too. When he at last managed to extricate himself and was able to run into his master's room, he saw that Raiko had also been the victim of the Goblin Spider.

The Goblin Spider was eventually discovered in a cave writhing with pain, blood flowing from a sword-cut on the head. He was instantly killed, and with his death there passed away the evil influence that had caused Raiko's serious illness. From that hour the hero regained his health and strength, and a sumptuous banquet was prepared in honour of the happy event.

Another Version

There is another version of this legend, written by Kenko Hoshi, which differs so widely in many of its details from the one we have already given that it almost amounts to a new story altogether. To dispense with this version would be to rob the legend of its most sinister aspect, which has not hitherto been accessible to the general reader.

On one occasion Raiko left Kyoto with Tsuna, the most worthy of his retainers. As they were crossing the plain of Rendai they saw a skull rise in the air, and fly before them as if driven by the wind, until it finally disappeared at a place called Kagura ga Oka.

Raiko and his retainer had no sooner noticed the disappearance of the skull than they perceived before them a mansion in ruins. Raiko entered this dilapidated building, and saw an old woman of strange aspect. She was dressed in white, and had white hair; she opened her eyes with a small stick, and the upper eyelids fell back over her head like a hat; then she used the rod to open her mouth, and let her breast fall forward upon her knees. Thus she addressed the astonished Raiko:

"I am two hundred and ninety years old. I serve nine masters, and the house in which you stand is haunted by demons."

Having listened to these words, Raiko walked into the kitchen, and, catching a glimpse of the sky, he perceived that a great storm was brewing. As he stood watching the dark clouds gather he heard a sound of ghostly footsteps, and there crowded into the room a great company of goblins. Nor were these the only supernatural creatures which Raiko encountered, for presently he saw a being dressed like a nun. Her very small body was naked to the waist, her face was two feet in length, and her arms were white as snow and thin as threads. For a moment this dreadful creature laughed, and then vanished like a mist.

Raiko heard the welcome sound of a cock crowing, and imagined that the ghostly visitors would trouble him no more; but once again he heard footsteps, and this time he saw no hideous hag, but a lovely woman, more graceful than the willow branches as they wave in the breeze. As he gazed upon this lovely maiden his eyes became blinded for a moment on account of her radiant beauty. Before he could recover his sight he found himself enveloped in countless cobwebs. He struck at her with his sword, when she disappeared, and he found that he had but cut through the planks of the floor, and broken the foundation-stone beneath.

At this moment Tsuna joined his master, and they perceived that the sword was covered with *white* blood, and that the point had been broken in the conflict.

After much search Raiko and his retainer discovered a den in which they saw a monster with many legs and a head of enormous size covered with downy hair. Its mighty eyes shone like the sun and moon, as it groaned aloud: "I am sick and in pain!"

As Raiko and Tsuna drew near they recognised the broken sword-point projecting from the monster. The heroes then dragged the creature out of its den and cut off its head. Out of the deep wound in the creature's stomach gushed nineteen hundred and ninety skulls, and in addition many spiders as large as children. Raiko and his follower realised that the monster before them was none other than the Mountain Spider. When they cut open the great carcass they discovered, within the entrails, the ghostly remains of many human corpses.

LITTLE CREATURES
& TINY FOLK

Introduction

'THE ELFIN MAIDENS were already dancing on the elf hill, and they danced in shawls woven from moonshine and mist, which looked very pretty to those who like such things. The large hall within the elf hill was splendidly decorated ... In the kitchen were frogs roasting on the spit, and dishes preparing of snail skins ...' Such is the festive fare on offer in Hans Christian Andersen's 'The Elfin Hill', for a miniaturized version of a human ball.

All the beasts in this book are in some sense stand-ins for human subjects, but those in this section take an anthropomorphic form. That makes the parallels they offer with the human realm that much closer and the ironies they afford that bit more telling. This is even more so because these beings tend to live alongside mortal humans, interacting with them as they go about their daily lives – though their interventions may be mischievous as well as helpful. The Dutch Kabouters – little people who worked in mines and forges underground – took it upon themselves to make church bells for their country's churches.

The Netherlands' Elves, we are told, 'sewed shoes for poor cobblers, when they were sick, and made clothes for children, when the mother was tired', but they also enjoyed cruel fun at the expense of the pompous or the mean. Hans Christian Andersen's 'Elf of the Rose', taking pity on a grieving maiden, helps to expose the man who murdered her young lover. At the very least these Little People provide a gently satirical perspective on the life of mortals; at other times they involve themselves much more decisively.

The Legend of the Dwarf

AN OLD WOMAN lived alone in her hut, rarely leaving her chimney-corner. She was much distressed at having no children, and in her grief one day took an egg, wrapped it up carefully in cotton cloth, and put it in a corner of her hut. She looked every day in great anxiety, but no change in the egg was observable. One morning, however, she found the shell broken, and a lovely tiny creature was stretching out its arms to her.

The old woman was in raptures. She took it to her heart, gave it a nurse, and was so careful of it that at the end of a year the baby walked and talked as well as a grown-up man. But he stopped growing. The good old woman in her joy and delight exclaimed that the baby should be a great chief.

One day she told him to go to the king's palace and engage him in a trial of strength. The dwarf begged hard not to be sent on such an enterprise. But the old woman insisted on his going, and he was obliged to obey. When ushered into the presence of the sovereign he threw down his gauntlet. The latter smiled, and asked him to lift a stone of three arobes (75 lb). The child returned crying to his mother, who sent him back, saying, "If the king can lift the stone, you can lift it too." The king did take it up, but so did the dwarf. His strength was tried in many other ways, but all the king did was as easily done by the dwarf.

Wroth at being outdone by so puny a creature, the prince told the dwarf that unless he built a palace loftier than any in the city he should die. The affrighted dwarf returned to the old woman, who bade him not to despair, and the next morning they both awoke in the palace which is still standing. The king saw the palace with amazement. He instantly sent for the dwarf, and desired him to collect two bundles of *cogoiol* (a kind of hard wood), with one of which he would strike the dwarf on the head, and consent to be struck in return by his tiny adversary. The latter again returned to his mother moaning and lamenting. But the old woman cheered him up, and, placing a *tortilla* on his head, sent him back to the king. The trial took place in the presence of all the state grandees. The king broke the whole of his bundle on the dwarf's head without hurting him in the least, seeing which he wished to save his own head from the impending ordeal; but his word had been passed before his assembled court, and he could not well refuse. The dwarf struck, and at the second blow the king's skull was broken to pieces. The spectators immediately proclaimed the victorious dwarf their sovereign.

After this the old woman disappeared. But in the village of Mani, fifty miles distant, is a deep well leading to a subterraneous passage which extends as far as Merida. In this passage is an old woman sitting on the bank of a river shaded by a great tree, having a serpent by her side. She sells water in small quantities, accepting no money, for she must have human beings, innocent babies, which are devoured by the serpent. This old woman is the dwarf's mother.

The Passing of the Dwarfs

WHEN THE EARTH WAS FORMED, the first dwarfs were bred from the corpse of Ymir. Dwarfs were also called black elves, and they were such ugly creatures that it was decreed that they should not be allowed to show their faces above ground, for fear of frightening gods and men to death. They were dark of skin, which made them nearly invisible in the dark, and they were never seen, for they risked being turned to stone by appearing in the daylight. Dwarfs were fine craftsmen, and although they lacked the size and power of the gods, they were certainly more intelligent than any other form of life in the nine worlds, and they were called upon often by the gods to provide assistance when their own magic failed.

And so it was that the dwarfs became great friends to the gods, helping them out by producing the peerless ship *Skidbladnir*, the golden locks of Sif, the hammer Miolnir, the golden-skinned pig Gulinbursti, the ring Draupnir, the spear Gungnir, and Freya's exquisite necklace, Brisingamen. Without these aids, the gods would never have had the power to keep at bay their many enemies, and when the old gods finally succumbed, the dwarfs themselves lost interest in the world above, and disappeared. This was the passing of the dwarfs.

When the old gods were no longer worshipped in the north, the dwarfs formed a conference and it was decided that they could no longer offer any help to humankind. For centuries they had made themselves useful in households – appearing to knead bread, or help with the farming, or rock a baby when necessary. But the twilight of the gods had caused a change of heart. One night, the dwarfs hired a ferryman, and for the whole of that night he was kept busy, filling his boat with his invisible passengers, so that it nearly sank, and transporting them back and forth across the river. When his night's work was complete, he was rewarded with riches beyond his greatest imaginings. The next morning the dwarfs had vanished from the land of the dark elves, a cry of protest against the disbelief of the people. Left to his own resources, no man was capable of running a household as smoothly without the helpful dwarfs, and no weapon as wondrous or as invincible as those formed by the dwarfs was ever produced again. The passing of the dwarfs marked the end of an age, and the end of the camaraderie between the two worlds.

The Elves

BESIDES THE DWARFS there was another numerous class of tiny creatures called Lios-alfar, light or white elves, who inhabited the realms of air between heaven and earth, and were gently governed by the genial god Frey from his palace in Alfheim. They were lovely, beneficent beings, so pure and innocent that, according to some authorities, their name was derived from the same root as the Latin word 'white' (*albus*), which, in a modified form, was given to the snow-covered Alps, and to Albion (England), because of her white chalk cliffs which could be seen afar.

The elves were so small that they could flit about unseen while they tended the flowers, birds, and butterflies; and as they were passionately fond of dancing, they often glided down to earth on a moonbeam, to dance on the green. Holding one another by the hand, they would dance in circles, thereby making the 'fairy rings,' which were to be discerned by the deeper green and greater luxuriance of the grass which their little feet had pressed.

If any mortal stood in the middle of one of these fairy rings he could, according to popular belief in England, see the fairies and enjoy their favour; but the Scandinavians and Teutons vowed that the unhappy man must die. In illustration of this superstition, a story is told of how Sir Olaf, riding off to his wedding, was enticed by the fairies into their ring. On the morrow, instead of a merry marriage, his friends witnessed a triple funeral, for his mother and bride also died when they beheld his lifeless corpse.

These elves, who in England were called fairies or fays, were also enthusiastic musicians, and delighted especially in a certain air known as the elf-dance, which was so irresistible that no one who heard it could refrain from dancing. If a mortal, overhearing the air, ventured to reproduce it, he suddenly found himself incapable of stopping and was forced to play on and on until he died of exhaustion, unless he were deft enough to play the tune backwards, or some one charitably cut the strings of his violin. His hearers, who were forced to dance as long as the tones continued, could only stop when they ceased.

In medieval times, the will-o'-the-wisps were known in the North as elf lights, for these tiny sprites were supposed to mislead travellers; and popular superstition held that the Jack-o'-lanterns were the restless spirits of murderers forced against their will to return to the scene of their crimes. As they nightly walked thither, it is said that they doggedly repeated with every step, "It is right;" but as they returned they sadly reiterated, "It is wrong."

In Scandinavia and Germany sacrifices were offered to the elves to make them propitious. These sacrifices consisted of some small animal, or of a bowl of honey and milk, and were known as Alf-blot. They were quite common until the missionaries taught the people that the elves were mere demons, when they were transferred to the angels, who were long entreated to befriend mortals, and propitiated by the same gifts.

Many of the elves were supposed to live and die with the trees and plants which they tended, but these moss, wood, or tree maidens, while remarkably beautiful when seen in front, were hollow like a trough when viewed from behind. They appear in many of the popular tales, but almost always as benevolent and helpful spirits, for they were anxious to do good to mortals and to cultivate friendly relations with them.

No discussion of the elves is complete without a few words about Oberon. There are stories told far and wide of the fairy king Oberon, and his delicate queen Titiania. Oberon was so exquisitely handsome, that mortals were drawn into his fairy world after just one glance at his elegant profile. In every country across the world, there was a sense of unease on the eve of Midsummer, for this is when the fairies congregate around Oberon and Titiana and dance. Fairy dances are a magical thing, and their music is so compelling that all who hear it find it irresistible. But once a human, or indeed a god, succumbs to the fairy music, and begins to dance, he will be damned to do so until the end of his days, when he will die of an exhaustion like none other.

Oberon was also very powerful, and his tricks above ground became legend throughout many lands. With the passing of the dwarfs, humankind had no help with their work, and the little folk were no longer considered to be a blessed addition to a household. Many believe that Oberon harnessed the powers of Frey when he fell, and used them beneath the earth to set up a kingdom of fairies which was a complex and commanding as Asgard had once been. With his strength, and his overwhelming beauty, he was considered by man to be nothing more than a demon.

In Scandinavia the elves, both light and dark, were worshipped as household divinities, and their images were carved on the doorposts. The Norsemen, who were driven from home by the tyranny of Harald Harfager in 874, took their carved doorposts with them upon their ships. Similar carvings, including images of the gods and heroes, decorated the pillars of their high seats which they also carried away. The exiles showed their trust in their gods by throwing these wooden images overboard when they neared the Icelandic shores and settling where the waves carried the posts, even if the spot scarcely seemed the most desirable. "Thus they carried with them the religion, the poetry, and the laws of their race, and on this desolate volcanic island they kept these records unchanged for hundreds of years, while other Teutonic nations gradually became affected by their intercourse with Roman and Byzantine Christianity." These records, carefully collected by Saemund the learned, form the Elder Edda, the most precious relic of ancient Northern literature, without which we should know comparatively little of the religion of our forefathers.

The sagas relate that the first settlements in Greenland and Vinland were made in the same way – the Norsemen piously landing wherever their household gods drifted ashore.

Tales of the Nisses

THE NIS IS THE SAME BEING that is called Kobold in Germany, and Brownie in Scotland. He is in Denmark and Norway also called Nisse god Dreng (Nissè good lad), and in Sweden, Tomtegubbe (the old man of the house).

He is of the dwarf family, and resembles them in appearance, and, like them, has the command of money, and the same dislike to noise and tumult.

His usual dress is grey, with a pointed red cap, but on Michaelmas-day he wears a round hat like those of the peasants.

No farmhouse goes on well without there is a nis in it, and well is it for the maids and the men when they are in favour with him. They may go to their beds and give themselves no trouble about their work, and yet in the morning the maids will find the kitchen swept up, and water brought in; and the men will find the horses in the stable well cleaned and curried, and perhaps a supply of corn cribbed for them from the neighbours' barns.

There was a nis in a house in Jutland. He every evening got his groute at the regular time, and he, in return, used to help both the men and the maids, and looked to the interest of the master of the house in every respect.

There came one time a mischievous boy to live at service in this house, and his great delight was, whenever he got an opportunity, to give the nis all the annoyance in his power.

Late one evening, when everything was quiet in the house, the nis took his little wooden dish, and was just going to eat his supper, when he perceived that the boy had put the butter at the bottom and had concealed it, in hopes that he might eat the groute first, and then find the butter when all the groute was gone. He accordingly set about thinking how he might repay the boy in kind. After pondering a little he went up into the loft where a man and the boy were lying asleep in the same bed. The nis whisked off the bed clothes, and when he saw the little boy by the tall man, he said –

"Short and long don't match," and with this word he took the boy by the legs and dragged him down to the man's feet. He then went up to the head of the bed, and –

"Short and long don't match," said he again, and then he dragged the boy up to the man's head. Do what he would he could not succeed in making the boy as long as the man, but persisted in dragging him up and down in the bed, and continued at this work the whole night long till it was broad daylight.

By this time he was well tired, so he crept up on the window stool, and sat with his legs dangling down into the yard. The house-dog – for all dogs have a great enmity to the nis – as soon as he saw him began to bark at him, which afforded him much amusement, as the dog could not get up to him. So he put down first one leg and then the other, and teased the dog, saying –

"Look at my little leg. Look at my little leg!"

In the meantime the boy had awoke, and had stolen up behind him, and, while the nis was least thinking of it, and was going on with his, "Look at my little leg," the boy tumbled him down into the yard to the dog, crying out at the same time –

"Look at the whole of him now!"

* * *

There lived a man in Thyrsting, in Jutland, who had a nis in his barn. This nis used to attend to his cattle, and at night he would steal fodder for them from the neighbours, so that this farmer had the best fed and most thriving cattle in the country.

One time the boy went along with the nis to Fugleriis to steal corn. The nis took as much as he thought he could well carry, but the boy was more covetous, and said –

"Oh! take more. Sure, we can rest now and then!"

"Rest!" said the nis. "Rest! and what is rest?"

"Do what I tell you," replied the boy. "Take more, and we shall find rest when we get out of this."

The nis took more, and they went away with it, but when they came to the lands of Thyrsting, the nis grew tired, and then the boy said to him –

"Here now is rest!" and they both sat down on the side of a little hill.

"If I had known," said the nis, as they sat. "If I had known that rest was so good, I'd have carried off all that was in the barn."

It happened, some time after, that the boy and the nis were no longer friends, and as the nis was sitting one day in the granary-window with his legs hanging out into the yard, the boy ran at him and tumbled him back into the granary. The nis was revenged on him that very night, for when the boy was gone to bed he stole down to where he was lying and carried him as he was into the yard. Then he laid two pieces of wood across the well and put him lying on them, expecting that when he awoke he would fall, from the fright, into the well and be drowned. He was, however, disappointed, for the boy came off without injury.

* * *

There was a man who lived in the town of Tirup who had a very handsome white mare. This mare had for many years belonged to the same family, and there was a nis attached to her who brought luck to the place.

This nis was so fond of the mare that he could hardly endure to let them put her to any kind of work, and he used to come himself every night and feed her of the best; and as for this purpose he usually brought a superfluity of corn, both thrashed and in the straw, from the neighbours' barns, all the rest of the cattle enjoyed the advantage, and they were all kept in exceedingly good condition.

It happened at last that the farmhouse passed into the hands of a new owner, who refused to put any faith in what they told him about the mare, so the luck speedily left the place, and went after the mare to a poor neighbour who had bought her. Within five days after his purchase, the poor farmer began to find his circumstances gradually improving, while the income of the other, day after day, fell away and diminished at such a rate that he was hard set to make both ends meet.

If now the man who had got the mare had only known how to be quiet and enjoy the good times that were come upon him, he and his children and his children's children after him would have been in flourishing circumstances till this very day. But when he saw the quantity of corn that came every night to his barn, he could not resist his desire to get a sight of the nis. So he concealed himself one evening at nightfall in the stable, and as soon as it was midnight he saw how the nis came from his neighbour's barn and brought a sack full of corn with him. It was now unavoidable that the nis should get a sight of the man who was watching, so he, with evident marks of grief, gave the mare her food for the last time, cleaned and dressed her to the best of his ability, and when he had done, turned round to where the man was lying, and bid him farewell.

From that day forward the circumstances of both the neighbours were on an equality, for each now kept his own.

The Ainsel

DEEP IN THE HEART of the Border country, where the wind howls with cold, lived a wee boy called Parcie. He lived with his mother in a small, snug cottage where the fire burned bright and bathed the stone clad walls in a soft, cosy glow. They lived alone there for his father was long since gone, but they managed with little, living simply and happily among the trees and the wood folk who inhabited them.

Now like most small boys, Parcie plotted all day in order to avoid being sent to bed each night. He longed to sit by the hearth with his mother, watching the burning embers cast intriguing shadows which danced and performed a story that seemed to Parcie like it could go on forever. But each night it was cut short, as was the sound of his mother's mellifluous voice as she sang to him of fairies and sea-folk, and told of stories and legends of long ago. For it was it at this point that Parcie's mother would close up her bag of mending.

"It's time for your bed, Parcie," she would say, always the same thing, and Parcie would be packed neatly into his tiny box-bed where the fairies had laid a nest of golden slumberdust so potent that his eyes were shut and he was fast asleep as soon as his head touched his soft pillow. And there he'd sleep all the night, until the next morning he struggled to hatch a plan to stay awake all night, to carry on and on the drowsy contentment of the evening.

But one night Parcie's tired mother could argue no further and when the fire began to sink down into black-red embers, and she said,

"It's time for your bed, Parcie" he would not go. And so she picked up her mending, and tidied it away, setting a bowl of cool, fresh cream by the doorstep as she went along the corridor to her own bed.

"I hope to God the old fairy wife does not get to you, lad, but it will be your own fault if she does," whispered his mother as she disappeared into her room.

And suddenly the warm red room took on a more sinister cast, and the shadows no longer told a story but taunted him, warning him, tempting him until he was a jumble of fear and confusion. And just as he steeled himself to dash to his warm box-bed, filled with golden slumberdust, a tiny brownie leapt from the chimney and landed on his foot.

Now brownies were common in the days when Parcie lived in the stone cottage with his mother, and they came each day to every house that had the courtesy and the foresight to leave a bowl of cool, fresh cream by the doorstep. And if some foolish occupant forgot that cream one night, she would be sure to find a tumultuous mess the next day. For brownies came to tidy everything away, neat and clean, collecting specks of dust and laying things just so, so that in the morning the lucky household gleamed with shining surfaces and possessions all in order.

But Parcie knew nothing of the magic that dropped through the chimney each night and he was surprised and rather pleased to see this tiny fairy. The brownie was not, however, so pleased to see Parcie, for he was an efficient wee brownie and he liked to have his work done quickly, in order to get to the lovely bowl of cool, fresh cream which awaited him by the doorstep.

"What's your name?" asked Parcie, grinning.

"Ainsel (own self)," replied the brownie, smiling back despite himself. "And you?"

"My Ainsel," said Parcie, joining in the joke.

And so Parcie and the brownie played a little together, and Parcie watched with interest while the brownie tidied and cleaned their cottage in a whirlwind of activity. And then, as he neared the grate to sweep away some dust that had come loose from the hearth, Parcie took an inopportune moment to poke the fire, and what should fly out upon the poor brownie but a red-hot ember which burnt him so badly that he howled with pain.

And then, into the snuffling silence that followed, a deep frightening voice boomed down the chimney. It was the old fairy wife who Parcie's mother had warned of, and she flew into a rage when she heard her dear brownie's tears.

"Tell me who hurt ye," she shouted down the chimney, "I'll get him, so I will."

And the brownie called out tearfully, "It was My Ainsel." Parcie lost no time in hurling himself from the room and into his box-bed where the golden slumberdust did not cast its magic over the terrified boy, for he laid awake and shaking for a long time after his head touched his soft pillow.

But the old fairy wife was not concerned about Parcie, for she called out, "What's the fuss, if you did it yer ainsel" and muttering she thrust a long brown arm down the chimney and plucked the sniffling brownie from the fireside.

Now what do you think Parcie's mother thought the next morning when she found her cottage spic and span, but the bowl of cream still standing untouched, cool and fresh by the doorstep. How perplexed she was when the brownie stopped visiting her cottage, although she always left a bowl of cream to tempt him. But in the heart of the Border country, where the wind howls with cold, bad is almost always balanced by good, and so it was then when from that night onwards, Parcie's mother never again had to say to him, "Parcie, it's time for your bed," for at the first sudden movement of the shadows, when the fire began to sink down into black-red embers, he was sound asleep in his tiny box-bed, deep in the sleep of the golden slumberdust.

The Cauldron

THE LITTLE ISLAND OF SANDRAY juts firmly through the waves of the Atlantic Ocean, which spits and surges around it. No human lives there, although sheep graze calmly on the succulent green grass, freshened by the moist salt air, and kept company by the fairy folk who live in a verdant knoll. But once upon a time there were men and women on the island of Sandray, and one was a herder's wife, called Mairearad, who kept a tiny cottage on the northernmost tip.

She had in her possession a large copper cauldron, blackened with age and with use. One day, as she wiped it clean of the evening meal, she was visited by a Woman of Peace, a fairy woman who tiptoed quietly into the cottage and asked to take away the cauldron for a short time. Now this was an older fairy, with a nature that was gentle and kind, and she presented little danger to Mairearad. She had a wizened fairy face, and features as tiny as the markings of a butterfly, and she moved swiftly and silently, advising no one of her coming or going. Mairearad passed her the cauldron, and as the Woman of Peace retreated down the cottage path, towards the twin hills that marked the fairy's Land of Light, she said to the fairy,

> *"A smith is able to make*
> *Cold iron hot with a coal;*
> *The due of the kettle is bones,*
> *And to bring it back again whole."*

And so it was that the cauldron was returned that evening, left quietly on the cottage doorstop, filled with juicy bones.

The Woman of Peace came again, later that day, and without saying a word, indicated the cauldron. And as days turned into years, an unspoken relationship developed between the two women, fairy and mortal. Mairearad would loan her cauldron, and in exchange she would have it filled with delicious bones. She never forgot to whisper, as the fairy drew out of sight,

> *"A smith is able to make*
> *Cold iron hot with a coal;*
> *The due of the kettle is bones,*
> *And to bring it back again whole."*

Then one day, Mairearad had to leave her cottage for a day, to travel to Castlebay, across the sea on Barra.

She said to her husband before she left, "When the Woman of Peace comes to the doorstep, you must let her take the cauldron, but do not forget to say to her what I always say."

And so her husband worked his field, as he always did, and as he returned for his midday meal he met with a curious sight, for scurrying along the path in front of him was a wee woman, her face gnarled with age, her eyes bright and shrewd. Suddenly he felt an inexplicable fear, for most men have had fed to them as bairns the tales of fairies and the cruel tricks they play, their enchantments and their evil spells. He remembered them all now in a rush of tortuous thought, and pushed past the fairy woman to slam the cottage door. She knocked firmly, but he refused to answer, panting with terror on the other side of the door.

At last there was silence, and then, a weird howl echoed around the cottage walls and there was a scrambling on the roof. Through the chimney was thrust the long brown arm of the fairy woman, and she reached straight down to the fire upon which the cauldron sat, and pulled it with a rush of air, through the cottage roof.

Mairearad's husband was still pressed against the door when she returned that evening, and she looked curiously at the empty hearth, remarking, "The Woman of Peace always returns the cauldron before darkness falls."

Then her husband hung his head in shame and told her how he'd barred the door, and when the fairy had taken the cauldron, he'd forgotten to ask for its return. Well Mairearad scolded her husband, and putting on her overcoat and boots, she left the cottage, lantern in hand.

Darkness can play tricks as devilish as those of the fairies themselves, and it was not long before the dancing shadows, and whispering trees sent a shiver along the spine of the fierce wife Mairearad, but still she pressed on, safe in the knowledge that the Woman of Peace was her friend. She reached the threshold of the Land of Light and saw on a fire, just inside the door, her cauldron, filled as usual with tender bones. And so she grabbed it, and half-fearing where she was, began to ran, exciting the attention of the black fairy dogs that slept beside an old man who guarded the entrance.

Up they jumped, and woke the old man, who cried out,

> *"Silent woman, dumb woman,*
> *Who has come to us from the Land of the Dead*
> *Since you have not blessed the brugh –*
> *Unleash Black and let go Fierce."*

And he let the dogs free to chase the terrified woman right back to the door of her cottage, baying and howling, spitting with determination and hunger. As she ran she dropped the tasty bones, buying herself a moment or two's respite from the snarling dogs. For fairy dogs are faster than any dogs on earth, and will devour all human flesh that comes across their paths. Mairearad fled down the path, finally reaching her door and slamming it shut behind her. There she told her breathless story to her husband, and they held one another's ears against the painful wailing of the hounds. Finally there was silence.

Never again did the fairy Woman of Peace come to Mairearad's cottage, nor did she borrow the cauldron. Mairearad and her husband missed the succulent bones, but never again did they trouble the fairy folk. They are long dead now, buried on the grassy verge on the island of Sandray, where the sheep graze calmly on the succulent green grass, freshened by the moist salt air, kept company by the fairy folk who live in a verdant knoll.

The Fairy Dancers

IT WAS CHRISTMAS EVE and by the Loch Etive sat two farmers, longing for a drink but with an empty barrel between them. And so it was decided, on that icy Christmas Eve, that these two farmers would walk the road to Kingshouse, their nearest inn, and they would buy a barrel of the best whiskey there, a three-gallon jar that would warm them through the frosty months to come.

So they set off along the winding road, and over the hills that glistened with snow, all frosted with ice, and came to the warm wooded inn at Kingshouse. It was there that a cup of tea was shared, and a wee dram or two, and so the two men were quite merry as they set off home again, the three-gallon jar heavy on the back of the youngest man, for they would take turns carrying its weight on the long journey down the winding road and over the hills.

And over the hills they went but they were stopped there, by the need for a taste of that whiskey, and for a smoke. Then the sound of a fantastic reel grew louder and louder, and a light shone brighter over the hills, towards the north.

"Och, it's just a wee star," said one man, ready for his smoke and his tipple.

"Nah, it's a light, and there's a party there to be sure," said the other, who was a great dancer and loved a reel more than any other.

So they crossed the brae to the north, towards the light, and the sound of pipes, which played a fine tune. There in front of them were dancers, women in silk dresses, bowing and twirling, and men in highland dress, with pipes playing an enchanted, fine tune that drew them towards the hill.

The younger man, who carried the jar, went first, and as he entered the great door in the hillside, and joined the merry throng, the door was closed. When the other farmer, slower than the first, reached the site, there was nothing to be found. For his friend had disappeared and there was no trace of him.

It was a cold and lonely walk home, and the farmer puzzled over what had occurred on that moonlit hill, with a magical reel playing from a light that shone in the darkness. He went first to the farm of the other man, and he told his wife what had happened, but as he talked, faces closed, and brows became furrowed, and it was clear that he was not believed, that no man could lose his friend on a hill just a few miles from home.

And so it was that the policemen were called from Inveraray, and they took him away and asked him questions that made his head spin, and caused him to slump over in exhaustion, and he wished more than anything for a drop of the whiskey that was hung on the other man's back. They kept him there, the police, and he was sent to trial, but he told them all the same thing, how a magical reel had played from a light that shone in the darkness, and how his friend had disappeared without trace.

He was sent back to that prison, and when they asked him again, he could only tell the truth of that fateful night, so they asked him no more, and sent him home, for he would not budge from his story, and that story never changed.

And it was near twelve months before this man had cause to travel past that hill again, and with him this time were some lads from the village who had set themselves the task of catching some fish for the Christmas feast. And with a basket full of fish, they stopped on their way back to their homes, with the need for a smoke and a taste of the whiskey that the farmer had tucked in his belt. And there again they heard that fantastic music, and saw the light beaming from the darkness of the hills.

But the lads from the village had heard too much of this madness, and they struggled home with the fish, ahead of the farmer who wanted more than anything to find his friend, and that barrel of whiskey. So the farmer climbed over the hills, towards that light, and he heard there the sound of pipes, which played a fine tune. There in front of him were dancers, women in silk dresses, bowing and twirling, and men in highland dress, with pipes playing an enchanted, fine tune that drew him towards the hill.

And he stuck his fishing hook in the threshold of the door, for no fairy can touch the metal of a mortal man, and he entered the room which spun with the music, and threatened to drag him into its midst. But this farmer never liked a dance, preferring instead a good smoke and a dram of whiskey, and he resisted the calls on his soul, and struggled through the crowd to find his friend the farmer, who danced in the middle of the reel like a man possessed.

"Och, lad, we've only just begun," the dancer protested, as his friend dragged him away.

And since he had danced for near twelve months with that barrel on his back, he carried it home again, along the winding road and over the hills that glistened with snow, all frosted with ice. They came to the farm of the man who'd been dancing, and what a surprise met his poor lonely wife when she opened the door. For there was her husband, just skin and bones to be sure, but there nonetheless with his barrel of whiskey, just twelve months late.

And they sat up that night, the man and his friend, and each of their wives, and what a Christmas Eve they had with that barrel of whiskey, which had mellowed with the warmth of the fairy hill, and they drank it all, just twelve months late.

The Page-Boy and the Silver Goblet

THERE WAS ONCE A LITTLE page-boy, who was in service in a stately castle. He was a very good-natured little fellow, and did his duties so willingly and well that everybody liked him, from the great Earl whom he served every day on bended knee, to the fat old butler whose errands he ran.

Now the castle stood on the edge of a cliff overlooking the sea, and although the walls at that side were very thick, in them there was a little postern door, which opened on to a narrow flight of steps that led down the face of the cliff to the sea shore, so that anyone who liked could go down there in the pleasant summer mornings and bathe in the shimmering sea.

On the other side of the castle were gardens and pleasure grounds, opening on to a long stretch of heather-covered moorland, which, at last, met a distant range of hills.

The little page-boy was very fond of going out on this moor when his work was done, for then he could run about as much as he liked, chasing bumble-bees, and catching butterflies, and looking for birds' nests when it was nesting time.

So one night, when everyone else was asleep, he crept out of the castle by the little postern door, and stole down the stone steps, and along the sea shore, and up on to the moor, and went straight to the Fairy Knowe.

To his delight he found that what everyone said was true. The top of the Knowe was tipped up, and from the opening that was thus made, rays of light came streaming out.

His heart was beating fast with excitement, but, gathering his courage, he stooped down and slipped inside the Knowe.

He found himself in a large room lit by numberless tiny candles, and there, seated round a polished table, were scores of the tiny folk, fairies, and elves, and gnomes, dressed in green, and yellow, and pink; blue, and lilac, and scarlet; in all the colours, in fact, that you can think of.

He stood in a dark corner watching the busy scene in wonder, thinking how strange it was that there should be such a number of these tiny beings living their own lives all unknown to men, at such a little distance from them, when suddenly someone – he could not tell who it was – gave an order.

"Fetch the Cup," cried the owner of the unknown voice, and instantly two little fairy pages, dressed all in scarlet livery, darted from the table to a tiny cupboard in the rock, and returned staggering under the weight of a most beautiful silver cup, richly embossed and lined inside with gold.

He placed it in the middle of the table, and, amid clapping of hands and shouts of joy, all the fairies began to drink out of it in turn. And the page could see, from where he stood, that no one poured wine into it, and yet it was always full, and that the wine that was in it was not always the same kind, but that each fairy, when he grasped its stem, wished for the wine that he loved best, and lo! in a moment the cup was full of it.

"'Twould be a fine thing if I could take that cup home with me," thought the page. "No one will believe that I have been here except I have something to show for it." So he bided his time, and watched.

Presently the fairies noticed him, and, instead of being angry at his boldness in entering their abode, as he expected that they would be, they seemed very pleased to see him, and invited him to a seat at the table. But by and by they grew rude and insolent, and jeered at him for being content to serve mere mortals, telling him that they saw everything that went on at the castle, and making fun of the old butler, whom the page loved with all his heart. And they laughed at the food he ate, saying that it was only fit for animals; and when any fresh dainty was set on the table by the scarlet-clad pages, they would push the dish across to him, saying: "Taste it, for you will not have the chance of tasting such things at the castle."

At last he could stand their teasing remarks no longer; besides, he knew that if he wanted to secure the cup he must lose no time in doing so.

So he suddenly stood up, and grasped the stem of it tightly in his hand. "I'll drink to you all in water," he cried, and instantly the ruby wine was turned to clear cold water.

He raised the cup to his lips, but he did not drink from it. With a sudden jerk he threw the water over the candles, and instantly the room was in darkness. Then, clasping the precious cup tightly in his arms, he sprang to the opening of the Knowe, through which he could see the stars glimmering clearly.

He was just in time, for it fell to with a crash behind him; and soon he was speeding along the wet, dew-spangled moor, with the whole troop of fairies at his heels.

They were wild with rage, and from the shrill shouts of fury which they uttered, the page knew well that, if they overtook him, he need expect no mercy at their hands.

And his heart began to sink, for, fleet of foot though he was, he was no match for the fairy folk, who gained on him steadily.

All seemed lost, when a mysterious voice sounded out of the darkness:

"If thou wouldst gain the castle door, keep to the black stones on the shore."

It was the voice of some poor mortal, who, for some reason or other, had been taken prisoner by the fairies – who were really very malicious little folk – and who did not want a like fate to befall the adventurous page-boy; but the little fellow did not know this.

He had once heard that if anyone walked on the wet sands, where the waves had come over them, the fairies could not touch him, and this mysterious sentence brought the saying into his mind.

So he turned, and dashed panting down to the shore. His feet sank in the dry sand, his breath came in little gasps, and he felt as if he must give up the struggle; but he persevered, and at last, just as the foremost fairies were about to lay hands on him, he jumped across the water-mark on to the firm, wet sand, from which the waves had just receded, and then he knew that he was safe.

For the little folk could go no step further, but stood on the dry sand uttering cries of rage and disappointment, while the triumphant page-boy ran safely along the shore, his precious cup in his arms, and climbed lightly up the steps in the rock and disappeared through the postern. And for many years after, long after the little page-boy had grown up and become a stately butler, who trained other little page-boys to follow in his footsteps, the beautiful cup remained in the castle as a witness of his adventure.

The Legend of Knockgrafton

THERE WAS ONCE a poor man who lived in the fertile glen of Aherlow, at the foot of the gloomy Galtee mountains, and he had a great hump on his back: he looked just as if his body had been rolled up and placed upon his shoulders; and his head was pressed down with the weight so much that his chin, when he was sitting, used to rest upon his knees for support. The country people were rather shy of meeting him in any lonesome place, for though, poor creature, he was as harmless and as inoffensive as a new-born infant, yet his deformity was so great that he scarcely appeared to be a human creature, and some ill-minded persons had set strange stories about him afloat. He was said to have a great knowledge of herbs and charms; but certain it was that he had a mighty skilful hand in plaiting straw and rushes into hats and baskets, which was the way he made his livelihood.

Lusmore, for that was the nickname put upon him by reason of his always wearing a sprig of the fairy cap, or lusmore (the foxglove), in his little straw hat, would ever get a higher penny for his plaited work than anyone else, and perhaps that was the reason why someone, out of envy, had circulated the strange stories about him.

Be that as it may, it happened that he was returning one evening from the pretty town of Cahir towards Cappagh, and as little Lusmore walked very slowly, on account of the great hump upon his back, it was quite dark when he came to the old moat of Knockgrafton, which stood on the right-hand side of his road. Tired and weary was he, and noways comfortable in his own mind at thinking how much farther he had to travel, and that he should be walking all the night; so he sat down under the moat to rest himself, and began looking mournfully enough upon the moon.

Presently there rose a wild strain of unearthly melody upon the ear of little Lusmore; he listened, and he thought that he had never heard such ravishing music before. It was like the sound of many voices, each mingling and blending with the other so strangely that they seemed to be one, though all singing different strains, and the words of the song were these – *Da Luan, Da Mort, Da Luan, Da Mort, Da Luan, Da Mort*; when there would be a moment's pause, and then the round of melody went on again.

Lusmore listened attentively, scarcely drawing his breath lest he might lose the slightest note. He now plainly perceived that the singing was within the moat; and though at first it had charmed him so much, he began to get tired of hearing the same round sung over and over so often without any change; so availing himself of the pause when the *Da Luan, Da Mort*, had been sung three times, he took up the tune, and raised it with the words *augus Da Cadine*, and then went on singing with the voices inside of the moat, *Da Luan, Da Mort*, finishing the melody, when the pause again came, with *augus Da Cadine*.

The fairies within Knockgrafton, for the song was a fairy melody, when they heard this addition to the tune, were so much delighted that, with instant resolve, it was determined to bring the mortal among them, whose musical skill so far exceeded theirs, and little Lusmore was conveyed into their company with the eddying speed of a whirlwind.

Glorious to behold was the sight that burst upon him as he came down through the moat, twirling round and round, with the lightness of a straw, to the sweetest music that kept time to his motion. The greatest honour was then paid him, for he was put above all the musicians, and he had servants tending upon him, and everything to his heart's content, and a hearty welcome to all; and, in short, he was made as much of as if he had been the first man in the land.

Presently Lusmore saw a great consultation going forward among the fairies, and, notwithstanding all their civility, he felt very much frightened, until one stepping out from the rest came up to him and said –

> *"Lusmore! Lusmore!*
> *Doubt not, nor deplore,*
> *For the hump which you bore*
> *On your back is no more;*
> *Look down on the floor,*
> *And view it, Lusmore!"*

When these words were said, poor little Lusmore felt himself so light, and so happy, that he thought he could have bounded at one jump over the moon, like the cow in the history of the cat and the fiddle; and he saw, with inexpressible pleasure, his hump tumble down upon the ground from his shoulders. He then tried to lift up his head, and he did so with becoming caution, fearing that he might knock it against the ceiling of the grand hall, where he was; he looked round and round again with greatest wonder and delight upon everything, which appeared more and more beautiful; and, overpowered at beholding such a resplendent scene, his head grew dizzy, and his eyesight became dim. At last he fell into a sound sleep, and when he awoke he found that it was broad daylight, the sun shining brightly, and the birds singing sweetly; and that he was lying just at the foot of the moat of Knockgrafton, with the cows and sheep grazing peacefully round about him. The first thing Lusmore did, after saying his prayers, was to put his hand behind to feel for his hump, but no sign of one was there on his back, and he looked at himself with great pride, for he had now become a well-shaped dapper little fellow, and more than that, found himself in a full suit of new clothes, which he concluded the fairies had made for him.

Towards Cappagh he went, stepping out as lightly, and springing up at every step as if he had been all his life a dancing-master. Not a creature who met Lusmore knew him without his hump, and he had a great work to persuade everyone that he was the same man – in truth he was not, so far as outward appearance went.

Of course it was not long before the story of Lusmore's hump got about, and a great wonder was made of it. Through the country, for miles round, it was the talk of every one, high and low.

One morning, as Lusmore was sitting contented enough, at his cabin door, up came an old woman to him, and asked him if he could direct her to Cappagh.

"I need give you no directions, my good woman," said Lusmore, "for this is Cappagh; and whom may you want here?"

"I have come," said the woman, "out of Decie's country, in the county of Waterford looking after one Lusmore, who, I have heard tell, had his hump taken off by the fairies; for there is a son of a gossip of mine who has got a hump on him that will be his death; and maybe if he could use the same charm as Lusmore, the hump may be taken off him. And now I have told you the reason of my coming so far: 'tis to find out about this charm, if I can."

Lusmore, who was ever a good-natured little fellow, told the woman all the particulars, how he had raised the tune for the fairies at Knockgrafton, how his hump had been removed from his shoulders, and how he had got a new suit of clothes into the bargain.

The woman thanked him very much, and then went away quite happy and easy in her own mind. When she came back to her gossip's house, in the county of Waterford, she told her everything that Lusmore had said, and they put the little hump-backed man, who was a peevish and cunning creature from his birth, upon a car, and took him all the way across the country. It was a long journey, but they did not care for that, so the hump was taken from off him; and they brought him, just at nightfall, and left him under the old moat of Knockgrafton.

Jack Madden, for that was the humpy man's name, had not been sitting there long when he heard the tune going on within the moat much sweeter than before; for the fairies were singing it the way Lusmore had settled their music for them, and the song was going on; *Da Luan, Da Mort, Da Luan, Da Mort, Da Luan, Da Mort, augus Da Cadine*, without ever stopping. Jack Madden, who was in a great hurry to get quit of his hump, never thought of waiting until the fairies had done, or watching for a fit opportunity to raise the tune higher again than Lusmore had; so having heard them sing it over seven times without stopping, out he bawls, never minding the time or the humour of the tune, or how he could bring his words in properly, *augus Da Cadine, augus Da Hena*, thinking that if one day was good, two were better; and that if Lusmore had one new suit of clothes given him, he should have two.

No sooner had the words passed his lips than he was taken up and whisked into the moat with prodigious force; and the fairies came crowding round about him with great anger, screeching, and screaming, and roaring out, "Who spoiled our tune? Who spoiled our tune?" and one stepped up to him, above all the rest and said:

> *"Jack Madden! Jack Madden!*
> *Your words came so bad in*
> *The tune we felt glad in; –*
> *This castle you're bad in,*
> *That your life we may sadden;*
> *Here's two humps for Jack Madden!"*

And twenty of the strongest fairies brought Lusmore's hump and put it down upon poor Jack's back, over his own, where it became fixed as firmly as if it was nailed on with twelve-penny nails, by the best carpenter that ever drove one. Out of their castle they then kicked him; and, in the morning, when Jack Madden's mother and her gossip came to look after their little man, they found him half dead, lying at the foot of the moat, with the other hump upon his back. Well to be sure, how they did look at each other! But they were afraid to say anything, lest a hump might be put upon their own shoulders. Home they brought the unlucky Jack Madden with them, as downcast in their hearts and their looks as ever two gossips were; and what through the weight of his other hump, and the long journey, he died soon after, leaving they say his heavy curse to anyone who would go to listen to fairy tunes again.

The Leprechaun of Ardmore Tower

THE LEPRECHAUN – that flash from elf-land – was perched comfortably upon the west window ledge, high up in Ardmore Tower. Dawn was just beginning to send misty, grey lights over the rolling land. Winds that have blown since the world began were blowing around the old Irish tower. It was the south wind, this morning, that was blowing the strongest – the wind from the good sea that washed the coast of Ardmore and the high-lands of Ireland. The strong, stone tower, tapering skyward, stood, as it stands today, like a silent sentinel on the 'hill of the sheep' – the 'great hill.' Below its conical top, two windows, east and west, looked out, and it's on the ledge of the west one – mind you – that the Leprechaun was sitting. He had been sitting there since sundown. An iron bar, inside the tower, goes from the top of the west window to the top of the east window, and once, no one knows how long ago, seven small bells hung from this bar under the pinnacle. They are gone now, but in the old days they used to ring often.

("That's so," said the Leprechaun. He was always saying "That's so," to agree with himself or other people – himself oftenest.)

This little elf, in red jacket and green breeches who spends most of his days and some of his nights making shoes for the fairy folk, has been working the past night on a pair of riding boots for the fairy prince who wants the boots by sunrise. Tap, tap, tap – goes the Leprechaun's tiny hammer. Whish, whish, go his swift fingers. Hum, hum-m-m-m – goes his little singing tune, for the Leprechaun could no more work without singing than you could sleep without shutting your eyes.

("That's so!" said the Leprechaun.)

He is only six inches high, and harder to catch than a will-o'-the-wisp. If one could ever succeed in catching him, and then could keep looking at him, he might tell – though not a bit willingly – where a wonderful crock of gold is. But do you think you could keep looking at him and at him alone? Why, just as you think you are looking at nothing else, he, somehow, makes you look away from him, and, ochone, he is gone! He's that clever.

("That's so," said the Leprechaun.)

Many an enchantment the Leprechaun can perform, for all he appears so simple as he pegs away at the riding boots. Yes, himself it is that can blight the corn or snip off hair most unexpectedly. When he sits, crosslegged at his work, whether on a cornice of a roof or on a twig of the low bushes, it's just as well not to let him know you are watching him. The Irish fairy folk are all like that, and draw magic out of earth and sea and sky, or else draw it out of nothing at all.

("Do you hear that?" said the Leprechaun.)

Now this misty, windy dawn of a morning, thousands of days and nights ago, as the Leprechaun, up there on the grey, stone tower, tapped, tapped with his hammer, to finish the prince's boots, promised by sunrise, his elfin mind capered around with many thoughts. The mists were beginning to shine in the dim light of early morning, and the Leprechaun's thoughts, freshened by the south wind, were wafted over the whole land of Erin that stretched beyond the bogs and swamps, beyond the mounds and cromlechs, beyond the hills. He could tell you the colours of all the winds of Ireland. This south wind was white; the north wind, full of blackness; the west wind pale yellow, and the east wind was always a stirring, purple wind. The lesser winds, too, had their colours – yellow of furze, red of fire, grey of fog, green of meadow, brown of autumn leaves, and three more colours that mortals could not see. The Leprechaun, whenever he wished, could travel lightly on whatever wind was blowing and sing a tune as loud as any of them. This morning, in the misty dawn, it was his heart that did the travelling and it was his thoughts that sang tunes to match. When his eyes glanced from his work, toward the sea, his thoughts flew to Manannan Mac Lir, the old sea-god, riding along in his chariot, with thousands of his steeds shaking their manes as they galloped with him. For many a century, the great, slender, round tower had watched these steeds and the spirited charioteer. On many a moonlit night, it had seen invading bands crawl quietly to shore and stealthily march right up to the base of the tower with bad plans to surprise the unprotected people. Again and again the men of Ardmore had gathered their families, with provisions, safely, into the tall tower, barring the narrow door that was many feet high above the ground. There the weak ones and the women and children had lived, for days, until the invaders had been driven away. The Leprechaun laughed aloud as he thought of one stormy day when the old sea-god, Manannan Mac Lir, had bidden his horses keep the invaders from reaching the shore and the tower. The lively horses shook their manes and obeyed – ochone, but they obeyed!

Tap, tap, tap! The south wind, thought the Leprechaun, will be a strong one, this day! And the wind will draw music from the harps of all the Little Good Folk throughout Erin. As the Leprechaun, between his taps, looked westward, there was a break in the light morning vapour, like the gay snatch of song a maiden sings in the midst of her work; and, through the break, the elf's long gaze swept across the river Blackwater, and beside Watergrasshill, over the moor-land to the Bochragh Mountains, and even as far as Mt. Mish. There was a tale about Mt. Mish that rushed in now upon his thinking – a tale about his ancestors, the Tuatha-de-Danann, 'the folk of the god whose mother is Dana.'

On a day, in the early age of the world, when grey moor-land and steep mountains began to blaze brilliant with purple heather and yellow furze, the Danaans, covering themselves with a fog, crept along the east coast to possess the country near Mt. Mish. Fiercely they fought with the inhabitants, the Firbolgs, and won. For a thousand years they held sway – these tall, fair-haired men of Greek descent who had come from the North. After the thousand years and one day more, new invaders, the Milesians, entering along the bank of the Inverskena River, swept up into the land, like the knowing conquerors that they were, to overcome the Danaans.

The Leprechaun now sang, with a little humming chant, the words that Amergin, chief druid of the Milesians, sang when he set his right foot on the soil of Erin:

"I am the wind that blows over the sea,
I am the wave of the ocean,
I am the murmur of the billows,
I am the ox of the seven combats,
I am the vulture upon the rock,
I am a ray of the Sun,
I am the fairest of plants."

When the Danaans had been conquered by the Milesians, they promised that they would dwell inside the hills or under the lakes, and that they would be invisible to mortals, except on rare occasions. This promise they had kept.

("That's so," said the Leprechaun.)

The Leprechaun liked what the Danaans, his ancestors, had done next. The chief druid of the Danaans had raised his golden harp in the dazzling sunlight, the other druids had lifted their silver harps in the glittering morning air, and all the druids had played such deliciously enchanting melodies that the Danaans, in a long procession that seemed like a living green, had followed their leaders, laughing as they went, and singing like merry brooks or happy children. Into the mountains they had gone, disappearing before the very eyes of the Milesians. Forever afterwards they lived within the mountains and became the Ever-Living Living Ones in the Land of Youth.

The Leprechaun knew well that he, and all his elf kin, were descendants of those very Danaans, who still lived in their underground palaces that blazed with light and laughter. Hadn't the drean – the wise, small wren – that druid of birds, often told him what was going on down there? Hadn't he himself been below the tower of Ardmore, where, in a glorious hall that belonged to the Ever-Living Living Ones, the Danaans held many a gay carousal? Didn't he hear, at times, their bells ringing under the bog, on a quiet evening? And hadn't he, more times than once, rung the sweet bells of Ardmore – these bells which never had been rung except by one whose real home was in the Land of Youth? In the Land of Youth was the Leprechaun's home. (Ochone, I should say!) There it had been since the day that Oisin, son of Finn, journeyed to that land. For, on the same day, without Oisin's knowledge, the Leprechaun had sped from the green hills of Erin, through a golden haze, to the country of the Ever-Living Living Ones. Oisin was his hero, his great hero, whom he had helped, invisibly, more than he had helped anyone else. The most valiant Danaan of all was Oisin, and Oisin he would follow to the world's end.

("That's so," said the Leprechaun, as he began the fancy stitching on the prince's riding boots.)

Now, for the thousandth time, he told himself the story of Oisin, for he liked this tale best of all: how Oisin, when hunting, met the maiden, Niam of the Golden Hair, riding her snow-white steed; how, after she sang to him a song of the enchanting "land beyond dreams," Oisin had ridden with her to the Land of Youth (and the Leprechaun, in the shape of a butterfly, had perched on the horse's mane); how, in the realm of her father, the king, fearless Oisin had had brave adventures. He rescued a princess from a giant; subdued the three Hounds of Erin (helped by the Leprechaun who confused the hounds), and found the magic harp – a harp next in wonder to the Dagda's harp whose strings, when touched, would sing the story of the one who last touched them. He had even tilted with the king's cupbearer to win a gold-hilted sword, and had done other worthy deeds. No time at all, it seemed to Oisin, that magical time, in the Land of Youth, but, at last, his heart longed to see his old home. So Niam of the Golden Hair gave him her snow-white steed to ride, but charged him three times that, when he should reach the familiar places of Erin, he must not, once, set foot upon the ground or he would never be able to return to the Land of Youth. Oisin bade her farewell and, with the Leprechaun as a butterfly still on the horse's mane, he began his homeward journey.

As he was riding along, once more, through a beautiful vale of Erin, he saw men, much smaller than himself, trying in vain to push aside a huge boulder that had rolled from the hillside down upon their tilled land. In pity for these weaklings, he instantly jumped from his saddle to the ground (not heeding the Leprechaun who, in his own form, clung with all his might, to remind him of Niam's warning) and, with one push, he sent the boulder out of the way. Alas! Even as the men were shouting praises to their god-like helper, it seemed to Oisin that darkness bore him to the earth. When he opened his eyes, lo, he was an old man, feeble, grey-headed, grey-bearded! The men whom he had helped, had with one accord run away; but the Leprechaun, astride a twig close by, whispered words of cheer and sang part of the song of the Danaans when they went into the mountains. Oisin then roused himself and said faintly, "I hear the voice of bells." Then he added in a resolute tone, "Whenever I shall hear sweet bells ring, young will be my heart." Since that day, the Leprechaun had often rung bells, especially the bells of Ardmore Tower, because he knew that Oisin would hear them and feel young again.

Tap, tap, tap – and the Leprechaun's work is done. It's little that anyone can tell about him making shoes, or about Ireland's heroes, or about its grassy mounds of mystery. He stands up now and stretches himself. If he felt like it, he could blow a blast on the tiny, curved horn, hanging at his side, and call, from the Underland, as many merry-hearted Danaans as he chose. He could cast spells, too, on the sea, beyond the ninth wave from shore. Instead, he whisks from the west window into the tower and out again, through the east window. There he stands for a few moments – his feet braced on the highest circular cornice, his back leaning against the sloping roof top – watching the rim of the sun rise over a mountainous cloud. The sky of gold is changing to the pink of a wild rose. The grey mists, over moorland and mound, are scattering as quickly as the men whom Oisin helped.

The Round Tower of Ardmore again greeted the sun, as the Leprechaun, hugging tightly the riding boots promised to the fairy prince at sunrise, swiftly slid down a sunbeam to the top of the oak tree, where the prince was waiting.

"Here they are, Your Highness," said the elf, with a bow.

The prince smiled, as he took the boots, and gave the Leprechaun a piece of gold. "You've kept your promise," he said.

"That's so," answered the Leprechaun. Then he sprang up on the rollicking south wind and flew away.

The Yellow Dwarf

ONCE UPON A TIME there lived a queen who had been the mother of a great many children, and of them all only one daughter was left. But then she was worth at least a thousand.

Her mother, who, since the death of the King, her father, had nothing in the world she cared for so much as this little princess, was so terribly afraid of losing her that she quite spoiled her, and never tried to correct any of her faults. The consequence was that this little person, who was as pretty as possible, and was one day to wear a crown, grew up so proud and so much in love with her own beauty that she despised everyone else in the world.

The Queen, her mother, by her caresses and flatteries, helped to make her believe that there was nothing too good for her. She was dressed almost always in the prettiest frocks, as a fairy, or as a queen going out to hunt, and the ladies of the court followed her dressed as forest-fairies.

And to make her more vain than ever the Queen caused her portrait to be taken by the cleverest painters and sent it to several neighbouring kings with whom she was very friendly.

When they saw this portrait they fell in love with the Princess – every one of them, but upon each it had a different effect. One fell ill, one went quite crazy, and a few of the luckiest set off to see her as soon as possible; but these poor princes became her slaves the moment they set eyes on her.

Never has there been a gayer court. Twenty delightful kings did everything they could think of to make themselves agreeable, and after having spent ever so much money in giving a single entertainment thought themselves very lucky if the Princess said "That's pretty."

All this admiration vastly pleased the Queen. Not a day passed but she received seven or eight thousand sonnets, and as many elegies, madrigals, and songs, which were sent her by all the poets in the world. All the prose and the poetry that was written just then was about Bellissima – for that was the Princess's name – and all the bonfires that they had were made of these verses, which crackled and sparkled better than any other sort of wood.

Bellissima was already fifteen years old, and every one of the princes wished to marry her, but not one dared to say so. How could they when they knew that any of them might have cut off his head five or six times a day just to please her, and she would have thought it a mere trifle, so little did she care? You may imagine how hard-hearted her lovers thought her; and the Queen, who wished to see her married, did not know how to persuade her to think of it seriously.

"Bellissima," she said, "I do wish you would not be so proud. What makes you despise all these nice kings? I wish you to marry one of them, and you do not try to please me."

"I am so happy," Bellissima answered: "do leave me in peace, madam. I don't want to care for anyone."

"But you would be very happy with any of these princes," said the Queen, "and I shall be very angry if you fall in love with anyone who is not worthy of you."

But the Princess thought so much of herself that she did not consider any one of her lovers clever or handsome enough for her; and her mother, who was getting really angry at her determination not to be married, began to wish that she had not allowed her to have her own way so much.

At last, not knowing what else to do, she resolved to consult a certain witch who was called 'The Fairy of the Desert.' Now this was very difficult to do, as she was guarded by some terrible lions; but happily the Queen had heard a long time before that whoever wanted to pass these lions safely must throw to them a cake made of millet flour, sugar-candy, and crocodile's eggs. This cake she prepared with her own hands, and putting it in a little basket, she set out to seek the Fairy. But as she was not used to walking far, she soon felt very tired and sat down at the foot of a tree to rest, and presently fell fast asleep. When she awoke she was dismayed to find her basket empty. The cake was all gone! and, to make matters worse, at that moment she heard the roaring of the great lions, who had found out that she was near and were coming to look for her.

"What shall I do?" she cried; "I shall be eaten up," and being too much frightened to run a single step, she began to cry, and leant against the tree under which she had been asleep. Just then she heard some one say: "H'm, h'm!"

She looked all round her, and then up at the tree, and there she saw a little tiny man, who was eating oranges.

"Oh! Queen," said he, "I know you very well, and I know how much afraid you are of the lions; and you are quite right too, for they have eaten many other people: and what can you expect, as you have not any cake to give them?"

"I must make up my mind to die," said the poor Queen. "Alas! I should not care so much if only my dear daughter were married."

"Oh! you have a daughter," cried the Yellow Dwarf (who was so called because he was a dwarf and had such a yellow face, and lived in the orange tree). "I'm really glad to hear that, for I've been looking for a wife all over the world. Now, if you will promise that she shall marry me, not one of the lions, tigers, or bears shall touch you."

The Queen looked at him and was almost as much afraid of his ugly little face as she had been of the lions before, so that she could not speak a word.

"What! you hesitate, madam," cried the Dwarf. "You must be very fond of being eaten up alive."

And, as he spoke, the Queen saw the lions, which were running down a hill towards them.

Each one had two heads, eight feet, and four rows of teeth, and their skins were as hard as turtle shells, and were bright red.

At this dreadful sight, the poor Queen, who was trembling like a dove when it sees a hawk, cried out as loud as she could, "Oh! dear Mr. Dwarf, Bellissima shall marry you."

"Oh, indeed!" said he disdainfully. "Bellissima is pretty enough, but I don't particularly want to marry her – you can keep her."

"Oh! noble sir," said the Queen in great distress, "do not refuse her. She is the most charming Princess in the world."

"Oh! well," he replied, "out of charity I will take her; but be sure you don't forget that she is mine."

As he spoke a little door opened in the trunk of the orange tree, in rushed the Queen, only just in time, and the door shut with a bang in the faces of the lions.

The Queen was so confused that at first she did not notice another little door in the orange tree, but presently it opened and she found herself in a field of thistles and nettles. It was encircled by a muddy ditch, and a little further on was a tiny thatched cottage, out of which came the Yellow Dwarf with a very jaunty air. He wore wooden shoes and a little yellow coat, and as he had no hair and very long ears he looked altogether a shocking little object.

"I am delighted," said he to the Queen, "that, as you are to be my mother-in-law, you should see the little house in which your Bellissima will live with me. With these thistles and nettles she can feed a donkey which she can ride whenever she likes; under this humble roof no weather can hurt her; she will drink the water of this brook, and eat frogs – which grow very fat about here; and then she will have me always with her, handsome, agreeable, and gay as you see me now. For if her shadow stays by her more closely than I do I shall be surprised."

The unhappy Queen, seeing all at once what a miserable life her daughter would have with this Dwarf, could not bear the idea, and fell down insensible without saying a word

When she revived she found to her great surprise that she was lying in her own bed at home, and, what was more, that she had on the loveliest lace nightcap that she had ever seen in her life. At first she thought that all her adventures, the terrible lions, and her promise to the Yellow Dwarf that he should marry Bellissima must have been a dream, but there was the new cap with its beautiful ribbon and lace to remind her that it was all true, which made her so unhappy that she could neither eat, drink, nor sleep for thinking of it.

The Princess, who, in spite of her wilfulness, really loved her mother with all her heart, was much grieved when she saw her looking so sad, and often asked her what was the matter; but the Queen, who didn't want her to find out the truth, only said that she was ill, or that one of her neighbours was threatening to make war against her. Bellissima knew quite well that something was being hidden from her – and that neither of these was the real reason of the Queen's uneasiness. So she made up her mind that she would go and consult the Fairy of the Desert about it, especially as she had often heard how wise she was, and she thought that at the same time she might ask her advice as to whether it would be as well to be married, or not.

So, with great care, she made some of the proper cake to pacify the lions, and one night went up to her room very early, pretending that she was going to bed; but, instead of that, she wrapped herself up in a long white veil, and went down a secret staircase, and set off, all by herself, to find the Witch.

But when she got as far as the same fatal orange tree, and saw it covered with flowers and fruit, she stopped and began to gather some of the oranges – and then, putting down her basket, she sat down to eat them. But when it was time to go on again the basket had disappeared, and, though she looked everywhere, not a trace of it could she find. The more she hunted for it the more frightened she got, and at last she began to cry. Then all at once she saw before her the Yellow Dwarf.

"What's the matter with you, my pretty one?" said he. "What are you crying about?"

"Alas!" she answered; "no wonder that I am crying, seeing that I have lost the basket of cake that was to help me to get safely to the cave of the Fairy of the Desert."

"And what do you want with her, pretty one?" said the little monster, "for I am a friend of hers, and, for the matter of that, I am quite as clever as she is."

"The Queen, my mother," replied the Princess, "has lately fallen into such deep sadness that I fear that she will die; and I am afraid that perhaps I am the cause of it, for she very much wishes me to be married, and I must tell you truly that as yet I have not found anyone I consider worthy to be my husband. So for all these reasons I wished to talk to the Fairy."

"Do not give yourself any further trouble, Princess," answered the Dwarf. "I can tell you all you want to know better than she could. The Queen, your mother, has promised you in marriage—"

"Has promised me!" interrupted the Princess. "Oh! no. I'm sure she has not. She would have told me if she had. I am too much interested in the matter for her to promise anything without my consent – you must be mistaken."

"Beautiful Princess," cried the Dwarf suddenly, throwing himself on his knees before her, "I flatter myself that you will not be displeased at her choice when I tell you that it is to me she has promised the happiness of marrying you."

"You!" cried Bellissima, starting back. "My mother wishes me to marry you! How can you be so silly as to think of such a thing?"

"Oh! it isn't that I care much to have that honour," cried the Dwarf angrily; "but here are the lions coming; they'll eat you up in three mouthfuls, and there will be an end of you and your pride."

And, indeed, at that moment the poor Princess heard their dreadful howls coming nearer and nearer.

"What shall I do?" she cried. "Must all my happy days come to an end like this?"

The malicious Dwarf looked at her and began to laugh spitefully. "At least," said he, "you have the satisfaction of dying unmarried. A lovely princess like you must surely prefer to die rather than be the wife of a poor little dwarf like myself."

"Oh! don't be angry with me," cried the Princess, clasping her hands. "I'd rather marry all the dwarfs in the world than die in this horrible way."

"Look at me well, Princess, before you give me your word," said he. "I don't want you to promise me in a hurry."

"Oh!" cried she, "the lions are coming. I have looked at you enough. I am so frightened. Save me this minute, or I shall die of terror."

Indeed, as she spoke she fell down insensible, and when she recovered she found herself in her own little bed at home; how she got there she could not tell, but she was dressed in the most beautiful lace and ribbons, and on her finger was a little ring, made of a single red hair, which fitted so tightly that, try as she might, she could not get it off.

When the Princess saw all these things, and remembered what had happened, she, too, fell into the deepest sadness, which surprised and alarmed the whole court, and the Queen more than anyone else. A hundred times she asked Bellissima if anything was the matter with her; but she always said that there was nothing.

At last the chief men of the kingdom, anxious to see their Princess married, sent to the Queen to beg her to choose a husband for her as soon as possible. She replied that nothing would please her better, but that her daughter seemed so unwilling to marry, and she recommended them to go and talk to the Princess about it themselves; so this they at once did. Now Bellissima was much less proud since her adventure with the Yellow Dwarf, and she could not think of a better way of getting rid of the little monster than to marry some powerful king, therefore she replied to their request much more favourably than they had hoped, saying that, though she was very happy as she was, still, to please them, she would consent to marry the King of the Gold Mines. Now he was a very handsome and powerful Prince, who had been in love with the Princess for years, but had not thought that she would ever care about him at all. You can easily imagine how delighted he was when he heard the news, and how angry it made all the other kings to lose for ever the hope of marrying the Princess; but after all Bellissima could not have married twenty kings – indeed, she had found it quite difficult enough to choose one, for her vanity made her believe that there was nobody in the world who was worthy of her.

Preparations were begun at once for the grandest wedding that had ever been held at the palace. The King of the Gold Mines sent such immense sums of money that the whole sea was covered with the ships that brought it. Messengers were sent to all the gayest and most refined courts, particularly to the Court of France, to seek out everything rare and precious to adorn the Princess, although her beauty was so perfect that nothing she wore could make her look prettier. At least that is what the King of the Gold Mines thought, and he was never happy unless he was with her.

As for the Princess, the more she saw of the King the more she liked him; he was so generous, so handsome and clever, that at last she was almost as much in love with him as he was with her. How happy they were as they wandered about in the beautiful gardens together, sometimes listening to sweet music! and the King used to write songs for Bellissima. This is one that she liked very much:

> *In the forest all is gay*
> *When my Princess walks that way.*
> *All the blossoms then are found*
> *Downward fluttering to the ground,*
> *Hoping she may tread on them.*
> *And bright flowers on slender stem*
> *Gaze up at her as she passes,*
> *Brushing lightly through the grasses.*
> *Oh! my Princess, birds above*
> *Echo back our songs of love,*
> *As through this enchanted land*
> *Blithe we wander, hand in hand.*

They really were as happy as the day was long. All the King's unsuccessful rivals had gone home in despair. They said good-bye to the Princess so sadly that she could not help being sorry for them.

"Ah! madam," the King of the Gold Mines said to her, "how is this? Why do you waste your pity on these princes, who love you so much that all their trouble would be well repaid by a single smile from you?"

"I should be sorry," answered Bellissima, "if you had not noticed how much I pitied these princes who were leaving me for ever; but for you, sire, it is very different: you have every reason to be pleased with me, but they are going sorrowfully away, so you must not grudge them my compassion."

The King of the Gold Mines was quite overcome by the Princess's good-natured way of taking his interference, and, throwing himself at her feet, he kissed her hand a thousand times and begged her to forgive him.

At last the happy day came. Everything was ready for Bellissima's wedding. The trumpets sounded, all the streets of the town were hung with flags and strewn with flowers, and the people ran in crowds to the great square before the palace. The Queen was so over-joyed that she had hardly been able to sleep at all, and she got up before it was light to give the necessary orders and to choose the jewels that the Princess was to wear. These were nothing less than diamonds, even to her shoes, which were covered with them, and her dress of silver brocade was embroidered with a dozen of the sun's rays. You may imagine how much these had cost; but then nothing could have been more brilliant, except the beauty of the Princess! Upon her head she wore a splendid crown, her lovely hair waved nearly to her feet, and her stately figure could easily be distinguished among all the ladies who attended her.

The King of the Gold Mines was not less noble and splendid; it was easy to see by his face how happy he was, and everyone who went near him returned loaded with presents, for all round the great banqueting hall had been arranged a thousand barrels full of gold, and numberless bags made of velvet embroidered with pearls and filled with money, each one containing at least a hundred thousand gold pieces, which were given away to everyone who liked to hold out his hand, which numbers of people hastened to do, you may be sure – indeed, some found this by far the most amusing part of the wedding festivities.

The Queen and the Princess were just ready to set out with the King when they saw, advancing towards them from the end of the long gallery, two great basilisks, dragging after them a very badly made box; behind them came a tall old woman, whose ugliness was even more surprising than her extreme old age. She wore a ruff of black taffeta, a red velvet hood, and a farthingale all in rags, and she leaned heavily upon a crutch. This strange old woman, without saying a single word, hobbled three times round the gallery, followed by the basilisks, then stopping in the middle, and brandishing her crutch threateningly, she cried:

"Ho, ho, Queen! Ho, ho, Princess! Do you think you are going to break with impunity the promise that you made to my friend the Yellow Dwarf? I am the Fairy of the Desert; without the Yellow Dwarf and his orange tree my great lions would soon have eaten you up, I can tell you, and in Fairyland we do not suffer ourselves to be insulted like this. Make up your minds at once what you will do, for I vow that you shall marry the Yellow Dwarf. If you don't, may I burn my crutch!"

"Ah! Princess," said the Queen, weeping, "what is this that I hear? What have you promised?"

"Ah! my mother," replied Bellissima sadly, "what did you promise, yourself?"

The King of the Gold Mines, indignant at being kept from his happiness by this wicked old woman, went up to her, and threatening her with his sword, said:

"Get away out of my country at once, and for ever, miserable creature, lest I take your life, and so rid myself of your malice."

He had hardly spoken these words when the lid of the box fell back on the floor with a terrible noise, and to their horror out sprang the Yellow Dwarf, mounted upon a great Spanish cat. "Rash youth!" he cried, rushing between the Fairy of the Desert and the King. "Dare to lay a finger upon this illustrious Fairy! Your quarrel is with me only. I am your enemy and your rival. That faithless Princess who would have married you is promised to me. See if she has not upon her finger a ring made of one of my hairs. Just try to take it off, and you will soon find out that I am more powerful than you are!"

"Wretched little monster!" said the King; "do you dare to call yourself the Princess's lover, and to lay claim to such a treasure? Do you know that you are a dwarf – that you are so ugly that one cannot bear to look at you – and that I should have killed you myself long before this if you had been worthy of such a glorious death?"

The Yellow Dwarf, deeply enraged at these words, set spurs to his cat, which yelled horribly, and leapt hither and thither – terrifying everybody except the brave King, who pursued the Dwarf closely, till he, drawing a great knife with which he was armed, challenged the King to meet him in single combat, and rushed down into the courtyard of the palace with a terrible clatter. The King, quite provoked, followed him hastily, but they had hardly taken their places facing one another, and the whole court had only just had time to rush out upon the balconies to watch what was going on, when suddenly the sun became as red as blood, and it was so dark that they could scarcely see at all. The thunder crashed, and the lightning seemed as if it must burn up everything; the two basilisks appeared, one on each side of the bad Dwarf, like giants, mountains high, and fire flew from their mouths and ears, until they looked like flaming furnaces. None of these things could terrify the noble young King, and the boldness of his looks and actions reassured those who were looking on, and perhaps even embarrassed the Yellow Dwarf himself; but even his courage gave way when he saw what was happening to his beloved Princess. For the Fairy of the Desert, looking more terrible than before, mounted upon a winged griffin, and with long snakes coiled round her neck, had given her such a blow with the lance she carried that Bellissima fell into the Queen's arms bleeding and senseless. Her fond mother, feeling as much hurt by the blow as the Princess herself, uttered such piercing cries and lamentations that the King, hearing them, entirely lost his courage and presence of mind. Giving up the combat, he flew towards the Princess, to rescue or to die with her; but the Yellow Dwarf was too quick for him. Leaping with his Spanish cat upon the balcony, he snatched Bellissima from the Queen's arms, and before any of the ladies of the court could stop him he had sprung upon the roof of the palace and disappeared with his prize.

The King, motionless with horror, looked on despairingly at this dreadful occurrence, which he was quite powerless to prevent, and to make matters worse his sight failed him, everything became dark, and he felt himself carried along through the air by a strong hand.

This new misfortune was the work of the wicked Fairy of the Desert, who had come with the Yellow Dwarf to help him carry off the Princess, and had fallen in love with the handsome young King of the Gold Mines directly she saw him. She thought that if she carried him off to some frightful cavern and chained him to a rock, then the fear of death would make him forget Bellissima and become her slave. So, as soon as they reached the place, she gave him back his sight, but without releasing him from his chains, and by her magic power she appeared before him as a young and beautiful fairy, and pretended to have come there quite by chance.

"What do I see?" she cried. "Is it you, dear Prince? What misfortune has brought you to this dismal place?"

The King, who was quite deceived by her altered appearance, replied:

"Alas! beautiful Fairy, the fairy who brought me here first took away my sight, but by her voice I recognized her as the Fairy of the Desert, though what she should have carried me off for I cannot tell you."

"Ah!" cried the pretended Fairy, "if you have fallen into her hands, you won't get away until you have married her. She has carried off more than one Prince like this, and she will certainly have anything she takes a fancy to." While she was thus pretending to be sorry for the King, he suddenly noticed her feet, which were like those of a griffin, and knew in a moment that this must be the Fairy of the Desert, for her feet were the one thing she could not change, however pretty she might make her face.

Without seeming to have noticed anything, he said, in a confidential way:

"Not that I have any dislike to the Fairy of the Desert, but I really cannot endure the way in which she protects the Yellow Dwarf and keeps me chained here like a criminal. It is true that I love a charming princess, but if the Fairy should set me free my gratitude would oblige me to love her only."

"Do you really mean what you say, Prince?" said the Fairy, quite deceived.

"Surely," replied the Prince; "how could I deceive you? You see it is so much more flattering to my vanity to be loved by a fairy than by a simple princess. But, even if I am dying of love for her, I shall pretend to hate her until I am set free."

The Fairy of the Desert, quite taken in by these words, resolved at once to transport the Prince to a pleasanter place. So, making him mount her chariot, to which she had harnessed swans instead of the bats which generally drew it, away she flew with him. But imagine the distress of the Prince when, from the giddy height at which they were rushing through the air, he saw his beloved Princess in a castle built of polished steel, the walls of which reflected the sun's rays so hotly that no one could approach it without being burnt to a cinder! Bellissima was sitting in a little thicket by a brook, leaning her head upon her hand and weeping bitterly, but just as they passed she looked up and saw the King and the Fairy of the Desert. Now, the Fairy was so clever that she could not only seem beautiful to the King, but even the poor Princess thought her the most lovely being she had ever seen.

"What!" she cried; "was I not unhappy enough in this lonely castle to which that frightful Yellow Dwarf brought me? Must I also be made to know that the King of the Gold Mines ceased to love me as soon as he lost sight of me? But who can my rival be, whose fatal beauty is greater than mine?"

While she was saying this, the King, who really loved her as much as ever, was feeling terribly sad at being so rapidly torn away from his beloved Princess, but he knew too well how powerful the Fairy was to have any hope of escaping from her except by great patience and cunning.

The Fairy of the Desert had also seen Bellissima, and she tried to read in the King's eyes the effect that this unexpected sight had had upon him.

"No one can tell you what you wish to know better than I can," said he. "This chance meeting with an unhappy princess for whom I once had a passing fancy, before I was lucky enough to meet you, has affected me a little, I admit, but you are so much more to me than she is that I would rather die than leave you."

"Ah! Prince," she said, "can I believe that you really love me so much?"

"Time will show, madam," replied the King; "but if you wish to convince me that you have some regard for me, do not, I beg of you, refuse to aid Bellissima."

"Do you know what you are asking?" said the Fairy of the Desert, frowning, and looking at him suspiciously. "Do you want me to employ my art against the Yellow Dwarf, who is my best friend, and take away from him a proud princess whom I can but look upon as my rival?"

The King sighed, but made no answer – indeed, what was there to be said to such a clear-sighted person? At last they reached a vast meadow, gay with all sorts of flowers; a deep river surrounded it, and many little brooks murmured softly under the shady trees, where it was always cool and fresh. A little way off stood a splendid palace, the walls of which were of transparent emeralds. As soon as the swans which drew the Fairy's chariot had alighted under a porch, which was paved with diamonds and had arches of rubies, they were greeted on all sides by thousands of beautiful beings, who came to meet them joyfully, singing these words:

"When Love within a heart would reign,
Useless to strive against him 'tis.

> *The proud but feel a sharper pain,*
> *And make a greater triumph his."*

The Fairy of the Desert was delighted to hear them sing of her triumphs; she led the King into the most splendid room that can be imagined, and left him alone for a little while, just that he might not feel that he was a prisoner; but he felt sure that she had not really gone quite away, but was watching him from some hiding-place. So walking up to a great mirror, he said to it, "Trusty counsellor, let me see what I can do to make myself agreeable to the charming Fairy of the Desert; for I can think of nothing but how to please her."

And he at once set to work to curl his hair, and, seeing upon a table a grander coat than his own, he put it on carefully. The Fairy came back so delighted that she could not conceal her joy.

"I am quite aware of the trouble you have taken to please me," said she, "and I must tell you that you have succeeded perfectly already. You see it is not difficult to do if you really care for me."

The King, who had his own reasons for wishing to keep the old Fairy in a good humour, did not spare pretty speeches, and after a time he was allowed to walk by himself upon the sea-shore. The Fairy of the Desert had by her enchantments raised such a terrible storm that the boldest pilot would not venture out in it, so she was not afraid of her prisoner's being able to escape; and he found it some relief to think sadly over his terrible situation without being interrupted by his cruel captor.

Presently, after walking wildly up and down, he wrote these verses upon the sand with his stick:

> *At last may I upon this shore*
> *Lighten my sorrow with soft tears.*
> *Alas! alas! I see no more*
> *My Love, who yet my sadness cheers.*
> *And thou, O raging, stormy Sea,*
> *Stirred by wild winds, from depth to height,*
> *Thou hold'st my loved one far from me,*
> *And I am captive to thy might.*
> *My heart is still more wild than thine,*
> *For Fate is cruel unto me.*
> *Why must I thus in exile pine?*
> *Why is my Princess snatched from me?*
> *O! lovely Nymphs, from ocean caves,*
> *Who know how sweet true love may be,*
> *Come up and calm the furious waves*
> *And set a desperate lover free!*

While he was still writing he heard a voice which attracted his attention in spite of himself. Seeing that the waves were rolling in higher than ever, he looked all round him, and presently saw a lovely lady floating gently towards him upon the crest of a huge pillow, her long hair spread all about her; in one hand she held a mirror, and in the other a comb, and instead of feet she had a beautiful tail like a fish, with which she swam.

The King was struck dumb with astonishment at this unexpected sight; but as soon as she came within speaking distance, she said to him, "I know how sad you are at losing your Princess and being kept a prisoner by the Fairy of the Desert; if you like I will help you to escape from this fatal place, where you may otherwise have to drag on a weary existence for thirty years or more."

The King of the Gold Mines hardly knew what answer to make to this proposal. Not because he did not wish very much to escape, but he was afraid that this might be only another device by which the Fairy of the Desert was trying to deceive him. As he hesitated the Mermaid, who guessed his thoughts, said to him:

"You may trust me: I am not trying to entrap you. I am so angry with the Yellow Dwarf and the Fairy of the Desert that I am not likely to wish to help them, especially since I constantly see your poor Princess, whose beauty and goodness make me pity her so much: and I tell you that if you will have confidence in me I will help you to escape."

"I trust you absolutely," cried the King, "and I will do whatever you tell me; but if you have seen my Princess I beg of you to tell me how she is and what is happening to her."

"We must not waste time in talking," said she. "Come with me and I will carry you to the Castle of Steel, and we will leave upon this shore a figure so like you that even the Fairy herself will be deceived by it."

So saying she quickly collected a bundle of sea-weed, and, blowing it three times, she said:

"My friendly sea-weeds, I order you to stay here stretched upon the sand until the Fairy of the Desert comes to take you away." And at once the sea-weeds became like the King, who stood looking at them in great astonishment, for they were even dressed in a coat like his, but they lay there pale and still as the King himself might have lain if one of the great waves had overtaken him and thrown him senseless upon the shore. And then the Mermaid caught up the King, and away they swam joyfully together.

"Now," said she, "I have time to tell you about the Princess. In spite of the blow which the Fairy of the Desert gave her, the Yellow Dwarf compelled her to mount behind him upon his terrible Spanish cat; but she soon fainted away with pain and terror, and did not recover till they were within the walls of his frightful Castle of Steel. Here she was received by the prettiest girls it was possible to find, who had been carried there by the Yellow Dwarf, who hastened to wait upon her and showed her every possible attention. She was laid upon a couch covered with cloth of gold, embroidered with pearls as big as nuts."

"Ah!" interrupted the King of the Gold Mines; "if Bellissima forgets me, and consents to marry him, I shall break my heart."

"You need not be afraid of that," answered the Mermaid; "the Princess thinks of no one but you, and the frightful Dwarf cannot persuade her to look at him."

"Pray go on with your story," said the King.

"What more is there to tell you?" replied the Mermaid. "Bellissima was sitting in the wood when you passed, and saw you with the Fairy of the Desert, who was so cleverly disguised that the Princess took her to be prettier than herself; you may imagine her despair, for she thought that you had fallen in love with her."

"She believes that I love her!" cried the King. "What a fatal mistake! What is to be done to undeceive her?"

"You know best," answered the Mermaid, smiling kindly at him. "When people are as much in love with one another as you two are, they don't need advice from anyone else."

As she spoke they reached the Castle of Steel, the side next the sea being the only one which the Yellow Dwarf had left unprotected by the dreadful burning walls.

"I know quite well," said the Mermaid, "that the Princess is sitting by the brook-side, just where you saw her as you passed, but as you will have many enemies to fight with before you can reach her, take this sword; armed with it you may dare any danger, and overcome the greatest difficulties, only beware of one thing – that is, never to let it fall from your hand. Farewell; now I will wait by that rock, and if you need my help in carrying off your beloved Princess I will not fail you, for the Queen, her mother, is my best friend, and it was for her sake that I went to rescue you."

So saying, she gave to the King a sword made from a single diamond, which was more brilliant than the sun. He could not find words to express his gratitude, but he begged her to believe that he fully appreciated the importance of her gift, and would never forget her help and kindness.

We must now go back to the Fairy of the Desert. When she found that the King did not return, she hastened out to look for him, and reached the shore, with a hundred of the ladies of her train, loaded with splendid presents for him. Some carried baskets full of diamonds, others golden cups of wonderful workmanship, and amber, coral, and pearls, others, again, balanced upon their heads bales of the richest and most beautiful stuffs, while the rest brought fruit and flowers, and even birds. But what was the horror of the Fairy, who followed this gay troop, when she saw, stretched upon the sands, the image of the King which the Mermaid had made with the sea-weeds. Struck with astonishment and sorrow, she uttered a terrible cry, and threw herself down beside the pretended King, weeping, and howling, and calling upon her eleven sisters, who were also fairies, and who came to her assistance. But they were all taken in by the image of the King, for, clever as they were, the Mermaid was still cleverer, and all they could do was to help the Fairy of the Desert to make a wonderful monument over what they thought was the grave of the King of the Gold Mines. But while they were collecting jasper and porphyry, agate and marble, gold and bronze, statues and devices, to immortalise the King's memory, he was thanking the good Mermaid and begging her still to help him, which she graciously promised to do as she disappeared; and then he set out for the Castle of Steel. He walked fast, looking anxiously round him, and longing once more to see his darling Bellissima, but he had not gone far before he was surrounded by four terrible sphinxes who would very soon have torn him to pieces with their sharp talons if it had not been for the Mermaid's diamond sword. For, no sooner had he flashed it before their eyes than down they fell at his feet quite helpless, and he killed them with one blow. But he had hardly turned to continue his search when he met six dragons covered with scales that were harder than iron. Frightful as this encounter was the King's courage was unshaken, and by the aid of his wonderful sword he cut them in pieces one after the other. Now he hoped his difficulties were over, but at the next turning he was met by one which he did not know how to overcome. Four-and-twenty pretty and graceful nymphs advanced towards him, holding garlands of flowers, with which they barred the way.

"Where are you going, Prince?" they said; "it is our duty to guard this place, and if we let you pass great misfortunes will happen to you and to us. We beg you not to insist upon going on. Do you want to kill four-and-twenty girls who have never displeased you in any way?"

The King did not know what to do or to say. It went against all his ideas as a knight to do anything a lady begged him not to do; but, as he hesitated, a voice in his ear said:

"Strike! strike! and do not spare, or your Princess is lost for ever!"

So, without replying to the nymphs, he rushed forward instantly, breaking their garlands, and scattering them in all directions; and then went on without further hindrance to the little wood where he had seen Bellissima. She was seated by the brook looking pale and weary when he reached her, and he would have thrown himself down at her feet, but she drew herself away from him with as much indignation as if he had been the Yellow Dwarf.

"Ah! Princess," he cried, "do not be angry with me. Let me explain everything. I am not faithless or to blame for what has happened. I am a miserable wretch who has displeased you without being able to help himself."

"Ah!" cried Bellissima, "did I not see you flying through the air with the loveliest being imaginable? Was that against your will?"

"Indeed it was, Princess," he answered; "the wicked Fairy of the Desert, not content with chaining me to a rock, carried me off in her chariot to the other end of the earth, where I should even now be a captive but for the unexpected help of a friendly mermaid, who brought me here to rescue you, my Princess, from the unworthy hands that hold you. Do not refuse the aid of your most faithful lover." So saying, he threw himself at her feet and held her by her robe. But, alas! in so doing he let fall the magic sword, and the Yellow Dwarf, who was crouching behind a lettuce, no sooner saw it than he sprang out and seized it, well knowing its wonderful power.

The Princess gave a cry of terror on seeing the Dwarf, but this only irritated the little monster; muttering a few magical words he summoned two giants, who bound the King with great chains of iron.

"Now," said the Dwarf, "I am master of my rival's fate, but I will give him his life and permission to depart unharmed if you, Princess, will consent to marry me."

"Let me die a thousand times rather," cried the unhappy King.

"Alas!" cried the Princess, "must you die? Could anything be more terrible?"

"That you should marry that little wretch would be far more terrible," answered the King.

"At least," continued she, "let us die together."

"Let me have the satisfaction of dying for you, my Princess," said he.

"Oh, no, no!" she cried, turning to the Dwarf; "rather than that I will do as you wish."

"Cruel Princess!" said the King, "would you make my life horrible to me by marrying another before my eyes?"

"Not so," replied the Yellow Dwarf; "you are a rival of whom I am too much afraid: you shall not see our marriage." So saying, in spite of Bellissima's tears and cries, he stabbed the King to the heart with the diamond sword.

The poor Princess, seeing her lover lying dead at her feet, could no longer live without him; she sank down by him and died of a broken heart.

So ended these unfortunate lovers, whom not even the Mermaid could help, because all the magic power had been lost with the diamond sword.

As to the wicked Dwarf, he preferred to see the Princess dead rather than married to the King of the Gold Mines; and the Fairy of the Desert, when she heard of the King's adventures, pulled down the grand monument which she had built, and was so angry at the trick that had been played her that she hated him as much as she had loved him before.

The kind Mermaid, grieved at the sad fate of the lovers, caused them to be changed into two tall palm trees, which stand always side by side, whispering together of their faithful love and caressing one another with their interlacing branches.

The Goblins Turned to Stone

WHEN THE COW CAME TO HOLLAND, the Dutch folks had more and better things to eat. Fields of wheat and rye took the place of forests. Instead of acorns and the meat of wild game, they now enjoyed milk and bread. The youngsters made pets of the calves and all the family lived under one roof. The cows had a happy time of it, because they were kept so clean, fed well, milked regularly, and cared for in winter.

By and by the Dutch learned to make cheese and began to eat it every day. They liked it, whether it was raw, cooked, toasted, sliced, or in chunks, or served with other good things. Even the foxes and wild creatures were very fond of the smell and taste of toasted cheese. They came at night close to the houses, often stealing the cheese out of the pantry. When a fox would not, or could not, be caught in a trap by any other bait, a bit of cooked cheese would allure him so that he was caught and his fur made use of.

When the people could not get meat, or fish, they had toasted bread and cheese, which in Dutch is "geroostered brod met kaas." Then they laughed, and named the new dish after whatever they pretended it was. It was just the same, as when they called goodies, made out of flour and sugar, "nuts," "fingers," "calves" and "lambs." Even grown folks love to play and pretend things like children.

Soon, it became the fashion to have cheese parties. Men and women would sit around the fire, by the hour, nibbling the toast that had melted cheese poured over it. But after they had gone to bed, some of them dreamed.

Now some dreams may be pleasant, but cheese-dreams were not usually of this sort. The dreamer thought that a big she-horse had climbed upon the bed and sat down upon his stomach. Once there, the beast grinned hideously, snored, and pressed its hoofs down on the sleeper's breast, so that he could not breathe or speak. The feeling was a horrible one; but, just when the dreamer expected to choke, he seemed to jump off some high place, and come down somewhere, very far off. Then the animal ran away and the terrible dream was over.

This was called a nightmare, or in Dutch a "nacht merrie." 'Nacht' means night, and 'merrie' a filly or a mare. In the dream, it was not a small or a young horse, but always a big mare that squatted down on a man's stomach.

In those days, instead of seeking for the trouble inside, or asking whether there was any connection between nightmares and too hearty eating of cheese, the Dutch fathers laid it all on the goblins.

The goblins, or sooty elves, that used to live in Holland, were ugly, short fellows, very smart, quick in action and able to travel far in a second. They were first cousins to the kabouters. They had big heads, green eyes and split feet, like cows. They were so ugly, that they were ordered to live under ground and never come out during the day. If they did, they would be turned to stone.

The goblins had a bad reputation for mischief. They liked to have fun with human beings. They would listen to the conversation of people and then mock them by repeating the last word. That is the reason why echoes were called "week klank," or dwarf's talk.

Because these goblins were short, they envied men their greater stature and wanted to grow to the height of human beings. As they were not able of themselves to do this, they often sneaked into a house and snatched a child out of the cradle. In place of the stolen baby, one of their own wizened children was laid. That was the reason why many a poor little baby, that grew puny and thin, was called a "wiseel-kind," or changeling. When the sick baby could not get well, and medicine or care seemed to do no good, the mother thought that the goblins had taken away her own child.

It was only the female goblins that would change themselves into night mares and sit on the body of the dreamer. They usually came in through a hole or a crack; but if that person in the house could plug up the hole, or stop the crack, he could conquer the female goblin, and do what he pleased with her. If a man wanted to, he could make her his wife. So long as the hole was kept stopped up, by which the goblin entered, she made a good wife. If this crack was left open, or if the plug dropped out of the hole, the she-goblin was off and could never be found again.

The ruler of the goblins lived beneath the earth, as the king of the underworld. His palace was made of gold and glittered with gems. He had riches more than men could count. All the goblins and kabouters, who worked in the mines and at the forges and anvils, making swords, spears, bells, or jewels, obeyed him.

The most wonderful things about these dwarfs was the way in which they made themselves invisible, so that men were able to see neither the night mares nor the male goblins, while at their mischief. This was a little red cap which every goblin possessed, and which he was careful never to lose. The red cap acted like a snuffer on a candle, to put it out, and while under it, no goblin could be seen by mortal eyes.

Now it happened that one night, as a dear old lady lay dying on her bed, a middle-sized goblin, with his red cap on, came in through a crack into the room, and stood at the foot of her bed. Just for mischief and to frighten her by making himself visible, he took off his red cap.

When the old lady saw the imp, she cried out loudly:

"Go way, go way. Don't you know I belong to my Lord?"

But the goblin dwarf only laughed at her, with his green eyes.

Calling her daughter Alida, the old lady whispered in her ear:

"Bring me my wooden shoes."

Rising up in her bed, the old lady hurled the heavy klomps, one after the other, at the goblin's head. At this, he started to get out through the crack, and away, but before his body was half out, Alida snatched his red cap away. Then she stuck a needle in his cloven foot that made him howl with pain. Alida looked at the crack through which he escaped and found it quite sooty.

Twirling the little red cap around on her forefinger, a brilliant thought struck her. She went and told the men her plan, and they agreed to it. This was to gather hundreds of farmers and townfolk, boys and men together, on the next moonlight night, and round up all the goblins in Drenthe. By pulling off their caps, and holding them till the sun rose, when they would be petrified, the whole brood could be exterminated.

So, knowing that the goblin would come the next night, to steal back his red cap, she left a note outside the crack, telling him to bring several hundred goblins to the great moor, or veldt. There, at a certain hour near midnight, he would find the red cap on a bush. With his companions, he could celebrate the return of the cap. In exchange for this, she asked the goblin to bring her a gold necklace.

The moonlight night came round and hundreds of the men of Drenthe gathered together. They were armed with horseshoes, and with witch-hazel and other plants, which are like poison to the sooty elves. They had also bits of parchment covered with runes, a strange kind of writing, and various charms which are supposed to be harmful to goblins. It was agreed to move together in a circle towards the centre, where the lady Alida was to hang the red cap upon a bush. Then, with a rush, the men were to snatch off all the goblins' caps, pulling and grabbing, whether they could see, or even feel anything, or not.

The placing of the red cap upon the bush in the centre, by the lady Alida, was the signal.

So, when the great round-up narrowed to a small space, the men began to grab, snatch and pull. Putting their hands out in the air, at the height of about a yard from the ground, they hustled and pushed hard. In a few minutes, hundreds of red caps were in their hands, and as many goblins became visible. They were, indeed, an ugly host.

Yet hundreds of other goblins escaped, with their caps on, and were still invisible. As they broke away in groups, however, they were seen, for in each bunch was one or more visible fellow, because he was capless. So the men divided into squads, to chase the imps a long distance, even to many distant places. It was a most curious night battle. Here could be seen groups of men in a tussle with the goblins, many more of which, but by no means all, were made capless and visible.

The racket kept up till the sky in the east was grey. Had all the goblins run away, it would have been well with them. Hundreds of them did, but the others were so anxious to help their fellows, or to get back their own caps, fearing the disgrace of returning head bare to their king, and getting a good scolding, that the sun suddenly rose on them, before they knew it was day.

At the first level ray, the goblins were all turned to stone.

The treeless, desolate land, which, a moment before, was full of struggling goblins and men, became as quiet as the blue sky above. Nothing but some rounded rocks or stones, in groups, marked the spot where the bloodless battle of imps and men had been fought.

There, these stones, big and little, lie to this day. Among the buckwheat, and the potato blossoms of the summer, under the shadows and clouds, and whispering breezes of autumn, or covered with the snows of winter, they are seen on desolate heaths. Over some of them, oak trees, centuries old, have grown. Others are near, or among, the farmers' grain fields, or, not far from houses and barn-yards. The cows wander among them, knowing nothing of their past. And the goblins come no more.

The Goblin and the Sneeze

ONCE UPON A TIME there was a very powerful goblin, who haunted a little house just outside the gates of a city. Nobody else lived in this house. There was a big black beam that ran across from one side to the other, up in the roof; and there this goblin perched. For twelve years he had served the King of the Goblins faithfully, and as a reward he was now permitted to gobble up any man who sneezed inside that house; and, indeed, that is why these creatures are called goblins. But if, when a man sneezed, some one else said, "God bless you!" as people do say, or "May you live a hundred years!" then the man who said it was free; and if the other answered, "The same to you!" he was free too. Everybody but these the goblin might gobble up for a single sneeze.

Now it fell out that one day a father and son were travelling along the road, and they came to the city gates just as the sun went down. I must tell you that in those days the people used to shut the city gates fast at sunset, and nothing would make them open again till the morning – they were horribly afraid of robbers or wild soldiers, who might come and damage them in the night. So when these two wayfarers came up to the gates, and wanted to go in, the porter said no.

"Now, do we look like robbers?" asked the father. Certainly they did not, dusty and grimy with their trudge, and a bag of tools over the shoulder.

"Robbers or no robbers, orders are orders," said the porter, "and this gate doesn't open for the King himself."

"Well, what are we to do?" The poor fellow was in despair.

"Oh, there's an empty house outside; there it is among the trees. It is haunted, they say; but I daresay the goblin won't hurt you."

"Goblin! – well, we must take our chance, I suppose." Indeed, there was nothing for it; so to the house they went. They rested, and cooked a meal for themselves on a fire of sticks, and then prepared to go to sleep.

The goblin, however, was not going to let them off so easily; he wanted his dinner too. After waiting a long time, with never a sneeze from one or the other, he raised a cloud of fine dust; that was rather mean of him, but still he was very hungry, and did not stick at trifles. Sure enough, the father nearly sneezed his head off.

The goblin chuckled, and made ready to pounce from his perch and devour the pair of them. But the son happened to see him, and, being a sharp lad, he guessed the truth. "God bless you, father!" says he; "may you live a hundred years!"

How the goblin gnashed his teeth! However, if his pudding was lost, his meat was left; so he stretched out a great claw to clutch the father and tear him to pieces.

Just then the father cried, "Thank you, my son, and the same to you!"

He was only just in time; the claw was within an inch of his throat; but the goblin, baffled, flew up to his perch again, and sat mouthing and mumbling there.

Then the son began to talk to this goblin, and showed him the error of his ways, and how cruel he was to eat men; and the end of it was, he persuaded the goblin to become a vegetarian, and to follow him about, and be his errand-boy. You will think this was a very soft-hearted goblin. Perhaps no one had ever spoken kindly to him before; anyhow, whatever the reason was, he went out with the two travellers, as tame as a tabby cat; and for all I know, they may be travelling together to this very day.

The Goblin City

LONG, LONG AGO, in the island of Ceylon, there was a large city full of nothing but goblins. They were all She-goblins, too; and if they wanted husbands, they used to get hold of travellers and force them to marry; and afterwards, when they were tired of their husbands, they gobbled them up.

One day a ship was wrecked upon the coast near the goblin city, and five hundred sailors were cast ashore. The She-goblins came down to the seashore, and brought food and dry clothes for the sailors, and invited them to come into the city. There was nobody else there at all; but for fear that the sailors should be frightened away, the goblins, by their magic power, made shapes of people appear all around, so that there seemed to be men ploughing in the fields, or shepherds tending their sheep, and huntsmen with hounds, and all the sights of the quiet country life. So, when the sailors looked round, and saw everything as usual, they felt quite secure; although, as you know, it was all a sham.

The end of it was, that they persuaded the sailors to marry them, telling them that their own husbands had gone to sea in a ship, and had been gone these three years, so that they must be drowned and lost for ever. But really, as you know, they had served others in just the same way, and their last batch of husbands were then in prison, waiting to be eaten.

In the middle of the night, when the men were all asleep, the She-goblins rose up, put on their hats, and hurried down to the prison; there they killed a few men, and gnawed their flesh, and ate them up; and after this orgie they went home again. It so happened that the captain of the sailors woke up before his wife came home, and not seeing her there, he watched. By-and-by in she came; he pretended to be asleep, and looked out of the tail of his eye. She was still munching and crunching, and as she munched she muttered:

> *"Man's meat, man's meat,*
> *That's what goblins like to eat!"*

She said it over and over again, then lay down; and soon she was snoring loudly.

The captain was horribly frightened to find he had married a goblin. What was he to do? They could not fight with goblins, and they were in the goblins' power. If they had a ship they might have sailed away, because goblins hate the water worse than a cat; but their ship was gone. He could think of nothing.

However, next morning, he found a chance of telling his mates what he had discovered. Some of them believed him, and some said he must have been dreaming; they were sure their wives would not do such a thing. Those who believed him agreed that they would look out for a chance of escape.

But there was a kind fairy who hated those goblins; and she determined to save the men. So she told her flying horse to go and carry them away. And accordingly, as the men were out for a walk next day, the captain saw in the air a beautiful horse with large white and gold wings. The horse fluttered down, and hovered just above them, crying out, in a human voice:

"Who wants to go home? who wants to go home? who wants to go home?"

"I do, I do!" called out the sailors.

"Climb up, then!" said the horse, dropping within reach. So one climbed up, and then another, and another; and, although the horse looked no bigger than any other horse, there was room for everybody on his back. I think that somehow, when they got up, the fairy made them shrink small, till they were no bigger than so many ants, and thus there was plenty of room for all. When all who wanted to go had got up on his back, away flew the beautiful horse and took them safely home.

As for those who remained behind, that very night the goblins set upon them and mangled them, and munched them to mincemeat.

The Goblin and the Huckster

THERE WAS ONCE a regular student, who lived in a garret, and had no possessions. And there was also a regular huckster, to whom the house belonged, and who occupied the ground floor. A goblin lived with the huckster, because at Christmas he always had a large dish full of jam, with a great piece of butter in the middle. The huckster could afford this; and therefore the goblin remained with the huckster, which was very cunning of him.

One evening the student came into the shop through the back door to buy candles and cheese for himself, he had no one to send, and therefore he came himself; he obtained what he wished, and then the huckster and his wife nodded good evening to him, and she was a woman who could do more than merely nod, for she had usually plenty to say for herself. The student nodded in return as he turned to leave, then suddenly stopped, and began reading the piece of paper in which the cheese was wrapped. It was a leaf torn out of an old book, a book that ought not to have been torn up, for it was full of poetry.

"Yonder lies some more of the same sort," said the huckster: "I gave an old woman a few coffee berries for it; you shall have the rest for sixpence, if you will."

"Indeed I will," said the student; "give me the book instead of the cheese; I can eat my bread and butter without cheese. It would be a sin to tear up a book like this. You are a clever man; and a practical man; but you understand no more about poetry than that cask yonder."

This was a very rude speech, especially against the cask; but the huckster and the student both laughed, for it was only said in fun. But the goblin felt very angry that any man should venture to say such things to a huckster who was a householder and sold the best butter. As soon as it was night, and the shop closed, and every one in bed except the student, the goblin stepped softly into the bedroom where the huckster's wife slept, and took away her tongue, which of course, she did not then want. Whatever object in the room he placed his tongue upon immediately received voice and speech, and was able to express its thoughts and feelings as readily as the lady herself could do. It could only be used by one object at a time, which was a good thing, as a number speaking at once would have caused great confusion. The goblin laid the tongue upon the cask, in which lay a quantity of old newspapers.

"Is it really true," he asked, "that you do not know what poetry is?"

"Of course I know," replied the cask: "poetry is something that always stand in the corner of a newspaper, and is sometimes cut out; and I may venture to affirm that I have more of it in me than the student has, and I am only a poor tub of the huckster's."

Then the goblin placed the tongue on the coffee mill; and how it did go to be sure! Then he put it on the butter tub and the cash box, and they all expressed the same opinion as the waste-paper tub; and a majority must always be respected.

"Now I shall go and tell the student," said the goblin; and with these words he went quietly up the back stairs to the garret where the student lived. He had a candle burning still, and the goblin peeped through the keyhole and saw that he was reading in the torn book, which he had brought out of the shop. But how light the room was! From the book shot forth a ray of light which grew broad and full, like the stem of a tree, from which bright rays spread upward and over the student's head. Each leaf was fresh, and each flower was like a beautiful female head; some with dark and sparkling eyes, and others with eyes that were wonderfully blue and clear. The fruit gleamed like stars, and the room was filled with sounds of beautiful music. The little goblin had never imagined, much less seen or heard of, any sight so glorious as this. He stood still on tiptoe, peeping in, till the light went out in the garret. The student no doubt had blown out his candle and gone to bed; but the little goblin remained standing there nevertheless, and listening to the music which still sounded on, soft and beautiful, a sweet cradle-song for the student, who had lain down to rest.

"This is a wonderful place," said the goblin; "I never expected such a thing. I should like to stay here with the student;" and the little man thought it over, for he was a sensible little spirit. At last he sighed, "but the student has no jam!" So he went down stairs again into the huckster's shop, and it was a good thing he got back when he did, for the cask had almost worn out the lady's tongue; he had given a description of all that he contained on one side, and was just about to turn himself over to the other side to describe what was there, when the goblin entered and restored the tongue to the lady. But from that time forward, the whole shop, from the cash box down to the pinewood logs, formed their opinions from that of the cask; and they all had such confidence in him, and treated him with so much respect, that when the huckster read the criticisms on theatricals and art of an evening, they fancied it must all come from the cask.

But after what he had seen, the goblin could no longer sit and listen quietly to the wisdom and understanding down stairs; so, as soon as the evening light glimmered in the garret, he took courage, for it seemed to him as if the rays of light were strong cables, drawing him up, and obliging him to go and peep through the keyhole; and, while there, a feeling of vastness came over him such as we experience by the ever-moving sea, when the storm breaks forth; and it brought tears into his eyes. He did not himself know why he wept, yet a kind of pleasant feeling mingled with his tears. "How wonderfully glorious it would be to sit with the student under such a tree;" but that was out of the question, he must be content to look through the keyhole, and be thankful for even that.

There he stood on the old landing, with the autumn wind blowing down upon him through the trap-door. It was very cold; but the little creature did not really feel it, till the light in the garret went out, and the tones of music died away. Then how he shivered, and crept down stairs again to his warm corner, where it felt home-like and comfortable. And when Christmas came again, and brought the dish of jam and the great lump of butter, he liked the huckster best of all.

Soon after, in the middle of the night, the goblin was awoke by a terrible noise and knocking against the window shutters and the house doors, and by the sound of the watchman's horn; for a great fire had broken out, and the whole street appeared full of flames. Was it in their house, or a neighbour's? No one could tell, for terror had seized upon all. The huckster's wife was so bewildered that she took her gold ear-rings out of her ears and put them in her pocket, that she might save something at least. The huckster ran to get his business papers, and the servant resolved to save her blue silk mantle, which she had managed to buy. Each wished to keep the best things they had. The goblin had the same wish; for, with one spring, he was up stairs and in the student's room, whom he found standing by the open window, and looking quite calmly at the fire, which was raging at the house of a neighbour opposite. The goblin caught up the wonderful book which lay on the table, and popped it into his red cap, which he held tightly with both hands. The greatest treasure in the house was saved; and he ran away with it to the roof, and seated himself on the chimney. The flames of the burning house opposite illuminated him as he sat, both hands pressed tightly over his cap, in which the treasure lay; and then he found out what feelings really reigned in his heart, and knew exactly which way they tended. And yet, when the fire was extinguished, and the goblin again began to reflect, he hesitated, and said at last, "I must divide myself between the two; I cannot quite give up the huckster, because of the jam."

And this is a representation of human nature. We are like the goblin; we all go to visit the huckster "because of the jam."

The Elf of the Rose

IN THE MIDST of a garden grew a rose-tree, in full blossom, and in the prettiest of all the roses lived an elf. He was such a little wee thing, that no human eye could see him. Behind each leaf of the rose he had a sleeping chamber. He was as well formed and as beautiful as a little child could be, and had wings that reached from his shoulders to his feet. Oh, what sweet fragrance there was in his chambers! and how clean and beautiful were the walls! for they were the blushing leaves of the rose.

During the whole day he enjoyed himself in the warm sunshine, flew from flower to flower, and danced on the wings of the flying butterflies. Then he took it into his head to measure how many steps he would have to go through the roads and cross-roads that are on the leaf of a linden-tree.

What we call the veins on a leaf, he took for roads; ay, and very long roads they were for him; for before he had half finished his task, the sun went down: he had commenced his work too late. It became very cold, the dew fell, and the wind blew; so he thought the best thing he could do would be to return home. He hurried himself as much as he could; but he found the roses all closed up, and he could not get in; not a single rose stood open. The poor little elf was very much frightened. He had never before been out at night, but had always slumbered secretly behind the warm rose-leaves. Oh, this would certainly be his death. At the other end of the garden, he knew there was an arbor, overgrown with beautiful honey-suckles. The blossoms looked like large painted horns; and he thought to himself, he would go and sleep in one of these till the morning. He flew thither; but "hush!" two people were in the arbor – a handsome young man and a beautiful lady. They sat side by side, and wished that they might never be obliged to part. They loved each other much more than the best child can love its father and mother.

"But we must part," said the young man; "your brother does not like our engagement, and therefore he sends me so far away on business, over mountains and seas. Farewell, my sweet bride; for so you are to me."

And then they kissed each other, and the girl wept, and gave him a rose; but before she did so, she pressed a kiss upon it so fervently that the flower opened. Then the little elf flew in, and leaned his head on the delicate, fragrant walls. Here he could plainly hear them say, "Farewell, farewell;" and he felt that the rose had been placed on the young man's breast. Oh, how his heart did beat! The little elf could not go to sleep, it thumped so loudly. The young man took it out as he walked through the dark wood alone, and kissed the flower so often and so violently, that the little elf was almost crushed. He could feel through the leaf how hot the lips of the young man were, and the rose had opened, as if from the heat of the noonday sun.

There came another man, who looked gloomy and wicked. He was the wicked brother of the beautiful maiden. He drew out a sharp knife, and while the other was kissing the rose, the wicked man stabbed him to death; then he cut off his head, and buried it with the body in the soft earth under the linden-tree.

"Now he is gone, and will soon be forgotten," thought the wicked brother; "he will never come back again. He was going on a long journey over mountains and seas; it is easy for a man to lose his life in such a journey. My sister will suppose he is dead; for he cannot come back, and she will not dare to question me about him."

Then he scattered the dry leaves over the light earth with his foot, and went home through the darkness; but he went not alone, as he thought – the little elf accompanied him. He sat in a dry rolled-up linden-leaf, which had fallen from the tree on to the wicked man's head, as he was digging the grave. The hat was on the head now, which made it very dark, and the little elf shuddered with fright and indignation at the wicked deed.

It was the dawn of morning before the wicked man reached home; he took off his hat, and went into his sister's room. There lay the beautiful, blooming girl, dreaming of him whom she loved so, and who was now, she supposed, travelling far away over mountain and sea. Her wicked brother stopped over her, and laughed hideously, as fiends only can laugh. The dry leaf fell out of his hair upon the counterpane; but he did not notice it, and went to get a little sleep during the early morning hours. But the elf slipped out of the withered leaf, placed himself by the ear of the sleeping girl, and told her, as in a dream, of the horrid murder; described the place where her brother had slain her lover, and buried his body; and told her of the linden-tree, in full blossom, that stood close by.

"That you may not think this is only a dream that I have told you," he said, "you will find on your bed a withered leaf."

Then she awoke, and found it there. Oh, what bitter tears she shed! and she could not open her heart to any one for relief.

The window stood open the whole day, and the little elf could easily have reached the roses, or any of the flowers; but he could not find it in his heart to leave one so afflicted. In the window stood a bush bearing monthly roses. He seated himself in one of the flowers, and gazed on the poor girl. Her brother often came into the room, and would be quite cheerful, in spite of his base conduct; so she dare not say a word to him of her heart's grief.

As soon as night came on, she slipped out of the house, and went into the wood, to the spot where the linden-tree stood; and after removing the leaves from the earth, she turned it up, and there found him who had been murdered. Oh, how she wept and prayed that she also might die! Gladly would she have taken the body home with her; but that was impossible; so she took up the poor head with the closed eyes, kissed the cold lips, and shook the mould out of the beautiful hair.

"I will keep this," said she; and as soon as she had covered the body again with the earth and leaves, she took the head and a little sprig of jasmine that bloomed in the wood, near the spot where he was buried, and carried them home with her. As soon as she was in her room, she took the largest flower-pot she could find, and in this she placed the head of the dead man, covered it up with earth, and planted the twig of jasmine in it.

"Farewell, farewell," whispered the little elf. He could not any longer endure to witness all this agony of grief, he therefore flew away to his own rose in the garden. But the rose was faded; only a few dry leaves still clung to the green hedge behind it.

"Alas! how soon all that is good and beautiful passes away," sighed the elf.

After a while he found another rose, which became his home, for among its delicate fragrant leaves he could dwell in safety. Every morning he flew to the window of the poor girl, and always found her weeping by the flower pot. The bitter tears fell upon the jasmine twig, and each day, as she became paler and paler, the sprig appeared to grow greener and fresher. One shoot after another sprouted forth, and little white buds blossomed, which the poor girl fondly kissed. But her wicked brother scolded her, and asked her if she was going mad. He could not imagine why she was weeping over that flower-pot, and it annoyed him. He did not know whose closed eyes were there, nor what red lips were fading beneath the earth. And one day she sat and leaned her head against the flower-pot, and the little elf of the rose found her asleep. Then he seated himself by her ear, talked to her of that evening in the arbor, of the sweet perfume of the rose, and the loves of the elves. Sweetly she dreamed, and while she dreamt, her life passed away calmly and gently, and her spirit was with him whom she loved, in heaven. And the jasmine opened its large white bells, and spread forth its sweet fragrance; it had no other way of showing its grief for the dead. But the wicked brother considered the beautiful blooming plant as his own property, left to him by his sister, and he placed it in his sleeping room, close by his bed, for it was very lovely in appearance, and the fragrance sweet and delightful. The little elf of the rose followed it, and flew from flower to flower, telling each little spirit that dwelt in them the story of the murdered young man, whose head now formed part of the earth beneath them, and of the wicked brother and the poor sister. "We know it," said each little spirit in the flowers, "we know it, for have we not sprung from the eyes and lips of the murdered one. We know it, we know it," and the flowers nodded with their heads in a peculiar manner. The elf of the rose could not understand how they could rest so quietly in the matter, so he flew to the bees, who were gathering honey, and told them of the wicked brother. And the bees told it to their queen, who commanded that the next morning they should go and kill the murderer. But during the night, the first after the sister's death, while the brother was sleeping in his bed, close to where he had placed the fragrant jasmine, every flower cup opened, and invisibly the little spirits stole out, armed with poisonous spears. They placed themselves by the ear of the sleeper, told him dreadful dreams and then flew across his lips, and pricked his tongue with their poisoned spears. "Now have we revenged the dead," said they, and flew back into the white bells of the jasmine flowers. When the morning came, and as soon as the window was opened, the rose elf, with the queen bee, and the whole swarm of bees, rushed in to kill him. But he was already dead. People were standing round the bed, and saying that the scent of the jasmine had killed him. Then the elf of the rose understood the revenge of the flowers, and explained it to the queen bee, and she, with the whole swarm, buzzed about the flower-pot. The bees could not be driven away. Then a man took it up to remove it, and one of the bees stung him in the hand, so that he let the flower-pot fall, and it was broken to pieces. Then every one saw the whitened skull, and they knew the dead man in the bed was a murderer. And the queen bee hummed in the air, and sang of the revenge of the flowers, and of the elf of the rose and said that behind the smallest leaf dwells One, who can discover evil deeds, and punish them also.

The Elfin Hill

A FEW LARGE LIZARDS were running nimbly about in the clefts of an old tree; they could understand one another very well, for they spoke the lizard language.

"What a buzzing and a rumbling there is in the elfin hill," said one of the lizards; "I have not been able to close my eyes for two nights on account of the noise; I might just as well have had the toothache, for that always keeps me awake."

"There is something going on within there," said the other lizard; "they propped up the top of the hill with four red posts, till cock-crow this morning, so that it is thoroughly aired, and the elfin girls have learnt new dances; there is something."

"I spoke about it to an earth-worm of my acquaintance," said a third lizard; "the earth-worm had just come from the elfin hill, where he has been groping about in the earth day and night. He has heard a great deal; although he cannot see, poor miserable creature, yet he understands very well how to wriggle and lurk about. They expect friends in the elfin hill, grand company, too; but who they are the earth-worm would not say, or, perhaps, he really did not know. All the will-o'-the-wisps are ordered to be there to hold a torch dance, as it is called. The silver and gold which is plentiful in the hill will be polished and placed out in the moonlight."

"Who can the strangers be?" asked the lizards; "what can the matter be? Hark, what a buzzing and humming there is!"

Just at this moment the elfin hill opened, and an old elfin maiden, hollow behind, came tripping out; she was the old elf king's housekeeper, and a distant relative of the family; therefore she wore an amber heart on the middle of her forehead. Her feet moved very fast, "trip, trip;" good gracious, how she could trip right down to the sea to the night-raven.

"You are invited to the elf hill for this evening," said she; "but will you do me a great favour and undertake the invitations? you ought to do something, for you have no housekeeping to attend to as I have. We are going to have some very grand people, conjurors, who have always something to say; and therefore the old elf king wishes to make a great display."

"Who is to be invited?" asked the raven.

"All the world may come to the great ball, even human beings, if they can only talk in their sleep, or do something after our fashion. But for the feast the company must be carefully selected; we can only admit persons of high rank; I have had a dispute myself with the elf king, as he thought we could not admit ghosts. The merman and his daughter must be invited first, although it may not be agreeable to them to remain so long on dry land, but they shall have a wet stone to sit on, or perhaps something better; so I think they will not refuse this time. We must have all the old demons of the first class, with tails, and the hobgoblins and imps; and then I think we ought not to leave out the death-horse, or the grave-pig, or even the church dwarf, although they do belong to the clergy, and are not reckoned among our people; but that is merely their office, they are nearly related to us, and visit us very frequently."

"Croak," said the night-raven as he flew away with the invitations.

The elfin maidens we're already dancing on the elf hill, and they danced in shawls woven from moonshine and mist, which look very pretty to those who like such things. The large hall within the elf hill was splendidly decorated; the floor had been washed with moonshine, and the walls had been rubbed with magic ointment, so that they glowed like tulip-leaves in the light. In the kitchen were frogs roasting on the spit, and dishes preparing of snail skins, with children's fingers in them, salad of mushroom seed, hemlock, noses and marrow of mice, beer from the marsh woman's brewery, and sparkling salt-petre wine from the grave cellars. These were all substantial food. Rusty nails and church-window glass formed the dessert. The old elf king had his gold crown polished up with powdered slate-pencil; it was like that used by the first form, and very difficult for an elf king to obtain. In the bedrooms, curtains were hung up and fastened with the slime of snails; there was, indeed, a buzzing and humming everywhere.

"Now we must fumigate the place with burnt horse-hair and pig's bristles, and then I think I shall have done my part," said the elf man-servant.

"Father, dear," said the youngest daughter, "may I now hear who our high-born visitors are?"

"Well, I suppose I must tell you now," he replied; "two of my daughters must prepare themselves to be married, for the marriages certainly will take place. The old goblin from Norway, who lives in the ancient Dovre mountains, and who possesses many castles built of rock and freestone, besides a gold mine, which is better than all, so it is thought, is coming with his two sons, who are both seeking a wife. The old goblin is a true-hearted, honest, old Norwegian greybeard; cheerful and straightforward. I knew him formerly, when we used to drink together to our good fellowship: he came here once to fetch his wife, she is dead now. She was the daughter of the king of the chalk-hills at Moen. They say he took his wife from chalk; I shall be delighted to see him again. It is said that the boys are ill-bred, forward lads, but perhaps that is not quite correct, and they will become better as they grow older. Let me see that you know how to teach them good manners."

"And when are they coming?" asked the daughter.

"That depends upon wind and weather," said the elf king; "they travel economically. They will come when there is the chance of a ship. I wanted them to come over to Sweden, but the old man was not inclined to take my advice. He does not go forward with the times, and that I do not like."

Two will-o'-the-wisps came jumping in, one quicker than the other, so of course, one arrived first. "They are coming! they are coming!" he cried.

"Give me my crown," said the elf king, "and let me stand in the moonshine."

The daughters drew on their shawls and bowed down to the ground. There stood the old goblin from the Dovre mountains, with his crown of hardened ice and polished fir-cones. Besides this, he wore a bear-skin, and great, warm boots, while his sons went with their throats bare and wore no braces, for they were strong men.

"Is that a hill?" said the youngest of the boys, pointing to the elf hill, "we should call it a hole in Norway."

"Boys," said the old man, "a hole goes in, and a hill stands out; have you no eyes in your heads?"

Another thing they wondered at was, that they were able without trouble to understand the language.

"Take care," said the old man, "or people will think you have not been well brought up."

Then they entered the elfin hill, where the select and grand company were assembled, and so quickly had they appeared that they seemed to have been blown together. But for each guest the neatest and pleasantest arrangement had been made. The sea folks sat at table in great water-tubs, and they said it was just like being at home. All behaved themselves properly excepting the two young northern goblins; they put their legs on the table and thought they were all right.

"Feet off the table-cloth!" said the old goblin. They obeyed, but not immediately. Then they tickled the ladies who waited at table, with the fir-cones, which they carried in their pockets. They took off their boots, that they might be more at ease, and gave them to the ladies to hold. But their father, the old goblin, was very different; he talked pleasantly about the stately Norwegian rocks, and told fine tales of the waterfalls which dashed over them with a clattering noise like thunder or the sound of an organ, spreading their white foam on every side. He told of the salmon that leaps in the rushing waters, while the water-god plays on his golden harp. He spoke of the bright winter nights, when the sledge bells are ringing, and the boys run with burning torches across the smooth ice, which is so transparent that they can see the fishes dart forward beneath their feet. He described everything so clearly, that those who listened could see it all; they could see the saw-mills going, the men-servants and the maidens singing songs, and dancing a rattling dance – when all at once the old goblin gave the old elfin maiden a kiss, such a tremendous kiss, and yet they were almost strangers to each other.

Then the elfin girls had to dance, first in the usual way, and then with stamping feet, which they performed very well; then followed the artistic and solo dance. Dear me, how they did throw their legs about! No one could tell where the dance begun, or where it ended, nor indeed which were legs and which were arms, for they were all flying about together, like the shavings in a saw-pit! And then they spun round so quickly that the death-horse and the grave-pig became sick and giddy, and were obliged to leave the table.

"Stop!" cried the old goblin, "is that the only house-keeping they can perform? Can they do anything more than dance and throw about their legs, and make a whirlwind?"

"You shall soon see what they can do," said the elf king. And then he called his youngest daughter to him. She was slender and fair as moonlight, and the most graceful of all the sisters. She took a white chip in her mouth, and vanished instantly; this was her accomplishment. But the old goblin said he should not like his wife to have such an accomplishment, and thought his boys would have the same objection. Another daughter could make a figure like herself follow her, as if she had a shadow, which none of the goblin folk ever had. The third was of quite a different sort; she had learnt in the brew-house of the moor witch how to lard elfin puddings with glow-worms.

"She will make a good housewife," said the old goblin, and then saluted her with his eyes instead of drinking her health; for he did not drink much.

Now came the fourth daughter, with a large harp to play upon; and when she struck the first chord, every one lifted up the left leg (for the goblins are left-legged), and at the second chord they found they must all do just what she wanted.

"That is a dangerous woman," said the old goblin; and the two sons walked out of the hill; they had had enough of it. "And what can the next daughter do?" asked the old goblin.

"I have learnt everything that is Norwegian," said she; "and I will never marry, unless I can go to Norway."

Then her youngest sister whispered to the old goblin, "That is only because she has heard, in a Norwegian song, that when the world shall decay, the cliffs of Norway will remain standing like monuments; and she wants to get there, that she may be safe; for she is so afraid of sinking."

"Ho! ho!" said the old goblin, "is that what she means? Well, what can the seventh and last do?"

"The sixth comes before the seventh," said the elf king, for he could reckon; but the sixth would not come forward.

"I can only tell people the truth," said she. "No one cares for me, nor troubles himself about me; and I have enough to do to sew my grave clothes."

So the seventh and last came; and what could she do? Why, she could tell stories, as many as you liked, on any subject.

"Here are my five fingers," said the old goblin; "now tell me a story for each of them."

So she took him by the wrist, and he laughed till he nearly choked; and when she came to the fourth finger, there was a gold ring on it, as if it knew there was to be a betrothal. Then the old goblin said, "Hold fast what you have: this hand is yours; for I will have you for a wife myself."

Then the elfin girl said that the stories about the ring-finger and little Peter Playman had not yet been told.

"We will hear them in the winter," said the old goblin, "and also about the fir and the birch-trees, and the ghost stories, and of the tingling frost. You shall tell your tales, for no one over there can do it so well; and we will sit in the stone rooms, where the pine logs are burning, and drink mead out of the golden drinking-horn of the old Norwegian kings. The water-god has given me two; and when we sit there, Nix comes to pay us a visit, and will sing you all the songs of the mountain shepherdesses. How merry we shall be! The salmon will be leaping in the waterfalls, and dashing against the stone walls, but he will not be able to come in. It is indeed very pleasant to live in old Norway. But where are the lads?"

Where indeed were they? Why, running about the fields, and blowing out the will-o'-the-wisps, who so good-naturedly came and brought their torches.

"What tricks have you been playing?" said the old goblin. "I have taken a mother for you, and now you may take one of your aunts."

But the youngsters said they would rather make a speech and drink to their good fellowship; they had no wish to marry. Then they made speeches and drank toasts, and tipped their glasses, to show that they were empty. Then they took off their coats, and lay down on the table to sleep; for they made themselves quite at home. But the old goblin danced about the room with his young bride, and exchanged boots with her, which is more fashionable than exchanging rings.

"The cock is crowing," said the old elfin maiden who acted as housekeeper; "now we must close the shutters, that the sun may not scorch us."

Then the hill closed up. But the lizards continued to run up and down the riven tree; and one said to the other, "Oh, how much I was pleased with the old goblin!"

"The boys pleased me better," said the earth-worm. But then the poor miserable creature could not see.

The Elves and Their Antics

THE ELVES ARE THE LITTLE WHITE CREATURES that live between heaven and earth. They are not in the clouds, nor down in the caves and mines, like the kabouters. They are bright and fair, dwelling in the air, and in the world of light. The direct heat of the sun is usually too much for them, so they are not often seen during the day, except towards sunset. They love the silvery moonlight. There used to be many folks, who thought they had seen the beautiful creatures, full of fun and joy, dancing hand in hand, in a circle.

In these old days, long since gone by, there were more people than there are now, who were sure they had many times enjoyed the sight of the elves. Some places in Holland show, by their names, where this kind of fairies used to live. These little creatures, that looked as thin as gauze, were very lively and mischievous, though they often helped honest and hard working people in their tasks, as we shall see. But first and most of all, they were fond of fun. They loved to vex cross people and to please those who were bonnie and blithe. They hated misers, but they loved the kind and generous. These little folks usually took their pleasure in the grassy meadows, among the flowers and butterflies. On bright nights they played among the moonbeams.

There were certain times when the elves were busy, in such a way as to make men and girls think about them. Then their tricks were generally in the stable, or in the field among the cows. Sometimes, in the kitchen or dairy, among the dishes or milk-pans, they made an awful mess for the maids to clean up. They tumbled over the churns, upset the milk jugs, and played hoops with the round cheeses. In a bedroom they made things look as if the pigs had run over them.

When a farmer found his horse's mane twisted into knots, or two cows with their tails tied together, he said at once, "That's the work of elves." If the mares did not feel well, or looked untidy, their owners were sure the elves had taken the animals out and had been riding them all night. If a cow was sick, or fell down on the grass, it was believed that the elves had shot an arrow into its body. The inquest, held on many a dead calf or its mother, was, that it died from an "elf-shot." They were so sure of this, that even when a stone arrow head – such as our far-off ancestors used in hunting, when they were cave men – was picked up off the ground, it was called an 'elf bolt,' or 'elf-arrow.'

Near a certain village named Elf-berg or Elf Hill, because there were so many of the little people in that neighbourhood, there was one very old elf, named Styf, which means Stiff, because though so old he stood up straight as a lance. Even more than the young elves, he was famous for his pranks. Sometimes he was nicknamed Haan-e'-kam or Cock's Comb. He got this name, because he loved to mock the roosters, when they crowed, early in the morning. With his red cap on, he did look like a rooster. Sometimes he fooled the hens, that heard him crowing. Old Styf loved nothing better than to go to a house where was a party indoors. All the wooden shoes of the twenty or thirty people within, men and women, girls and boys, would be left outside the door. All good Dutch folks step out of their heavy timber shoes, or klomps, before they enter a house. It is always a curious sight, at a country church, or gathering of people at a party, to see the klomps, big and little, belonging to baby boys and girls, and to the big men, who wear a number thirteen shoe of wood. One wonders how each one of the owners knows his own, but he does. Each pair is put in its own place, but Old Styf would come and mix them all up together, and then leave them in a pile. So when the people came out to go home, they had a terrible time in finding and sorting out their shoes. Often they scolded each other; or, some innocent boy was blamed for the mischief. Some did not find out, till the next day, that they had on one foot their own, and on another foot, their neighbour's shoe. It usually took a week to get the klomps sorted out, exchanged, and the proper feet into the right shoes. In this way, which was a special trick with him, this naughty elf, Styf, spoiled the temper of many people.

Beside the meadow elves, there were other kinds in Elfin Land; some living in the woods, some in the sand-dunes, but those called Staalkaars, or elves of the stall, were Old Styf's particular friends. These lived in stables and among the cows. The Moss Maidens, that could do anything with leaves, even turning them into money, helped Styf, for they too liked mischief. They teased men-folks, and enjoyed nothing better than misleading the stupid fellows that fuddled their brains with too much liquor.

Styf's especially famous trick was played on misers. It was this. When he heard of any old fellow, who wanted to save the cost of candles, he would get a kabouter to lead him off in the swamps, where the sooty elves come out, on dark nights, to dance. Hoping to catch these lights and use them for candles, the mean fellow would find himself in a swamp, full of water and chilled to the marrow. Then the kabouters would laugh loudly.

Old Styf had the most fun with another stingy fellow, who always scolded children when he found them spending a penny. If he saw a girl buying flowers, or a boy giving a copper coin for a waffle, he talked roughly to them for wasting money. Meeting this miser one day, as he was walking along the brick road, leading from the village, Styf offered to pay the old man a thousand guilders, in exchange for four striped tulips, that grew in his garden. The miser, thinking it real silver, eagerly took the money and put it away in his iron strong box. The next night, when he went, as he did three times a week, to count, and feel, and rub, and gloat, over his cash, there was nothing but leaves in a round form. These, at his touch, crumbled to pieces. The Moss Maidens laughed uproariously, when the mean old fellow was mad about it.

But let no one suppose that the elves, because they were smarter than stupid human beings, were always in mischief. No, no! They did, indeed, have far more intelligence than dull grown folks, lazy boys, or careless girls; but many good things they did. They sewed shoes for poor cobblers, when they were sick, and made clothes for children, when the mother was tired. When they were around, the butter came quick in the churn.

When the blue flower of the flax bloomed in Holland, the earth, in spring time, seemed like the sky. Old Styf then saw his opportunity to do a good thing. Men thought it a great affair to have even coarse linen tow for clothes. No longer need they hunt the wolf and deer in the forest, for their garments. By degrees, they learned to make finer stuff, both linen for clothes and sails for ships, and this fabric they spread out on the grass until the cloth was well bleached. When taken up, it was white as the summer clouds that sailed in the blue sky. All the world admired the product, and soon the word 'Holland' was less the name of a country, than of a dainty fabric, so snow white, that it was fit to robe a queen. The world wanted more and more of it, and the Dutch linen weaver grew rich. Yet still there was more to come.

Now, on one moonlight night in summer, the lady elves, beautiful creatures, dressed in gauze and film, with wings to fly and with feet that made no sound, came down into the meadows for their fairy dances. But when, instead of green grass, they saw a white landscape, they wondered, Was it winter?

Surely not, for the air was warm. No one shivered, or was cold. Yet there were whole acres as white as snow, while all the old fairy rings, grass and flowers were hidden.

They found that the meadows had become bleaching grounds, so that the cows had to go elsewhere to get their dinner, and that this white area was all linen. However, they quickly got over their surprise, for elves are very quick to notice things. But now that men had stolen a march on them, they asked whether, after all, these human beings had more intelligence than elves. Not one of these fairies but believed that men and women were the inferiors of elves.

So, then and there, began a battle of wits.

"They have spoiled our dancing floor with their new invention; so we shall have to find another," said the elfin queen, who led the party.

"They are very proud of their linen, these men are; but, without the spider to teach them, what could they have done? Even a wild boar can instruct these human beings. Let us show them, that we, also, can do even more. I'll get Old Styf to put on his thinking cap. He'll add something new that will make them prouder yet."

"But we shall get the glory of it," the elves shouted in chorus. Then they left off talking and began their dances, floating in the air, until they looked, from a distance, like a wreath of stars.

The next day, a procession of lovely elf maidens and mothers waited on Styf and asked him to devise something that would excel the invention of linen; which, after all, men had learned from the spider.

"Yes, and they would not have any grain fields, if they had not learned from the wild boar," added the elf queen.

Old Styf answered "yes" at once to their request, and put on his red thinking cap. Then some of the girl elves giggled, for they saw that he did, really, look like a cock's comb. "No wonder they called him Haan-e'-kam," said one elf girl to the other.

Now Old Styf enjoyed fooling, just for the fun of it, and he taught all the younger elves that those who did the most work with their hands and head, would have the most fun when they were old.

First of all, he went at once to see Fro, the spirit of the golden sunshine and the warm summer showers, who owned two of the most wonderful things in the world. One was his sword, which, as soon as it was drawn out of its sheath, against wicked enemies, fought of its own accord and won every battle. Fro's chief enemies were the frost giants, who wilted the flowers and blasted the plants useful to man. Fro was absent, when Styf came, but his wife promised he would come next day, which he did. He was happy to meet all the elves and fairies, and they, in turn, joyfully did whatever he told them. Fro knew all the secrets of the grain fields, for he could see what was in every kernel of both the stalks and the ripe ears. He arrived, in a golden chariot, drawn by his wild boar which served him instead of a horse. Both chariot and boar drove over the tops of the ears of wheat, and faster than the wind.

The Boar was named Gullin, or Golden Bristles because of its sunshiny colour and splendour. In this chariot, Fro had specimens of all the grains, fruits, and vegetables known to man, from which Styf could choose, for these he was accustomed to scatter over the earth.

When Styf told him just what he wanted to do, Fro picked out a sheaf of wheat and whispered a secret in his ear. Then he drove away, in a burst of golden glory, which dazzled even the elves, that loved the bright sunshine. These elves were always glad to see the golden chariot coming or passing by.

Styf also summoned to his aid the kabouters, and, from these ugly little fellows, got some useful hints; for they, dwelling in the dark caverns, know many secrets which men used to name alchemy, and which they now call chemistry.

Then Styf fenced himself off from all intruders, on the top of a bright, sunny hilltop, with his thinking cap on and made experiments for seven days. No elves, except his servants, were allowed to see him. At the end of a week, still keeping his secret and having instructed a dozen or so of the elf girls in his new art, he invited all the elves in the Low Countries to come to a great exhibition, which he intended to give.

What a funny show it was! On one long bench, were half a dozen washtubs; and on a table, near by, were a dozen more washtubs; and on a longer table not far away were six ironing boards, with smoothing irons. A stove, made hot with a peat fire, was to heat the irons. Behind the tubs and tables, stood the twelve elf maidens, all arrayed in shining white garments and caps, as spotless as snow. One might almost think they were white elves of the meadow and not kabouters of the mines. The wonder was that their linen clothes were not only as dainty as stars, but that they glistened, as if they had laid on the ground during a hoar frost.

Yet it was still warm summer. Nothing had frozen, or melted, and the rosy-faced elf-maidens were as dry as an ivory fan. Yet they resembled the lilies of the garden when pearly with dew-drops.

When all were gathered together, Old Styf called for some of the company, who had come from afar, to take off their dusty and travel-stained linen garments and give them to him. These were passed over to the trained girls waiting to receive them. In a jiffy, they were washed, wrung out, rinsed and dried. It was noticed that those elf-maidens, who were standing at the last tub, were intently expecting to do something great, while those five elf maids at the table took off the hot irons from the stove. They touched the bottom of the flat-irons with a drop of water to see if it rolled off hissing. They kept their eyes fixed on Styf, who now came forward before all and said, in a loud voice:

"Elves and fairies, moss maidens and stall sprites, one and all, behold our invention, which our great friend Fro and our no less helpful friends, the kabouters, have helped me to produce. Now watch me prove its virtues."

Forthwith he produced before all a glistening substance, partly in powder, and partly in square lumps, as white as chalk. He easily broke up a handful under his fingers, and flung it into the fifth tub, which had hot water in it. After dipping the washed garments in the white gummy mass, he took them up, wrung them out, dried them with his breath, and then handed them to the elf ironers. In a few moments, these held up, before the company, what a few minutes before had been only dusty and stained clothes. Now, they were white and resplendent. No fuller's earth could have bleached them thus, nor added so glistening a surface.

It was starch, a new thing for clothes. The fairies, one and all, clapped their hands in delight.

"What shall we name it?" modestly asked Styf of the oldest gnome present.

"Hereafter, we shall call you Styf Sterk, Stiff Starch." They all laughed.

Very quickly did the Dutch folks, men and women, hear and make use of the elves' invention. Their linen closets now looked like piles of snow. All over the Low Countries, women made caps, in new fashions, of lace or plain linen, with horns and wings, flaps and crimps, with quilling and with whirligigs. Soon, in every town, one could read the sign 'Hier mangled men' (Here we do ironing).

In time, kings, queens and nobles made huge ruffs, often so big that their necks were invisible, and their heads nearly lost from sight, in rings of quilled linen, or of lace, that stuck out a foot or so. Worldly people dyed their starch yellow; zealous folk made it blue; but moderate people kept it snowy white.

Starch added money and riches to the nation. Kings' treasuries became fat with money gained by taxes laid on ruffs, and on the cargoes of starch, which was now imported by the shipload, or made on the spot, in many countries. So, out of the ancient grain came a new spirit that worked for sweetness and beauty, cleanliness, and health. From a useful substance, as old as Egypt, was born a fine art, that added to the sum of the world's wealth and pleasure.

The Kabouters and the Bells

WHEN THE YOUNG QUEEN Wilhelmina visited Brabant and Limburg, they amused her with pageants and plays, in which the little fellows called kabouters, in Dutch, and kobolds in German, played and showed off their tricks. Other small folk, named gnomes, took part in the tableaux. The kabouters are the dark elves, who live in forests and mines. The white elves live in the open fields and the sunshine.

The gnomes do the thinking, but the kabouters carry out the work of mining and gathering the precious stones and minerals. They are short, thick fellows, very strong and are strenuous in digging out coal and iron, copper and gold. When they were first made, they were so ugly, that they had to live where they could not be seen, that is, in the dark places. The grown imps look like old men with beards, but no one ever heard of a kabouter that was taller than a yardstick. As for the babies, they are hardly bigger than a man's thumb. The big boys and girls, in the kabouter kingdom, are not much over a foot high.

What is peculiar about them all is, that they help the good and wise people to do things better; but they love to plague and punish the dull folks, that are stupid, or foolish or naughty. In impish glee, they lure the blockheads, or in Dutch, the 'cheese-heads,' to do worse.

A long time ago, there were no church spires or bells in the land of the Dutch folks, as there are now by the thousands. The good teachers from the South came into the country and taught the people to have better manners, finer clothes and more wholesome food. They also persuaded them to forget their cruel gods and habits of revenge. They told of the Father in Heaven, who loves us all, as his children, and forgives us when we repent of our evil doings.

Now when the chief gnomes and kabouters heard of the newcomers in the land, they held a meeting and said one to the other:

"We shall help all the teachers that are good and kind, but we shall plague and punish the rough fellows among them."

So word was sent to all little people in the mines and hills, instructing them how they were to act and what they were to do.

Some of the new teachers, who were foreigners, and did not know the customs of the country, were very rude and rough. Every day they hurt the feelings of the people. With their axes they cut down the sacred trees. They laughed scornfully at the holy wells and springs of water. They reviled the people, when they prayed to great Woden, with his black ravens that told him everything, or to the gentle Freya, with her white doves, who helped good girls to get kind husbands. They scolded the children at play, and this made their fathers and mothers feel miserable. This is the reason why so many people were angry and sullen, and would not listen to the foreign teachers.

Worse than this, many troubles came to these outsiders. Their bread was sour, when they took it out of the oven. So was the milk, in their pans. Sometimes they found their beds turned upside down. Gravel stones rattled down into their fireplaces. Their hats and shoes were missing. In fact, they had a terrible time generally and wanted to go back home. When the kabouter has a grudge against any one, he knows how to plague him.

But the teachers that were wise and gentle had no trouble. They persuaded the people with kind words, and, just as a baby learns to eat other food at the table, so the people were weaned away from cruel customs and foolish beliefs. Many of the land's folk came to listen to the teachers and helped them gladly to build churches.

More wonderful than this, were the good things that came to these kind teachers, they knew not how. Their bread and milk were always sweet and in plenty. They found their beds made up and their clothes kept clean, gardens planted with blooming flowers, and much hard work done for them. When they would build a church in a village, they wondered how it was that the wood and the nails, the iron necessary to brace the beams, and the copper and brass for the sacred vessels, came so easily and in plenty. When, on some nights, they wondered where they would get food to eat, they found, on waking up in the morning, that there was always something good ready for them. Thus many houses of worship were built, and the more numerous were the churches, the more did farms, cows, grain fields, and happy people multiply.

Now when the gnomes and kabouters, who like to do work for pleasant people, heard that the good teachers wanted church bells, to call the people to worship, they resolved to help the strangers. They would make not only a bell, or a chime, but, actually a carillon, or concert of bells to hang up in the air.

The dark dwarfs did not like to dig metal for swords or spears, or what would hurt people; but the church bells would guide travellers in the forest, and quiet the storms, that destroyed houses and upset boats and killed or drowned people, besides inviting the people to come and pray and sing. They knew that the good teachers were poor and could not buy bells in France or Italy. Even if they had money, they could not get them through the thick forests, or over the stormy seas, for they were too heavy.

When all the kabouters were told of this, they came together to work, night and day, in the mines. With pick and shovel, crowbar and chisel, and hammer and mallet, they broke up the rocks containing copper and tin. Then they built great roaring fires, to smelt the ore into ingots. They would show the teachers that the Dutch kabouters could make bells, as well as the men in the lands of the South. These dwarfish people are jealous of men and very proud of what they can do.

It was the funniest sight to see these short legged fellows, with tiny coats coming just below their thighs, and little red caps, looking like a stocking and ending in a tassel, on their heads, and in shoes that had no laces, but very long points. They flew around as lively as monkeys, and when the fire was hot they threw off everything and worked much harder and longer than men do.

Were they like other fairies? Well, hardly. One must put away all his usual thoughts, when he thinks of kabouters. No filmy wings on their backs! No pretty clothes or gauzy garments, or stars, or crowns, or wands! Instead of these were hammers, pickaxes, and chisels. But how diligent, useful and lively these little folks, in plain, coarse coats and with bare legs, were! In place of things light, clean and easy, the kabouters had furnaces, crucibles and fires of coal and wood.

Sometimes they were grimy, with smoke and coal dust, and the sweat ran down their faces and bodies. Yet there was always plenty of water in the mines, and when hard work was over they washed and looked plain but tidy. Besides their stores of gold, and silver, and precious stones, which they kept ready, to give to good people, they had tools with which to tease or tantalize cruel, mean or lazy folks.

Now when the kabouter daddies began the roaring fires for the making of the bells, the little mothers and the small fry in the kabouter world could not afford to be idle. One and all, they came down from off the earth, and into the mines they went in a crowd. They left off teasing milkmaids, tangling skeins of flax, tearing fishermen's nets, tying knots in cows' tails, tumbling pots, pans and dishes, in the kitchen, or hiding hats, and throwing stones down the chimneys onto the fireplaces. They even ceased their fun of mocking children, who were calling the cows home, by hiding behind the rocks and shouting to them. Instead of these tricks, they saved their breath to blow the fires into a blast. Everybody wondered where the 'kabs' were, for on the farms and in town nothing happened and all was as quiet as when a baby is asleep.

For days and weeks underground, the dwarfs toiled, until their skins, already dark, became as sooty as the rafters in the houses of our ancestors. Finally, when all the labour was over, the chief gnomes were invited down into the mines to inspect the work.

What a sight! There were at least a hundred bells, of all sizes, like as in a family; where there are daddy, mother, grown ups, young sons and daughters, little folk and babies, whether single, twins or triplets. Big bells, that could scarcely be put inside a hogshead, bells that would go into a barrel, bells that filled a bushel, and others a peck, stood in rows. From the middle, and tapering down the row, were scores more, some of them no larger than cow-bells. Others, at the end, were so small, that one had to think of pint and gill measures.

Besides all these, there were stacks of iron rods and bars, bolts, nuts, screws, and wires and yokes on which to hang the bells.

One party of the strongest of the kabouters had been busy in the forest, close to a village, where some men, ordered to do so by a foreign teacher, had begun to cut down some of the finest and most sacred of the grand old trees. They had left their tools in the woods; but the 'kabs,' at night, seized their axes and before morning, without making any noise, they had levelled all but the holy trees. Those they spared. Then, the timber, all cut and squared, ready to hold the bells, was brought to the mouth of the mine.

Now in Dutch, the name for bell is 'klok.' So a wise and grey-bearded gnome was chosen by the high sounding title of klokken-spieler, or bell player, to test the bells for a carillon. They were all hung, for practice, on the big trestles, in a long row. Each one of these frames was called a 'hang,' for they were just like those on which fishermen's nets were laid to dry and be mended.

So when all were ready, washed, and in their clean clothes, every one of the kabouter families, daddies, mothers, and young ones, were ranged in lines and made to sing. The heavy male tenors and baritones, the female sopranos and contraltos, the trebles of the little folks, and the squeaks of the very small children, down to the babies' cooing, were all heard by the gnomes, who were judges. The high and mighty klokken-spieler, or master of the carillon, chose those voices with best tone and quality, from which to set in order and regulate the bells.

It was pitiful to see how mad and jealous some of the kabouters, both male and female, were, when they were not appointed to the first row, in which were some of the biggest of the males, and some of the fattest of the females. Then the line tapered off, to forty or fifty young folks, including urchins of either sex, down to mere babies, that could hardly stand. These had bibs on and had to be held up by their fond mothers. Each one by itself could squeal and squall, coo and crow lustily; but, at a distance, their voices blended and the noise they made sounded like a tinkle.

All being ready, the old gnome bit his tuning fork, hummed a moment, and then started a tune. Along the line, at a signal from the chief gnome, they started a tune.

In the long line, there were, at first, booms and peals, twanging and clanging, jangling and wrangling, making such a clangour that it sounded more like an uproar than an opera. The chief gnome was almost discouraged.

But neither a gnome nor a kabouter ever gives up. The master of the choir tried again and again. He scolded one old daddy, for singing too low. He frowned at a stalwart young fellow, who tried to drown out all the rest with his bull-like bellow. He shook his finger at a kabouter girl, that was flirting with a handsome lad near her. He cheered up the little folks, encouraging them to hold up their voices, until finally he had all in order. Then they practiced, until the master gnome thought he had his scale of notation perfect and gave orders to attune the bells. To the delight of all the gnomes, kabouters and elves, that had been invited to the concert, the rows of bells, a hundred or more, from boomers to tinklers, made harmony. Strung one above the other, they could render merriment, or sadness, in solos, peals, chimes, cascades and carillons, with sweetness and effect. At the low notes the babies called out "cow, cow;" but at the high notes, "bird, bird."

So it happened that, on the very day that the bishop had his great church built, with a splendid bulb spire on the top, and all nicely furnished within, but without one bell to ring in it, that the kabouters planned a great surprise.

It was night. The bishop was packing his saddle bags, ready to take a journey, on horseback, to Rheims. At this city, the great caravans from India and China ended, bringing to the annual fair, rugs, spices, gems, and things Oriental, and the merchants of Rheims rolled in gold. Here the bishop would beg the money, or ask for a bell, or chimes.

Suddenly, in the night, while in his own house, there rang out music in the air, such as the bishop had never heard in Holland, or in any of the seventeen provinces of the Netherlands. Not even in the old lands, France, or Spain, or Italy, where the Christian teachers, builders and singers, and the music of the bells had long been heard, had such a flood of sweet sounds ever fallen on human ears. Here, in these northern regions, rang out, not a solo, nor a peal, nor a chime, nor even a cascade, from one bell, or from many bells; but, a long programme of richest music in the air – something which no other country, however rich or old, possessed. It was a carillon, that is, a continued mass of real music, in which whole tunes, songs, and elaborate pieces of such length, mass and harmony, as only a choir of many voices, a band of music, or an orchestra of many performers could produce.

To get this grand work of hanging in the spire done in one night, and before daylight, also, required a whole regiment of fairy toilers, who must work like bees. For if one ray of sunshine struck any one of the kabouters, he was at once petrified. The light elves lived in the sunshine and thrived on it; but for dark elves, like the kabouters, whose home was underground, sunbeams were as poisoned arrows bringing sure death; for by these they were turned into stone. Happily the task was finished before the eastern sky grew grey, or the cocks crowed. While it was yet dark, the music in the air flooded the earth. The people in their beds listened with rapture.

"Laus Deo" (Praise God), devoutly cried the surprised bishop. "It sounds like a choir of angels. Surely the cherubim and seraphim are here. Now is fulfilled the promise of the Psalmist: 'The players on instruments shall be there.'"

So, from this beginning, so mysterious to the rough, unwise and stupid teachers, but, by degrees, clearer to the tactful ones, who were kind and patient, the carillons spread over all the region between the forests of Ardennes and the island in the North Sea. The Netherlands became the land of melodious symphonies and of tinkling bells. No town, however poor, but in time had its carillon. Every quarter of an hour, the sweet music of hymn or song, made the air vocal, while at the striking of the hours, the pious bowed their heads and the workmen heard the call for rest, or they took cheer, because their day's toil was over. At sunrise, noon, or sunset, the Angelus, and at night the curfew sounded their calls.

It grew into a fashion, that, on stated days, great concerts were given, lasting over an hour, when the grand works of the masters of music were rendered and famous carillon players came from all over the Netherlands, to compete for prizes. The Low Countries became a famous school, in which klokken-spielers (bell players) by scores were trained. Thus no kingdom, however rich or great, ever equalled the Land of the Carillon, in making the air sweet with both melody and harmony.

Nobody ever sees a kabouter nowadays, for in the new world, when the woods are nearly all cut down, the world made by the steam engine, and telegraph, and wireless message, the automobile, aeroplane and submarine, cycle and under-sea boat, the little folks in the mines and forests are forgotten. The chemists, miners, engineers and learned men possess the secrets which were once those of the fairies only. Yet the artists and architects, the clockmakers and bellfounders, who love beauty, remember what their fathers once thought and believed. That is the reason why, on many a famous clock, either in front of the dial or near the pendulum, are figures of the gnomes, who thought, and the kabouters who wrought, to make the carillons. In Teuton lands, where their cousins are named kobolds, and in France where they are called fée, and in England brownies, they have tolling and ringing of bells, with peals, chimes and cascades of sweet sound; but the Netherlands, still, above all others on earth, is the home of the carillon.

The Oni on His Travels

ACROSS THE OCEAN, in Japan, there once lived curious creatures called onis. Every Japanese boy and girl has heard of them, though one has not often been caught. In one museum, visitors could see the hairy leg of a specimen. Falling out of the air in a storm, the imp had lost his limb. It had been torn off by being caught in the timber side of a well curb. The story-teller was earnestly assured by one Japanese lad that his grandfather had seen it tumble from the clouds.

Many people are sure that the onis live in the clouds and occasionally fall off, during a peal of thunder. Then they escape and hide down in a well. Or, they get loose in the kitchen, rattle the dishes around, and make a great racket. They behave like cats, with a dog after them. They do a great deal of mischief, but not much harm. There are even some old folks who say that, after all, onis are only unruly children, that behave like angels in the morning and act like imps in the afternoon. So we see that not much is known about the onis.

Many things that go wrong are blamed on the onis. Foolish folks, such as stupid maid-servants, and dull-witted fellows, that blunder a good deal, declare that the onis made them do it. Drunken men, especially, that stumble into mud-holes at night, say the onis pushed them in. Naughty boys that steal cake, and girls that take sugar, often tell fibs to their parents, charging it on the onis.

The onis love to play jokes on people, but they are not dangerous. There are plenty of pictures of them in Japan, though they never sat for their portraits, but this is the way they looked.

Some onis have only one eye in their forehead, others two, and, once in a while, a big fellow has three. There are little, short horns on their heads, but these are no bigger than those on a baby deer and never grow long. The hair on their heads gets all snarled up, just like a little girl's that cries when her tangled tresses are combed out; for the onis make use of neither brushes nor looking glasses. As for their faces, they never wash them, so they look sooty. Their skin is rough, like an elephant's. On each of their feet are only three toes. Whether an oni has a nose, or a snout, is not agreed upon by the learned men who have studied them.

No one ever heard of an oni being higher than a yardstick, but they are so strong that one of them can easily lift two bushel bags of rice at once. In Japan, they steal the food offered to the idols. They can live without air. They like nothing better than to drink both the rice spirit called saké, and the black liquid called soy, of which only a few drops, as a sauce on fish, are enough for a man. Of this sauce, the Dutch, as well as the Japanese, are very fond.

Above all things else, the most fun for a young oni is to get into a crockery shop. Once there, he jumps round among the cups and dishes, hides in the jars, straddles the shelves and turns somersaults over the counter. In fact, the oni is only a jolly little imp. The Japanese girls, on New Year's eve, throw handfuls of dried beans in every room of the house and cry, "In, with good luck; and out with you, onis!" Yet they laugh merrily all the time. The onis cannot speak, but they can chatter like monkeys. They often seem to be talking to each other in gibberish.

Now it once happened in Japan that the great Tycoon of the country wanted to make a present to the Prince of the Dutch. So he sent all over the land, from the sweet potato fields in the south to the seal and salmon waters in the north, to get curiosities of all sorts. The products of Japan, from the warm parts, where grow the indigo and the sugar cane, to the cold regions, in which are the bear and walrus, were sent as gifts to go to the Land of Dykes and Windmills. The Japanese had heard that the Dutch people like cheese, walk in wooden shoes, eat with forks, instead of chopsticks, and the women wear twenty petticoats apiece, while the men sport jackets with two gold buttons, and folks generally do things the other way from that which was common in Japan.

Now it chanced that while they were packing the things that were piled up in the palace at Yedo, a young oni, with his horns only half grown, crawled into the kitchen, at night, through the big bamboo water pipe near the pump. Pretty soon he jumped into the storeroom. There, the precious cups, vases, lacquer boxes, pearl-inlaid pill-holders, writing desks, jars of tea, and bales of silk, were lying about, ready to be put into their cases. The yellow wrappings for covering the pretty things of gold and silver, bronze and wood, and the rice chaff, for the packing of the porcelain, were all at hand. What a jolly time the oni did have, in tumbling them about and rolling over them! Then he leaped like a monkey from one vase to another. He put on a lady's gay silk kimono and wrapped himself around with golden embroidery. Then he danced and played the game of the Ka-gu'-ra, or Lion of Korea, pretending to make love to a girl-oni. Such funny capers as he did cut! It would have made a cat laugh to see him. It was broad daylight, before his pranks were over, and the Dutch church chimes were playing the hour of seven.

Suddenly the sound of keys in the lock told him that, in less than a minute, the door would open. Where should he hide? There was no time to be lost. So he seized some bottles of soy from the kitchen shelf and then jumped into the big bottom drawer of a ladies' cabinet, and pulled it shut.

"Namu Amida" (Holy Buddha!), cried the man that opened the door. "Who has been here? It looks like a rat's picnic."

However, the workmen soon came and set everything to rights. Then they packed up the pretty things. They hammered down the box lids and before night the Japanese curiosities were all stored in the hold of a swift, Dutch ship, from Nagasaki, bound for Rotterdam. After a long voyage, the vessel arrived safely in good season, and the boxes were sent on to The Hague, or capital city. As the presents were for the prince, they were taken at once to the pretty palace, called the House in the Wood. There they were unpacked and set on exhibition for the prince and princess to see the next day.

When the palace maid came in next morning to clean up the floor and dust the various articles, her curiosity led her to pull open the drawer of the ladies' cabinet; when out jumped something hairy. It nearly frightened the girl out of her wits. It was the oni, which rushed off and down stairs, tumbling over a half dozen servants, who were sitting at their breakfast. All started to run except the brave butler, who caught up a carving knife and showed fight. Seeing this, the oni ran down into the cellar, hoping to find some hole or crevice for escape. All around, were shelves filled with cheeses, jars of sour-krout, pickled herring, and stacks of fresh rye bread standing in the corners. But oh! how they did smell in his Japanese nostrils! Oni, as he was, he nearly fainted, for no such odours had ever beaten upon his nose, when in Japan. Even at the risk of being carved into bits, he must go back. So up into the kitchen again he ran. Happily, the door into the garden stood wide open.

Grabbing a fresh bottle of soy from the kitchen shelf, the oni, with a hop, skip and jump, reached outdoors. Seeing a pair of klomps, or wooden shoes, near the steps, the oni put his pair of three toes into them, to keep the dogs from scenting its tracks. Then he ran into the fields, hiding among the cows, until he heard men with pitchforks coming. At once the oni leaped upon a cow's back and held on to its horns, while the poor animal ran for its life into its stall, in the cow stable, hoping to brush the monster off.

The dairy farmer's wife was at that moment pulling open her bureau drawer, to put on a new clean lace cap. Hearing her favourite cow moo and bellow, she left the drawer open and ran to look through the pane of glass in the kitchen. Through this, she could peep, at any minute, to see whether this or that cow, or its calf, was sick or well.

Meanwhile, at the House in the Wood, the princess, hearing the maid scream and the servants in an uproar, rushed out in her embroidered white nightie, to ask who, and what, and why, and wherefore. All different and very funny were the answers of maid, butler, cook, valet and boots.

The first maid, who had pulled open the drawer and let the oni get out, held up broom and duster, as if to take oath. She declared:

"It was a monkey, or baboon; but he seemed to talk – Russian, I think."

"No," said the butler. "I heard the creature – a black ram, running on its hind legs; but its language was German, I'm sure."

The cook, a fat Dutch woman, told a long story. She declared, on honour, that it was a black dog like a Chinese pug, that has no hair. However, she had only seen its back, but she was positive the creature talked English, for she heard it say "soy."

The valet honestly avowed that he was too scared to be certain of anything, but was ready to swear that to his ears the words uttered seemed to be Swedish. He had once heard sailors from Sweden talking, and the chatter sounded like their lingo.

Then there was Boots, the errand boy, who believed that it was the Devil; but, whatever or whoever it was, he was ready to bet a week's wages that its lingo was all in French.

Now when the princess found that not one of her servants could speak or understand any language but their own, she scolded them roundly in Dutch, and wound up by saying, "You're a lot of cheese-heads, all of you."

Then she arranged the wonderful things from the Far East, with her own dainty hands, until the House in the Wood was fragrant with Oriental odours, and soon it became famous throughout all Europe. Even when her grandchildren played with the pretty toys from the land of Fuji and flowers, of silk and tea, cherry blossoms and camphor trees, it was not only the first but the finest Japanese collection in all Europe.

Meanwhile, the oni, in a strange land, got into one trouble after another. In rushed men with clubs, but as an oni was well used to seeing these at home, he was not afraid. He could outrun, outjump, or outclimb any man, easily. The farmer's vrouw (wife) nearly fainted when the oni leaped first into her room and then into her bureau drawer. As he did so, the bottle of soy, held in his three-fingered paw, hit the wood and the dark liquid, as black as tar, ran all over the nicely starched laces, collars and nightcaps. Every bit of her quilled and crimped head-gear and neckwear, once as white as snow, was ruined.

"Donder en Bliksem" (thunder and lightning), cried the vrouw. "There's my best cap, that cost twenty guilders, utterly ruined." Then she bravely ran for the broomstick.

The oni caught sight of what he thought was a big hole in the wall and ran into it. Seeing the blue sky above, he began to climb up. Now there were no chimneys in Japan and he did not know what this was. The soot nearly blinded and choked him. So he slid down and rushed out, only to have his head nearly cracked by the farmer's wife, who gave him a whack of her broomstick. She thought it was a crazy goat that she was fighting. She first drove the oni into the cellar and then bolted the door.

An hour later, the farmer got a gun and loaded it. Then, with his hired man he came near, one to pull open the door, and the other to shoot. What they expected to find was a monster.

But no! So much experience, even within an hour, of things unknown in Japan, including chimneys, had been too severe for the poor, lonely, homesick oni. There it lay dead on the floor, with its three fingers held tightly to its snout and closing it. So much cheese, zuur kool (sour krout), gin (schnapps), advocaat (brandy and eggs), cows' milk, both sour and fresh, wooden shoes, lace collars and crimped neckwear, with the various smells, had turned both the oni's head and his stomach. The very sight of these strange things being so unusual, gave the oni first fright, and then a nervous attack, while the odours, such as had never tortured his nose before, had finished him.

The wise men of the village were called together to hold an inquest. After summoning witnesses, and cross-examining them and studying the strange creature, their verdict was that it could be nothing less than a Hersen Schim, that is, a spectre of the brain. They meant by this that there was no such animal.

However, a man from Delft, who followed the business of a knickerbocker, or baker of knickers, or clay marles, begged the body of the oni. He wanted it to serve as a model for a new gargoyle, or rain spout, for the roof of churches. Carved in stone, or baked in clay, which turns red and is called terra cotta, the new style of monster became very popular. The knickerbocker named it after a new devil, that had been expelled by the prayers of the saints, and speedily made a fortune, by selling it to stone cutters and architects. So for one real oni, that died and was buried in Dutch soil, there are thousands of imaginary ones, made of baked clay, or stone, in the Dutch land, where things, more funny than in fairy-land, constantly take place.

The dead Japanese oni serving as a model, which was made into a water gutter, served more useful purposes, for a thousand years, than ever he had done, in the land where his relations still live and play their pranks.

The Tragedy of the Gnomes

MANY, MANY AGES AGO this fair old world of ours wore a solemn and forbidding aspect; no carpet of thick, green grass eased the footfall of man as he climbed the hills; no human voice was heard amid the desolation – ice, ice everywhere – from the North Pole to the centre of that which is now the temperate zone, and only such life peopled this region as could endure the rigour of a more than arctic condition. Vast sheets of ice, in depth immeasurable, covered the surface of the hills and valleys, broken toward the tropics into serrated edges – the verdure running up an occasional valley, as though in laughing derisions of its neighbours the ice-imprisoned mountains.

In those days there existed only hideous animals and reptiles of size great and awful; animals whose terrible voice shook the mountains like an earthquake; slimy or scaly reptiles who walked on many feet, or dragged a hideous length along the ice-covered rocks. It seemed as if the great Creator must have fashioned all existent things in an hour of wrath, or that man, having existed, had been for some sin exterminated by that icy inundation, and that animal creation had so displeased him that he had fashioned them in grotesque caricature upon all grace and beauty.

Man esteems himself higher than all other created things; who shall say that the great, buzzing bluebottle fly does not think the same of himself, and perhaps, with as much reason; it is at most but a grade of intelligence; and what do we understand of that intelligence which is above us?

In one of the green valleys running up into the foothills of what is now called the Rocky Mountains, frisked and played a band of gnomes. These were but a fairy people, differing only from the fairies of woodland glade and dell in this; those fairy folk were things of beauty like imprisoned sunbeams; lighter than gossamer, they floated hither and thither, always trending toward the tropics, where the sun shone radiantly warm, and the silvery moon lighted the verdant carpet of grass, and the sweet south wind rang the lily bells in merry chime; there they idled away each sunny day – creatures of light and frivolity.

These gnomes were a sturdier, darker folk, short in stature, but with a breadth of shoulder, a depth of chest, and muscles fit for giants. Though for an occasional frolic they danced and roughly tossed each other about in the valley, they better loved their homes in the heart of the ice-covered mountains, where they forged beautiful things from the yellow metal, or decked their cavern homes with softly glowing, or fiery-eyed jewels; thus from earnest labour their faces gained a look of firmness and determination; they were homely, but were good to look upon, lighted as their faces were by love and kindliness.

One among them was wondrously fair: Lilleela they called her. Her hair was like silk as it winds from the cocoon; her eyes were blue as the sky when it shows between the fleecy clouds of summer; her cheeks were as though they had been kissed by the wild rose blooms, which left their dainty stains upon the fair skin. She was as sweet and pure as the breath of the dawn.

Walado was her lover; a short, deep-chested giant, with a face like a ripe walnut – all seams and puckers; not with age, but with jolly laughter, and intent, hard work. Lilleela must have the finest of rubies, on strings of beaten gold; tiny silver bells must be made, to ring their sweet chimes with every joyous movement; dainty chains of gold – set with amethyst, rubies and diamonds – must be wrought to bind the floating cloud of hair. Away down in the heart of the mountain Walado plied his little hammer of polished stone – clink-clink-clink all day long like a refrain it accompanied his happy song.

One fair day the troop of gnomes went down into the green valley for a holiday.

Walado objected: "No, no! You can go, but I must finish this golden girdle for my Lilleela, and then, there are sandals of gold to be set with precious stones for her feet – they are too sweet and fair to be bruised by the rocks," he had answered, screwing up his face into a funny little smile.

"Oh, do come, Walado! The girdle and sandals can wait! The sun is so cold and sorrowful up here, but down in the valley it is so beautiful!" pleaded Lilleela.

Her blue eyes moulded his will like warm wax, and over the ice they sped away many, many miles, to where its broken edges lay like icicles flattened out with huge rollers; some having sharp, sword-like points, others rounded and scalloped, as though in fanciful adornment. All along the border of the valley, reaching in places high up on the mountain side – wherever there were breaks in the ice – hardy trees had planted their feet, and lifted their heads to catch a breath of the warmer air of the tropics; some few, essaying to climb still higher, or being less hardy – reached their dead arms abroad, or pointed with ghostly fingers toward the icy desolation in warning to their kind.

These happy, childlike beings, instead of walking, had a gliding movement which carried them over the ground very rapidly; laughing, tumbling, pushing one another in merry sport, they sped on as though wings were attached to their feet. Hand in hand went Walado and Lilleela; his nut-brown face drawing into a nest of comical wrinkles, which were so many happy smiles; her look was like the sun, bright and warm.

Of a sudden she stopped and shivered: "Oh, my Walado, what was that?" From off the mountain height had come a long, low wail, and a chill was borne with it which froze them with fear.

Walado gathered her in his embrace, and shading his eyes with one hand, looked back over the mountain: "Fear not, my Lilleela, 'tis but the voice of the storm on its way from the far north. See! We shall soon be in the beautiful valley, where he cannot come!"

"Let us hasten, then, for in my heart I feel a chill which is like death."

Walado gathered her closer to him: "Little sun beam! Am I not able to shield you from the shadow of the dark cloud?"

She patted his brown face with her wee, rose-leaf palms, and kissed the wrinkles on his brown cheeks lovingly.

"Yes, my Walado; your arm is as strong as your heart is brave, but—" she broke off abruptly: "Let us fly!" she finished with a sound between a laugh and a sob as the wailing came borne from the mountain heights once more.

Turning their affrighted glance backward, they saw the tall pines at the foot of the hills swaying wildly; some which stood so tall and straight were snatched off like a brittle weed and tossed down the mountain side.

Lilleela shivered again, remembering the look the fearful Ice King had given her as he rode above the mountain height upon which she stood at twilight hour; he was seated upon a cloud of inky blackness; his eyes shot forth red and yellow flame, like the terrible light which streamed up from the far north; his lips were blue and hideous, and his matted hair, and long, tangled beard, were a mixture of frost and ice. He pointed a finger at her which looked as though belonging to the hand of one long since dead – so rigid and bloodless it appeared – the nails showed blue and ghastly. With a voice like the whistling north wind, he said, "You'll make a bonny bride for the Ice King! Your youth will warm my old blood finely! o-We-ee, Y-e-ss!" The cloud passed on, and bore him from her view, but the deadly chill remained, for well Lilleela knew that his love meant death, as his hate meant destruction.

For this reason the wailing sound shook her with an awful fear, but she dared not tell Walado; she feared that he would turn and seek the terrible monarch whose simple touch was death; once more she caught Walado's hand, crying gayly, "Come, come, before the storm god overtakes us!"

They romped and played through all that happy day; they climbed the steep inclines, and sitting on the glittering ice dashed down to the valley below, tumbling over and over, with laughter sweet as the tinkling of silver bells; it seemed strange to hear such sweet and musical sounds issuing from those queer little bodies, but the sound fitfully represented the sweet harmonious souls within.

At last, worn out with play, they climbed the long, icy hills; they wound around the towering rocks, they clung to dizzy precipices; they crept by the lairs of horrible animals with noiseless tread; ever upward and onward toward the North Pole, where life had grown old and dead, while the new life had slipped down toward the equator.

"Oh, why do we journey so far to-night, Walado?" said Lilleela wearily.

"There is a mountain lying in the light of the northern star, which is filled with yellow gold; its caverns are lined with jewels; I seek them for you, my Lilleela."

As he ceased speaking, again that wailing sound filled with awful menace smote their ears: "o-o-W-ee" a sound that rose from fretful discontent into fiercest anger, then died away like a long sigh of satisfied hate.

"I am afraid, Walado! Oh do return!" cried Lilleela in terror.

"'Tis but the wind, beloved one," answered Walado stoutly, though he too shivered.

"Nay! nay! It is the Ice King passing by in his chariot of storm, and drawn by his slaves – the winds of the hurricane," she cried frantically, fear making her pallid lips tremble.

Walado's wrinkled visage grew stern – all the pleasant lines drawn out of it; he understood more than her words told him.

"Has he dared to look upon you, with a desire to possess you? Knows he not that you are mine? I am not worthy of you – except as love for you makes me worthy—" his voice dropping into tender cadence, "but he – the monarch of all cruelty – is not of our kind. His very kiss is death; let him find a bride in his own frozen empire – the North Pole!" He shook his clinched hand in the direction of the swift rushing shadow, which so depressed them all: "Haste! haste, men and maidens! Let us flee to our own mountain home, where we can defy the monster! Our Lilleela has just cause for fear, for none upon whom he has looked with the desire for possession ever escaped him; and it is only by speedily reaching our caverns that we may hope for safety."

They turned about, and like a flock of frightened birds they flitted away, with no more noise than would be made by the rustle of a bat's wing, and were lost in the gloom.

The moon shone out cold and pale, as though grieving over the dread desolation and lighted up the angry face of the Ice King with a pallid luster; he puffed out his gaunt cheeks menacingly; his eyes darted flame like the quick thrusts of a sword blade in deadly battle; as he saw that the gnomes had fled he shrieked in wrath. He swayed the tall trees, and tossed their dead branches in every direction; he fiercely threw the rocks from the lofty mountain summits, and as they went crashing down, down, with thunderous noise, they splintered and tore up the ice like a silver foam, which glittered and flashed with pale prismatic glow as it caught the moon's sad, cold ray.

Faster, faster flew the tiny band; closer clung Lilleela to Walado's hand as that wrathful shriek reached their ears; dashing wildly past the brow of the darkly towering mountain, as the crashing of rocks smote them with wild affright; leaping across the roaring torrent, to slip and sprawl on the glassy ice of the further bank; up and away, bruised and sore; past lifeless trees, whose dead branches were falling all about them, until at last they reached a mountain home seldom used by them. Nothing was to be seen save a tiny crevice between the rocks; one after another they lay down, and silently slid through; then, and not until then, Walado spoke:

"We are safe! Even the Ice King cannot enter here! We are safe, quite safe!"

"Are you sure? Ah, my Walado, he is so vengeful!" sighed Lilleela. Walado laughed, all his funny little puckers laughing as well:

"He knows nothing of our hiding place, and he could not force his great rigid body through the narrow opening. Oh, we are quite safe!" he reiterated gleefully.

But Lilleela sighed.

Walado felt the hopelessness of that sound, and it grieved his tender heart; he passed his rugged, brown hand over her flossy hair, with a touch as soft as the brushing of a butterfly's wing.

"My treasure, if ill befall us here in this our vaulted hall, there are still the lower caverns, where none can possibly come save 'we who know.'"

They soon regained confidence, and joked and made merry; they were such trusting, childlike beings, taking the comfort and joy of each hour at its utmost worth.

Their enjoyment was at its height, when faintly heard came that long chilling wail. Two of their number had gone outside unnoticed by Walado; they came shooting in through the entrance, their brown faces bleached an ashen grey, their teeth chattering, their eyes protruding. All sprang up in wild affright.

"Where have you been? What is the matter?" cried Walado, as sternly as the gentle soul could speak.

"We but crept out for the birds we had snared! We thought to help out the feast!" said Tador, the hairy one.

"And I had a skin of berries that I gathered in the valley below; they were very sweet, Walado!" answered Sudana, the good.

"Tell me what you saw," replied Walado sadly, his anger melted away by their deprecating looks and words.

Sudana answered: "We saw the Ice King; his cloud chariot so low that it touched the top of the mountain, he was so angry that the frost flew in great clouds from his nostrils; his breath reached us and chilled us through."

Walado opened his lips to speak, when – "O-o-W-W-ee," filling all that vaulted chamber with the dread sound, it came borne on a wind so chill that it pierced the hearts of each with cold and fear.

These loving souls had never felt the need of a ruler, each doing his utmost through love for all, thus there had been no dissensions; now all turned instinctively to Walado for guidance. They were growing benumbed with the chill of that icy breath.

Walado silently pointed to the narrow passage leading deep into the bowels of the earth. Each took his beloved by the hand and prepared for the descent; before they had taken so much as one step, there came a crash so awful that it shook the great mountain to its centre; the falling of rocks resounded in deafening commotion; the Ice King's snarling wail echoed and re-echoed throughout the cavern; bitter, bitter cold grew the air; crash – crash – crash, came the sound of falling mountains heaped upon them; covering them deeply beneath the debris.

Then was a new horror added; the roaring and growling of many horrible beasts, as they fought and struggled for entrance through the narrow passageway, to escape the falling ruins, and the deadly cold.

There was the shrieking and tumult of the tempest; the hiss and roar of the struggling reptiles, but higher and shriller than all else was the fierce wailing menace of the angry Ice King; it shrieked to them insolently: "You defy me, do you? We'll see! We'll s-e-e!"

Grey and pallid grew the little brown faces as they silently followed Walado down into the bowels of the earth until they came to a lofty room; here they huddled silently together.

Thus they remained day after day, night after night, no ray of light to distinguish the one from the other; but as time passed on the pangs of hunger assailed them fiercely. Tador's birds were divided, and by morsels eaten; Sudana's berries were parceled out by ones and by twos, Walado adding all his share to Lilleela's, although she knew not that it was so; greyer grew his little, wrinkled face, but ever it smiled tenderly upon Lilleela, and with patient kindness he answered all questions in unselfish endeavour to comfort and cheer the others. For a time they could feel the earth quiver and vibrate as though in shuddering fear, then came a time of awful calm, when the sound of a voice smote the deadly silence with all the horror of thunder tones, until they shrank affrighted, and spoke only in awed whispers – afraid of the awful echo which answered sound. Paler and more spiritlike grew Lilleela; sadder, sadder grew Walado as he pillowed her head upon his broad breast. The sighs of all rose incessantly!

At last Tador whispered, "Shall I not descend further toward the centre of the earth? It will be warmer than it is here – it grows so very cold!" shivering.

"As you wish, Tador," replied Walado sadly.

Hearing Walado's answer all clamoured to accompany him – anything seemed preferable to this inaction.

As they prepared for the descent, Sudana said: "We do not know what we may find, Walado," trying to speak hopefully.

"Gold and jewels in plenty, but all that lies hidden in the whole mountain range, are not worth as much as one juicy berry," and he glanced at Lilleela's wan face. She was far too weak to accompany the party, and all insisted that Walado must remain with her; he silently folded her in his arms; he would not have left her.

She raised her sad eyes to his face: "Better had I have given myself to the Ice King; then I only should have perished," she said.

"No! no! no!" whispered they, as with one voice.

Wearily, wearily time passed on, but they did not return. Lilleela dozed and whispered fitfully, but Walado sat with staring eyes, and listened intently for sounds of his comrades, he was afraid to move lest he disturb his precious burden.

At last she raised herself up on her elbow, her eyes full of agony: "Oh, Walado, take me up above – I cannot breathe here! Oh, I must get one breath of air!" her chest heaving convulsively, her hollow cheeks palpitating with the struggle for inhalation.

One great tear rolled down Walado's cheek, and fell splashing on the rocky floor.

Around his waist he wore a rope made of the hide of animals, which served to hold his stone hammer and axe; with this rope he bound Lilleela to him, passing it under her arms and around his neck.

"Dear one, put your arms about my neck to steady yourself all that you are able, and I will carry you safely up."

Her chest rose and fell spasmodically; her heart fluttered faintly, or thumped with wild, irregular motion.

The walls of the shaft were covered with ice, rendering it almost impossible to obtain a foothold; inch by inch he made slow headway, every muscle strained to its utmost tension; his hands leaving stains of blood with every grasp. He could at last see a ray – scarcely of light, but a little less gloom; he was so exhausted that he was gasping for breath; he placed his hands upon a slight projection for one more effort – it may have been that his eagerness was too great, or that he grasped but brittle ice which broke off – for he fell. Down, down he slipped, with inconceivable rapidity; weak from want of food, and frightened lest he injure his beloved, he lost his presence of mind.

Lilleela recalled his wandering faculties; after one frantic scream, she made no outcry – indeed she had little breath for speech – but with her lips close to his ear she whispered: "Throw out your hands and feet against the wall, and I will do the same; we may at least break the fall!" Little by little the speed decreased, until as Walado's foot touched another projection they stopped altogether. He waited long enough to recover breath and a little strength. Lilleela's head fell over sidewise; she had fainted, and hung a dead weight about his neck; he dared not loose his hands, though he madly longed to caress the cheek which felt so cold to his trembling lips. Once more, nerved by desperation, he made an effort to reach the upper cave; slowly and carefully he climbed; resting often – a hand or foot slipping – clinging frantically as the ice became thicker, and the ascent more difficult. At last, just as his fingers were over the upper edge his foot slipped, and threw the other from its resting-place; for one breathless instant he hung suspended by his fingers – Lilleela's lifeless weight dragging him down! Sparks of fire shot before his eyes! A noise as of rushing water sounded in his ears: His breathing became laboured and stertorious! A bitter cry rose to his lips as Lilleela's cold cheek touched his drooping face; he made one supreme effort, and half unconscious he lay upon the floor of the upper cavern, Lilleela's cold form clasped in his embrace!

The chill at length restored him to consciousness; he sat up and unbound Lilleela; he struck two pieces of flint rapidly together, and ignited the punk which he carried in a bag about his neck. He observed that the cold wind had ceased blowing in, thus he knew that the Ice King must have departed, probably believing that all were dead. Well, so they were – all but himself – and – perhaps Lilleela!

He felt for her heart, but could find no pulsation; he kissed her cold cheeks, and blew his warm breath between her parted lips; at last the madness of despair took possession of him. He grovelled on the icy floor! He shrieked aloud, to be answered only by a thousand hollow echoes! He ran to the opening through which they had entered, and found the passage barred by rocks and dirt; he tore at the rubbish with his hands as an animal digs with its claws, only to fall back in despair with the tears coursing down his cheeks.

"Oh, my Lilleela! If I could but reach the air! If I could only carry you into the sunshine and let it warm your cold face! Oh, my Lilleela. Oh, my Lilleela!" he cried, gathering her once more into his arms. All the cave was now lighted with a dim, red light, from a few slivers of wood ignited with the burning punk. Water had oozed through the rocks from above and formed long, glittering icicles, frozen by the fierce breath of the Ice King; the floors and walls were likewise of ice, cold and scintillating. The sighs which had arisen from the imprisoned gnomes had congealed into forms of wonderful beauty, as pure as the white souls of the passing spirits; all over that arched ceiling hung fairy curtains of frost, wonderful jewels, each like a frozen tear, ornamented each jutting point. Walado sat down with his back against an angle of the wall, and clasped Lilleela in loving embrace; he smiled sadly yet lovingly as his eyes rested upon walls and dome: "It is a fitting tomb for thy fair body, my beloved! Thy spirit, not even the Ice King can imprison; and I – thine even in death – I go with thee, to serve thee still!"

He bowed his face against her fair hair, and as he so rested his spirit left his homely little body.

It seems almost a pity that they could not have known how fully their wrongs were avenged. Hot waves washed up from the tropic seas and melted the crust of ice with which the cruel monarch had encased all the hills; and he was driven by the south wind to his lair at the North Pole, there to remain in expiation forever. Thus the hills became fertile, and with the passing of those pure souls there sprang to life on the mountain side – the primrose, for Lilleela's pink-white skin; the columbine, for the azure of her eyes; the gentian, for the crimson of her lips; and the tall, white lily, for the stately grace of her body; and always the brown-coated robin, with his warm breast, sings lovingly by day and sleeps in their midst by night, and thus Walado's soul still faithfully serves his beloved.

Text Sources & Biographies

The stories in this book derive from a multitude of original sources, often from the nineteenth century and often based on the writer's first-hand accounts of tales narrated to them by native and indigenous peoples, while others are their own retellings of traditional tales. Authors, works and contributors to this book include:

Tok Thompson (Foreword)
Tok Thompson is Professor of Anthropology and Communication at the University of Southern California. Born and raised in rural Alaska, at age 17 he began studying at Harvard college, where he graduated with a degree in Anthropology. Later, he received an MA in Folklore and a PhD in Anthropology, at University of California, Berkeley, studying under the late great folklorist Alan Dundes. A popular lecturer, active editor, and well-known author, Tok has published numerous articles and books on various topics in folklore and mythology from around the world.

Marie-Catherine d'Aulnoy
Marie-Catherine Le Jumel de Barneville, Baroness d'Aulnoy (1650/1651–1705) was a French aristocrat and writer. She published memoirs and novels but is most famous for her collections of fairy tales (*Les Contes des Fées*, 1697, and *Contes Nouveaux, ou Les Fées à la Mode*, 1698) – indeed, she originated the term. Her tales seem to follow and be heavily influenced by folkloric material and oral tradition, and five of them were later collected by Andrew land in his *Blue Fairy Book* (1889).

Peter Christen Asbjørnsen and Jørgen Moe
Arguably Norway's most famous folklorists, Peter Christen Asbjørnsen (1812–1885) and Jørgen Moe (1813–1882) began gathering fairy tales and folk legends from an early age, having discovered a shared interest after meeting at school. Both would travel extensively across their homeland in search of new tales during their lifetimes, and while Asbjørnsen would go onto become a zoologist and Moe a bishop, it is for their volumes of folk stories, published as *Norske Folkeeventyr* (*Norwegian Folk Tales*) and later translated into English by George Dasent, that they are best remembered.

Hans Christian Andersen
Hans Christian Andersen (1805–75) was born in Denmark in 1805. When he was fourteen years old, he moved to Copenhagen with the intention of becoming an actor, but it was his writing that would earn him success. Although he published poetry, plays and sketches based on his travels, he is now most remembered for his fairy tales, which have influenced generations of children's authors. The first two volumes of *Fairy Tales Told for Children* were published in 1835, and when his fairy tales were translated a decade later he received long-lasting recognition in the field.

R. Nisbet Bain
R. Nisbet Bain (1854–1909) was born in London, England. As a historian and linguist with the ability to read over twenty languages, Bain was a prolific translator, especially of folklore and fairy tales, working often with folklore from Ukraine, Russia, and Turkey. He is known for his translation of *Weird Tales from Northern Seas* (1893), a Norwegian classic by Jonas Lie, in which the tales 'Finn Blood' and 'The Huldrefish' appear. Bain also contributed to the *Encyclopaedia Britannica* and worked for the British Museum.

Thomas Bulfinch

Thomas Bulfinch (1796–1867) was an American author born in Newton, Massachusetts. Having published three books of popular mythology and fable in his lifetime – *The Age of Fable, or Stories of Gods and Heroes* (1855), *The Age of Chivalry, or Legends of King Arthur* (1858), and *Legends of Charlemagne, or Romance of the Middle Ages* (1863) – Bulfinch's writing was later posthumously compiled into the classic *Bulfinch's Mythology* (1867). His versions of numerous well-known myths and tales became the standard still taught in many American schools today.

Frank T. Bullen

British author Frank T. Bullen (1857–1915) spent much of his childhood and early adulthood at sea, first setting out at the age of twelve and sailing throughout the world for fifteen years. He served as the second mate of the *Harbinger* and the chief mate of the *Day Dawn*. His time at sea inspired him to write extensively on the subject, producing such works as *The Cruise of Cachalot* (1898), *Sea Wrack* (1903), and *The Call of the Deep* (1907). One of his most well-known works is *Idylls of the Sea*, which includes such tales as 'The Kraken'.

Margaret Compton

Margaret Compton was born in 1852 and is best known as the author of *Snow Bird and the Water Tiger and other American Indian Tales*, a collection of Native American folk tales written for children and young adults that was based on authentic Native American lore. Originally published in 1895, the book was republished four years after Compton's death in 1903 under the new title *American Indian Fairy Tales*.

T. Crofton Croker

T. Crofton Croker (1798–1854) was born in Cork, the son of an army major. Although he had little education, he always made time to read while working in merchant trade. When his father died in 1818, Croker moved to London where he held a position in the Admiralty. Throughout his youth, Croker collected Irish legends, folk songs, and keens, some of which he sent to the poet Thomas Moore. This collection formed the basis of Croker's first major publication, *Researches in the South of Ireland* (1824). His next work, *Fairy Legends and Traditions of the South of Ireland*, was so greatly received he decided to write a second series. Passionate about his findings, Croker's fairy tales are filled with his notes, emphasizing the similarities between Irish legends and those of other countries.

Frank Hamilton Cushing

Born in 1857, Frank Hamilton Cushing was an American anthropologist and ethnologist who pioneered a new method of study – one which saw him actively participate in the cultures he studied, rather than merely observing from afar. Cushing's work was focused primarily on the Zuni Indians of New Mexico; he would live among them for a period of five years from 1879–84, and go on to write a number of books about them, including *Zuni Folk Tales* (1901). Cushing would continue to lead expeditions up to his death in 1900.

G.W. Dasent

British author G.W. Dasent (1817–1896) was born in St. Vincent, British West Indies. After studying Classical literature at university and then serving in a diplomatic role in Sweden, Dasent discovered his great passion for Scandinavian mythology and literature. Going on to become an assistant editor at *The Times*, and then a professor of English literature and modern history at King's College London,

Dasent also worked as a translator of Scandinavian folk tales. Among his best-known translations are those of Peter Christen Asbjørnsen and Jørgen Moe's folktales (*Norske Folkeeventyr*) in *Popular Tales from the Norse* (1859) and *Tales from the Fjeld* (1874).

F. Hadland Davis

Frederick Hadland Davis was a writer and a historian – author of *The Land of the Yellow Spring and Other Japanese Stories* (1910) and *The Persian Mystics* (1908 and 1920). His books describe these cultures to the western world and tell stories of ghosts, creation, mystical creatures and more. He is best known for his book *Myths and Legends of Japan* (1912).

H.S.C. Everard

H.S.C. Everard (1848–1909) was a British author with extensive expertise in golf and folklore. Having written in both subjects, his works include *Golf in Theory and Practice* (1896), and the various discussions of fantastical beasts, such as 'The Phoenix', which appeared in the 1899 collection *The Red Book of Animal Stories*, selected and edited by Andrew Lang. Everard also competed in and won several golfing competitions, including The Royal and Ancient Golf Club and the Calcutta Cup.

Juliana Horatia Ewing

Juliana Horatia Ewing (1841–85) was a prolific author of children's stories and novels. Born in Sheffield, England, she was herself the daughter of a children's author. Ewing's work has been noted by author Roger Lancelyn Green as the 'first outstanding child-novels' within English literature. She is known for her 1882 collection *Old-Fashioned Fairy Tales*. Her other works include *Melchior's Dream and Other Tales* (1862) and *The Land of Lost Toys* (1900). In addition to writing, she was also a skilled artist and worked as an editor for several magazines that published stories for children, including *Nursery Magazine*.

J. Sheridan Le Fanu

The remarkable father of Victorian ghost stories Joseph Thomas Sheridan Le Fanu (1814–73) was born in Dublin, Ireland. His gothic tales and mystery novels led to him become a leading ghost story writer of the nineteenth century. Three oft-cited works of his are *Uncle Silas*, *Carmilla* and *The House by the Churchyard*, which all are assumed to have influenced Bram Stoker's *Dracula*. Le Fanu wrote his most successful and productive works after his wife's tragic death and he remained a relatively strong writer up until his own death. The tale in the present volume ('What Was It?') was published in *A Stable for Nightmares* of 1896.

Eugene Field

Eugene Field (1850–95), of St. Louis, Missouri, was known as the 'poet of childhood'. He was a journalist for the *St. Joseph Gazette*, followed by various editorial and authorial roles at other newspapers including the *Morning Journal* and the *Times-Journal*. His humorous essays were often published in newspapers throughout the country, and in 1879 he also began publishing poetry. His collections include *A Little Book of Profitable Tales* (1889) and *Second Book of Tales* (1896).

Parker Fillmore

Parker Fillmore (1878–1944) was an American author born in Cincinnati, Ohio. Upon taking a job as a teacher in the Philippines, Fillmore was given no textbooks to teach his students English, and so he crafted his own stories for this purpose, launching his career in writing. Returning to the US and moving to a primarily Czech neighbourhood in New York City, he gained a great passion for the Czechoslovakian folklore that his neighbours shared with him. This led to his publication of several collections of these stories including *Czechoslovak Fairy Tales* (1919) and *The Shoemaker's Apron* (1920).

Charles Gould

Charles Gould (1834–93) was a British geologist and author. He is famed for being the first geological surveyor of the island of Tasmania, where he conducted three expeditions throughout the 1860s. He also worked as a land surveyor and consultant geologist in Tasmania, New South Wales, and the Bass Strait Islands. He was also an amateur naturalist and held a strong interest in 'cryptozoology'. This passion led to his publication of *Mythical Monsters*, one of the earliest works in that genre.

Elizabeth Grierson

Elizabeth Grierson (1869–1943) was born on a farm near Hawick, in the Scottish Borders. Throughout the course of her life she published more than thirty books, many of which covered Scottish fairy tales and folklore. In addition to these, she also published travel guides to the cities of Edinburgh, Scotland, and Florence, Italy. Her best-known works are her collections *The Scottish Fairy Book* (1910) and *Children's Tales from Scottish Ballads* (1906).

William Elliot Griffis

Born in Philadelphia, William Elliot Griffis (1843–1928) went on to serve as a corporal during the American Civil War. He studied at Rutgers University after the war and graduated in 1869. He tutored Latin and English to a samurai from Fukui and then travelled around Europe for a year prior to studying at what is now known as the New Brunswick Theological Seminary. In 1870, Griffis went to Japan and worked in education as well as writing for many newspapers and magazines. On returning to the United States in 1874 he worked in several churches on the east coast but retired in 1903 to write. With the help of his extensive knowledge of Japanese and European culture, he produced a number of books, such as *Japanese Fairy World* (1880), *The Fire-fly's Lovers and Other Fairy Tales of Old Japan* (1908), *Dutch Fairy Tales* (1918), *Belgian Fairy Tales* (1919), *Welsh Fairy Tales* (1921), *Japanese Fairy Tales* (1922), *Korean Fairy Tales* (1922) and many more.

Jacob and Wilhelm Grimm

The German academics, folklorists and authors Jacob Ludwig Karl Grimm (1785–1863) and Wilhelm Carl Grimm (1786–1859) are best known for their collection of fairy tales. The brothers excelled in their studies and developed an interest in philology whilst attending the University of Marburg, and as well as university teaching and librarian posts, they carried out extensive research on the history of the German language and its literature. They began collecting folk tales around their mother's death in 1808, and gradually established a method of recording fairy tales that has become a standard among folklorists. Their first edition of *Children's and Household Tales* was published in two volumes, in 1812 and 1815 respectively, and underwent a number of revisions culminating in the seventh and final editions in 1857.

Frank Hamel

Frank Hamel was a British author who was interested in mythology and the occult. His book *Human Animals* (1915) explored the belief found in many cultures that humans can transform into animals, and vice-versa. This can be found in folk tales throughout Europe, as well as the mythology of

Ancient Egypt and the oral traditions of some Native American tribes, among other cultures. Hamel focused his work especially in the subject of werewolves, as seen in 'The Werewolf in Myth and Legend' and 'The Werewolf Trials'.

Nathaniel Hawthorne

The prominent American writer Nathaniel Hawthorne (1804–64) was born in Salem, Massachusetts. His most famous novel *The Scarlet Letter* helped him become established as a writer in the 1850s. Most of his works were influenced by his friends Ralph Waldo Emerson and Herman Melville, as well as by his extended financial struggles. Hawthorne's works often incorporated a dark romanticism that focused on the evil and sin of humanity. Some of his most famous works detailed supernatural presences or occurrences, as in his *The House of the Seven Gables* as well as many of his short stories. The tales in this present volume of Hawthorne's are 'The Gorgon's Head' (from *A Wonder-Book for Boys and Girls*, 1851) and 'The Minotaur' (from *Tanglewood Tales*, 1853, 1921 edition).

Lafcadio Hearn

After being abandoned by both of his parents, Lafcadio Hearn (1850–1904) was sent from Greece to Ireland and later to the United States where he became a newspaper reporter in Cincinnati and later New Orleans where he contributed translations of French authors to the *Times Democrat*. His wandering life led him eventually to Japan where he spent the rest of his life finding inspiration from the country and, especially, its legends and ghost stories. Hearn published many books in his lifetime, informative on aspects of Japanese custom, culture and religion and which influenced future folklorists and writers whose writings feature in this collection – standout examples of Hearn's output include *Glimpses of Unfamiliar Japan* (1894), *Kokoro: Hints and Echoes of Japanese Inner Life* (1896), *Japanese Fairy Tales* (1898, and sequels), *Shadowings* (1900), *Kottō: Being Japanese Curios, with Sundry Cobwebs* (1902) and *Kwaidan: Stories and Studies of Strange Things* (1903). In 1891 Hearn married and had four children but later died of heart failure in Tokyo in 1904.

William Hope Hodgson

William Hope Hodgson (1877–1918) was born in Essex, England but moved several times with his family, including living for some time in County Galway, Ireland – a setting that would later inspire *The House on the Borderland*. Hodgson made several unsuccessful attempts to run away to sea, until his uncle secured him some work in the Merchant Marine. This association with the ocean would unfold later in his many sea stories. After some initial rejections of his writing, Hodgson managed to become a full-time writer of both novels and short stories, which form a fantastic legacy of adventure, mystery and horror fiction. The tale in the present volume ('Demons of the Sea') was first published in *Sea Stories*, 1923.

Clara H. Holmes

Clara H. Holmes (1838–1927) was an American author born in Ohio. Later moving to Cripple Creek, Colorado, she began contributing to the *Midland Monthly* from 1896. Her best-known work is the collection *Floating Fancies Among the Weird and the Occult* (1898), in which 'The Tragedy of the Gnomes' appears. Her other works include *Scattered Autumn Leaves* (1926), as well as several short stories that were published in various newspapers.

Margaret Hunt

Margaret Hunt (1831–1912) was a British author and translator during the Victorian period. She wrote several novels, some under the pen name Averil Beaumont, but she is now chiefly remembered for her comprehensive translation of Grimm's *Household Tales* in 1884. She was married to the artist Alfred William Hunt (1830–96) and they had three daughters, one of whom, Violet Hunt (1862–1942), also became a novelist.

Vuk Stephanovic Karadzic

Vuk Stephanovic Karadzic (1787–1864), was deemed by *Encyclopaedia Britannica* as 'the father of Serbian folk-literature scholarship'. He is best known for his careful collection and preservation of Serbian folktales, and for his story 'The Prince and the Dragon', which appeared in Andrew Lang's collection *The Crimson Fairy Book* (1903). A philologist and linguist, Karadzic is also regarded as being a significant reformer of the modern Serbian language.

Nicholas O'Kearney

Nicholas O'Kearney (*c.* 1802–65) was born in Thomastown, west of Dundalk, County Louth. A poet, scribe and editor, O'Kearney would go on to co-found the Irish Celtic Society with John O'Daly and be responsible for translating manuscripts including W.B. Yeats' *Fairy and Folk Tales of the Irish Peasantry* (1888).

Patrick Kennedy

Born in County Wexford, Ireland, Patrick Kennedy (1801–73) worked as a teacher before later establishing a bookshop in Dublin. As a writer, Kennedy would contribute articles and tales to several periodicals of the time, but it is as a collector and publisher of Irish folk tales and legends that he is best known. His work to record everything from tales to ballads and even children's games in such books as *Fictions of Our Forefather* (1855), *Legendary Fictions of the Irish Celts* (1867) and *The Fireside Stories of Ireland* (1870), has been hailed as being vitally important in helping preserve traditional Irish folklore for future generations.

Charles Kingsley

Charles Kingsley (1819–75) was an English priest, professor, social reformer, historian, novelist and poet, whose most famous works are probably the novels *Westward Ho!* (1855) and *The Water-Babies, A Fairy Tale for a Land Baby* (1863). Though he held some questionable views, his knack for storytelling is evident in *The Heroes, or Greek Fairy Tales* (1856).

Gertrude Landa

Gertrude Landa (1892–1941) was a journalist and writer often referred to simply by her pseudonym Aunt Naomi. Landa wrote a number of plays and novels with her husband, the writer Myer Jack Landa, and published a collection of classic tales and folklore stories in the book *Jewish Fairy Tales and Legends* (1919).

Bertha Palmer Lane

Little is known about Bertha Palmer Lane, author of *Tower Legends* (1932), a book that brings together classic tales and folklore stories about towers in myth and legend, such as 'The Leprechaun of Ardmore Tower'.

Andrew Lang

Poet, novelist and anthropologist Andrew Lang (1844–1912) was born in Selkirk, Scotland. He is now best known for his collections of fairy stories and publications on folklore, mythology and religion. Inspired by the traditional folklore tales of his home on the English-Scottish border, Lang complied twelve coloured fairy books (such as *Red, Blue, Crimson* and *Yellow*) which collected 798 stories from French, Danish, Russian and Romanian sources, amongst others. This hugely successful series further encouraged the increasing popularity of fairy tales in children's literature.

Cyrus MacMillan

Cyrus MacMillan (1882–1953) was an academic at McGill University in Montreal, Canada, where he was Chairman of the English department before eventually rising to the position of Dean of the Faculty of Arts and Science. MacMillan also served as a politician in Mackenzie King's government from 1930, and was the author of several books including *Canadian Wonder Tales* (1918), *McGill and Its Story* (1921) and *Canadian Fairy Tales* (1922).

H.E. Marshall

The British author Henrietta Elizabeth Marshall (1867–1941) is best remembered for her history books for children, most notably *Our Island Story* (1905), which was long considered the standard for educating children about the history of England in the United Kingdom. Marshall's extensive travels around the world led to further books exploring the histories of other countries, including the *Our Empire Series*, as well as a translation of *Beowulf* (1908) and *Stories of Robin Hood Told to the Children* (1912).

Frederick H. Martens

Frederick Herman Martens (1874–1932) was an author, lyricist and translator, whose work includes a translation of Pietro Yon's 1917 Christmas carol 'Gesu Bambino', a biography of the musician A.E. Uhe (1922), *A Thousand and One Nights of Opera* (1926), *Violin Mastery (Talks with Master Violinists and Teachers)* (1919), and fairy-tale translations in *The Chinese Fairy Book* (ed. Dr. R. Wilhelm).

Mrs. E.B. Mawr

Little is known of Mrs. E.B. Mawr, who collected and translated over a dozen folklore stories and historical tales for her book *Roumanian Fairy Tales and Legends* (1881).

Abraham McCoy

Abraham McCoy was the original story-teller who shared 'The Story of Conn-Eda; or, The Golden Apples of Lough Erne' with Nicholas O'Kearney for the book *Fairy and Folk Tales of the Irish Peasantry* (1888).

William Frederick Travers O'Connor

William Frederick Travers O'Connor (1870–1943) was an officer in the British and British Indian armies. In a distinguished career lasting thirty-five years, he would be decorated numerous times, including The Most Eminent Order of the Indian Empire and the Royal Victorian Order. He travelled extensively across Asia, and it was during two years spent in Tibet that he was inspired to collect and translate a number of folk tales and verse for the book *Folk Tales from Tibet* (1906).

Mrs. H. B. Paull

Susannah Mary Paull (1812–88) was born in St James Parish, Middlesex, England as Suzannah Mary Peakome, the daughter of the saddler William Peakome. She married Henry Hugh Beams Paull (hence the "H. B.") and we know little else about her other than that she seems to have become a fairly prolific writer of religious and children's fiction, possibly to support herself after her husband got into financial difficulties. She began in 1855 with *The Doctor's Vision: An Allegory* and her last fiction work appears to have been *Mabel Berrington's Faith: and Other Stories* (1886). She also of course successfully translated the fairy tales of Hans Christian Andersen (the first edition of which was published in 1867), as well as those of the brothers Grimm.

Norman Hinsdale Pitman

Norman Hinsdale Pitman (1876–1925) was an author and educator, born in Lamont, Michigan. His works include: *The Lady Elect: A Chinese Romance* (1913), *A Chinese Wonder Book* (1919), *Chinese Fairy Tales* (1924) and *Dragon Lure: A Romance of Peking* (1925).

Theodore Roosevelt

History remembers Theodore Roosevelt (1858–1919) – also known as Teddy – as the twenty-sixth president of the United States. Roosevelt was also the youngest man to ever take office when, at the age of forty two, he succeeded William McKinley following McKinley's assassination in September 1901. A renowned writer, naturalist and conservationist, Roosevelt wrote extensively on a broad range of subjects throughout his life, publishing almost fifty books that covered everything from historical matters (his two volumes of *The Naval War*, 1882) to the great American outdoors (*The Wilderness Hunter*, 1893) and his travels abroad (*African Game Trails*, 1910).

W.H.D. Rouse

William Henry Denham Rouse (1863–1950) was a British teacher who was born in Calcutta before his family returned to the United Kingdom. An acclaimed school master who author Arthur Ransome once cited as an inspiration, Rouse is remembered for his use of the direct method of teaching Latin and Greek and his translations of *The Odyssey* (1937) and *Illiad* (1938).

Ivan T. Sanderson

Ivan T. Sanderson (1911–1973) was a Scottish-born biologist and writer who travelled extensively from an early age and would go on to write about the natural world in books such as *Animal World* (1937), *The Continent We Live On* (1961) and *How to Know the American Mammals* (1951). He is perhaps best known for his work in the field of cryptozoology and the paranormal, however, where he explored subjects ranging from unidentified flying objects to mythological creatures in titles such as *Abominable Snowman: Legend Come to Life* (1961), *Uninvited Visitors: A Biologist Looks at UFOs* (1967) and *Investigating the Unexplained* (1972).

Henry Rowe Schoolcraft

Henry Rowe Schoolcraft (1793–1865) devoted a significant portion of his life to interactions with Native American people. In 1822 he served as an Indian agent for the US government covering Michigan, Wisconsin and Minnesota, before later marrying Jane Johnston, who was herself the daughter of an Ojibwa war chief. From his wife Schoolcraft would learn the Ojibwa language and much about their history and way of life. His works include *The Myth of Hiawatha, and other Oral Legends, Mythologic and Allegoric, of the North American Indians* (1856) and a comprehensive six-volume series titled *Historical and Statistical Information Respecting the History, Condition, and Prospects of the Indian Tribes of the United States* that was published between 1851 and 1857.

Feodor Sologub

Feodor Sologub (1863–1927), born Fyodor Teternikov, was a Russian novelist, poet and playwright. His literary career would begin in 1884 while he was working as a teacher, with the publication of his first poem, and he would go on to increasing success in the years that followed. He retired from teaching in 1907 and married the translator Anna Chebotarevskaya the following year. Sologub would write prolifically, but for several years his work would go unpublished in his homeland as a result of the Bolsheviks. Among his many works were the novels *Bad Dreams* (1896) and *The Petty Demon* (1907), the short story collections *The Sweet-Scented Name and Other Stories* (1915) and *The Old House and Other Tales* (1916), as well as numerous plays, poems and tales.

Clara Stroebe

Clara Stroebe (1887–1932), also known as Klara Stroebe, was the editor of several collections of fairy tales from around the world that were published by the Frederick A. Stokes Company. Among her books were *The Swedish Fairy Tale Book* (1921) and *The Norwegian Fairy Tale Book* (1922).

Percy Amaury Talbot

Botanist, anthropologist and researcher Percy Amaury Talbot (1877–1945) was a British colonial district officer in southern Nigeria between 1902 and 1931, ascending to the post of District Commissioner in 1911. He was the author of many studies about the peoples of Nigeria, including *In the Shadow of the Bush* (1912), *Life in Southern Nigeria* (1923), *Some Nigerian Fertility Cults* (1927) and *The Tribes of the Niger Delta* (1932).

C.J.T. (Charles John Tibbits)

Charles John Tibbits (1861–1935), often known simply as C.J.T., was a journalist and newspaper editor who is best remembered for his collections of folklore tales from around the world. Among his books were *Folk-Lore and Legends: English* (1890), *Folk-Lore and Legends: Scandinavian* (1890) and *Folk-Lore and Legends: Russian and Polish* (1890).

John Vinycomb

John Vinycomb (1833–1928), was an artist and writer from Newcastle-Upon-Tyne. He was a founding member and president of the Belfast Art Society and a vice president of the Ex-libra Society of London, and an authority on heraldry. Among his published works were *On the Processes for the Production of Ex Libris (Book-Plates)* (1894) and *Fictitious and Symbolic Creatures in Art* (1909).

Abbie Phillips Walker

Abbie Phillips Walker (1867–1943 or '51) was an American writer hailing from Rhode Island, New England. She is most well-known for writing the Sandman series of fairy tale books, including *The Sandman's Hour: Stories for Bedtime* (1917) and *Sandman's Goodnight Stories* (1921).

H.G. Wells

Herbert George Wells (1866–1946) was born in Kent, England. Novelist, journalist, social reformer and historian, Wells is one of the greatest ever science fiction writers and, along with Jules Verne, is sometimes referred to as a 'founding father' of the genre. Wells created over 50 novels, including his famous works *The Time Machine*, *The Invisible Man*, *The Island of Dr. Moreau* and *The War of the Worlds*, as well as a fantastic array of gothic short stories. The tale in the present volume ('The Sea Raiders') was published in *The Plattner Story and Others* (1897).

Dr R. Wilhelm

Richard Wilhelm (1873–1930) was a German theologian, missionary and sinologist. He is best known for his translations of philosophical works, from Chinese into German, including his translation of the *I Ching* and *The Secret of the Golden Flower*. He also edited *The Chinese Fairy Book* (1921).